DENNIS WHEATLEY

THE LAUNCHING
OF ROGER BROOK

Original Frontispiece by
MARK GERSON

Original Illustrations by
RICHARD DALKINS

Distributed by
HERON BOOKS

4121

FOR

My darling wife
J O A N :

This, my first historical novel—inspired by "Cosey Cott",
which she has done so much to make the smallest stately
home—with all my love.

CONTENTS

CHAPTER I

THE HAPPIEST DAYS . . .(?)

W H I T E - F A C E D and tense, his blue eyes smouldering under their dark lashes, young Roger Brook glared at the older and much sturdier lad who stood grinning at him in the narrow corridor.

"Give me my cap, Gunston! Come on; give me my cap!" he demanded angrily.

George Gunston was a broad-shouldered youngster of sixteen with a crop of coarse red curls which grew low down on his forehead, and a round, freckled face. He showed the mortar-board that he had just snatched from Roger's head provocatively for a moment, then thrust it again behind his back as he began to chant:

"Bookworm Brook, bookworm Brook. He's a toady to the ushers, is bookworm Brook."

"That's a lie!" exclaimed Roger, "I don't toady."

"So you give me the lie, do you, you little swot. All right! Come outside and fight."

Roger strove to control the fear that suddenly made his heart beat faster, passed the tip of his tongue over his dry lips, and muttered: "I only said I don't toady—and I'm not a swot. I've simply found that it saves trouble in the long run to do my prep properly and keep my books neat. It's not my fault that you're always in hot water because you're too lazy to do either. Now stop behaving like a second-form kid, and give me back my cap."

"If you want it, come and get it."

For a moment Roger considered the challenge. On two previous occasions, baited beyond endurance by Gunston, who was the bully of his year, he had fought him, and each time received a thorough licking. To fight again was only to court disaster; yet he must have his mortar-board back, and quickly, as his House Master had just sent for him, and there would be trouble if he did not present himself before "Old Toby" decorously clad in cap and gown.

As they stood there eyeing one another, Roger with the hot, bitter resentment of one who knows himself to be superior in every way to his tormentor, except for physical strength, and George, taking an oaflike delight in the power that physical strength gave him to humiliate his cleverer class-mate, a jumble of sounds came to them, muted by the thick walls of the one-time Benedictine monastery, that for countless generations had housed Sherborne School in Dorset.

Normally, at this evening hour, the school was hushed while its scholars unwillingly bent their minds to construe the passages of Caesar, Horace or Cicero that they had been set for their prep, but this was the last night of term and the boys were packing to leave next morning for their summer holidays.

1

Sherborne is a very early foundation, its charter having been granted by Edward VI in 1550; yet there is evidence to show that its roots go much farther back, and that it had its beginnings in the days of St. Aldhelm, who lived in the eighth century.

Already, therefore, on this 28th day of July, in the year 1783, the venerable buildings had known the joyous atmosphere that pervades a school on the last night of term for something like a thousand years.

Such term endings differ little with the passing of the centuries, except in the very gradual change in the clothes worn and the language used by masters, staff and pupils—and such minor points as that, where the boys had once washed down their supper with a draught of mead, they now took strong ale and in less virile times yet to come, would drink plain water. The boys themselves altered not at all, and now that discipline was relaxed they were shouting, playing pranks and throwing their hated lesson books at one another in the exuberance engendered by this eve of freedom. Snatches of song, squeals of mirth and running footsteps penetrated faintly to the secluded corridors in which Gunston had met Roger and seized this last chance to provoke him to a fight that would mean an easy victory.

"Well! What are you waiting for?" Gunston sneered.

Roger still hesitated, torn between the urgent necessity to get back his cap and his dread of physical pain. His hatred of Gunston was such that he would have risked a fight if only he could have been certain of landing one good hard blow on his tormentor's fat, stupid face, but he knew that the odds were all against his being able to get in first. Moreover, he was loath to go home to his mother next day with a black eye or a badly cut lip.

It seemed that Gunston had almost read his thoughts, as he said suddenly: "So you're afraid you'll have a bitten tongue to-morrow night when you drink the health of that old Popish schemer 'over the water,' eh?"

The gibe, Roger knew, was directed at his mother, as she was of Scottish parentage, and so obviously suspect of Jacobite sympathies. It was still less than forty years since Bonnie Prince Charlie had had his father, the Old Pretender, proclaimed King in Edinburgh, and civil war had sown bitter discord through the length and breadth of Britain. Gunston's shot had been fired at random, but it was all the more telling because Roger's mother did still regard the now elderly Stuart Prince who lived in Rome as her legal sovereign, and, at times, toasted him in silent symbolism by passing her glass of wine over the water in her finger bowl.

Roger's own vivid imagination also inclined him secretly towards the romantic Stuart cause. The fact that his mother had often told him that he must not prejudice his career by championing the side that had lost in this quarrel of an older generation, but should follow the loyalty of his English father to the Hanoverian line, made no difference. Political hatreds and the persecution resulting from them died hard in those slow-moving times, and Roger knew that he dared not allow the imputation of Jacobitism to pass.

Tensing his slender body he clenched his fists and suddenly struck out at Gunston with a yell of: "You dastard! I'll teach you to speak ill of my family!"

After their two previous encounters Gunston had actually had small hope of inciting young "Bookworm Brook" to fighting pitch, so when the attack came it took him by surprise. He was, moreover, temporarily at a disadvantage in that his right hand was still behind him holding Roger's cap.

Dropping it he stepped back a pace, but not quickly enough to avoid a savage jab on the nose. Tears started to his eyes and the mocking grin was wiped from his pudgy face. But George Gunston was not the type of bully who is a coward, and promptly caves in when stood up to. Swiftly throwing himself into the attitude he had often admired in semi-professional pugs during knuckle fights at fairs and on village greens, he easily parried the unscientific rain of blows that Roger aimed at his head.

After a moment Roger stepped back to regain his breath. Instantly his red-headed antagonist took the initiative. Closing in he landed a heavy punch on Roger's chest that drove him back another pace towards the angle of the corridor. Following up Gunston swung a right hook to Roger's jaw, missed it by a fraction, but landed another left on his body.

Roger gasped, threw up his arms to protect his head and retreated another couple of steps. His one advantage lay in the fact that he was much the nimbler of the two and, had he had more space he might have dodged some of Gunston's blows, but here, in the narrow corridor, he was deprived of any chance to use his agility.

He knew, too, that without losing his balance, he could easily have thrown his adversary into confusion by giving him a swift kick on the shin, and he had never been able to understand why, if one was set upon by a bigger fellow, one should not resort to any such trick for one's own protection. But a strange unwritten law of England forbade such tactics, just as it also ordained that he must not turn and run. To have done either would have been thought worse than spitting on the floor of the Chapel during Holy Communion.

Yet he was seized now with a blind, despairing misery. He fought on automatically, but knew that he had no hope of escaping a thorough drubbing. In another moment Gunston would have him in the corner and lam into him with those freckled, brutal fists until he fell to his knees and cried for quarter.

As through a haze he saw that Gunston's nose was bleeding, but before he had any chance to feel elation at the sight he received a terrific wallop on the ear that knocked him sideways and made his head sing. For a moment he was deafened and as he ducked to avoid another blow he did not hear a quiet voice drawl:

"What's this? Fighting on end of term night? For shame now! Desist at once! Who have you in that corner, Gunston?"

As the expected blow did not fall, Roger lowered his arm, raised his head and realised the cause of his deliverance.

A tall, thin young man, with an elegant air, narrow shoulders and a pronounced stoop had appeared on the scene. He had a large fleshy

3

nose and a pair of very pale blue eyes, which now surveyed the still breathless combatants with an expression of indolent disapproval. Although he was some two years older than either of them, he was so frail that Gunston could have laid him out with a single blow; yet the habitual bully almost cringed before him.

The interrupter of the fight was known as "Droopy Ned" and he held a highly privileged, if curious, position in the school. This was not alone because he was a member of one of those great families which, in that heyday of the aristocracy, collectively wielded a far more potent power in the governance of England than the occupant of the throne. In fact, the century was approaching in which any son of a peer was to be given an extra kick at his public school, just because he was the son of a peer; so, even in this era when patronage counted for so much, Droopy Ned's prestige had little connection with the fact that he was the younger son of the Most Noble the Marquess of Amesbury, and that his proper style was Lord Edward Fitz-Deverel.

His real, although quite unorthodox, authority—since for some reason best known to themselves the school authorities had repeatedly passed him over in their selection of prefects—was based upon his most unusual personality. He differed so abnormally from his school-fellows that they were quite incapable of understanding him but, recognising instinctively that he possessed the brain of a mature man, they accepted his idiosyncrasies and deferred to his judgments without question.

In some ways he shocked them unutterably. In an age when blood sports occupied nine-tenths of the thoughts and leisure of every English gentleman, Droopy Ned made no secret of the fact that he abhorred bull-baiting, fox-hunting and cock-fighting; he also displayed an aloof disregard for all schoolboy crazes, ball games and field sports. Instead, he concerned himself with strange expensive hobbies, such as the collecting of antique jewellery, the study of ancient religions and experimenting on himself with eastern drugs: the latter then being neither forbidden by law nor frowned on morally. Without appearing to concern himself with his studies he mastered them with ease and would always give his help to more backward class-mates with the utmost readiness. He possessed great charm of manner and was extremely generous but, on occasions when provoked by the bumptious or offensive, his lazy good nature gave place to a bitter, devastating wit, of which both the masters and his school-fellows went in dread.

Droopy airily waved a fine cambric handkerchief under his big nose and both the boys caught a whiff of the French scent that was on it, as he inquired: "What were you two fighting about?"

Gunston would no more have challenged the speaker's right to put the question than he would have thrown an inkpot at the Head.

"I took the little fool's cap," he answered sheepishly.

"Why, may I ask?"

"Oh, it was just a rag."

Droopy's pale blue eyes hardened. "I vow you had a deeper reason. You did it to force a fight upon young Brook. The love of fighting for fighting's sake is forgivable in the little savages of Lower

4

School, but you will be moving into Upper School next term, and it ill becomes a fellow of your age to act the bully and the bore. Retrieve Brook's cap now, and give it to him."

Gunston hesitated only a second, then he picked up Roger's cap and handed it over.

"Now shake hands," Droopy ordered.

As they obeyed, with ill-concealed reluctance, he looked at Roger and went on: "You are about to wait on Old Toby, are you not? I have just come from him and he was speaking of you. He was saying that you show great promise, particularly in languages and English composition. Such gifts may incline you to enter public life. As you may know, I am leaving this term to start on the Tour, but I shall be back in England in three or four years' time. If in the future I can be of any service to you, pray command me. You will always be able to obtain news of my whereabouts from Amesbury House, in Arlington Street."

Roger made him a little formal bow. "That is most kind of you, Lord Edward." His quick wit led him to use the title deliberately in recognition of the fact that Droopy Ned was virtually no longer a schoolfellow, but, on leaving, had become a man.

A smile of appreciation showed in the pale blue eyes. "I see you have the making of a man of parts, Mr. Brook, but I shall always remain 'Droopy' to my friends, and I hope that I may count you among them."

Gunston had been standing by with a surly look on his face, and he now shuffled his feet awkwardly. Droopy glanced at him and went on: "I must continue my farewells, so I will not detain either of you longer."

As Gunston turned away with a muttered "Good-bye" Roger said: "I envy you vastly going abroad. I would give anything to travel."

Droopy nodded. "No doubt you will, one day. In the meantime all good fortune to you. Pray remember to come and see me on my return."

"Indeed, I will. The best of fortune on your journey and my duty to you for rescuing me just now."

" 'Twas a pleasure." With another airy wave of his scented handkerchief Droopy Ned followed Gunston down the corridor.

The three were not destined to meet again for several years, but if Roger could have seen into the future it would have been revealed to him that both the others were to enter his life at many of the most important crises in it.

Again and again he was to come up against the pig-headed stupidity of Gunston, as Lieutenant, Captain, Major, Colonel, and, finally, as General Sir George on the field of Waterloo. While Droopy Ned was to prove a powerful friend and wise counsellor in the tortuous path that he, Roger Brook, was to tread, as Mr. Pitt's principal secret agent during the dark days of the French Revolution and the mighty struggle against Napoleon.

5

CHAPTER 11

A KNOTTY PROBLEM

T H E Reverend Mr. Tobias Chapwode, or "Old Toby" as he was called by the boys of his House, was by no means one of the most popular masters. His real interest lay in his own special subject, English History, upon which he had written several scholarly books. Had he had an income of his own he would have retired to devote himself exclusively to these studies, but he was dependent on his stipend and so compelled to remain at Sherborne although his duties there often conflicted with his private work.

In consequence, whenever he was immersed in a particularly tricky passage of his writings he became extremely lax and discipline suffered. Then, suddenly becoming aware of this, to restore the situation he would pounce and punish with considerable severity. As the boys were unaware of the cause of this inconsistency in his treatment of them, they were naturally apt to resent it, and some even regarded him as a malicious old man who delighted in deliberately playing a cat and mouse game for his own amusement.

The belief was fostered owing to the fact that few of his pupils ever got to know him. He regarded boys in the main as young animals, whom time alone could change from barbarous little savages into reasoning human beings. Moreover, he considered that his responsibility consisted only in keeping the worst of their natural vices in check and sending them out into the world stuffed with enough knowledge, acquired parrot fashion, to form a basis for further education should they later choose to develop any talents they might have.

Yet to the few of whom he took conscious notice he presented a very different personality. In the seclusion of his untidy, book-bestrewn study he was no longer the reserved and apparently dreamy individual, who nine times out of ten failed to take notice of minor misdemeanours but on the tenth occasion would deal out birchings and impositions with startling suddenness. Those whom he invited there occasionally for purposes other than inflicting punishment, always found him both tolerant and kindly; moreover, he had a strange facility for setting them at their ease and talking to them, not as their House Master, but as a friend.

These favoured few were always boys who had attracted his notice by the promise they showed of becoming something worthwhile later in life. His historical studies had long since made him aware that these were by no means always the youngsters who did best at their lessons and he had an uncanny knack of singling out those showing incipient strength of character, regardless of their talents or lack of them. Among those with whom during the past year he had felt it worth while to bother was Roger Brook.

6

Roger, therefore, had been in no trepidation on being sent for and, even had he not just been reassured by Droopy Ned, would have felt no qualms as he knocked on Old Toby's door.

"Come in," boomed a sonorous voice, and on entering the study, Roger saw that, as usual for such interviews, Old Toby had dispensed with all formality. He was a fat, elderly man, with a round face, sharp nose and rather fine green eyes. The desk behind which he sat was covered with a disorderly mass of parchments, his ill-curled grey wig reposed on a wig-stand beside his chair, the double lappets of his white clerical collar were undone and his rusty black gown was stained with spilt snuff.

"Ah, 'tis you, Brook," he said. "Come in and sit down. Take that armchair and make yourself comfortable."

As Roger obeyed, Old Toby scratched his shaven pate and went on with a smile: "Now, why did I send for you? For the life of me I can't remember, but 'twill come back in a minute; that is, if you don't grudge me the time from your packing for a little conversation."

"Of course not, Sir," Roger replied politely, marvelling, not for the first time, that his House Master could be so affable when in the seclusion of his own room. "I've naught left to do but cord my boxes to-morrow morning."

"Have you far to go?"

"Only some forty odd miles, Sir. I live at Lymington, on the Solent."

"Ah, yes. That is something of a cross-country journey, though, and the coaches would serve you ill. You've bespoken a post-chaise, no doubt?"

"No, Sir, I prefer to ride. Jim Button, our groom, will have arranged a change of horses for us on his way over to-day, and my baggage will go by carrier."

"That should be pleasant if the weather is clement, as it has been these few days past. You'll take the turnpike road to Poole and so on through Christchurch, I suppose?"

Roger shook his head. "We go by way of Blandford, and then through the New Forest. The tracks are quite passable at this time of year, and the forest glades are wondrous beautiful."

"You're not afraid of footpads then," Old Toby smiled. " 'Tis common knowledge that the forest is rarely free of such dangerous gentry."

"I've never met any, Sir. But if we do we'll hope to give a good account of ourselves. Jim always ports his blunderbuss and he'll bring me my brace of pistols."

"You would stand and fight, then?"

"Why not, Sir?" Roger's dark eyes gleamed with excitement at the thought. "I can shoot the pip out of an ace at fifteen paces, but I've had no opportunity to try my pistols on a human target, yet. I'd like the chance."

Old Toby chuckled. "You young spitfire! Our Master-at-Arms tells me, too, that you are becoming quite a dangerous antagonist with the foils. But this recalls to me the matter about which I wished to

7

talk. Does the interest you display in weapons incline you to the profession of Arms?"

Roger hesitated only a second, then he decided that Old Toby would not resent it if he was absolutely frank. "To be honest, Sir, there is nothing that I would hate more than going into the Navy or Army. You see, I know 'tis very wrong of me, but I just can't bear to be ordered about. I don't mean that I resent being told what to do by people I respect, like yourself. But some of the other Masters—well, they often make rules to suit their own convenience without a thought as to how they will affect us boys. That's the privilege of their position, of course, and one accepts it as philosophically as one can—as long as one remains at school. But I think anyone a fool who, on leaving, deliberately saddles himself with a new lot of masters for the rest of his life."

It was an exceptionally strong statement from a boy not yet sixteen, in an age when the word of all parents was a law against which there was no appeal and rigid discipline was regarded as the essential backbone of the whole structure of society. But Old Toby's face showed no sign of disapproval at this declaration of heresy. He was thinking, 'I was right to take an interest in young Brook, he has moral.as well as physical courage, and may go far.'

Still uncertain of the effect his rash words might have had, and wishing to strengthen his argument, Roger hurried on: "Some of the older boys are worse than the masters, and they can't even claim to know best because they are grown up. They fag the younger fellows to do all sorts of stupid time-wasting things, often out of pure malice, and I see no reason why their natures should change when they become older. Take Gunston, Sir. I'm not complaining about him, but he is going into the Army. Just think of having a stupid oaf like that for one's senior officer, and being unable to question his decisions. Life would be positively unbearable."

Old Toby took a pinch of snuff. "Your views are unorthodox, Brook, and I would advise you to keep them to yourself. There is, I admit, something in what you say; yet discipline is a necessary ingredient in all our lives. *Rectique Cultus pectora roborant.* To succeed in any career, you must school yourself to accept that fact. But tell me, why, if it is not your intention to adopt the profession of Arms, do you spend so many hours in the fencing school and shooting gallery each week?"

"To make myself proficient, Sir. Then when I am older no man will be able to gainsay me with impunity."

"I had not realised that you were of such a quarrelsome disposition."

"I trust that I am not. I would not seek to force a quarrel on anyone. But a gentleman should know how to defend himself, and the ability to do so is the best means of assuring full independence of both spirit and action."

"You must be aware that edicts inflicting severe penalties for duelling have been in force for many years now."

Roger smiled and gave a slight shrug. "Yet duels occur with some frequency just the same, Sir, and they are not forbidden in many places on the Continent. I hope to travel in due course."

"Ah," Old Toby shuffled with some papers. "That brings us back to the reason for my asking you to wait upon me. You will be moving into Upper School next term, and I see that I have no note here as to the career which your parents desire you to follow. The time has come when I should be informed of it in order that I may allocate a certain portion of your time to the most appropriate studies."

"Nothing definite has been settled yet, Sir. My father wanted me to go into the Navy, but there was some hitch. My mother——" Roger flushed and broke off.

Old Toby gave him a shrewd look. "Your mother was Lady Marie MacElfic before her marriage, was she not? And all her family are still irreconcilable Jacobites. Were you about to say that the King had refused entrance to the Navy to you on that account? It is common knowledge that the Government is still averse to appointing officers to either Service who have even remote connections with the Stuart cause."

"Well, yes, Sir. That is what happened. As a Captain in the King's Navy, himself, my father did not think that there would be any difficulty about my appointment, but there was. He was furious, but said there was plenty of time and that before I was old enough to go to sea he would make their Lordships at the Admiralty see reason. That was soon after the American war broke out. Then when the French intervened in seventy-eight, his ship was ordered to sea, and, thanks be to providence he has not been home since; so has been unable to do aught about it."

" Seventy-eight," murmured Old Toby, "Why, that is five years ago. And so, young man, you have been a stranger to parental discipline for all that time. If you have been allowed to have your head at home for so long 'tis little wonder that you have come to find the restraints of school irksome. Has your father made no mention of this matter in his letters?"

"Yes; from time to time. But he felt, I think, that little could be done by writing to their Lordships, and he has no personal influence at Court. He was counting on the patronage of Admiral Rodney when the Fleet got home, but the war dragged on for so long and his ship was one of those left on the West Indies Station after our great victory last year off the Isle of Saints."

"And meanwhile, you have been growing up. It is not too late yet for you to enter the Navy, but it very soon will be. As you have no inclination for the life I take it that you are congratulating yourself already on having escaped your father forcing you to it."

Roger grinned sheepishly. "Even if he were ordered home to-morrow he has to get here; then 'twould take him months of lobbying finally to overcome the old objections, and once I'm sixteen I shall be safe. For me the late war has proved a miraculous preservation. The Army would have been bad enough, but to be a midshipman, boxed up in a ship for months, living on weevilly biscuits and kicked around by every Tom, Dick and Harry! It makes me shudder to think of it."

"Quæ fuit durum pati, meminisse dulce est, was Seneca's very wise remark on that, you will remember. But, have you made any plans of your own?"

"No, Sir, and I'd willingly be guided by you. In any event, as far as entering Upper School is concerned, I'm sure my mother would be agreeable to your putting me to any studies that you think most suitable."

"Outside the usual curriculum you are already taking French. Few boys show any interest in Modern Languages, and I remember thinking it strange this time last year when you asked to be allowed to do so. What was your reason, Brook?"

"Because I hope to travel."

"Both your Latin and Greek are exceptionally good for one of your years; and the former being the common tongue of all educated people I should have thought that would have filled your need anywhere on the Continent."

"No doubt it would, Sir; but with Latin, English *and* French, I shall stand a better chance of making myself fully understood by people of all classes, wherever I may go."

Old Toby regarded the slim figure and thin, eager face in front of him thoughtfully. The boy had great self-assurance for his age, was well proportioned and when fully grown should make a fine figure of a man. Those dark blue eyes, a gift no doubt from his Highland mother, coupled with the short, straight nose, strong white teeth and resolute chin, would play the very devil with the women. The fat, worldly-wise old man caught himself thinking that it would not be long before the lad seduced some ripe young chambermaid or dairy wench. In the days before he had taken orders to assure himself a sinecure he had done quite a bit of whoring himself; and to his way of thinking any young man of sixteen who had not started to roll the girls in the hay was neither healthy nor normal. People began both to fight and love young in those days.

As his glance fell on Roger's hands his thoughts shifted. They were fine hands, none too clean at the moment, but long and firm, sensitive yet strong. They had, however, one peculiarity: the little fingers on both were of exceptional length, their tips reaching almost to the nails of the third fingers.

Cheirognomy or the science of reading character from the shape of the hands, is as old as fortune-telling and at one time Old Toby had interested himself in it. He now recalled that unusually long little fingers acted as a balance to the impulsiveness given by strong thumbs, and indicated the power of their possessor to influence others. Not without reason, too, the ancients had associated the qualities of the god Mercury with the little finger and averred that when abnormally developed it showed great ability of expression in both writing and speaking, and that the owner was one who could interest and command people by the manner in which he would apply facts and knowledge to the treatment of anything that strongly concerned him.

He wondered that he had not noticed young Brook's long little fingers before, but was pleased that he had done so now, as the boy's flair for languages and the ease with which he expressed his thoughts was one more proof of the correctness of the ancient, though now discarded, science.

"I think," he said slowly, "that during this holiday you should consult your mother and ascertain if she has any views as to your future."

"I will, Sir; but I'd be mighty obliged if you could offer some suggestions that I might put to her."

"Have you, or are you likely to have, any money of your own?"

Roger shook his head. "Such money as there is in the family lies with my mother's people, and they cut her off when she married my father against their will. My father has only a few hundreds a year apart from his pay."

" 'Tis a pity, that; since few careers are open to a gentleman lacking fortune; other than learning and the sword. Are you irrevocably set against entering one of the Services?"

"I fear so, Sir. I'll not submit myself to be dragooned all my life by people for many of whom, I am convinced, I should have no respect."

"*Far est et ab hoste doceri*," Old Toby quoted, and added: "While 'tis true that a certain number of the King's officers are men of little merit whose lack of education is deplorable, in the main they are honest, courageous fellows of good will, who do their duty as they see it. At times you might have the misfortune to find yourself under an ignorant martinet, but 'tis morbid to assume that you would always do so. In these days, too, promotion is rapid for young men who show ability; so I feel you should strive to overcome this arrogant prejudice of yours. Even if you are set against the Navy you could canvass such patronage as the gentry round Lymington would no doubt give to a neighbour's son, to overcome this lingering Jacobite taint, and secure you a commission in the Army. That, I am sure, in these war-like times, would afford you the best chance of making a name for yourself."

"But we are no longer at war, Sir," Roger protested. "What with the French, the Spaniards, the Dutch, and the Colonists we have enjoyed only some fifteen years of peace out of the last forty-four, and they must be as exhausted as we are. Surely, after the last seven years of strife, we should be able to count now on a long period of tranquillity."

Old Toby grimaced, and took snuff again. "I doubt it, Brook. 'Tis true that the signing of the Peace of Versailles last January secured the pacification of Europe and the final Independence of America, but it leaves many grounds for contention still outstanding. During the past two centuries we have humbled the might of Spain and ground down the power of the Dutch, so that both are now reduced to second-class nations. But France, our inveterate enemy, still remains immensely strong and a constant menace to our interests in every corner of the world."

"Permit me to observe, Sir, that we've had the upper hand in India for some twenty years past now," Roger remarked deferentially. "And that by the Quebec Act Lord North gave Canada a charter that

11

has deprived King Louis of the allegiance of the Canadian French so it seems that we have little further trouble to face in either."

"That may be so, but these long-drawn-out contentions over distant continents are merely the skin of the apple, not its core. As for my Lord North's measure; by securing the monastic lands in Canada to the Roman Church and granting complete freedom of worship to all sects, he may have won over the Canadian Papists, but its repercussions both in New England and at home were disastrous. The storm it raised, culminating in the Gordon riots a few years back, bids fair to delay all hope of religious toleration in England, and even more so in Scotland, for another generation. It also played no small part in the fall of his own ministry fifteen months ago. "

"Surely, Sir, his loss of the Premiership after twelve years of office is another reason for anticipating a long period of peace? As the King's protégé, my Lord North represented the war party, but now that he has been compelled to accept a minor place in the new Coalition his colleagues, and particularly Mr. Fox, will prevent him from allowing us to become involved again."

"I greatly doubt if the Coalition will live out the year. Lord Rockingham's death and Lord Shelburn's resignation have already caused two reshuffles since Lord North's own fall. His Grace of Portland is no more than a figurehead and the present arrangement with Lord North and Mr. Fox as joint secretaries under him is too unnatural to last. The two men have been bitter enemies for years and have not a thought in common. But reverting to yourself, Brook. Do politics attract you?"

"They would, Sir; if I could see my way to enter them."

"'Tis a great field for young men, these days. There are many members of the House who are still in their early twenties, and an outstanding example of unusual talent being recognised is afforded us by young Mr. Pitt. Only last year Lord Shelburn took him into his Ministry as Chancellor of the Exchequer at the age of twenty-three."

Roger smiled. "But he had the advantage of being the son of the Great Commoner, and his mother is a Grenville so he has the backing of the most powerful connections in the realm."

"Such influence counts for much, particularly in politics now that Parliament has virtually become a club, half the members of which are nominated by our oligarchic aristocracy that controls the pocket Boroughs. But no influence, however powerful, would have alone sufficed to induce Lord Shelburn to make young Billy Pitt his Chancellor. He owes that to his capacity for business and his gift for oratory."

Old Toby paused for a moment, then went on: "You have too good an opinion of yourself already for me to further swell that young head of yours by suggesting that you might become another Mr. Pitt. And I fear your poor grasp of mathematics would soon bring ruin to us all if you were ever made responsible for the Exchequer. But you have application and a most ready tongue, so you might well aspire to some remunerative minor office, if you could find a means to enter Parliament."

"Alas, Sir, that's the rub." Roger shrugged despondently. "One needs both patronage and money to secure a pocket Borough, and, as I have told you, I have neither."

"Um! I had forgotten that you lack money of your own. *Hiatus maximé deplendus.* Patronage is by no means impossible to win, given a pleasing presence and fair speech, but a good private income is essential to any man having political aspirations. We are thrown back then to a choice of learning or the sword. When you leave Sherborne could your parents afford to send you to one of the Universities?"

"Yes, I'm sure they could do that, and in many ways I'd like it, Sir. But where would it lead in the event of my doing well?"

"To preferment and some well-paid sinecure in which you could follow your own inclinations—if you are prepared to take orders. To do so is still regarded as a pre-requisite to becoming a Fellow. You could then remain on as one if you wished or, in due course, accept a warm living or the headmastership of a school, since a great number of the best of these are within the gift of the Colleges."

"With due respect to your cloth, Sir, I feel no inclination to enter the Church. But I should welcome the chance of pursuing my studies in History, and I was under the impression that a B.A. could prove a valuable asset in securing profitable employment."

Old Toby grunted. "Then dismiss the thought, Brook. As I have said, we live in an age of war, and learning is at a discount. A degree in itself could open no better prospect to you than tutor to some nobleman's son at forty pounds a year, or, at best, an appointment as usher in a school. As for such studies as you have in mind I fear you would be grievously disappointed. During the past century both the Universities have fallen into a sad decline and only a few of the more conscientious Fellows bring themselves to lecture now and then. Such is the sloth that has gripped our seats of learning for many decades that no Regius Professor of Modern History at Cambridge delivered a lecture between 1725 and 1773, and the last holder of that Chair died from a fall from his horse while riding home drunk to his Vicarage at Over. Conditions at Oxford are as bad, or worse, and the students at both are of two kinds only. Those who are prepared to take orders to the end of later obtaining a benefice, and young rake-hells with time to waste, who are sent up from family tradition by rich parents."

"That rules out Oxford or Cambridge for me, then," Roger sighed. "I've no particular wish to go to the Colonies, but it looks as if that is all that remains to me. In the new lands no stigma attaches to a gentleman who engages in trade, and I might, perhaps, become a rich merchant."

Old Toby nodded. "That certainly is a possibility; although to engage in commerce successfully one requires capital. You might, however, obtain a post with the India Company or, if you prefer Canada, seek employment with that which controls the vast territories round Hudson's Bay. With either I doubt your sword being likely to rest for long in its scabbard. But neither will it if you remain at home for that matter. In the event of another war against the French every man will be needed, and you would hardly be able to avoid service with the Army, however much you may now dislike the idea."

"You seem very confident that there will be another war, Sir."

"I am, alas! After the French and ourselves have had a few years to lick our wounds I regard it as inevitable. For seven hundred years they have been our hereditary enemies, yet neither of us have succeeded in destroying the other. With the constant expansion of our interests a final decision becomes more imperative with every year that passes. The loss of our oldest colonies in the Americas has been more than compensated for in the last few decades by our gains in Canada and India and the great new lands that Captain Cook has opened up to us by his voyages in the southern seas. Britain has now become an Imperial Power unrivalled since the days of Rome; but our hold upon these great possessions is still fragile in the extreme. The French, too, need 'living room' and their population is twice as large as ours. The far-flung bases over which new fly the flag of the Union gives us a strangle-hold upon their commerce. They know that they must break that hold or lose the leadership of Europe and degenerate into a second-class Power, where poverty will take the place of affluence. Overseas the game has gone to us, but only a narrow strip of water divides us from King Louis's numerous and well-armed legions. Believe me, Brook, before ten years are gone the French will make another great effort to overwhelm us and obtain the Empire of the World. For them 'tis either that or stagnation, bankruptcy and death."

For a moment there was silence in the quiet room, then Old Toby glanced at the clock on the mantel, and said:

"Good gracious me! I had no idea 'twas so late. I fear I have detained you overlong. Well, speak with your mother as to your future when a suitable opportunity arises, and let me know any fresh thoughts you may have upon it on your return next term. A happy holiday to you."

"Thank you, Sir; the same to you." Roger stood up and added with a smile: "And permit me to thank you for your interest in me." Then he made a formal bow and left the room.

As he walked back along the corridor, where earlier that evening he had had his affray with Gunston, he realised that the time had come when he ought to face up to this business of choosing a career for himself. For years the nightmare of being forced into the Navy against his will had haunted him, yet he had not dared to think of any other future. Then, as with the passing of time the shadow had lifted, he had gradually begun to savour the joy of escape without formulating any alternative. But now Old Toby had precipitated matters, and it seemed a much more knotty problem than he had imagined would be the case.

He was an only child, but, even so, his inheritance would amount to no more than a moderate-sized house with a few acres of garden and meadows and something less than a thousand a year; and in the meantime he must find some way to support himself honourably in the quality of gentleman to which he was bred. The Church would give him leisure to read and the service of the Crown would ensure him travel; and he wanted both, but was most strongly averse to entering either;

14

yet, without money of his own every other prospect seemed barred to him. It was indeed a poser.

On opening the door of the Junior Common room, a burst of riotous sound almost deafened him. Scores of his companions were ragging together as they cleared out their lockers. The thought that he would be at Sherborne for another two years, so there was really ages of time before he would have to burn his boats, drifted through his mind; then he was struck sharply on the cheek with a pea blown from a pea-shooter. Forgetting all else, with a high-spirited yell he rushed upon his attacker.

Next morning he was up and dressed soon after four. For all but the *haute monde* of London and such fashionable spas as Bath, who could literally afford to burn money in the constant consumption of many candles, the sun governed most people's lives in those days, and "early to bed and early to rise" was still the general rule; but, anxious to be on their homeward way the boys had risen of their own accord an hour earlier than usual.

The great courtyard of the school and the road outside it was now the scene of immense bustle and activity. Scores of grooms with led horses, some in smart liveries, others in plain home-spuns, jostled one another for place while seeking their young masters. The road for half a mile was blocked by a double line of private coaches, hired post-chaises, gigs, cabriolets and phætons. While the drivers swore at their neighbours and strove to quieten their restive horses the boys ran amongst them, each seeking the familiar equipage that had been sent the day before, or overnight, to fetch him; and an army of servants struggled through the crowd bent under the weight of heavy corded boxes.

Entering the turmoil Roger raised himself on tiptoe, looking eagerly to left and right in search of Jim Button. As he did so he caught a glimpse of Droopy Ned, standing beside a splendid gilded coach with postilions, outriders and a great coat of arms emblazoned on its door.

Not a cap or gown was now to be seen, and the boys were all dressed in holiday attire, like little replicas of their fathers. Most wore good suits of broadcloth, riding-breeches and unornamented three-cornered hats, but the richer among them swaggered in brightly coloured coats of silk or satin, with embroidered waistcoats and lace ruffles at throat and wrists; Droopy Ned outshone them all.

He was wearing a long-skirted coat of yellow watered silk, the huge cuffs and pockets of which were braided with gold. The curls of a great white wig tumbled down between his narrow shoulder-blades and perched on the top of it was a tricorne hat edged with more gold lace and a thin ruching of feathers. From one hand he dangled a large lace handkerchief and with the other, while he directed the liveried footman in the stowage of his baggage, he leaned negligently on a five-foot long malacca cane topped with a huge opal.

Roger was just thinking how fine it must feel to be the Lord Edward Fitz-Deverel, now a man, rich beyond the dreams of avarice and just about to set off on the Grand Tour, when he caught the sound of a familiar voice.

"Hey, Master Roger! Here I be! I thought ye was never a-coming."

Turning, he pushed his way through the crush to an angle of the yard where Jim Button was waiting, holding the reins of a hired led horse for him.

With a laughing "Good morning, Jim; all well at home?" Roger caught the reins of the led horse, thrust a foot into the stirrup and swung himself into the saddle.

As he reached it Jim leant over with a grin. "Aye, all's well, Master Roger. And I've great news for 'e. The Captain's back. 'Twas only yester-e'en but y'r father's at last come home from the sea."

CHAPTER III

AN ENGLISHMAN'S HOME

T H I S startling news put a damper on Roger's high spirits as effectively as a snuffer douses a candle. It was not that he disliked his father. Far from it; until the announcement that he was destined for the Navy had engendered in him a secret fear of his parent he had had a warm affection and high admiration for that hearty, vigorous man who could tell such fascinating stories of buccaneers and the hazards of the ocean. That early attachment would still have been strong enough to make him rejoice at the thought of the Captain's return had it not been marred by a sudden wave of renewed anxiety as to his own future.

He had counted on their having news that his father was about to sail for home before his ship actually left the Indies. The voyage took from six to eight weeks and, normally, even had he been ordered home that summer, which from his letters had seemed most improbable, Roger had reckoned that he could hardly reach England before September. That would have left him only a little over three months in which to pull such few strings as he had with the Admiralty; and, knowing the appalling delays to which officialdom customarily subjected such unimportant applications, Roger had felt confident that January the 8th, 1784, his sixteenth birthday, would still see him unfettered by a Midshipman's commission. But now that the Captain had six months to work in Roger had serious grounds for alarm.

Nevertheless, by the time they had changed horses at Blandford, the lovely morning sunshine and the feel of his own little mare between his knees again had done much to dispel his gloom; and when, an hour later, they left the King's highway to strike through leafy lanes towards the New Forest he thrust his misgivings into the back of his mind.

The road, if it could be called one, that ran through the forest, was merely a rutty track, confined at times by mossy banks feathered with ferns and bracken, but for the most part barely furrowing the flat surface of broad grassy glades that ran one into another. At the end of each the track curved a little to open up a new prospect of giant oaks, chestnuts and beeches, the lofty branches of which in some places met overhead and in others were separated by several hundred yards, so that their green crests could be seen towering to the sky.

Roger had always loved the forest for its silence and the mystery that seemed to lurk waiting for discovery in the depths of each shadowed cavern of undergrowth. Leaving Jim to amble along he frequently cantered ahead or explored byways where the green sward beneath his mare's hooves was dappled with golden sunlight flickering through its branches. Here and there he startled a rabbit or squirrel into a headlong retreat and more than once set little groups of fallow deer loping away from him.

When they reached the ferry over the Avon they made a hearty second breakfast off the provender that Jim had brought with him, then, fording the stream, continued their way through the seemingly endless forest. They encountered no footpads but came upon an encampment of Egyptians, as the gipsies were then called. These strange dark folk, with their black locks, gold earrings and brightly coloured scarves seemed very alien to England, yet they had dwelt there in the forest in apparent contentment for centuries. It was said that they sometimes kidnapped children and they were certainly horse thieves, but they never molested travellers. Roger gave them a friendly wave and the white teeth of their women flashed as they smilingly waved in reply. The children ran beside him for a little way, shouting for largess in their strange Bohemian tongue. He threw them a few small coins and cantered on.

The sun was high overhead by the time they left the forest and crossed Setley Heath. Shortly after one o'clock they walked their horses into Lymington.

The town was opposite the western end of the Isle of Wight but lay about four miles from the sea. It consisted of some half-hundred houses grouped round the quays, where a widening of the river Lym formed a small natural harbour, and a single long street that ran up a steep hill to westward of the old town. Just above the crown of the hill the High Street divided into two narrow alleys passing either side of the Town Hall, with its stocks, blind house and butchers' shambles, then uniting again in a broad thoroughfare as far as the church. Beyond this lay a straggling ribbon of houses, known as St. Thomas's Street.

It was from this western end that Roger entered the little town and on reaching the church he turned seaward, down Church Lane, a few hundred yards along which lay his home. The house was situated on a gentle slope to the south of the High Street and separated from it by gardens, a strip of woodland and a large meadow.

From time immemorial there had been a dwelling there and part of the last remained; a low-roofed building faced with old red tiles which was now used as the kitchen quarters. Roger's grandfather had bought the property, demolished most of the earlier structure and built the main portion of the present house. It formed a solid square block with tall, white-painted windows most of which faced south and had a fine view of the Island. There were two storeys only but the rooms were spacious and on both floors twelve feet in height. It was not a mansion according to the times, but if for sale would have been advertised as a commodious residence, suitable to persons of quality.

A small orchard lay to west of it, an acre of walled kitchen garden to its north, stabling and outhouses to its east; along the south front of the house ran a long balustraded terrace, ornamented with carved stone vases and with two sets of steps leading down to a wide lawn beyond which a number of fine trees and shrubberies formed shady walks. The whole was enclosed by a high brick wall which, although the property was so close to the town, gave it as much seclusion as if it were a mile or more from its nearest neighbour.

Eager to greet his mother, Roger dismounted at the orchard gate, leaving Jim to take his mount round to the stables, and, running up the path burst into the house by its side entrance. As he had guessed would be the case, at such a time, she was in the kitchen superintending her maids in the preparation of a gala dinner for her returned hero.

Lady Marie Brook was then forty-six. The dark hair, partly hidden by her lace cap, was now turning grey, but in her deep blue eyes and fine profile, it was still easy to recapture the ravishing beauty that, eighteen years earlier, had caused the dashing Lieutenant Christopher Brook to declare that he must have her even if he died for it. And he very nearly had, since both her brothers had called him out and in the second duel he had been seriously wounded.

At the time of their meeting Jacobite plots had still been rife, and he had come upon her, white-faced and indignant, while he was leading a naval landing-party in the forced search of her home in Scotland for a concealed store of arms. She had been only seven when her father, the Earl of Kildonan, had joined Prince Charles Edward's ill-fated rising and after the battle of Culloden been butchered by the Duke of Cumberland's brutal Hanoverian horsemen; but had been old enough to remember the grief of her devastated clan at their losses in battle and the merciless hunting for fugitives that had succeeded it. The passing of twenty years had made no difference to the extreme hatred that she and her family bore to all who wore the uniform of the Hanoverian King; yet the very first sight of Christopher Brook had caused in her an overwhelming emotion. Her first love had been killed as a result of a shooting accident and she had felt the blow so deeply that she had rejected all other offers, but the dashing young Naval Lieutenant had dissipated her old loyalties as swiftly as mist is dispersed by strong sunshine and, in spite of all arguments, entreaties and threats, she had broken with her family to run away with him.

Lady Marie was not only a beautiful, but also a very practical, woman; and her housekeeping was a model of industry and efficiency, even for those times. Not a fruit, herb or vegetable in her garden was ever allowed to go to waste and the shelves of her storeroom groaned under their loads of conserves, pickles, spices and syrups.

In the old kitchen where she now stood, making pastry herself while she kept a watchful eye on her ample-bosomed cook and her two maids, Polly and Nell, the time-blackened beams overhead were festooned with hams, tongues, and flitches of bacon, while the tables could hardly be seen for joints, game, pudding-basins and vegetables.

18

As Roger ran in she swiftly dusted the flour from her hands and, laughingly submitting to his wild embrace, kissed him on both cheeks; then she held him from her and exclaimed:

"My darling boy, you're looking wondrous well, and I can see that you're much excited by the great news. Your father is out on the terrace with some other gentlemen. He's just mad to see you, so run to him now and leave me to my cooking."

After kissing her again Roger did as he was bid, and slipping from the old to the new part of the house, he came out through the pillared portico that gave on to the terrace.

His father was there, a big, brown-faced, jovial-looking man of fifty-two, surrounded by a group of neighbours who had called to welcome him home. Roger knew most of them; old Sir Harry Burrard, the richest man in the district, who lived across the river at Walhampton; General Cleveland of Vicar's Hill; John Bond of Buckland Manor; Mr. Eddie of Priestlands and Mr. Robbins of Pylewell. Captain Burrard was there, too, talking to Harry Darby, the Mayor of Lymington whom he hoped to succeed, in that ancient and honourable office which had been held by no less a person than the Duke of Bolton only ten years earlier; and Sam Oviatt, the local wine-merchant, present by virtue of his calling, which was considered of such importance at that date that wine-merchants were freely admitted to country society, which rigorously excluded all other tradesmen.

As Roger's father caught sight of him, he cried: "Why, Roger, boy, thou hast become a man! Stand not on ceremony but come hither, lad."

Roger had been about to make a bow but instead he ran down the steps and his father kissed him heartily.

"What a surprise you gave us," he laughed up at the bronzed, heavy jowled face just above his own. "Where is the *Bellerophon*? Did you dock at Plymouth or is she in Portsmouth Roads?"

"Nay, I left her in the Indies, and came home as a passenger in the frigate *Amazon*. I carried dispatches, and having a fair wind behind us we made all sail up channel to anchor at the Nore. 'Twas half a day saved, though it meant my jolting all the way from London in a plaguey post-chaise yesterday. But you know the company, Roger?"

Recalling himself, Roger made a deep sweeping bow which, beginning with Sir Harry Burrard, included all those present.

"Your servant, gentlemen."

As they returned his bow, he noticed for the first time that there was a stranger among them. He was a paunchy little man with a fat face, double chin, small pursed-up mouth and snub nose, but he had large, luminous eyes. Many of the older men were wearing wigs, but evidently he preferred the newer fashion, as his own brown hair was curled in two rolls above his ears and tied with a black bow at the back of his neck.

At that moment he stepped forward and spoke in a sonorous, rather pompous voice.

"Captain, pray do me the honour to present me to your son."

"On the contrary, Sir, I am flattered that you should take notice

19

of him. Roger, make your service to Mr. Edward Gibbon, who has recently become our Member of Parliament on the retirement of Sir Harry, here. But keep your schoolboy Latin tags for other company, since that is his second tongue, and his learning upon ancient times puts us all to the blush."

Roger's eyes opened wide as he bowed again. "Indeed, I'm honoured, Sir. My House-master at Sherborne lent me the first volume of your *Decline and Fall* but I had not thought to have the happiness of meeting its distinguished author."

Gibbon's fat face broke into a smile. "Nor I, young Sir, that my cherished labours should already have reached so youthful a public."

"Strap me, Roger!" beamed his father, "you have the laugh of us, for I'll vow that few others of us here have as yet had the courage to tackle so weighty a work, much as we may admire Mr. Gibbon's industry. For that you deserve a glass of wine. What shall it be— Madeira, Malaga or Sack? But I forget, you're old enough now to drink as and when you please."

"Thank you, Sir," Roger turned away to a table that old Ben, the house-man, now elevated by the wearing of his best black to the rank of butler, had carried out on to the terrace. On it were three decanters and a tray of tall, slender, trumpet-shaped glasses. Choosing the Madeira, as the sweetest wine, he was pouring himself a glass when Mr. Bond cried:

"I take you up on that, Chris! I've read all three volumes that Mr. Gibbon has so far published, and am a-thirst for more."

"Ah, John, your nose was ever in some book while the foxes at Buckland made a Roman holiday in your hen roosts," responded the captain, and his sally raised a hearty laugh among the fox-hunting squires of which the company mainly consisted.

"I, too, am happy to say that I have read Mr. Gibbon," declared Sam Oviatt.

"I'll not gainsay you," said his host, with a broad wink at the others. "With no lands to look to and the scandalous profits you make on your smuggled liquor, you must be the richest man among us and the one with most leisure."

Another gust of laughter followed, then Mr. Gibbon held up a plump hand. "Come, come, gentlemen! No more disputing over the rival claims of my poor work and other pursuits, I beg. Three readers among ten of you is so handsome a proportion that could I boast the same of the population of England I should be so well endowed that I could afford to found a free library for the enlightenment of poor sailors returned from the wars."

The laugh this time was against Captain Brook but it was interrupted by the arrival of two newcomers, the Vicar and Mr. Sutherland, who lived at Grosvenor House in the High Street, the meadow behind which ran down to abut on the Captain's orchard. After greetings had been exchanged and they had been furnished with drinks, the gay, inconsequent talk went on.

Soon after three o'clock old Sir Harry Burrard asked that his coach might be summoned, so that he could drive home to dinner;

but Captain Brook would not hear of it, insisting that the whole company should remain to dine with him, and that his wife had prepared against them doing so. Heads were counted and Roger sent to tell his mother that, besides themselves, there would be eleven guests; and as she had already bidden her nearest and dearest neighbour, Mrs. Sutherland, to join them, to keep her in countenance with so many gentlemen, covers were prepared for fifteen.

Roger helped old Ben put the extra leaves in the dining-room table, but they had no need to use them all, as it was a good modern one made only a dozen years before in Mr. Chippendale's London workshop and could, as Roger knew from their Boxing Night parties, seat twenty, when fully extended.

By four o'clock its highly polished mahogany mirrored a brave array of china, glass, gleaming silver, white napery, crystal bowls of fruit and filigree baskets holding bonbons, comfits and candied peel, while the side tables were filled to capacity with steaming dishes and rows of bottles.

Polly and Nell, now smart in their frilled aprons and mob caps, took their places on either side of the table; old Ben announced that his master was served, and the company went in to dine.

Lady Marie had Mr. Gibbon on her right and Sir Harry on her left; the Captain had Mrs. Sutherland on one side and old General Cleveland on the other; Roger sat between Sam Oviatt and Captain Burrard.

For a first course Lady Marie gave them a dish of perch and trout, another of lobster patties, three fowls broiled, a fore-quarter of lamb, and a fillet of veal roasted with Morella cherries and truffles. And for a second course, sweetbreads, a green goose roasted and peas, a pigeon pie, apricot tart, cheesecakes, and a trifle.

Few ate of all these things, but many of most; everyone choosing what they preferred and often having their plates piled high with helpings from several different dishes at the same time. The meal was good, but by no means pretentious as nine dishes to each course were often served in larger houses and even when alone few of those present ever sat down in their own homes to a dinner of less than a single course of five. All of them took unabashed enjoyment in their food and washed it down with copious draughts of Rhenish, Claret and Anjou. Such heavy eating and drinking brought internal troubles to most people in middle life and was largely responsible for the early death rate but they lived too fully and violently to give a thought to that.

With the interval between courses this cheerful guzzling continued for the best part of three hours, then the port was put on the table and the ladies withdrew.

Behind a tall, brocaded screen in one corner of the room was a commode with two chamber pots, in order that the gentlemen might be spared the inconvenience of interrupting their conversation by leaving the room. Most of them now made use of these and, as they settled down again, the Captain told Roger to take his mother's place at the foot of the table; the decanters were passed round and the jovial talk went on.

21

"You have told us little yet, Sir, of the state in which you left the Indies," remarked Mr. Gibbon to his host, "and no small part of our prosperity hangs upon the Sugar Islands."

"Things are well enough there now, Sir," promptly replied his host. "The enemy caused some destruction in the towns where our people put up a resistance to him; but in such islands as fell to his assault he burnt few of the plantations, thinking to profit from them himself in years to come."

Captain Burrard laughed. "After the French recapture of St. Eustatius, and with only Jamaica, Barbados and Antigua left to us, he had some reason to count his chickens. Things there were in a parlous state until my Lord Rodney's victory off the Saints restored the situation."

"Were you present at the fight, Chris?" asked Mr. Sutherland.

"Aye, Jack," nodded Captain Brook, "and a bloody business it was; the enemy's ships being crammed to bursting with soldiers for his projected invasion of Jamaica. As you may have heard tell, my Lord Rodney made naval history by deliberately disrupting his own line of battle to break clean through the enemy centre. This new manœuvre enabled us to get to windward of the French and encircle five of their biggest ships, including the *Ville de Paris*, in which Admiral de Grasse was flying his flag. After a monstrous gruelling he hauled down the flag of France with his own hands and surrendered himself to Hood on the *Barfleur*. Rodney then called off the fight, and although we took four prizes, in Hood's view had we kept at them we might have taken many more. So, although a fine victory, 'twas not so conclusive as Quiberon Bay, where I served as gunnery Lieutenant of the middle deck in *Augusta*. I count Lord Hawke's action there in 'fifty-nine as our greatest naval victory since the Armada; it gave us undisputed command of the seas for a decade."

"Those were the days!" muttered old Sir Harry reminiscently. " 'Twas in the same year that General Wolfe's victory at Quebec secured Canada to us, and but two years earlier that Lord Clive had bested the French at Plassey. By 'sixty-one both the Mogul Empire and the Americas were ours, and we had naught to fear from any man."

"The cause of our late disaster, Sir, is not far to seek," put in Mr. Gibbon. "Had not the King's rebellious subjects in what they are now pleased to term the United States forced a war upon us and engaged our forces overseas, the French and their allies would not have dared once more to challenge our supremacy for another decade at least."

"Oh, come, Sir," cried Mr. Robbins, "The American war was a thing apart, and the Colonists had right on their side in their contention that they should not be subject to taxation without representation in our Parliament."

"That contention, Sir, was both illegal and impractical," boomed back Mr. Gibbon. "The time and distance separating the two continents would have made representation in our legislature of little value. Moreover, it is ancient practice that the distant Provinces of an Empire should in part bear the financial burden of their own defence. We had but recently preserved the New Englanders from falling under the tyranny of the French who, at that time, were dominant in Canada and a constant menace to them, so I count their refusal to accept that just liability as base ingratitude; an opinion which is shared by no less erudite and thoughtful men than Dr. Samuel Johnson and Mr. John Wesley."

"Yet, Lord Chatham, Mr. Burke, Mr. Fox and Mr. Walpole were all against you, Sir," said Sam Oviatt, "and the City of London so opposed to this taking up of arms against our kin that they refused to vote funds for the war."

"As for Mr. Wesley, Sir," said the Vicar truculently, "you can scarce expect those of us who are loyal to the Church Established to attach much weight to the opinions of such a firebrand."

"On the contrary, Sir," hit back Mr. Gibbon acidly, "You and your brethren would do well to adapt yourselves to many of the precepts of that great preacher's teaching unless you wish to lose what little credit is still left to you. In the past forty years his Methodism has gained such a legion of converts that unless you bestir yourselves the movement bids fair to deprive you all of your congregations."

Seeing that tempers were rising Captain Brook intervened. "There is much to be said on both sides. The real tragedy lay in our Government's failure to compose the quarrel in its early stages, as could so easily have been done."

"Aye," agreed Harry Darby, "and the blame for that lies with the King, whose wish to rule us as an autocratic monarch caused him to ignore all sager counsels and entrust the Government to a weakling like my Lord North, solely because he knew that he could make a catspaw of him."

"True enough!" chimed in Captain Burrard, "The King's crazy pig-headedness has been the root of all our troubles."

Mr. Gibbon frowned. "Crazy pig-headedness, Sir, is a strange term to apply to one who has the courage of his convictions, when those convictions have the support of law, the undeniable rights of sovereignty and also form the opinion of the great majority of a people. The Colonists' defiance of Parliament shocked the nation and by the election of 'seventy-four it clearly confirmed the King in his policy."

"The King has a long purse and there are always a plenitude of pocket Boroughs for sale," laughed Captain Burrard.

"Say what you will, Sir," retorted Mr. Gibbon, "Unlike the first two Georges, the King is by birth, education and inclination, an Englishman. Affairs of state are no longer subject to the corrupt and venal influence exercised by German harlots and from the inception of his reign King George III has ever placed what he considers to be the true interests of England before all else."

"Aye, the King's well enough," nodded Captain Brook, "and 'twas Lord North's mismanagement that so embittered the Colonists. They would have been content with their early successes and glad enough to patch up the quarrel had he not offered the negro slaves their freedom if they enlisted with us, and despatched Hessian troops to fight against our own flesh and blood."

Sir Harry Burrard banged the table with his fist. "You've hit

23

upon it, Chris! That was the crowning blunder of them all, and well do I remember the Great Commoner's attack upon the Government at the time, when he thundered 'You have ransacked every corner of Lower Saxony, but forty thousand German boors never can conquer ten times that number of British freemen.' And he was right."

"Yet, 'twas Lord Chatham himself who two years later opposed the Duke of Richmond's motion to withdraw all forces by sea and land from the revolted provinces," countered Mr. Gibbon.

"I grant you that, Sir, and I well remember that occasion, too, since 'twas my Lord Chatham's dying speech and he collapsed but a half hour later. I was again in the Lords gallery at the time, and although it is all of five years ago I recall his words as well as if he'd spoke them yesterday. 'Shall we,' he asked, 'tarnish the lustre of this nation by an ignominious surrender of its rights and fairest possessions? Shall a people that fifteen years ago was the terror of the world now stoop so low as to tell its ancient, inveterate enemy—take all we have, only give us peace.' But remember, Sir, he spoke them in a very different case. The French were about to intervene on behalf of General Washington and the thought of a European conflict being added to our woes had caused something near to panic. Lord Chatham would have supported my Lord North in making any terms with the Americans, short of giving them their independence, since to do so at that juncture would only have laid us open to other so-called, 'positively last demands' by the French. How could he, to whose leadership we owed our splendid victories over them in the Seven Years' War, refrain from rising, even from a bed of death, to protest against such ignominious folly?"

"Yet his Grace of Richmond had wisdom on his side," argued Mr. Eddie. "The extension of the war in 'seventy-eight compelled us to evacuate Philadelphia in order to protect New York and defend the Indies from the French; and our case became even worse when the Spaniards, too, came in against us in 'seventy-nine."

" 'Twas worse still in 'eighty," added General Cleveland, "when our blockade had maddened the Russians, Swedes, Prussians, Danes and Austrians into a common policy of armed neutrality against us, and the Dutch added themselves to our active enemies."

"Nay, General," Captain Brook took him up quickly, "I pray you say nothing against the blockade. 'Tis England's greatest weapon. With it we've many times brought the Continent to reason and under Providence will do so many times again."

The old General grunted. "Let us pray then that should such a case arise we'll have no major conflict raging overseas. Since, saving your presence, Captain, 'twas bad naval strategy and naught else that lost us our fairest possessions in America."

"That I contest, Sir, and, saving yours, I count the Army more to blame. On no less than four occasions our Generals bungled badly. At the very outset of the war General Gage locked himself up in Boston for eleven months instead of engaging the Colonists before they could become organised. Then in 'seventy-six, had they been active, Generals Howe and Cornwallis could have crushed Washington between them;

but they frittered away their opportunity. In both 'seventy-seven and 'eighty-one, had two large British forces not dallied but made their junction on the Hudson, as was intended, they could have cut off the North from the South and so still preserved the Southern Colonies to the Crown. Yet, as we know, their dilatoriness resulted, in the first case, in General Burgoyne being trapped and compelled to surrender at Saratoga and, in the second, in General Cornwallis laying down his arms at Yorktown, and with them our last hope of victory. Had we had a Commander of General Washington's quality on our side I am convinced that the conflict would have ended very differently."

"I admit that there was some misdirection in the early stages," the General agreed, "but Cornwallis out-generalled and defeated Washington on numerous occasions; and you have ill-served your case by referring to the surrender that was forced upon him. He deployed his Army in the Yorktown peninsular for the sound purpose of being able readily to reinforce New York. Had the British Fleet not dallied in the Indies, no French battle squadron could have occupied Chesapeake Bay, and enabled Washington's Army to achieve a junction with General Lafayette by landing on the neck of the peninsular."

"The Fleet cannot be everywhere at once, Sir," protested the Captain.

"No, Sir," the General rapped back, "but it should be at the right place at the right time; and its first duty in war is to protect the lines of communication of the Army."

"Would you have had us then let the French have the Indies for the taking and leave the shores of Britain unprotected? We had to contend with the fleets of no less than four enemy powers, remember, and in that year we both hammered the Dutch off the Dogger Bank and relieved General Elliot at Gibraltar."

"God forbid that I should impugn the Navy's gallantry, Captain. I contend only that its strategy was ill-designed. Our Admirals followed a policy of dealing with local attacks as and when they occurred instead of seeking out the enemy fleets to destroy them, and the dispersion of our sea forces proved our undoing."

"I am with General Cleveland in that," declared Mr. Gibbon. "Our Army made no great showing, yet it would not have been reduced to asking for terms had not the Navy failed it at a critical time. Nevertheless our host's excuse is valid, in that our preoccupation in Europe and particularly with Gibraltar, were given first place by the Government. It has been very truly said that 'to save a rock we lost a continent,' but no blame for that can be laid to either service."

Mr. Gibbon's diplomatic summary saved the faces of both protagonists. The tension eased and the Captain laughed. "I am well content to leave it at that; and at least we can all agree that Lord Rodney's victory at the Saints, by restoring our supremacy at sea, enabled us to make none too bad a peace."

"Indeed, without it, we would have been hard put to it to obtain terms at all," said Sam Oviatt. "As it is we have come off monstrous well. The loss of the Colonies is a thing apart, but giving up St. Lucia,

Tobago and Goree to France, and Minorca and Florida to Spain, is little enough to pay for the consolidation of our position in Canada and India and all our other gains."

"For that a good share of thanks are due to Lord Shelburne's fine diplomacy," remarked Sir Harry.

Captain Brook turned quickly to him. "Yet he was forced from office after only a few months, and when I was in London I heard it said that the Coalition is far from secure."

"Its fall at any time would not surprise me," Sir Harry answered. "The King is still determined to rule the roost. After twelve years of virtual dictatorship, through Lord North, he can hardly be resigned to allowing power to slip from his grasp; and since the country demanded North's dismissal the fleeting Ministries of the past seventeen months have been little more than experiments. The Marquess of Rockingham's death last summer alone made way for Shelburne, whom the King neither liked or trusted, and he likes the Coalition even less. He shares the national disgust at his old minister having entered into this unnatural partnership with the man who has been his bitterest critic for so many years and will, I am convinced, have them both out of office as soon as a suitable pretext presents itself. His real problem is to find a man malleable to his own interest who will yet prove of sufficient stature to dominate the House. 'Tis reported that with this in mind he even offered young Billy Pitt the Treasury before reconciling himself to accepting Mr. Fox. That Pitt refused the offer is to his credit. At least he had the sense to see that the House would give short shift to anyone so lacking in experience."

"I consider it more likely that it was not lack of self-confidence but astuteness that caused Pitt to reject office for a time," remarked Mr. Gibbon. "From all I have seen of him he shows exceptional promise. His grasp of business is at times uncanny for one of his years, his repartee is scathing and his oratory is superb."

Sir Harry nodded. "He speaks monstrous well, I grant you, and in that he is my Lord Chatham's son without a doubt. I recall his maiden speech when he first took his seat in the House at the age of twenty-one. One of our oldest members said of it 'There was not a word or a gesture that one would have sought to correct' and Mr. Burke, seated nearby me, remarked, 'He is not a chip of the old block, but the old block itself.' "

"Then, should we be forced to take up arms against the French, may he play as glorious a part as did his great father," said Captain Brook. "But come, gentlemen, 'tis time we joined the ladies."

They had been sitting over their wine for the best part of an hour and a half, so it was now close on half-past eight and dusk was falling. Squire Robbins and Harry Darby, who were a little unsteady on their pins, excused themselves, but the others trooped into Lady Marie's cool green and white drawing-room, where the conversation took a lighter tone and local gossip was mingled with talk of charities and entertainments.

Soon after nine, Mrs. Sutherland declared for home, and her leaving was the signal for the breaking up of the party. The Sutherlands walked back across the meadow to their house up in the High Street, and the Vicar went with them, while old Ben, now flushed from his exertions as host these past two hours to a dozen visiting servants in the kitchen, summoned the carriages and horses of their masters. Invitations were poured upon the Brooks from all sides, then with a cheerful shouting of good-byes, their guests drove or rode away.

By a quarter to ten, father, mother and son were at last alone and reassembled in Lady Marie's drawing-room.

"It's been a great homecoming, Chris," she smiled, "and you can see now how your friends have missed you."

The Captain swayed slightly on his feet. He was not drunk but his long years at sea had left him out of training for such heavy drinking, and he had had a little more than he could carry comfortably. He was smiling broadly, and declared with a laugh:

"The best is yet to come, m'dear. I've two fine surprises for you."

"Oh, tell us, do," she leaned eagerly forward in her chair, and Roger added his urging.

"You'd never guess," the Captain grinned. " 'Tis far more than I hoped for, as I thought myself forgot after my long absence from home, and I said nothing of it to the company as it may be a month or more before it appears in the *Gazette*. But I'm to fly my flag. Their Lordships have made me a Rear-Admiral."

"Chris! Is it really true? Oh, how prodigious fine!" Lady Marie jumped up and kissed him on his flushed cheek.

"Hurrah!" cried Roger, "Three cheers for Admiral Brook! Hurrah! Hurrah! Hurrah!"

Not wishing to make a fool of himself he had gone as carefully as he could with the wine, but having been granted the status of a man, he had also not liked to appear less than one by passing the port untouched too frequently. So he too, had had as much as he could carry, as was evident from his flushed face and unnaturally bright eyes.

"But you said you had two surprises for us," Lady Marie went on. "I can scarce bear the suspense to hear the other. Is it that they've given you a ship of ninety-eight guns to fly your flag in?"

"Nay," replied the Captain. " 'Tis something that I value more. With me I brought despatches from the Indies and the First Lord did me the honour to instruct me to lay them personally before His Majesty."

"What! You actually talked with the King?" exclaimed Roger.

His father put an arm affectionately round the boy's shoulders. "Aye, lad, and he was mighty civil to me; so I took the bull by the horns and went in to the attack. I asked him for a commission for you, and, praise God, he was graciously pleased to grant it to me there and then."

The blood drained from Roger's face. In the excitement of the last few hours he had temporarily forgotten his own anxiety, and the bomb now exploded beneath his feet with startling suddenness.

Lady Marie too, paled a little, but for a different reason. She knew that Roger was averse to the sea as a career, but thought his attitude no more than the unreasoning prejudice of a boy, that could soon be overcome; and her husband's wishes were to her the law. Yet Roger was her only child and she was most loath to part with him at such an early age and see him in future only at long intervals.

"So Roger will not be returning to Sherborne next term?" she said slowly.

The Captain gave him a hearty slap on the back. "Nay. His school days are over, and he'll be posted as a midshipman on the recommissioning of one of our ships now in dock within the next month or two. Well, Roger, hast thou naught to say?"

"Indeed, I'm very grateful, Sir—both to you and to His Majesty," Roger managed to stammer.

Captain Brook's perceptions were too blunted by the wine he had consumed to note the lack of enthusiasm in Roger's tone, and he hurried on: "Next week we'll go into Portsmouth and see to the ordering of your kit. You'll cut a brave figure in a uniform and all the gels will be casting sheep's eyes at you." He converted a mild belch into a yawn. "But enough for now. 'Tis time we sought our beds. Strap me! but it's good to be home again and see to the locking-up of one's own home for the night.

"I'd best come with you, Sir," Roger volunteered. "A new door has been made to the still-room, since you went away, and 'tis concealed behind a curtain."

Lady Marie led the way out into the spacious hall and, turning, kissed Roger good-night at the foot of the white-painted, semi-circular staircase, then father and son made the round of the ground floor, fastening the shutters, putting up chains and shooting bolts.

As Roger followed his father from room to room, his mind was in a turmoil. The wine and the shock he had sustained had now combined to bemuse his brain and make him feel that he wanted to be sick. On the news of the Captain's return that morning he had thought that at worst he would have several months in which to wage a campaign of resistance against any renewal of the project to send him to sea. His father was both good-natured and affectionate, so by waiting for such times as he was in his most calm and responsive moods it might have been possible to argue him out of it. But the time for seizing such opportunities had now been cut from beneath Roger's feet.

He saw himself within the next few weeks being shipped off like a victim of the press-gangs to a life of slavery in the hideous discomfort inseparable from serving in a man-o'-war. Midshipmen were then treated little better than the sailors before the mast and worked to the limit of their endurance. They took watch for watch and were sent aloft with the hands to help furl the sails, under the blistering tropic sun or in the icy, blinding rain of the worst tempests. The common seamen at least had leisure to yarn, carve models, or laze about in their off-duty hours, but not so the midshipman, who, in the intervals of scrubbing decks, cleaning brass fitments and hauling on great tarry ropes were herded into the ship's schoolroom to receive instruction in navigation, gunnery, trigonometry and ship's management. Their fare was a rarely varied diet of salt pork and hard biscuits washed down with unsweetened lime juice to prevent scurvy; their quarters a single low cabin in which there were constant comings and goings, their sleep limited to three and three-quarter hours at any one time before they were roughly woken to roll out of their dirty blankets and scamper up the ladders for the muster of a new duty-watch on deck. They were kept on the run from morning to night and for half the night semi-frozen while acting as look-outs in the crow's nest high above the ship. Their title of "Mister" was a mockery; the officers were as far above them as the gods and it was considered that the harder the tasks they were given the better officers they would make later on. Bugle calls and the ship's bell ruled their every hour; they had no privacy or recreations and were bullied unmercifully.

Knowing all this Roger was engulfed in a black wave of despair, yet felt that he would rather die than submit to such a fate. Blindly he followed his father's unsteady footsteps from room to room, seeking a way out but finding none. His alcohol-laden brain refused to work although it was seething with revolt. At length they reached the conservatory on the west side of the house. A dim light filtering through from the hall was enough to show the glass double-doors leading out to the orchard, but it was now pitch dark outside. Admiral Brook had walked forward to lock the door, when Roger suddenly exclaimed in a choking voice:

"Sir, may I speak with you for a moment?"

"Yes. What is it, Roger?" the Admiral flung cheerfully over his shoulder.

"This Commission, Sir, I've no wish for it."

"What's that!" The Admiral swung round and peered at him in the uncertain light. "What didst thou say? Surely I can't have heard aright?"

Only his half-drunken state had given Roger the courage to take the plunge but, having taken it, he hurried on. "I'm sorry to disappoint you, Sir, seeing you're so set on it, but I don't want to take up this Commission."

"In God's name, why?" gasped the Admiral in blank astonishment.

"I—I've a dozen reasons, Sir," Roger stammered now. "I don't want to go to sea. I—I——"

"You're drunk, boy," exclaimed his father, sharply. "You don't know what you're saying. Get to bed this minute."

"I'm not drunk, Sir," Roger protested. "At least, not so drunk as all that. I made up my mind years ago. I'd hate the life, I swear I would. I pray you don't force me to it."

"So this is what an expensive schooling has done for you!" His father was angry now. "Or is it lack of discipline because I've been so long from home? How dare you question my decisions. I know what's best for you. Get to bed now and let's hear no more of this."

"Please!" Roger begged, "Please! You must remember your own days as a midshipman. You've often told me how they worked you until you were often almost asleep on your feet. And of the cold and the storms and the bullying."

"Bah! That's nothing. You'll soon get used to it and come to love it."

"I shan't, Sir. I've dreaded this for years and I'll loathe every moment of it."

"Hell's bells, what schoolgirl vapourings!" the Admiral cried in a fury. "Am I but come home to find that I have a coward for a son?"

"I'm not a coward, Sir. I'll take on any fellow of my own weight, but I don't want to go to sea."

"D'you dare to stand there and defy me?"

Roger was white to the gills and feeling desperately sick again, but the gross injustice of disposing of him against his will had driven him, too, into a fury.

"Yes, since I must," he cried. "It's my life and I'll not be condemned to a slavery worse than the plantations. I won't go to sea, and you shan't make me."

"God!" roared the Admiral, "Such insolence as this is something I never dreamed to meet, and for it I'll leather the hide off you." Suiting the action to the word he snatched up a cane from a potted plant and thrust out a hand to grab Roger by the collar.

Roger dodged the blow by stepping sideways and, in the semi-darkness, the Admiral tripped over some large flower-pots that were standing on the tiled floor. He fell among them with a clatter but was up again in a moment and made another grab at Roger with a hearty curse.

" 'Tis discipline you need, you presumptuous young fool and I'm the man to give it to you. I'll soon show you who is master in this ship."

Next moment he had Roger by the scruff of the neck and forcing him over brought the cane down with a resounding wallop on his buttocks.

Roger let out a yell and tensed himself for another blow, but it did not come. While the stick was still raised in mid-air, the Admiral's action was arrested by three sharp, clear knocks that came out on the night on one of the panes of the conservatory door.

CHAPTER IV

THE MAKING OF A MAN

F o r a moment they remained as inanimate as though posed in *tableau vivant*, then with a muttered curse the Admiral released his hold on Roger and, turning, strode to the door. It was still unlocked and pulling it open he stared out into the warm darkness of the summer night.

A tall, bearded figure stood there and the Admiral's eyes, already accustomed to the gloom of the conservatory, swiftly took in the knitted stocking cap, woollen jersey, leather breeches and heavy seaboots of his belated visitor.

"E'en" Cap'n," said the man in a gruff voice, "Hearin' ye was back from the wars I thought ye could do with a keg of the best."

"Why, Dan!" exclaimed the Admiral, "I scarce knew you for the moment, but 'twas good of you to think of me. What have you brought us, brandy or schnapps?"

The smuggler tapped with his boot the little two-gallon cask that he had set down beside him. " 'Tis French cognac, and none better ever came out of the Charente."

The smuggling of wines, spirits, lace and perfume from France had been rife for the past eighty years—ever since Lord Methuen had imposed such heavy discriminating duties against the French that the British people, resenting them as an unjust imposition, had resorted to openly flouting the law and become ready buyers of illegal cargoes. For sheep stealing, a man could still be hanged and the sentences inflicted on poachers were often of a barbarous ferocity, but, despite the utmost pressure of the Government, no bench of magistrates would convict a smuggler, however strong the evidence against him.

The Admiral had now got back his breath and his good humour. "How fares it with you, these days?" he asked. "Is the old game as beset with pitfalls as ever, or are the Excise men grown slack?"

Dan Izzard shook his massive head and the gold earrings in his ears glinted in the half-light. " 'Twas easier while the war were on, Cap'n. Most o' the revenue cutters were impressed for the Navy then, but now they're freed ag'in they're doing their darnedest to put us down."

"So the war was good for business, then?"

"Aye! Wars make no difference to the likes o' us on either side o' the Channel. An' all open trading being cut off put prices up. 'Tis fine pickings we've had these past few years, but a man has to take his life in his hands to run a cargo now the fighting's over."

Roger knew Dan well, but although he was now standing close behind his father he scarcely took in what they were saying. He felt ghastly and the conservatory seemed to be rolling round him as distressingly as if it were Dan's lugger in a heavy sea.

The Admiral stooped and tilting the little cask rolled it in through the open doorway, as he said: "Well, thanks, Dan. Look in and see me any time you're passing, and I'll settle up with you."

"Aye, aye, Cap'n, I'll do that. But 'twon't be for a day or two, as 'tis overlong since I made a trip. Good-night to 'e."

As the door closed Roger drew back, fearing a renewed assault from his father; and he had good cause to do so, as the Admiral suddenly said with cold wrath: "And now, Sir, I'll deal with you!"

At that instant Roger lurched forward, grasped uncertainly at the wooden staging on which stood several rows of pots, and was violently sick.

Baffled, the Admiral stared at him. He could hardly give the boy a leathering while in such a state. After a moment he turned away to bolt the door, and muttered angrily: "Oh, get to bed. I'll teach you manners in the morning."

Stuffing his handkerchief in his mouth, Roger slunk away and stumbled up to his room.

Having been up at four and it now being two hours past his usual bedtime, neither the tempestuous scene nor his unhappy physical state kept him long awake. After rinsing out his mouth, and sponging his face with cold water he pulled off his clothes and flopped into bed. Ten minutes later he was sound asleep.

From habit he woke soon after dawn and, but for a slight heaviness in his head, felt little the worse for his violent emotions of the previous night. When he had washed, dressed and done his brown hair as was his custom, by combing it off his forehead and tying the ends with a bow at the back of his neck, he left his room and went up by a short flight of steps to the roof.

That of the newer portion of the house had two triangular eaves filling the bulk of a square, but a leaded walk ran right round them and a breast-high parapet concealed the eaves from anyone looking up from the gardens below. It was a good place to laze if one favoured solitude on a sunny day and the views from it provided a never-failing interest.

To the north, farther up the slope, lay the gardens and backs of the largest houses of the old town, in which some activity was always to be seen; to the west lay open, wooded country and to the east, beyond the double row of limes that formed the drive up to the house, lay the little harbour. But the most engaging prospect was to the south. There, through low-lying meadows and mud-flats, where in spring innumerable gulls' eggs were to be had for the collecting, the river Lym wound its way to the Solent. Across the three-mile-wide stretch of open water rose the island, sometimes so sharply visible that one felt one had only to reach out to touch it with the hand and the jetties of Yarmouth were easily discernible to the naked eye, at others with its heights shrouded in mist, so that only its tree-clad foreshore was visible and it took on the appearance of some mysterious jungle coast in a tropical sea.

This morning there was a faint haze which gave promise of another glorious day. Roger could see Hurst Castle on the low-lying spit that jutted out from the mainland, but he could only just discern Worsley's Tower, opposite it on the island. There, the Solent was at its narrowest and for over a thousand years it had been the ill-omened road to the invasion of England. Vespasian had made the crossing in his galleys before capturing Lymington and launching his Roman legions on their conquest of Britain. Right up to Queen Elizabeth's time the French had frequently held the vulnerable island for months at a stretch, and from it despatched forays that had pillaged and burnt the coast towns as far west as Devon.

It was for that reason that Baldwin de Redvers, second Earl of Devon and feudal lord of Lymington, finding this little outpost of his vast domains too expensive to defend, had granted the town its freedom in the year 1150, thus making it one of the first free Boroughs in all England. But for the past two centuries, despite frequent periods of acute alarm, the Burgesses had remained safe behind the shield of the Royal Navy; and day in day out all through the year the vista was now a never-failing reminder that the power of Britain was based upon the sea. Brigs and brigantines, frigates, sloops and great three-deckers were ever to be seen as they tacked and veered on their way to protect our commerce in distant seas, or bringing the wealth that was the envy of the world to England's shores.

But to-day, Roger had no eyes for the barque that was beating to seaward against the gentle sou'-westerly wind. Plunged in misery, his lively imagination was already conjuring up the dreaded interview with his father that was to come. That he was in for a licking, and a hard one, he had no doubt at all. It would be worse too than the spontaneous beating with a bamboo that he has escaped the previous night, since, now that he was on the way to being fully grown, his father would take a whip to him and not spare his blows. That was a foregone and nerve-shaking conclusion, but what was to befall after the licking had been administered? Should he humbly retract or risk further punishment by sticking to his guns?

He felt terribly alone and wished desperately that he had someone with whom he could talk over his wretched plight. It was useless to go to his mother for, much as she loved and would be sorry for him, she adored his father to distraction and considered that his every decision was for the best. Jack Bond of Buckland, Roger's best friend, had not yet returned from Eton, and Dick Eddie of Priestlands was, so he had learned the day before, down with the smallpox. He knew a number of other boys in the neighbourhood but did not feel that any of them were intimate enough friends to fill his present need.

It was then that Georgina Thursby crossed his mind. It would never have occurred to him to go to any ordinary girl for sympathy and support in such a crisis, but Georgina was very far from being an ordinary girl. The Thursbys played no part in local society, for a very good reason, and Roger was the only neighbour who ever visited their house. He had first met Georgina out riding alone in the forest, some two years previously; in itself a most unusual thing for a young girl to be allowed to do, but the Thursbys were a law unto themselves. Roger had struck up an acquaintance with her which had soon ripened into a warm friendship. She was, he knew, a bare-faced coquette, vain, self-willed and tempestuous, but Colonel Thursby had no other children and the solitary existence that she led, uncontrolled by any women, had made her boyish in her outlook, forthright in her opinions and courageous in her acts.

The more Roger thought of Georgina the more certain he felt that she would understand and with her quick mind even, perhaps, find some way out for him. His father had named no hour for the dreaded interview and was still abed. There was nothing to prevent his leaving the house and he was not even called on to let the servants know where he had gone. To ride over to the Thursbys now would at least be a respite from the ordeal of meeting his parents at a silent and sultry breakfast table. Turning, he made his way cautiously downstairs and out to the stables, saddled his mare himself and trotting up the lane to the town took the road to Highcliffe.

A seven-mile ride brought him to his destination. The name applied not to a village but the district in which lay the castle where Lord Bute, the King's ex-tutor and minister, was spending his declining years, and a number of scattered houses. Highcliffe Manor, in which the Thursbys lived, was a comfortable cream-brick mansion with large double mullioned windows looking out on to a well-kept lawn and gardens. The house itself did not stand on high ground but its location could be fixed for many miles in any direction, owing to what was locally regarded as an eccentric foible of the Colonel's. He was much interested in all new inventions and to test the strength of iron bars, as opposed to wooden beams, as a framework for building had, a few years earlier, erected in that medium a tower a hundred and fifty feet in height, at no great distance from his house. There, tall, thin and square, it reared up from a naked field but it now provided a fine landmark for ships out at sea and the whole surrounding countryside.

As Roger entered the hall Colonel Thursby was just coming down-stairs to breakfast, and he at once invited the visitor to join them. The Colonel was a thin-faced, studious-looking man in the middle fifties. He did not look in the least like a soldier and, in fact, had only been one in his youth because a wealthy father had bought him a Lt.-Colonelcy. On his father's death he had promptly sold it and spent several years in travelling, visiting even such distant places as Turkey and Russia. On his return he had fallen violently in love with a beautiful girl who was then the toast of the county and, to the delight of all their acquaintances, married her. But their happiness had been short-lived. One night an overturned candle had set the curtains of the poor girl's bed alight and she had been burned to death before anyone could come to her assistance.

For some months the Colonel had shut himself up, refusing all consolation. Then scandalous rumours had begun to circulate. It was said that he had a gipsy girl living in the house. With the easy morality of the times none of his neighbours would have condemned him for endeavouring to console himself with a pretty mistress, though it was thought in ill taste to keep the woman in the home to which he had only eighteen months before brought his young bride; but when a few months later he openly announced that he had married the gipsy, the depths of their disapproval were beyond plumbing.

Henceforth the Colonel was ostracised by all who had known him, and to complete his apparent discomfiture, his gipsy wife had died in bringing a daughter into the world. Actually he was little affected by the county's condemnation, since he was richer than most of his neighbours, spent much of his time in London and—as he had never been a sporting man—when at his country home was perfectly content to amuse himself pottering in his well-stocked garden or browsing among his fine collection of books.

If anyone had suffered it was his daughter, since, even when she reached her teens, he had made no attempt to reopen social relations with his neighbours on her account and, although many of them were sorry for the motherless girl, they felt that it was not for them to take the first step.

Yet Georgina would not have had matters otherwise. She was shrewd enough to know that had local society been open to her she would have had to accept the authority of a governess, and been expected to conform to the simpering manners and unexciting lady-like pursuits of her contemporaries. Her father was wealthy, generous and a man of taste. He ordered her clothes in London, so that her wardrobe put those of the local belles to shame, and had provided her with an education far above that of the average girl of her age by the simple process of long intimate talks and encouraging her to read widely, no book in his library being barred to her.

The Colonel had scarcely given orders for Roger's mare to be taken round to the stables when there came a cry of delight from behind them. Turning, he saw Georgina, as fresh and pretty as a red rose with the morning dew still on it, come running down the staircase and with his three-cornered hat still in his hand he made her a most gallant leg.

She was now seventeen, over a year older than Roger, and well developed for her age. It is doubtful if, when they first met, she would have bothered with him but for her instinctive urge to captivate every male she set her black eyes upon, and the fact that he filled the need she unconsciously felt for a companion who could share her youthful enthusiasms. She had inherited the dark, lush beauty, big dewy eyes and full ripe mouth of her gipsy mother; had a splendid figure and a graceful freedom of carriage born of unrestrained activity in the open air. She rode like a female centaur, swam like a dryad and could climb trees with the agility of a monkey.

Roger was not in love with her but the feelings she aroused in him were as near love as he had so far got. He admired her dark beauty and at times was conscious of an uneasy feeling when he touched her; but she was too abrupt in her changes of mood and too dominating a personality to fit into his vague imaginings, which centred round a dreamy, fair-haired blue-eyed, creature reclining indolently on a settee. His attachment to her was much more in the nature of an honest comradeship, yet flavoured with a romantic desire to be her champion against the slight that he felt her neighbours had put upon her.

Georgina fully reciprocated the comradeship and accepted his awkward attempts at chivalry with secret mirth. She was, however, fully conscious that he was an embryo man and, for lack of more mature material to practise on, took delight in trying out his reactions to her latest toilettes and, on rare occasions, seeking to see how near she could get to rousing his apparently dormant passions.

Those passions were actually by no means so dormant as she supposed. Roger had little left to learn theoretically about the tender passion and had so far refrained from its practice only on account of a certain fastidiousness. In those days of easy morals no one thought the worse of a youngster for giving free rein to his budding desires, providing he did not attempt his friends' sisters, and there were few country girls who did not consider it an honour to be seduced by a son of the quality. Roger knew half a dozen boys of his own age at Sherborne who had found willing initiators into the mysteries in their mother's maids, and one much-admired young coxcomb who had even successfully invaded the bed of his married cousin.

But Roger, having toyed with the idea of both Polly and Nell during his last holidays, had decided to wait until he came across a young girl of less buxom charms and one who would prove more mentally exciting. As far as Georgina was concerned he knew that to think of her in that way was to play with fire, and, since he placed her automatically in the same category as he would have one of his friend's sisters, he rarely allowed himself to do so.

Yet now, as they all went into the dining-room, he could not help remarking how much more beautiful she seemed to have become since he had last seen her, and the laughter in her wicked dark eyes gave him a sudden half-guilty thrill.

The dining-room was furnished with the new tulip-wood which was just then coming into fashion and the two sideboards were laden, one with half a dozen hot dishes, the other with a cold ham, pig's face and crystal bowls of peaches, nectarines, apricots and grapes from Colonel Thursby's glass-houses.

The Colonel and Roger helped themselves lavishly, but after surveying the tempting array uncertainly for a moment, Georgina declared with a pout: "The very sight of food so early in the day gives me the vapours. 'Twill be as much as I can do to face a bowl of bread and milk."

Roger looked at her in astonishment, but the Colonel gave him a sly wink. "See, Roger, what a London season has done for your old playfellow. Had we had notice of your coming, I vow she would have had her hair dressed a foot high and used a sack of flour upon it; 'tis only overnight that she has lost that fine appetite of hers."

Then he turned to his daughter and gave her a friendly slap on the behind. "Don't be a fool, girl, or you'll be famished by mid-morning. Pretend to live on air when you're in London, if you will, but spare us these conceits here in the country."

Georgina suddenly burst out laughing. "Oh, well, give me some salmon pasty then, and an egg; but no bacon; the fat makes me queasy, and that's the truth."

Roger had been so occupied with his own concerns that he had temporarily forgotten that Georgina must have only just returned from her first London season, and so now should be definitely regarded as grown up. With a smile he asked her how she had enjoyed herself.

" 'Twas a riot," she declared, enthusiastically. "Balls, routs and conversaziones tumbled a-top of each other with a swiftness you'd scarce credit possible. For all of ten weeks I was never up before midday or abed before two in the morning."

"I wonder you didn't die of your exertions, but I must say you look none the worse for it," remarked her father. " 'Tis your poor aunt that I was sorry for, though. I wouldn't have had the chaperoning of you for a mint of money."

Georgina shrugged. "Since you paid her five hundred guineas to take me out, and footed the bill for her to present that milk-sop daughter of hers into the bargain, she has no cause to complain."

"Was Queen Charlotte's drawing-room as splendid as accounts of it lead one to believe?" asked Roger.

" 'Twas a truly marvellous spectacle. All the gentlemen in their fine uniforms and the ladies with tiaras and great ostrich feathers in their hair. And you should have heard the buzz when I made my curtsy. I near died of gratification."

Her father glanced at her with unconcealed pride. "Yes, you certainly took the town by storm; 'tis not many girls who become one of the reigning toasts in their first season."

"You did not lack for beaux, then?" Roger said, feeling a distinct twinge of jealousy.

"Lud, no!" she laughed. "I had a score of proposals, and am half committed to three young bucks; but I doubt if I'll take any of them."

"What did you enjoy most—apart from all these flirtations?" inquired Roger, with a faintly malicious grin.

Her black eyes sparkled. " 'Tis hard to say. The ball father gave for me at our own house in Bedford Square was a roaring success. Then there was our grand day at the Derby, where I won twenty guineas. I loved His Grace of Queensberry's water party down at Richmond, and the night we all went masked to Vauxhall Gardens. But I think my most prodigious thrill, apart from my presentation, was to see Mrs. Siddons play Lady Macbeth at His Majesty's theatre in Drury Lane."

For half an hour she rattled on, dazzling Roger with descriptions of the great world as yet beyond his ken, then her father left them to go out and see his gardeners.

"Well! How shall we spend the day?" she asked, after a pause to regain her breath. "Shall we ride in the forest, go down the cliff and provide a fresh scandal for the neighbours by bathing from the beach, or take luncheon up to our old haunt in the tower?"

Roger had intended only to spend an hour with her and then return to face his irate parent, but the more he thought of doing so the more unnerving the prospect became. The gravity of the issue was such that his father's anger could scarcely be increased whatever he did now; so he decided that he might as well be hung for a sheep as a lamb and spend the day with Georgina, as she obviously expected him to do.

From his ride through the forest on the previous day he knew that the flies were now hatching out in such numbers as to prove irksome during a picnic. The promised heat of the day made a swim sound attractive, and he cared little for the fact that for a young man to bathe with a fully grown girl was frowned upon, but the tower offered the best prospect of a long talk entirely free of any possibility of interruptions, so, after a moment, he voted for it.

Although they had only just finished breakfast Georgina went off to the kitchen to procure supplies; since it entailed no small effort to climb the three hundred odd stairs to the little room at the top of the tower and, once there, to descend and reascend for any purpose would have been a foolish waste of time and energy.

A quarter of an hour later she rejoined him in the garden and as she came towards him across the lawn, a well-laden basket over her arm, he thought how seductive she was looking. As always, except when about to go out riding, she was wearing more diaphanous clothes than were usual in the country. A full skirt of sprigged India muslin billowed about her legs and, as the gentle breeze pressed it against her, gave a hint of the shapely limbs beneath it. The sleeves were cut very wide, showing her well-made brown arms to the elbows and a double fichu goffered of white organdie crossed on her breast accentuated the outline of her rounded bosom.

Roger took the basket from her and a few minutes' walk brought them to the base of the tower. Square and unornamented it rose starkly to the sky, the small round cupola which crowned it no longer visible from where they stood. Georgina led the way in through its narrow door, and they began the ascent.

The stairs were narrow and the atmosphere abominably stuffy, being relieved only by air holes consisting of narrow slits at every twenty feet, through which no more than a glimpse could be obtained of the surrounding country. Three times on the way up they paused, hot and panting, to regain their breath, but at last they came out into the turret chamber.

It was a small square apartment, large enough only to contain a brocaded settee, two chairs and a table, but its windows provided an outlook that was probably unrivalled in southern England. Inland. Meadows and cornfields were spread below them, merging into forest and heath, as far as the eye could reach, finally to blend with the sky in purple distances; while to seaward the white coast-line from Durlston Head, beyond Poole, to St. Catherine's Point, at the southern extremity of the Isle of Wight, lay unrolled to their gaze like some gargantuan map; and the white sails of ships could be seen far out at sea.

They knew that the tower was quite safe, although it always seemed to sway slightly as the wind moaned round its top in winter and summer alike. Yet this, and being so far above the earth, had never failed to give them a rather queer feeling ever since they had come to favour it as a retreat on account of its absolute privacy. Since Colonel Thursby received no visitors, no one except themselves ever came there and, even had strangers done so, the echo of their footsteps on the stone stairs would have given warning of their approach at least several minutes before they could have reached the turret chamber. It was, therefore, an ideal place for two young conspirators to make plans and exchange confidences.

Having gazed their fill at the view, they settled themselves side by side on the settee.

"Well, little boy," said Georgina with an air of superiority. "Tell me about yourself? Hast thou done well at thy lessons this term or been the recipient of many birchings?"

"I'm not a little boy," Roger protested hotly, "And don't you try to play the fine lady with me, just because you've been to Court and done a season."

She laughed. "Oh, Roger! Should I live to be a hundred I'll never forgo teasing you, and I vow you'll still rise to it. All the same, you may like it or not, but having been presented makes a woman of me."

"It takes more than that to make a girl into a woman," he scoffed.

"That's as maybe, m'dear, but at all events you can lay no claim yet to being a man."

"Another few weeks will see me one—unless———"

As he broke off her big eyes opened wide. "Unless what? Whatever do you mean?"

"Oh, God!" he burst out. "How much rather I'd remain a boy and be going back to Sherborne!" Then he suddenly buried his face in his hands.

"Why, Roger, dear!" She threw a warm arm round his shoulders and pulled his head down into her lap. "What is it? Do tell me. We've never had any secrets from each other, and never shall."

For a moment, conscious of her soft thigh against his forehead, he allowed that pleasant but disturbing sensation to distract his thoughts, then he muttered: "Of course I'll tell you. It's all right. I'm not blubbering. I'm too scared and angry to do that."

She released him, but seeing his distress, took one of his hands between her own, seeking by their firm pressure to give him strength, as she commanded: "Out with it, now!"

Roger gulped back the tears he had denied, and that neither Gunston nor his father had been able to draw from him. Then, bit by bit, half incoherently at first but graduating to a fierce, steady monologue of pent-up resentment, he poured out to her the story of the day before and the hideous fate that he now felt menaced him.

Her dark eyes fixed intently on him she let him ease himself of his burden without interruption, until he at last fell silent; then she said:

"But Roger, this is monstrous. Can you not appeal to your mother to make your father see reason?"

He shrugged. "My mother thinks more of him than she does of God. She loves me, but she'd never intervene; and 'twould be useless if she tried."

"Your other relatives, then?"

"I have none, except my mother's people whom I've never seen. My father, like myself, was an only son."

"But you cannot submit to this?"

"What other course is open to me?"

"God knows, m'dear; but the injustice of it makes my blood boil."

For the best part of another hour they talked round and round the subject without coming any nearer to a solution. The sun was now well up in the heavens and striking down on the stone cupola of the tower made the turret room close and hot. Roger got up to open one of the windows and stripping off his long-skirted coat flung it over the back of a chair.

They had fallen silent again. The wind had dropped and up there in their eerie no sound reached them from the earth far below. Roger felt, as he had often felt before in the turret, as if he was in a different world that had no connection with the life he knew. There was something God-like in being at that high altitude from which the men working in the fields looked to be no more than pigmies. Time seemed to be standing still, and even the interview that he so dreaded coming no nearer despite the steady mounting of the sun which, with the passing of a few more hours, must inevitably set.

Suddenly Georgina spoke: "Roger! There's but one thing for it. You must run away."

"What's that!" he swung round to stare at her. "Run away! How can I? Where to?"

"Romantic young fools are always running away to sea," she declared. "Why shouldn't you run away from it?"

"But there is nowhere I could go?" he faltered.

She tossed her black ringlets impatiently. "The world is wide and you are strong and healthy. These summer months you might do worse than go to live with the Egyptians in the forest, or you could make your way to London and find some employment there."

"No," he shook his head glumly, " 'tis too drastic a measure that you propose, and the remedy would prove a greater affliction than the illness. By it I'd cease to be all that I am and lose such small advantages as my birth and education give me. I'm determined to make something worth while of my life, and 'twould be the height of folly to throw away the best years of my youth scraping a living as a tinker."

"I don't mean run away for good, stupid, but just for a month or two; until this threat to your happiness has blown over, or your father has been given another ship and ordered back to sea."

For the first time he considered her suggestion seriously and, crossing the narrow room, sat down again beside her.

"I might do that," he murmured. " 'Tis certainly a possibility. But the forest is no good. The Egyptians might have you but they wouldn't have me. They'd think that I'd been sent to spy on them."

"Go to London, then. 'Tis less than a hundred miles and you could walk there in a week."

"Maybe, but I have not a single friend there, or even an acquaintance."

"Had it been last month I could have given you a score of introductions; but, alas! town will now be as empty as a drum and all my friends of the season gone back to their places in the country. Still, you're a likeable fellow, Roger, and would soon find plenty of people to help you."

"I fear your wish is father to the thought, m'dear," he said despondently. "Among persons of quality the making of friendships is always easy, but in such a case I'd have put all that behind me. The poor live hard and for the most part are driven by their needs to batten upon one another. I know no trade and could be of little use to anyone except as a scrivener. I'd find myself starving within a week."

"Nonsense!" she flashed at him. "Where there's a will there's a way! You've a pair of hands and they could be put to a dozen different uses."

Roger's fatal imagination was again working overtime. He had never been to London, but he knew enough about it to realise that the gilded world in which she had disported herself so gaily for a few weeks was very far from being the metropolis that a patronless and penniless young man would find should he go there. Old Ben, the Brooks' houseman, was a Londoner by birth, and he had often told Roger horrifying tales of the debtors' prison at Newgate, the Fleet, and the madhouse at Bedlam, where the lunatics, beating their heads against the walls and eating the filthy straw on which they lay, were exhibited in chains to anyone who cared to tip the warder a shilling. From Old Ben's stories, too, he conjured up the noisome alleys haunted by disease-ridden Molls, the filth, the stench and the cut-purses who haunted the thieves-kitchens on the lookout for some greenhorn from the country whom they might despoil.

"No," he said, after a moment, "I wouldn't dare to go to London."

"Then tramp the country," she replied tartly. " 'Tis high summer, and 'twon't harm you to sleep under a hedgerow now and then."

"Not now and then, perhaps; but I'd have to live, and I couldn't beg my bread all the time. I've no trade, I tell you! and I'm not strong enough yet to do the full days' labour of a man. I'd face it if I had sufficient money to ensure me food for the time we have in mind, but I haven't—that's the rub."

"I can set your mind at rest on that score," swiftly volunteered Georgina. "My Derby winnings have gone, alas, on furbelows, likewise my quarter's allowance from papa. But I've pretty trinkets that should fetch a tidy sum, and you shall have them. You could dispose of them with ease in Winchester or Southampton."

"I couldn't take them from you," Roger demurred.

"Be not a fool! I'll not give you the best or most valuable. Those I shall keep for my own adornment; but in my grandmother's box which has come to me there is a plenitude of old gewgaws that I'd ne'er be seen dead in. Yet they are of gold and should fetch a good price in a county town."

"No, no! I'll not rob you. 'Tis part of your inheritance and you may need them some day to raise money for some project of your own."

"Stuff and nonsense! As my father's heir I don't lack for fortune; and even if I did, my face and figure would soon make it for me. These oddments are but a bagatelle, and you must take them, Roger. 'Tis the only way to save yourself from the nightmare of this life at sea."

Her words recalled Roger to his impending fate; yet he still hesitated. Even provided with a little store of gold, to abandon everyone he knew and the only way of life he understood, for a lonely and perhaps perilous existence, was no light undertaking. Certain aspects of the unknown had always had greater terrors for him than the known, and to be cast out of the world of security and comfort that had been his ever since his birth, into one of uncertainty and hardship, filled him with misgiving.

"No," he said. "No, Georgina, I can't do it. You forget that I've led an even more sheltered life than you and am not yet sixteen. That is too young to face the world alone, even for the few months that you suggest."

"Ah!" she sneered, "There you've hit upon it. You're not a man, as you would like to think. Only a timorous little boy."

"I'm nothing of the kind!" he declared angrily.

"Well, you behave like one," she retorted. "And you are certainly not a man yet; any girl could tell that with half a look at you."

"What the devil do you mean?"

"What I say! And disabuse yourself of the idea that a midshipman's uniform could turn you into one. It couldn't; any more than being presented at Court turns a girl into a woman."

Roger flushed to his temples. "Oh, you mean that!" he said softly.

For a moment they sat there staring at one another. The tower was now swaying slightly again and they both had that strange feeling of being utterly alone, entirely divorced from the everyday existence that was going on far below them. As the blood mounted to Roger's face he could feel his heart beating wildly. Georgina's dark eyes were unnaturally bright. Her red lips were a little parted and she was smiling at him; a queer, enigmatic, mocking little smile.

Suddenly he pulled her towards him and their mouths met in a violent kiss. Her lips seemed to melt under the pressure of his and the feel of the soft contours of her body against his own set his brain on fire. The kiss ended only when they were forced to draw breath, and a second later he exclaimed:

"By heaven! I'll show you if I'm a man, or not!" Then, as their mouths hungrily closed on each other's again, he thrust her back against the cushions and crushed her to him in a fierce embrace.

For several minutes they lay there, now lost to all sense of time, place, age, or convention; their youthful passions rising to fever pitch from a series of avid caresses during which his trembling hands became ever more audacious.

Suddenly she pushed him roughly away from her with a breathless cry of: "Fie, Roger! Stop it now! I'll let no man handle me so unless he loves me."

"But I do! I do!" he blurted out, now wrought up to an ungovernable pitch of excitement. "Georgina, I've always loved you! I've loved you since the very first moment I set eyes on you!"

"It isn't true! I'll not believe it!" she whispered, her face now as flushed as his. But she did not attempt to repel his renewed caresses, only whispered again: "Roger! You mustn't! Desist now, I beg. You're not a man, only a boy, and 'tis folly to pretend otherwise."

"I'll show you that I'm a man," he muttered, and as their lips met again he pressed her down beneath him. For a moment their two hearts palpitated wildly against one another and he stared down into her face with eager yet fearful eyes; then he gasped: "Do you want me to prove it?"

Her only reply was a half-hysterical laugh and a tightening of her soft arms round his neck.

CHAPTER V

THE ROAD TO FORTUNE

ROGER sat staring out of the turret window that overlooked the vast sweep of the bay, but his eyes no more took in the ancient Abbey of Christchurch or the waves creaming against the jagged rocks of the Needles, than they had the details of the view from the roof of his own home first thing that morning.

His face was red, his hair tumbled and he had great difficulty in keeping his hands from trembling. Never before had his young soul plumbed such depths of abject misery. Only a short time before he had been fired with a mad elation and almost swooned with rapture in the intoxication of a hitherto unexperienced pleasure. It had been all too short, yet, while it lasted, far beyond his wildest imaginings. But now, the awful consciousness of all that his act implied was fully borne in upon him. It seemed that for the past twenty-four hours his evil angel had held undisputed sway over his affairs. A midshipman's commission had been sprung upon him without warning; he had got drunk and defied his father; and now he had seduced Georgina.

He did not dare to look at her, as he was desperately afraid that she would either burst into floods of tears or wither him to the very soul with one outraged glance from her black eyes.

Then she whispered: "Roger, what ails thee, m'dear? Doest thou not like me any more?"

Her whisper brought him some relief. She was not angry, only frightened. "Indeed I do," he gulped, still not daring to turn his face to hers. "I—I think you're adorable. And have no fear. I'll make an honest woman of you. We'll have to wait until I'm old enough to marry, but I'm willing to wait as long as need be, if you are."

"Roger," she said, in a much firmer voice. "Come here. Come back and sit beside me."

He turned then, and was staggered to see that she had already tidied her hair, smoothed out her skirts, and was sitting there, a picture of demure amusement, quietly laughing at him.

"Don't you—don't you mind?" he faltered.

"Of course not, you silly fellow. "For me, it wasn't the first time."

"D'you mean you've done that sort of thing before?" he said incredulously, his relief struggling with a sudden new-born jealousy.

"Why not?" she shrugged. "It has just as much attraction for a woman as a man, and it's absurdly unfair that men should love where they list while girls are supposed to go through life like marble images."

"Who was it with?" he demanded truculently.

" 'Tis none of your business. Yet I don't mind telling you. In London I favoured one of my beaux far above the rest. Old Aunt Sophie was so exhausted from sitting up for me to all hours on rout seats and stiff-backed gilded chairs that she slept most afternoons. My little fool of a cousin, Dorothea, took some evading but two or three times a week I managed to give her the slip and go out shopping with my maid. Jenny was a sensible gel and easily bribeable, so I used to send her to do my shopping and spend the time pleasuring my lover in his rooms in Jermyn Street."

Quite illogically, in view of his recent act, Roger was frankly horrified. "D'you really mean that you actually went to a man's rooms of your own free will and let him seduce you?"

"Well, what if I did," she shrugged. "I see no reason why *you* should look so shocked about it. But as a matter of fact, he didn't seduce me. I'd lost all I had to lose last spring, before I went to London."

Roger's new feeling of jealousy returned with redoubled force at the thought that someone in the neighbourhood had been the first to enjoy Georgina's charms, and the not unnatural assumption that on that first occasion she must have been forced to it against her will, made him positively seethe with anger.

"Tell me his name," he cried. "Tell me his name, and, by heaven, I'll kill him."

"You won't; and you couldn't if you tried, my littlest gallant. 'Twas Captain Coignham."

Roger's eyes almost popped from his head. "What!" he gasped, "Not the highwayman?"

"Yes, indeed. I know of no other."

He groaned. "Oh, Georgina; and I've warned you so often that 'tis dangerous for you to ride alone in the forest."

His fervid imagination swiftly conjured up a wild scene of the screaming Georgina being dragged from her horse, pulled in among the bushes, brutally raped and left dishevelled and swooning. Yet his morbid curiosity got the better of him and he could not resist adding: "It must have been simply terrible for you; but how did it happen?"

" 'Twas not so terrible," she smiled reminiscently. "We came face to face no great distance from the Queen's Elm. I've always felt that jewellery was made to be worn, not kept locked up in a box. I had that day a fine sapphire ring on my finger and a diamond aigrette in my hat. He greeted me most polite, but bade me hand them over. I parleyed with him a little and begged him to let me at least keep the ring, since it had been my mother's. He declared that I could keep both the ornaments if I was willing to ransom them with a kiss a-piece. He was a personable fellow, well groomed and of good address, so I considered the saving of my jewels cheap at the price. We both dismounted and he gave me the first kiss. 'Twas a long one and the fellow knew his business. Then he picked me up in his strong arms and carried me through the trees to a mossy bank, as he said, to give me the other in surroundings more suited to my beauty. Call me a brazen hussy if you will, but I've not a shadow of regret over that sunny day last spring when I came upon Captain Coignham in the forest. 'Twas a fine romantic way to lose one's maidenhead."

Roger remained silent for a few moments. He had often heard of the notorious highwayman but never seen him. Georgina's story of the encounter was so unlike anything he had expected that he found the grounds for anger cut from beneath his feet. The fellow was reputed handsome and, despite his monstrous impertinence, appeared to have behaved with the utmost civility; while Georgina had clearly proved his willing victim. Roger was wondering now if, in view of her previous adventures, he was still called on to pledge himself to her. Convention demanded that any girl a gentleman took to wife should go to her bridal chamber as spotless as an angel; no matter what pranks she might get up to later if the couple decided to go their separate ways, providing only that she cloaked her amours with a reasonable decency in order to protect his name.

Yet, he reflected, she had not been called upon to tell him anything, and he had made his avowal before she had spoken. Even if she was not the languorous, golden-haired creature of his dreams she was still one of the loveliest people he had ever set eyes on, and her soft embrace so recently enjoyed had given her a new enchantment for him. More, where would he ever find a girl whose interests tallied so closely with his own; in all their many hours together he had never known a dull moment in her company. The episode with the highwayman was a misfortune that might have happened to any imprudent girl and, once seduced, the affair with the London buck could be excused by the unconventional way in which she had been brought up, coupled with her zest for any form of daring and adventure. With sudden resolution he decided that convention could be damned, and that in any case a gentleman must stick by his word, so, from every point of view he should go through with it.

"A penny for your thoughts, Roger," she said softly.

"I was just wondering," he replied with a smile, "how soon we can get married. I fear we won't be allowed to until I'm seventeen, but that isn't very long to wait. The devil of it is, though, that I've got no money."

"Oh, Roger, you darling," she sighed. "You haven't really been thinking of marrying me, have you?"

"Of course. That is unless you've promised yourself to the fellow in London?"

She shrugged her shoulders airily. "What, Harry! Lud, no! He's married already; and even if he weren't I wouldn't have him. He's devilish handsome, but a hopeless wastrel."

"You'll promise to forget him, then. And we'll consider it a settled thing. God alone knows what the future holds for me, but as soon as I'm in any situation to do so I'll speak to your father."

Taking his hand she drew him down beside her, and said seriously: "Roger, m'dear, I'm deeply sensible of the honour that you do me. More especially since I've been unmaidenly enough to declare myself a piece of shop-soiled goods. But I've no intention of pledging myself to any man as yet."

"But you can't go on like this," he protested. "After taking three lovers while barely seventeen, 'tis over-time already that you became respectable."

"Four," she corrected, with a little laugh. "I met the wickedest, handsomest young spark that ever I did see at the Lansdowne House

Ball, and we met again while attending old Q's water-party at Richmond. He tumbled me in a punt and I simply could not bring myself to resist him."

"Georgina!" he suddenly wrung his hands, "how could you! It needs but such looseness through another season for your name to become a byword. Then none will marry you."

She shook her dark curls. "Dear Roger! You don't understand. What if I have had four lovers? I hope to have forty more, should I find forty men that please me. Nay, I'll take a hundred before I die, and the finest and handsomest men in the realm among them. As for marriage, set thy fears for me at rest. Do'st thou not realise that I am an heiress?"

"Your father is reputed a warm man, I know," he nodded.

"He is far richer than you think. This place and the house in Bedford Square represent but a small fraction of his fortune."

"How so? I have heard it said that old Mr. Thursby died in good circumstances, but never that he left your father great riches."

"True, but papa has brains, and has made a mint of money for himself. 'Tis his interest in engineering and machinery—the very things people count him crazy for—that have brought him his wealth."

"You have never told me of this before."

"I did not know it myself until he presented me during the season to the Duke of Bridgewater, who, it seems, is one of his partners in a company. 'Twas His Grace who made the first canal, to supersede the system by which coal was carried on pack horses from his mines at Worsley to Manchester. But 'twas Mr. Josiah Wedgwood who first interested papa in such schemes."

"What, the Mr. Wedgwood who makes such lovely plaques and urns of pottery?"

"The same. 'Twas Mr. Wedgwood who discovered the engineering genius of young James Brindley, then a workman in his employ. Together they constructed the Grand Trunk canal that links the Trent and the Mersey, so that Mr. Wedgwood's pottery could be carried from his works at Etruria to the ports at a saving of no less than seventy per cent. Then papa also has an interest in Mr. Samuel Compton's spinning mule, which, 'tis said, will prove vastly superior to the spinning jenny. 'Tis from such undertakings that of late years papa has piled up a great fortune."

Roger looked at her in astonishment. "It seems then that you are indeed an heiress, and a fine prize for any man, quite apart from your beauty."

"Yes," she said seriously. "With me, when I marry, will go a hundred thousand pounds. Papa told me so in order that I might not pledge myself lightly to some good-looking nobody. And who in their-senses would not be prepared to overlook a few peccadilloes on my part when the securing of such a fortune is in question. With it I can buy myself an Earl any time I wish. But I'll not be content with some old dotard. I require one who will both be complaisant and do me credit. I've a mind, just as you have, Roger, to cut a fine figure in this world of ours. Money alone is not enough. I want influence and power and,

Royalty apart, to be the first lady in the kingdom. If the husband I choose has it in him to carry me that high, maybe I'll be faithful to him. If not I'll use my beauty with the same skill as a great general handles his battalions. I'll slip into bed with one man or twenty, providing they can lift me a rung up the ladder towards the things I crave. Perhaps I'll become the mistress of a King, and make and unmake statesmen at my will; but whate'er befall I vow I'll be a Duchess before my hair turns grey."

As she spoke, her great eyes lifted unseeing towards the blue horizon; her gipsy blood was calling up a prophetic vision of the tempestuous and amazing career that was indeed to be hers.

The violence of her declaration left Roger temporarily without words; then, recovering himself he said: "Oh, come, Georgina, I doubt not that your money will buy you a coronet, if you've set your heart on one, but Kings don't make Duchesses of their mistresses in these days."

Bringing herself back with a jerk, she laughed up at him. "They have before; there's no reason that they shouldn't again. Charles II made Castlemaine into Cleveland and French Louise into Portsmouth with other Duchies for all their sons; while George I created that greedy German whore that he brought over Duchess of Kendal."

Roger's relief that he had not, after all, been called on to commit himself was now almost outweighed by pique at having, seemingly, won only to lose this flamboyant creature who, at the same time, both shocked and attracted him so strongly.

"Oh, well," he muttered sulkily, "Since you've no use for me, and prefer this mad plan to go whoring after a Duchy for yourself, good luck to you."

She regarded him with a rather sad little smile. "Be not angry, Roger, nor foolish in thy speech. 'Twould be a madder thing by far, for both of us, were I to accept you here and now as my spouse-to-be. As for whoring after a Duchy, I'll be no ordinary whore, and it takes much more than that to achieve the strawberry leaves of a ducal coronet. I'll have a use for you too, never fear. I'll have a fondness for you beyond all my lovers, and, if you will, ever count you my earliest and most faithful friend."

He brightened at once. "Do you really mean that, Georgina?"

"Indeed I do." She took his hand again and her smile deepened to one of mischievous amusement. "What will you have as your share of the plunder? Will you be Northern or Southern Secretary? But no! I'll make you Paymaster to the Forces, since 'tis the most lucrative post of them all."

Lifting the hand that held his own he kissed it, with a laugh. "Your Grace's most obliged, obedient and humble servant, Ma'm."

Quite suddenly she became serious again and, releasing his fingers, looked him squarely in the face. "Roger, I've seen enough of the young London bucks to know that you are no ordinary lad. Together we may go far. Don't think that I have told you of my most intimate affairs idly or from a perverted pride in having had several lovers while still so young. 'Twill remain my jealously guarded secret from every other soul. But I'll need someone in the days to come who knows me better than I know myself; someone to whom I can give my whole confidence and who will advise me rightly in the crises with which I am bound to be faced. It may seem to you now a far cry from this room to London and the power that moves armies from behind a throne; but I have no shadow of doubt that you and I will get there, and I will make your every interest my own. For the moment I have done all I can for you. The next step must be yours. But I have given you something that no other woman will ever be able to give you, for this day I have made of you a man."

It suddenly flashed upon him that although he was not committed to her in one way he had committed himself in another. The inference was plain. He had pleaded his youth to excuse his fear of facing unknown perils and hardships, but she had given him manhood and now expected him to act upon it. Panic seized him and, in a fresh effort to escape, he muttered uneasily:

"Yes, you've made a man of me. But, somehow, I don't feel the least bit different. Perhaps that's because I didn't prove a very good one."

"Oh, yes, you did, m'dear," she reassured him sweetly. "For a first attempt you did your part nobly. And now you must begin to play a man's part in the world."

He saw that his honour was at stake. To draw back would be to shame himself before her in a way that was unthinkable. Yet the more he thought about it the less regret he felt at having fallen into the silken snare that he now realised she had deliberately laid for him. The awful decision as to if he should succumb to his father's will or continue his defiance had been taken for him. As the fact sank in it was as though a great burden had been lifted from his shoulders. His course was now clear, and he was vaguely surprised that he had not jumped at it in the first instance as the only sensible way out of his difficulties.

"So be it then!" he exclaimed. "I'll start this very night."

"Well done!" she cried, clapping her hands. "Whither wilt thou make for?"

"London, I think, but with luck some chance to secure work may befall on the road." His glance fell on the basket of provisions, and he added: " 'Tis still early yet, but all the same I feel plaguey hungry."

"And so do I," laughed Georgina, jumping up to unpack the basket. " 'Tis but natural after our exertions. I would we had a bottle of sparkling Sillery here on which to celebrate; but there is cider and lots of things to eat."

They settled down to demolish the good things she had selected from the larder and after half an hour their two hearty young appetites had left not a crumb.

It was not yet eleven o'clock; but the heat of the tower room and their meal had made them drowsy, and Georgina said: "If you mean to take the road to-night 'twould be a good preparation to sleep a while. What say you to a nap?"

He nodded. "Yes, I had a plaguey long day yesterday, and already feel as if I had been up a week."

She arranged a pile of old cushions at one end of the settee, and, stretching herself on it luxuriously, drew him down beside her so that his face was pillowed on her breast, and her soft chin rested against his forehead. For a while they exchanged gentle caresses, then they both fell asleep.

When they awoke it was after two o'clock. Still drowsy, and warm from their long embrace, they kissed again, then sat up and put their rumpled clothes to rights.

"We'd best go down, I think," said Georgina, "and see what we can find in my jewel box for you to take with you."

"Nay, I beg——" he began. But she waved his protests aside.

"Be not a fool, Roger. Money in thy pocket will mean the difference between happiness and misery. Few people will give worthwhile employment to a pauper who begs his bread, but a full purse begets confidence and the man who has one can make his own terms. You must not waste your time sawing wood for a living but make your way to London and seek a secretaryship with some great nobleman who may be useful to us, later on."

"But I plan to be away no more than two or three months," he objected.

"That will depend on events; and you will be ill-advised to set out with that idea, as 'twould lead to your frittering away your time and getting nowhere. If your father relents and fortune has served you ill, clearly you should return. But if you secure some post of promise, as I pray you may, 'twould make you independent of your family and it might well pay you best to stick to it."

There was no gainsaying such sound common sense and as Georgina gathered her billowing skirts about her Roger picked up the basket to follow her down the seemingly endless flight of spiral stairs.

Leaving Roger in the orchard, Georgina went into the house, with the intention of smuggling her jewel box out under cover of some rugs and going through it with him under the trees. But on going indoors she learned that her father had driven into Christchurch on some business, so she went back to collect Roger and took him up to her room.

In the drowsy heat of the afternoon the house was very quiet, as the servants were taking their ease after their morning labours. Unlocking a cabinet, Georgina took from it a large box covered in crocodile skin and two smaller caskets. Opening all three she emptied their contents on the gay patchwork quilt of her bed.

Roger had always known that she loved trinkets, as she bedecked herself with them on every occasion, but he was amazed at the size and variety of her collection. Much of it was trashy stuff that she had bought herself with her pin-money in the neighbouring towns, but three-quarters of her treasure consisted of items of considerable value.

With deft fingers she began to sort the heap into two piles and as Roger saw that intended for himself rapidly increase in size he began to protest again. But she refused to listen to him and with prodigal generosity continued to throw gold chains, cameo brooches and paste shoe-buckles upon it, as she said:

"Believe me, I have no further use for these old-fashioned gewgaws, and as I never wear such things, papa will not suspect that I have parted with them. Besides, 'tis my wish that you should have much more than will merely keep you from hunger. When you reach London you should put up at some good inn. The 'Swan and Two Necks' in Lad Lane, or the 'Turk's Head' in the Strand are reputed good. Either would serve, but if you put up at the latter you'll be near Hoare's Bank, and 'tis there I'd advise you to place the money that you'll get by the sale of these jewels. Then you should get yourself made some London clothes, so as to cut a good figure, and frequent the coffee houses in Whitehall and St. James's. You will be taken for a young man of wealth and soon fall in with somebody who will introduce you to persons of good standing. Make yourself agreeable to their women, Roger, m'dear, and in no time at all some good opening will be offered to you."

As she rattled on all Roger's unhappy forebodings of hard manual labour and sleeping under haystacks gave place to rosy visions of ease, comfort and success. It all seemed so simple now, and this going out into the world a joyous adventure instead of a thing to dread.

When the division of the treasure had been completed, Georgina found a piece of strong satin to wrap Roger's share up in and stuffed it into one of his capacious pockets.

"I'll never be able to thank you enough," he murmured, kissing her again.

"Stuff and nonsense!" she declared, pushing him away from her. "Your sword is mine, remember, and that good brain of yours, too. Maybe I'll call upon them sooner than you think. Once you are settled let me have your address and I'll seek some excuse to accompany papa on his next visit to London."

As they were about to leave her room he halted suddenly, and said: "Georgina! The strangest thought has just occurred to me. D'you recall last Christmas-tide when you told my future in a glass of water. You said then that high summer would bring a great change into my life, and that I'd be burdened with new cares and responsibilities. I thought then it must be my move to Upper School at Sherborne that you predicted. I little guessed that you were foretelling my leaving school for good."

"Yes, I remember now," she nodded. "Would you like me to look into the glass for you again? 'Tis a risk, though. For I can tell only what I see, and it may not be good."

"I'll take that risk," he declared boldly. "Come—do it for me."

"As you will, then." While he cleared an array of fans and perfumed gloves from a small Buhl table, and moved it from the muslin-draped bow window farther into the room, she filled a toothglass with water from the jug on her washstand. Setting it down in the centre of the table, she drew up a chair and he took another opposite to her.

"Take my hands," she ordered.

On his obeying, she dropped her eyes to the glass and concentrated their gaze upon it. After a minute or two she began to speak in a lower voice than usual.

"There is water, Roger. You will cross water many times and always be in danger from it. I see you as several years older, near drowning, and with a parchment you value clenched between your teeth. But the scene changes. I see you now with your sword in your hand, and this will be soon. Oh, m'dear, be careful. Wait though, I see no blood. No blood is spilled and you are laughing with a tall man. I cannot see his face but it seems that there is something amiss with his left eye. He gives me an uneasy feeling. There is now another with him; an old man with white hair. He is a cunning rogue but he is looking at you with affection. You will go into some sort of partnership together and profit from it greatly; yet 'tis a dangerous game and will not lead you to fortune."

She paused for a moment, then went on: "I see you in the dusk upon a lonely heath with trees nearby. You are older now, much older. A halted coach stands in the road and you are conversing angrily with its occupants. They have a foreign look, but these are persons of quality, richly dressed and with jewel-hilted swords. Alack! They have got out and you are fighting with them now. The older of the two attacks you ferociously. To deal death lies in both your hearts. The wraith of a woman rises between your flashing swords. She is fair-haired, slim of figure, and has a haughty, aristocratic face. 'Tis over her that you are fighting. There is blood now, a mist of blood obscures all. Alas! Alas! I can see no more. I cannot tell if you live or die." With a little wail she snatched her hands from Roger's, and burying her face in them, let her head fall forward on the table.

He had gone a trifle pale, but he quickly recovered himself and began to stroke her hair, murmuring softly as he did so.

"There, there, Georgina, darling. Don't cry. Please don't cry. I'll be all right. I vow I will. You were speaking of some years hence, and by the time I'm fully grown I'll be a match with the rapier for any man."

She raised her head, her eyes still swimming. "Oh, Roger, dear, do take care. You seemed furiously angry. But you must keep calm. You *must* keep calm; your life will hang on that. And you'll need all your skill. Your antagonist will be one of the finest swordsmen in France."

"In France?" he echoed.

"Yes," she shook herself. "Why did I say that? I know not. Yet I am certain 'twas in France that I saw you, as a man of maybe twenty, fighting this frightful duel."

Georgina had discovered when still quite young that she had inherited the gift of second sight from her gipsy mother, and she had often told Roger's fortune on previous occasions, but generally half playfully, and never with such an outpouring of emotion.

"You've never told me half as much, or described people that I'm going to meet when you've looked in the glass for me before," he remarked, thoughtfully.

She shrugged. "Perhaps I'm getting better at it now I'm older.

But I don't think it's that. There is little to foresee in a schoolboy's dull existence, whereas from now on all sorts of things may happen to you."

"Are you not jealous of the fair-haired girl," he laughed, trying to make light of the matter.

"Why should I be?" she answered seriously. "I've had you first and I'll have you last, if I've a mind to it. That is—if you live to come back to me."

He nodded. "Yes, I'll never forget you, Georgina, wherever I may go. I may fall in love with other women for a season, but you will ever hold a special place in my heart."

"And you in mine, dear Roger. Our comradeship these two years past has meant more to me than you can ever know. But the day marches. 'Tis near four o'clock, and you'll need to buy a few things in Lymington before you set out; so you should be on your way if you mean to take the road to London to-night."

"So be it then. Let us go down, and we can say farewell while my horse is being brought round from the stables."

"Nay," she shook her head. "I'll not come down. Kiss me good-bye here. Then I can have a good cry about you on my bed as you ride away. 'Tis monstrous foolish of me, but I almost think I love you at this moment."

"Then pledge yourself to me," he cried impulsively. "You're wondrous beautiful, and if I feel not love for you I know not what it is. Your kisses fire me as naught else has ever done, and I would give my life to protect your happiness.

"Nay, sweet Roger. 'Tis you who are being foolish now, and we are pledged to something far more lasting than a summer's passion. Kiss me now and go. May God protect you."

Once more her soft arms were round his neck and their mouths crushed together. Then she broke from him and, stifling a sob, turned away.

A moment later he was clattering down the stairs on his way out into the world to seek fame and fortune.

CHAPTER VI

VENDETTA

ROGER had now adopted Georgina's plan, that he should go to London, cut a fine figure on the proceeds of her jewels and trust to his natural gifts to secure him a promising opening, without reservation; and, had he there and then turned his mount towards Lyndhurst and the London road, his future would have been entirely different.

Fate decreed, however, that unreasoning instinct should impel him to ride back to Lymington as his natural starting-point on this great adventure. For one thing, although the little mare he was riding was always regarded as his in the holidays, it never even occurred to him to deprive his parents of her in order to facilitate his journey; for another, Georgina had put it into his mind that, before setting out, he should buy a few things that he was bound to need, in the town; and for a third, he felt that he could not leave his mother the prey to most appalling anxiety by simply disappearing without a word.

Entering Lymington from the west he rode past the church, up the High Street and through the low arch that gave on to the stable yard of the Angel Inn. As he handed his mare over to the ostler for a rub down and a feed he knew that she would be quite safe there and, when he failed to claim her, be duly returned to her own stable the following morning. Realising that it was the last he would see of the skittish little chestnut, he gave her an extra pat, and turned, rather sorrowfully, into the tap-room.

At this hour of the afternnon, as it was not a market day, the low-raftered tap-room was deserted. He rapped his riding-crop sharply on one of the stout oak tables until a fresh-cheeked girl appeared, then he asked her for a glass of Ratifia and writing things. She brought him the cordial, an inkhorn, quill pen, sand-shoe and paper. Sitting down he composed a letter to his mother, which ran:

My dear Mother,

Please do not think too hardly of me, but I have formed an unshakeable determination not to go to sea. The only course that is open to me is to leave home for a while. Yet do not think of me, I beg, as penniless or hungry. A good friend has furnished me with ample funds and now that I am a man in all but stature I am quite capable of taking good care of myself. Do not be uneasy should I not write to you for some little time but I will do so as soon as I am settled in some profitable employment and, if by then my father has relented, I will gladly return home to discuss any other project for my future.

Your very loving, if undutiful, son,

Roger.

Having sanded his missive he sealed it with a wafer and put it in his pocket, knowing that he could give it to anyone in the town just before his departure and be quite certain of its safe delivery.

He next considered how best to set about his journey. To walk all the way to London seemed a stupid and time-wasting proceeding now that he could well afford to go by coach; yet there was a snag to that, since his new-found wealth was not in coin and on counting over his money he found that he had only five and eightpence on him.

To endeavour to turn some of Georgina's trinkets into cash at the local silversmiths seemed a risky venture. The man was a sour creature and would be certain to wonder how a lad had come into possession of a woman's jewellery. He would probably think that Roger, having got into difficulties, had purloined them from his mother's jewel-box, say that he must have a little time to assess their value and take them along for Lady Marie's inspection that very evening.

The thought of his money-box at home began to tantalise Roger.

In it there was gold as well as silver, and more than enough to pay his coach fare to London—if only he could manage to collect it. On more than one occasion he had been out on a ramble at night with his friend Jack Bond, when his mother thought him safely tucked up in his bed asleep, and had got back into the house, in the small hours, by way of his bedroom window. He wondered if he dared risk a clandestine visit to his room that night for the purpose of burgling his own money-box, and decided that it would be worth it, as he could at the same time collect a dozen other things that would be useful to him and that he had not the ready cash to buy at the moment. It would mean waiting until the household was fast asleep, but a few hours' delay in the time of his setting out would make little difference.

Once he had secured the money he would walk into Southampton. It was thirteen miles; a longish trudge but no great matter for an active and healthy youngster. He could get there easily, before dawn, secure a seat in the morning coach, and be in London by the following evening.

At the thought of London, his optimism suffered a sharp decline. All Old Ben's stories of cut-purses and thieves' kitchens came back to him. He had very little idea what Georgina's jewellery should fetch, but, at a guess, he put its worth at anything from two to five hundred guineas. To enter London with such a treasure seemed to be tempting providence; yet how could he dispose of it otherwise?

There were goldsmiths in Southampton, or at Winchester if he chose to break his journey there, who would give an honest price for what he had to sell; but the question was, would any of them do a deal with him? Would they not wonder where a youngster of his age had obtained this small fortune in gold chains, brooches, buckles and bangles? He could think of no plausible explanation as to how he had come into possession of such property. If he were detained and an inquiry made, it could only result in his being ignominiously returned to his father.

The more he thought of the difficulty of dispersing of his spoil, the more worried he became about it. If only there had been someone to whom he could go immediately on reaching London—someone he knew and could trust—the transaction might have been arranged with safety and despatch, but he had not a single acquaintance there; and it now seemed to him that even endeavouring to sell single pieces in provincial towns would be fraught with a certain danger. Each attempted sale would expose him to the risk of questioning and detention.

The elegant figure of Droopy Ned drifted across his mind, bringing him fresh hope for a moment. He felt that he would be perfectly safe in confiding his whole story to Droopy and that the eccentric young nobleman, having a passion for jewels, would probably buy the whole collection from him; or at least, arrange a sale and see that he was not cheated. But the question was, would Droopy be in London?

All the odds were that he would not. At this season it was as good as certain that the Marquess of Amesbury would be at his seat, Normanrood, in Wiltshire, and that Droopy would spend at least a fortnight there taking leave of his family before setting out on the Grand Tour. It was probable that he would spend some days in London before actually leaving for the Continent but when that would be it was impossible to guess and it was even probable that he might elect to cross to France by the more direct route from Southampton.

In any case, it seemed to Roger, it would be a poor gamble to count on Droopy being at Lord Amesbury's London house before mid-August and, in the meantime, a country boy with little ready money but a hoard of jewels stood a terrible risk of becoming the prey of the sharks that infested the poorer quarters of the capital.

While he was still pondering the thorny problem of converting his treasure into cash the outer door was thrust open and Dan Izzard came in. With a cheerful "Good day, young Squire" to Roger, the smuggler advanced to the narrow counter and banged upon it with an empty pewter pot. The serving maid came out of the back room and greeted him with a smile.

"Is Master Trattle in?" asked Dan; and on the girl nodding, he added: "Then go fetch he, wench, and I'll thank thee for it."

A moment or two later the burly, red-faced landlord appeared and asked Dan's business.

The smuggler cast a casual glance over his shoulder at Roger, then leaned over the counter and, lowering his gruff voice, began to talk to the landlord.

Roger was still absorbed in his own affairs and, at first, did not pay much attention to the conversation. It was evident that Dan, knowing him to be "safe" was indifferent as to if he listened or not, and he had jumped to it at once that the smuggler was arranging the shipment of a new supply of illicit spirits for the inn. But as his gaze rested idly on Dan's broad back a sudden idea came to him.

For some minutes the two men continued their low-voiced talk; then, with a muttered: "That suits me, well enough; us'll make it four nights from now," Dan turned away.

"Dan!" Roger called. "Wilt join me in a glass?"

The smuggler paused, halfway across the room. "Aye, Master Roger; I never say nay to a dram o' good liquor. I'll drink 'e's good health in a noggin' o' rum."

Mr. Trattle poured the drink and disappeared to resume his afternoon nap. Dan picked it up and, with a smile, came and sat down at the table.

Lifting his glass he said: "Well, here's long life to 'e, young Master. 'E've grown quite a bit since I last clapped eyes on 'e, and soon it'll be Mister Brook that us'll all be touchin' our caps to."

"That's it, Dan," Roger smiled back, as he sipped his own cordial. The spontaneous lead that he had been given lent itself to the idea he was developing, and an easy distortion of facts came quite readily to his tongue. "My father is by way of getting me a midshipman's commission, and I hope to be at sea in a month or two."

"Well, jus' think o' that now! 'Tis a fine life though; 'tis a fine life, Master Roger."

"I've never doubted that," Roger lied, adding after a second: "But it will take a lot of getting used to, and it's that which worries me. I'll just die of shame, Dan, if I'm sick the first time my ship leaves port on a voyage."

"Why should 'e be, Master Roger?" Dan asked him in surprise. " 'I's seen 'e often in they little yachts sailin' round the island when it were blowin' quite a bit, an' 'e seemed merry as a grig."

"But that's different," Roger objected, "I may be sick as a dog in a big ship once she's out in the open sea."

"Nay, 'tis not as different as all that. In a tempest, now, many a strong man's belly turns over on 'im 'fore it's blowed itself out; but 'e've naught to fear given normal weather."

Roger sighed and looked down into his glass. "I would that I felt as certain as you do that I'll not make a fool of myself. You see, I've never sailed farther than along the coast to Poole, or up to Southampton, and I haven't an idea what it's like in mid-channel."

" 'Tis no different, I tell 'e," Dan assured him; but he was now regarding the boy with thoughtful sympathy, assuming that some old salt must have scared him with tales of waves as high as mountains; and, to his simple mind, there was nothing strange in a land-lubber believing that it was always rough out in unprotected water.

Having planted this seed in the smuggler's mind, Roger pretended to shrug away his own worries and asked: "How are things with you, Dan?"

"Oh, well enough, Master Roger. There's only one real worry I got. That bastard Ollie Nixon 'as swore to get me, an' 'e's darn nigh done it a brace o' times since Whitsuntide."

Roger knew that the man referred to was the Chief Excise Officer of the district, whose main business it was to put down smuggling, but a special bitterness in Dan's tone impelled him to ask:

"Why has Mr. Nixon got his knife into you, particularly, Dan?"

" 'Tis on account of an affair last winter, over Poole way. Ollie Nixon's young brother were the leader of a squad o' Preventive Men. They catched some chaps comin' up a chine wi' pack-horses, havin' jus' landed a cargo, an' there were a real set-to."

"I remember hearing of it," Roger put in. "One of the gang hit young Mr. Nixon over the head with a cudgel and he died of it. The Justices have never been down on smuggling, but they won't stand for murder, and 'twas murder, right enough. There was a big reward offered."

"Aye; fifty guineas, no less, for any of 'em who'd turn King's evidence, an' a free pardon into the bargain; but they ne'er laid hands on the wicked devil that done it."

"Does Ollie Nixon think that you were mixed up in that affair, then?"

"That's the rig of it, Master Roger. Though as God is my witness, my order to my lads has ever been to jettison the cargo an' take to their heels at first sight o' the Preventives. Better by far lose a cargo than be forced into a fight where a killing may happen."

"You're right there, Dan, and 'tis hard that Nixon should be endeavouring to pin it on you, since you're innocent."

"He'll not pin it on me. There be no way he can do that. But 'tis fixed in his mind that 'twas my lugger lying off shore that night, an' that one o' my lads dealt the blow. So he's swore he'll get me, be it by fair means or foul."

"You're off again soon, aren't you? I was just behind my father in the conservatory when you came to the house last night, and you said something to him of another trip."

"Aye, aye; an' to-night it is. I'll be droppin' down the river wi' the turn o' the tide soon arter midnight."

Roger sprang his mine. "Take me with you, Dan."

The smuggler's eyes opened wide at the request, and he quickly shook his head. "Nay, Master Roger. 'Tis a crazy thing you ask. Should the Cap'n learn of it he'd ne'er forgive me."

"He won't learn of it," Roger said firmly, and added with swift invention: "He believes I'm lying away from home to-night at Colonel Thursby's house; and as they are not on speaking terms he'll never find out that I didn't."

Again Dan shook his head. "Nay, that will not serve 'e. Us'll be gone three days, and unable to land 'e again till four nights from now."

"Oh, but it will," Roger parried, "I'd planned to stay with the Thursbys for a week. I can easily ride over to Highcliffe this evening, make my excuses, and say that I'll not be coming to them till Saturday."

"My lads would be again' it. They know the quality be our good friends, but they'd be strong against the likes of 'e bein' let into the secrets o' the game."

"Please, Dan," Roger begged. "The making of such a trip would be a vast boon to me. 'Twould give me just the chance I need to prove myself before entering the Navy."

"Nay, Master Roger, 'tis too great a risk to take. Were anything to happen to 'e I'd have half the gentry o' the county down on me."

"Why should anything happen—unless we're all caught. And in such a case having me with you would prove to your advantage. The Justices would never convict if it involved sentencing Captain Brook's son to transportation."

"Aye, there's something in that. Still, I'm agin' it."

"Look!" said Roger suddenly, "I'll make it worth your while, Dan. I'll pay you a five-pound bounty to take me on the trip."

The smuggler's dark eyes showed a gleam of cupidity. In spite of the good profits he made after each successful run he was by no means a rich man. Periodically he was compelled to jettison a cargo from fear of capture, and each time that happened it robbed him of the earnings of many months' hard and dangerous work. Owing to Mr. Nixon's vendetta against him it was much longer than usual since he had made a trip and he was only driven to it now by the grumbling of his penniless crew. He had to pay cash for his goods on the other side and being in low funds himself was not taking over as much money as he could have wished; so an additional five pounds would come in very handy. Yet he still hesitated.

Seeing his hesitation Roger leapt into the breach. "Please, Dan! I beg you to. If 'tis as you say and the sea no rougher in mid-channel than off the island, a voyage to France and back is the very thing I need to give me confidence. 'Twould make a world of difference to me when I join my first ship this autumn."

Dan Izzard was a good-hearted man and deeply touched by the appeal. It overcame the last scruples of his better judgment, and he said: "So be it then. I'll take 'e. But no skylarkin', mind. 'E'll not be young Master aboard the *Sally Ann*, but do as 'e's bid."

"I will, Dan; I will. I promise," agreed Roger enthusiastically.

"Then be down by Nothover's quay sharp on midnight," Dan added. " 'Tis from there we sail, an' time an' tide wait for no man."

The matter now being agreed the smuggler finished his drink, pulled the tassel of his woollen cap a little further over his left ear, and, with a gruff word of good-bye to Roger, left the inn.

Roger's eyes were still shining from his success in having persuaded the smuggler to take him, as he was confident the trip would prove the solution to the problem that had been worrying him so much. The French authorities, he knew, were entirely indifferent as to if cargoes of spirits shipped from France were for legal or illegal tender when they reached England. Therefore it was certain that Dan would pick up his shipment quite openly in one of the French ports—probably the great city of Le Havre. They would be there for a full day at least, and Roger felt that there should be no difficulty in his going ashore and disposing his treasure to a French goldsmith in the town.

Every Englishman of good appearance and address was, he had often heard, regarded as a fabulously rich Milord in France, so his possession of a pocketful of jewels would not excite the same suspicion there as it was likely to do in England. Moreover, even if the goldsmith to whom he offered them did suspect that they were stolen goods, he would see at once that they were of English origin and, having nothing to fear from the English law, have no hesitation in buying them, provided that he could make a profitable bargain.

Already Roger saw himself safely back in England on the coming Saturday night with several rouleaux of gold coin that he could place with a banker in London for safe keeping on the following Monday. Congratulating himself on this excellent stroke he summoned the maid, paid her eightpence for the drinks and left the "Angel."

He had been considering what he should do with himself for the next few hours when Dan had come in. As he could hardly remain in the tap-room till nightfall and had no wish to spend the time loitering about the town, in case he should run into someone from home who would tell him that his father was seeking him, he decided to go into hiding. The woods outside the town offered a score of good places where he could lie up but he did not wish to go too far afield and unnecessarily fatigue himself with a longish walk back after dark, so it had occurred to him that the churchyard would be a good place to conceal himself during the long summer evening.

Having walked back along the High Street, he turned into it and found, as he had supposed would be the case, that it was completely deserted. Making his way to its extreme end he selected a grassy dip between a large box-like stone tomb and the hedge, and settled himself down there. For a little he thought about Georgina, then, tired out with the excitement of the day, he fell asleep.

He awoke with a start to find it quite dark. As the rendezvous he had made with Dan flashed back to him he stumbled to his feet in panic, fearing that it might now be so late that he had missed it. A moment later the bell of the Town Hall clock began to strike. Anxiously he counted the strokes and sighed with relief when they ended; it was only a quarter past ten.

A little shiver ran through him and he was suddenly conscious of an eerie feeling from being there alone, at night, in the graveyard. Vaguely now he could see the white tomb stones, and each one seemed like a ghost. Hastily stumbling between them he ran back to the road, arriving in the High Street quite breathless and with his heart beating like a hammer. The street was empty; most of the townsfolk had been in bed for the past hour and the only light that was to be seen came from an upper window in Monmouth House, on the corner of Church Lane.

When his breathing had eased, Roger crossed the street and made his way along it, past the bow windows of the now shuttered shops and the few private dwellings interspersed among them; but some way before reaching the Town Hall he turned right, entering a narrow gap between two buildings. The alley, known as Aishley's Lane, was less than a hundred yards in length but continued as a footpath which led straight down the hill between an open field on the one hand and the meadow and walled kitchen garden of his own home on the other.

Now that his eyes were accustomed to the semi-darkness of the summer night he could make out the square pile of the house rising from the lower ground and the outline of the tall trees beyond it. Two minutes' walk brought him to the end of the footpath and into the road on to which the stable gates of the house opened. They were locked, as he expected, but he made short work of hoisting himself up on them and dropping down inside. As he did so the Town clock chimed the half-hour.

Curly, the Irish wolf-hound, came out of his kennel and growled ominously. Roger spoke to him softly and at the sound of the well-known voice the dog fell quiet, shook himself with a rattle of his chain, and retired once more to his kennel. Tip-toeing across the yard Roger entered the garden and, taking to the grass, began to make a cautious circuit of the house for any signs of wakefulness of its occupants.

As he came out on to the lawn he saw, to his intense annoyance, that there was a light behind the curtains of the library window. Evidently his father was waiting up for him. He stood there irresolute for a moment, the terror of what would happen to him if he were caught by his infuriated parent surging through him. He positively dared not go in, yet, somehow he had got to get hold of his money-box before midnight. The only thing to do was to wait a while and hope that his father would go to bed.

Retracing his steps he sat down in the summer-house and, forcing himself to go slowly, counted a thousand. Then he walked round the corner of the house again. The light was still burning. Returning to the summer house he vowed to himself that he would not take another look until some moments after the next chiming of the Town clock, as it seemed to him hardly likely that his father would continue his vigil beyond eleven.

Consumed with impatience, he waited. At last the melodious chimes rang out but, to his amazement and dismay, the bell did not toll eleven; it was only a quarter-to. All the same he went round the house, but only to meet with another disappointment.

Back in the summer-house once more it suddenly came to him that he had had no dinner and was very hungry. There was plenty of fruit in the garden and, although not very sustaining, it was better than nothing; moreover going in search of it would occupy a little time during the enforced waiting. Tip-toeing up the path he went through the arch to the kitchen garden and made for the west wall, which was covered with fan-trained plum trees. Most of the gages were not yet ripe but he knew every tree in the garden and went straight to a purple plum that was just ready for picking. Having eaten several, he went into the netted cage and attacked the raspberry canes. But they did not taste half as good without sugar and cream, so he abandoned them and, leaving the cage, walked up to the south wall on which grew the peaches and nectarines. Finding that the only early trees had been denuded of their fruit for his father's home-coming dinner of the day before, he fell back on the apricots and ate of them until he was satisfied.

It seemed as if he had been listening for the clock to strike for half an hour, but at last it chimed eleven. Controlling his impatience he made himself count another thousand, then he left the kitchen garden and walked cautiously round the corner of the house again. The light was still burning in the library.

He wondered desperately if he dared enter the house while his father was still up. As his own room was at the back of the house he thought that he would be able to get into it unheard, but, to collect his things he would have to kindle a light, and the door of his room opened on to the half-landing of the staircase. Should his father decide to go up to bed while the light was on he would see it under the door and the fat would then be in the fire with a vengeance. Roger decided that he dared not risk it.

Yet, if he failed to get his money-box in time to be at Northover's quay by midnight, his whole plan would be ruined. He had promised Dan five pounds and, if he could not show the colour of his money Dan might refuse to take him. A prey to the most appalling indecision he hovered there, taking his weight first on one foot then on the other. Suddenly the light went out.

His relief was soon swamped in a new wave of impatience. He must give his father time to lock up and get to bed and, fearing that he might be seen from one of the windows he quickly tiptoed back to the shelter of the summer-house. With his hands clasped he sat there counting the seconds as the interminable minutes dragged away. At last the clock chimed a quarter past. He could bear to wait no longer and, getting up, stole round to the courtyard at the back of the house.

Old Ben's pantry consisted of a single storey passage room connecting the old wing of the house with the new building. By getting on to its roof Roger could easily reach the window of his bedroom. His heart hammering wildly again now, he climbed on to a rain butt and hauled himself up on to the low roof. His window was open a foot. It creaked a little as he raised it further and he paused there listening intently for a moment; but no sound came and he slipped inside.

The room was in pitch darkness but his groping fingers soon found his tinder box and he lit a candle. He had already made a mental list of the things he wanted to take and with quick soft steps he set about collecting them, the solitary candle casting a giant shadow of him on the walls and ceiling.

First he broke open his money-box. He had not added anything to its contents for the past few years, but it had in it most of the cash presents he had received during his childhood. A swift count showed that he had fifteen guineas in gold and a fist full of silver crowns, which was considerably more than he had thought. Next, he stripped off his outer clothes and hurriedly changed into his best blue broad-cloth suit, pulling on top of it his winter overcoat. Taking a roomy leather satchel from a chest he crammed into it a change of linen, the pair of silver-mounted pistols that his mother had given him on his fifteenth birthday, a pair of court shoes with silver buckles and a number of other items that he thought might come in useful. Thrusting his money in one pocket and the fat packet of Georgina's jewels into another he left the letter he had written to his mother propped up on the dressing-chest, gave a last hurried look round, blew out the candle and climbed out of the window.

Having regained the garden he hastened along the grass verge of the terrace to its eastern end, withdrew the bolts of a small postern door in the high wall and let himself out. Turning into the avenue of limes that formed the drive up to the main gate of the house he broke into a run, fearful now that he had been so long in collecting his things that it would be midnight before he could reach the quay. But before he was half way along it the Town clock chimed again, eleven strokes and the three quarters, so with a gasp of relief he dropped back into a walk. Beyond the avenue there lay only a short lane ending in a steep street of old houses that ran down to the water.

At the quayside he found the *Sally Ann*. Only the silhouette of her mast and rigging now showed against the night sky, but having often seen her in full daylight, he knew her well as a long, rakish, swift-moving craft.

No attempt was being made to conceal her departure, as she normally made one of the fishing fleet, solitary boats of which often sailed from Lymington at the turn of the tide late at night or in the small hours of the morning.

A gruff voice hailed Roger as he reached the lugger's side and a lantern was raised from behind a pile of tarpaulins. By its light Roger saw that the man who had challenged him was Nick Bartlett, a fellow of ill repute, who picked up a dubious living on the waterfront.

As Roger asked for Dan, Nick said in a grumbling tone: "So it be 'e, be it? Dan said 'e was a-coming wi' us, though what he be after wi' the likes of e' aboard Satan knows."

After this ill reception Roger was glad to see Dan's bearded head emerge from the hatchway and hear him call: "Stow that, Nick Bartlett! What I does be my affair. 'Tis none of 'e's business an' the young gentleman is paying his footing handsome. Come aboard, Master Roger an' don't pay no heed to yon fellow's cussedness."

Scrambling over the lugger's low bulwark Roger joined Dan aft and was taken by him down to the cabin. Three other men were there, whiling away the time until the tide should fall, by gambling for half-pence with a greasy pack of cards. Roger knew two of them by sight: Fred Mullins, a brawny, open-faced man, who, in his youth, had been impressed into the Navy and had later deserted; and Simon Fry, a grizzled, weather-beaten fisherman who had had the ill luck to lose his boat some winters before. The third was a dark, wiry fellow with a sly, cunning look. The others addressed him as Ned, and it later transpired that he came from Boscombe way, where he had quarrelled with and left another gang.

While Roger sat watching them from a corner of the smelly ill-lit cabin, the minutes seemed to drag again. He had a frightening vision of his father paying a last visit to his room before going to sleep, to see if he had come home by the window, and, on seeing the disorder there, coming hot-foot in pursuit of him. But he quickly reassured himself with the thought that even if his father did now discover the empty money-box and the scattered clothes he could not possibly guess where their owner had got to.

Thirty long minutes ticked away before Nick thrust his head over the edge of the hatchway and called: "Tide's on the ebb, Cap'n."

Abandoning the cards they all went on deck, a lantern was hoisted on the forestay and at a word from Dan the hawsers were cast off. Two of the men got out long sweeps and, as the lugger drifted away from the quayside, began to pole her out into open water. Dan took the tiller and gave another order, the sweeps were drawn inboard and the jib was set. It slapped for a moment, then bellied out, soon giving the ship enough way for Dan to steer her into the channel, and with the water barely rippling along her sides she dropped smoothly down river.

Roger looked back towards Lymington. Across the marshes he could see the two small beacons that marked the entrance to the harbour and the vague outline of the massed houses behind them; but the long, low salt-pans, from which for centuries the town had supplied half England and made a handsome revenue, were hidden by the darkness, as was the roof of his own home which he would have been able to make out easily, between its sheltering trees, had it been day-time.

Quarter of an hour of gentle tacking round the bends of the creek brought them to its mouth. The breeze seemed fresher now and Dan gave orders for the mainsail to be hoisted. Roger joined the others in hauling on the sheet; the wooden rings rattled against the mast, the boom swung over and the great spread of canvas rose above them. Leaving the land on their starboard beam they headed out towards the western extremity of the Isle of Wight.

After his long sleep Roger was not the least tired and he sat by Dan staring out with eager eyes into the darkness. Ahead he could see the warning beacon flashing on the cruel rocks of the Needles, to his left the friendly lights of Yarmouth harbour but to the right the great sweep of the mainland showed no signs of human occupation. In vain he searched the dark horizon there for a glimpse of Highcliffe Tower, but it was hidden by the night, so he could only gaze at a spot where he imagined it to be, as he thought of the beautiful Georgina, and wondered if she was still awake and thinking of him, or sound asleep in the big warm bed on which they had shared out her treasure that afternoon.

Giving the Needles a wide berth Dan turned the lugger out to sea and it was some half-hour after this new course had been set that Roger, chancing to glance astern, suddenly saw the faint shimmer of foam creaming at one solitary place in the gloom behind them.

"Dan!" he gasped in an excited whisper: "We're being followed! Look astern there! Naught but a ship's bow cutting through the wake could churn it up so steadily."

"Be easy, lad," Dan replied with unaccustomed familiarity, "There be more mysteries to this trade o' ours than 'e would wot of." Then, to Roger's surprise, he gave orders to douse the lights and lower the sails, and the lugger hove to.

The shimmer of foam rapidly grew to what seemed a quite abnormal height, until it was sufficiently near for Roger suddenly to realise that only the base of the pyramid at which he was gazing was formed of water and that from it rose the brow of a white-painted ship. A moment later her masts and sails were visible, and, checking her speed as she came up with them, she emerged like a ghost-ship out of the night, a trim little two-masted schooner.

Hails were exchanged with the newcomer, then Dan hoisted his jib and after a certain amount of manœuvring the two ships were brought alongside one another. The schooner's counter was slightly higher than that of the lugger, but by leaning over it the men in her could converse with Dan and his mates without raising their voices.

There was a brief interchange of questions and answers and on both parties ascertaining that all was well with the other Dan said to Roger, "Run, get thy bag, lad. We be goin' aboard her."

Roger hesitated. He had already given Dan the five pounds and he wondered unhappily if the smuggler, having been so averse to taking him in the first place, had later thought up some trick for getting his money but not taking him after all. He had now recognised the white schooner as the *Albatross*, out of Yarmouth, and suspected that he was to be put aboard her for shipment back to the island.

"What's toward, Dan?" he asked, striving to keep the uneasiness he felt out of his voice. "Why must I board her?"

" 'Tis not for 'e to ask questions," Dan replied gruffly. "Do as 'e's bid, an' smart about it, now."

Being in no position to argue, Roger turned away. If they intended to send him back there was nothing he could do about it, and no way in which he could recover his money from Dan, either. It was the first dealing he had had with lawless characters and he felt again how incompetent he was to hold his own outside the secure world he knew, in that where poverty made men unscrupulous.

The thought that he still had some fourteen pounds in cash upon him was some consolation. That was enough to get him to London and keep him for a week or two there. But suddenly it flashed upon him that the smugglers might rob him of the rest of his money before putting him ashore.

Hastening his steps he dived down into the cabin, pulled off his boots and poured his guineas and crowns into them, leaving only some small change in his pocket. In something of a panic now he pulled out the bulky packet of Georgina's jewels and wondered how he could possibly manage to conceal it. After a second he tore the silk scarf he was wearing from around his neck, spread it out on the table, undid the packet of jewels and poured them on to it. Rolling the scarf up he tied each of its ends in a knot and the middle with a strand of hemp that was lying handy; then he undid his clothes and arranged the long uneven sausage round his waist next his skin, in such a way that the leather belt of his breeches would keep it in position. He was still stuffing back his shirt over it when Dan's stentorian voice came to him.

"Below there! What the hell's keeping 'e?"

"Coming!" called Roger, and he stumbled up on deck again.

To his surprise he saw that several strange men from the schooner were now aboard the lugger and that her own crew were in the process of climbing over the schooner's counter. Evidently the two ships were exchanging crews and this, though queer, seemed somewhat reassuring; so, without further attempt to secure an explanation, he followed Dan aboard the *Albatross*.

The exchange having been made the two ships cast off. Amidst a chorus of muttered farewells from their crews the bumpers were hauled in and they drew apart.

When the *Sally Ann* had been swallowed up in the darkness Roger made his way down to the schooner's cabin. It was roomier and somewhat cleaner than that of the lugger, and it had eight bunks instead of only four. Depositing his satchel on one of them he went up again to seek out Dan, now feeling a twinge of remorse at his recent fears that the smuggler intended to cheat and rob him.

The crew were busy setting the sails and Dan was standing at the break of the shallow poop behind the big wheel.

"I've no wish to pry, Dan," Roger said as he joined him, "but

I'm all agog to know the reason for the exchange we've just made. Won't you tell me what lies behind it?"

The smuggler laughed. "Aye, why not. 'E'll find out for 'e's self soon enough. 'Tis this way. The Riding Officers be mighty spry these days roun' Mudeford and Bourne Heath; but the Isle o' Wight has quiet covers a plenty, so 'tis there we now run our cargoes. Then the Yarmouth lads bring 'em over piecemeal, a few kegs at a time, in the little boats that be always plyin' to an' fro from the island."

"So that's why 'tis done," murmured Roger. "But why couldn't you land your cargo on the island direct from the lugger?"

"I could, lad; an' always did in the good days. But as I've telled 'e Ollie Nixon's out to have my blood. 'Tis to fox he that we make the change o' craft. Come daylight should he sight the *Sally Ann*, 'tis her he'll keep his weather eye on, while she does a bit o' harmless fishin' an' we take the *Albatross* to France."

" 'Tis monstrous clever, that, Dan."

"Aye; 'tis a ruse that has worked twice afore, an' pray God 'twill work again."

For the best part of two hours Roger remained on deck, while the little schooner, lifting and falling gently to the swell, cleaved her way through the night; then he thought that he would turn in for a bit. The knobs and points of the jewel-filled bandage round his waist irked him somewhat but their weight was better distributed than it had been as a heavy packet in his pocket, so he decided to leave them as they were, and, adjusting them more comfortably, lay down on his bunk in his clothes. Youth can do with far more sleep than age, and, in spite of his long nap that evening, he had hardly closed his eyes before he dropped off.

When he awoke it was daylight and a strong smell of cooking assailed his nostrils. On sitting up he saw that Fred Mullins was busy cooking bacon, onions and pigs' fry in the tiny galley that formed the far end of the cabin. Tidying his hair as best he could in a cracked mirror nailed to the bulkhead, he joined the ex-naval jolly and helped lay up the table for breakfast.

The men came down for their meal in relays, Dan being last, and when he had eaten he turned in for a spell while Roger went on deck. The old fisherman, Simon Fry, was now at the wheel and the schooner was scudding along on a fine breeze. The weather promised well and on looking round the horizon Roger could see no sail except the *Sally Ann*, which apparently had kept them company all through the night, and now lay about a mile away on their port quarter.

There was nothing to do but laze in the sunshine and, making himself as comfortable as he could on a coil of rope Roger took his ease there all through the morning. At midday he joined the crew in another rough and ready meal and, after it, Dan took the wheel again.

As he did so he asked Roger how he was feeling, and Roger, having entirely forgotten the plea by which he had induced the smuggler to take him on the trip, replied cheerfully: "I never felt better, Dan. I'm as fit as a fiddle."

" 'Tis just as I told 'e," Dan laughed. "Tain't no different in mid-channel, here, than 'tis huggin' the coast in a bit o' a yawl. An' we's nigher to France than England now. Come six o'clock we should make a landfall."

The early hours of the afternoon drifted by uneventfully but soon after four o'clock Nick Bartlett, who was acting as lookout, called: "Sail astern, Cap'n."

Slipping a noose of rope over one of the spokes of the wheel to keep it in position Dan picked up a spy-glass and focused it on the speck that the surly longshoreman had reported.

After a few moments he lowered his telescope with a curse and added: " 'Tis the Revenue cutter *Expedition*; Ollie Nixon be after us again."

"Well, you've naught to fear," Roger said in an effort to reassure him. " 'Tis the *Sally Ann* that he'll be interested in, not us."

"Aye, let's hope so," Dan muttered, "may God rot his guts."

The captain of the *Sally Ann* had also evidently sighted the Revenue cutter, as she began to play her part as a decoy and draw away, while the *Albatross* held on her course.

All the crew had now assembled on deck and for the next half-hour they watched the Revenue cutter anxiously. She was considerably faster than either of the other ships, and soon began to overhaul them. In order to avoid arousing the Revenue men's suspicions the *Sally Ann* had not taken any drastic action that would have been immediately perceptible to them but only adopted a slightly divergent course a few more points to westward; so it was at first impossible to tell whether the cutter was in pursuit of the schooner or the lugger.

Then, to their dismay, the issue became certain. The *Sally Ann* was now a good two miles away and had dropped some distance astern; but the *Expedition* was ignoring her and, with all sail spread, coming up in the wake of the *Albatross*.

"Darn his eyes!" Dan swore. "He've smelled our red herring once too often, an' he means to board us."

"What if he does?" said Roger. "You've not loaded your contraband yet, so he can't lay a finger on you."

"Nay," Dan muttered uneasily, "To-night we've naught to fear 'cept from the Frenchies. But Ollie Nixon havin' tumbled to our ruse bodes ill for our homeward run. Once he have satisfied hisself that 'tis me an' my lads is aboard the *Albatross* he'll patrol these waters for days to get us."

While they had been talking the cutter had come up to within hailing distance of the schooner and a faint but clear call came to them from across the water:

"Heave-to, there! In the King's name, heave-to!"

With another curse Dan gave the wheel a spin, bringing the schooner round within six points of the wind, so that her sails emptied and began to flop idly against her stays. Her crew scattered quickly to reef them in, and while they were still busy at it the cutter drew abreast. No sooner had she checked her way than some of her people began to get out a boat. It was easy to see that they were used to the business, from the despatch they used, and five minutes later a smart gig was making fast to the schooner's stern.

A heavy, red-faced man hauled himself aboard and his sharp black eyes swept the little group of sullen-looking sailors.

"Arternoon, Mr. Nixon," said Dan, with the best grace he could muster.

"So, 'tis you, Dan Izzard," Nixon muttered, "I guessed as much. What are you and your culleys doing aboard the *Albatross?*"

"Cap'n Cummings giv' me the loan o' her, Sir. 'E'll allow there's naught illegal in that."

Nay, naught illegal, but 'tis monstrous fishy seeing that I know you to have sailed from Lymington last night in the *Sally Ann*. What cargo are you carrying; or are you in ballast?"

"In ballast, may it please your honour," replied Dan sarcastically.

Nixon turned to a petty officer who had scrambled aboard after him. "Nip down into her hold, Higgins, and take a look-see."

As the man moved to obey Dan threw up a hand to restrain him and grumbled: "Easy, easy. If 'e must stick 'e's nose into other folks' business 'tis a cargo o' salt we have aboard, an' we're bound for Le Havre."

"So that's the lay, is it?" Nixon's heavy face broke into a sly grin. "All right, Higgins, we'll take his word for it."

"B'ain't naught illegal in that, neither," said Dan with a scowl.

"Not if you land your salt openly at Le Havre; but I'm not in King Louis's pay, so that's not my affair."

As Nixon turned to regain his boat he suddenly caught sight of Roger who, up till then, had been standing half-concealed from him by the big wheel. Halting, he exclaimed in surprise:

"Why, 'tis Master Brook! What would you be doing here?"

"I'm shortly going into the Navy, Sir," Roger replied promptly. "And I came on this trip to try out my sea legs."

" 'Tis strange company to find a young gentleman in," Nixon frowned. "I'll make no accusations I can't prove: but if there's contraband in the vessel next time I board her 'twill be my duty to take you, if you're among her crew, and charge you with the rest."

Roger flushed slightly as he lied: "I'm sure Dan Izzard and his men intend nothing illegal, Sir."

"I am entitled to my doubts of that, and if you're here for a lark it has lasted long enough. If 'tis no more than a sea trip you sought come with me, and I'll give you passage home."

"Thanks, Sir, but I've never been abroad and I'm all agog to see Le Havre, so, if you'll excuse me, I prefer to stay with Dan."

"Unless my wits deceive me, should you remain aboard the *Albatross* there's a chance of you finding yourself in a French galley instead of seeing Le Havre. Come now! Come home with me, and let me earn your mother's gratitude."

Roger did not fully take in the meaning of this allusion to a French galley and, even had he done so, it seemed to him now that so much depended on his being able to land in France, that it is doubtful if he would have allowed the warning to influence him. As it was he simply shook his head and said again: "Thanks, Sir, but I prefer to stay with Dan."

Nixon shrugged his broad shoulders. "So be it then; but I fear you'll have cause to repent of your folly before you're much older."

With a curt nod to Dan he went over the ship's side, followed by his man, and a moment later the gig's crew were giving way lustily as they pulled him back to the *Expedition*.

The sails of the *Albatross* were re-set and, leaving the Revenue cutter behind, she was soon skimming over the water towards the French coast once more.

A little belatedly, and uneasily now, Roger was thinking over Mr. Nixon's sinister remark, that he might find himself in a French galley instead of seeing Le Havre. If Dan had a cargo of Lymington salt aboard it was obviously destined for France. The French, so Roger had heard, were forced to pay an exceptionally high price for this simple commodity, owing to an exorbitant tax that their king had put upon it. The tax was called the *gabelle*, and was one of the French people's principle reasons for discontent against the monarchy. Since Dan had for years earned his living by smuggling illicit spirits into England it seemed most unlikely that he would willingly pay a heavy import duty in order to land a cargo of salt in France.

Having reached the conclusion that Dan contemplated making a big illegal profit at both ends of his trip, Roger was not particularly perturbed by the additional risk in which he had unwittingly involved himself, because Dan had for so many years proved himself a capable and canny smuggler, but he became extremely worried at the thought that the *Albatross* might both unload her cargo of salt and take on a new one of spirits in some secluded cove, and not enter the port of Le Havre at all.

Striving to conceal his new anxiety he went up to Dan and asked: "What time should we make Le Havre, Dan?"

"First light to-morrow morning, all bein' well, lad," Dan replied quite casually. "We've a rendezvous, as the Frenchies call it, wi' some friends o' mine farther down the coast to-night. Then we beats up channel to the port to pick up our nice drop o' liquor, an' sails for home at dusk."

This was highly reassuring, and Roger smothered a sigh of relief, as it now seemed clear that they were not only really going to Le Havre, but that he would have the whole day in which to go ashore and dispose of his jewels.

"Do the French Preventives give you much trouble?" he asked after a moment.

"Nay. They's nothin' nigh so smart as our chaps, nor so numerous. 'Tis good money for old rope so long as 'e don't fall foul o' one o' they's men o' war. Look, lad! Do'st see the dark streak on the horizon, yonder? 'Tis the coast of France."

All else forgotten, Roger picked up Dan's spy-glass and, glueing his eye to it, endeavoured to make out the features of that strange land where lived England's traditional enemies, and of which he had heard so much.

Occasionally Dan glanced over his shoulder at Mr. Nixon's cutter. He had thought that after boarding him she would put back towards England, if only temporarily, but to his annoyance she continued to follow in the wake of the *Albatross* under three-quarter sail. Now, as he luffed and brought the schooner round on to a westward course so that she should run down the Normandy coast while still some miles distant from it, the cutter ignored his action and, somewhat to his surprise, continued on a course towards Le Havre.

Soon after this they took their evening meal, and when Roger came on deck again the cutter had disappeared from sight. But now they were considerably nearer the French coast and here and there could see small craft working their way along it.

About nine o'clock, just as the summer dusk was beginning to fall, they discerned twenty or thirty dots on the horizon astern, which Dan said were the Le Havre fishing fleet putting out to sea. Roger watched them idly through the spy-glass for a while. They too, seemed to be on a westward course as, although they grew no larger, they did not drop from view; and one of them that seemed to be much larger than the rest even appeared to be gaining on the *Albatross*.

He was just about to draw Dan's attention to this bigger ship when he was distracted by the smuggler giving orders for the lowering of the main and fore sails; as they had now come opposite that part of the coast where he had his rendezvous and he intended to lay off there until full darkness would cover his landing operation.

When Roger looked through the glass again he saw that not one but two of the ships in the fishing fleet were of different build and, clearly now, much larger than the rest. Both had detached themselves from the scattered line of dots and were coming on ahead of them under full sail. Running over to Dan he pointed them out to him.

Dan took the glass and studied them for a moment. " 'Tis two traders, what have sailed out o' Le Havre on the tide, like as not," he declared. "But take the glass, lad, and keep 'e's eye upon they."

Again Roger focused the two oncoming ships for a few moments. There seemed something vaguely familiar about the rig of the smaller of the two, and suddenly he recognised her.

"The smaller one," he cried, " 'Tis Mr. Nixon's cutter."

Dan snatched the telescope from him. "Aye, lad, 'e's right!" he grunted. "What devil's work would he be up to now? And what be other craft? Hi! Fred Mullins! What make 'e of yon ship? The bigger o' the two."

The ex-naval rating took the glass and, steadying it against a stay, took a long look at the approaching ships. Identification was not easy, owing to the falling twilight and the fact that the stranger craft being dead astern only her bows and fore sails were visible.

"She's a Frenchie," he muttered. "And if I mistake not, a thirty-six gun frigate."

"God's death!" swore Dan. " 'Tis as I feared. That bastard Nixon has betrayed us. Just think on it. What sort o' Englishman is he who would bring the Frogs upon us, an' send we to a daily floggin' in they's galleys. Avast, there! Avast! Up sail an' away."

Instantly every member of the crew flung himself into feverish activity. To be caught smuggling contraband into England was one thing, except on overwhelming evidence no bench of magistrates would convict; to be captured by the French quite another—it meant a hideous and long drawn-out death, rotting in chains shackled to an oar, in one of the French war galleys. In a bare ten minutes every sail the schooner could carry was set and she was standing out to sea, their one hope now being to escape in the gathering darkness.

As the light deepened they watched their pursuers with terrible anxiety. Both ships had altered course and were now beating seaward on lines converging with that of the schooner in the hope of cutting her off. The frigate and the *Expedition* were both faster ships than their prey and it was soon perceptible that they were gaining on her.

Roger prayed for darkness as he had never prayed before, yet it seemed that the long summer twilight scarcely deepened and that night would never fall. Dan stood grimly by the wheel getting every ounce of way out of the schooner of which she was capable. His crew had wrenched aside her hatches and, working like madmen, were now jettisoning her cargo, in the hope that if they could only get all the great blocks of salt overboard before the frigate came up with her they would be able to show a hold free of contraband.

As Roger lent a hand, he kept an anxious eye on the frigate. Staggering under the weight of one of the blocks he was just about to tip it overboard when he saw a little cloud of white smoke issue from her fo'c'sle head. A moment later he heard a sharp report. He did not see the shot but guessed that their pursuer had fired a round from her long gun at some point ahead of their bows to bring them to.

The shadows had deepened now and, ignoring the warning, Dan held on his course, still hoping that night might cover their escape from French waters.

The gun boomed again and Roger saw the second shot ricochet across the waves within ten yards of the schooner's starboard quarter. Still Dan doggedly held on and gave no order to lower sail.

A third time a little white cloud issued from the frigate's fo'c'sle and the report echoed across the water, to be followed almost instantly by the crashing of woodwork in the schooner's stern. The roundshot had found a mark in her poop, and, crashing through it, bounded along her deck.

As to what happened next Roger was not quite sure. He heard the gun fire a fourth time, then there was a frightful splintering of wood. The schooner's main mast heeled over and came crashing down. Sails, ropes and spars seemed to be flying in all directions. Something hit him a terrific buffet in the back, knocking him off his feet and throwing him forward. Next moment he found himself in the water struggling for his life.

CHAPTER VII

THE MAN IN RED

R o g e r was a good swimmer, but never before had he been plunged into the sea fully dressed; within a moment he found that his sodden clothes hampered him enormously. In addition he had coins in his boots and several pounds weight of precious metal around his waist. As he felt the pull of them dragging him down he was overtaken by panic and opened his mouth to let out a yell. His shout for help was cut short by a wave crest slapping into his face. Choked by sea water, he gulped, and went under.

The next minutes were a nightmare to him. Lack of breath caused a suffocating pain in his chest and as he sank he thought that he was done for. In a violent effort to save himself he attempted to kick off his boots; they did not come off but his frantic kicking brought him back to the surface.

Gasping in air he struck out wildly, with no thought of direction or husbanding his strength but simply with the animal instinct to keep himself from drowning. After a dozen flailing strokes he saw that he was heading towards the French frigate. Seen from low down on the water she seemed much larger now and she was still coming on under full sail.

By swimming with all his strength he found that he could keep afloat and make a little headway; but he knew that the frigate would pass him at some distance and that, in the gathering gloom, it was most unlikely that anyone on her deck would see him struggling there in the water.

Thrusting himself round he looked towards the *Albatross*. He was now about two hundred yards astern of her, since her way had carried her on that far before the shattered main mast, that now hung over her side, had dragged her to a standstill.

He wondered desperately if he would have the strength to gain her. Georgina's treasure now threatened to be his death; it hung like a thick belt of lead resting on his hips, and, as it was under his clothes, there was no way in which he could get rid of it. With every stroke he took its weight seemed to increase and it kept him so low in the water that every wavelet broke over his face, filling his eyes and nostrils with salty spume. Despair now gripped his heart and he felt that each moment would be his last.

His range of vision was very limited and he had only glimpsed the schooner by heaving himself up with a special effort, so he did not even see the big spar that had come adrift from her main mast until it was washed right on top of him. With a gasp of relief he threw his arms over it and hung there, panting.

Having got his breath back and shaken the water from his eyes he hoisted his head above the spar and took a quick look round. He was still a good hundred and fifty yards astern of the disabled *Albatross*.

The frigate was now coming up abreast of her and in the failing light he could just make out the *Expedition* a quarter of a mile astern of the frigate. Dropping back he remained for about five minutes swaying gently in the water while his agitated mind sought a way of getting himself rescued.

When he looked again he saw that the frigate and cutter had both hove to. Their lanterns were lit and the former was lowering a boat. It was too dark to make out any details but faintly he could hear a French officer shouting orders and then the splash of the oars as the boat was pulled towards the *Albatross* to take the smugglers in her prisoner.

At that thought his heart sank even lower. As long as he could cling to the heavy spar he was safe from a watery grave but rescue meant the frightful prospect of being sent as a slave to the French war galleys. For a few moments he was racked with indecision whether to hang on there, on the chance of being washed ashore or picked up by another ship, or to put all his strength into shouts for help, and accept the grim alternative.

The summer night had now closed down, and when he bobbed up he could make out the stricken *Albatross* only as a vague whitish blur; the positions of the frigate and cutter were indicated by their lights. For a few moments more he wavered, then he decided that he dared not ignore this chance of rescue, however frightful the future that it portended, and he began to shout.

After a minute he thought he heard an answering cry, and paused to listen, but it did not come again and he realised that an altercation was going on between Dan and his men and the Frenchmen in the boat. Panicking again at the thought that he might not be able to make himself heard he began to yell with all the force of his lungs.

Again he paused to listen, there was silence now. The *Albatross* was no longer visible and the lights of the frigate and cutter seemed farther off. Grimly it came to him that the tide must be carrying him away from them, and frantically now, he called again and again; but there was no response.

After ten minutes, his throat sore and his breath coming in gasps from the effort, he gave up. Full darkness had come and as he could now see only the mast lights of the two ships in which his hope of rescue lay, he knew that he must have drifted at least half a mile away from them.

His one hope was that he would be able to cling on to the spar until he was washed ashore or daylight came with a new chance of rescue. Fortunately it was high summer and the water was quite warm but, even so, he feared that his hands would grow numb and lose their grip on the spar before many hours had passed.

With the idea of finding an easier hold he began to pull his way along the spar and soon came upon a length of rope that was trailing from it. Hanging on, first with one hand then with the other, he got the rope under his arms and managed to lash himself to the spar sufficiently firmly for only a light hold on it to be necessary to keep his head above water. Slightly relieved in mind he relaxed a little but now that he had leisure to think for the first time since he had been thrown overboard his thoughts brought him little comfort.

The thing that had made the greatest impression on him in the past hectic hour was Mr. Ollie Nixon's betrayal of his compatriots to the French. It was obvious now that the *Expedition* had left the *Albatross's* tail only to make for Le Havre, and that Nixon had tipped off the authorities there that a smuggler craft was just down the coast well inside French territorial waters. He had then followed the frigate in order to gloat over the ill fate that he had brought upon the unfortunate Dan and his companions. Roger would never have believed that an Englishman could be capable of such baseness and he made a mental vow that, if he lived, he would somehow get even with Nixon on Dan's account as well as his own. But, at the moment, the chances of his surviving to carry out his vow looked far from good.

The mast lights of both the ships had now disappeared below Roger's limited horizon and, although the stars had come out, there was no hint of human life whichever way he peered through the surrounding gloom.

For what seemed an eternity he hung there, submerged up to his armpits in water, his dangling legs swaying gently with the motion of the waves. Georgina's prophecy that water would always be dangerous to him reoccurred to his mind. He thought how surprised she would be if she knew how swiftly it had been fulfilled; as by this time she no doubt fondly imagined him to be lodged at some comfortable inn in London having safely deposited the proceeds of her jewels in Messrs. Hoare's bank. He sought such comfort as he could from the idea that her other prophecies had yet to be fulfilled, but he remembered with misgiving her once having told him that things seen in the glass would come to pass only if the subject pursued a path made natural to him through his character and environment—as indeed most people did—but that an abnormal exercise of free will might cause deviations from it, or the whole future suddenly be rendered void by a higher power decreeing death for the subject.

As he tried to weigh the pros and cons of the matter in his mind he was temporarily cheered again by the thought that he was off the coast of France, and it was in France that Georgina had seen him fighting a duel. Yet she had been very definite that the duel would not take place for several years, and if he was washed ashore he meant to get back to England as soon as he possibly could, so that did not get him anywhere either.

He had now been in the water for an hour and a half and with the advance of the night he was becoming chilly. As he began to jerk his limbs about to restore his circulation he turned his head, and suddenly saw a moving light no more than fifty yards distant from him. Instantly he began to shout.

A French voice answered his cries, excited shouts followed; the direction in which the light was moving changed, now coming towards him, and the bulk of a small craft, with her sails set, loomed up out of the darkness. A few minutes later he was being hauled aboard her.

Roger's French consisted only of what he had picked up at school during a year of lessons, and the handful of sailors who crowded round him as he was dragged squelching on to the deck questioned him in their Normandy patois, which he found it almost impossible to understand. But his flair for languages had enabled him to make good use of his comparatively slender instruction. He managed to convey to them that he had fallen overboard unnoticed in the darkness from an English merchantman an hour earlier, and to gather that their boat was one of the fishing fleet which he had seen after they had put out from Le Havre, just before dusk that evening.

A short, swarthy man with gorilla-like shoulders, who appeared to be the Captain, took him below to the tiny cabin. He had borne up so far, but now the reaction from the shock and strain of the last few hours set in and he practically collapsed. It was all he could do to swallow the fiery Calvados that was poured down his throat and to keep his senses while his soaking garments were peeled from his body. Within a quarter of an hour of his rescue he was wrapped up like a mummy in four thicknesses of rough blankets and sound asleep.

When he woke it was daylight and he found the swarthy Captain staring down at him. They exchanged a few more sentences with difficulty, from which Roger learned that the smack had had a good night's fishing and was now heading back to Le Havre. The man then gave him a basin of gruel and left him.

Roger's first thought was for his possessions, but with great relief he saw that the sausage-like bundle, containing Georgina's jewels, had been laid, still tied by the piece of hemp, beside him, and that near it in a small crockery pot were the gold and silver coins that he had had in his boots. His rescuers were evidently honest men, or, perhaps, having recognised that he was a person of quality by his clothes, had been afraid to rob him; but he felt that on discovering his wealth they must have been highly tempted and might well have thrown him back into the sea after despoiling him, so he blessed their integrity.

As he looked round the mean little cabin he thought it all the more striking from their evident poverty. That of Dan's lugger had smelt almost as evilly, but there had been an air of rough comfort about it; bits of spare clothing, worn but of good thick material, stout leather sea-boots, a flitch of bacon and a cask of rum. Here, there was nothing but the refuse of semi-destitution. Even the Captain, Roger had noticed, wore ragged trousers of some thin cotton stuff and wooden clogs, while the gruel he had been given was obviously the crew's normal fare, as there was no good English odour of liver, onions and bacon lingering about the cabin.

The blankets, too, in which he was wrapped were little better than sacking; but, since his clothes had been taken away, there seemed no alternative to lying there until they were returned to him.

For some two hours he dozed and meditated on his own miraculous preservation, the strange sequence of events that had led to his being where he was and the wretched fate which he had good reason to suppose had overtaken the crew of the *Albatross*. Then the Captain clattered down the ladder, bringing him his clothes.

They had been rough-dried on deck in the morning sunshine and, apart from the fact that they were sadly rumpled, appeared to be little the worse for their immersion. As he put them on he thought sadly of the fine warm greatcoat, and of the satchell with his silver-mounted pistols and other items he valued in it, all of which he had left behind in the cabin of the *Albatross;* but he swiftly upbraided himself for worrying about such comparative trifles when a merciful Providence had spared him his life, liberty and little fortune.

On going on deck he found that the smack and some two score of her fellow craft were running before a fair breeze towards a smudge on the horizon which must be the coast of France. The bulk of the little ship was occupied by its hold and this was now more than half-filled by a great heap of shiny silver fish, mainly haddocks, whiting and plaice. While he was looking at it one of the crew leant over and gathered a few of them into a small basket, which he took below. Then, half an hour later, the Captain came to Roger, took off his cap, bowed to him and invited him down to the cabin.

In it he saw that some food had been put ready on a rough pine table, but to his surprise the Captain did not sit down with him. Indicating a bench to Roger he tipped the fish from a saucepan out on to a large earthenware dish, cut from a loaf a great hunk of rye bread which he laid beside it, then stood back, respectfully.

Seeing that he was expected to eat with his fingers, Roger set to. The fish had been plain boiled with a clove of garlic and, owing to their freshness, Roger found them excellent. He would have much preferred them fried, but guessed that these poor fisher-folk could not afford the luxury of fat. There was a jug on the table, but no glass, and on drinking from it, Roger found that it contained still cider of an incredible sourness; and it was all he could do, in deference to his host, to prevent his face screwing up into an agonised grimace.

When he had done the Captain bowed him up on deck again and calling to two of his men they went down to eat their share of the mess of fish.

Roger now found that the coast was clearly visible and an hour later the masts of the shipping in the great port of Le Havre could be clearly made out. The fishing fleet duly put into its own harbour, which was some little way from the big naval dock and the basins in which the merchantmen were berthed.

There were no landing formalities to go through here so it remained only for Roger to thank his rescuers. Having Georgina's jewels safely round his waist again he felt that he could well afford to be at least as generous as he had been with Dan, so he gave the swarthy Captain five out of the fourteen pounds that remained to him. The Frenchman did not appear to have expected so handsome a present and with many barely understandable expressions of gratitude bowed Roger on to the wharf as though he had been a veritable Prince.

Roger had yet to learn that the poor of France were in such a sad condition of slavery to the nobility that, far from daring to lay a finger on him, they would almost certainly have executed any reasonable order that he cared to give without expecting to be rewarded in any way for their services. As it was, he walked off into the town with the happy feeling that he had satisfactorily maintained the honour of England and the belief that every English gentleman was a *milor* rich beyond the dreams of avarice.

The clocks of the city were chiming half-past three as he landed and it was again a pleasant sunny afternoon. Turning into the *Rue Francois 1er*, which, as it chanced, was the busiest and most fashionable thoroughfare of the town, he entered its turmoil, turning his head swiftly from side to side as each new sight or sound of this strange foreign town caught his attention. Although the street was comparatively broad for the times the upper storeys of the houses that lined it projected so far above the lower that they almost met overhead. In this it differed little from the streets that he knew well in Winchester and Southampton, but its occupants seemed to him almost as if they were all got up in fancy dress.

In France, a much richer and more colourful standard of attire was still maintained among the upper classes than had of recent years become the fashion in England. Few gentlemen had as yet abandoned wigs unless their own hair was prolific and in that case they still wore it powdered. Cloth was still regarded as a bourgeois material, except for wear when travelling, and the men from the smart equipages who were shopping in the street were nearly all clad in satin or velvet, while their ladies were dressed in flowered silk skirts with bulging panniers and wore absurd little hats perched on elaborate powdered coiffures, often as much as a foot and a half in height.

Even the common people seemed more colourful than those in English provincial cities, as the grisettes aped the fashions of their betters, the postilions and footmen were all dressed in gaudy liveries, and the sober black of the countrywomen who had come into market was relieved by their picturesque local head-dresses of white lace.

The goods of the shopkeepers in this busy centre were displayed not only in the bow windows but also on trestles outside their shops and the wealth of articles they offered struck Roger as in strange contrast to the dire poverty of the fishermen he had just left.

The street was so crowded with vehicles and its sides so cluttered with stalls that half-a-dozen times Roger had to dodge beneath the heads of horses, or swerve to avoid the wheel of a coach, in order to escape being run over. But at every opportunity he paused to sniff up the spicy scent that came from an *epicerie* or to stare into a shop window in which, to him, unusual goods were displayed.

Behind the narrow panes of one halfway down the street he saw an array of swords, and stopped to look at them. In England, civilians no longer wore swords habitually, but he had been quick to notice that here in France, every man who, from his raiment, had any pretension to quality carried a sword at his side: in fact it was obviously the hallmark by which the gentry distinguished themselves from their inferiors.

His delight in arms had often led him to regret that the fashion of carrying a sword had gone out at home; and the next day or two, until he could get a passage back to England, offered an excellent opportunity to indulge himself in such a foible. For a moment he hesitated, the carefulness inherited with his Scots' blood causing him to wonder if the expense was really justified for a few hours' amusement, but he found a ready pretext in the thought that nothing could make a more satisfactory and lasting souvenir of both his first day alone in the world and of his visit to France; so he entered the shop and, in a carefully chosen phrase, asked to look at some of the swords.

The armourer at first produced several court swords suitable to Roger's height, but as he would have to put his purchase away on his return to England he decided to buy a proper duelling weapon of a man's length which he could use when fully grown if ever he was called out.

The man hid a smile and laid a number on a long strip of velvet for Roger's inspection. They varied in price from a *pistol* to six *louis*, according to their condition and the ornamentation of their hilts, so most of them were beyond Roger's pocket. After testing several he selected one that had been marked down to a *louis* and a half, on account of its plain old-fashioned hilt, but had a blade of fine Toledo steel.

On his taking out his money to pay for it he explained that he had only just landed in France and the armourer readily agreed to send one of his apprentices along the street to have it changed at the nearest bank, so Roger asked for three of his remaining guineas to be changed.

While the lad was gone Roger chose a frog, which cost a *crown*, for attaching the sword to his belt, and buckled it on. The change arrived as twenty-four *crowns* and at first Roger was a little puzzled by it. He knew that a French *louis* was the equivalent of an English pound, but a crown in England meant five shillings so it looked as if his three guineas had miraculously turned into six *louis*. The armourer smilingly explained to him. A *louis* was worth twenty-four *livres*, or *francs* as they were now beginning to be called; a *pistol* twenty and a French *crown* only three, or half the value of an English one; so he had been given the French equivalent for his money less a shilling in the guinea, which had been deducted for the exchange.

Having paid thirteen *crowns* for his purchases he pocketed the remaining eleven three-*franc* pieces, thanked the armourer and left the shop with a little swagger at the thought of the fine figure he must now cut with the point of his long sword sticking out behind him.

A few doors farther down he noticed a hat shop and suddenly realised that, having lost his own, he probably did not cut such a fine figure after all. The defect was soon remedied by the purchase of a smart high-brimmed tricorne with a ruching of marabout which cost him another three *crowns*. It was somewhat elaborate by contrast with his plain blue cloth coat but definitely in the fashion of the French gentlemen who were passing up and down the crowded street.

It next occurred to him that he would need a few toilet articles for the night and a change of linen, so he turned back towards the quay and visited several other shops he had noticed, including a tanner's where he bought himself a leather bag, and a mercer's, at which, amongst other things, he selected a fine lace jabot that he put on there and then in place of his own crumpled linen neck-band.

His purchases completed, he suddenly realised that he was very hungry so he turned into a *patisserie*. On looking round he was astonished at the wonderful variety of cakes and sweets displayed, most of which he had never seen in England. Seating himself at a little marble-topped, gilt-edged table, he ordered hot chocolate and soon made heavy inroads into a big dish of cakes, sending in due course for more chocolate éclairs, as he found this admirable invention of Louis XIV's most famous chef particularly delightful.

To his relief he had found on his shopping expedition that, whereas the Normandy patois of his rescuers had been almost incomprehensible to him, he had little difficulty in understanding the French spoken by the townsfolk. By asking them to speak slowly he could usually get their meaning, anyhow at a second attempt, and by thinking out carefully what he wished to say himself before speaking he had succeeded quite well in making himself understood.

On paying his score he asked the white-coated pastrycook behind the counter if he could recommend a good clean inn which was not too expensive.

"Monsieur," declared the man with a smiling bow, "You could have asked no one better than myself. Go to *Les Trois Fleur-de-Lys*, down on the *Quai Colbert*. There your lordship will find soft beds and excellent fare for the modest sum of a *crown* a day; also a cellar renowned and company of the most distinguished. The host, Maître Picard, is an honest man and will serve you well. He is my uncle by marriage, so I can vouch for him. Please to mention me and you will lack for nothing."

The recommendation sounded so good that Roger did not hesitate to accept it and, having secured directions from the pastry-cook, he set off to *Les Trois Fleur-de-Lys*.

When he reached it he was a little disappointed. The inn was a small one in an old and poor part of the town, and its exterior had long lacked paint, but it overlooked the *Bassin Vauban* where much interesting shipping activity was in progress and Roger felt that he could not expect to lodge in a palace for three francs a day; so he went in and asked for the host.

Maître Picard proved to be a fat, oily-looking man of lethargic habits, but he was quick enough to smell money in Roger's smart feathered hat and fine lace jabot. Washing his hands with invisible soap and bowing at every sentence with the servility of his tribe he confirmed the terms that Roger had been given and took him up to an attic room. As he saw his prospective guest's look of distaste at such poor accommodation he hastened to explain that there were rooms more suitable to a gentleman of his quality on the lower floors, but they ran from six *francs* to a half *pistol* a day.

Having turned down the bed and seen that the cotton sheets were clean, Roger decided that even small economies now would help him to make a better show when he got to London; so he told the landlord that as he would not be staying for more than a few nights the room would serve.

Maître Picard then inquired about supper. A *pot-au-feu* followed by a dish of vegetables and *petit cœurs à la Reine*—the cream cheese of the locality—were in with the price of the room. But the English *milor* would not find such simple bourgeois fare at all to his taste. No doubt he would wish a turbot and a chicken cooked to supplement them?

Full as he was with cream-filled chocolate éclairs, Roger felt that at the moment there was nothing he would wish less, and he said so; adding that when supper-time came he felt sure that a bowl of soup and some cheese would prove ample for his needs.

Resentful now that he should have been deceived into believing his customer a man of wealth by the feathers and lace he wore, the landlord gave a surly nod and shuffled from the room.

Roger unpacked his few belongings, then, bolting the door, undid his clothes and took the knobbly sausage of gold trinkets from round his waist. It had chafed him considerably so he was much relieved to be free of it, but he wondered now what to do with his treasure. As he knew, its bulk and weight made it awkward to carry done up in a packet in one of the pockets of his coat yet if he distributed it about his person he felt that here, in this crowded city, he would run a considerable risk of losing some of it through having his pockets picked. After a little thought he decided that if he could find a safe place his best course would be to hide it for the night somewhere in the room.

A careful inspection of the floor revealed a loose board under the deal washstand, so he prized it up and thrust his hoard as far under it as he could reach. He had hardly got the board back into place when there came a knock on the door.

Swiftly adjusting his clothes he opened it to find outside a spotty, depressed-looking little chambermaid who had come up to ask if he required anything.

Taking off his crumpled blue coat he asked her if she could press it for him and let him have it back as soon as possible.

When she had gone he re-examined his business-like-looking sword with the keenest pleasure and made a few passes with it; but he soon wearied of this and began to wonder how best to amuse himself. The window of the attic did not look out on the *Bassin Vauban* but on to the narrow, dirty stableyard of the inn. The dinner hour was long since past and that of supper, even if he had wanted it, not yet come. So he decided to take a turn along the quays and look at the shipping, while it was still light. As soon as the chambermaid brought back his coat he put it on and, going downstairs, went out on to the wharf.

After an hour's walk he returned to *Les Trois Fleur-de-Lys* and went into its parlour. The "company of the most distinguished" promised by the pastry-cook turned out to consist of two men engaged in a game of backgammon, who looked like ill-paid sea captains, an old man in a blue cloth suit, with a shock of white hair, a fine forehead and watery blue eyes, and a lanky fellow of about thirty dressed in a red velvet coat that looked somewhat the worse for wear. The old man was staring vacantly in front of him while he toyed with a tot of spirits and Roger decided that he was either dotty or three-parts drunk; the man in the red velvet was reading a badly-printed news-sheet through a quizzing glass, but he lowered it as Roger came in, gave him a sharp glance, and, bowing slightly, said:

"Good evening to you, Monsieur."

As Roger returned the bow and the greeting, the man went on in an amiable tone: "Pray, pardon my apparent curiosity, but are you a casual visitor here? Or have you, perchance, taken a room in this pestiferous hostelry?"

Roger admitted to the latter and asked: "And you, Monsieur?"

"For my sins I have been lying here some ten days," came the prompt reply. "And I am near dying of boredom; so 'tis a most welcome diversion to see a new face."

"If you dislike it here, why do you remain?" Roger inquired with a smile.

"I am forced to it," the lanky individual answered, his long face breaking into a wry grin. "I owe the plaguey landlord a trifling sum— a mere bagatelle of eighty *crowns* or so—and he has had the impudence to seize my baggage as surety for its payment. So I must needs remain here till the funds that I am expecting daily, reach me."

Roger had to ask for parts of this to be repeated more slowly, explaining that he was an Englishman who had only that day arrived in France.

"You astound me," exclaimed his new acquaintance. "The little French you have spoken is so excellent that I had no idea you were a foreigner."

"You flatter me, Monsieur," said Roger, a flush of pleasure mounting to his face. "But 'tis the fact."

The man in red stood up and bowed: "Permit me to introduce myself. I am the Chevalier Etienne de Roubec. Your servant, Monsieur. I am charmed to welcome you to my country. My only regret is that this temporary lack of funds deprives me of the happiness of doing its honours towards you in a fitting fashion."

Standing up Roger bowed and introduced himself in turn, then as they sat down again he said: "You were telling me, Monsieur le Chevalier, why it is that you remain on at *Les Trois Fleur de-Lys?*"

"Ah, yes," the Chevalier smiled and using simple phrases he went into a somewhat longer explanation, including an account of how he had had his pocket picked of a purse containing a hundred and twenty *Louis*, this being the original cause of his present embarrassment.

As Roger listened, striving to get the meaning of the less usual words through their context, he had ample opportunity to study the Chevalier's face. His brown eyes were quick and intelligent; a small scar on his left cheek ran up to the corner of one of them pulling it down a little and giving him a faintly humorous expression. His mouth was full and sensual, his chin slightly receding and his teeth bad, but he had a cheerful, vivacious manner and, as Roger had been feeling distinctly lonely during his hour's walk, he was glad to have someone with whom he could talk as a friend.

De Roubec, was, it transpired, the younger son of the Marquis

of that name, and he obviously expected Roger, even though an Englishman, to have heard of this rich and powerful *Seigneur*. The family
had great estates in Languedoc but his father was, of course, at
Versailles, where he held a high appointment near the person of the
King. On being robbed of his money the Chevalier had at once written
to his parent and expected any day now to receive a considerable
remittance from him. In the meantime his principal worries were, that
he was ashamed to appear in the clothes he was wearing, since he had
had on his oldest things and been out on a fishing expedition when the
pestiferous landlord had confiscated all his better garments; and that
lack of cash made it impossible for him to buy Roger a drink.

Roger obligingly stepped into the breach, and, on the Chevalier
declaring that Malaga was his favourite tipple, ordered a couple of
glasses. He then gave a somewhat fictitious account of himself;
saying that he had come to Le Havre, only to transact some business
for his father, who was an English Admiral, and that having arrived
by the packet boat from Southampton that morning he hoped to complete his business next day and return to England the following night.

After they had been talking for about half an hour supper was
announced by a wizened little fellow who did duty, both as waiter
and barman. The old man in the blue suit, who, in the meantime, had
been drinking steadily, remained where he was; but the two seafarers,
De Roubec and Roger, crossed the narrow hallway of the inn to the
coffee room, and the two latter agreed to share a table.

Having by this time digested his surfeit of cream cakes Roger was
agreeably surprised by the meal that was now served to them. In
England, where few people except the poorest considered that a meal
was not a meal at all unless it included an ample portion of red meat,
the repast would normally have given rise to aggrieved complaint.
But the soup had an excellent flavour, the dish of vegetables cooked
in fresh butter proved a revelation as to how good vegetables could be
when not swamped in water, and the cream cheeses were delicious.
For the modest sum of a *franc* Roger found that he was able to buy
a bottle of Bordeaux, and by the time it was empty the two new
acquaintances were in splendid spirits, laughing together as though
they had known each other for years.

De Roubec set down his glass with a little sigh. "'Tis now," he
said, "that I find my lack of funds provoking almost beyond endurance.
'Twould have been such a pleasure this evening to take you forth and
show you something of the town. Le Havre is a poor place compared
to Paris or Lyons but, even so, it has a few passably diverting establishments and 'tis a sad pity that as you are leaving for England again so
soon you should not see them while you are here."

" 'Tis monstrous good of you to suggest it," Roger replied "Unfortunately I'm plaguey short of cash myself for the moment. I'll
have ample when I've completed my business to-morrow, but I
brought over only some twenty *louis* for my immediate expenses
and I laid out considerably more than half of that on my passage and in
purchases this afternoon."

The Chevalier shrugged his lean shoulders. "For twenty or thirty *crowns* we could have quite a good evening's sport. That is if you care to act as banker? But it must be on the firm understanding that I am host and will repay you any sum we expend when my money arrives. If you are already gone I will send it to you to England by a safe hand."

Roger barely hesitated. His native caution warned him that it would be tempting providence to run himself right out of cash before he had sold Georgina's jewels; but he reflected that he still had over six pounds so would have an ample safety margin if he blew three of them, and the idea of celebrating his first night as a free, grown man by going on the spree in this strange, foreign city, was tremendously exciting.

"If twenty *crowns* will serve, I'm your man, and mighty obliged to you into the bargain," he declared with a laugh.

So they left the table and collecting their hats and swords, went out on to the dark quay.

Turning westwards along it De Roubec led Roger past the Arsenal into the narrow *Rue de Paris* and there knocked loudly on the door of a tall, shuttered house. The door was opened by a pock-marked manservant in a grey and silver slivery. He evidently knew the Chevalier and ushering them into the hall asked them to wait a moment while he fetched his master.

A dapper little man clad in white breeches and a sky-blue silk coat then appeared.

"Ah, my dear Chevalier!" he exclaimed with an elegant bow and a quick glance at Roger. "What a pleasure to see you again. You are, I take it, once more in funds and come to challenge Dame Fortune at my tables?"

"Your servant, Monsieur Tricot. We intend only a mild flutter," De Roubec replied nonchalantly. "But permit me to present milord Brook, the son of the distinguished English Admiral. It is my privilege to show him the few amenities of Le Havre, and your establishment being one of them I have brought him to see it; but we'll risk a *louis* or two for the good of the house."

Roger thought it pointless to repudiate the sudden elevation he had been given and he much admired the skilful way in which De Roubec had disguised the fact that their purses were so ill-lined.

The gaming-house keeper begged him to consider the house as his own whenever he was in Le Havre and led them upstairs.

The whole of the first floor consisted of one big salon. In it about thirty people were assembled, all of them men, grouped round four large baize-covered tables. The room was lit adequately, but not brightly, by two-score of shaded candles set on the tables, or held by sconces centred in the gilt-outlined panels of the white painted walls. The floor was covered with a thick Aubusson carpet and at the far end from its tall, heavily curtained windows there was a buffet for food and drinks, and a small separate table with neat piles of gold and silver coins on it, behind which sat a dark-browed man. The atmosphere was orderly and subdued, the only sounds being the clink of coins, the quick flutter of cards and an occasional murmur from one of the players.

De Roubec led the way over to the cashier and Roger produced two of his guineas. The black-browed man gave only seven *crowns* and two *francs* each for them, but at a sharp word from the Chevalier he shrugged his shoulders and pushed across another *crown;* which made Roger feel that he had been very lucky to find such a worldly wise friend to protect his interests. As they walked over to the tables he slipped eight of the *crowns* into De Roubec's hand, retaining the rest for himself.

For ten minutes or so they moved quietly about watching the play. There were two tables of *Vingt-et-un* and two of *Trente-et-quarante;* those nearest the window being in each case for higher play with a gold *demi-pistol* as the minimum stake, whereas at the other two, players could stake anything from a *franc* upwards. Roger was fascinated by the sight of the little piles of double *Louis, Louis* and *pistols* on the high-play tables, as he had never seen so much gold in his life, but he was not a gambler by nature and, even had he had the money, he would have played at one of the lower tables from choice.

Both the games were entirely strange to him so on De Roubec's asking him which he wished to play he chose the *Trente-et-quarante*, since it seemed much the simpler of the two, and they took two of the gilt chairs at the lower table.

Quickly picking up the idea of the game Roger began to punt a *franc* a time on each hand, and for a quarter of an hour won and lost more or less alternately, but the Chevalier refrained from playing and appeared content to watch his protégé, having quickly realised that the young Englishman was new to the game and feeling that he might in due course be blessed with beginner's luck.

De Roubec's hunch proved correct. For some minutes Roger's little pile of silver steadily increased, then the Chevalier came in, following his lead but staking *crowns*, and later, double-*crowns*, instead of *francs*. For the best part of an hour their run of luck continued, then fortune seemed to turn against them and their gains began to dwindle; but after twenty minutes and while they were still well in hand the luck came back. They played for another half-hour then De Roubec suddenly sat back, swept up his winnings and poured them into his pocket.

Roger looked at him in surprise but he smiled, and said: "Continue if you wish, *mon ami*. But I shall not tempt fortune further, and I would advise you, too, to withdraw before the fickle jade ceases to smile upon you."

The advice was sound and again Roger congratulated himself on having found so pleasant and wise a mentor. On counting his money he found that he had made fifty-five *francs* and he wished now that he had been playing in *crowns* as De Roubec must have cleared at least three times that sum; but he felt that he certainly had no cause to grumble.

Leaving the table they went over to the buffet for a drink and the Chevalier, now in tremendous good humour, ordered and paid for two goblets of champagne. Roger had heard of the wine but never drunk it, as it was still a great luxury in England and rarely seen except at private supper parties given in London by the richer members of the fashionable world. He found it rather too thin for his taste but the effervescence intrigued his palate and when he had drunk it a warm glow ran through him.

"This is no place to celebrate our good fortune," remarked De Roubec, as he finished his champagne. "What say you now to paying our respects to the ladies?"

The generous wine and his luck at the tables had made Roger feel that this was the best of all possible worlds and ripe for anything, so, without a thought as to what he might be letting himself in for, he readily agreed.

Following De Roubec's example he made a generous contribution to a box "for destitute gamblers"—which was actually one of Monsieur Tricot's sources of income—before leaving, and tipped both the cashier and the doorman who let them out, thereby relinquishing fourteen of his *francs*, but that seemed a small price to pay for two hours of such profitable entertainment.

Out in the ill-lit street once more, they took a side turning, which led off from the *Rue de Paris* past the Church of Notre Dame and brought them back to the water-front. A hundred yards along it, De Roubec halted in front of a house where bright lights showed through the chinks of nearly all the shutters and from which came the sound of fiddles and laughter.

On knocking, they were let in by a coal-black negro, but De Roubec seemed to know the place well and waving the grinning black aside led the way upstairs. The whole of the first floor here was also one big salon, but it had none of the subdued elegance of Monsieur Tricot's apartment. Its decorations were both gaudy and tawdry and instead of quiet decorum a spirit of dissolute abandon pervaded the place.

As a hugely fat woman, who appeared to be bursting out of her black satin dress, came forward to greet them Roger took in the scene, his eyes almost popping from his head. He had, of course, heard that such houses existed in London and other great cities but none of his friends had ever been to one and he had never imagined them to be like this.

In one corner three fiddlers on a low dais were sawing away at their violins; the other corners and sides of the room were occupied by small tables at most of which sat men with girls in varying states of semi-nudity, while in the centre of the floor, eight or ten others, mostly women, were executing a wild version of a country dance; in which, every time the partners met, instead of simply taking hands they embraced, kissed and mauled each other.

The Chevalier tapped Roger on the arm, drawing his attention back to the fat woman and said, "This is the Widow Scarron," but he did not give Roger's name. and added with a sly grin: "She is called so, after the puritanical mistress of Louis XIV's old age, in ironical jest."

"The Madame" had little black eyes half hidden in rolls of fat, her cheeks were white sacks heavily daubed with rouge and her fleshy mouth was painted a violent red. She gave a hideous leer at Roger then said to the Chevalier:

"What a handsome young man! Why, my girls will claw one another's eyes out to get at him," and, as she led them to a corner table, she added, *sotto voce*, some lewd jest that Roger did not catch but which caused De Roubec to burst out laughing.

They were no sooner seated at the table than a hunchbacked waiter hurried over to them bringing an ice bucket in which was thrust a bottle of champagne.

" 'Tis indifferent stuff," remarked De Roubec, "and the price charged for it exorbitant; but custom demands that we should buy it by way of entrance fee to this Temple of Venus." As the Chevalier had paid for the drinks at the gaming-house Roger felt that it was up to him to pay for the bottle and with a tip to the waiter it cost him twelve *francs*.

He was already half regretting that he had accepted De Roubec's suggestion that they should pay "their respects to the ladies"; as he had had a vague idea that the Chevalier simply meant to take him to some public assembly rooms where they could join in the dancing, and this water-front brothel was much stronger meat than he had bargained for. The place held for him all the excitement of something new and wicked but at the same time it was vaguely frightening. It reminded him of some of Mr. Hogarth's pictures, and might well have been one of them brought to raucous and sordid life.

But he was given little time to decide whether he was glad or sorry that this experience had, willy-nilly, been thrust upon him. Having seen them to their table, madame had at once left them to whip up the disengaged among her team, and the waiter had scarcely opened the champagne before the table was surrounded by a dozen young women immodestly displaying their charms and loudly vying with one another for the patronage of the newcomers.

They all looked young by candlelight but close inspection showed most of them to have left their teens far behind and all of them had hard, tired eyes. Some wore voluminous but tatty dresses, from beneath which they skittishly kicked up bare legs to show that they had nothing on underneath, while others wore only draperies of gauze that left nothing whatever to the imagination. All of them were heavily painted and in several cases Roger noticed that the paint had not been laid on quite heavily enough to hide old pock marks on their cheeks and foreheads. But as far as he was concerned the "Widow Scarron" proved a true prophet. In his youth and freshness, even more than his good looks, they all saw something to excite their jaded appetites and entered into a violent contest to secure his favour.

"*Voilà!*" said De Roubec, eyeing him quizzically. "I'll wager there's little to choose for naughtiness between them, but take your pick."

As Roger hesitated the Chevalier leaned forward and catching a short, dark, plump girl by the wrist drew her towards him. With a laugh she fell into his lap and putting her arms round his neck kissed him, leaving the red imprint of her lower lip just below his mouth.

"And what is your name, my pretty?" he asked.

"Fifi," she replied gaily. "And yours?"

"Etienne," he smiled. "Come now, a glass of wine, and you shall tell me your life's history. I doubt not that you are the daughter of a Marquis, or a Count at the least, and ran away from home with some handsome young buck who betrayed you?"

Roger still hesitated while the other girls clamoured round him. He did not particularly fancy any of them, but he saw that he must choose one if only to be rid of the rest, so he smiled and beckoned to a slim, fair-haired girl who looked a little more refined than her companions and attracted him on account of her colouring and figure.

She saw that he was nervous so did not embarrass him by kissing him at once, but quietly took the chair next to his and poured herself some wine. The others instantly stopped laughing and posturing before the table and with sullen looks at not having been chosen moved away.

Fifi was saying to De Roubec: "You are wrong, *cheri*, I am just one of the people—the people who will rule France one day. I am a Marseillaise and my father was a fisherman. I was brought up in a hovel and when I was thirteen, times were so bad that he sold me to a brothel-keeper."

Roger turned his attention to his own companion and asked her name.

"They call me Mou-Mou here," she replied, "and it serves as well as any other. By what name would you like me to call you?"

"My name is Roger," he said at once.

"*Rojé*," she repeated, "that is a nice name. Monsieur is a foreigner, is he not?"

"Yes, English. And you, mam'selle? You are French, of course, but are you a native of these parts?"

She shook her fair head. "No, monsieur, I am a Flamande. My husband brought me here from Antwerp in his ship; but he left again without doing me the courtesy of saying good-bye. I had no money and here I am."

"What a monstrous thing to do," Roger exclaimed in quick sympathy.

The corners of her hard mouth turned down in a cynical little smile. "He was not really my husband; but I had had a child by him and hoped that he might make me his wife one day. But why should I bore you with my past misfortunes? Drink up your wine and tell me some naughty stories."

Roger had never told a dirty story to a woman in his life and he would have felt embarrassed about doing so now, even if his French had been up to it, and he excused himself on that account.

Fifi was continuing her story for De Roubec's benefit, and both the others turned to listen to her.

"A young journalist bought me out of the brothel. He gave me a good home and taught me about politics. Ah, he was clever; but too clever for our happiness in the end. He wrote a lampoon on the Queen, and the seventy thousand *louis* of the people's money that she had frittered away in a single year by gambling. The agents of Monsieur de Crosne seized him and carried him off to one of the dungeons in the

Chateau D'If. Poor wretch, he is there still for all I know. As for myself, I took up with a bos'un in the Navy, and he brought me here as a stowaway; but the officers found us out. They had him tied to a grating and gave him two-hundred lashes—the brutes, and put me ashore. Then a pimp got hold of me and sold me to madame, here, for a hundred *francs*."

"Perchance someone else may take a fancy to you and buy you out," remarked De Roubec.

She shrugged. "Who would want me for a keep after five years of this? I've little doubt now but that I'll die as I was born—in a ditch. But the good God may grow tired of Queens so mayhap Marie Antoinette will die in a ditch, too. In the meantime, I have no complaints. Madame is no more greedy and harsh than others of her kind, and I console myself for my lot by enjoying myself when I am fancied by a handsome gentleman like you. Come, Monsieur Etienne, now you have heard my story let us join the dance."

As they stood up Mou-Mou laid her hand on Roger's and said: 'Would you not like to dance, too?"

The big room was stifling hot and heavy with the reek of cheap perfume, mingled with even less pleasant odours. Her fingers were slightly clammy yet he did not like to offend her by disengaging his hand; but he shook his head. The last thing he desired was to enter the bacchanalian mêlée in the middle of the floor and be kissed and mauled by the painted harridans dancing there.

"What lovely eyes thou hast, *Rojé*," she said suddenly, and adopting the *tu-toi* towards him. "They would be worth a fortune to any woman."

He gave an embarrassed grin. "You have very nice eyes yourself."

"*Merci*," she smiled. "I am so glad thou chosest me. So many of the men who come here are middle-aged and horrid; and a girl can give so much more of herself to a young man like thyself. Tell me, hast thou loved many girls? But no, I do not think thou can'st have, as yet."

He was spared a reply by the arrival of the hunch-backed waiter at their table. The man picked up the bottle which was now empty and looked at Roger interrogatively: "*Encore, Monsieur?*"

Mou-Mou nodded for him and a few minutes later the waiter put a second bottle on the table for which, as De Roubec was still dancing, Roger had to pay.

As it was being opened a little girl aged about twelve came up to them. She was dressed as Cupid and suspended by blue ribbons from her shoulders carried a tray of sweets.

Roger was shocked by the sight of a child in such surroundings and repelled by the wicked knowing look in her prematurely-aged face, but Mou-Mou said at once: "Please, *Rojé*, buy me some bon-bons."

He obliged and bought her a box for the outrageous price of five *francs;* upon which she put her arm round his neck and kissed him on his cheek. Her breath smelt faintly of garlic, but he did not like to draw away from her.

After a moment, she said: "Thou dos't not like it here? Am I not right? Come up to my room with me; or if thou preferrest we will command a *salon privé* where we can sup together."

"No, not—not yet," he stammered, "Let us wait until my friend comes back." But when he looked again at the dancers he saw that De Roubec and Fifi had already left the room.

Mou-Mou had also noticed that De Roubec was no longer among the whirling, stamping crowd, and she said: "Thy friend has gone upstairs with Fifi. Come, *Rojé*, or Madame will give me a beating for wasting my time. Which would'st thou prefer, my room or supper first in a *salon privé?*"

CHAPTER VIII

THE DISPOSAL OF THE JEWELS

ROGER felt desperately ill at ease. He thought Mou-Mou a kind girl and was deeply sorry for her. The last thing he wished to do was to put a slight upon her and get her into trouble with Madame, yet he had no inclination to make love to her. In other surroundings and less heavily painted she might have passed in a crowd as quite attractive. But closer inspection showed that her fair hair was coarse and brittle; it was really mousey, as showed near the roots where it had grown since she had last dyed it. Her hands, though small, were fat and the nails had been bitten down. The garlic on her breath seemed to increase in pungency each time she leaned towards him. There were deep shadows under her eyes and her cheeks had a flaccid, unhealthy look. Her pleasant manner, soft voice and youth saved her from being actually repugnant to him but she was a little moulting water-hen compared to a beautiful white swan by contrast with Georgina, and the whole business seemed to him forced and sordid.

He wished now that he had pleaded tiredness and said that he wanted to go home, while De Roubec was still with them, but now that he had gone off with Fifi he might be away for an hour, and Roger had not the courage to walk out on his own from fear of pre-cipitating a row. Seeking to put off the unpleasant decision that he knew he would soon be forced to take, he said:

"Before we go up let's finish our wine."

Mou-Mou shrugged and poured him another glass. "As thou wilst. 'Tis not very good, though, and too much of it is apt to give one the wind, so I beg thee to excuse me."

They sat silent for a few moments, then she said quietly:

"At least, *Rojé*, thou mightest make up thy mind if thou would'st sup or no, as if so I will order it."

It was on the tip of his tongue to say "Yes," as supping with her would gain him another postponement, but he remembered in time that the cost of a meal would prove too severe a strain on his slender resources. If a box of bon-bons cost five *francs* supper might easily run him into a couple of *louis*.

"No," he blurted out. "Thank you, but I'm not hungry. I'd rather go up to your room."

Now that the decision was taken he felt somewhat better about it, and endeavoured to get as much enjoyment as possible out of his wine which, although sweet and insipid, he did not find unpalatable. But directly he set down his glass she stood up and, instinctively, he stood up with her.

Having skirted the dancers they went out into the passage and she led the way upstairs. The salon had been shoddy enough but the upper part of the house seemed like a decayed tenement. Above the first floor the staircase was not carpeted and each of the three flights they ascended grew narrower and more rickety. As he followed her up he saw by the faint light coming from under the ill-fitting doors of the rooms they passed that her shoes were worn down and turned over, and he caught glimpses of rat-holes in the bottom of the wainscoting.

At last, as he paused breathless behind her on a dark and narrow landing, she threw open a door, fumbled for a tinder box, lit two candles and called over her shoulder: "Come in, *cheri*."

On entering he saw that her bedroom was an attic in a state of repellent filth and disorder. The shaded candles, which were on a small dressing-table before a low window, shone on a jumble of rouge pots, hares' feet and soiled face-cloths. The bed was a divan on which the coverings were already rumpled and a half-filled chamber-pot stood unconcealed in one corner. The room looked larger than it actually was owing to a huge mirror that occupied the whole of its one unbroken wall, but it smelt abominably of stale scent and seemed the very antithesis of the sort of place that anyone would have chosen in which to make love.

"Please forgive the untidiness," Mou-Mou said, on seeing the look of repugnance on his face. "I have to share this chamber with another girl. We use it turn and turn about, and she is a veritable slut; but I will soon make thee forget all about that."

As she spoke she undid a single hook at the top of her bodice and her striped blue and white frock slid to the ground, revealing her stark naked.

There was a big bluish bruise on one of her hips and a vivid scar disfigured her stomach. She held out her arms to Roger but he knew now that he could not go through with it. His whole soul revolted at the very thought of touching her.

Swiftly turning his back he pulled out his purse and by the light of the candles fished a guinea from it. Tossing the coin down on the bed he turned, wrenched open the door and fled from the room.

He had hardly gained the stairs before she had sprung out on to the landing after him.

"Come back!" she cried. "Of what are you afraid? How dare you treat me thus! *Ce n'est pas gentil!*"

Then, as he did not heed her, she began to shrill in louder tones: "*A moi! A moi!* We have a rat in the house! Stop him! Bar the door!"

Blindly Roger crashed his way down the rickety stairs as though all the devils in hell were behind him. By the time he reached the second landing doors were opening on every side and heads poking out to see what all the commotion was about. Mou-Mou's cries, now mingled with the foulest abuse, had roused the house. The doors of the salon were flung wide and the "Widow Scarron" came lumbering through it followed by half a score of her girls and patrons.

As Roger made to dive past her she grabbed him by the arm and with surprising strength jerked him towards her whilst screaming obscenities in his ear.

"Let me go!" he yelled. "Damn you! Let me go!" and wrenching himself free he bounded towards the last flight of stairs.

"Zadig!" she shouted over his shoulder. "*En garde!* Don't let him go until he has paid! A *louis*, and no less! Do you hear?" And Roger saw that he now had to get past the big negro down in the hall.

For an instant he thought of drawing his sword and attempting to fight his way out into the street, but he realised at once that in such confined quarters he would have little space to use it. Zadig was half crouching there below him with a stout cudgel held ready in his hand, and with bitter fury Roger realised that unless he wanted a smashed pate he must pay up. Pulling forth his purse again he counted out eight *crowns* and thrust them into the hand of the negro.

"And one for me, Monsieur," said Zadig, now grinning from ear to ear once more.

Hastily Roger paid the toll, and the big black unbarred the door.

Out in the street he gulped in the fresh air with indescribable relief; but he had not yet either felt or smelt the last results of his unpremeditated visit to this house of ill-fame. Mou-Mou, whom he had thought so kindhearted and of better instincts than her companions, was waiting for him at her attic window. Immediately he appeared in the street below, with a gutter-bred yell of derision, she emptied the contents of her chamber-pot out on to his head.

The main douche missed him by a couple of feet but he was splashed by the disgusting mess from head to foot and took to his heels with rage and hatred in his heart. The length of his sword proved his final undoing as he had covered only a hundred yards down the nearest side-turning when it got between his legs and sent him a cropper into the gutter.

Picking himself up with a curse he went on more slowly, but his night's adventures were far from over as, having walked the length of two short streets which he thought would bring him to the Arsenal, he then discovered that he was hopelessly lost and had not the faintest idea how to get back to *Les Trois Fleur-de-Lys*.

In those times the civic authorities had not yet taken upon themselves the responsibility for either maintaining a proper street-lighting system or for clearing away refuse. The only light came from dimly burning lanterns on occasional street corners or over the porches of the richer private houses, and most of the latter were extinguished when their inmates went to bed. At this hour long canyons of pitch blackness separated the widely-dispersed little pools of yellow light; so the midnight wayfarer had to grope his way from one to another, as best he could, through pavementless streets often so narrow as to permit the passage of one coach only at a time and all littered by the accumulation of household rubbish that had been thrown out into the gutters.

Few honest citizens ever ventured out at night, unless compelled to do so, and Roger knew that the only people he was likely to meet were drunken roisterers or lurking thieves, so it would be an added peril to show himself unnecessarily and there would be a certain risk in asking his way of anyone he might come upon.

The cool night air had at first refreshed him after the sickly heat of the brothel, but it now began to affect him unexpectedly, and he realised that owing to his having consumed the best part of a bottle of indifferent champagne he was now a little drunk.

Pulling himself together on the corner of the street which he had believed would bring him to the Arsenal he decided that, although it had already been dark when he left the inn with De Roubec, if he could regain the waterfront he should be able to find his way back. After trying two streets he came out on a quay and turned in what he believed to be the right direction. The faint sound of violins caught his ear and soon guided him back to the "Widow Scarron's." Giving the house a wide berth he continued onward but, having visited Monsieur Tricot's gaming-rooms before going to the brothel had confused him in his bearings, so he was now actually walking away from the inn instead of towards it.

The docks and quays of Le Havre are very extensive so he went on quite confidently for some twenty minutes before he began to suspect that he had somehow gone wrong. Now and then he had heard footsteps in the distance or seen a lurking figure momentarily emerge from the shadows, but nobody had attempted to molest him as, in the gloom, with his long sword sticking out from under the skirts of his coat he had the appearance of a well-armed, if somewhat short, man. But now he felt that he simply must chance an encounter to find out where he was and, some five minutes later, coming on a party of sailors belatedly returning to their ship, he hailed them in as gruff a voice as he could manage. To his relief, though hilariously tipsy, they proved friendly enough and gave him verbose directions how to find the *Bassin Vauban*.

The moon was now rising above the masts of the shipping so his long tramp back was made somewhat easier from his being able to avoid the frequent potholes among the cobbles and the heaps of stinking garbage with which the wharfs were littered.

At length, fairly sober again now, but tired and still seething with anger at his night's misadventures, he recognised the sign of *Les Trois Fleur-de-Lys*. Then, with the cessation of his own footsteps as he paused before the door he heard others, and realised that someone must have been walking along behind him. Turning, he looked in the direction from which he had come and saw a lanky figure approaching. With a fresh wave of anger he recognised De Roubec, the author of all his troubles.

After a moment the Chevalier saw him too, and his greeting showed

91

that he was in an equally ill humour. "So 'tis you, my little cock without spurs," he remarked acidly. "Methought that failing a mother to tuck you up in bed you would have gone to spend the night in a convent."

"What the devil d'you mean?" Roger exclaimed, flushing hotly, although he knew perfectly well at what De Roubec was driving.

"You know what I mean," declared the Chevalier, mouthing his words thickly. "And a fine return you made for my interest in you. Not only do you insult a poor girl and upset a well-conducted house to which I introduced you; but by going there as my friend and behaving as you did you put a shame upon me publicly."

"If you consider that thieving rabble a public worthy of consideration, God pity you," flared Roger.

"So now you have the impudence to call in question the company I keep?"

"Yes, when 'tis composed of whores, bawds and lechers. And what blame to me if, having no stomach for such scum, I choose to leave it?" Roger was now speaking in mangled French and English but anger sent enough scarce-remembered French words to his tongue for his meaning to be clear.

"Well enough, my little anchorite," came the swift retort. "But no gentleman occupies a wench's time, then leaves his friend to pay for the dish he leaves untasted."

"I did no such thing. I gave the girl a guinea before I left her room, and that old bitch of a Madame made me disburse a further *louis* before they would let me out of the house."

"I find it difficult to believe that, since I am an old habitué of the place and they made me pay up on your behalf."

"D'you call me a liar?"

"What of it, if I did? You are but a tom-tit dressed in the fine feathers of a peacock, and have not the guts to tumble a woman, let alone fight a man."

"I'll not suffer being called a liar, though," Roger stormed, "I tell you I paid that trollop."

"And I tell you I did."

"Why should you have done so? 'Twas not your affair."

" 'Tis you who are calling me a liar now," cried the Chevalier furiously. "If you carried that long sword of yours as anything but an ornament, *Corbleau*, I'd compel you to use it!"

" 'Tis not an ornament," yelled Roger, half-mad with rage.

"In that case apologise or draw it, you ill-mannered brat!"

As De Roubec placed his hand upon the hilt of his own sword Roger's impulse to continue the violent altercation suffered a sharp check. He felt certain that the Chevalier, like himself on leaving the brothel, was a little drunk, and that his own brain was still somewhat heated by the fumes of the bad wine. It was fair enough to maintain one's own view-point in a heated argument, particularly when one felt oneself to be in the right, but very different to risk a sword-thrust through the body. De Roubec was a head taller than himself and, for all he knew, an expert swordsman; so, although he was loath to retreat absolutely he was scared enough to attempt a postponement of the issue.

"Hold!" he exclaimed. "Take thought, I beg. We cannot fight like this. If one of us were killed the other would be taken for murder. If fight we must at least proceed like gentlemen and arrange a proper duel with seconds as witnesses, in the morning."

"Who spoke of a duel," sneered De Roubec. "I'll not make myself the laughing stock of Le Havre by challenging a puppy such as you. As for killing, dismiss the thought. I mean but to cut your ears off and send them to Mou-Mou as a salve to her wounded pride. Come, draw, or I'll slice them from your head as you stand there."

Roger was aghast and realised that the Chevalier must be much drunker than he had at first thought him. Street brawls in which drunken rakes quarrelled and drew their swords upon one another without seconds, while staggering home in the small hours of the morning, were still quite common in all large cities; but De Roubec's cause for offence seemed absurdly trivial and his proposal about sending Mou-Mou her recent visitor's ears positively fantastic.

"Stop!" cried Roger, "you can't be serious. You must be drunk to talk like this of making yourself the champion of a harlot!"

"Drunk, am I?" De Roubec roared. "We'll soon see if I'm drunk or not. And if for naught else I'll slit your ears to teach you manners." Upon which he lurched forward and wrenched his blade from its scabbard.

Roger was frightened now. An exciting bout with foils in the fencing school was one thing; to fight in deadly earnest with naked steel quite another. But there was no escape. Springing back a pace he drew his sword and threw himself on guard.

The blades came together with a clash and circling round each other shimmered in the moonlight. For a moment, with added apprehension, Roger felt that the unaccustomed length of his weapon would tell against him, but he suddenly realised that not only was the fine Toledo blade much more resilient and easier to wield than he supposed, but its length cancelled out the natural advantage that De Roubec would otherwise have had from his longer reach.

In a formal duel both of them would have spent a few cautious moments in getting the feel of the other's steel before going in to the attack; but the Chevalier was in no mood to waste time trifling with his young antagonist. Within a minute he had delivered three swift lunges and advancing with each strove to force down Roger's guard by the sheer weight of his stronger arm.

Roger knew that if he allowed these tactics to continue he would never be able to stay the course. If he remained on the defensive his more powerful opponent would soon tire him out and have him at his mercy.

He was dead sober now and fighting skilfully. Almost to his amazement he found that he could hold his own, at least for a limited period, but he knew that he must attempt to end the fight before he felt the first signs of exhaustion.

How to do so was now his problem. They had twice circled round one another, their blades close-knit and flashing like living fire. Roger side-stepped twice in order to get the moon behind him and in the Chevalier's eyes. He was almost as afraid of killing his antagonist, for fear of what might befall him later if he did, as of being killed himself; so he essayed a pass that the old Master-of-Arms at Sherborne had taught him.

With a sudden spring forward he ran his sword up De Roubec's until the hilts met with a clash; he then gave a violent twist. The Chevalier let out a gasp of pain and his sword flew from his hand as the result of a half-sprained wrist.

It somersaulted through the air to fall with a clatter on the cobbles twenty feet away. As Roger had been taught that a disarmed man might run after his weapon, pick it up and renew the fight, he dashed over to the fallen sword himself and put his foot upon it. Then, seeing that the Chevalier had made no move, he picked it up and walked slowly back.

De Roubec seemed momentarily stunned by his defeat and when he spoke his voice no longer carried any hint of the liquor he had consumed.

"Monsieur Brook," he said soberly, "my service to you. Believe me I had no real intent to do you harm; but I was a little in wine, and a stupid impulse urged me to give a young man, whom I felt had been guilty of some rudeness towards me, a lesson. As it is I have been taught one myself."

The apology was so handsome that Roger could not but accept it, and it was not in his nature to bear malice. So, with a bow, he handed the Chevalier back his sword, and said:

"Pray, think no more of it, Monsieur le Chevalier. I admit now that I was much at fault myself. You had, I am sure, the best intentions in taking me to these places of entertainment and 'twas kind of you to seek to provide amusement for a stranger. That I could raise no zest for little Mou-Mou was no fault of yours, and I should have made myself clear on that head much earlier. But I give you my word that I paid not once but twice for the dubious privilege of spending an hour in her company."

"And I willingly accept it, as I feel sure you will accept mine that I also paid the young harpy."

"Indeed, I do; so let us both thank God that we have no cause for more serious regrets on the matter than are occasioned by a few squandered guineas."

De Roubec took Roger's arm. "I swear to you, *mon ami*, that even in a drunken temper I would never have harmed you seriously. Indeed I vow I drew upon you only with the intent of scaring you into running away."

He spoke with such earnestness that Roger found it difficult to doubt his sincerity and he flushed with pleasure as the Chevalier went on:

"But what address you showed, and what courage! Having scratched a Chinaman I found a Tartar, and I was hard put to it to defend myself. Come now, my mouth is as dry as a bin of sawdust from that villainous champagne, and I am sobered up entirely. To show that there is no ill-feeling left between us let's drink a bottle of good Burgundy together before we go to bed."

Roger's throat now also felt dry and parched so he readily assented, and they began to hammer with their sword hilts on the nail-studded door of the inn.

After a while it was opened by the wizened little serving-man who, having been aroused from his sleep in a cubby-hole under the stairs, grumblingly admitted them.

De Roubec pulled out a fistful of *crowns* and showed them to the man, as he said, "Stir your stumps, knave, and get us up a bottle of Burgundy from the cellar. And a good one, mind; a Chambertin or a Hospice de Beaune, if you have it."

Having lit the lantern in the parlour for them the man disappeared, to return a few minutes later with a dust-encrusted bottle and glasses. After uncorking the wine and taking the money for it he shambled off back to his cubby-hole out in the hall.

The two recent antagonists now toasted one another with most friendly phrases and both felt considerably better after a good drink of the clean, generous Burgundy. The sight of the Chevalier's pocket full of *crowns* had recalled to Roger that even if the later form of entertainment to which his companion had introduced him had proved a fiasco the earlier had been an unqualified success, and he remarked:

"You must have made a pretty sum at Monsieur Tricot's, since towards the end you were staking double *crowns*."

" 'Tis but indifferent sport playing at a low table," shrugged De Roubec grandly. "But 'twas none too bad a haul, and 'twill serve to keep me in wine for a day or two; with luck until my funds arrive. My sole regret is that you plan to leave Le Havre so soon, otherwise 'twould have been a pleasure to afford you some entertainment of your own choosing out of my winnings."

"I hope to complete my business to-morrow," said Roger, "but it may be a day or two before I can secure a passage home, and if so I will certainly avail myself of your kind invitation."

De Roubec nodded. "Pray do not think that I have any desire to pry into your affairs, but I know Le Havre well, and if you feel that I might be of any assistance to you in this business of yours, do not hesitate to command me."

Roger was now feeling in great fettle. The fact that he had actually fought in earnest for the first time and emerged victorious from the encounter filled him with elation; and, since the cause of the affray now appeared to have been no more than a stupid misunderstanding brought about by the fumes of dubious liquor, he was, not unnaturally, drawn towards his late antagonist. The Chevalier had, he felt, gone out of his way to take an interest in him as a young and lonely stranger, had seen to it that he got a good exchange for his English money and had enabled him to win a nice little sum. Moreover, it now seemed to him that the expedition to the "Widow Scarron" should not be held against his new friend, since it might have appealed to many young men as the high-spot in an evening out. The Chavalier had, too, taken his defeat like a gentleman and was at the moment playing the generous host.

None of the excitements of the past twenty-four hours had caused Roger to forget for long that his sole purpose in coming to France was the satisfactory disposal of Georgina's jewels, and this had yet to be accomplished. It struck him now that instead of seeking out a goldsmith for himself and dealing with one who might or might not give him a good price, he could both save himself time in the morning and make certain of securing a fair deal by consulting De Roubec, so he asked:

"Do you perchance know of an honest goldsmith here in Le Havre?"

"Why, yes," replied the Chevalier, after only a moment's hesitation. "I know of several. Do you wish to make a purchase or have you something to sell?"

"I wish to dispose of some trinkets, mainly gold items, but a few with gems set in them and a number of cameos. To do so was, in fact, my reason for coming to France."

De Roubec's eyes narrowed slightly, and Roger, seeing this, did not wonder, as the bare statement might have put all sorts of ideas into anyone's head. With his usual quick inventiveness he went on to offer an entirely false explanation.

"These jewels belonged to my mother's twin sister, who died recently. The two were prodigiously devoted to one another and my father felt that should my mother perchance see any of them being worn by one of her neighbours the shock would affect her most severely. Yet he has need of the money they will bring; so, not wishing to dispose of them locally, he decided that the best course would be to send them abroad. As he was recalled to his ship unexpectedly and could not cross to France himself he charged me with this mission. Unfortunately I have little experience in such matters and if you could assist me in it I'd be mighty obliged to you."

Having listened attentively to Roger's somewhat mangled French, De Roubec nodded. " 'Twill be a pleasure. I know the very man and will take you to him in the morning."

Roger thanked him and they talked for a while on other topics, the Chevalier having apparently dismissed the matter of the jewels from his mind; but both of them were now feeling tired so as soon as they had finished their wine they went upstairs to bed.

After looking under the loose board in the floor to make certain that his treasure was still there, Roger undressed to his shirt and slipping between the coarse cotton sheets was soon asleep.

He woke late in the morning, as he judged from the angle of the sun that it must be near nine o'clock, and after a hurried toilet transferred the jewels from their hiding-place to his pockets, then went downstairs.

The coffee room was deserted and to his surprise he found that rolls, butter and *confiture* were the only food provided for breakfast. Not being accustomed to such meagre fare he asked for something more substantial, and after a wait of ten minutes he was brought an *omelette fines herbes;* a dish entirely new to him but one which he thoroughly enjoyed.

On finishing his meal he went in search of De Roubec, and found that lanky gentleman lazily sunning himself on the front porch.

"Ah, there you are!" said the Chevalier, displaying his bad teeth in a friendly smile, "I trust you had a good night?"

"Excellent, I thank you," Roger smiled back. "Except that I fear I slept over late, and I am naturally anxious to get my business settled as soon as possible. Would it be troubling you too much to take me this forenoon to the goldsmith you spoke of?"

"Willingly; but I have been giving some little thought to the matter, and an idea upon it has occurred to me. I take it you are not so pressed for time as to be unable to afford me a few moments' private converse in the parlour. There is no one about, so we shall have it to ourselves."

"By all means," Rogers agreed. So they went into the parlour together and, having closed the door carefully behind him, De Roubec fastened the latch so that they should not be interrupted.

Wondering a little what these mysterious precautions portended, Roger sat down at one of the tables, but the Chevalier reassured him by saying: "There is no cause for alarm, yet one cannot be too careful when discussing transactions in which large sums of money are involved."

Seating himself on the settee at Roger's side he went on in a low voice: "May I ask if you have mentioned this matter to anyone else?"

"No," said Roger. "Not a soul in France knows of it other than yourself. I thought it unwise to noise it about that I was carrying upon me anything of such value."

De Roubec nodded approvingly. "I am relieved to hear it, and 'twas fortunate that in myself you chose an honest man to confide in. After all, you know little enough about me as it is, and great seaports such as this abound in rogues who would not scruple to cut your throat for a handful of *louis*."

"If one both drinks and fights with a man yet remains friends with him afterwards, one has fair reason to trust him," Roger laughed. "And I certainly trust you."

The Chevalier bowed. "I am sensible of it, and should be prodigious distressed if it were not so. Have you the jewels perchance upon you now, or did you deposit them yesterday with a banker?"

"No, at the moment I have them spread about in pockets all over my person, as together they make quite a bulky bundle."

"May I have a sight of them?"

"Certainly, if you wish."

As Roger began to produce the trinkets and lay them out on the table the Chevalier added: "I ask only that I may get some idea as to their value, as it would be well if we fixed a price in our own minds before offering them to a goldsmith; and, although you are doubtless aware of their worth, I may be able to assist you in assessing what they are likely to fetch in France."

One by one he picked up the items of the collection and examined them through his quizzing glass then, as Roger began to stow them back in his pockets again, he asked: "What price had you in mind?"

"Five hundred guineas," said Roger, thinking it best not to show his ignorance by naming too small a sum.

De Roubec shook his head. "They may be worth that in England, where everyone is very rich; but I doubt if you will get that for them in France. I am no expert in such trifles, but if they were mine I should be glad to accept three hundred and eighty *louis* for the lot. They are mostly old-fashioned pieces and of little value apart from their weight as gold."

Roger was far from disappointed, as he had been quite prepared to let them go for two hundred and fifty if he could get no better offer; and he congratulated himself again on having consulted the Chevalier, as, by having done so, he felt that he had as good as made himself an additional hundred and thirty pounds.

"So be it," he said, endeavouring to appear a little crestfallen, "I'll take three-eighty for them, since you advise it."

"Nay, we will ask four-fifty for them as our opening shot and only come down gradually. 'Tis all against a gentleman's inclination to quibble over money, but one needs must for one's own protection in a case like this; and by so doing we might screw the knave up to parting with four-hundred *louis*. But I have yet to tell you my disturbing thought."

"What is it?" inquired Roger anxiously.

De Roubec hesitated a moment, then he said: "You will not take offence, I trust, at anything I may say?"

"Nay, why should I do so if 'tis for my benefit."

" 'Tis this, then. Your age is your own affair, but when I first set eyes on you last night I put you down as scarce seventeen. The fact that you handle your sword as well as a man makes no difference to the youthfulness of your appearance. Your account of how you came by these trinkets is fair enough, and 'twould not enter my head to cast doubt upon your word. Yet others, who have not had the happiness of your acquaintance, may not prove so credulous. For so young a man to be offering for sale all these women's gewgaws would strike any goldsmith as strange, to say the least; and, God forbid that such a thing should occur, but he might even think that you had stolen them and are being hunted in England by the agents of the Minister of Police. 'Twill be obvious to him at a glance that the stuff is of English make and I gather that you know no one in Le Havre who could vouch for your honesty. Perhaps my forebodings are no more than moonshine, but I felt it my duty as your friend to warn you of what may befall. Since 'twould be monstrous unpleasant to find yourself clapped into prison on suspicion, for a month or more while inquiries were being made."

Roger's face fell in earnest now. It had never occurred to him that he might be faced with the same difficulties in disposing of Georgina's jewels in France as he would have been in England. He had taken it for granted that a French goldsmith would be prepared to buy without asking questions; but now it seemed that in offering them for sale here he would be running a far greater risk than he would have in some county town at home. There, the worst that could have befallen him would have been to pass a night in the lock-up and be ignominiously returned to his irate parent next day, whereas here he might be held a prisoner for weeks on end before tedious official inquiries led to his identity being fully established and his family in England securing his release.

"I am much indebted to you," he said in a rather small voice, "I had not thought of that, and there is much in what you say."

"Of course, if you care to risk it," hazarded the Chevalier, "I will accompany you to a goldsmith's with pleasure. But, willing as I am to help, I could not honestly say that I had independent knowledge as so how you came by these jewels, or swear to it that I had known you for more than a day; since if further inquiry were made I should soon be in a trouble myself for perjury."

"Yes, I fully appreciate that," said Roger thoughtfully, but a new idea had come to him and he went on with some diffidence: "My father needs this money with some urgency, though, and I am most loath to return to England without it. Would you—would it be asking too much of you to sell the stuff for me? I give you my solemn word of honour that it was come by honestly, and is mine to dispose of as I think fit. You are a grown man and well known in Le Havre, so the goldsmith would never question your right to dispose of such goods."

The Chevalier considered for a moment. "Yes, it could be done that way," he said slowly. "Maître Blasieur knows me well, and we have oft done far larger deals together."

"Please!" Roger urged. "Please help me in this and I'll be eternally grateful to you."

: De Roubec smiled at him. "I believe you have a greater interest in this matter than you pretend?"

Roger coloured slightly. "Well, as a fact, my father promised me a portion of the proceeds of the deal if I showed my capabilities by handling it with credit. 'Tis in a way a test, too, as to if he will or no henceforth regard me as an equal and allow me to manage his affairs while he is away at sea."

"In that case I can scarce bring myself to disoblige you."

"This is stupendous!" Roger laughed again, now once more confident of success. "Let us lose no time but start at once and get the matter over."

"A moment, I beg." De Roubec raised his hand. " 'Twill not appear to Maître Blasieur that 'tis I who am the seller if the goods for sale are produced by you, one by one, out of your pockets. I fear you will have to trust me with them for a short time at the least."

Roger's hesitation was barely perceptible. He was most strongly averse to parting with his treasure, and he had not known De Roubec long enough to place complete faith in him. Yet it seemed clear that he must accept this risk or offend the Chevalier and say goodbye to any hope of this deal on account of which he had been to such pains in getting to France.

"I fully appreciate that," he agreed, wondering at the same time how he could manage to keep a safety line on his property. "How would you suggest that we arrange the matter?"

"Any way that suits yourself," replied the Chevalier casually. "But to start with I am sure you will see the advantage of making the jewels up into one convenient packet, so that they can be handed to Maître Blasieur without your hunting about your person as though you were seeking fleas in the coat of a dog."

Seeing the sense of this Roger began to get out his collection again while De Roubec sought for something suitable in which to put it. On the lower shelf of a cupboard he came across a long, flat bon-bon box, and, finding it to be empty, threw it on the table with a muttered: "This will serve."

Having packed all the chains, brooches, bangles and rings into the box, Roger looked up at him and inquired: "What now?"

"Why, put it in the big pocket of your coat, *mon ami*," laughed the Chevalier, "I have no desire to be responsible for your property for a moment longer than the occasion demands; and we will now go together to the goldsmith's."

His last lingering doubts of the Chevalier's probity thus being dispelled, Roger got to his feet and, unlatching the door, they left the room.

Outside, the hot August sunshine glared upon the quay and as Roger walked along beside his companion his heart was high. Four-hundred pounds would be a nice little fortune on which to start life in London. For five pounds a week a young man could live in considerable comfort at a modest yet respectable hostelry and have half that sum over to spend on getting about. At that rate Georgina's present would keep him for over a year and a half, but long before that he expected to have some profitable employment, so he could well afford to cut a good figure and take more expensive lodging in the meantime if, having acquired well-to-do friends, it seemed advisable to do so.

On reaching the *Rue Francois* 1er they walked some way along it, then De Roubec halted and pointed with his cane to a corner shop with a low bow window.

"That is Maître Blasieur's," he said. "T'would be best, I think, if I go in while you wait outside for me, otherwise he may suspect that I am acting only as an intermediary, and that the goods are really yours, which might lead to his asking embarrassing questions."

"You foresee everything," Roger smiled and wriggling the long heavy box out of his pocket he handed it to De Roubec, as he added: "I am indeed grateful to you. I will wait here and pray meanwhile that you may have good fortune on my behalf."

"Be sure I will do my best for you," laughed the Chevalier, "and I will be as speedy as I can. But do not be too impatient, as for a gold-smith to weigh and assess so many articles is certain to take not less than twenty minutes."

He was about to turn away when he paused and added:

"'Tis understood that I am authorised by you to accept three hundred and eighty *louis*, or at the worst a close offer to that, is it not?"

Roger nodded and the Chevalier disappeared into the shop.

For a time Roger amused himself by watching the smart equipages with which this fashionable street was as crowded as it had been on the previous afternoon. A clock above the mercer's at which he had bought a change of linen and his smart lace jabot had shown it to be just on a quarter to eleven when De Roubec had left him, and every few minutes he glanced impatiently at its dial.

The hands of the clock seemed to crawl but at last they reached the eleven and the bells in the steeples of the town rang out the hour. Roger was standing no more than a couple of yards from the doorway of Maître Blasieur's shop and his glance now rarely left it although he told himself that after the gold had been weighed De Roubec would require at least a further ten minutes to drive a good bargain.

He was wondering now if the Chevalier would manage to get for him four hundred *louis* or only three hundred and eighty. Perhaps he might even be driven to accept three-seventy? On the other hand he seemed a shrewd fellow and might persude the goldsmith into parting with four-hundred and ten. In any case, Roger felt, he must give him a handsome present for all the trouble he had taken, and as the hands of the clock over the mercer's crawled on from eleven to ten past he turned over in his mind various gifts that he might make his friend.

He thought of lace ruffles, a more elegant cane, and a new sword-belt but decided that none of these were good enough, and finally settled on a pair of silver-mounted pistols, similar to those he had lost himself in the *Albatross*, and would have liked to possess again.

A clock chimed the quarter and still De Roubec had not emerged from the goldsmith's. Roger began to fret now at his friend being so long, and endeavoured to peer into the shop, but the door was of stout wood and behind the window hung a plain black velvet curtain which cut off all view of the interior.

Striving to muster such further patience as he could he began to walk agitatedly up and down. That De Roubec could not yet have come out was certain as the place had one entrance only and no second door round the corner of the street.

For a further ten minutes Roger waited with ever-mounting impatience, then he could smother his half-formed fears no longer, and turning the handle of the shop door pushed it a little open. The shop was empty except for a man in a grey wig who stood behind the counter examining some gems.

Thrusting the door wide, Roger almost fell inside, exclaiming breathlessly: "The Chevalier de Roubec! Where is he? Where has be gone?"

The man in the wig stared at him stupidly for a moment then he said: "What do you mean, Monsieur? The Chevalier De Roubec. I know no one of that name."

"But you must!" insisted Roger wildly. "He came into your shop half an hour, nay, nearly three-quarters of an hour ago, with some gold ornaments that he wished to sell."

"Ah, Monsieur means a tall gentleman, no doubt. A gentleman in a red velvet coat having a scar on his cheek that dragged down the corner of his left eye a little?"

"Yes, yes! That is he!" Roger panted. "Where has he gone to?"

The shopman spread out his hands. "I have no idea, Monsieur. He offered no gold ornaments for sale, but bought a cheap scarf pin for three *crowns*. Then he asked if he might use the privy out in the yard at the back, and said that when he had done he would leave by the alley on to which the yard abuts. But why is Monsieur so excited? Has he been robbed?"

"No," stammered Roger with sudden visions of a police inquiry which he felt would do him little good and might even land him in further trouble. "No, but I wanted to speak with him most urgently, and he said—he said if I'd wait outside he would attend to my business as soon as he had done with you. How long has he been gone?"

"Half an hour, at least, Monsieur; more by now. He spent but a few moments choosing his pin, then left at once."

"Perchance he was suddenly taken ill and is still out there," Roger suggested, snatching at a wild hope.

"If Monsieur wishes we will go and see," replied the man in the wig, moving out from behind the counter. "But I can hardly think that it is likely to be so."

Together they visited the back of the premises. The earth closet was empty and the gate in the yard which gave on to a narrow alley slightly open. With a heart as heavy as lead Roger realised that it would be futile to attempt a chase. The purchase of the scarf pin alone was enough to convince him that he had been deliberately tricked, and by now the Chevalier might be a mile or more away.

Thanking the jeweller in a subdued voice he accompanied him back to the shop and walked out into the street. The sun was still shining and the gay equipages of the local French nobility still edging past each other in the congested thoroughfare, but he no longer had any eyes for their elegantly clad occupants.

His little fortune was gone, just as surely as if it had dropped overboard when he had been flung from the *Albatross* into the sea. He was alone and friendless in France. His winnings of the previous night had been eaten up by the money he had been forced to disburse in the brothel, and more with them. With added bitterness he recalled that De Roubec had not paid him back the *louis* he had lent him to finance his play at Monsieur Tricot's. In one way and another his cash capital had dwindled to only a little over four pounds, and he still had his bill at the inn to settle. Near panic seized him at the sudden, awful thought that he was now stranded in this strange foreign city, and had not even enough money left to pay for a passage back to England.

CHAPTER IX

THE MAN IN BLUE

S L O W L Y and sadly Roger made his way back to *Les Trois Fleur-de-Lys*. If there had been the faintest hope of catching the Chevalier there, anger and the acute anxiety he was feeling as to his future would have lent wings to his feet, but he knew there was none. De Roubec had now a clear three-quarters of an hour's start and, even if he had returned to the inn to pick up a few belongings, assuming that the irate Roger was certain to make for it as soon as he discovered the fraud that had been put upon him, would have left it again by this time.

As it was it seemed unlikely that the Chevalier had gone back to the inn even for a few moments, or would ever show his face there again. Knowing the man now for the plausible rogue that he was Roger began to see him in an entirely new light. His shoddy finery consorted ill with the tale that he really possessed a handsome wardrobe which had been impounded by a distrustful landlord. His story that he was a scion of a great and wealthy family who had had his pocket picked and was waiting for a lavish remittance was, no doubt, all moonshine. No real gentleman, Roger realised all too late, would be a regular habitué of a low waterside brothel such as the "Widow Scarron's." His anxiety that morning, too, to know if anyone else in Le Havre was aware that Roger was in possession of a hoard of valuable trinkets showed that he had premeditated and deliberately planned the theft.

Yet, badly as he had been taken in, Roger felt that a more experienced person than himself might equally have fallen a victim to the Chevalier's wiles. His face had been a weak rather than vicious one, and he had shown great vivacity, sympathy and apparent generosity; in fact, all the characteristics calculated to win the interest and friendship of a stranger quickly. But that anyone else might have been fooled as easily as himself was little consolation to Roger now.

As he walked on he wondered desperately how he could possibly get back to England, then, swiftly on top of that came the even more distressing question as to what would happen to him if he did succeed in securing a passage across the Channel. Gone were the bright dreams of comfortable lodgings and cutting a fine figure in London. If he got back at all it would be to land there near penniless. It would be a choice then between hedgerows and hard manual labour or going home to eat humble pie before his father; and the thought of being forced to the latter made him almost sob with rage.

On reaching the inn he met the oily Maître Picard on the doorstep and inquired at once if he had seen the Chevalier during the past hour.

The landlord shook his head. "I've not set eyes on him since he went out with you this morning, Monsieur."

"Has he any other address, or have you any idea where I could find him?" asked Roger.

"No, none, Monsieur. He comes and goes as he lists, that one. He said nothing this morning of leaving, but 'twould not be the first time that he has walked out on me. He is, as you may know, a professional gambler, and often in low water. If I may offer a word of advice, Monsieur, he is not a good companion for a young gentleman like yourself."

"Would that you had said as much before," Roger muttered ruefully.

"Why so," asked Maître Picard. "Has he then robbed you of something? I have heard tell that he can be light-fingered on occasion."

Visions of a police inquiry with himself held for weeks as a material witness, again flashed before Roger's mind, so he said hastily, "No—at least nothing of great value. Only a pair of shoe buckles that he promised to get valued for me; but they were not of sufficient consequence to make a fuss over. Is it true that you hold his wardrobe as surety for his reckoning?"

"Nay, Monsieur," the landlord smirked, "that is an idle tale. Sometimes he pays before he leaves, at others he settles his old score on the next occasion that he asks for a room. He has worn naught but that old red velvet coat of his since he first came here last Hallowe'en and I'd have thought anyone would have spotted him for a slippery customer."

"Why do you suffer such rogues to lodge at your inn, and mingle with your other guests?" snapped Roger, his temper getting the better of him.

Maître Picard bridled. "I am a poor man, Monsieur, and cannot afford to turn away a patron without proof that he has actually been dishonest. As for the others, 'tis for them, not me, to mind their purses. And had you been more circumspect in your choice of a companion, doubtless you would still be in possession of your buckles." Upon which he turned huffily away and slouched off through the hall to his quarters at the back of the premises.

Swallowing this rebuff, which he felt that he had asked for, Roger went into the parlour and sat down. It was empty except for the old man in the blue suit with the shock of white hair and watery blue eyes, who had been there the night before. He was no longer drunk or drinking, but was sitting with a woebegone expression on his face staring at his boots.

Roger gave him only a glance, then fell once more to seeking a way out of the frightful mess in which he had landed himself. It was true that Georgina had made no great sacrifice in giving him a lot of old-fashioned jewellery for which she had no use; yet she had given it to him for a definite purpose and the theft now made that purpose impossible of achievement, so by allowing himself to be robbed he felt that he had let her down badly.

He was not old enough or strong enough to get himself taken on as a hand in a ship sailing for England; but it occurred to him that for his few remaining pounds he might induce some freighter captain to take him aboard and let him work off the balance of the fare by serving as cabin boy on the trip. But such a proceeding would still leave him face to face with the far higher fence of what to do when he landed. On one thing he was determined; he would not go home and ask pardon of his father since, if he did so, he would never be able to look Georgina in the face again. The alternative now seemed grim in the extreme yet having lost the means to a fine start she had given him he felt that by hook or by crook he must, somehow, make good without it.

Suddenly the voice of the old man broke in upon his thoughts.

" 'Twould be a most courteous gesture, Monsieur, if, with the generosity that I see in that fine open face of yours, you cared to buy a dram for an old and ailing fellow human."

Realising that, since they were alone in the room, the appeal must be addressed to him Roger's first reaction was one of angry withdrawal. He had suffered enough at the hands of a chance acquaintance met with in that very room to teach him a lesson for a lifetime. With all too recent memories of De Roubec having expressed such flattering amazement at his French, and Mou-Mou's compliment upon his blue eyes, this old codger's reference to his handsome face struck him instantly as a most suitable opening gambit for a further attack on his now all too slender resources; but the old fellow went on:

"When you reach my age, Monsieur, you will have learned how to read men's thoughts from their faces. To me yours is an open book of misfortune and distress. I, too, am sad because I have been weak and foolish. I am far from being a worthy son of the Church, and have not been to confession now for many years; yet there is much truth in the priestly doctrine that 'a sorrow shared is but half a trouble'. Why, then, should we not confess the reasons for our sadness to one another and, if you would be so kind, seek the cheer, however, temporary, that lies at the bottom of every glass of Marc, Calvados or Cognac?"

The old man spoke clearly, slowly, and with a certain dignity, so Roger got the drift of all he had said quite easily. The expenditure of another few francs could make little difference to his depleted fortunes now, and he felt a strong urge to unburden himself to someone. Getting up, he called the serving man and, moving over to the old man's table, he bowed before sitting down at it, and said:

"You are right, Monsieur. Fortune has served me a scurvy trick, and I regret to hear that she has also turned her back on you. My name is Brook—Roger Brook; and I am happy to offer you the refreshment you desire. What will you take?"

"A Cognac, I thank you, and er—a double portion would not come amiss if 'tis not trespassing too far upon your generosity. As to the kind I am not particular. The potent spirit that they term *'fine maison'* in this dubious caravanserai is good enough for such as me."

Roger ordered a glass of Malaga for himself, and as the servant disappeared to fetch the drinks the old man went on:

"My name is Aristotle Fénelon and for business reasons I style myself Doctor. I will not tell you, as I tell many others, that I have taken the highest degrees at the most famous universities; but simply that I am a student of mankind. I make a living and, when fortune smiles upon me, a tolerably good one by pandering to the vanity of women and the credulence of men. In his wisdom the good God has so designed nature that every part of it is sustained by some other part; and by inspiring large numbers of men and women with the wish to improve upon His handiwork by making themselves more vigorous or more beautiful than they are, He provided me with an adequate means of support."

The drinks arrived at that moment and when Roger had settled for them, the "Doctor" lifted his glass with a hand that trembled a little, as he said:

"To your health, O kind and generous young man. And, believe me, 'tis the best toast I could drink to you. Given a healthy body there are few distempers of the mind that cannot be overcome, and given a healthy mind laughter cannot long remain absent from the lips."

"To your health too, then!" Roger replied, and as he set down his glass he added: "I fear my French is far from good. Am I right in assuming you to be a dealer in cosmetics?"

"Aye, and more than that." Aristotle Fénelon shook back his mop of white hair, "I can provide a panacea for a thousand ills. I can draw teeth, set sprains and cure malignant eruptions of every variety. The penalties which Venus inflicts upon her incautious votaries are my especial province, and I can brew a potion that will make any maid look fondly on her lover. But enough about myself for now. The aged are accustomed to sorrow and can philosophically await the turning of its tide; whereas youth is ever impatient for the solacing of its troubles. Tell me now the reason for that angry cast-down look that I saw upon your face when first I had the temerity to address you."

"You are perhaps acquainted with the Chevalier de Roubec?" Roger began. "He was the man in red, who was in here yestere'en."

The Doctor nodded. "I have had no speech with him, but have seen him about here in these past few days. A merry-looking fellow enough but one in whom, from his physiognomy, I would put little trust."

Roger made a grimace. "Alas, I lack your capacity for judging faces, *Monsieur le Docteur*. I put my faith in him at sad cost to myself." He then went on to describe his previous night's adventures and the manner in which he had been robbed that morning. Warming to the tale as he told it he realised that there was no longer any point in concealing the manner in which he had obtained the jewels, and that if the Doctor's advice was to be of any value to him he would be wise to give a complete picture of his circumstances; so he told him the reason for his leaving home and that he was now stranded in France with very little money.

When he had done, old Aristotle assessed the position shrewdly. "I fear, my young friend, that you have little prospect of recovering your property unless you go to the police, and your reasons for not wishing to do so are soundly conceived. As to your future, it should not be impossible for you to find a Captain who would let you work your passage across the Channel, more especially if you can offer him a *pourboire* of a *louis* or two for allowing you to do so. But once in England you will indeed be between Scylla and Charybdis. Life is a hard taskmaster for those who, having no trade by which to make a livelihood, must beg or earn their bread as best they can. My earnest advice to you is to sink your pride and make your peace with your father."

"Nay, that I'll not do," said Roger stubbornly. "Few fates that could befall me would be worse than being sent to sea. Moreover, my honour is involved in this. I set too much store by the opinion of the lady who gave me the jewels to return home with my tail between my legs after an absence of a bare four days, even if I could find anyone to give me passage this very evening."

"While I admire your spirit I deplore your reasoning," replied the Doctor. "Would that I could propose a further alternative, but alas! I see none."

For a few moments they sat in silence, then Roger said: "But tell me now in what way fortune has done you a mischief?"

"I am, alas! the author of my own misfortunes," Aristotle Fénelon held up his now half-empty glass of brandy. "Youth has many pleasures, age but few; and it has become my habit at certain seasons to indulge myself with this amber fluid which removes all care. More, I must confess it or the tale lacks point, at such times one dram begets the desire for another dram, and that for yet another. My virtuous resolutions gradually become things of little consequence. I remain addlepated for sometimes days at a stretch, and at last woefully regain full consciousness of my circumstances to realise that I have drunk away my last *sou.*"

"I take it," put in Roger, "that this morning is such a day, since you are beyond question sober now?"

"You are right, my young friend," the Doctor acknowledged. "Yet this morning finds me in a far worse pass than is usual on such occasions."

"How so?"

"As you may have already assumed, I am a journeyman doctor. Few men know France better than myself, since I have tramped its length and breadth many times in the past two-score years. I go from village to village selling my simples and my remedies to all whom I can induce to buy. I'll not deny that many of them are drastic in their effects. They needs must be, or the poor folk who buy them would feel that they had been cheated of their money. Often one must put gunpowder in their stomachs quite unnecessarily to persuade them that they have been treated at all. It is on occasion a question of kill or cure, and sometimes their last case is worse than their first. Yet, as God is my witness, I rarely make mistakes, and bring much relief from suffering to the less fortunate of our fellow-creatures who could not afford a treatment at all were it not for such wayside physicians as myself."

There was nothing new to Roger in all this, since quack doctors who stumped the countryside and put up their booths at fairs were then as common in England as in France, and for some little time past he had guessed the way in which Dr. Aristotle Fénelon earned his living. So he said:

"Why, then, having come to the end of your profits do you not set out again to earn some more?"

"Ah, that is just the trouble, Monsieur." The doctor's watery blue eyes held his for a moment. "At the end of every month or so, on reaching a large town, it is my custom to give myself a little holiday. Of the pleasant but profitless way in which I spend these brief seasons of leisure I have already told you. But each time before I set out again I must buy drugs, greases and potent waters, pots, bottles and vials wherewith to make up the stock in trade that I carry with me. It has always been my practice to put aside a few *louis* from my last journey especially for this purpose. But now I am undone, for in a tipsy moment I raided my reserve and have drunk that away, too."

" 'Twas a most unfortunate impulse. Did some special circumstance lead to it? Or was it an urge that at times has overcome you before?"

" 'Tis only on rare occasions that I have been so far lost to all good sense; but not the first time, I confess."

"It seems then, that your remedy lies in proceeding as you have done on similar awkward occasions in the past?"

Doctor Aristotle sighed. "A sound if uninspired judgment, my young friend, and one that brings me little comfort. It condemns me to fall back on straightforward surgery for a while, and sometimes one can visit half-a-dozen hamlets without finding a tooth to draw, or a broken bone to set. In the meantime I must eke out a most miserable existence until I can build up a small capital wherewith to buy drugs and ointments once more."

Again there fell a short silence and it seemed that neither of these companions in misfortune had been able to benefit the other, except in the slight comfort gained from the relation of their woes.

At length the Doctor twiddled his now empty glass and coughed. "Would you, Monsieur? I hesitate to ask. But no; it would be ungenerous in me to take advantage of the good nature of one to whom every *franc* must now be a matter of concern."

Roger had taken a liking to the old man, instinctively feeling him to be kind and wise, if weak; and the price of another couple of drinks could make little difference to his prospects of getting back to England; so he went out of the room and ordered them.

When he returned the Doctor thanked him gravely and added, as if on a sudden thought, "Would it be indiscreet, Monsieur, to inquire how much money you have left?"

Seeing no harm in disclosing his resources, Roger replied: "Something over four *louis*—about thirty-seven *crowns* to be exact."

" 'Twould be enough," the Doctor murmured.

"Enough for what, Monsieur?"

"Why, to purchase a new stock of medicines and unguents."

Roger smiled. "Much as I would like to relieve you of your cares, you must see that it is out of the question for me to lend you any money at the moment."

"Nay, I had no thought of begging a loan," the Doctor hastened to reassure him. " 'Twas a very different project that I had in mind. You say you are fully resolved that, come what may, you will not throw yourself upon the mercy of your father, and the only alternative that you can suggest is to seek a precarious livelihood tramping the English countryside. Yet living is far cheaper and more agreeable in France. Moreover, I could at least guarantee you a roof over your head, victuals of fair quality and an occupation which never lacks for interest and variety. I have the knowledge, you have enough capital to set us on the road. Why should we not form a partnership?"

For a moment Roger did not reply. Nothing could have been further from his own vague imaginings about his future, and such a course could certainly not lead to securing an influential position in London.

"Come now!" Doctor Aristotle went on more eagerly, "I would not seek to persuade you against your better judgment, but surely this is the solution to both our difficulties. The moment I set eyes on you I had a feeling that you were a young man with quick wits and of good address. It is not only your capital that I crave, but also your company. When your French is improved, you can harangue the little crowds that gather round my stand in curiosity, and you will find it most fascinating sport to talk even the most sceptical among them into buying one of our remedies for some, oft-imagined, complaint. And the women, too, why I would more than double my sales of skin creams and eye lotions were I able to point to that handsome counten-ance of yours as proof of their efficacy. 'Tis not winter either, so we'll not have to tramp through mud and rain, but 'tis a good season of the year; and by autumn we'll have made enough to take our journeys easily, lying up for the day at a warm fireside whene'er the weather proves inclement."

It was the last argument that decided Roger. By autumn his father would almost certainly have gone to sea again, and if he could then return home with a pocket full of *louis* honour would be satisfied. England offered no such prospect of a face-saving return, and during August and September what could really be more pleasant than a walking tour through France with its stimulating newness to him, its exciting foods and its volatile people?

"So be it," he said with a smile. "I'll come with you, but I make one stipulation."

"What is it?"

"That I keep the purse."

The Doctor gave him a rueful look. "Do'st grudge me my dram of Cognac?"

"Nay, not in reason; but for your sake as well as my own I wish to ensure that by autumn our pockets are tolerably well lined."

" 'Tis said that old heads do not grow upon young shoulders, but methinks yours will serve you well enough."

"Maybe I have aged somewhat swiftly overnight," commented Roger drily. "Is it agreed?"

"Yes; and in truth I should be grateful to you, since you propose to do for me that which I doubt my having the strength of will to do for myself."

"When do we set out?"

"To-morrow morning, if you will. After *déjeuner* we will go forth into the town to purchase our requirements. This evening we will make some of them up in Maître Picard's brewhouse, which he has on numerous previous occasions lent me for the purpose, and will no doubt again."

It was now a little after midday and, at that moment, the serving man put his head round the door to say that *déjeuner* was ready; so Roger and Dr. Aristotle went through to the coffee room and sat down to it together.

Being accustomed to the English fashion of making a hearty breakfast then taking the main meal of the day at four o'clock, Roger was somewhat surprised to find this midday repast more substantial than that he had been given the previous evening; but he was quick to realise that as the French eat only rolls and *confiture* on rising they must sadly need something more filling before mid-afternoon; so their so-called "breakfast" was really their dinner, and the evening meal considered by them to be of secondary importance.

When they had finished Dr. Aristotle took Roger out to the stable and presented him to Monsieur de Montaigne, a quiet and elderly mule, so named, the Doctor explained, on account of his wisdom and sagacity. It was Monsieur de Montaigne's function to transport from place to place, in a pair of capacious panniers, his master's few personal possessions and stock-in-trade, and to carry strapped lengthwise on top of them a contraption made of wood and canvas which could swiftly be erected into a street pulpit. Saddling the mule with his panniers they led him out on to the quay and bent their steps towards the centre of the city.

Roger had no intention of laying himself open to being tricked twice in one day, so when the Doctor halted in a side street before an apothecary's, he made no move to produce his money, but the old man did not even suggest it; he simply tied his mule to a ring in the wall and beckoned Roger to follow him inside.

Half an hour went by while the apothecary weighed and measured a score of ingredients ranging from great jars of fat to little phials of crude but pungent scent. After some haggling on the Doctor's part Roger parted with one *louis* seven *crowns* and a *franc*, then they carried their purchases outside and loaded them on to Monsieur de Montaigne.

Their next visit was to an *épicerie* where the Doctor added to their store a quantity of soap, sugar, cheap sweets and spices, including a good supply of peppercorns, for an outlay of three *crowns* six *sous*. After this they went to the warehouse of a wholesale china and glass dealer from whom they purchased several score of containers for their wares; bottles of various sizes, jars, pots and little hand-painted vases, which cost a further five *crowns*.

Roger thought that their business was now completed, but he proved mistaken. Instead of turning back towards *Les Trois Fleur-de-Lys* Doctor Aristotle led the way farther into the city, and they walked on for the best part of a mile until they had passed through it and were in a leafy *Faubourg* leading up to the *Bastion de Tourneville*. Some way along it the Doctor halted opposite a squat, ivy-covered cottage with a thatched roof, and said:

"I have to make another purchase here and I shall require a *louis*."

"But we have only some thirteen *crowns* left," expostulated Roger, "and if I give you eight of them, after we've settled up at the inn, we'll have next to nothing left for emergencies."

The Doctor shrugged. "My score is already settled; since, knowing my sad habits, Maître Picard makes me pay always in advance; and having been there but a day yours cannot be a heavy one. Give me the money, I beg. 'Tis to acquire a drug which is ever one of my most profitable lines and at nowhere else do I know a place to obtain it nearer than Rouen."

Roger half suspected that the old man wanted to obtain the *louis* for some purpose of his own, but he had so far had no grounds for doubting his honesty and felt that as long as the mule, with its now valuable cargo, remained in his charge he had ample security; so with some reluctance he counted out the money.

The door of the cottage was opened by a repulsive old crone with a bent back, hairs upon her bony chin and a black cat perched upon her shoulder. Roger felt sure she was a witch, and hastily averted his gaze as the Doctor went inside with her.

The thought that his partner was about to purchase some rare and expensive decoction from this sinister old woman gave Roger furiously to think. What kind of drug could the Doctor possibly require that was not obtainable at an apothecary's? Could it be that he was not merely an old quack whose worst fault lay in selling remedies, many of which he knew to be worthless?

In the time of Louis XIV all Europe had been horrified by the disclosures at the trials of the infamous La Voisin and the Marquise de Brinvilliers. A vast conspiracy had been uncovered in which hundreds of people had been involved, including the King's favourite, Madame de Montespan. Her young rival, Mademoiselle de Fontanges, had died in agonised convulsions after drinking a cup of fruit juice on her return from hunting with the King. The inquiry, on which her family had insisted, had revealed the existence of a great organisation fostering the practice of Satanism and willing to ensure the death of unwanted husbands, parents and rivals for a price, in many cases as low as ten *Louis*. Although the King had refused to allow a case to be brought against his old favourite, on account of the children he had had by her, it had led to her downfall, and a number of her associates had been broken on the wheel. Hundreds of mysterious deaths had been traced to their evil machinations and, as a result, France had not even yet lived down the reputation of being a land where poisoning was rife. Could it be that Doctor Aristotle Fénelon made the more remunerative part of his precarious living as a poisoner?

When the Doctor came out of the cottage he showed Roger a fair-sized bottle three parts full of liquid.

"What is that?" asked Roger, striving to conceal his perturbation.

" 'Tis Ergot of Rye," replied the Doctor shortly, "an invaluable

111

specific for the ills to which many young women become subject,'' but he refused to amplify his statement, so Roger was left only partially satisfied as to the purpose for which this expensive acquisition was intended.

As they walked back towards the centre of the town Georgina's prediction recurred to him. She had said that he would be in grave danger from water; and he had been. She had said that he would meet with a man that boded no good to him and had something the matter with his left eye; and, wondering that he had not thought of it before, Roger now recalled the scar running up to the eye corner on De Roubec's left cheek. She had said that he would go into some form of partnership with an old man who would prove a good friend to him, yet that no permanent good would come to him from it.

But it was too late now to speculate on whether or no the Doctor was the old man she had seen in the glass. Roger realised that his last chance of getting back to England had vanished with the completion of their purchases that afternoon and only a few *francs* now stood between him and starvation. The die was cast and, for better or for worse, he must take the road with old Aristotle Fénelon the following morning.

CHAPTER X

THE MAN IN GREY

T H E Y got back to *Les Trois Fleur-de-Lys* with some hours of the long afternoon still to spare, so they at once set about turning the brew-house into a dispensary. While Roger stabled Monsieur de Montaigne and unloaded his panniers the Doctor brought down from his room two battered old portmanteaux, containing his medical instruments, a few crude laboratory appliances and the oddments of stock that he had over from his last journey. A fire was soon lighted under the big copper and a supply of fresh water drawn from the well in the yard; then Dr. Aristotle entered upon the performance of his dubious mysteries.

Roger, his coat off and his shirt sleeves rolled up, watched him fascinated, and lent his aid by washing and drying the pots and bottles, then filling them with the Doctor's sinister concoctions. Many of their purchases needed no further treatment than watering down and the principal business resolved itself into two main operations each followed by a number of subsidiary ones. The first was the blending of a foundation grease to which was added a variety of scents, some fragrant and some abominably foul, to give it the semblance of a number of quite different ointments; the second was the blending of a clear fluid, containing 90 per cent water, to varying proportions of which colouring matter or pungent flavourings were added for a similar purpose.

They broke off for supper then returned to finish their labours by candlelight, spending an additional hour rolling pills made of soap and a dash of cascara, then they packed their wares into the panniers and retired to bed.

In the morning Roger woke with the awful thought that during the night the Doctor might have absconded with the lotions and unguents which now represented his small capital, leaving him near destitute. Hurriedly pulling on his clothes he dashed downstairs and out to the stable. To his immense relief he found his fears to be groundless; Monsieur de Montaigne was quietly munching away at the hay in his manger and the panniers lay nearby packed and strapped as they had been left the night before.

Half an hour later, still feeling a little guilty about his unjust suspicions, he met his partner in the coffee room and they sat down to their *petit déjeuner*. Over the meal they discussed the itinerary for their journey and the Doctor having come down from Picardy via Dieppe, visiting all the villages along the coast on his way, it was decided to continue on into southern Normandy; but as they could not afford to take passage in a ferry across the wide estuary of the Seine they would follow its northern bank east as far as Rouen and then strike south from there.

Roger's bill for the eventful thirty-eight hours he had spent at *Les Trois Fleur-de-Lys* came to eight *francs* fourteen *sous*, so after a *pourboire* to the serving man and the chambermaid he was reduced to a single *crown* and a little small change; but he was not unduly perturbed by the depletion of his resources as the day was fine and it held for him ample promise of new scenes and interests.

Having hoisted the panniers on to Monsieur de Montaigne's back and strapped on top of them the Doctor's collapsible street pulpit they left the inn soon after eight o'clock and took the road to Harfleur.

It was on the way there that the Doctor spoke tactfully to Roger about his sword. The old man told him that in France it was forbidden to carry arms unless of noble birth; the only exception to the rule being that barbers were allowed to do so, as a special concession on account of their peculiarly intimate relations with the nobility and their clients' dependence upon them. In the towns, of course, many soldiers of fortune, and scallywags such as the Chevalier, wore swords in support of their pretensions to an aristocratic lineage that they did not in fact possess, and they were so numerous as rarely to be called to account for this misdemeanour, but in the country it was different.

As the Doctor pointed out, should some nobleman drive up to an inn and halt there for the horses of his coach to be watered he might see Roger wearing a sword while assisting to peddle their medicines. This would appear so incongruous to him that he would most probably set his lackeys on to give Roger a whipping.

Having worn his sword only for a day, Roger was somewhat loath to take it off; but he saw the sense of the Doctor's remarks and felt that as he had never carried one in England, to go without it would be no great deprivation, so he removed it from its frog and stowed it among the baggage on the mule.

113

By ten o'clock they reached the still battlemented walls of Harfleur, made famous by King Henry V's siege and reduction of it, but they did not pause there, and continued on along the main highway to the north-east, until an hour after midday they entered the village of St. Romain.

Hungry now, after their twelve-mile tramp, they went to the inn and, for a *franc*, procured a meal of bread and cheese washed down by a coarse *vin du pays*. During the afternoon they rested in an orchard, then towards five o'clock when the peasants, their day's work done, began to drift back from the fields, the partners proceeded to set about their business.

While the Doctor put up his stand outside the inn, Roger brought from the stable an assortment of bottles and pots which he set out on a small folding table beside the stand. The Doctor then mounted it and picking up a large handbell began to ring it loudly to attract the handful of people who were to be seen doing errands or gossiping in the village street.

In a few moments he had a dozen children round him and a few grown-ups, and Roger had to admire the cleverness with which he opened the proceedings. Producing a packet of the cheap sweets from his pocket he addressed himself to the children.

"My little ones, you see in me a wise man skilled in all medicines. Many of you must have mothers, fathers, and other relatives who are suffering and in pain from one cause or another. Run now to your homes and tell them that the good Doctor Aristotle Fénelon has arrived here for the special purpose of curing their complaints, and that it will cost them no more than a few *sous*. But before you bear these good tidings to your folks look what I have here for you, a sweet a-piece as succulent as it is colourful. Forget not my message; and those of you who have pretty sisters should add that for a trifle I have lotions and unguents here which will make red hands as white as alabaster and dull eyes sparkle like the stars."

He then handed out the highly-coloured sweets amongst them and they scurried away to spread the news of his visit through the village.

After ringing the bell again for a while he had a crowd of some twenty people assembled and more were drifting up every moment. As Roger looked at them he greatly doubted if they could raise a *louis* between them, as they were mostly dressed in rags, and it struck him most forcibly how much poorer the people here appeared to be than would have a similar crowd in an English village. But his attention was soon distracted from the comparison as he endeavoured to follow the flowery phrases in which the Doctor now addressed them.

"My friends!" he cried, in a sonorous voice, "To-day is a day of good fortune for this ancient and populous township of St. Romain. Never, I make bold to say, since the good Saint who founded it passed to his holy rest, has such a unique opportunity been offered to its intelligent inhabitants to be swiftly relieved of their ills, both physical and mental.

"I am the great Doctor Aristotle Fénelon, of whom many of you must have heard; since I spend my life ministering to suffering humanity, and my name is reverenced from far Muscovy to even more distant Cathay for the miraculous cures and good works that I perform —yet I am also your most humble servant.

"I was educated at the Sorbonne in Paris, and also at the famous universities of Leyden, Oxford, Pavia and Heidelberg. At these great seats of learning I took all the degrees which it was possible to take, while still quite young, and my wisdom became so renowned that elderly professors travelled from such distant cities as Danzig, Palermo and Madrid to hold converse with me.

"Having completed my studies I spent twenty years in travelling the world in search of medicines and remedies so far unknown in Europe. From the Moorish doctors of the Orient I learned the secrets by which the ladies of the Great Turk's harem preserve their beauty from decay for almost unbelievable periods, so that at the age of sixty they are no less desirable than when at seventeen they first attracted the notice of their munificent master. Journeying on to Hind, I traversed the empire of the Grand Mogul from end to end, studying the methods by which the fakirs prolong their lives to the span of three-hundred years, as did the Patriarchs in holy writ, and are still capable of begetting a child upon a virgin when two-hundred and fifty years of age.

"But think not that my search for the secrets of healing, longevity, beauty and vigour have been confined only to Europe and the East. I have also visited the Americas, where I learned of the Redmen how to seal open wounds by fire almost painlessly, and to cure the pox by a decoction made from the bark of a tree that grows only on the tops of the Andes mountains. In short, I am the living compendium of all knowledge concerning bodily ailments and the satisfaction of physical desire.

"Yet, lest you may think me boastful I will freely confess that there is one thing I cannot do. I am an honest man and would never seek to deceive so distinguished and critical an audience. Death is still the master of us all, and although I can prolong life I cannot do so indefinitely. It is your great misfortune, as it is also mine, that although I once possessed a rare parchment on which an Atlantian alchemist had inscribed the method of distilling the Elixir of Life, a rascally Egyptian priest stole it from me; and, alas! the recipe was too complicated for any human brain to remember.

"But, even though I cannot offer you the divine gift of immortality, I can provide a panacea for a thousand ills. I draw teeth, set sprains and apply electric fluid after the principles of Doctor Mesmer, who, as you may have heard, is now all the rage in fashionable Paris, and, 'tis said, has even treated Queen Marie Antoinette herself. I can cure boils, warts, tumours, goitre, suppurating ulcers, irritant rashes, eczema, catarrh, lumbago, anæmia, a persistent cough, acidity, headaches, sleeplessness, sore nipples, affections of the eyes, deafness, night-sweats, wind, bad breath and foot rot.

"There are too, those results of amatory imprudence which for some purpose of His own the good God has seen fit to inflict upon us poor mortals. I refer, in the first place, to those dangerous diseases which, praise be, are rarely met with in the country, and particularly in towns of such high morality as St. Romain, but can be caught by even the best-intentioned during visits of curiosity to the dubious haunts of our great cities; in the second, to that process in nature which, as the result of a few moments' indulgence, oft inflicts upon a girl or woman a burden that she is either unfitted or unwilling to bear. Finally, there are those distempers of the mind and brain which call for special treatment. Unrequited love is such a one, loss of sexual vitality and an inability to beget children are others. For all of these I have most efficacious remedies; but such are private matters, and should any of you wish to consult me on them I shall be at your service in my room here, at the inn, between eight o'clock and midnight. I make no extra charge for these confidential consultations and your secrets will be as safe with me as if made to your *Curé* in the confessional."

As the Doctor finished this long and grandiloquent harangue, Roger would not have been surprised if the crowd had broken into cries of anger and derision. Never had he heard so many palpable lies rolled off in so few moments, and it seemed impossible that any collection of sane men and women would believe one-tenth of them. Yet, as he looked at the dull and stupid faces of the peasant audience he realised that their ignorance must be abysmal, and that it was doubtful if they even understood half the allusions the Doctor had made to his mythical journeyings. They just stood quietly and patiently there like a herd of animals. There was hardly a movement among them and their faces remained quite expressionless.

As no one came forward the Doctor went on: "Now, good folk, have no fears, but seize upon this all-too-fleeting opportunity, for by dawn to-morrow it will be too late. The world is wide and there are many sufferers in it, so I must be on my way to give the great benefit of my experience to others. But for this evening my encyclopædic knowledge is yours for the asking. To produce an example, and thus overcome your reluctance to voice your needs, I will give a free treatment to whoever first consults me."

This offer produced an immediate reaction. The peasants were not so deaf and dumb as they appeared, and there was a little surge forward of the crowd as several people, all speaking at once, endeavoured to push their way to the front.

"That's better," purred the Doctor, as a lean, determined-looking woman gained first place. "Well, mother! What ails thee?"

It was the woman's eyes that were troubling her. Stepping down from his stand the Doctor screwed a pocket-lens into his own eye, took a quick look at them, and gave her a bottle which Roger knew to contain plain salt dissolved in water; as he remembered the Doctor remarking when they made it up that no better eye lotion had ever been discovered, and that it was a pity they had to pander to their customer's stupid belief that no medicine was ever efficacious unless it was coloured, since the colouring matter rendered it much less soothing than would have been an unadulterated solution.

The next applicant was a man with a horrid suppurating ulcer on his forearm, for which the Doctor sold him a pot of ointment; the third a woman who complained of splitting headaches; the fourth, another carrying a child that had croup: and so it went on for an hour or more. After a brief examination of each patient the Doctor pointed out the bottle or pot that Roger was to hand them and told him how much to charge. The fee was generally three *sous* and rarely more than six, while for drawing a tooth or extracting the core of a malignant boil by the application of the neck of a heated bottle, the Doctor charged only half a *franc*, so Roger, greatly disappointed in this collection of half-pence, began to fear that they would not even make enough clear profit to pay for their night's lodging.

Yet his pile of greasy little copper coins gradually grew, and presently the young men and girls of the village began to mingle with the afflicted, having raided their savings to buy the vigour-inducing tonics and beauty preparations which the Doctor had mentioned in his opening address.

For each he had some special name and story. "Paris drops" were the very same elixir which had enabled the hero of antiquity to rape one hundred virgins in a night and yet remain with his desire unappeased next morning. "Helen's cream" was the secret of the beauty which had made the knees of old men turn to water as they watched her pass by on the battlements of Troy. "Cleopatra's ointment" was that same kohl with which the Egyptian Queen had painted her black eyebrows when she went out to meet and ensnare Cæsar, and so on, *ad infinitum*.

As Roger handed out these nostrums, balms and potions, he was amazed that the village wenches among his customers should be so far removed from the score or so of elegant ladies he had seen shopping in the *Rue Francois 1er* two afternoons earlier, and even from the shop girls of Le Havre, as to appear almost of a different race. They were bedraggled, dirty and slovenly, with their hair unkempt and their ugly feet thrust naked into wooden *sabots*. Yet it seemed, as they carefully counted out their hoarded *sous*, they were as anxious to obtain some little aid to beauty as their more fortunate sisters in the city.

At length, as twilight deepened, the crowd dwindled and the last customer was served with a little phial of "Oil of Hercules," that the Doctor assured him would enable him to win the village ploughing contest in the coming spring; and having packed up their goods and chattels they went into the inn.

It was a poor place but the simple food was well cooked and, after they had eaten, the partners received three visitors, at intervals, in the room they were sharing. Dr. Aristotle had been averse to his young companion being present at these interviews but Roger, still a little suspicious from his sad experience of the previous day, thought it possible that the old man might secrete a portion of the fees wherewith to buy brandy on the sly, so he insisted.

The proceedings made him feel slightly sick in all three cases, as the first two patients were suffering from advanced stages of venereal disease, and the third was a bent but lecherous-looking old man who

117

wanted a potion that would make him capable of deflowering a girl who worked on his holding. But the Doctor took a *franc* a-piece off the two former and a *crown* off the latter, so Roger felt that he had been wise to remain.

Next morning they struck away from the high road and walked at an easy pace for five miles down by-lanes until they came to the smaller village of Tancarville, at the mouth of the Seine. Here the performances were repeated with still more meagre results and at a penalty of having to sleep in a miserable inn where the beds were alive with fleas; but on the following day they turned north-east again and, arriving at the township of Lillebonne by midday, spent the following three nights there in reasonable comfort. On the first two they did good business and the third day of their stay being Sunday they rested from their labours.

On the Monday they set out again, zig-zagging eastward through the villages of Candebec and Duclair to another little township called Barentin, which they reached on the Wednesday. Thursday, Friday and Saturday they slept in the nearby adjacent villages of Le Houlme, Maromme and Deville, and on the Sunday morning they walked into the ancient city of Rouen.

By this time Roger had picked up the game, and on entering a place where they intended to pass the night was able to form a fair estimate of what their takings in it were likely to be. Any village, however small, seemed good enough for a night's bed and board with a few *crowns* over, but in the small towns they had made much bigger profits. For one thing the crowds they attracted were considerably larger and, for another, the general run of the inhabitants being somewhat better off, the Doctor was able to charge more for his wares. So on entering Rouen Roger had high hopes of their garnering a bumper harvest.

On his mentioning this, however, his partner was quick to disabuse him of the idea. The Doctor emphasised that only from the poor and ignorant could they hope to exact unquestioning belief in his own powers, and consequent tribute. In the larger towns and cities there were properly qualified doctors, apothecarys' shops and barbers' establishments which dealt in beauty preparations much superior to his own. Moreover, a good part of their inhabitants were educated people or, worse, cynical riff-raff who thought it good sport to throw rotten eggs and decayed garbage at such poor street practitioners as himself. This visit to Rouen, he added, must be regarded only as a holiday and the occasion for a little relaxation.

Contrary to Roger's expectations the old man had, so far, been very good in refraining from asking for nips of Cognac; but, on hearing this, his young partner rightly suspected that the Doctor now had it in mind to indulge his weakness. In ten evenings' work they had, somewhat to Roger's surprise, managed to amass, mainly in *sous* and *francs*, some nine *louis* over and above their expenses, and he had no intention of seeing this small nucleus to their future fortunes frittered away. So he took the bull by the horns and said at once:

" 'Tis not yet two weeks since we set out upon our journey, so the time has not yet come for us to take a holiday."

"Why should we not take just a *little* holiday?" the Doctor pleaded. "Two or three nights, no more; but long enough for me to show you the site upon which the Maid of Orleans was burnt as a witch and the tombs of the Crusaders in the great Cathedral?"

"That we can do to-day," said Roger firmly. "And, since you say that we should only invite trouble by setting up our stand here, to-morrow morning we will continue our progress southward to lesser places where profits are to be made."

"So be it," sighed the Doctor. "But thou art a hard taskmaster for one so young. I intended to ask no more than a little rest for my old bones and, perhaps, a few *crowns* from our profits with which to purchase the wherewithal to warm the lining of my stomach."

"I knew it," Roger replied. "But one little dram leads to another little dram, as you yourself have said; and once you fall to drinking in earnest I'll never be able to get you on the move again. I've naught against our treating ourselves to a good dinner and a decent bottle of wine to go with it, but I pray you be content with that, and let us take the road again to-morrow."

The Doctor brightened a little and now seemed quite willing to let Roger fight his failing for him; but although they did not set up their stand in Rouen they were fated to meet trouble there.

Le Pomme D'Or, at which they put up, because the Doctor was known at it, proved to be a small inn down by the river. Having stabled Monsieur de Montaigne and taken their things up to their room, they went down to the parlour and found it to be full of sailors, who had recently been discharged from a man-o'-war. As in England, most of them had originally been pressed into the service, and many of them had spent the best years of their youth sailing the seas and fighting in the late war; yet now that the French Navy was gradually being reduced they had been paid off with a pittance which would barely keep them for a month, and comparatively few of them knew a trade by which they could earn a living ashore.

Naturally they were in an angry mood, and Roger, on learning the reason for their discontent, was indiscreet enough to remark that the French King's finances must be in a very poor state compared to those of the King of England, since the latter gave his sailors handsome bonuses on their discharge, and they went ashore with their pockets full of gold from their share of the prize money earned by the ships in which they had served.

On it emerging that he was English himself, they showed a sudden and alarming hostility. They knew nothing of the real causes of the late war; only that as a result of it they had been seized by the press-gangs and forced to spend years of hardship and danger far from their families. They had, moreover, been taught to believe that the perfidious English, desiring to dominate the world, had forced the war upon peaceful France, and that every Englishman was a fit object for the blackest hatred. In consequence they now regarded Roger as a visible cause of their past miseries and present anxieties.

With menacing looks half a dozen of these dark, wiry, uncouth-looking sailors now gathered round, shouting obscene abuse indiscriminately at him and everything that England stood for, and the street women they had picked up on landing added to the clamour with shrill, vindictive cries.

Only the Doctor's intervention saved Roger from a nasty mauling. In his sonorous voice the old man quelled the tumult. He upbraided the sailors for their discourtesy to a citizen of a country with which France was now at peace, and pointed out that since the late war had begun in '78 no one so young as Roger could possibly have had a hand in the making of it.

A blue-eyed shrew, attracted by Roger's good looks, also took his part and turned her screaming abuse upon the now hesitant sailors, calling them a pack of great, misbegotten bullies for attempting to browbeat so young a lad.

At the Doctor's suggestion Roger stood the company a round of drinks, and there the matter ended. But, when they had gone up to their room that night, he told Roger that among the ignorant in France there was still much resentment against the English, on account of the additional taxes and other hardships that the war had brought upon them; so he thought it would be a wise move if his young companion took another name and gave himself out to be a native of some other country.

As he was very proud of being English Roger was, at first, most loath to adopt the Doctor's suggestion, but eventually he was persuaded of its wisdom, and, after some discussion, it was decided that to account for his poor French and heavy accent he should pass himself off as a Frenchman hailing from Alsace; since most of the inhabitants of that province were brought up to speak only their mother tongue, which was German.

It was then agreed that Roger should keep his Christian name, which, pronounced as *Rojé*, was not uncommon in France, and change his surname to *Breuc*, that being the nearest French spelling to Brook.

On the Monday they set out again, crossing the Seine and journeying from village to village through central Normandy by way of Bernay and Lisieux to Caen. The August days were warm and pleasant, the life never lacking in variety and interest. Their stock was dwindling but Roger's money-bag grew satisfactorily heavier and when they reached Caen on the thirtieth of the month their takings totalled twenty-three *louis*.

Now that they had once more reached a city the Doctor again pressed for a "little holiday." But after some trouble Roger managed to argue him out of it on the grounds that another two days would see them in September, so they could count on only five or six weeks more good weather, and therefore should make the most of it.

The Doctor admitted that there was sound sense in this, as journey-man-doctoring in winter was a poor business, and the more they were able to put by while the good weather lasted the more frequently they would be able to lie up when storms were turning the roads into quagmires.

That afternoon, instead of remaining in the stuffy city, they walked out to a meadow, from which they could see the spires of the great Norman churches, and lay there for a while in the sunshine.

They dozed for a little, then, on their rousing, the Doctor asked Roger, apropos of nothing, how he liked the life he was leading and if he would be willing to continue their partnership as a permanency.

" 'Tis well enough," Roger replied, "and I am mighty grateful that I fell in with you. But as soon as I have saved sufficient to make me independent for a while I plan to return to England."

"Had you not that in view, would you be content to remain with me?" inquired the Doctor.

Roger had developed a great fondness for the old man and while he knew that his ambitions could never be satisfied by such a life, he was loath to hurt his companion's feelings, so he said:

"We get on so well together that I would hate to part with you, and the life itself has many attractions. Even if we fool some people and endanger others by selling them drastic remedies, the good we do to the great majority is out of all proportion to the harm we may do the few. Yet at times it saddens me."

"How so?"

" 'Tis the sore straits in which those from whom we make a living, live themselves. They herd together like animals in their miserable, broken-down cottages, many of which have leaking roofs and hardly any of which even have windows to keep out the bitter winds of winter. Often I am ashamed to take from them the miserable *sous* they bring us."

"I'll not gainsay that they are poor," replied the Doctor, "but the majority of them are by no means as poor as you might think. In most cases 'tis for quite a different reason that they refrain from patching their roofs and putting windows in their houses. As you must have seen, on Sundays and Feast-days the village women bedeck themselves in very different raiment to that which they wear in the fields. Their layers of striped petticoats and lace headdresses have cost good money, and few of them are without gold chains and crosses for their necks, so they can well afford to part with a few *sous* for a beauty ointment."

"Why, then, do they live in such miserable conditions?"

" 'Tis on account of the *taille*, my young friend, the most monstrously stupid form of taxation that was ever devised by a government of fools. The King's Intendants assess each village at whatever lump sum they may judge it to be worth, and the village syndics, whether they like it or not, are forced to collect the money from the villagers. The syndics, in turn, are empowered to assess each householder quite arbitrarily, not upon his actual capacity to pay, but simply on the amount they think they can squeeze out of him. Each man is taxed, therefore, upon his presumed wealth, and this is judged by his mode of living and apparent prosperity. As a result every villager makes an outward show of the direst poverty in order to get off as lightly as he can. This not only leads them to the self-infliction of many hardships which there would otherwise be no call for them to bear but it also

121

strikes most savagely at the true interests of the country, since the peasants leave much of their land untilled from fear that bigger crops would land them with a higher tax assessment."

"What incredible folly," said Roger. "But why do not the nobles who own so much of the land make representations to the King, and get the tax laws altered?"

The Doctor shook his head. "The nobility of France still retains its privileges. Most unjustly all persons of rank are exempt from taxation, and they still possess the sole rights in shooting and snaring game, which is hard on the peasantry; but for many decades past they have lost all power of influencing the government. 'Twas the great Cardinal de Richelieu who destroyed the power of the feudal lords, and Le Grand Monarque completed the process by compelling them all to leave their estates and live as idlers at his court of Versailles in order to make a splendid background for himself. From that time on the running of the country fell into the hands of the Kings almost entirely, and they could know little of its state, as they were advised only by a small clique of greedy favourites and Finance Ministers who depended on the Farmers of the Revenue to suggest ways of raising money as best they could."

"They seem to have made a pretty mess of things," Roger commented. "Our nobility in England would not stand for such mismanagement, nor would the people, either. Why, they cut off the King's head with less reason a hundred and forty years ago."

" 'Twas neither the nobility nor the people who cut off King Charles's head," corrected the Doctor gently. " 'Twas the *bourgeoisie;* the lawyers and the rich tradespeople of the cities. And 'twill be the same here if the present discontents come to a head. The peasantry are too apathetic and too cowed to rise; the nobility has all to lose and naught to gain by so doing. But there is money in the towns, and money begets both ambition and jealousy of the privileges of the ruling caste. Of late years the reading of books by such as can read has spread apace, and such works as those of Messieurs de Quesnay, de Mirabeau, de Morelly and Jean Jacques Rousseau have spread abroad this cry for equality. Yet those who shout loudest have not in mind equality for the peasant with themselves but equality for themselves with the nobility."

"Have you no body the like of the English Parliament that could put matters to rights without disrupting the country by a great rebellion?"

"We have no Parliament in your sense, to which the people elect their own representatives. There are the local Parliaments, which we term Estates. Each of these consists of three chambers, the Church, the Nobility and a third Estate composed of the representatives of the city corporations and the trade guilds; but they have never been aught but provincial municipalities. Time was, though, when they used to send their representatives to Paris to sit in the States-General and advise the Kings of France whenever there arose a major crisis in the affairs of the nation. But the States-General has not now been summoned for nearly a hundred and seventy years. The last time they met was in 1614; and since then the Monarchy has become so all-powerful that it ignores them. As for the provincial Estates, from one cause and another most of them have ceased to function these many decades past, and only those of Artois, Flanders, Burgundy, Brittany and Languedoc continue to assemble regularly."

"How is the kingdom governed, then?" asked Roger, "for if the nobles play no part and these Estates you speak of are moribund, how can the King, hedged about as he is by a crowd of ill-informed wasters, know what is happening to his subjects?"

"Alas! he does not; though 'tis said that he is good-intentioned. By theory he rules through the governors of his provinces, but these are all great nobles who live in luxury at his Court on the huge incomes that their governorships bring them. In fact, the land is ruled by the Intendants appointed by the Comptroller-General of Finance, most of whom are clever upstarts with but one concern—to line their own pockets at the expense of both the King and the people."

"But can the gentry do nothing to better matters?" asked Roger. "In England all people who have estates, whether large or small, feel it incumbent on them to protect and succour their dependants. A landlord who allowed his tenants' cottages to fall into disrepair or left his village folk starving in a bad winter would at once be cold-shouldered by his neighbours."

"Ah, and 'twas so here in the good old days. But the gentry are now almost as helpless as the peasants. All the wealth of the land is drawn either to Versailles in taxes or into the pockets of the lawyers and rich merchants in the cities. The upper tenth of the nobility, that which lives at Court near the King and grabs up the rich plums that fall from his table, does monstrous well; the other nine-tenths lives on its estates, mostly small properties that bring in barely enough to keep a roof on the Chateaux of their owners. They are mostly proud, aloof, hidebound in their ideas and jealous of their privileges; and they have lost both the inclination and the means to help their unfortunate peasantry."

" 'Tis a parlous state the country has come to, in very truth; and what you tell me interests me mightily. Yet it affects not the fact that I find it ever increasingly repugnant to take their savings off these wretched villagers."

"If 'tis that which worries you," the Doctor said, after a moment, "we will proceed yet further south into Brittany. The ancient kingdom is one of the few provinces in France where the Estates still function to some purpose. Moreover, the nobility there have never brought themselves to feel any strong allegiance to the Crown, and both rich and poor among them rarely leave their properties. I do not say that you will find the Breton peasants wealthy, but at least you will find them more prosperous and better cared for than those in the villages you have so far visited with me."

So it came about that, having replenished their stock of unguents, balms and 'sovereign remedies" in Caen next day, they followed the road south-west through Vire and Avranches towards Brittany. It was the 20th of September before they paid toll to enter the province and, since leaving Caen, in spite of their outlay there, the funds of the

123

partnership had mounted to forty *louis*, partly as a result of several profitable private consultations that the Doctor had given to patients coming to him after dark.

Roger now no longer participated in these harrowing and gruesome interviews. Apart from the disgust they caused him he had reached the conclusion that there was little point in his doing so, since he knew how many private visitors the Doctor received each evening and approximately what he was likely to make out of them. Moreover, he now felt convinced that the only time his partner was at all likely to attempt to cheat him was when they were in a town and the craving for brandy overcame the old man's better nature.

From the frontier of the province they struck south towards Rennes, intending to make a wide circuit of its interior after they had once more replenished their store of drugs in its capital.

As the Doctor had foretold, Roger found the Breton peasantry much more alive and human than their neighbours to the north. They showed more independence and even, at times, heckled the great Aristotle Fénelon, questioning his encyclopædic knowledge and his much-vaunted wisdom. At times, too, the *Curés* of the villages came out and drove the human benefactor away, upbraiding him as a godless charlatan. But, in spite of this, the Bretons proved a credulous folk and their women bought much more freely of the Doctor's toilet preparations; so, when they reached Rennes on 5th of October, Roger had fifty-four *louis*, tucked, literally, under his belt, as he now kept their funds, as he once had Georgina's jewels, in an elongated pouch round his waist.

On arriving in Rennes they went to the *Du Guesclin*, a good inn, overlooking the *Champe de Mars*, as they intended to do themselves well. Having reached the town by mid-morning they were in time to enjoy an excellent *déjeuner*, but it struck Roger that during it his companion was unusually silent.

After the meal, as had become their custom on reaching any town of importance, they went out for a walk in order that the Doctor might show Roger such items of historic interest as the place contained. As they proceeded towards the Cathedral of St. Pierre the old man's quite abnormal uncommunicativeness continued, so Roger asked him if he was not feeling well.

"I'm well enough in myself, but a trifle worried," the Doctor replied.

"About what?" Roger inquired.

"I trust 'twill prove a matter of no moment; but did you, perchance, notice the man in the grey coat who was sitting alone at a small table in the coffee room, at its far end on the left side of the hearth—a tall, thin, angular fellow with red hair and a somewhat sour expression?"

"Yes," said Roger. "I glanced at him more than once because I was struck by the exceptional pallor of his face. I thought him not unhandsome, but there was something vaguely repellent about that small mouth of his, and his heavily lidded eyes that avoided my glance each time I looked at him. Who is he?"

"His name is Joseph Fouché. He is a lay preacher of the Oratorian

Order and a native of Nantes. His father was, I believe, a sea-captain and left him both some small properties in Brittany and a plantation in San Domingo, so he is of independent means. However, as a hobby he interests himself in police affairs, playing the rôle of a private investigator for his own amusement, then acting as an informer. 'Twas in such a matter that I met him."

"What part did you play in this?" asked Roger with some apprehension.

"I was in Nantes towards the end of last winter and, er—my funds were unusually low. 'Twas on that account that, against my better judgment, I agreed to treat a somewhat stubborn case. 'Twas through no lack of care on my part that I lost my patient. Even then no harm would have resulted to myself had not a wealthy family been involved and Monsieur Fouché, as a friend of theirs, taken it upon himself to investigate the matter. He traced the cause of death to me, then browbeat me into certain admissions, and on his information the police issued a warrant for my arrest."

"Phew! That was indeed a tight corner to be in. How did you manage to get out of it?"

The Doctor sighed. "By sacrificing the handsome fee that I had received. As you may have gathered police-agents are almost universally corrupt. I bribed the agent sent to arrest me to connive at my escape. But I must confess that seeing Monsieur Fouché again has temporarily unnerved me."

"That I can well understand," Roger agreed. "Yet it does not seem to me that you have aught to fear from him. From what you tell me it appears that his only interest in such affairs is the sport he derives from tracing up a case. If that is so, in yours, he has already had all the satisfaction it could afford him."

"It may be that I have allowed myself to be scared without reason, but the warrant for my arrest must still be in existence. If Monsieur Fouché chose to be vindictive——"

"The devil!" exclaimed Roger. "I had thought that as this all happened months ago, and we are many leagues from Nantes, you were not in any actual danger.'D'you mean that he might inform again and cause the police of Rennes to arrest you?"

"If he did I would be hard put to it to escape a hanging."

"Then we must leave Rennes as speedily as possible," said Roger with decision.

"He may not have recognised me," hazarded the Doctor. "And, even if he did, I may be doing him a great injustice to suppose that, having no personal score against me, he would pursue me with such vindictiveness."

"Nevertheless I'm sure we'd be wise to quit the town before there is any chance of your running into him again. I have our money on me and if we set out at once we could reach some village to the south or west before nightfall."

"But how can we do business without our stock in trade?" the Doctor protested.

"We have ample funds and can buy more at the next town we come to; we are certain to reach one within a few days."

"You forget Monsieur de Montaigne. Never could I bring myself to abandon that faithful beast. Besides, there are my instruments. Many of them are not easy to come by and it would be weeks before I could replace them all. 'Twould prove a most serious handicap were we to leave them behind."

Roger thought for a moment, then he said: "I too should be loath to let poor old Monsieur de Montaigne fall into the knackers' hands; and since we must go back for him, how would it be if we wait till dusk? We could slip into the side door of the inn, collect our things, get him from the stable and be off again, with small chance of meeting this police-cheat on the stairs or being seen by him from one of the windows?"

On the Doctor agreeing that this proposal seemed to offer the best prospect of avoiding any risk of trouble, they proceeded about their inspection of the ancient monuments in the Breton capital. But for both of them it proved an uneasy afternoon, and they were glad when the falling shadows gave them notice that the time had come to go back to the inn.

When they reached it Roger felt that he had chosen this hour for their flitting well, as the twilight had deepened sufficiently to obscure the faces of passing pedestrians when they were at a little distance, yet the windows of most of the houses still remained unlighted, so the hallway and staircase of the inn would be in semi-darkness.

They went to the stable first, and swiftly saddled up Monsieur de Montaigne; then they entered the inn by its yard door and went cautiously along a gloomy passage. As they had treated themselves to a special *déjeuner* they had paid for it at the time, so they had no bill to settle. The *Du Gueselin* was an expensive place so they had taken one of the cheaper rooms beneath its eaves. It only remained for them to collect the two old portmanteaux containing the Doctor's implements from their attic and get down the staircase without running into Monsieur Fouché.

Roger reached the room first. As it had only a dormer window it was now almost dark in there and on his opening the door he could barely distinguish the outlines of the furniture. The Doctor followed him in and began to fumble with his tinder-box.

"Hurry!" exclaimed Roger, snatching up a candle and holding it out to him. " 'Tis a pity we must strike a light, but we'll see the better to pack our things and so the more quickly get away."

"We will need a light to see each other by; but why this hurry?" said a quiet voice from the bed, and as the wick of the candle flared they swung round to see the tall form of the man in grey reclining on the bed.

"Surely, *Monsieur le Docteur*, you were not thinking of leaving Rennes without allowing me the opportunity of paying my respects to you?" he went on mockingly. "That would have been churlish indeed."

"Why, no, Monsieur Fouché: I—I would not have dreamed of such a thing," stammered the Doctor, as Roger set down the candlestick on the chest of drawers.

"That is admirable; and, as you see, I have spared us both the trouble of arranging an interview by coming to your room. In fact, I have been waiting for you here most of the afternoon. But I am happy to be able to tell you that I found your bed quite passably comfortable. Tell me, *Monsieur le Docteur*, what have you been doing all this time. Are you still upon the road?"

"Yes, Monsieur."

"So I gathered on finding that old mule of yours in the stable, and the panniers he bears stuffed with the noisome messes that you peddle to the peasantry. Whence have you come?"

"From Le Havre, Monsieur, by way of Rouen and Caen."

"A nice step that; and I trust profitable. After so long a tour your pockets should be positively bursting with shekels." After a moment the man in grey added quite casually: "Have you killed anybody recently?"

"Monsieur, you do me a great injustice," the Doctor burst out. "My medicines do no one any harm if taken as directed. That tragic accident in Nantes last winter came about through the poor girl taking too much of the drug I gave her."

" 'Twas the sort of accident that leads to old men like you meeting the executioner one fine morning before breakfast. You knew well that the Demoiselle Bracieux was five months gone with child, and that the odds were all against your being able to save her from the results of her indiscretion so late in her pregnancy."

"I have known similar cases where success was achieved, Monsieur; and the poor girl begged of me so hard to help her."

" 'Twas the ten *louis d'or* she offered you that softened that rogue's heart of yours."

"Nay, Monsieur, 'twas not only that. She swore to me that her parents would put her into a convent for life if they discovered her shame. I warned her that there was some risk, but both she and her lover decided that for her the lesser evil was to take it. 'Twas her foolish impatience in taking an overdose that killed her, and a terrible misfortune for all concerned."

"Your misfortune, my friend, was not the killing but in the person whom you killed. Had you made corpses of a dozen village wenches you'd have heard no more of it, but 'twas the height of folly to run such a risk with the daughter of a Councillor of Parliament."

Again Fouché remained silent for a moment, then he went on: "But 'tis all over and as good as forgotten now, is it not, *Monsieur le Docteur?*"

"Why, yes, Monsieur Fouché," sighed the Doctor with obvious relief. "Thanks to a fortunate explanation I was able to give the police, they refrained from executing the warrant that Councillor Bracieux took out against me."

"But the warrant is still valid, so I would not show your face in Nantes for a year or two if I were you."

"No, no. Be sure I shall give that fine city a wide berth in future."

"That would be wise, but I thought I should warn you."

" 'Twas most kind of you, Monsieur Fouché."

"Then there remains little more to be said."

"No; only for me to thank you again for having spent the afternoon here in order to warn me not to return to Nantes."

" 'Twas a pleasure," murmured the man in grey, but he made no move to get off the bed and continued to lie there propped up on one elbow with his head resting on his hand.

By the light of the candle Roger could now see his features clearly. He looked about twenty-four and was handsome in a way. His features were well cast though long and bony and the high cheekbones in conjunction with his deathly pale face suggested that, although tall and wiry, he might be delicate. The most disturbing thing about him was his hooded eyes and the fact that whenever he spoke he seemed to deliberately avoid the gaze of whoever he was addressing.

"Then if there is nothing else——" hazarded the Doctor suggestively.

Fouché's thin lips broke into a smile. "You seem very impatient to be rid of me."

"No, no, Monsieur, not in the least. But my young friend here and I made a change in our plans this afternoon. Big places like Rennes are no good for our business and we—well, we decided to push on to a smaller place to-night, and darkness is already falling."

"Indeed! You wish to get on with your packing, then. Well, do so by all means. I am quite comfortable here, and there will be ample time for me to mention another little matter before you go."

Roger saw that their sinister visitor was only playing with the poor old Doctor, so he blurted out:

"What do you want, Monsieur? Give it a name, or leave us!"

Without a second's warning Fouché sprang from the bed, seized Roger's wrist and twisted it up behind his back, causing him to let out a cry of pain.

"I'll tell him what I want in my own good time, you impudent young puppy," snarled Fouché. "Meanwhile, let's have your name, and hear how you came to join this old codger?"

"My name's Rojé Breuc!" gasped Roger. "Let me go! You're hurting!" Then, as he felt the tall man's grip ease a little, he went on: "I come from Alsace. I'm a native of Strasbourg and I ran away from home to seek adventure."

"You lie!" Fouché snapped. "You're no Frenchman of German stock. You are English. I could tell it by your accent from the first words you spoke on entering this room. Try again. But I want the truth, now, or it will be the worse for you." And to emphasise his point he gave Roger's arm another savage twist.

"All right, then!" Roger panted, as the pain caused tears to spring to his eyes. "I am English, and my name is Roger Brook. It's true, though, that I ran away from home."

"Where is your home?"

"At Lymington, in Hampshire."

"You mean the little port near Southampton?"

"Yes."

"You look like a youth of good family. Are you well-born?"

"Yes."

"What is the name of your father?"

"Christopher Brook. He is an Admiral in the English Navy."

"Is that the truth?" Fouché again exerted his full strength on Roger's arm, forcing him up on tiptoe with it twisted behind him.

"Yes, yes!" moaned Roger, "I swear it!"

"And when did you become the apprentice of this old charlatan?"

"About eleven weeks ago. I met him soon after I landed at Le Havre."

Fouché suddenly released Roger, flinging him with a contemptuous jerk half across the room and turned to the Doctor, who, during Roger's swift interrogation, had been standing impotently by, wringing his hands.

"Now!" said the man in grey, "I have amused myself long enough. I know how you succeeded in escaping your due deserts in Nantes. You bribed the police-agent with the ten *louis* that you received in payment for the Ergot of Rye that you sold to the demoiselle Bracieux. 'Tis my policy never to persecute people or make enemies needlessly, and the matter would have ended there, as far as I am concerned, had we not met again to-day and it so chances that the moment finds me in dire need myself. The annual remittances from my plantations in the Indies have failed to reach me this year, and I am committed to heavy expenses in connection with certain experiments in ballooning, in which I am interested. But why should I tell you all this? The fact is that I need money urgently and, after your long summer journey, you must have a nice sum put by. I trust you will see the wisdom of lending me fifty *louis* without argument."

The Doctor spread out his hands in a pathetic gesture and looked at Roger.

Still nursing his twisted arm, Roger muttered angrily: " 'Tis naught but blackmail!"

Fouché's small mouth broke into a thin smile. "Call it by any name you like, but I need the money. Either I get it or I'll lay an information with the police of Rennes. *Monsieur le Docteur* will be held upon my affidavit, the warrant will then be forwarded by courier from Nantes, and executed."

Roger saw that there was no way in which they could escape the demand and, with bitter reluctance, began to undo his shirt to get out his money belt. As their funds were all in the one long narrow sack he could not pretend that they were incapable of paying the full sum but in an effort to save part of the amount he announced with such firmness as he could muster: "Half of this belongs to me."

"Does it so?" said Fouché quietly. "How much have you there altogether?"

"Fifty-four *louis*," Roger replied as he took off the belt.

"I'll have the lot, then!" cried Fouché with another sudden display of brutality. "The extra four as a penalty for your impudence."

As he spoke he snatched at the end of the belt that dangled free. But Roger had firm hold of the other end and, springing back, endeavoured to wrench it from his grasp. The thought of all their savings from two long months of toil being taken from them by the unscrupulous amateur crime-investigator lent him strength and he almost jerked the tall young man off his feet.

"Let go!" shouted Fouché, his white face flushing with anger. "For rogues like you what I say is the law! D'you hear me! And learn that I'll take this but as an interim payment. We'll meet again from time to time, never fear. And each time we meet I'll empty your pockets for you, if I've a mind to it. Let go, now, or I'll swear you both into jail this very evening."

It was perhaps the threat to his future earnings, the thought of a never-ending blackmail, that stirred the Doctor into sudden, violent action. As the other two swayed wildly back and forth, struggling for the belt, they had moved round so that Fouché's back was now turned to him. Grabbing up Roger's sheathed sword from a chest nearby he struck the blackmailer a heavy blow on the back of the head with its hilt.

Fouché gasped and fell, half stunned, to the floor. But he still had hold of the belt and the sudden pull upon it dragged Roger down with him.

The Doctor, his watery blue eyes now mad with desperation, raised the sword to strike again. But Fouché was too quick for him. Letting go the belt he rolled over and pulled a small double-barrelled pistol from inside his grey coat. As he cocked it Roger heard the click. Next second there came a blinding flash and a loud report.

Roger staggered to his feet. He saw the Doctor drop the sword; then that one of his eyes had become a hideous red patch. The blood began to trickle from it. He had been shot clean through the head, and with a long, low moan sank slowly to the floor.

Still holding the belt Roger stood for a second, transfixed with horror, staring down at the Doctor's crumpled body. Then he heard Fouché cock the second barrel of his pistol. The sound released a spring in his momentarily petrified brain, and in one bound he reached the door.

He was barely through it and out on the landing when he heard the informer begin to shout: "Help! Murder! A man has been killed here. Stop, thief! Below there! Stop the murderer!"

In a flash Roger realised that Fouché intended to pin the Doctor's killing on to him and, in a panic of terror from a vision of the hangman's rope, he launched himself down the stairs.

CHAPTER XI

L'ANCIEN RÉGIME

S O M E eleven weeks previously Roger had gone crashing down the rickety stairs at the "Widow Scarron's" in Le Havre. Then, his flight had been actuated by a sudden wave of physical revulsion; now, he knew that he was flying for his very life. There, with a hand on the banister rail he had gone down three steps at a time; here, he jumped the first short flight in one swift bound. Yet here, as there, he had barely crossed the upper landing before the sound of opening doors and excited voices coming from below told him that the cries from the attic had already roused the house.

The money-belt still dangling from his hand, he hurled himself down the second flight. Suddenly his foot slipped on the highly polished wood. His legs shot from under him and sprawling on his back he slithered down towards the next landing. In an effort to save himself he flung out his hands. One end of the long purse caught round a banister. In his fall he had relaxed his grip and the precious belt was jerked from his grasp.

At the bottom of the flight he rolled over, jumped to his feet and swung round to regain the belt. In the faint light from the landing-window he could just see it as a whitish blur where it now lay, a few feet beyond his reach. One end of it was on the stairs, the other hanging over in the gulf beyond the banisters. Springing up two stairs he thrust out a hand to grab it. At that second he heard Fouché's heavy footsteps on the upper stairs. The sound threw him into fresh panic. In his haste, instead of grasping the end of the belt firmly, he overshot it, merely knocking it with his hand. Before his fumbling fingers could catch at it again it had slid from under them. The weight of the coins in its far end carried it over the edge into the dark abyss of a passage below which lead to the kitchen quarters.

All hope of recovering it for the present had gone, but life was infinitely more precious than money. Without wasting another second, Roger turned to resume his flight. Dashing across the landing he reached a broader staircase that led to the ground floor. The sound of Fouché's pursuing footsteps spurring him to fresh recklessness he charged down it. At its bottom, attracted by Fouché's cries, three men and a serving-maid were standing; he glimpsed their excited faces staring up at him.

With a final bound he reached the hall, stumbled and fell again. It was his fall that temporarily saved him. The two nearest men had sprung forward to seize him, but neither had anticipated his mishap. Going down head first he slithered along the boards between them and they came into violent collision above his prostrate body.

His hands stinging, his knees bruised, gasping for breath, Roger rolled away from them and stumbled to his feet. He was hardly up before the third man came at him. Instinctively Roger put up his fists. The Frenchman not understanding this manœuvre ignored it and came charging in. With a fleeting memory of George Gunston, Roger struck out at the man's face. The blow took him on his fleshy nose, bringing him up with a jerk. Pain, surprise and indignation showed in his eyes as they suddenly began to fill with water and the blood came gushing from his injured member.

The two men who had collided wasted a moment cursing at one another, but they now simultaneously turned on Roger. To avoid their grasp he dodged behind a large table that stood in the centre of the hall. For a second he thought himself temporarily safe from a renewed attack, as all three men were on the far side of it; but he had reckoned without the serving-wench. She had snatched a copper bed-pan from the wall. Lifting it, she now struck at his head from behind.

His eyes riveted on the men, he had not even seen her. It was pure chance that he moved a little sideways at that instant. The heavy bed-warmer missed his head but struck him on the shoulder. Swinging round he seized it by the middle of its handle and wrenched it from the woman's grasp.

Less than a minute had elapsed since he had arrived sprawling in the hall. His wild career down the stairs had left the more cautious Fouché well behind; but now he had arrived on the scene and was bellowing orders to the others for Roger's capture.

"Quick, get round that side!" he shouted. "I'll take the other!" and he ran round the table to the serving-maid's assistance, just as Roger snatched the bed-pan from her.

Caught between two fires Roger now seemed lost; but, once again, his agility temporarily saved him. Since he was holding the bed-pan by the middle of its handle he could not wield it as a weapon, but he flung it with all his force in Fouché's face. As the informer ducked to avoid it, Roger side-stepped and darted past him. The rest, following instructions, had raced round the other end of the table, so the whole group was now upon its far side, leaving Roger a clear run to the door. Without pausing to glance behind him he dashed through it and out into the street.

It was now nearly dark outside and there were lights in the windows of many of the houses. Dashing across the road he gained the deeper gloom of a double row of plane trees that lined the south side of the *Champe de Mars*. Turning west, between them, he pelted along the avenue that they formed.

Already he could hear the shouts of his pursuers as they streamed out of the inn. Then came a cry from Fouché: "There he goes! There he goes!" and he knew that he had been seen entering the shadow of the trees.

For a moment they lost him in the gloom and, thinking that he had struck straight across the square, charged in a ragged line through the trees towards its open centre. Then, not seeing him ahead of them in the half-light, they halted uncertainly; but only to catch the patter of his flying footsteps farther along the avenue to his left. With renewed cries of "Stop, thief! Stop, murderer!" they came pounding after him.

The avenue was three hundred yards in length and their false start on leaving the inn had given him a hundred yards' lead, but it was all that he could do to keep it. With his head down and his arms tucked in to his sides, as he had been taught to run at Sherborne, he sped on. The ground flew from beneath his light, swift feet. But they had the longer pace and, still shouting, came thundering on between the trees behind him.

The end of the avenue loomed into view. From his walk with the

Doctor that afternoon Roger knew that the big building he was now approaching, on the south-west corner of the square, was the barracks. Through the lower branches of the trees he could see a hanging lantern above its gate. The thought flashed upon him that if there were any soldiers lounging there, he would be caught between two fires. He had scarcely had it when there came a sudden stir of movement beneath the light, and shouts ahead of him answered those in his rear.

Swerving violently he dashed from between the trees and across the street again. The soldiers at the barrack gate had not yet caught sight of him. For a precious moment they remained where they were, peering into the shadows of the avenue. He had reached the corner of the *Rue du Colombier* and shot round it before one of them spotted him; then, with excited cries, they joined the chase.

Roger's breath was coming fast now; his heart was thumping wildly. Up to the time of his leaving the avenue he had managed to keep his lead on Fouché and the people from the inn, but the soldiers had entered the chase at an angle and turned into the *Rue du Colombier* barely fifty yards behind him. Their nearness lent him fresh vigour and he tore on in terror of his life.

For a brief interval he was hidden from them by the curve of the street. During it, he looked desperately to right and left for an alley into which he could dive, but the houses on both sides of the street formed solid blocks; none of them had even an open doorway offering some chance of sanctuary.

As the street straightened out the soldiers caught sight of him again. They gave a yell that told him how close upon his heels they were. Ahead he could now see a crossroads. Rallying himself for a final effort, he spurted towards it in the vague hope that he would be able to elude his pursuers there.

The crossroads proved to have five streets radiating from it. He was hidden again for a second from his pursuers by an outjutting building on the corner of the *Rue de Colombier*. Instead of dashing across the open space ahead of him he swivelled round the hairpin bend to his right, almost doubling back on his pursuers. The street he had entered was a narrow one and it was almost blocked by a big, stationary coach.

The coach was facing away from him. A footman, holding a lighted torch, was waiting in the doorway of the house before which the coach stood. Both he and the coachman on the box had their backs turned. It flashed into Roger's mind that the occupant of the coach must have gone into the house, so it would be empty. If only he could get inside it unobserved and remain there for two minutes his pursuers would run past, he would then have a new chance to elude them in the darkness.

He knew that if the lackey turned and saw him the game would be up; but his chest was now paining him so badly that he also knew he could not run another hundred yards. It was a choice of attempting to conceal himself in the empty coach, or of capture.

From fear of attracting the man's attention he dropped into a walk; he had no more than ten paces to cover. In a moment he had reached the offside of the coach. Now that it was between him and the lackey he felt more confident. Seizing the curved door handle he turned it and pulled the door open. To his horror there was a sudden movement in its shadowy interior. It was not empty after all.

The heavy boots of the running soldiers striking against the cobbles could be heard clearly now. The lackey in the doorway turned and lifted his flambeau on high to find out the cause of the approaching clamour. The light from it shone into the coach and Roger could see its occupant plainly.

It was a girl; a girl so young that she still carried a doll, and so could not yet have fully left childhood behind. Yet, all his life long, Roger was to remember the staggering impression her beauty made upon him in that first brief glimpse before he scrambled into the coach and fell panting at her feet.

Her eyes were a bright china blue; her hair, golden and unpowdered, fell in thick, silky ringlets about her small shoulders. She wore no paint but her skin was flawless and her complexion of milk and roses. Her mouth was small and delicately modelled, the upper lip short, the lower a little full. Her nose was thin and of Roman cast; her face oval, ending in a firm, determined chin. She sat bolt upright and so looked taller than she was in fact. Every feature of her face, and her whole attitude, expressed a completely natural imperiousness and absolute right to command immediate obedience to her slightest whim.

"Save me!" gasped Roger. "They're after me for a killing that I didn't do! I swear I didn't! For God's sake, hide me!"

The clamour at the street corner could now be heard by them both. Voices, amongst which Roger could distinguish Fouché's, were calling: "Where is he? Which way has he gone?"

As Roger stared up at the girl the light from the torch now lit his face too. She did not appear the least frightened and had made no attempt either to shrink away from him or to cry out. Her arched eyebrows had risen in a little frown, creasing her smooth forehead, but as she saw his face, nearly as young as her own, and gazed straight into his deep blue eyes fringed by their dark lashes, her lips broke into a smile, showing two rows of white, even teeth.

"What is it to me if you have done a killing?" she laughed suddenly. "I like your face, so I'll protect you. Quick! Get over there and draw your feet up!"

The cushioned seat opposite, to which she pointed, was both wide and deep, and as on speaking she snatched up a large fur rug, Roger saw that she meant to hide him under it. Flopping into one corner he pulled in his legs and next moment the fur blanketed his sight but not his hearing.

Two seconds later he caught a loud voice: "Has a young fellow passed this way? He wore a blue coat, and would be running!"

The inquiry was evidently addressed to the lackey with the torch, and the voice hurried on: "What of the coach? If 'tis empty he may have hopped inside it while your back was turned. With your leave I'll ascertain."

As the near door was pulled open the girl's high treble came:

swift, haughty, dominating: "Hands off my coach, villain! How darest thou push past my lackey to have speech with me! I have seen no fugitive. Close that door instantly and get about thy business!"

With a muttered apology the man closed the door, but the high childish voice went on now, evidently calling to the footmen. "Up on thy stand, Pierre! I've a mind to get home and will not wait for Madame Velot. The coach can return to pick her up later."

Then, unseen by Roger, she gave a violent jerk to a silk cord attached to the coachman's little finger and, as he lifted the hatch in the roof of the coach, trilled up at him: "*A l'hôtel, Baptiste! Depêche-toi!*"

The footman sprang up on his stand at the back of the coach, the coachman shook the reins of his horses, and the great cumbersome vehicle rumbled into motion. It had not covered twenty yards before the girl pulled the rug from off Roger and said: "You can sit up now, and tell me about yourself."

On his jerking his feet from the seat one of them struck a dark object in a far corner of the foot space, near the door opposite to that by which he had entered. The object gave a little bark of protest and, until that moment, owing to the deep shadows, he had not realised that a dog was lying there. As it reared up he saw that it was a black poodle.

"Down, Bougie! Down!" cried its young mistress. "Quiet now, or I will order the Englishman to eat you!"

For a second Roger thought that she was referring to him, and stared at her in astonishment, wondering how she could possibly have guessed his nationality so quickly. But at that moment they were passing a street corner lantern and she held up her doll for him to see, as she said:

"This is my Englishman. Is he not hideous? And the English do eat dogs, you know. My uncle, the Count, commanded the last expedition that we sent to aid Monsieur de la Fayette in the Americas and he told me so on his return. They are a most bloodthirsty and barbarous people."

The doll was certainly a fearsome monstrosity. It differed only from the later caricature of John Bull in having a cocked hat instead of a squat topper. A Union Jack waistcoat covered its great protruding paunch, its forehead was so low as to be almost entirely lacking and a most alarming row of upper teeth protruded from its gaping jaws.

Roger was about to repudiate the charge indignantly, when he thought better of it. Since he was now being hunted for murder and his young protectress believed all Englishmen to be bloodthirsty by nature, to disclose that he was one himself might easily throw her into such a panic that she would abandon him and turn him over to his enemies.

"Well! Tell me of yourself!" she demanded. "I am all agog to hear about this killing of which you are accused. What is your name?"

Had Roger but known it the fate of nations hung upon his reply; and the simple fact that a young French girl, although already budding into glorious womanhood, was still sufficiently amused by dolls to carry one, was in a few years' time to have immeasurably far-reaching

effects on European politics. Had it been otherwise he would have told
the truth about himself and given his real name. As it was, he decided
to stick to the story to which he was now well accustomed through his
journeying with old Aristotle Fénelon these past two months, and he
replied:

"My name is Rojé Breuc, and I am a native of Alsace. I ran away
from my home in Strasbourg to seek adventure early last July. I have
since been following the road with a journeyman-doctor whom I met
with in Le Havre." He then went on to describe the Doctor's murder
that evening and how a rascally teacher, named Joseph Fouché, who
acted as an informer to the police, was attempting to pin the murder
on to him.

The coach had meanwhile crossed the river Vilaine by the single
bridge in the centre of the town, passed the Cathedral of St. Pierre and
entered the *Rue St. Louis*. Halfway along the street it halted, until
at the shouts of the footmen a pair of great gates in a high wall were
thrown open, so that it could drive into a spacious courtyard.

Roger just had time to say: "May I know the name of the beautiful
young lady to whom I owe my life?" when the coach pulled up before
a broad flight of steps leading up to a heavily carved pair of double
doors.

"I am Athénaïs de Rochambeau," the girl replied, "and this is the
Hôtel de Rochambeau, the town house of my father, the Marquis."

On the footman opening the door Roger sprang out and handed
her down. The double doors of the mansion had now been opened and,
going up the steps together, they entered a wide, lofty hall. It was
paved with marble, and a splendid horseshoe staircase of elaborate
iron scrollwork, picked out with gold, led to a landing, then divided
again to sweep towards the upper floors. At either side of the doorway
stood three tall footmen with powdered wigs and dressed in the same
violet and gold livery as the lackey who had accompanied the coach.
They stood there like statues, rigidly immobile, but a seventh servant,
considerably older and dressed in a more sombre livery than the others,
came forward, bowing almost to the ground before Mademoiselle de
Rochambeau.

"The coach is to return to the *Rue de Nantes*, to pick up Madame
Velot, Aldegonde," she told him. "Meanwhile, take this gentleman
somewhere where he can tidy himself, then bring him to the small
salon. He is to dine with us." Without deigning to glance at either the
major-domo or Roger, she lifted the front of her full skirts a little and
tripped upstairs as lightly as a bird.

Monsieur Aldegonde gave Roger one swift glance of appraisal, noted
that his clothes were of cloth, which now showed the wear of his eleven
weeks' wanderings, and that he wore no sword, gave the very faintest
sniff of disapproval, and bowed very slightly, as he said: "This way,
Monsieur. Please to follow me."

He led Roger between two of the eight great pillars that supported
the gallery round the hall and threw open a door concealed in the
panelling under one side of the staircase. It gave on to a small room

in which there was a marble washbasin, towels and a variety of toilet articles laid out on the shelves of a shallow recess.

Roger washed, combed his hair and brushed down his clothes. As he did so, he wondered with some misgivings what would happen next. He was still shaken and immeasurably distressed by the old Doctor's death, and he knew that he had only escaped capture by a piece of remarkable good fortune. But he was now acutely anxious as to what view Mademoiselle de Rochambeau's father would take of the matter. Would he support his beautiful little daughter's high-handed action or promptly hand his unexpected visitor over to the police?

Having made himself as presentable as possible Roger came out and waited for some time in the hall until, eventually the major-domo returned and led him upstairs. The whole of the first floor appeared to be one long suite of rooms, each being of splendid proportions and magnificently furnished, their walls hung with Gobelins tapestries and the parquet of their floors polished to a mirror-like brilliance. After passing through two of them the major-domo ushered him into a third, somewhat smaller than the other two and panelled in striped yellow silk.

As the door opened Roger nerved himself to meet the Marquis, but at the first glance he saw that he was not yet called upon to face this ordeal. There were four people in the room; an elderly Abbé with graceful white locks falling to the shoulders of his black cassock; a portly woman of about forty, well but soberly dressed; Mademoiselle Athénaïs and a handsome boy who, from his features, appeared to be her brother.

Athénaïs waved a little white hand negligently towards the woman: "Madame Marie-Ange Velot, my governess, whom we left behind in the *Rue de Nantes*; and this is my brother, Count Lucien de Rochambeau."

Roger made a leg to the woman then bowed to the boy, who returned his bow a little stiffly. The young Count's features were in the same cast as his sister's but distinctly heavier, his eyes, although also blue, lacked the brightness of hers, and both his nose and mouth were much thicker. Roger put him down as about two years younger than himself, and formed a first impression that he was of a somewhat sullen nature and dull-witted. However, with formal politeness, Count Lucien said:

"I have not the pleasure of knowing your name, Monsieur," and added, half-turning towards the priest, "but I should like to present you to my tutor, Monsieur l'Abbé Duchesnie."

As Roger and the Abbé exchanged salutations Athénaïs said, quickly: "Monsieur is one, Rojé Breuc, a native of Strasbourg. As I was telling you, they are after him for a killing. I have given orders that he is to dine with us, and over dinner he shall entertain you with his story."

At this announcement the governess and the Abbé exchanged a somewhat disturbed glance and the little Count, eyeing Roger's clothes disdainfully, said in a haughty voice: "Was it necessary to invite Monsieur to eat with us, sister? Surely Aldegonde could have attended to his wants, and he could have told us his story afterwards."

"Hold thy tongue, little fool," replied the girl, tartly. "Thou would'st do better to spend more time studying thy books and less in thinking of thy sixty-four quarterings."

But evidently Madame Marie-Angé Velot was of the boy's opinion as she said: "I hardly think, Mademoiselle, that Monseigneur your father would approve."

"My father, Madame, is in Paris," snapped Athénaïs. "And in his absence I am the best judge of what takes place here."

"Even so, Mademoiselle," hazarded the Abbé, "I feel sure Monsieur Breuc would find himself more at home below stairs, and I support the suggestion that he should be conducted there."

Athénaïs stamped her small foot. "I'll not have it! I found him; and he is mine, to do what I will with!"

Roger, now flushed with mortification at this unseemly wrangle as to if or no he was fitted to eat at their table, was about to declare hotly that he was an English gentleman and as good as any of them, when he was saved from this imprudence by the door opening to disclose Monsieur Aldegonde, who cried in a loud voice:

"Monsieur le Comte et Mademoiselle sont servis!"

Athénaïs looked at Roger and said with extraordinary dignity in one so young: "Monsieur Breuc, your arm, if you please."

With his most courtly bow he proffered it to her; then, following the pompous Aldegonde, who held aloft a six-branched silver candelabra to light them, they traversed the big rooms again and crossed the landing to enter a lofty dining-room. At the table in it five places were laid and behind the chair set for each stood one of the tall footmen. Athénaïs took one end of the table, motioning Roger to a seat on her right, while her brother took the other. The Abbé said a short grace and the meal began.

The dishes were lighter and more varied and sumptuous than anything that Roger had encountered in England, but his good table manners soon showed the Abbé and Madame Marie-Angé that they had been wrong to judge him by his worn cloth suit as fitted only to eat downstairs in the kitchen, and both of them began to regard him with more friendly attention.

At their request he retold his story, giving additional details. His eleven weeks in France had improved his French out of all recognition, so that although he still had a noticeable accent he could talk with unhesitating fluency; and, since he was by nature a born raconteur, he kept the small company enthralled through several courses.

Athénaïs both fascinated and intrigued him. He thought her quite the most beautiful thing he had ever seen, and could only compare her in his mind to a fairy, from the top of a Christmas tree. It may be that she put the idea into his head herself as she seemed fond of fairy stories and made frequent references to them, chaffingly remarking that she felt sure he must be a Prince in disguise, or at least, a miller's youngest son, since they always leave home in search of dragons to kill and end up with a Princess for their bride.

Yet he found it extraordinarily difficult to place her satisfactorily. She was so small and slight of build that she could well have been taken at first sight for no more than thirteen; moreover, she frequently showed the most abysmal ignorance on many matters of common interest, and spoke with the petulant, dictatorial manner of a spoilt child. But, against this, the air of dignity and authority that she equally frequently assumed, and her rather surprising fund of knowledge upon certain subjects, suggested that she might easily be a physically undeveloped seventeen.

Roger had yet to learn the reason for these strange anomalies, which were by no means uncommon among young people of her class in France at that time. Among the French nobility family life had degenerated to such an extent that it was the common practice for parents to leave their offspring during the whole period of childhood in the care of servants on their country estates, or often, even put them out to board with some almost illiterate family. There they were left, rarely seeing their parents and frequently entirely forgotten by them, until they reached their teens. They were only then belatedly given tutors and governesses, to fit them for the high stations in life they were to occupy; but, once they emerged from the sad neglect to which they had been subject, they were given rich clothes, money, fine apartments and a horde of servants to wait on them, and were, in fact, expected to behave like grown-ups with the full exercise of the authority over all inferiors which was assumed to be theirs by right of birth.

Athénaïs de Rochambeau was at this time actually fourteen and a quarter, while her brother Lucien was just one year younger, and it was a bare two years since they had been removed from their foster-parents to begin their education; yet in those two years they had both learned to regard themselves as people of great importance in the small world they occupied, and born to be obeyed. Normally, despite the fact that he was the younger of the two, the boy would have been the dominant partner of the pair but, as Roger had rightly assessed, he was a dullard, so she, conscious that she was one of the greatest heiresses in Brittany, had made herself the pivot round which the life of the great mansion revolved during her father's absence.

They had reached a marvellous confection of violet ice-cream topped by a mass of spun sugar when the Abbé said to Roger:

"And what is it your intention to do now, Monsieur Breuc?"

"I hardly know, *Monsieur l'Abbé*," replied Roger, but having by now had a chance to sort out his ideas to some extent he went on: "After some little thought, this man Fouché may realise that, as I could have no possible motive for murdering my poor old friend, his case is a weak one, and decide not to pursue it. If that occurs, as I pray it may, I feel under a natural obligation to arrange for Doctor Fénelon's burial. Then, too, I am most anxious to return to the *Du Guesclin* for the purpose of recovering the purse I dropped. It may still be lying in a dark corner of the passage or, if someone has picked it up, unless they are downright dishonest, they will have given it for safe keeping to the landlord. Yet I greatly hesitate to go there until I feel a little more confident that I'll not be putting my head in a noose. Would you, *Monsieur l'Abbé* do me the favour of giving me your advice?"

"I am no man of the robe," the old priest replied, "so 'tis outside my office to offer an opinion on legal matters. Yet it does seem to me that this purse containing fifty-four *louis* would have been motive enough to incite a young man in your situation to the crime, had he the nature of a murderer. According to your own account you fled with it, and I should not have thought it usual for one so many years junior to his partner to be entrusted with the whole resources of a partnership."

"There was an especial reason for that," Roger broke in quickly. "As I have told you——"

The Abbé Duchesnie raised his hand. "I know, I know, my young friend. I do not seek to question your own explanation but, as I understand it, you have no one whom you can bring forward to give evidence of the Doctor's habits, and I am simply putting to you the view that the police may take of this matter."

From having regained some degree of optimism Roger was suddenly cast back into the depths of gloom. He realised now that the good food and wine and rich surroundings had given him a false sense of security and that in the cold light of impartial examination his case must look very black indeed. The Doctor had died by violence and he, Roger, had made off with what would undoubtedly be assumed to be his partner's money.

Madame Marie-Angé saw his look of misery and, being a good-natured, motherly woman, strove to comfort him, by saying:

"I do not see what this Monsieur Fouché has to gain by fixing the assassination on Monsieur Breuc."

"Why, to prevent it being fixed upon himself, Madame," promptly replied the Abbé.

"But he could equally well say that the Doctor took his own life to save himself from being arrested," urged the governess. " 'Twould be beyond reason vindictive in any man, however ill-natured, to send another who had done him no harm to the rope."

"A thousand thanks, Madame!" Roger exclaimed eagerly. "There is much in what you say. And in my own mind, I feel confident now, that Fouché called 'Murder' after me not so much with a view to getting me hanged, but to have me stopped so that he might secure the purse."

"Is he likely, though, once having made the charge, to withdraw it?" pessimistically remarked the Abbé.

" 'Twould be easy for him to say that people had misunderstood his cries," Madame Marie-Angé retorted. "He could claim that by his cry of 'Murder' he had meant no more than that a violent death had just occurred, and that those who heard him had confused it with his shouts of 'Stop, thief'!"

"By so doing he could save himself from the sin of perjury and avoid the burden of attending at a lengthy trial," the Abbé agreed. "And as you, Madame, have very rightly pointed out, there seems no particular cause for him to carry vindictiveness to the point of endeavouring to bring about our young friend's death."

Athénaïs shrugged her slim shoulders. "You have admitted, Monsieur l'Abbé, that you know little of such matters, and I know nothing. Why should we not send for the notary—what is his name—Maître—Maître——?"

"Léger," supplied the Abbé.

"Yes, Maître Léger. Let us summon him and find out."

She had no sooner had the idea than she turned to Aldegonde and ordered him to send a messenger with instructions that she required Maître Léger to wait on her at once. Then, having toyed a little with the desserts, they all retired to the yellow salon to await the lawyer's arrival.

Within a quarter of an hour Maître Léger was announced. He proved to be a man of about sixty and something of a dandy. His green suit was of cloth but very well cut, with padded shoulders and silver buttons. His cravat and wristbands were of fine lawn and his hair, which had been black, now being flecked with grey had the smart appearance of having been lightly dusted with powder. Beneath a broad forehead he had a pair of lively brown eyes, a very sharply pointed nose and a firm, thin mouth.

Having bowed to Athénaïs he thanked her deferentially as she waved him to a chair.

"In my father's absence, Monsieur, I require your services," she began at once, and with a slight turn of her head towards Roger, went on: "This is Monsieur Breuc of Strasbourg. He is accused of killing some old man. Please see to it that the charge is withdrawn."

The lawyer coughed. "I am entirely at your disposal, Mademoiselle; but I am sure you will permit me to remark that the law is made by the King, and is therefore above and beyond us all. Once set in motion its processes cannot be stopped by a mere request, even should the request be made by such a distinguished personage as Monseigneur, your father. However, I will assuredly do all I can if I may be permitted to know the full circumstances of the case."

Without replying Athénaïs waved her fan in Roger's direction and he once more related the nerve-racking sequence of events that had befallen him earlier that evening.

When he had done, Maître Léger slightly inclined his handsome head. "If all that you have told me is correct, I think there is a fair hope that you are mistaken in your belief that Monsieur Fouché intended to charge you with the Doctor's murder. It seems to me more likely that his attempts to have you stopped were actuated by his desire to get possession of the money-belt, and that in your own excitement you confused his cries announcing that a killing had taken place with those calling upon the other occupants of the inn to stay your flight."

"There," exclaimed Madame Marie-Angé in triumph, " 'tis the very thing I said myself towards the end of dinner."

"I only pray that you may be right," Roger murmured, as the lawyer continued:

"Moreover, if a trial results, Monsieur Fouché will be forced to resort to statements containing much perjury in order to make a case against you. If one of them is proved false not only might the whole case break down but he would find himself in serious trouble. I can see no reason why he should elect to run such a risk when he can terminate the issue by frankly admitting that he killed the doctor himself in self-defence. That was in fact what happened, was it not?"

"Yes, it would be difficult to contend otherwise," Roger agreed, after a moment. " 'Twas all so sudden and so horrible that the thought had not occurred to me; yet I must admit that the Doctor had struck him down with the hilt of my sword, and was about to strike at him again just as he fired his pistol."

"Are you prepared to swear to that before a magistrate?"

"Yes; if I must."

"That is well. You must remember that in the moments succeeding your friend's death Monsieur Fouché had no reason at all to suppose that you would be willing to give evidence which would clear him of a charge of murder. It may be that he believed that you would attempt to get him hanged, if you could, and instantly made up his mind that his best prospect of escape lay in accusing you of the killing. It would then have been your word against his, and as you had taken the money the odds would have been in his favour. But there will be no official inquiry into the Doctor's death until to-morrow morning, and I will see Monsieur Fouché before the inquiry opens. If I inform him that you will come forward to give evidence that he killed the Doctor in self-defence, I feel there is every reason to hope that he will see the wisdom of admitting to it."

"I am indeed grateful, Monsieur," smiled Roger, now much comforted. "What you have said takes a great load from my mind."

"You are not out of the wood yet," Maître Léger warned him. "And if complications arise it may be that you will be detained while further inquiries are made; but at least it does not appear that you have any grave reason to fear that you will be hung."

"I thank you, Monsieur," said Athénaïs. "You have cheered us mightily, and I rely on you to do your best for Monsieur Breuc."

The elderly lawyer bowed. "Your wishes, Mademoiselle, are my commands."

Madame Marie-Angé then turned to him and said: "Did I not hear that you are but just returned from Paris, Maître Léger. What news have you brought with you from the capital?"

"The talk is all of His Majesty's appointment of Monsieur de Calonne to be the new Comtroller-General of the Finances," replied. the man in green, " 'Tis to be hoped that he will make a better showing than those who have held brief office during these past eighteen months; for public confidence has suffered a sad decline since the dismissal of M. Necker."

"Who was M. Necker, Monsieur?" inquired Athénaïs, and Roger looked at her in some surprise; since even he knew that Necker was the great Swiss banker whom Louis XVI had called to his assistance in the hope of straightening out the incredible tangle of debt and disorder into which the finances of France had fallen.

"He was for five years His Majesty's principal adviser, Mademoiselle," smiled the lawyer, "and a man of great ability. Before he was driven from office, getting on for two years ago, he published his *Compte Rendu du Roi*, which, for the first time in the history of our country, gave to the public a balance sheet showing how the King derives his revenues and how they are expended. 'Twas a sad pity that the Court prevented his continuing his progressive measures."

Count Lucien frowned. "I see no reason why the King should render an account to anyone of how he spends his money."

" 'Tis money obtained from the taxation of the people," *Monsieur le Comte*, "and surely they have some right to know what is done with it."

"That, I think, is generally accepted now," put in the Abbé. "But am I not right in believing that M. Necker's *Compte Rendu* was misleading? Did it not show a credit balance which was later proved to have no real existence?"

Maitre Léger inclined his head. "Alas, *Monsieur l'Abbé*, that is so. Our state is far worse than we were led to suppose; yet the publication was a step in the right direction, and the alarming deficit was mainly due to our having taken up arms on behalf of the Americans against the English."

"That burden, at least, is lifted from us now," Madame Marie-Angé remarked. " 'Tis true, is it not, that the final ratification of the peace was signed last month?"

"Yes, Madame. And in Paris there were great rejoicings; particularly on the withdrawal of the English Commissioners from Dunkirk, which formed one of the stipulations of the treaty. It annulled the clause in the treaty of 1763, by which we were compelled to demolish the fortifications of Dunkirk and accept an English Commission there to assure that they were not re-erected. 'Twas a humiliation that the nation was well justified in resenting as long as it continued."

Athénaïs was looking bored, and asked suddenly: "Did you see my father, Monsieur, when you were in Paris?"

"Yes, Mademoiselle. *Monseigneur le Marquis* was much occupied, as he spends a great part of his time with the Count de Vergennes, His Majesty's Foreign Minister; but he did me the honour to receive me twice, and I am happy to be able to tell you that he is in excellent health."

"And did you go to Versailles?"

The lawyer smiled. "I have not the privilege of the *entrée* to the Court, Mademoiselle."

"Yet you must have news of it; and such news is much more exciting than all this dreary talk of money and of foreign treaties?"

" 'Tis said to be as gay as ever. There are amusements from dinner at one each day until one the next morning. Three plays or operas are put on for their Majesties' entertainment each week and two balls, on Tuesdays and Thursdays, with great suppers, and cards for those who prefer the tables. The Queen has just recommenced the weekly masked balls that she gives throughout the winter, and the principal occupation of the courtiers during the other six days is the preparation of the costumes in which they intend to appear. For some time past, both Paris and Versailles have been full of English visitors, and 'tis reported that Her Majesty shows them especial favour."

"Why should she?" Athénaïs demanded, "since but eight months ago we were at war with them!"

The lawyer coughed and replied discreetly: "The Queen is a law unto herself, Mademoiselle, and 'tis not always her pleasure to align herself with popular prejudice. In this case popular opinion is represented by many of the younger nobility, who served with Monsieur de la Fayette and the Count, your uncle, in the Americas. They found the way of life there much to their liking. They were greatly impressed by the free and easy manners, the sense of equality and the lack of restrictions on personal liberty, that are enjoyed by the Americans. Who can blame them for desiring reforms which would bring about the same state of affairs in France? On the other hand there are many at Court who are strongly opposed to such reforms, as they feel that change would result in their having to sacrifice their ancient privileges. These last consider that our intervention on behalf of the Americans was a great mistake, since we aided them to defy their King and overthrow all established custom. Quite naturally they regard the English nobility who come to Versailles as the true representatives of law, order, and the countenance of a privileged caste. Therefore, headed by the Queen, they receive them with all friendliness and sympathy."

"The Queen is right then," declared Athénaïs promptly, "and my uncle wrong. Henceforth I'll take a better view of the English."

Maître Léger made no comment, and there was a short silence before he said: "If Mademoiselle has no further use for my services to-night, may I beg leave to make my adieux?"

She nodded regally to him and, having promised Roger that he would endeavour to see Monsieur Fouché first thing in the morning, he bowed himself out of the room.

When he had gone they talked for a little, until Athénaïs put up her fan to hide a yawn, then announced her intention of going to bed.

Aldegonde was summoned and ordered to conduct Roger to a suitable chamber in which he could pass the night; and, having kissed the hand of his protectress, he followed the major-domo to a comfortable but plainly furnished room on the third floor of the mansion.

As he undressed he endeavoured to sort out his impressions. He was still badly shaken by the Doctor's death and his own precarious position, yet his thoughts never wandered for long from Athénaïs de Rochambeau.

She was, he knew, abominably spoilt and self-willed, but he attributed that entirely to her upbringing; and she possessed both courage and self-confidence—qualities which he greatly admired. But, beyond all, she was the most perfect expression of beauty that he had ever seen. The play of emotions on her face, and her every movement, were a joy to watch; and the strange mixture of child and woman that she embodied he found entirely fascinating. No other girl that he had met even remotely resembled her, and he knew now that he had never been in love with Georgina.

As he fell asleep his last thought was of the bright blue eyes and golden hair of Athénaïs, and he realised that he was already profoundly, desperately in love with her.

Yet neither his anxieties nor his new-found passion disturbed his slumbers, and he slept right on until one of the footmen called him by bringing his breakfast up to him on a tray. Except when ill of childhood complaints he had never had a meal in bed in his life, so he was considerably surprised at this, and he was not quite sure if he liked the custom; but it did not interfere with his appetite. He would have much preferred a good, meaty English breakfast to eat either upstairs or down, but he had to admit to himself that a *petit déjeuner* in the house of a French nobleman was not without its attractions. Instead of the simple rolls, butter and jam served at the inns where he had stayed, his tray was loaded with a pot of frothy chocolate, rolls with caraway seeds in them, feather-light *brioches*, crisp horseshoe *croissants*, honey, three kinds of *confiture* and a dish of fresh fruit.

Having tried them all he got up, dressed and went downstairs. A score of servants were sweeping and cleaning in the great apartments, and the yellow drawing-room proving untenable he descended to the hall, since he was anxious now to be on hand and learn Maître Léger's news the moment the lawyer should arrive.

Aldegonde, appearing on the scene, seemed to regard his presence there with surprised disapproval, and when Roger asked him what time Mademoiselle de Rochambeau would be down he replied stiffly: "Mademoiselle is rarely visible before ten o'clock."

Since it was only just after eight, this was small comfort, and Roger found his wait a dreary business as he was compelled to hang about for the best part of an hour. But, at last, a bell jangled somewhere and one of the footmen, slipping on his coat, went to the front door.

When the man threw it open, to Roger's amazement, not only Maître Léger, but also Monsieur Fouché, walked in.

"Good day to you, Monsieur Breuc, " said the lawyer, as they bowed to one another; then, turning to Fouché, he added; "Would you be good enough to wait here while I have a word in private with my client."

Leaving Fouché he came over to Roger, led him further away into an embrasure behind two of the tall marble pillars, and said in a low voice:

"I think matters will arrange themselves satisfactorily, but that now largely depends upon yourself. The Court sits to inquire into the death of Doctor Fénelon in half an hour and if Monsieur Fouché and yourself tell the same story I doubt not that they will be satisfied and discharge you both. However, this desirable result depends on you both giving the same account of the way in which Doctor Fénelon met his death, and Monsieur Fouché has already stated to the police that the doctor committed suicide."

He paused for a moment then went on: "You will appreciate, I am sure, that it is not for me, a lawyer, to suggest that you should attempt to deceive the Court, but what you choose to say before the magistrates is entirely your own affair. Mademoiselle de Rochambeau

145

has given me implicit instructions to save you from trouble if I can'
and while such a step is highly unorthodox, it occurred to me that the
best hope of doing so lay in bringing Monsieur Fouché and yourself
together for a private conversation before the Court opens. I need
scarcely add that your interests in this matter are now absolutely
identical. Namely that the whole affair should be dismissed without
further inquiry. Do you consent to talk with him?"

"If you advise it, and 'tis unavoidable," Roger agreed with some
reluctance.

"Very well, then; come this way."

Recrossing the hall, and beckoning to Fouché to join them, Maître
Léger led the pair into a lofty room which, from the rows of shelves
filled with ledgers that lined its walls, looked like an office. Having
ushered them in he closed the door behind him and left them together.

Fouché walked over to the wide fireplace, turned, and with his
back to the carved mantel stood there for a moment, his hands clasped
behind his back, then, without looking at Roger, he said:

"It has always been against my principles to make enemies needlessly. Your lawyer tells me that you are willing to compose this
matter. If that is so, I am your man."

"I am naturally anxious to avoid being held for a lengthy period
while an exhaustive investigation takes place," replied Roger frankly.
"Yet I find it difficult to regard the murderer of my old friend as
anything but an enemy."

"Your assumption that I murdered Doctor Fénelon has positively
no foundation," said Fouché, his pale face remaining quite inscrutable.
"I killed him in self-defence. You were a witness to it, and must have
seen that had I not shot him he would have brained me with the hilt
of the sword with which he had already struck me down."

Roger was forced to admit to himself the justice of this and asked:
"Well, what is it that you propose?"

"I have already informed the officers of the law that some eight
months ago I caused a warrant to be taken out for the Doctor's arrest.
That can easily be verified by reference to the authorities in Nantes.
I went on to state that finding the Doctor still to be at large I told him
last night that, in the interests of justice, I intended to raise the matter
with the authorities here. And that, in a fit of despair, he then pulled
out a pocket pistol and before either you or I could stop him, shot
himself through the head. As I had the good sense to leave the pistol
beside the body such an account of the matter provides a loophole for
us both; so all you will be called on to do is to verify my statement and,
perhaps, testify that you knew the pistol to be the Doctor's property."

"It seems that you thought better of accusing me of murder," said
Roger shrewdly. "And I see no reason why I should tell lies to get you
out of trouble."

"Do you not, *Monsieur Breuc?*" Fouché's small mouth broke into a
thin smile. "Yet on entering this house this morning I found you still
to be living a lie. You have passed yourself off here as a native of
Alsace. As for last night, I took such measures as I thought might
get you stopped and enable me to obtain possession of your money-belt.

I failed in that, but to-day is another day. Do you wish me to inform your noble friends, the de Rochambeaux, that they have taken up the cause of an impostor?"

Roger had been under no compulsion to deceive Athénaïs at the time of their meeting and it flashed upon him how utterly shamed he would feel if he were now shown up as having lied to her.

By a swift sideways glance from his heavily lidded eyes Fouché saw Roger's discomfiture and pressed home his advantage. "Besides, *Mister Brook*, I have not yet said my piece before the magistrates, and I have long made a practice of trimming my sails to every emergency. I can still tell them that, touched by your youth, on an impulse of compassion for you, when questioned last night, I sought to shield you from the results of your criminal act; but, to-day, my conscience smiting me, I feel constrained to tell the truth: That is, that, on informing the Doctor I intended to have him arrested you attempted to shoot me, but missed your aim and shot him instead, then panicked and endeavoured to escape with his money."

With growing trepidation Roger realised that behind the pale high forehead of this red-haired Oratorian teacher there lay a subtle and cunning brain. Such a story would square quite well with what Fouché had told the police the previous night, yet leave him, Roger, to face a charge of attempted murder or manslaughter, at the very least. He knew that he dared not face it, and said slowly:

"So be it. I will do as you suggest."

Fouché smiled down at his boots. "You may not have inherited the boldness associated with English Admirals, but in this you show a wisdom which will prove more profitable to you than any rash display of courage. You can leave me to do the talking. All you need do is to say that I have given a full and true account of the affair and, if you are asked, state that for as long as you had known him the Doctor had always carried that little two-barrelled pistol. 'Tis time now that we went, for the Court will soon be sitting."

On their leaving the room young Monsieur Fouché's pale smile was enough to tell Maître Léger that they had reached agreement, and he hurried them both into his carriage.

At the Court House everything went according to plan. In a quarter of an hour the inquest was over. There was no jury, but after consulting for a few moments the magistrates declared their verdict: that Doctor Aristotle Fénelon had taken his own life while his mind was temporarily deranged owing to his having just been told that he was to be arrested on a charge involving the death penalty.

Afterwards, without a glance at Roger, the tall, thin Fouché left the Court House and walked away. As Roger watched him go Maître Léger said: "What have you in mind to do now, my young friend?"

"I'm monstrous eager to get back to the inn, in order to collect my money," Roger replied. "But I feel that first I should let Mademoiselle de Rochambeau know that I have come safe out of this business."

"In that case I will drop you at the Hôtel de Rochambeau," volunteered the lawyer.

Roger thanked him and, as they went out to the carriage, said a little diffidently: "And to you, Monsieur, I can never render thanks enough. My funds, unfortunately, are limited; but if your fee is within my means I will be most happy to pay it."

"Nay, I'll not deprive you of your money," replied the lawyer kindly. "It needs but half an eye to see that you are an honest youth and that Fouché is a rogue who deserves to hang. Think no more of it, I beg. 'Twas a pleasure to have been of service to you; and, in any case, 'tis a part of my livelihood to handle all legal matters in which the de Rochambeau family are concerned. The Marquis is rich enough to pay me a *louis* or two for my morning's work and never miss it."

Ten minutes later they were back at the Hôtel de Rochambeau. Maître Léger set Roger down there and drove away. Roger at once inquired if Mademoiselle Athénaïs would receive him.

After a short wait she came downstairs. With the sunshine streaming on her golden hair he thought his newly acquired divinity more beautiful than ever. Swiftly he told her of the morning's events and thanked her once more, both for the protection and the legal aid that she had afforded him.

He thought she took the matter very calmly and even seemed a little distrait, as she asked him what he intended to do now that he was no longer menaced by a charge of murder.

"I've hardly had time to think," he replied quickly. "But first I must return to the inn to see to the Doctor's burial, and to secure my money."

"Of course," she agreed. "If the occasion arises you must let me know if I can be of any further service to you." Then, having given him her hand to kiss, she turned away to issue orders about some bandboxes that two of her maids were carrying downstairs.

Roger was torn between the desire to linger with her and his urge to get back to the inn, but, seeing that she was now busy with other matters, he succumbed to the latter. With a farewell wave he left the mansion and, half running, half walking, made his way to the *Du Guesclin*.

On his arrival he learned from the landlord that the Doctor's body had been removed to the city mortuary. He then inquired about his purse. The man averred that he had neither found it nor had it been given to him, and together they went to the dark passage under the stairs to look for it.

The passage was a straight one with no niches in which such a thing could have remained concealed for long. In vain Roger stared at first one end of it then the other, and ran several times up and down the stairs to ascertain the exact point at which the purse had dropped, and if it could possibly have got caught up on something during its fall. After a quarter of an hour of frantic searching he had to admit that it was not there, and that whoever had picked it up must have made off with it.

It occurred to him that Fouché might have seen it drop, and, after the abortive chase, returned to the inn to make a search for it that had proved successful; but he had no proof of that and any one of the servants of the inn, the landlord or a visitor, might equally well have picked it up and decided that fifty-four *louis* were worth straining one's conscience to keep.

Sadly depressed, he gave up the hunt and set about making arrangements for the Doctor's funeral. Having no other resources than the few francs in his pocket he saddled Monsieur de Montaigne and, taking him to an apothecary, sold the remaining contents of his panniers for two *louis*. Then, he hardened his heart and disposed of the old mule for a further four *crowns*.

That afternoon he managed to raise two more *louis* on the Doctor's medical instruments; then he went in search of a priest who would give his poor old friend decent burial. As the verdict of the Court had spread about the town this proved far from easy; but by nightfall he found a poor priest in the parish of St. Helier de Vern who was broad-minded enough to undertake the business for a payment of three *louis*.

Next morning he was the sole mourner at the Doctor's funeral, and he came away from it with only four *crowns* and two *francs* in his pocket; the expenses of the funeral having absorbed the remainder of the money he had succeeded in raising from the sale of his late partner's effects.

Yet he was not unduly downhearted regarding his own prospects. He felt certain that his beautiful little protectress would find a means to open for him a new and much more promising career.

On leaving the cemetery he hurried to the Hôtel de Rochambeau. At its door he was met by the supercilious Aldegonde. In less than a minute that pompous functionary shattered his hopes and took obvious delight in so doing.

"Mademoiselle left yesterday for *Monseigneur le Marquis's* chateau in the country," he announced with evident enjoyment. "And she will not be in Rennes again for several weeks." Upon which he rudely slammed the door.

Sadly Roger turned away. Once again Georgina's foretelling of his future had proved correct. No good had come to him from his partnership with old Aristotle Fénelon. He was back where he had started eleven weeks ago. In fact, his situation was somewhat worse, as the summer had gone; he was again almost penniless, and considerably further from home. At his age he could not conceivably set up to be a journeyman-doctor who had travelled the world in search of a hundred miraculous remedies, and he knew no other trade. Once more he was destitute in a strange land without either prospects or friends.

CHAPTER XII

THE MAN IN GREEN

As Roger walked aimlessly away from the Hôtel de Rochambeau one fact emerged clearly from his unhappy musings; it was imperative that within the next few days he should find himself some sort of work.

Rennes was the best part of fifty miles from St. Malo, its nearest seaport. Even had he now been prepared to admit defeat and endeavour to beg a passage home on promise of payment the other end, his few *crowns* would not support him for so long a tramp; and the poverty of the French countryside made it, unlike England, no place in which one could with any ease pick up a night's board and lodging here and there in return for casual work. Whatever he might decide to do later, he saw that, for the time being, he must somehow secure employment in Rennes which would enable him, by careful saving, to build up a capital of at least five *louis* before taking any further decision as to his future.

It then occurred to him that he was not altogether friendless. Maître Léger had not only given him very shrewd legal advice the day before on Athénaïs's instructions, but behaved towards him in the most pleasant and kindly manner.

Turning about he retraced his steps to the Hôtel and once more bearded the supercilious Monsieur Aldegonde, who told him that the lawyer lived in the Rue d'Antrain a few doors from the *Hôtel de Ville*, and that the street lay only just across the *Place*.

Following these directions Roger soon found the house. It proved to be a commodious old building serving both as home and office, as could be seen from the green wire blinds in the ground floor room and the heads of several young men bowed over ledgers that were visible above them. Going in, Roger gave his name and asked to see Maître Léger.

A youth, a little older than himself, with fiery red hair and a spotty face, took his message, and asked him to wait in a small musty-smelling ante-chamber. Ten minutes later he returned and conducted Roger to a room on the first floor, where he found the immaculately dressed lawyer seated at a big desk strewn with parchments and law books.

"Good day to you, my young friend," said the man in green affably. "In what way can I be of service to you?"

"I want your advice and help, if you would be kind enough to give it to me," replied Roger, sitting down in a comfortable elbow chair to which the lawyer waved him; and without beating about the bush he explained the precarious position in which Doctor Aristotle Fénelon's death had left him.

Maître Léger adjusted a pair of steel-rimmed spectacles which were now perched upon his thin, sharp nose, sat back with the tips of his fingers placed together and listened attentively. When Roger had done, he said:

"Your position is certainly a difficult one, and I think that much your best course would be to return to your parents. If I advance you the necessary money for your journey to Strasbourg can you give me an honourable undertaking as to my reimbursement, in due course?"

Roger flushed slightly. For a moment he thought of taking the money and using it to return to England, but his whole mind still revolted at the thought of reappearing penniless at home to throw himself on his father's mercy; so he said, a trifly awkwardly:

"Your offer, Monsieur, is most kindly meant, and I deeply appreciate

150

it. But I left home on account of a most bitter quarrel with my step-father, who had made my life unbearable, so I am most loath to go back as long as there is the least possibility of my being able to earn my own livelihood."

The lawyer nodded sympathetically. "Well, in that case, if you will tell me your qualifications, I will see if I can suggest anything."

"At school, Monsieur, I did well at composition and I write a fair hand. Unfortunately, I know nothing of bookkeeping, but I am strong in languages; my Greek is fair and my tutor was good enough to compliment me many times upon my Latin."

Maître Léger looked at him with a sudden increase of interest. "A good understanding of Latin is a valuable asset; and, of course, you speak and write fluent German?"

This was a facer that Roger had not expected, and to have denied it would have immediately disclosed his story of being a native of Alsace to be false, so he avoided telling a direct lie by saying quickly: "I also did well in English; in fact, 'tis said that I have quite a gift for that tongue."

"These languages, coupled with a legible hand and the ability to compose, clearly fit you to enter one of the learned professions," Maître Léger announced. "Has it ever occurred to you to take up the law?"

Again Roger was slightly nonplussed. He had wanted a life of excitement and travel, and few things could have been further removed from that than the dry-as-dust occupation of poring over legal documents. But in his mind at this moment there was no thought of choosing a permanent career, only of obtaining some temporary work which would stave off starvation; so he answered tactfully: "No, Monsieur, but it is an honourable profession, and no doubt interesting."

The lawyer smiled drily. "It gives one as good a status in France as one can have if not born of the *noblesse*. But whether so high-spirited a young man as yourself would find it interesting is quite another matter. How old are you?"

"Seventeen," lied Roger, stretching his age as far as he thought he could do so with plausibility.

"You are a little old, then, to be bound as an apprentice; and 'tis the custom for parents whose boys are articled to me to pay a consideration for their learning the profession. So 'twould be resented by the others if I took you without a fee."

On seeing Roger's face fall, Maître Léger went on tactfully: "However, that might be overcome. I have formed the impression that you have a quick and intelligent mind, and if your Latin is as good as you say I may be able to offer you employment." Sorting quickly through his papers he selected one and, passing it across his desk, added: "See what you can make of this?"

For a moment Roger was sadly baffled by the legal terms with which the document was besprinkled, but he soon found he could understand enough of it to pronounce it to be a mortgage on some fields and a small vineyard, and to state the terms of interest and repayment.

151

"Since one can hardly expect you to be acquainted with our legal jargon, that is none too bad," Maître Léger declared, "and most of the papers with which we are called on to deal are in Latin. I have recently lost my second Latin copyist, so I could offer you his place; but the renumeration would not be large."

"What figure have you in mind?" asked Roger anxiously.

"Twelve *louis* a year."

Again Roger's face fell. It was less than five shillings a week. He had always known that clerks were a down-trodden and ill-paid class, but had not imagined the remuneration of their most junior grade to be quite as miserable as this.

" 'Tis very kind of you," he murmured unhappily, "but I fear I could barely live on that."

"You would not have to," the lawyer replied. But perhaps I did not make my whole thought plain. We had been speaking of my apprentices and, while circumstances do not permit of your being articled to me, in view of your youth I was thinking of you in those terms. That is to say, you would bed and board with them here at my cost, and the *louis* a month would be yours to spend as you willed on small enjoyments or keeping some young woman in ribbons."

This put a very different complexion on the matter. A *louis* a month was no fortune and, Roger felt, a sad decline in his earnings after the near half a *louis* a *day* that he had been making as his share in his recent partnership. It seemed all wrong that the rewards of honest work should be so infinitely less than those of merry charlatanism, but that was to be expected; and the present offer at least meant security from want throughout the winter with a prospect of having saved enough to return to England by the spring if no better approach to fortune had occurred in the meantime. In fact, as the lawyer was usually paid to take his apprentices and in this case was offering a wage, it seemed he was behaving very generously; and Roger, with his usual honesty when not forced by circumstances to conceal his motives, said so when accepting the proposition.

Maître Léger smiled again. " 'Tis true that I was in part prompted by the thought that no man works well and happily unless he has a few *francs* for his private necessities in his pocket, yet I believe that I have the reputation in Rennes of a shrewd man at a bargain. You will learn soon enough that my apprentices are an idle, slovenly lot, with scarce a peck of brains or learning between them; whereas you, Monsieur Breuc, are clearly a young man of superior education and if you choose to apply yourself with even moderate endeavour to the tasks which are set you will, I have no doubt, earn your twelve *Louis* a year and show me a good profit in addition."

"I shall certainly do my best to repay your kindness," Roger replied with genuine sincerity. "When do you wish me to start?"

"Why, the sooner the better, since you have only to fetch your things from the *Du Guesclin*. Come with me now and I will present you to your future colleagues; then you can collect your belongings and settle in this evening."

As he stood up the lawyer paused a moment, staring down at his papers thoughtfully; then he said: "My senior apprentices are older than yourself and are still working without a wage after three years here. You will be sharing their accommodation and be one of them in all but name. I am anxious to avoid any jealousy arising from the fact that you are being paid, so I think it would be wise to resort to a small deception. My wife is a native of Artois and has many relatives in the northern provinces. I propose to give out that you are a distant cousin of hers, as the relationship will appear an adequate reason for the special arrangement I have made in your case."

"It is good of you to provide against my being subject to unpleasantness," said Roger. "But to carry the matter through would it not be advisable for you to present me to Madme Léger before I meet any of your employees, in order that we may arrange some details of this cousinship against anybody questioning me concerning it?"

"I would do so, but Madame Léger accompanied me on my recent visit to Paris, and is not yet returned. I will inform her by letter of the arrangement, so that when she gets back she may greet you at once as her relative; but for the moment all you need tell anyone who questions you; is that your mother was a Colombat, since that was my wife's maiden name." As he finished speaking, Maître Léger led the way downstairs and proceeded to introduce Roger to his new colleagues.

The chief clerk was a bent old man named Fusier, but Brochard, his number two, a broad-shouldered, thick-set man of about forty, struck Roger as having much more personality. Three other clerks were employed, Guigner, Taillepied and Ruttot, the latter being the senior Latin copyist under whom Roger was to work. He thought all of them dreary, depressed-looking men, and was thoroughly glad that he had no intention of making the law his permanent profession.

The apprentices were introduced as Hutot, Quatrevaux, Douie, Monestot and Colas; that being the order of their seniority. Roger judged that the age he had given himself, of seventeen, made him younger than the two senior, about the same age as Douie and older than the two who had most recently joined the firm; but that in actual fact he was probably about of an age with the youngest.

Hutot was a big, fair-haired, stupid-looking lout; Quatrevaux a dark thin fellow of better dress and appearance than the others; Douie the youth with the violent red hair who had shown him up to Maître Léger, Monestot a pimply-faced youngster who looked as if he had outgrown his strength; and Colas a bright-eyed, impish-looking lad.

Roger found that the whole of the ground floor appeared to be offices. The apprentices all worked in a room at the back, under the supervision of the thick-set second head, Brochard. The clerks occupied the front room, with the exception of the old chief clerk Fusier, who had an office to himself on the opposite side of the stairs, next to the waiting-room. It was decided that as Roger was to be employed copying documents it would be best for him to work in the clerks' room at a desk next to that of his senior, Ruttot.

When the introductions had been completed Roger was handed

153

over to the junior apprentice, Colas, to be shown his living quarters. The mischievous-looking youngster took him upstairs to the top of the house where, beneath the roof, two attics had been converted into one room for the apprentices. Even so, the space seemed extraordinarily small; the six truckle beds were no more than a few inches apart and the low ceiling made the crowded chamber appallingly stuffy.

"That's yours," said Colas, pointing to a bed in the far corner. "And, by all the saints, I'm pleased to see you."

"Thank you," replied Roger giving him a slightly suspicious look, at this somewhat curious welcome.

Colas grinned. "You don't know what you are in for yet. 'Tis you who are the junior apprentice now, and a dog's life you'll find it, till some other poor greenhorn is articled and takes your place."

"But I have not been articled," said Roger firmly, "so I am not an apprentice."

"To the devil with that!" Colas declared truculently. "As you are to share our room you'll count as one. 'Twill be for you in future to get up an hour before the rest of us and fetch up the pails of water for our washing. You'll have to run errands for us, too; get us our tucker from Julien, the pastrycook, and carry *billet-doux* from Hutot and Monestot to their mistresses. You'll empty the slops and make our beds in the midday recess. You won't have time for that in the mornings since 'twill be for you now to sweep out the office, clear the wastepaper baskets and fill the inkpots, unless you choose to do that overnight; but I've always been too tired by evening after eight hours of that old brute Brochard's driving."

Roger's mouth hardened. When he had accepted Maître Léger's offer he had expected to be faced with long hours of dreary and uninteresting work, but not to be sent back to school again; and young Colas had painted a picture of a more exacting life than that led by the most junior fags at Sherborne.

"I'll do all there is to do in the office, if 'tis required of me," he said, "but you can all get your water for yourselves and run your own errands."

"We'll see about that," scoffed Colas. "Hutot is as strong as a bull, and as easily angered. Cross him if you like but 'twill be the worse for you. And don't think 'twill do you any good to go tale-bearing to Maître Léger. If you do we'll make your life hell for you."

He paused for a moment, then went on more kindly. "Take my advice and do as Hutot tells you without complaining. You'll soon get used to it, and I will lend you a hand now and then. I'll give you a good tip, too. Keep on the right side of Brigitte, the cook, and she'll give you a decent portion at meals."

Roger accepted this belated olive branch but reserved his decision as to how far he would make himself a slave to the other apprentices; then, as the day was now well advanced, he said he would go and fetch his belongings from the *Du Gueselin*.

He had already settled up there that morning, so he had only to collect his bag, and, on the way, he decided to take a walk through the town in order to think over the new situation in which he found himself.

Apart from the personal loss he felt over the death of old Aristotle Fénelon he was just beginning to realise how much he would miss the free life of the road, as the constant change of scene and interest had suited his temperament. By comparison the lawyer's office offered not only a narrow life but one of drudgery. Yet to settle down there for a time at least offered security and seemed his only way of escape from the perils which beset a life of homeless vagabondage.

There was, too, the question of Athénaïs. Even with his other pre-occupations during the day she had never been far from his thoughts and, although Monsieur Aldegonde had said that she would be absent from Rennes for some weeks, she was certain to return there in due course. He felt that, come what might, he could not possibly bring himself to leave Rennes without seeing her again; so the obvious course was to make the best of things for the time being at Maître Léger's.

One point about his new position worried him considerably. His master had naturally assumed that he knew German, and, although it seemed unlikely that much German correspondence passed through the office, he did not want to be caught out; not only for his own sake but because of the awkward position in which it would place his benefactor, now that he was presumed to be one of Maître Léger's relatives by marriage.

It was clear that he could not hope to master the language in a few weeks without proper tuition, but he felt that with the aid of a German grammar, for such secret study as he could get in during his spare time, he might be able to learn sufficient of it to make out the contents of a letter; so he walked the streets until he found a bookshop on the *Quai de Lamennais*, where he managed to buy a "First Steps in German" and a French-German dictionary.

Darkness was now falling, so, quickening his pace, he collected his things at the *Du Guesclin* and made his way back to the lawyer's house in the *Rue d'Antrain*.

Up in the attic he found his new room-mates tidying themselves up before going down to supper. They immediately all crowded round him with a spate of questions. He did his best to answer civilly but without committing himself too far on the score of his past circumstances.

The dark, well-dressed Quatrevaux proved his most persistent questioner, but it was the surly-looking Hutot who said:

"So; you're a relative of Madame Léger's, are you? Well, don't imagine that we shall treat you any differently on that account. You are now the junior here and will consider yourself as our servant."

"Nay, nay," Quatrevaux protested in a mocking voice, "how crudely you put things, Hutot. Monsieur Breuc is not our servant, but a friend who will be delighted to render us certain services; and, as an earnest of his friendship, he was just about to suggest procuring half a dozen bottles of good wine in which we could drink his health to-night."

Roger knew that the custom of paying one's footing was a common one on entering many walks of life, so he replied at once: "I will do so with pleasure, Messieurs, if you will be good enough to tell me where best to buy them."

"After supper I will take you to a good place round the corner," volunteered Quatrevaux. "But there is supper, so let us go down."

A handbell had begun to clang as he was speaking and, on hearing it, all the others made a dash for the door, leaving Roger and Quatrevaux to bring up the rear.

"Ill-mannered brutes," murmured the dark young man. "By the way they rush for their food anyone could tell that they come from peasant families; but I saw at the first glance, Monsieur Breuc, that you are a person of some breeding."

" 'Tis true, Monsieur, and I am happy to be able to return the compliment."

"I trust we shall be friends, then. In these times persons who have any pretensions to quality should stand together. But I warn you to have a care how you cross Hutot. He is cunning as well as strong and in a position to make your life a misery if you refuse to obey his slightest whim."

"Thanks for the warning," said Roger gratefully. "As for your offer of friendship, Monsieur, I am most happy to accept it. If my lot is to be a hard one here 'twill be a great consolation to have someone to whom I can talk freely."

On their reaching the ground floor Quatrevaux led Roger through a short passage at the back of the hall to a one-storeyed wing of the house that jutted out along the side of a small courtyard. It contained Maître Léger's dining-room and the kitchen quarters.

Roger had supposed that the apprentices would eat with the master of the house, but Quatrevaux told him that only Brochard enjoyed that privilege, and that of being waited on by Aimée, the little fifteen-year old maid. The rest of the staff lived out, and to fend for themselves in the kitchen was considered good enough for the apprentices.

The others were already seated at a big deal table and Brigitte, the ample-bosomed young cook, was ladling stew from a saucepan on to their plates. Roger wished her good-evening and, as soon as she had helped him, set to; but before he was a third of the way through, the others had guzzled their portions and were calling for a second helping. By the time his turn came Hutot had demanded a third and the saucepan was empty, which provoked a general laugh at Roger's expense. There was only bread and cheese to follow, but ample of that, so he made up on it and did not leave the table hungry.

When they had finished they all went out into the town and, leaving their companions, Quatrevaux took Roger to a small tavern nearby: on entering which he at once suggested that they should drink a bottle together on their own.

" 'Twill take us half an hour or more to dispose of a bottle," Roger hazarded, thinking of his extremely small store of *crowns*. "Will not the others become angry at being kept waiting for so long?"

"Nay, we have ample time," Quatrevaux shrugged. " 'Tis perhaps some excuse for the way they bolt their food that on weekdays after supper is our only time of recreation. All of us have a tryst with some wench most evenings, but must be in by ten, as Brochard locks up at that hour and has a dozen unpleasant ways of taking it out of late-comers. 'Tis on that account we are forced to celebrate by taking bottles up to our room; but you can depend upon it that none of them will be back before St. Pierre's bells have begun their chiming."

"In that case what wine will you drink?" asked Roger, endeavouring to hide his anxiety as to whether his funds would run to this evening's entertainment.

To his relief his new friend answered: "They have a good *Chateau Neuf du Pape* here that is not expensive, and for the wine we are to take back the *Vin Ordinaire* will serve. Those clowns have no palates for a good vintage. They scarce know one wine from another and require only something upon which they can sozzle themselves."

At a table in one of a line of partitioned recesses they enjoyed their bottle and, meanwhile, Quatrevaux gave Roger quite a lot of information about Maître Léger's household. The lawyer himself was a shrewd man and a not unkindly master. His wife, as Roger no doubt knew, was much younger than himself, a pretty creature and a born coquette. Old Fusier knew his law but otherwise was a dotard and rarely interfered with anybody. Brochard, who aspired to a partner-ship, really ran the place. He was both clever and exacting. His only interest outside the firm was politics. He was a reformer of the most rabid type and if the present discontents ever came to a head would prove dangerous. Douie, the third apprentice, on the other hand, was deeply religious, and the Church still wielded immense power in Brittany. He, Quatrevaux, was not himself a Breton; he hailed from Provence. As Brochard was a freethinker he and Douie often had terrific arguments.

As the catalogue went on Roger gathered that these two were, apart from Maître Léger, the only serious people in the house. The others either lived the lives of cabbages or were solely concerned with a succession of ever-changing love affairs.

"How is it that you have no tryst to-night?" Roger inquired, after he had listened to Quatrevaux's revelations about several of his colleagues' illicit amours, made with evident approval.

The handsome young Provençal gave him a sly look. "You have not met Manon Prudhot yet, have you? She is a niece of Maître Léger's, and keeps house for him in Madame's absence. She is a Parisien and infinitely superior to these little Rennes trollops with whom the others amuse themselves. Why should I go outside the house when such good fare is to be had within it?"

As the Cathedral clock struck the quarter they collected the six bottles of *Vin Ordinaire*, which to Roger's relief cost only half a *franc* a-piece, and carried them back to their lodging. A few minutes later the rest of the apprentices began to arrive, pewter mugs were pro-duced, the corks of the bottles were drawn and the small company settled down on their beds to toast Roger's initiation.

For some time the talk was general, with many allusions to the other inmates of the house and various girls of the town, which meant nothing to Roger; but then they began to ask him again about himself and he had to call largely upon his powers of invention.

From the crosstalk that ensued he soon discovered that they were just primitive and boorish rather than malicious, and that, apart from Quatrevaux, he already knew far more of the world than all of them put together. They had all been brought up in narrow parochial surroundings; none of them had ever been in a town larger than Rennes and his English public school education far surpassed anything they had received at the hands of Catholic priests in small town colleges.

By the time five out of six bottles had been consumed he knew that he had created something of an impression and that they now regarded him with a certain respect, even if their admiration was somewhat offset by a grudging envy; so he felt that if he played his cards well he might be able to secure a reasonable deal from them. With a view to further enhancing his prestige he launched into an account of his sword fight with De Roubec, although retailing the affair as though it had occurred in Strasbourg and had resulted from a chance encounter with a drunken rake on the way home one night.

At first they obviously believed him to be boasting and soon began to taunt him with half-drunken sneers of derision; but, quite good-humouredly, he pulled his long sword from under his bed, displayed it to their surprised gaze and said:

"Believe me or not as you like, but I am perfectly prepared to fight anyone here, either in a fencing school with buttoned foils or somewhere outside the town with naked steel."

His half-playful announcement was followed by a brief, strained silence. He doubted if any of them had ever handled a sword in their lives, and felt certain that his challenge would not be accepted; but he waited with interest to see how they would take it.

After a moment the hulking Hutot spoke up for the rest:

"I am of the people and the rapier is not for such as us; but I am strong enough to break you in half, my little man, and you would remember a good kick from me for a month afterwards. While I am here you'll show me the respect and service due to your elders."

Roger was quick to seize upon the point. He had known all along that he would never be able to intimidate Hutot, or overawe the others as long as they had the support of their senior; so he launched a project that he had in mind for splitting the party.

"Monsieur Hutot," he said with sudden gravity, "Believe me, you will never find me lacking in respect to you or unwilling to oblige you in anything you may require of me. But I am sure you will agree that, since I am not an articled apprentice, I am entitled to suggest that my age should be the governing factor in whom I serve here and whom I do not."

" 'Tis an innovation that I'll not stand for," declared Douie.

"You will hold your peace and do as you are bid," said Quatrevaux sharply. "How old are you, Breuc?"

"Seventeen and three months," Roger lied, once more stretching his age to the maximum which he thought might pass as credible; yet, had he known it, he could safely have added another six months, since so impressed were they by his *savoir-faire* and comparative breadth of knowledge, they would still have believed him.

"We celebrated Douie's name-day towards the end of September," Quatrevaux remarked, "so he can be but seventeen and a few weeks. I am eighteen and a half, and Hutot nearly twenty."

"Very well, then," said Roger. "I will serve you, Monsieur Quatrevaux, and Monsieur Hutot, to the best of my ability, but the other three must arrange matters among themselves."

" 'Tis all against our custom," demurred Hutot.

"And what of the cleaning of the office?" cried little Colas angrily. "I've done it daily for eight months and thought my time was nearing its end. Yet now, the sixth bed here is occupied, Maître Léger cannot take another apprentice until Hutot leaves, and that will not be till next Whitsuntide. 'Tis unjust that I should be saddled with it for sixteen months when the normal period is something less than a year."

For a moment it looked as though Roger's plan for saving himself from becoming the general drudge hung again in the balance, but he said quickly:

"The office work I am prepared to share with you." Then picking up the last bottle of wine he refilled the glasses of the two seniors and added: "The decision rests with you, Monsieur Hutot, but in view of my age and the fact that I am not an articled apprentice I appeal to your sense of fairness."

Quatrevaux suddenly came to his assistance. "Breuc has made a good case. We are all lawyers here, and our rulings should be just ones."

"I'll not start to run my own errands again," Douie put in suddenly, and the silent, stupid-looking Monestot nodded agreement.

"Colas will continue to serve you two while Breuc looks after us," said Quatrevaux. "That is fair enough, is it not, Hutot?"

The burly Hutot shrugged his broad shoulders. "As you will. So long as my needs are attended to without question I care not how the juniors arrange matters between themselves."

So the question was settled and now, half befuddled by the wine they had drunk, they went to bed: Roger feeling no little pleased with himself that his skilful diplomacy had succeeded in at least reducing his new masters from five to two.

Next morning, having carried up the washing-water with Colas and helped him to clean out the office, Roger breakfasted with the others in the kitchen and, immediately afterwards, was set to work under Ruttot's supervision on copying Latin documents.

The senior copyist was a frail looking, bespectacled fellow of about thirty-five, who suffered from an habitual and irritating cough. He was a man of no ambition, having been a copyist for the past ten years and expecting to continue as one all his life. But he was competent at his work and evidently anxious that Roger should become so, too; as he took the trouble to make out a list for him of Latin legal expressions and helped him without grumbling whenever he found himself in difficulties.

As Roger had feared, the work proved extremely monotonous and, as soon as its newness had worn off, he began to feel more than ever that Fate had played him a scurvy trick in forcing him to earn a pittance in such a manner.

He soon found, too, that although he had saved himself from becoming the slave of all his colleagues, fagging for Hutot alone was worse than anything he had endured as a new boy at Sherborne. The only interests of this coarse and powerfully built young Breton were drink and women. Brigitte, the fresh-faced cook, was his permanent stand-by, but on such nights as he did not creep down to the little room that she occupied on the ground floor, and they were many, he left the house by stealth after it had been locked up to spend the best part of the night with other girls of loose morals who lived in the neighbourhood.

His method of doing so was to lower himself by a rope from the attic window to the roof of the out-jutting kitchen and, from there, scramble down into the courtyard. But lest the rope should be seen from one of the lower windows during his absence it had to be hauled up after his descent and lowered again on his return. This now became one of Roger's duties and, since Hutot rarely returned till the early morning, his abettor had to sleep with a piece of string attached to his little finger, the other end of which, having been passed through the window, hung down into the yard so that Hutot could pull it as a signal that he had returned.

Roger intensely resented being violently woken three or four nights a week by a painful jerking of his hand, and even more the fact that Hutot often returned drunk, which necessitated putting him to bed and afterwards clearing up the disgusting mess he had made when he had been sick. Yet there was nothing to be done about it as, on the only occasion that he had had the temerity to protest, Hutot had knocked him down and kicked him savagely.

Another less unpleasant but irritating duty that Roger was called on to perform was, during the midday recess, to carry Hutot's *billet-doux* to his latest conquests. As the senior apprentice was not the least particular about looks or class these ranged from washerwomen to girls who were known to be the common property of the town.

They were a coarse and vicious lot, and several of them, having made advances to Roger himself without success, then took a special delight in jeering at him as a prude and trying to make him blush by obscene remarks every time he had to visit them. Not only did he come to hate these missions but they took much of his free time that he would have otherwise employed in studying his German. He dared not let his books be seen by anyone at Maître Léger's, so his only opportunity of getting down to them, except on Sundays, was on fine days when he could spend an hour after *dejeuner* sitting on a bench in the *Jardin des Plantes*.

Quatrevaux continued to treat him as a friend when the others were not about but, possibly from fear of losing his own prestige, was also exacting in his requirements of service. Nevertheless, his demands were much less onerous than Hutot's and mainly consisted in buying ribbons, bonbons and other presents for Mademoiselle Manon Prudhot.

Roger met Manon occasionally, going in or out of the house or on the stairs, and he did not consider her particularly pretty; but she had a beautiful figure, dressed with great elegance and had dark, roguish eyes. She was about twenty-two and, for those times, old not to be already married; but rumour had it that a scandal resulting from her having had an illegitimate child had hampered her chances in Paris; hence her coming to live with her uncle at Rennes. In any case, Roger knew that she could be no prude as often, when he was roused in the early hours of the morning by Hutot returning home, he saw that Quatrevaux's bed was empty.

After three weeks of his boring and humiliating existence at Maître Léger's Roger felt that he could not possibly bear it much longer. The thought of Athénaïs had alone sustained him so long, but he had known her for only one evening and even the indelible impression made upon him by her fairy-like yet imperious beauty was becoming slightly blunted in his memory. She would, he knew, remain his dream divinity for years to come, yet his prospects of seeing much of her in the future now seemed remote, and those of his ever being able to make her his wife, positively nil.

While pondering his unhappy state one day towards the end of October it occurred to him that it was now just on three months since he had left home. By this time his father should have been re-posted and, if despatched to a distant station, would not be back in England for another year or more. If that were the case the coast was now clear for his own return. His homecoming, it was true, would not have the glamour with which he had once hoped to invest it, but at least he could say that he had succeeded in supporting himself in a foreign country for three months, which, at his age, was no small achievement. And while he was still not prepared to face his outraged father he felt that he could quite well bring himself to eat humble pie before his mother.

With this in mind he decided to write to her and, as he was apt to act at once on any impulse he felt to be a good one, he set about it that very day.

In his letter he said nothing of his nearly disastrous crossing with the smugglers, or of poor old Aristotle Fénelon, and he made his position sound considerably better than it was in fact. He once more begged pardon for the anxiety that his running away must have caused her, then went on to say that he was in excellent health and had obtained a good position with the leading lawyer in Rennes. It was, he admitted, a come-down for a gentleman to serve in a lawyer's office as a clerk, but even that was, in his eyes, an infinitely better condition of life than the miserable existence led by a midshipman in a man-o'-war. He added that while he had no intention of making law his career he should certainly stick to it until something better offered rather than return if his father was still at home. But that if the Admiral had been given a command and gone to sea again he was quite willing to take ship for England and discuss with her any ideas which she might have as to a more promising future for him. He refrained from informing her that he lacked the necessary funds to get back as he did not wish to admit that he was practically penniless, and he felt that it would be time enough to ask her to send him the money for his passage if her reply was favourable.

Having completed his letter he was anxious to get a reply to it as speedily as possible. On inquiring at the *Hôtel des Postes* he learned that his missive might take anything up to a month to reach England, but that if he sent it by express it should get there, depending on the state of the weather, in a week to ten days; so he spent his last two crowns in sending it by the faster service.

His father having so recently been made a Rear-Admiral could be taken as a sure sign that he would be fairly speedily re-posted, so Roger felt that all the odds were on his parent being already once more at sea. It had cost him a lot to propose returning, as he would still have to face a possibly scornful Georgina and tell her what a poor figure he had cut in the matter of her jewels. But now that he had taken the decision he was glad of it and, much comforted by the thought that he would, almost certainly, be back in his own comfortable home by the end of November, he returned to face his daily drudgery and Hutot's outrageous demands with a more cheerful countenance than he had been able to put upon them for some time.

It was eight days after he had written and despatched his letter that he again saw Athénaïs. His flair for foreign languages made his study of German sufficiently interesting for him to continue working at it after lunch each day, although he now counted on getting home in the near future; and, having left the *Jardin des Plantes*, he was on his way back through the *Rue St. Mélaine* when he recognised her coach. He knew it at once from the liveries of the servants, and as it passed him a moment later at a fast trot he caught sight of her inside. She did not see him, as she was sitting bolt upright, beside Madame Marie-Angé Velot, staring straight in front of her, but the one glimpse of her lovely and imperious profile was enough to set his heart thumping like a sledge-hammer.

As he turned to gape after the coach he felt that she was ten, nay a hundred, times more beautiful than the picture he had kept of her in his memory; a little goddess who had descended to this sordid earth on which no mortal was even fitted to be a footstool for her feet. Yet, before the coach had turned the corner of the street he had determined that he must kiss her hand that very night.

That afternoon, for the first time, Monsieur Ruttot had to upbraid him severely for really slipshod work in his copying, but he simply could not keep his mind on his task and, that evening, having smartened himself up as well as he could, he bolted his dinner with the avidity of the other apprentices in order the more quickly to get out of the house.

On his arriving at the Hôtel de Rochambeau one of the footmen answered the door to him and went to summon Monsieur Aldegonde. The major-domo greeted him with his usual look of haughty disapproval and when Roger asked for his name to be taken up to Mademoiselle de

Rochambeau replied that Mademoiselle could not be disturbed at present as she was still at dinner.

His ardour somewhat damped by this rebuff Roger set to slowly pacing back and forth across the great marble-floored hall, while Aldegonde reascended the staircase to resume supervising the service of the meal. For over half an hour he waited, at first somewhat consoled for the delay from having learned that his divinity was definitely at home and had not merely been in Rennes on a flying visit that afternoon; then with ever-growing impatience to have sight of her.

At last footsteps sounded again at the top of the stairs and, to his surprise, he saw young Count Lucien, followed by Aldegonde, coming down towards him. Ceasing his pacing he greeted the Count with a smile and made him a low bow.

The little Count halted two steps from the bottom of the staircase and returned the bow only with the faintest inclination of the head, then he said in a shrill voice:

"I am told that you have requested an audience with Mademoiselle, my sister, Monsieur. For what purpose do you require it?"

"Why, *Monsieur le Count*, to pay my respects to her," Roger replied a trifle uneasily.

"Is it true that you have become a clerk in our lawyer's office?"

"Yes, and I do not seek to hide it. But 'tis only a temporary measure. You will recall, no doubt, the straits in which I was left on the death of Doctor Aristotle Fénelon, and I was forced to take the only employment that offered, or starve."

"I care not if you starve or no," cried the young Count, giving vent to his anger. "How dare you presume on the fact that Mademoiselle de Rochambeau was impulsive enough to bring you here one night out of charity. You were then naught but a penniless vagabond, and you are little better now. The de Rochambeaux do not consort with lawyer's clerks and your request to wait upon Mademoiselle is an outrageous insult."

Roger had gone pale to the lips. "You stuck-up little fool!" he suddenly burst out. "Whatever work I may do I'm as much a gentleman as you any day. Keep your tongue between your teeth, or 'twill be the worse for you!"

Count Lucien's hand shot out, and he shrilled to Aldegonde: "Seize that impudent upstart and throw him out!"

At Aldegonde's signal the tall footman advanced upon Roger, grasped him by the shoulders and, swivelling him round, thrust him towards the door.

"By God!" he shouted over his shoulder, "I'll get even with you for this!"

Next moment he was at the top of the steps. He heard Count Lucien cry: "If you dare to show your face here again I'll have you whipped by my lackeys."

Then the footman's knee caught Roger a hefty biff on the behind. He pitched forward down the short flight of steps and fell sprawling in the courtyard; the door was slammed to behind him.

Picking himself up he turned round and shook his fist in impotent fury at the dark façade of the mansion; then, literally sobbing with rage, he staggered out into the street.

For a week he could scarcely think of anything but the abominable humiliation to which he had been subjected. He came from a country where there were still very marked class distinctions, but in which there had grown up during the centuries a feeling that all classes were necessary to a well-ordered society, and that each was worthy of respect from the others as long as in the main its representatives contributed their quota to the common good. The better educated and more fortunately placed planned and ordered the way of life of the majority. They gave of their blood unstintingly in leading the defence of the country in time of war, meted out impartial, unbribable justice to their equals and inferiors alike, and tided the country people over times of difficulty whenever there was a failure of the crops. The others gave loyal service in peace and war and did not question the wisdom of their intellectual superiors in directing the affairs of the nation. Yet all stood fairly on their own feet with a true sense of their own dignity as individuals and proper rights as free men; and all had a ready word of good cheer for the others in their daily lives. The humblest labourer would talk as an equal about the prospects of crops or village affairs with his landlord and the noblest in the land was not ashamed to crack a joke with the yokels over a cup of ale in the village inn.

Here in France everything was utterly different. The country people lived in the direst poverty and were treated, not like human beings but like animals, by a stupid, hidebound and stony-hearted nobility of whom, Roger felt, little Count Lucien was a typical representative. Even the townsfolk were a race apart, despising the peasants and in turn despised by the aristocracy. Owing to the decay of feudalism the whole system had become hideously false and distorted so that the links binding one class to another had now utterly disappeared, leaving gaping voids of hatred and envy where good will, trust and mutual service had once held sway.

In this week of personal bitterness he became an inarticulate but fervid revolutionary; and, while quite illegally divorcing Athénaïs de Rochambeau from her caste, hoped that the day would soon come when the whole decadent French nobility might be stripped of its antiquated privileges and thrown upon a dungheap. Yet, beyond all, he longed as he had never longed before to return to the green and smiling fields of England.

Morose and silent he laboured on at his work and did as he was bid by the senior apprentices without a murmur of complaint, but he was now counting the hours until a letter from his mother should bring him release from his bondage.

At last, on the 16th of November, it arrived. Brochard handed it to him on his entering the office first thing that morning and gave him a look of curiosity as he remarked:

"You must have friends who travel far afield, young man, to correspond with them in England."

But Roger ignored the implied question, stuffed the letter in his pocket and, excusing himself hurriedly, dashed upstairs to read it. He was already cursing his short-sighted policy in not having asked his mother for funds with which to return, as now he would have to write again, and another three weeks must elapse before he could receive her reply with the money which would enable him to set out. In his mind he made a swift calculation. Three weeks would bring him to the 7th of December and allowing another four days, which should be ample for his journey, he should reach Lymington by the 11th. Even with unforeseen delays he would be home in plenty of time for Christmas.

With hasty, fumbling fingers he tore the letter open, and ran his eye swiftly down the close-written pages. The letter was only mildly reproachful and full of loving phrases. As he skimmed through it a paragraph near its end suddenly riveted his attention.

In it, his mother urged him to write frequently, and said how relieved she was to hear that he was comfortably settled as, much as she would love to see him, it would be most ill-advised to return as yet. With time she hoped to bring about a softening of his father's heart, but Roger's conduct had angered him to such a degree that he had sworn never to receive him into the house again. As to the Admiral's going to sea, to her own great joy, apart from the fact that it would deprive her of seeing Roger, there would be no prospect of that for a long time to come. He had, early that month, been appointed C.-in-C., Portsmouth, and his command being so near Lymington would enable him to practically live at home for the next two years.

CHAPTER XIII

FIRST LOVE

Two years! At Roger's age that sounded like a life sentence. Aghast and dumbfounded, tears welled up into his eyes. As they misted over he could no longer make out his mother's fine writing and he dropped the letter on to his truckle bed. This then, was the price he must pay for his liberty. To slave for eight hours a day, week after week, in a musty office, to feed in a kitchen and sleep with five others in the sordid, depressing attic room. No holidays, apart from the principal Saints' days, were ever given; Saturday was a working day like all the rest and, even had there been some periods of leisure to look forward to, he had neither the money nor the friends with which to enjoy them. Yet, where could he go? What could he do? Other than continue to face this dreary round, which appeared to be his sole means of securing the bare necessities of life.

Gamely he fought back the tears, blinked his eyes clear and picked up the letter again to read it through properly, in the hope that he might yet discover in it some ray of comfort. But there was none. Evidently his mother had read into his overdrawn picture of the position he had secured that he was content to remain where he was for the present unless his father was prepared to forgive and forget the past. She praised him for his initiative in having obtained a post of responsibility while still so young and said how fortunate he was to have been taken into the house of a kindly and respectable lawyer. The rest of the letter contained only local news and much good advice as to how he should care for his health through the winter.

Her reference to the winter brought back to Roger's mind a problem that had been causing him much concern of late. Apart from a change of linen he had no clothes other than those he stood up in; and, now that it was mid-November, he sadly needed a warm coat.

As his prospects of returning home had been so rudely shattered, it occurred to him that, while he could not ask his mother to send him money without loss of face, he could ask her to send him his wardrobe. Monsieur Brochard, who acted as cashier as well as second head in the office, would, he felt sure, give him his November pay in advance if he asked for it. Then he could buy himself a coat at once, still have cash in hand and, by selling some of his things that he did not particularly require when they arrived from England, make good the outlay he contemplated at the moment.

This project helped a little to take his mind off the sad blow he had just received and, during the course of the day, he carried it out. The possession of the new coat, a good warm garment of maroon cloth with a big triple collar, cheered him considerably; and the next day being Sunday, he went to Mass in it.

Roger had been brought up with a horror of Popish mummery, as the practices of the Roman Catholic church were then termed in England; but upon going to live at Maître Léger's he had found himself in a most invidious position. None of the household, apart from the red-headed Douie, appeared to be particularly religious, and from their conversation it was clear that a number of them were actually free-thinkers; yet everyone in the household went to at least one service in the Cathedral every Sunday, and Roger was obviously expected to go too.

As he was supposed to have come from a German province he had thought of saying that he was a Lutheran, but he soon realised that he would be inviting serious trouble for himself if he did. During his two months in France he had already learned that all Protestants were penalised there even more rigorously than were Catholics in England, and that Brittany was the most rabid of all Catholic strongholds. Not being of the stuff of which religious martyrs are made and fearing to add to the many difficulties with which he was already beset, he had decided, like King Henry of France and Navarre before him, that a quiet life was worth a Mass, and, taking the line of least resistance, had accompanied Julien Quatrevaux to St. Pierre.

To his relief he found that most of his colleagues neither took Communion or went to Confession with any regularity; so, not being called upon to imperil his immortal soul, as he would have regarded so doing, he was able to attend the service simply as an interested spectator. The gorgeous robes of the priests, the pageantry of the ceremonial, the incense and the music all appealed to his imagination; and he thought the short but colourful ritual a great improvement on the long and uninspiring services he had been accustomed to attend in England; so he had formed the habit of going to Mass without a qualm.

On this occasion a surprise was in store for him. There were no pews in the nave of the great Cathedral and the bulk of the congregation stood about in little groups, only the richer among them using stools or *prie-dieu* which were brought to church and carried home again by the servants who accompanied them. This led to people often changing their position during the course of the service and, about halfway through the Mass, a tall man having planted himself in front of Roger, he moved to a less congested place. From it, he suddenly caught sight of Athénaïs.

For the remainder of the service he could not take his eyes off her and, at its end, he moved again so that she would have to pass close to him on her way to the door.

Flushed and excited he nerved himself to meet her glance as, having moved on an impulse, he was suddenly beset by an awful fear that he had deliberately offered himself to a new humiliation. Count Lucien was not with her, only Madame Marie-Angé and a footman, but her brother might have told her how he had had her uninvited visitor thrown out of the house and Roger, burning with shame at the memory, now dreaded that on seeing him her look would hold only contempt.

Panicking at the thought he sent up a swift prayer that she would not see him after all; but it was too late—their eyes had met.

For a second hers showed only surprise, then she made a slight inclination in response to his deep bow. When he raised his head again she was passing within a foot of where he stood. Suddenly she turned her dazzling smile full upon him. His heart missed a beat and he barely suppressed a gasp of astonished delight. By the time he could draw breath again, she was gone.

For several moments he remained standing where he was, his eyes unseeing and quite unconscious of the crowd that was streaming about him towards the doors of the Cathedral. He knew that he was trembling but he could not collect his wits, then suddenly it dawned upon him how much difference that single radiant smile had made in his life.

He might be condemned to daily drudgery and nightly irritations; he might be penniless and with only the most slender prospects of bettering his condition for a long time to come. But he still held the interest and friendship of the loveliest and most adorable person in the whole world. By remaining in Rennes, he could see her from time to time. If only he were patient Fate could not be so unkind as to fail to provide him with an opportunity of talking to her again.

All Sunday afternoon and evening his mind was filled with delicious daydreams. Some powerful noble would besmirch the beautiful Athénaïs's name and he, Roger, would call the fellow out. As he thought of it he could feel the stretch of his shoulder muscles in the furious lunge by which he would drive his blade clean through the villain's black heart. Her coach would be beset by footpads one dark night and, single-handed, he would drive off the whole brutal gang, to receive as his reward for her rescue Count Lucien's apologies and the grateful thanks of the Marquis, her father. Better still, he would render some amazing service to his own country, for which King George would make him an Earl, or perhaps, a Duke; and he would then return to France as a resplendent nobleman himself to demand from the Marquis, Mademoiselle de Rochambeau's hand in marriage.

But on the Monday, to the obvious surprise of Ruttot, he threw himself with an entirely new enthusiasm into his work. Overnight he had abandoned his wild imaginings. He had suddenly realised that as long as he remained a copyist he would be tied to his office stool all day, but if he could make himself really useful to Maître Léger he might, like the senior clerks, sometimes be entrusted to conduct outside missions; he might even be given the de Rochambeau papers to handle, and thus be provided with an adequate reason for making frequent visits to Athénaïs's home.

For some days, apart from Ruttot's praise, the great improvement in his work gained no recognition; but towards the end of the week it brought him a quite unexpected amelioration of his lot.

It so chanced that Maître Léger, who was generally so absorbed in his own affairs that he had hardly spoken to Roger since engaging him, had to go out on the Saturday morning to keep an exceptionally early appointment. On his return he found Roger and Colas still cleaning out the front office. Pausing in the doorway, a frown of disapproval on his sharp features, he said to Roger:

"Why are you down so early, Breuc, and thus engaged? 'Tis for the junior apprentice to clean out the offices. And, even if they have counted you as such so far I will have it so no longer. Your work has greatly improved of late and 'tis not right that a competent copyist should be put to such menial tasks."

Flushing with pleasure, Roger thanked him and determined to redouble his efforts. Little Colas was furious, but there was clearly no appeal from this decision of the master, so, henceforth, Roger was enabled to enjoy an extra half-hour in bed each morning.

Next day he was at the main door of St. Pierre half an hour before High Mass was due to begin, but, although he stood there until the service had got well under way, he did not see Athénaïs arrive. Thinking she might have entered the Cathedral by one of the other doors he went in and moved about as discreetly as he could among the crowd, but his search for her was in vain. This was a grievous disappointment as the whole of his leisure during the past week had been given to the anticipation of seeing her again and being the recipient of another of her divine smiles.

In bed that night he tortured himself with all sorts of probable and improbable reasons for Athénaïs's non-appearance at Mass. She had been taken ill; was perhaps at death's door, and he was powerless to help her. Madame Marie-Ange had seen her smile at him the previous Sunday and, like Count Lucien, disapproving of the association, had insisted on taking her to hear Mass somewhere else. She had repented of her kindness and later, feeling angered at his presumption in forcing himself upon her notice, had determined not to allow such a situation to arise again. On the other hand, she had, perhaps, been looking forward to seeing him as much as he had been to seeing her, but Madame Marie-Angé had told Count Lucien of the episode and he had told his father; upon which Athénaïs's harsh and brutal parent had locked her up on a diet of bread and water. This last fantasy filled him with hot indignation and, at the same time, an almost unbearable thrill from its wild assumption that she might conceivably love him and have accepted suffering rather than agree to give him up.

A surly order from Hutot, to get the rope from under the bed as he meant to go out, brought Roger back to earth. Then, shivering from the cold night air, he snuggled down into his narrow bed again, and told himself that it was no good building "castles in the air" and that he must get through the coming week with such patience as he could, till next Sunday brought him another possibility of seeing Athénaïs.

Yet, when the longed-for day came he had no luck. Neither did he on the following Sunday, although he attended every service at the Cathedral from dawn onwards and searched each crowd of worshippers, with frantic eyes, for his beloved.

In the week that followed, however, he met with real good fortune in another direction. On the Tuesday word ran round the house that Madame Léger was at last expected back from Paris on the coming Friday, and from the pleased looks of his colleagues it was clear to Roger that this lady was universally popular with her household. She arrived by the diligence that set its passengers down at the *Hôtel des Postes* at six in the evening, and at that hour the whole staff crowded into the hallway to welcome her on her return.

As one of the most junior among them Roger modestly took his place right at the back of the hall, so on her entrance his view of her was obscured by the tall, pimply Monestot, who was standing in front of him. It was only by peering round Monestot's shoulder that he managed to see that she was a woman of about twenty-seven, with remarkably fine blue eyes but a sadly receding chin.

For the past few days Roger had been anticipating her home-coming with considerable uneasiness. Although on his first arrival Maître Léger had given him out to be his wife's cousin no further reference had been made to this fictitious relationship, and Roger was now afraid that by this time the lawyer might have either forgotten all about it or neglected to prime his wife upon the point.

His fears were soon set at rest. While Madame's baggage was being carried in by willing hands she seemed to have a kind word for every-body; then, suddenly pausing in her loquacious greetings, she looked round the crowded hall and cried: "But where is my young cousin, Rojé Breuc?"

Much relieved, Roger came forward, and was about to make her his most gallant leg, but, after one quick look of approval, she placed her hands on his shoulders and gave him a hearty kiss on either cheek.

Next moment she broke into a spate of swift questions about people

169

of whom he had never even heard. How had he left Aunt Berdon? Was Cousin Marote married yet? How was Uncle Edmond's gout? It was so long since she had seen them all and she was positively dying to hear all the news.

Since none of her questions called for an answer that he could not easily invent, Roger entered into the game with zest, and even went so far as to give her tidings of entirely non-existent people. She appeared much amused at his quick wit and, before going upstairs to change out of her travelling clothes, tapped him on the arm and said: "Thou shalt tell me more of the gossip of Strasbourg, little cousin, over dinner." And when dinner-time came Maître Léger sent the servant girl Aimée to fetch him.

The party consisted of Maître Léger and Madame Léger, Manon Prudhot, Brochard and Roger. The meal was a gala one and all of them were in high good humour. At first, Roger was a little nervous that he might over-play his hand and arouse the suspicions of the sharp-eyed Brochard, but he had ample time to get accustomed to his new surroundings since, to begin with, Madame almost monopolised the conversation by regaling them with an account of her last weeks in the capital.

In due course, however, obviously enjoying the part she was called on to play, she asked him further questions about her relatives in Strasbourg. His replies were as prompt as before and once more he invented a few amusing stories, but he was suddenly disconcerted by Manon saying:

"I am, of course, of the Léger side of the family, but I must confess that I have never heard of half these relatives you mention."

Quickly recovering himself he smiled at her. "That is quite understandable, Mademoiselle. My family is an exceptionally large one and even Madame, here, may scarcely remember some of these people of whom I have been speaking."

"Have you, perhaps, also relatives in England?" Brochard inquired with apparent unconcern.

Roger instantly realised that the question was inspired by a still unsatisfied curiosity about the letter he had received and, knowing that others would be arriving for him as time went on, he determined on a bold course.

"Why, yes, Monsieur," he replied, amiably. "My godmother married an Englishman by the name of Jackson, and she now lives there. Only last spring I spent some months at their home in Hampshire and 'tis to that visit I owe my slight knowledge of English."

"I had quite forgotten that," remarked Maître Léger with his dry smile and, evidently wishing to amuse himself by testing Roger's powers of invention further, he began to question him about his visit.

Here, although it remained unrealised by anyone present, Roger was naturally on much safer ground, and he was able to provoke much hearty laughter by relating what he knew they would regard as some of the strange and barbarous customs of their hereditary enemies. But he also took occasion to establish the fact that he and his "godmother" doted on each other and kept up a regular correspondence.

At the close of the meal Maître Léger took occasion to say that he found his young protégé such excellent company that he must dine with them again sometime.

On this Madame raised the well-marked eyebrows above her big blue eyes and exclaimed: "Do'st mean to tell me that thou hast allowed my young cousin to feed all this while with the apprentices in the kitchen! For shame, Monsieur! In future he must take his meals with us."

"You are most kind, Madame," Roger demurred, fearing that Maître Léger might not approve, "but I have no wish to intrude, or to slight my colleagues by appearing to have sought a place above them."

"Nay," said the lawyer, with a kindly smile, " 'twill be no intrusion, as Madame likes to have young people about her. You can tell the others that it is Madame's desire on account of the relationship you bear her."

Thus, through Maître Léger's original prevarication and Roger's own ready wit, a new, broader and far happier life suddenly opened out for him. He dined each night at leisure in comfortable surroundings and enjoyed good talk. In addition he was granted the use of the parlour afterwards, where he sometimes played cards with Madame and Manon, and at others read books from Maître Léger's well-stocked shelves. Sometimes, too, the family invited friends in for a musical evening, so Roger took up the bass-viol; but he had no ear and did little credit to the Léger quartet in their renderings of chamber music.

In the first week of December he saw Athénaïs again, but, once more, only a fleeting glimpse of her as she drove past him in her coach, and she was not looking in his direction. The mystery of her non-reappearance at the Cathedral remained unsolved, but, at least he had the satisfaction of knowing that it was not due to illness. Her little face, framed now that winter had come in a fur hood, looked as lovely as ever and remarkably healthy.

That afternoon he was further cheered by receiving a reply to his second letter to his mother; in it she said that she had despatched all his clothes and other things that she thought might be useful to him in a spare sea-chest of his father's, as it had a stout lock and being strongly made would travel well. Then, on the twentieth of the month, he had a note from the authorities to say that it had arrived by barge from St. Malo and was down at the quay awaiting collection.

To his annoyance he found that he had to pay a heavy duty upon certain of the articles it contained, but Brochard advanced him the money to cover this, and it was a great joy to have a good store of clothes and certain possessions of his own again. He explained the arrival of the chest and its contents by saying that they were the things he had taken with him to England on his visit to his godmother the previous spring, and he had expected them to have reached Rennes by the time of his own arrival; hence his arriving there so ill-provided, but for several months the chest had been lost in transit.

After a careful sorting out he sold about a third of his things, which enabled him to repay the advance he had had and left him enough money over to buy small Christmas presents for the Légers, Manon, Brochard and Quatrevaux. As they were accustomed to exchange gifts at the New Year they were somewhat surprised at receiving his presents on the 25th, but Maître Léger unconsciously saved him from the slip by remarking that the Germans always kept *Weihnachtsfest* instead of *Nouvelle Année*.

When the New Year came his tactful gifts at Christmas were more than repaid. Quatrevaux had told Manon something of the dance that Hutot led Roger and she had told Madame Léger. In consequence the two women had cleared out a little boxroom on a half-landing and furnished it as a bedroom; then on New Year's morning they blindfolded Roger, led him upstairs and removed the bandage when he was in his new abode.

It was a tiny place and had no window, but it was his own and meant an end of getting up at all sorts of godless hours to lower the rope for Hutot; so Roger could not have been more delighted, and his two laughing benefactresses were amply repaid for the trouble they had taken by the pleasure he showed.

Thus, with the New Year of 1784 Roger entered on a far happier period than he had known for some time. His work was still monotonous, his prospects entirely uninspiring and his affair with Athénaïs at a standstill; but he was free of Hutot; well fed, comfortably clothed and housed, and accepted as a member of a pleasant, laughter-loving family.

His open adoption by the Légers as their cousin also led to his making many other acquaintances, since, when they had friends to dine, the visitors often included Roger in their return invitations, and when Manon Prudhot was invited to a young people's party he was now generally asked to accompany her.

It was at her suggestion that he took up dancing. He assented willingly, as at home he had learnt only a few country dances and he felt that he was now reaching an age where he should be able to lead a lady out to a minuet, quadrille or gavotte without embarrassment. Manon was in the habit of going once or twice a week to the Assembly Rooms or other public dance places with Julien Quatrevaux, but she was anxious not to make her affair with him too conspicuous, so they welcomed Roger as a third. They were able to introduce him to plenty of partners and he soon attached himself to one girl in particular, named Tonton Yeury.

Tonton was the daughter of a goldsmith, and a dark, vivacious little thing. She had a retroussé nose, brown almond-shaped eyes and was never serious for a moment. Few girls could have been in stronger contrast with Athénaïs, and that was perhaps one of the reasons why Roger was attracted to her. His love and longing for the imperious Mademoiselle de Rochambeau remained unabated, but in Tonton's merry company he was able temporarily to forget his secret passion.

By early January one of the severest winters that France had known for many years developed with extreme rigour, so that the canals and the river Vilaine were frozen a foot thick, and after Mass each Sunday the richer inhabitants of Rennes made carnival on the ice. Roger and his friends joined in the skating, sledging and tobogganing with great zest; but in all other respects they suffered considerably from the severity of the weather. None of them had any heat in their bedrooms and the offices in which Roger and Julien laboured for long hours each day had only small wood-burning stoves. In consequence they had to work in the frowsty cold, muffled up in their overcoats, and each time they dressed or undressed their teeth chattered from the icy blast that seemed to whistle in through every crevice.

On his third skating expedition Roger again saw Athénaïs. Count Lucien and a dark, good-looking young man somewhat older than himself were with her, so he did not dare approach; but, to his joy she gave him a friendly wave as the two youths propelled her swiftly past in a lovely little single-seated sleigh fashioned like a swan.

That night he was torn between bliss at her recognition of him and agonising jealousy at the thought that the dark young man must inevitably be in love with her and that she, quite probably, returned his love. Yet the sight of her served to revive all his old ambitions and he began to seek for an opportunity to secure advancement in the firm.

It came a few evenings later. Towards the end of dinner, Maître Léger and Brochard were discussing a case in which one of the firm's richest clients was involved and, seizing on a point that did not appear to either of them, Roger felt that without appearing impertinent he might draw their attention to it.

The point was quite a minor one but both men looked a little surprised that he should have sufficient shrewdness to appreciate that it might be of some value. Maître Léger would no doubt have thought no more of the matter had not Brochard remarked, quite with a smile:

"You display good reasoning powers, Monsieur Breuc, and we shall make a lawyer of you yet," which gave Roger the opening to reply:

"Thank you, Monsieur, but 'twill take a long time, I fear, from the little experience I gain as a Latin copyist."

"I would that we could give you something of more interest," said Maître Léger, "but to set anyone without proper training to the drafting of documents usually results in additional labour for someone else later on."

Brochard gave a somewhat spiteful little laugh. " 'Twould be easy enough for me to teach Monsieur Bruec the rudiments of the business in the evenings, but I am sure he is much too occupied in gallivanting about the town with his friends to desire that!"

"On the contrary, Monsieur," Roger took him up swiftly. "If you would be so kind, I place my leisure entirely at your disposal."

A new interest suddenly showed in Brochard's alert eyes and, with a shrug of his broad shoulders, he replied:

"So be it, then. Two evenings a week should suffice. Let us say Tuesdays and Thursdays, and after dinner we will adjourn to old Fusier's office. Being smaller it is warmer than the others and I will have the fire kept up after he has gone."

The legal coaching that resulted from this arrangement did not seriously interfere with Roger's amusements and made him feel that at last he was getting somewhere, if only towards a better job than the wearisome monotony of endless copying. He found, too, that beneath Monsieur Emile Brochard's rather severe and taciturn manner there lay a very vital and likeable personality.

Brochard was a Bordelais, and he had inherited a strong share of that tradition which made the great city of Bordeaux, from having been a fief of the English Crown for so many centuries, still markedly English in customs and sympathies. He had a passionate admiration for the British, formed mainly from the quite erroneous belief that everything they did was based on reason and, as a freethinker, he regarded "Reason" as the Supreme Deity. He was, like the great majority of educated people in France at that time, convinced that his country was on the verge of ruin, and that only the granting of a liberal Constitution by the King, coupled with the abolition of all aristocratic privileges, could possibly save it from complete disaster. And, again and again, he pointed out to Roger legal cases where the verdict would go to a noble, simply because he was a noble, whereas under English law the verdict would have gone to a commoner, not because he was a commoner, but because reason and justice were on his side.

Roger proved so attentive and appreciative an audience to these disquisitions that they fell into the habit of talking for an hour or so on such matters after the evening's lessons were concluded.

On one occasion, towards the end of February, Brochard remarked that the English were sensible enough to turn even their apparent misfortunes to advantage, as was instanced by the swift reorientation of their policy towards the United States. Having lost the war they had wasted no time in bitterness and rancour, but had at once set about relieving the acute shortage of manufactured goods that had resulted from their own five-year blockade of the Americas. Before there had even been time for the British Army to be evacuated British merchants by the hundred had crossed the Atlantic to offer the hand of friendship and, as the Americans possessed hardly any industry of their own, Britain was now enjoying a tremendous trade boom.

Roger replied a little dubiously: "That may be so, but when I was in England last year I heard many people express the opinion that the country was showing grave signs of decadence and was, in fact, pretty well on its last legs. It is the general view here, too, that, while England succeeded by the skin of her teeth in securing a reasonably good peace, the American war cost her exceeding dear, both in money and prestige; and that the many victories of the Continental Allies during it have more than made up to France for the defeats she suffered in the earlier Seven Years' War."

"You have been listening to the talk of wishful-thinking fools," scoffed Brochard. "In the war of '56-'63, we lost our hold on India and were thrown out of Canada for good. Nothing we have gained in the more recent conflict is one-tenth the value of either of those great dominions. And Britain still controls the seas to the detriment of our commerce. As for the English having become decadent, I am amazed to hear that any among them are pessimistic enough to think it. Decadence comes only to countries that are governed by the old, and since last December Britain has had for her Prime Minister young

Mr. Pitt, who is not yet twenty-five years of age. What greater proof of vitality and will to develop new ideas could any country give than that?"

It was the first that Roger had heard of this remarkable appointment of so young a man as Billy Pitt to the highest office under the British Crown. His mother now corresponded with him regularly, but her letters contained little other than local news and she never mentioned politics.

As long as the fierce frosts held the land in their grip he got what fun he could skating every Sunday. Twice more in February and March he saw Athénaïs in her little white and gold swan sleigh, but each time she was accompanied by several people so he did not dare to approach her.

The bitter cold continued right up to April so that people almost began to despair of the winter ever ending, and in many parts of the country starvation was widespread. Paris had for two months been without wood for fires and the situation there was said to be desperate. The King had given lavishly from his private purse to succour the thousands who were starving and ordered a great acreage of the royal forests to be cut down for fuel. He had also forbidden the use of private horse-drawn vehicles in the streets of the capital, since the recklessly-driven *cabriolets* of the younger nobility had knocked down and killed hundreds of poor people who were unable to get out of the way in time owing to the slipperiness of the icy roads. But these measures did little to alleviate the general distress or lessen the ever-growing hostility of the masses towards the warmly-clothed and well-fed upper classes.

Brochard declared that the worst evil lay in the infamous *Pacte de famine* by which a group of unscrupulous financiers and nobles controlled the grain supply of the whole country, and released it only in comparatively small quantities in times of shortage, such as the present, in order to make enormous profits. He said that the old King, Louis XV, had himself taken the lead in this iniquitous traffic, to which had been due the three years' famine of '67-'69, and that although Louis XVI had done his best to suppress it the monopolists had proved too powerful for him, and continued to make vast fortunes from the sufferings and death of the people. Roger was horrified, and agreed that the mere depriving of their privileges of these highly-placed criminals was far too lenient a punishment for such inhumanity.

With May there came several changes in the Léger household. A new apprentice at last arrived to relieve Colas of his drudgery; and Hutot left, regretted by none, to take up a position with a lawyer at Dinan. The following week Maître Léger took on a junior Latin copyist and to Roger's great satisfaction he was promoted to the drafting of documents under Brochard with an increase of salary to eighteen *louis* per annum.

Now that he had a chance to set his wits to work, Roger found a new interest in the law, but his love affair could hardly have been in a worse state. He had not even had a distant glimpse of Athénaïs during the past two months and, as he had learned in casual conversation from Maître Léger that the de Rochambeau family always spent the summer on their country estate, he had little hope of doing so for another five.

He had already tired of Tonton Yeury's empty, facetious laughter, and for some time past had been striving to console himself with a tall, serious-minded blonde named Louise Ferlet. When the weather was fine on Sundays they went for picnics and read poetry together; but as he lay on the grass beside Louise he could never for long escape a secret craving that, instead of her golden head, it was Athénaïs's that rested on his shoulder.

In August their picnics came to an end on account of bad weather, accompanied by exceptionally high winds. A few days after the most devastating of several bad storms there was some excitement in Rennes, on account of the Marquis de Castries spending a night in the town on his way through to Cherbourg. De Castries was a Marshal of France and the Minister for the Navy, and he was going in person to inspect the damage that the storms had caused to some new works that were under construction at the Breton port.

From various conversations Roger learned that this fine natural harbour was in process of conversion into a huge new naval base. A mole was to be formed of eighty immense cases of conical form filled with stones, sunk close to one another, each costing twelve thousand *louis*. When completed, as it was hoped that it would be in eight years, the anchorage would be capable of sheltering no less than one hundred ships of the line; and it was further proposed to build a great watch-tower on the high ground behind the port, from which, through a glass, the coast of England would be visible, and, in clear weather, British squadrons entering or leaving Portsmouth roads could be kept under constant observation. Quite clearly this vast labour and expenditure could have been undertaken with only one object—the determination of the French to dominate the Channel.

As Roger continued to spend two evenings a week studying with Brochard, he took an early opportunity of asking him why, in view of the recent treaty of peace and France's deplorable financial situation, she should undertake such a stupendous outlay in preparation for another war.

The Bordelais shrugged his broad shoulders. " 'Tis said that the King wishes for peace, yet he never ceases to build ships of war with every few *francs* that he can scrape together. The truth is that he is weak as water and swayed in his opinion from one side to the other by every person that he talks to. One day he supports M. de Vergennes, his Foreign Minister, who desires a better understanding with England, the next M. de Castries and M. de Ségur, the Minister of War, who naturally desire to set their dangerous toys in motion. The Peace of Versailles stipulated that within a year France and England should enter into a Commercial Treaty. 'Twould greatly benefit both countries by a reduction of the present crushing duties that they level on one another's merchandise. If 'tis concluded the peace party should triumph. But the nobles, in the main, look to war as a pleasurable excitement from which they may win personal glory and the bulk of the spoil from any victorious campaign, so they are ever eager for it.

Others, like our client, the Marquis de Rochambeau, consider that France should by right dominate the world, and spend their lives intriguing to embroil us with one country or another in the hope of bringing a new slice of territory under the banner of the *Fleur-de-Lys*. But, make no mistake, if they force us into another conflict within the next ten years France will become bankrupt on account of it."

The idea of spying on behalf of his country had never entered Roger's head, and to send home a chance come-by military secret of a people who were affording him hospitality seemed a mean thing to do; yet, having thought the matter over, he decided that the Cherbourg project was so flagrantly a pistol levelled at the very heart of England that he could not possibly rest easy while his own country remained in ignorance of it; so he wrote to his mother giving her as full particulars as he could gather, and asked her to pass them on to his father for submission to their lordships at the Admiralty.

Although he was totally unaware of it he had pulled off a coup that any professional spy would not have stuck at murder to achieve. His mother acknowledged the letter and a week later, greatly to his surprise, he received a terse note from his father, which ran:

I cannot find it in me to forgive the unpardonable affront you put upon me personally and the deliberate wrecking of all my cherished hopes in you. Yet I am pleased that you have not so far forgotten yourself as to fail in your duty as an Englishman. Their Lordships were mightily pleased with what you sent and have commanded me to convey their thanks to you, hence this letter. I may add that any more of the same or similar that you may be able to send will be received with appreciation; but, since I may be from home on a round of inspections, 'twould be better that you write direct to one Gilbert Maxwell, Esq., of No. 1 Queen Anne's Gate, Westminster, to whom your name has now been given.

On re-reading the note it was clear to Roger that his father would never have written to him at all had he not been commanded to do so by their Lordships, and, as there was no other information worth reporting, that appeared to end the matter.

Summer merged into autumn and the only change that it made for Roger was that he gave up reading poetry with the fair-haired Louise to resume dancing; this time with another brunette, named Geneviève Boulanger. But now he was looking forward to Athénaïs's return from the country and daily his hopes rose of once more catching sight of his little goddess.

In October all Europe was electrified by a war scare, caused by Marie Antoinette's brother, the Emperor Joseph II of Austria, manifesting most bellicose intentions towards the Dutch. The news sheets were full of most contradictory reports about the grounds of the quarrel, so Roger, as usual in such matters, went for enlightenment to the knowledgeable Brochard.

" 'Tis the well-being of the great port of Antwerp that is at the bottom of it," Brochard informed him. "Long ago, after the Dutch had rebelled against the Spaniards and gained their independence in the United Provinces, the Treaty of Munster gave them the land on each side of the mouth of the river Scheldt, while the Spaniards retained the city of Antwerp, which lies some way up it. In due course Antwerp and the Belgian Netherlands passed from Spain to Austria, and, as you know, they still form part of Joseph II's Empire, although separated from its main part by numerous German Principalities. The Dutch built forts on both sides of the river mouth and for many years have levied the most crushing tolls on all merchandise either going up to Antwerp or coming seaward from the port. In short, they have virtually levied a tax on the whole sea trade of the Austrian Netherlands and, in consequence, Antwerp has declined from one of the greatest cities in Europe to a town of a mere forty-thousand souls of whom, 'tis, said, twelve-thousand are now reduced to living on charity."

"And the Emperor has formed a resolution to open up the port?" put in Roger.

Brochard nodded. "Precisely. Unlike his sister, Joseph II is a great reformer. He has spent most of his reign travelling to all parts of his dominions, and in others, to see things for himself; and to find out in what way he can better the lot of the many races that go to make up his people. When he visited the Austrian Netherlands he was infuriated to find that his subjects there had become desperately impoverished solely to enrich the Dutch. He demanded that they should open the Scheldt to his traffic. Since, after a year's arguing, they still refuse to do so, this month, as a test case, he sent two Austrian ships up the river with orders to refuse to halt at the forts. The Dutch fired on both ships and drove them back, so the Emperor is now reported to be mobilising an army with a view to invading the United Provinces."

" 'Tis surely unfair that one nation should be in a position to tax another out of existence," observed Roger. "So it would seem to me that the Emperor's cause is just."

"One cannot but sympathise with it," Brochard agreed. "Yet as legal men we should be the last to approve the ignoring of the sanctity of a solemn treaty; and 'tis that which the Emperor asserts his right to do."

" 'Tis a nice point: but why, if the Austrians and the Dutch do decide to fight it out, should all Europe become involved, as the news sheets would have us believe?"

"The Low Countries have ever been the scene of the greatest European conflicts, and for that there are many causes. For one thing they form a racial no-man's-land where the Latin and Teuton stocks are mingled together. For another, the two great blocks of southern Catholic Europe, and northern Protestant Europe, meet head on there. Then it has always been a cardinal factor in English foreign policy that they should not be allowed to fall into the hands of any great power, since their possession by such would prove a constant menace to England's safety. And for that same reason the war party in France has always hankered after them."

"Yet none of these reasons apply to the present quarrel."

"They might. Austria is a great power and the English may well decide to support the Dutch by force of arms, rather than see Joseph II master of the United Provinces. Again, our own war party is no doubt inciting the Dutch to resist in the hope of being called in to their support."

"But in that case France and England would be allied in a common cause against the Emperor."

Brochard shook his head. "Nay. It goes deeper than that, for the Dutch are divided against themselves. The Stadtholder, William V of Orange, has little power. The States-General, as the Dutch Parliament is called, practically ignores him and has strongly revolutionary tendencies. Yet, like all his family, he is the protégé of England and, if the English come in, 'twould be to maintain him on his throne. France, on the other hand, is behind the rich burghers who wish to establish a republic, and if she came in would use them as a cat's-paw to secure the domination of Holland to herself."

Long afterwards Roger was to recall this conversation with intense interest, as it made plain things of the utmost importance to him which he would not otherwise have understood.

In November he saw Athénaïs in her coach once again, and the sight of her rearoused all the violent emotions that had lain dormant within him throughout the summer. But she still did not reappear at the Cathedral of St. Pierre.

Nevertheless, seeking among the crowd for her there on the following Sunday gave him a sudden idea, and he was furious with himself that it had never occurred to him before. Athénaïs must go to Mass somewhere each Sunday. Why should he not wait outside the Hôtel de Rochambeau until her coach came out, then run after it until it reached the church that she attended?

A week later he posted himself in the Rue St. Louis, a good half-hour before there was the least hope of Athénaïs appearing. When at last her coach emerged from the courtyard he slipped out from the archway in which he had been lurking and pelted hot-foot in pursuit. As he had foreseen, in the narrow streets of the town the cumbersome vehicle was unable to make any great pace, so he was easily able to keep up with it; and it had covered scarcely a quarter of a mile before it halted outside the church of St. Mélaine.

Breathless and excited he followed Athénaïs, Madame Marie-Angé, and the footman who carried their *prie-dieux* inside, and took up a position in which he could keep his eyes glued to the face of his beloved during the whole service. Except on the evening of their first meeting he had never had the opportunity of observing her for so long at a stretch, and by the end of the Celebration he felt positively intoxicated by the sense of her beauty. So bemused was he that he forgot to leave his place in time to catch her glance as she left the church, and he returned home still in a state of half-witted exultation.

He could hardly wait for next Sunday and counted the hours till it came round. This time he was waiting on the church steps for her arrival and, noticing him as she was about to enter the sacred building, she gave him a smile. Towards the close of the service he moved quietly over to the stoop, as he had often seen gentlemen in Catholic churches dip their hands in the Holy Water and offer it to ladies of their

179

acquaintance who were about to leave, and he meant to boldly adopt this courtesy towards her.

As she approached she smiled again and, seeing his intention, withdrew her hand from her muff. Only with the greatest difficulty could he keep his hand from trembling as he dipped it in the water and extended it to her. For a second their fingers touched. Lowering her brilliant blue eyes she crossed herself and murmured, "*Merci, Monsieur*"; then she had, passed and was walking on towards the door. Again bemused with delight Roger left the church. After nearly fourteen months of longing he had once more touched her hand and heard her voice.

Geneviève Boulanger had already gone the way of Louise Ferlet and Tonton Yeury, and he was now spending a few evenings a week with an attractive young woman named Reine Trinquet, but he determined to see no more of her. He could not bear the thought of letting any other girl even touch the hand that Athénaïs had touched. Henceforward he must keep it as sacred as though it were a part of her.

The next Sunday and the next he went through the same ritual with his adored at the church of St. Mélaine, but he was terrified that if he made any further advance he might lose the precious privilege that he had gained. At the same time, having given up the two or three evenings a week dancing to which he had become accustomed, for all his marvellous day-dreaming about Athénaïs, he found time begin to hang heavily on his hands.

As a remedy for this, taking out his sword one night to clean it provided him with an idea. It was over a year since he had done any fencing, and he had no intention of remaining a lawyer's clerk all his life. If he meant to become a really first-class swordsman it was high time that he got in some practice.

Inquiries soon provided him with the address of a fencing-master; one M. St. Paul, an ex-trooper of His Majesty's Musketeers. M. St. Paul's academy proved to be mainly a resort of the local aristocracy, but in this one matter of practising with weapons they seemed to have no class prejudices whatever; many old soldiers went there for an occasional bout and anyone who could handle a rapier or sabre efficiently was welcome. Roger's first visit resulted in the wiry little ex-Musketeer taking him on himself and, after expressing his satisfaction, agreeing to his coming whenever he wished on payment of a *franc* an evening.

In December the Emperor Joseph was reported as moving through the German States towards Holland with an army of 50,000 men, and, to the perturbation of the peaceable citizens of Rennes, all leave for the French army was cancelled as from the 1st of January. But Roger was now too taken up by thoughts of his weekly meetings with Athénaïs to bother his head any more about whether or no Europe was on the point of bursting into flames.

As Christmas approached he thought of sending her a New Year's gift, but could think of nothing that he could afford to buy which, in his eyes, would be worthy of her acceptance. Then, on further thought, he realised that in any case it might be extremely ill-advised to send her a present. Madame Marie-Ange no doubt regarded his offering Athénaïs the Holy Water each Sunday as a harmless courtesy inspired by gratitude; but if he sent a present the duenna might guess that he had a much stronger feeling for her charge and adopt Count Lucien's attitude towards him. Yet he felt that he could not allow the season of good will to pass without showing Athénaïs some mark of his feelings for her.

The inspiration then came to him to write a poem as, folded up into a small packet, he felt sure he could manage to slip it into her hand on the Sunday nearest New Year's day without Madame Marie-Ange seeing him do so.

Roger had a definite gift for expressing his thoughts clearly on paper and using French as a medium was no handicap to him as, after seventeen months in France without speaking a single word of English, he now habitually thought in French; but he had no flair for poetry. The result was that after several nights of cudgelling his brain he produced only a strange effusion which any serious critic would have regarded with scornful amusement. Nevertheless it did not lack for feeling and, being no critic himself, he was rather proud of it.

Without Madame Marie-Ange apparently noticing anything he managed to slip his verses into Athénaïs's hand, then he waited with the greatest impatience for the next Sunday in the hope that she might reward his efforts by some acknowledgement of them. In this he was disappointed, yet she gave him her usual gracious smile so he at least knew that she was not offended. In consequence, he set to work on another, longer, poem and, although the correspondence continued to be one-sided, he henceforth produced one a week for her.

This winter of 1784-85 the river did not freeze hard enough for there to be any skating, so he saw his beloved only at church and occasionally driving through the streets; but on none of these occasions was she accompanied by the young man he had seen pushing her sleigh on the ice the previous winter, so he had no cause for jealousy.

By February two French armies were being mobilised, one in Flanders and another on the Rhine, and war was now thought to be inevitable. But Roger took scant notice of such news, since he was wholly absorbed in his weekly poems for Athénaïs.

Spring came at last and with it, on a Sunday in mid-April, an event that created a drastic change in his whole outlook. As usual at the end of Mass he had, concealed in his hand, a poem for Athénaïs. Just as he was about to hand it to her she dropped her missal and stooped to recover it. He, too, bent swiftly to pick the book up for her. While they were both bent above it she stretched out both her hands, took his poem with one and, with the other, pressed into his free hand a little three-cornered *billet-doux;* then she retrieved her missal and, with a smiling bow to him, walked on towards the door.

Trembling with delight and impatience to read this, her first love letter to him, he hurried into a side chapel and unfolded the single sheet of paper. On it were a few scrawled lines in an untidy, illiterate hand that looked more like the laborious effort of a child of nine than the writing of a girl of nearly sixteen. It read:

Dear Monsieur Breuc,

This is to tell you how much I have enjoyed your poems. I think it very clever of you to write them. I wish that it was possible for us to meet so that we could talk again. I found you very unusual. You interested me very much because you have seen a side of life that I shall never know. But social barriers forbid us the pleasure of such conversations. This letter is also to bid you farewell. To-morrow I leave for our Château at Bécherel where we always spend our summers. Next winter I do not return to Rennes. 'Tis the desire of my father that I should join him at Versailles where I am to be presented and live at Court. So we shall not see one another any more. Good fortune to you Monsieur Breuc and may God have you in His Holy keeping.

Athénaïs Hermonaie de Rochambeau.

Had the roof of the church fallen upon Roger he could hardly have been more shaken. The fact that she had written to him at last, the pleasure she had derived from his poems, and her obvious liking for him all went for nothing beside the one heartbreaking thought that he was never to see her again. In all his previous trials he had managed to restrain his tears but, although he was now seventeen, he leant against a pillar of the chapel and wept unrestrainedly.

For a fortnight or more he could take no interest in anything. Madame Léger, Manon, Julien and Brochard all saw that he was desperately miserable about something, but he would not confide in any of them and their efforts to cheer him up were of no avail.

In the spring of that year there had been exceptionally little rain and May was a month of glorious sunshine, but it brought upon France the evil of a terrible drought. Even in Brittany, normally rich in dairy produce, butter, milk and cheese rose to phenomenal prices. The dearth of cattle fodder was so great that the King took the unprecedented measure of throwing open the Royal Chases to the livestock of his suffering people. Yet, as usual, while the rich went short of nothing the poor had to go without, and discontent against the ruling caste caused sullen murmurings in all the great cities.

It was one day in May that Roger saw sixty wretched men all manacled together being marched through the streets under a strong guard of soldiers. They had barely passed him when they were halted on the *Champ de Mars*, outside the barracks; so out of curiosity he turned back a few paces and asked one of the Sergeants of the guard who the unfortunate creatures were.

"They are felons, friend," replied the Sergeant. "We've marched them all the way from the Bicêtre prison in Paris, and are taking them to Brest. They are to be put on one of M. de la Perouse's ships. As you may know he is the great explorer, and he is shortly making a voyage to a strange land called New Zealand. 'Tis said that there are fine hardwood trees there for making ships' masts and such-like. 'Twas Admiral de Suffren's idea, I'm told, to dump this lot there as colonists. They'll hew the wood and each year one of our ships will pick it up, then we'll be a move ahead of the English.''

Roger thanked the man and turned away. He knew that Captain Cook had hoisted the British flag in New Zealand some fifteen years earlier and this looked as if the French intended making a secret attempt to jump the British claim. The matter certainly seemed worth reporting, so he wrote an account of it to his father's friend, Mr. Gilbert Maxwell, and in due course received a formal acknowledgement.

Austria and the United Provinces were still wrangling over the opening of the Scheldt, while their armies and those of France marked time on the frontiers, but it was now definitely felt that open hostilities would be averted, at least for this summer's campaigning season.

Gradually Roger's grief grew less poignant and he began to take up his amusements of the previous summer. At first he did so only half-heartedly but, finding that the society of other young women gave him a temporary respite from the gnawing longing he felt for Athénaïs, he plunged recklessly into a bout of dissipation, in an attempt to banish her altogether from his mind.

To a limited degree this violent medicine had the desired effect, but by the middle of July he was both disgusted with himself and utterly wearied of making love to girls for whom he did not give a fig.

One Sunday he went again to St. Mélaine, where Athénaïs had caused him so many violent heart-throbs and, after Mass, remained on there when the church had emptied, taking stock of his situation. It was two years, all but a few days, since he had run away from home, and where had he got to? Where were all the fine high hopes with which his dear, ambitious Georgina had imbued him? Where would the road that he was treading lead him? Certainly not to fortune. He had become a lawyer's junior clerk, working for a pittance.

He realised that in some ways he was very fortunate and that few young men of the *bourgeoisie* would have found any reason to complain at his lot. He lived in reasonable comfort with a family and friends who were kindness itself to him. His salary was small but, actually, more than sufficient for his needs, since life was very cheap in Rennes. As there were no theatres, except for occasional travelling shows, and the French did not either indulge in, or go to watch, any sports the young people were, perforce, thrown back on love-making as almost their sole amusement. They thought and talked of practically nothing else and, as only the girls of the upper classes were at all strictly chaperoned, there was abundant opportunity to indulge in casual affairs. But he, as some variety to that, also had his fencing and his interesting talks with Brochard on politics and international affairs.

He felt that he really had no right to be discontented yet he could not escape the worrying thought that this life of *laissez-faire* was leading him nowhere. When he had first started in Maître Léger's office it had been his intention to work there only until such time as he could save enough either to return to England or set out in search of more promising employment. He could have done so many months ago, and he suddenly realised that it was only his love for Athénaïs which had kept him in Rennes for so long. Now that she had gone why should he remain there longer? He had six *louis* put by. That was ample to keep him on the road for the best part of two months; and it was high summer again. Before he left the church he had made up his mind to give in his notice to Maître Léger and set out once more to seek a better fortune.

After dinner that evening he asked the lawyer if he could spare him a few minutes in his office. Immediately they were settled there he went straight to the point, and said:

"I trust you'll not think me ungrateful, Monsieur, for all the kindness and hospitality you have shown me; but I feel that the time has come when I should make a change and seek some other employment."

Maître Léger placed the tips of his fingers together and regarded Roger thoughtfully through his steel-rimmed spectacles.

"I'll not say that I am altogether surprised to hear this, *Rojé*. In fact, for some time past I've observed that you have become somewhat unsettled. I need hardly add that I am loath to lose you, and you will leave a sad gap in our little family circle. But you have an excellent intelligence and should go far. I take it that the cause of your wishing to leave us is that you feel there are not sufficiently tempting prospects for you here?"

"I must admit that is the case, Monsieur; but I am deeply touched by the kind things you say, and I, too, shall miss all of you prodigiously, wherever I may go."

"That sounds as if you have no plans as yet?"

Roger nodded. "I have nothing in view at all, but I have saved a few *louis;* enough to support me for some weeks, and during then I hope to find a fresh opening which at least may add to my experience."

"I admire your courage, but is that not rather rash?"

"Maybe it is," Roger agreed. "But the urge to try my luck again has come upon me."

"When do you wish to depart?"

"As soon as I have tidied up such matters as I have in hand and it is convenient to yourself, Monsieur."

"Will you seek employment here in Rennes, or elsewhere?"

"I had it in mind to go to Paris, Monsieur, and try my luck there at securing a secretaryship to some rich nobleman."

For a moment Maître Léger remained silent, then he said, "I much dislike the idea of your leaving us so ill-provided, and going to the capital with no security whatever as to some future means of livelihood. I am sure that if I recommend you to my Paris correspondent, Maître Jeurat, he would be willing to furnish you with similar employment to that which you have had here while you look round for something that may please you better. Would you like me to do so?"

"You overwhelm me," Roger replied with real gratitude. "In fact, you make me feel a positive ingrate for proposing that I should leave your service. If that could be arranged it would give me ample time to search for a really promising opening."

"So be it then," Maître Léger smiled, "I will write to Maître Jeurat to-morrow. We should hear something from him in a fortnight or so."

Despite its pleasant termination the interview had been something of a strain on Roger, so he decided to say nothing of his proposed departure for the time being to the other members of the Léger family and, wanting to think things over again, he went early to bed.

He could not help wondering if he had not been a fool to burn his boats like this. As he had never lived in a large city the idea of endeavouring to establish himself in Paris now frightened him a little. True, he would not be altogether without friends there if Maître Jeurat consented to accept him into his office as a temporary clerk; yet it was too much to expect that he would again have the luck to be adopted into a delightful family; and the memory of his first months in Rennes flooded back to him with horrid clarity. He felt that he would be unlucky indeed if he was forced once more to become a slave to another Hutot, but common sense told him that the best he could anticipate was loneliness in a cheap, uninspiring lodging-house. Beset by renewed uncertainty as to the wisdom of the step he had taken and dark forebodings as to his probable future, he fell asleep.

Yet he was not, after all, destined to go to Paris and work in Maître Jeurat's office. Fate once again took charge of his affairs in a most unexpected manner. The following afternoon Maître Léger sent for him and, looking up from his papers with a smile as Roger entered his office, said:

"My young friend, I think you must have been born under a.lucky star. Did you not say only last night that you would like to obtain a secretaryship to someone of importance?"

"Indeed I did, Monsieur," replied Roger with quick interest.

Maître Léger picked up a letter from his desk. "Then I think I have here the very thing for you. One of our most distinguished clients writes to me asking if I will find for him an assistant secretary to undertake some special work. The qualifications required are a certain amount of legal experience and a good knowledge of Latin. Board and lodging will be provided and the remuneration offered is forty *louis* per annum. If you like the idea I feel confident that I can recommend you for such a position with a clear conscience."

"I'd like nothing better!" Roger exclaimed with a happy laugh. "But tell me, Monsieur; where am I to take up this new situation, and what is the name of my proposed master?"

"Ah, yes!" said the lawyer. "Did I not mention it? You will proceed to the Château de Bécherel and make your service to *Monseigneur le Marquis de Rochambeau.*"

CHAPTER XIV

THE BARRIER

F o u r days later Roger arrived at Bécherel. The village lay about twenty miles to the north-west of Rennes and some five miles off the main road from the Breton capital to St. Malo. It consisted only of a single street of houses and a small stone church; half a mile beyond it, on the far side of a belt of trees, lay the château.

The building was E-shaped and had been designed by François Mansard about one hundred and forty years earlier. The two wings of the E formed an open courtyard, and the recessed central block contained the main entrance. It was of three storeys, the windows of the third being set in its high, steeply sloping slate roofs, from which projected an array of tall, symmetrically-placed chimneys. The long façade at its back gave on to a balustraded terrace below which there was a formal garden. Beyond this and to either side stretched wide parklands.

Roger would have liked to make his appearance cavorting gracefully on a mettlesome horse with a servant riding behind him, or at least, in a hired coach. But he could not afford such luxuries and he hoped that Athénaïs was not looking out of one of the windows as the one-horse cart, in which he and his heavy sea-chest had travelled from Rennes, slowly ambled past the front of the château and drew up at the stable entrance round its east side.

A servant found his old enemy, Monsieur Aldegonde, for him and the pompous major-domo showed considerable surprise on learning that Roger had come to take up his residence at the château; but he took the letter for the Marquis that Roger presented and twenty minutes later returned to give orders for his accommodation. A footman named Henri took him up to a bedroom on the third floor, under the Mansard roof, in the east wing, then led him down to a small chamber on the ground floor and told him to make himself comfortable there.

It was already evening and when he had sat there for some time the footman returned bringing him a meal on a tray. This was a sad disappointment, as Roger had thought that, as a private secretary, he would rank with the duenna and tutor, and feed with the family.

When he had eaten he expected to be sent for by the Marquis but two hours drifted by without his receiving any summons. Not knowing whether to wait up or go to bed, he pulled the bell and when the footman came asked to be taken to Aldegonde. Henri led him down several echoing passages and showed him into a room where the major-domo was sitting in a comfortable elbow chair, his wig and coat off, his feet up on a hassock and with a bottle of wine beside him on a small table.

It had already occurred to Roger that he might save himself many minor irritations during his stay at Bécherel if he took the trouble to placate the vanity of this arrogant head-servant, so he bowed politely and said:

"Pardon me for disturbing you at this hour, Monsieur Aldegonde, but I wondered if you could give me any idea if Monseigneur is likely to send for me to-night?"

" 'Tis most improbable," replied the fat major-domo, without stirring from his chair, "since Monseigneur is five miles away dining with his neighbour, Monsieur de Montauban. Normally, no doubt Monseigneur's secretary, M. L'Abbé d'Heury would have given you your instructions, but he too, is from home, and not expected back from Dinan until Friday."

"Thank you, Monsieur," murmured Roger; then, flushing slightly he took the big fence that he thought it wise, however painful, to get over once and for all.

"Last time we met it was in circumstances most embarrassing to myself. As you will recall, M. le Comte Lucien had me thrown out of the house; but I wish you to know, Monsieur, that this was only owing to my ignorance of social observances in this part of the world. You see, I come from one of the German provinces where life is vastly different; but while I am here, I shall endeavour to observe Breton customs, and I should be grateful if I may seek your guidance when I find myself in any difficulty."

Aldegonde gave him a sharp sideways glance. "That is a wise decision, Monsieur Breuc, as it is a good thing that senior *servants* should have a mutual respect for one another. On the score of Count Lucien you need trouble yourself no further, as he left us for the Military School at Brienne over a year ago. For the rest we will do what we can to make you comfortable."

To Roger, this was most excellent news and, after some further, rather stilted, small talk, Henri was summoned to show him the way up the back stairs to his bedroom.

In the morning Henri called him and said that his *petit déjeuner* would be served in half an hour in the room where he had eaten the night before. When he had had it he sat there all through the morning. He would have liked to explore the house and grounds, but did not like to do so from fear that, at any moment, he might be sent for.

He was still too excited at the thought that he would soon see his adorable Athénaïs again to be unduly depressed by this neglect of him, and whiled away the hours by browsing through some books in an old press that occupied one wall of the room. It was not until an hour after the midday meal that a footman he had not seen before came to say that Monseigneur required his presence.

The servant led him across a great echoing hall with balustraded balconies and, opening one-half of a pair of high double doors, ushered him into a room at the back of the house. It was a splendidly proportioned library with tall windows looking out on to the garden. In front of a great carved mantel, his hands clasped behind his back, stood the Marquis.

He was a tall, well-built man of about fifty, and one glance at his strong, haughty features was enough to show how Athénaïs had come by her imperious manner and good looks. His coat and knee-breeches were of rich, dark-blue satin, his stockings were of silk and his hair was powdered, being brushed back from his broad forehead and having set rolls above the ears. A pale-blue ribbon of watered silk came from each of his shoulders down to his chest then, forming a double V, ascended again to be clasped at its centre by a great diamond cluster in the fine lace jabot at his throat. He was an imposing and resplendent figure.

Roger made a deep bow: "Your servant, Monseigneur."

The Marquis took a pinch of snuff and raised one eyebrow. "You seem very young for the work I have in mind. How old are you?"

"Nineteen, Monseigneur," Roger lied, adding, as had long been his custom, two years to his age. "And I have worked in Maître Léger's office for twenty-two months."

"He gives you a good recommendation for intelligence and states that your Latin is excellent. Do you consider that you are capable of deciphering a mass of old documents and making a competent précis of their contents?"

"I trust so, Monseigneur. I had frequently to deal with old mortgages and contracts in my late employment."

"Very well then; come with me."

The Marquis led Roger upstairs to a sparsely-furnished room on the third floor, near his own. Against one wall there was a huge, old, iron-bound chest with a great, cumbersome triple lock. Walking straight over to it the Marquis unlocked it and, with his strong, capable hands, lifted the heavy lid. It was full to the brim with hundreds of neatly tied rolls of parchment, the majority of which were yellowed with age.

"These papers," he said, with a swift glance at Roger, "all have some bearing on a large estate in Poitou, named the *Domaine de St. Hilaire.* 'Tis my contention that through the marriage of my great-aunt this property should belong to me; but my claim is denied by the de Fontenay family, who still retain possession of it. The estate is valued at a million and a half *livres;* so 'tis worth some trouble to obtain sufficient data on which to base an action for its recovery. It will take many months, perhaps a year or more, of industrious application to extract all that may be of value from these documents, and I did not wish them to pass out of my possession for so long a period. Hence my idea of asking Maître Léger to recommend some suitable person to enter my employ and go through them here. This is your task. If you can produce enough evidence for me to establish my claim you will not find me ungrateful."

"I thank you, Monseigneur," Roger replied. "If the evidence is there you may rest assured that I will find it for you."

For the first time the Marquis looked at him as though he was a human being, and not merely an automaton with some legal training who might, or might not, serve his purpose.

"You show great self-confidence for one so young," he said, his beautifully modelled mouth breaking into a faint smile. "I think that, perhaps, Maître Léger was right to send you to me, rather than some dried-up old fogey. Shortly I am returning to Paris. I have no idea when I shall visit Bécherel again; but wherever I may be I do not wish to be bothered with this matter until your work is completed. In the meantime this room is yours to work in and my major-domo will pay you your salary and furnish you with anything you may require to facilitate your task."

"Am I—er—to continue to take my meals alone?" Roger hazarded.

The Marquis's eyebrows lifted. "Why, yes, I suppose so. Surely you would not prefer to eat them in the kitchen?"

"Oh, no, Monseigneur," said Roger hastily. "It was only—well, that I fear I shall find such a life a little lonely."

Again the Marquis regarded him with human interest. He was not used to his employees raising the question of their well-being with him and found himself, for once, rather at a loss.

"You could make a friend of the *Curé* in the village," he suggested after a moment, "then there is Aldegonde, and Chenou, my chief huntsman. The last is an excellent fellow. Are you town or country bred?"

"I was born in the country, and have lived in it most of my life."

"In that case you can ride, then. I am no votary of the chase, myself, and the coverts here are always overthick with game. Tell Chenou that I have given you permission to ride the horses in the stables, and to take out the falcons or go coursing when you wish."

"I am indeed grateful, Monseigneur. And in the long winter evenings? I am very fond of reading, particularly history. Would it be possible for me to borrow a few books?"

"Eh! Yes, why not. I prefer that my books should not be removed from the library; but no one ever uses the room when I am not here. In my absence you may read there if you like."

The Marquis was a man of quick perceptions and it had already struck him that Roger was a young man much above the run of the ordinary lawyer's clerk; otherwise it would never have occurred to him to make such concessions. But now his mind passed to another matter with which he was concerned and, as Roger thanked him, he murmured: "That will be all, then. The sooner you get down to work the better. Report to me when you have finished." Then, with a brief nod, he walked out of the room.

That evening Roger began to list the documents in the chest and, anxious as he was to see Athénaïs, he felt that he would be wise not to attempt to do so until her father was well out of the way; so for the next few days he continued his solitary existence and concentrated on his task.

When Sunday came the footman who looked after his simple requirements told him that Mass would be celebrated in the chapel of the château at eleven o'clock and informed him how to get there. Having donned his best suit and dressed with care he made his way across the great hall downstairs to the west wing, in which the chapel was situated. On learning that he was not, after all, to act as a private secretary to the Marquis, he had been greatly disappointed, but that did not affect his happiness at having become a permanent resident under the same roof as Athénaïs and now, at last, he would be able to gaze his fill at her once more.

On his reaching the chapel, Aldegonde beckoned him to a place between himself and a tall, black-bearded man, whom, in a whisper, he introduced as Monsieur Chenou. They were occupying the third pew; the two in front remained empty, while those behind were rapidly filling up with two or three score of other servants, all of whom took their places in order of rank, the back pews being filled with scullions and laundry girls. The men occupied the right-hand side of the aisle, the women the left. When everyone had taken their places the music began, then the Marquis came in with Athénaïs on his arm. At the top of the aisle they separated, stepping into the front pews, and Madame Marie-Ange, who had followed them in, took her place in the second pew, behind Athénaïs.

From his position Roger was able to look at his divinity's cameo-like profile from a slightly sideways angle, and he watched her all through the service, only wishing that it had been longer. On coming in she had not noticed him but as she came out on her father's arm her glance met his. It showed surprise, then a little frown that he had no means of interpreting, but which worried him all through the rest of the day.

As he left the chapel, however, his thoughts were temporarily diverted by Chenou asking him if he would like to see round the stables. Although he was in no mood to show as much interest as he normally would have done he accepted politely, as it was the first kind word that had been addressed to him since his interview with the Marquis three days previously.

The chief huntsman was a handsome-looking man in his late thirties, with clear grey eyes and a fine black beard and moustachios. He told Roger that he had formerly been a Sergeant in the Breton Regiment of Dragoons and that he controlled all the outside staff of the château while Monsieur Aldegonde was responsible for running the inside of it. He lamented the fact that his master was not the least interested in venery, but was delighted to hear that Roger had received permission to ride and the freedom of the chases. That afternoon they went out for a ride together and Chenou became even more well-disposed when he found that Roger was a competent horseman, with, for a young lawyer, a quite remarkable knowledge of hunting, shooting and fishing.

This new and promising friendship did something to take his mind off Athénaïs's unexpected coldness, but he was still worrying about it next morning when he received a visitor.

After an abrupt knock, a gaunt, stooping priest with thin, greying hair, a high forehead and piercing black eyes, came with a catlike step into his room.

Roger had seen him in the chapel the previous day assisting the *Curé* in the Celebration of the mass, and guessed that he must be the Marquis's secretary.

"I am L'Abbé d'Heury," the priest introduced himself, confirming Roger's guess, "and I felt that I must make your acquaintance before leaving for Paris, in case there is any way in which I can be of assistance to you."

After Roger had thanked him and assured him that he had everything he wanted, the Abbé lingered for only a few moments to make a few general remarks on the difficulties of the task that Roger had undertaken, then quietly withdrew.

The following morning, with two coaches, the first for himself and the Abbé d'Heury, the second for his personal chef, barber and valet, and preceded by a troop of outriders to clear his way through towns

and villages, the Marquis set out for Paris. In consequence, when evening came, Roger decided to avail himself of the permission he had received to occupy the library, and went down the main staircase in the hope that somewhere in that part of the house he might happen upon Athénaïs.

Having hung about the hall for a little, and, not liking to enter any of the other rooms uninvited, he went into the library and half-heartedly began to examine some of the shelves of beautifully bound books. He had been thus engaged for some half-hour when he heard a faint sound behind him and, turning, saw Athénaïs standing in the tall doorway.

She was in simple country clothes with her golden hair unpowdered, and to him she looked absolutely ravishing. But she did not acknowledge the leg he made her or return his smile. Instead, she said sharply:

"Monsieur Breuc! What are you doing here?"

"Your father gave me permission to use this room and to read his books," Roger replied in surprise.

"I do not mean that. What are you doing at Bécherel, living in the château?"

"I am analysing the contents of some documents for Monseigneur."

She made an impatient gesture. "Yes, yes! I learned that on Sunday after seeing you at Mass. Do you not understand that I resent, intensely, your following me here and insinuating yourself into my home?"

"But Athénaïs——!" he began in a hurt and puzzled voice.

Her blue eyes flashed. "How dare you call me Athénaïs! To you I am Mademoiselle de Rochambeau."

"But Mademoiselle!" he protested. "What have I done to bring upon myself your displeasure? Maître Léger offered me this post and I naturally accepted it."

"Would you have done so had you not thought that it offered you an opportunity to seek my society?"

Roger hesitated only an instant. "No, I would not. But I thought that you would be pleased to see me."

"On the contrary; your presence here embarrasses me exceedingly."

"Why should it?"

"Because you have taken advantage of a kind interest on my part to attempt to force yourself upon me."

"I don't understand," Roger held out his hands in a pathetic gesture. "In those poems I wrote for you I made clear my feelings, and in the note you gave me before leaving Rennes you said how much you wished that we could talk together."

"Surely you had the sense to realise that I meant that only if our circumstances were different?"

"Well, they are different," Roger cried desperately. "Good fortune has provided me with a way through the barrier that kept us apart. I now have a right to be in your house, so why should we not develop our friendship?"

Athénaïs tapped her foot impatiently upon the floor. "Since you force me to it I see that I must speak more plainly. That night, nearly two years ago, when you took refuge in my coach, I was only a little girl. I carried you home and, with a childish lack of values, insisted that you should dine with us. Even my small brother had the sense to see the unfitness of such a proceeding, but I was always headstrong. Later, it amused me to receive your verses. It had all the strangeness of a fairy tale; 'twas like receiving the homage of a man on Mars. But now, things are entirely different. I am grown up and you are no longer a man living in some strange other world. You are here, in this house, and simply as one of my father's servants. That fact has killed for ever any absurd romantic thoughts that I may have indulged in about you."

Roger stared at her in dismay. It was true that she was no longer a child. She had grown a lot in the past two years, her figure, although not yet fully formed, had filled out in gentle contours; her voice had lost its shrill note and become more melodious. He thought her more than ever desirable but he could not understand her attitude.

"How can you be so unkind!" he burst out. "That I work for your father makes me no other than I was. I am still the same person, and your most devoted slave."

"Monsieur!" she said haughtily. "Will you kindly understand that Mademoiselle de Rochambeau does not accept devotion, in the sense you mean it, from one who sits behind her in the chapel of her home. A person, in fact, who has placed himself on a par with people like Chenou and Aldegonde. 'Tis unthinkable; and your coming here was the worst possible error in good taste. If you wish to revive any spark of good feeling that I may have left for you, the best thing you can do is to pack your bag and leave here to-morrow morning."

Roger went as white as though someone had struck him. For a second he did not reply, then his blue eyes hardened and he snapped: "I'll do no such thing. Your father has given me work to do, and I'll remain here till I've done it."

"So be it!" she snapped back. "But I give you fair warning! If you seek to force yourself upon me I'll secure your dismissal by writing to my father. In the meantime, should we chance to meet about the château, you will speak only should I first address you; and you will keep your eyes lowered, as befits your position."

Snatching up a book that she had come to fetch, from a nearby table, she turned on her heel and marched regally from the room.

Poor Roger was quite shattered. In a brief three minutes his whole object in coming to Bécherel had been completely nullified. He felt that he would have done better by far to have gone to Paris, where new scenes and people might finally have worked Athénaïs out of his system. But, having said that he meant to stay on he determined to stick it out, rather than give her the satisfaction of having driven him away.

When Sunday came again it brought him at least the comfort of an unexpected kindness. Madame Marie-Ange met him in the garden. She returned his bow with a pleasant smile and suggested that he should walk with her for a while as she would like to talk to him.

Somewhat surprised he fell into step with her and, after a moment, she said: "I fear, Monsieur Breuc, that you find yourself in a somewhat difficult position here?"

"Not more so, Madame, than I would in any other strange household," he replied, colouring slightly.

"Oh, come!" she tapped his arm lightly with her fan. "You need have no secrets from me, and I know what is troubling you. Do you suppose I am so blind that I did not see you slip those little notes to Mademoiselle Athénaïs each Sunday last winter, in St. Mélaine?"

Roger's colour deepened to a brilliant pink. "Madame!" he stammered, "Madame, I——"

"Do not seek to excuse yourself," she went on quietly. "Athénaïs is a haughty and wilful girl, but she has many good qualities and a kind heart. As no harm could come of it I saw no reason why I should deprive either of you of this small pleasure. But, now that you have come to live at the château, I trust you will appreciate that, in my position, I could not countenance the continuance of what I have hitherto regarded as a childish frolic."

"Be at rest, Madame," Roger replied gloomily, "Mademoiselle Athénaïs has already made it clear to me that, now she is grown up, she no longer has any time for my romantic attentions. "

"I guessed as much. Hence your doleful looks, no doubt."

"I take it hardly, Madame, that Mademoiselle will no longer regard me as a friend."

"Did you expect it, then?" asked Madame Marie-Angé, raising her eyebrows.

"Why should I not?" he grumbled. "Because I have taken service with Monseigneur I have not, overnight, acquired bugs in my hair, or lost such culture as I formerly possessed."

"But surely, Monsieur, you realise that the difference in your stations renders such a friendship out of the question?"

"Why should it? You, Madame, are talking to me now with courtesy and kindness. Why should she not treat me in the same fashion?"

"Ah, but her situation and mine are far from the same. If I remember, you come from one of the German provinces, do you not? There is in them, I am told, much more freedom of intercourse between the classes; but here etiquette is still most strict upon such matters. My late husband, Monsieur Velot, was a Councillor of the Parliament of Rennes, and so a noble of the robe. Had I a house of my own I might, if it so pleased me, occasionally entertain Maître Léger to dinner, but Monseigneur would never dream of doing such a thing. He might, perhaps, have entertained my late husband now and then, as a mark of favour; but he accepts me regularly at his table only because I am his daughter's duenna. And you, my young friend, are not even Maître Léger; you are naught but one of his clerks. So you see what a great gulf there is fixed between you and Mademoiselle Athénaïs? In view of the little passages which I was indulgent enough to allow to pass between you, I hope you now see what an embarrassment your sudden arrival here has caused her?"

" 'Twas very different where I come from," Roger said, more

reasonably. "But now that you have explained matters I do see that Mademoiselle has some excuse for her sudden change of front towards me. To tell the truth she even suggested that I should relieve her of my presence altogether. But I did not feel inclined to leave Bécherel except on a direct order from Monseigneur."

"Whether you go or stay is your own affair, providing you do not attempt to overstep the bounds of your position. Be advised by me, Monsieur Breuc, and either leave here now, or make up your mind once and for all that Athénaïs can never be anything to you."

"Having undertaken certain work for Monseigneur, 'twould be difficult to find a suitable excuse for my sudden departure. I feel that I should stay on, at least until I have made some progress in it."

"In that case, continue to adore Athénaïs from a distance if you will, but I beg you to refrain from any rash act which would necessitate my asking for your dismissal. 'Twould be wise to engage your thoughts with other interests, as far as possible."

"I will endeavour to do so, Madame."

As they regained the terrace, Madame Marie-Angé turned and smiled at him. "That is well. It may be that I can help you in that, a little. Athénaïs practises upon her harpsichord between four and five each afternoon. At that hour you will always find me alone in my boudoir. I usually employ it to read the latest news sheets while drinking a cup of chocolate. If you feel lonely at any time come and join me, and we will talk of the doings of the great world together."

"Madame, you are of the true noblesse," said Roger, and bowing over her hand he kissed it.

In the next fortnight or so he settled down to a steady routine. The documents gave him plenty of mental occupation, as some of them were in semi-archaic writing several centuries old, and needed prolonged study before he felt confident enough about their contents to set down a précis of it in French. When, after several hours of work, he found himself badly stuck he broke off to take a walk round the garden, go for a ride, or, if it were round four o'clock, take a cup of chocolate with Madame Marie-Angé.

The garden he found most disappointing. He had expected that it would be something like those of Walhampton, Pylewell and other big houses near his own home; instead it occupied somewhat less ground than the château itself. It had no fine lawns with gracious trees, no shady walks through flowering shrubberies, no herbaceous borders, nor ornamental lakes; it consisted only of a score of formal, box-edged beds, intersected by gravel paths and arranged geometrically about two large stone fountains.

The house, on the other hand, with its marble staircases, painted ceilings and elaborately carved doors must have cost a fortune; and, as he began to find his way about it, he never tired of admiring the splendid tapestries, furniture and *objets d'art* that it contained.

When he visited Madame Marie-Angé they never spoke of Athénaïs but discussed the contents of the news sheets, and towards the end of August they learned of an affair that had set all France in a dither. On the fifteenth of that month the Cardinal Prince, Louis de Rohan,

Grand Almoner to the King, had been publicly arrested as he left the chapel of Versailles in his pontifical robes and, by His Majesty's order, imprisoned in the Bastille.

Nothing was known for certain, but the report ran that the Cardinal was accused of having forged the Queen's signature on an order to the Court jewellers, and thereby fraudulently obtaining a diamond necklace valued at one million six hundred thousand *livres*. What made the affair seem so extraordinary was that de Rohan was one of the richest nobles in France; so rumour already had it that some deep intrigue unconnected with money lay at the bottom of this mysterious affair.

The wrangle between the Austrians and the Dutch had gone on all through the summer, but now Louis XVI had offered himself as a mediator; so it was hoped that with the aid of France a definite settlement might be reached. But Dutch anxieties were, at the moment, being added to by grave internal troubles amongst themselves.

The Stadtholder, William V of Orange, had succeeded his father at the age of three, and his long minority had enabled the Republican party—which was in fact a body of rich, ambitious merchants who wished to replace the throne by an oligarchy—to gain great power. On attaining his majority, in 1766, the Stadtholder had entered into a pact with the Duke of Brunswick, who had previously acted as his Regent, to assist him in governing the country. This was regarded by the Republicans as unconstitutional and, after years of intrigue they had, the previous October, at last forced the Duke's resignation. Abandoned by his minister the weak and inept William now found himself at the mercy of his enemies. A tumult had broken out in the Hague and the States-General had deprived him of the command of the garrison; upon which he had taken refuge in Gelderland, one of the few States remaining loyal to him.

From time to time Roger came face to face with Athénaïs in the house or garden and, while nothing would have induced him to show the servility of lowering his eyes in her presence, as she had ordered, he made no attempt to speak to her. He always bowed politely and she acknowledged his salutations with calm aloofness. But towards the end of September he was destined to see her in an entirely new guise.

It was on a Sunday morning and, on his way to chapel, he slipped on the marble stairs. By grabbing at the balustrade he managed to save himself from falling, but his nose came in violent contact with a nearby pillar, and started to bleed. Thinking it would soon stop he went on to his usual seat between Aldegonde and Chenou, but all through the service the bleeding continued and by its end his handkerchief was soaked through with blood.

Immediately they came out Chenou said: "You must do something to stop that bleeding. 'Tis Mademoiselle's hour in her surgery, so you had best go there at once and let her attend to it for you."

"Surgery!" snuffled Roger, "I did not know she had one."

"Why, yes! 'Tis in the west wing, round by the Orangery. Come, I will take you there."

Roger would have liked to refuse but, as his nose was still bleeding profusely, he did not very well see how he could do so, and as he accompanied Chenou across the courtyard he asked: "How long is it since Mademoiselle has taken to practising medicine?"

"From the time she was quite little, when she used to help her mother," Chenou replied. 'But since Madame la Marquise died, three years ago, she has continued to run the surgery with the aid of Madame Velot. The sick poor from the village come up to the château each Sunday after Mass, and she tells them what to do for their ailments."

At the entrance to the surgery they found a little crowd of village people patiently waiting their turn, but Chenou insisted that Roger needed immediate attention and pushed him in ahead of them. The walls of the room were lined with shelves carrying an array of big jars and bottles; behind a heavy oak table Madame Marie-Angé and the *Curé* were busy handing out ointments and medicines; Athénaïs, her clothes covered by a white smock, was dressing an ugly ulcer on the leg of an old peasant.

As Roger came in she looked at him in surprise, then, seeing the bloodstained handkerchief he was holding to his face she told the *Curé* to bandage up the old man's leg for her, and beckoned Roger over.

His nose had now swollen up and his eyes were still watering, so he presented a most woebegone appearance and, although for a moment she tried to restrain her mirth, she could not help laughing at him. He hardly knew whether he was pleased or annoyed, but she could not have been kinder or more gentle as she bathed his face, anointed the injured member with a soothing ointment and, having put a cold-water compress on it, made him lie down on a couch until the bleeding should cease.

It was this episode which convinced him that, if he could only find some way of breaking down this absurd social barrier that lay between them, he might yet gain her friendship and affection. But how to do so seemed an almost insoluble problem.

He thought of seeking her out and telling her the whole truth about himself—that he was, in fact, the son of an English Admiral and the grandson of an Earl; but he had carried on his imposture as a native of Strasbourg for so long that he did not think she would believe him. Once more he began to conjure up fantastic day-dreams in which she was beset by some dire peril from which he rescued her in the nick of time; yet in the quiet, sheltered life that she led at Bécherel it seemed that no event could possibly occur that would enable him to draw his sword in her defence.

Nevertheless he began, almost unconsciously at first, to neglect his work in order to seek opportunities of watching her from a distance; and he soon discovered that his best chances of this were when she went out riding. She was always accompanied by a groom and, in any case, he had no intention of forcing himself upon her. But she drew him like a magnet, and, as he could take a horse from the stable at any time, it was easy for him to ride out after her and, while unobserved himself, follow her at half a mile or so for the joy of looking his fill at her slim, elegant figure.

He was following her in this way one afternoon in mid-October, when he saw that her groom's horse had cast a shoe. After a short colloquy with her the man turned back, and it was obvious that Athénaïs meant to finish her ride alone, so Roger continued to follow her at a distance.

Some twenty minutes later a peasant child ran out of a hedge, causing the mettlesome mare that Athénaïs was riding to shy violently. Next moment the mare had bolted.

Roger's heart seemed to leap up into his throat with apprehension, but it was just the chance he had been waiting for to show his prowess and devotion. Spurring his own mount into a gallop he set off after her in wild pursuit.

But for the double hedge, bordering a lane, from which the child had run out, the country was open pasture land. Both horses made good going, but Roger's was the more powerful animal and after covering half a mile he was already gaining on Athénaïs. She had lost her three-cornered hat and her golden ringlets were flying in the wind, but she seemed to have a good grip of her saddle.

As Roger decreased his distance to her he saw that she was pulling hard on her right rein. Evidently she was trying to steer her runaway mount in the direction of a belt of woodland that lay some three-quarters of a mile away. He imagined that she was counting on the mare slackening her pace, or coming round in a circle, when she saw the barrier of trees. It flashed upon him that Athénaïs might be carried in among them and dashed from her saddle by one of the low branches.

Spurring his own horse to fresh efforts he came charging up on her right. Heading her off from the trees he forced her mare towards the open country, which continued to the left.

Athénaïs shouted something to him but her voice was drowned in the thunder of the hoof-beats. Leaning forward he made a snatch at her bridle. At that moment the mare veered still more towards the left, and he missed it.

Again Athénaïs shouted, but again he failed to catch her words. For two hundred yards they raced on neck to neck. Suddenly he saw a break in the ground ahead. Instantly he realised what Athénaïs had been shouting at him. Her cry had been a warning: "The river! The river lies ahead!"

He remembered then that a tributary of the Rance made a wide loop there, running along a concealed gully that threaded the flat plain. Next instant he saw it. The sluggish stream lay between two steeply shelving banks and the horses were now no more than a dozen yards from the verge of the nearest.

There was no time left to bring Athénaïs's mare down to a canter. Leaning forward again Roger seized her rein and jerked upon it with all his strength. The mare, too, had seen the water. Splaying her forefeet she suddenly stopped dead. Athénaïs was shot straight over her head and landed with a resounding splash in the river.

Roger was flung forward on his horse's neck, but managed to regain his saddle and, still holding both bridles, slid to the ground. With horrified eyes he watched Athénaïs. She was in no danger, as the water was shallow, yet had been deep enough to break her fall.

Drenched to the skin, her lovely face blotched with mud and her hair hanging in damp rat's-tails she had picked herself up and, struggling with her long sodden skirts, was plodding through the slimy mire back to the bank.

He knew that it was his own misdirection of affairs that had led to her receiving this ducking, yet he could not even go to her assistance without risking the horses bolting and leaving them stranded there, miles from home.

Still clutching her riding-switch she staggered from the water and up the slope. Then, her face chalk-white beneath the smears of slime and her blue eyes blazing, she flared at him.

"You miserable fool! I've checked a runaway before now! I would have had my mare under control a mile back, had not the hoof-beats of your horse following behind urged her to gallop faster. And then, of all the senseless idiocy, to ride me into the river! This comes of your spying upon me. Oh, don't deny it! Of recent weeks you've done naught but lurk behind corners and goggle at me from the windows. Think you the servants, too, have no eyes to see such things. I doubt not there is many a jest coupling your name with mine cracked in the kitchen. Oh, 'tis intolerable! I die for very shame to think that such scum should bandy my name about on account of a nobody like you. I hate you for it!"

For a second she paused for breath. Then, lifting her riding-switch, she struck him with it, as she cried: "You wretched upstart! Take that, and that, and that! Then go back and show them your miserable face with the marks of my displeasure."

Again and again her swift-cutting strokes descended on Roger's face, head, hands and shoulders. Letting go the bridles of the horses he strove to protect himself from her furious onslaught, but he could neither fend off nor evade her slashes.

There was only one thing to do. Stepping forward he grabbed her arm and twisted the riding-switch from her grasp.

"How dare you lay hands on me!" she gasped. " 'Tis a crime to lay hands on one of noble blood. I'll have you flogged for that! I'll have the hand that touched me cut off at the wrist!"

"Then have my head cut off as well!" cried Roger, angered beyond endurance. "By God! I'll teach you that you can't strike a free man with impunity! What's more, you arrogant little fool, I'll punish you in a way that will be a lesson to you. Aye, even if I die for it."

Seizing her round the waist he pulled her to him. Grasping her chin with his left hand he forced up her face. Then, he kissed her hard and full upon the mouth.

CHAPTER XV

THE DREAM

F O R a long moment she lay passive in his arms, then she wrenched herself away and stood staring at him. Her eyes were round, not with fright, but with some emotion that he could not analyse.

198

Slowly drawing the back of her hand across her mouth, she whispered: "You shouldn't have done that. No man has ever done that to me before."

"Then there is less chance that you'll forget it," he said harshly. His face and hands were stinging abominably and thin red weals were springing up in the dozen places where the switch had lashed them. He felt not a twinge of remorse as he went on: "However many Dukes and Princes may kiss you in the future you'll always remember that your first kiss was given you by a servant, an upstart, a nobody. That is, unless you have the sense to realise that if we both cut ourselves your blood would show no bluer than mine; and that 'tis no disgrace to be kissed by a man who loves you."

"If I tell my father of this, he will have you branded with red-hot irons and thrown into prison afterwards," she said slowly.

His bruised lips pained him as he gave a twisted smile. "I know it. I've lived here long enough to realise that the nobility has devised the most fiendish punishments for anyone who lays a finger on their womenfolk. So it seems that my love for you must be mighty desperate for me to have risked that kiss."

" 'Twas not love, but hate, that inspired you at that moment."

"Maybe, you're right. Maybe, though, 'twas contempt for all you stand for; coupled with the wish to melt that stony heart of yours."

"Mount me on my mare," she ordered suddenly.

Obediently, he held out his hand about two feet from the ground; she placed a small foot in its palm and, as he took her weight, sprang into the saddle.

"My whip," she demanded, and added as he gave it to her: "You are not to follow me for an hour." Then, turning her mare, she galloped away.

Left to himself Roger descended to the river's edge and bathed his smarting face and hands. When the pain had eased a little he sat down to consider the possible outcome of his rash act.

Soon after his arrival at the château Athénaïs had had one of the footmen thrashed for spilling a cup of chocolate down her gown; so he felt that she was quite capable of having him branded and imprisoned for his infinitely more serious offence.

At the moment he was still a free man, and so not compelled to return to the château. Twilight was now falling, and he had a good horse upon which he could put many miles between himself and Bécherel during the night. But he had only a little silver on him and if Athénaïs requested the authorities to arrest him there was little chance of his being able to get clean away.

He felt, too, that it would be the act of a coward to attempt to run away. By returning to face whatever fate she might decree for him, he could at least show her that he was not lacking in courage; and there was always the possibility that, furious as she might be, she would shrink from humiliating herself further by telling anyone what had occurred, and, rather than that, let the matter drop.

When the hour was up he rode slowly back through the deepening shadows, handed his mount over to a stable boy and went up by the back stairs to his room. On looking in the mirror he saw that his face was a network of angry red weals and he wondered how to account for its condition to the servants. The easiest way seemed to give out that his horse had bolted with him and carried him full tilt into a grove of alders, the springy shoots of which had whipped fiercely at his face as he was swept wildly through them. As the weals were straight, short lines and not the least like scratches the story was somewhat thin, but he was too tired and depressed to worry further over it and decided that it must serve.

However, instead of going downstairs for his supper he went straight to bed, with the idea that the bedclothes would serve to partially conceal his injuries, and that he would remain there till they were better.

In due course, Henri came to inquire why he had not come down for his evening meal, and Roger gave his explanation, adding that he had also hurt his leg, so would probably stay in bed for a day or two. The man brought his supper on a tray and, after eating it, while still wondering what the outcome of the afternoon's events would be, he dropped asleep.

After his *petit déjeuner* he spent the morning hours in considerable anxiety, listening for any heavy footfalls in his lonely corridor which might herald the approach of a group of servants sent by Athénaïs to apprehend him. At last, just before midday, the footfalls came.

There was a knock on his door, then, to his amazement, Athénaïs's clear voice called: "Monsieur Breuc, may we come in?"

"Come . . . come in," he stammered, wondering what on earth was about to happen.

Followed by Madame Marie-Angé, she walked in and said calmly: "I am told that you met with an accident when out riding yesterday. I trust that it is nothing serious, and we have come to attend to your hurts as well as we can."

There was not a trace of expression in her eyes or voice and with a muttered, "No, no, Mademoiselle, it is nothing serious, I assure you," he went on to tell them his version of how he had come by his now empurpled face.

"My, my! How those alder shoots must have stung you!" exclaimed Athénaïs, after one close look at his injuries. "But this will soothe the angry places they have made," and taking a pot from Madame Marie-Angé she began to apply some of the ointment it contained.

The sympathy of her words was swiftly belied by her actions; as, with her back turned to Madame Marie-Angé, she proceeded to rub the ointment into his cuts as though she was scrubbing a floor.

When she had done, both of them talked to him for a little, then, bidding him stay where he was until he was fully recovered, they left him to his thoughts.

One cardinal fact emerged from this visit. Athénaïs had evidently decided that it would be best to let sleeping dogs lie; so he was not yet destined to have his hand cut off, be branded on the shoulder with a red-hot iron, or cast into a dungeon. Yet he felt that he could hardly regard her ministrations as the offering of an olive branch. They had been much too painful for that. On thinking it over he came to the conclusion that she was very far from being a little fool and, having decided to keep her humiliation to herself, had realised that she must continue to behave towards him in a normal manner; and, in consequence, had treated him just as she would any other member of the château staff who had been reported to her as in bed as the result of an accident.

Nevertheless, he now began to feel a slight twinge of guilt at his own behaviour, and, as the day wore on, it grew. He did not believe that most girls of sixteen would have been so shattered by a kiss, even if it was their first. He knew that, as she saw things, she had a perfect right to strike him, and he realised now that he had given her real cause for anger by dogging her footsteps, as he had. It had never occurred to him at the time that his actions would be noticed and commented on by the servants, but, of course, they must have seen him lurking in the corridor outside her boudoir and riding out after her in the afternoons. Naturally they would have talked among themselves, and she had good cause to resent that. In view of the traditional chastity in which young French girls of noble birth were brought up she no doubt regarded his kiss almost in the nature of a rape, and that was far beyond anything that he had intended.

By the following day he had reached the conclusion that she had really acted with extraordinary forbearance in not sobbing out the truth on Madame Marie-Angé's broad bosom, and, without anyone else knowing the cause of the matter, leaving her duenna to order his locking up until the Marquis could be informed of his crime.

In spite of its harsh application, the ointment Athénaïs had applied to his cuts both soothed and healed them rapidly; so, on the third morning after his whipping, on looking at himself in the mirror, he decided that he might show his face downstairs without arousing undue comment.

Another night of solitude and reflection had reduced him to a definite state of remorse, for what he now thought of as his churlish brutality, so he determined to seek out Athénaïs and, at the first suitable opportunity, humbly beg her pardon.

His surprise and dismay can, therefore, be imagined when he learnt that she and Madame Marie-Angé had taken coach for Paris on the previous day. According to their plans, as he had understood them, they had not been due to leave Bécherel for the capital for another fortnight; so it seemed that Athénaïs, unable to bear the thought of being reminded of the shame he had put upon her, by seeing him about the place, had devised some way of manœuvring Madame Marie-Angé into advancing the date of their departure.

Only too clearly he recalled the contents of the note that Athénaïs had pressed into his hand the previous April. It had said that she would not be seeing him again, as next winter, instead of returning to Rennes she was to be presented at Court. And, as he now realised, once she was established there, the chances of her returning to Bécherel for the following summer were extremely slender. Not only had he lost her but she had left before he had had a chance to beg her pardon for his outrageous conduct, and must have carried away with her a bitter, angry memory of him in her heart.

After a few days of acute depression he flung himself into his work again with renewed energy, in an attempt to make up for lost time and keep himself from brooding over her; and soon the mass of old documents were occupying most of his thoughts. As he delved deeper into them the problem of the rightful ownership of the *Domaine de St. Hilaire* began to take on a deep fascination for him. In a few weeks he became a positive mine of information on the genealogical trees of half the great families in western France. Each time he unearthed a new link in the chain he felt a thrill of excitement, and each time he came upon a settlement or will that blocked the claim he was endeavouring to establish he felt as though he had lost a battle.

Now and again the tall, black-bearded Chenou came upstairs to invade his workroom and insist that it was high time he got some exercise. Sometimes they rode together, at others, when the weather was inclement, as the ex-Dragoon was a fine swordsman, they practised their skill with rapier and sabre in the tennis court adjacent to the stables. Monsieur St. Paul had taught Roger some useful thrusts in his academy at Rennes, the previous winter, but Chenou taught him more; and now that the strength of a well-set-up young man was added to his agility he was rapidly becoming a really dangerous antagonist.

Occasionally on their rides they halted to take a glass of wine with Monsieur Lautrade, the Marquis's bailiff who lived in a little house in a clearing of the woods some distance from the château. Lautrade was a fat, elderly, bespectacled man, kind by disposition but firm by habit, as he had to be in order to extract his master's rents at the dates they were due from the ever-complaining farmers.

On one such visit Roger asked him if the case of the peasants was really so hard as it appeared, and he replied:

"Monsieur Breuc, it varies greatly in different parts of the kingdom. Here in Brittany, in Languedoc and in the German provinces, things are not too bad, because the nobility have managed to retain something of their independence. That makes for good conditions on some estates and bad ones on others; but at least it is better than the rule that maintains in the greater part of France. There, the Intendants wield almost absolute power, and the thousands of petty government servants who work under them is each a little tyrant, producing nothing and living like a parasite on the labour of people who are hard put to it to support themselves.

"Again different systems of tenure have grown up in various areas. In Picardy, Flanders and other provinces of the north, the nobles and clergy are accustomed to let their land in large farms. That is a good thing; such farms are the best cultivated, the farmers become men of substance and their hired labourers are paid a wage which often enables them to save enough to buy a small plot of land of their own. The peasant is always hungry for land, of course. But I am not of the opinion that its possession profits him."

"Why do you say that, Monsieur?" asked Roger. "I should have thought it a good thing for a man to have a piece of land of his own."

"Experience does not go to show that as far as smallholders are concerned. 'Tis estimated that two-fifths of the kingdom consists of little plots owned by the peasants and 'tis they, not the hired labourer, whose condition is most wretched. Apart from the north all France is honeycombed with these smallholdings which have been acquired piecemeal from the nobles, either on outright payments or on the *métayer* system."

"What is that, Monsieur?"

"A *métayer* is one who acquires the right to cultivate a piece of land in return for a share of its produce. The system is always unsatisfactory, as the cultivator is naturally tempted to conceal the true bulk of his crops and the landlord, rightly or wrongly, always believes that he is being cheated."

"Even so," remarked Roger, "if the peasants have succeeded in buying nearly half the land in France it does not seem that their condition can be so deplorable."

Monsieur Lautrade nodded. "They would be no worse situated than the peasantry of other countries were they left to go about their work as they wished, and allowed to dispose of their produce as they thought fit. 'Tis the *corvée* and the *droits de seigneur* which deprive them of any hope of prosperity and fill them with discontent. By the *corvée* they may at any time, perhaps at such important seasons as the sowing or the harvest, be taken from their land for enforced labour on the roads, bridges and other government construction. And in many places the *droits de seigneur* are extremely oppressive.

"Do they vary then? I thought the *droit de seigneur* was the right of a noble to send for any girl living in one of the villages on his estate, on the night of her marriage, and have her sleep with him whether she was willing or no."

" 'Tis one of the *droits*," agreed the bailiff, with a smile. "And 'twas exercised, no doubt, in the middle ages. But can you see a fastidious gentleman like Monseigneur taking one of our uncultured village wenches into his bed?"

"I know one or two that I would not mind taking into mine," Chenou grinned.

"You do so, anyhow, you handsome rogue," laughed Lautrade. " 'Tis said that not one of them is safe from you, and that they fall willing enough victims to your fine black moustachios."

"Aye! I have my share of fun," the chief huntsman acknowledged. ,But you're right about Monseigneur, and his kind. They have no stomach for such strong, garlic-flavoured dishes and have long since ceased to exercise their privileges."

"I was referring to numerous other *droits*," Lautrade went on. "There are many and they vary with each manor, but some are common to all. There is the *droit de colombier*, by which the *seigneur* may keep as many pigeons as he chooses, which find their food as much in the peasants' fields as in his own; the *droit de chasse*, which reserves all game exclusively for the *seigneur's* amusement. Then there are the *banalités* which oblige the peasant to send his corn to the *seigneur's* mills, his grapes to the *seigneur's* wine-press, and his flour to the *seigneur's* oven. For each such operation a fee is exacted and on badly run estates the work is often ill-done or subject to irritating delays against which there is no redress. In addition there are the *péages*, or tolls that the peasant is called on to pay whenever he takes a cart-load of produce more than a mile or so from his home. To use every road or cross any river he must pay something either to the Crown, the Church, or to some noble. But you must know this yourself, and that one must also pay to cross each line of customs barriers that separate the provinces from one another. 'Tis this infinity of little outgoings that rob the peasant of his substance."

"It sounds a most burdensome catalogue," Roger agreed. "But surely the *noblesse* could well afford to give some relief from this local taxation?"

Lautrade shrugged. "The rich ones who live at Versailles know little of the peasants' lot and care less. The rest, and they form the great majority, are mostly too poor themselves to make such a sacrifice. For hundreds of years such families have sent their menfolk to France's wars, and to ·equip themselves for each campaign they have been compelled to part with a little more of their land to the thrifty peasants. Now, thousands of them have naught left but a château and a few acres of grazing ground. 'Tis that which makes them so insistent on the retention of their privileges. I know of noble families who eke out a miserable existence on as little as twenty-five *louis* a year; and if they gave up their *droits* they would be faced with starvation."

"To my mind, 'tis the restrictions on selling produce that hit the peasant hardest," cut in Chenou. "In a bad season he garners scarce enough to feed himself, so 'tis but fair that when he has a good one he should be allowed to make a bit for putting by. Yet the corn laws forbid him to sell his surplus to the highest bidder, and he is compelled to turn it in at the Government depôt for whatever skinflint price the grain ring have agreed to give for it. But come, I must be getting back to take a look at a mare that should be foaling some time to-night."

As he stood up Roger rose with him, and said angrily: "Such measures are iniquitous, and I no longer wonder that so many people curse the government. I doubt if people in any other country would suffer its continuance."

"Nay, take not an exaggerated view," demurred Lautrade, as he escorted them to the door. "Serfdom is now almost abolished in France, and the whole country is far richer than it was half a century ago. The peasants live a hard life but their condition here is better than in any other part of Europe, except perhaps in England and the United Provinces. If you would see real poverty, you should go to Spain as I did, not many years ago, to bring back a fresh supply of trees for Monseigneur's orangery."

Still thinking of these things Roger rode back to the château, to find that a letter had arrived from his mother. In it she told him that, after two years at Portsmouth, his father had now been reposted as Rear-Admiral, Channel Squadron; so, as long as no war broke out, his ships would spend a great part of the year in harbour and, to her joy, he could continue to be much at home.

Roger took the news quite casually. Occasionally he still longed to be back in England, but the time had passed when he would have given almost anything to return and have the chance of starting his career again. He now had not only good food and comfortable quarters, but servants to wait on him, horses to ride and a splendid library at his disposal. His task was a fascinating one and he was not tied to it by any regulated hours. His pay of forty *louis* a year was the equivalent of the salary that, on his last night at Sherborne, old Toby had told him he might hope to receive after getting his B.A. as a tutor to a nobleman's son. It was no fortune, but it was clear gain as he could not spend a single *sou* of it as long as he remained at Bécherel. In the meantime he was, for all practical purposes, his own master and, enjoying as he did the *droit de chasse*, led a life not far removed from that of the *petit noblesse*, yet without any of its cares and responsibilities.

By the approach of Christmas he found himself a little jaded from his long hours of poring over the old parchments, and while Chenou was the best of companions with whom to hunt or fence, Roger began to feel an oppressive sense of loneliness during the long dark evenings; so he decided to take a holiday and spend Christmas with the Légers.

He could have ridden in to Rennes but he wanted to take a good supply of Christmas fare to his friends, so Chenou made no difficulty about placing a coach at his disposal; and when he left on the morning of Christmas Eve the coach carried more than his own weight in venison, hares and partridges.

The Légers, Brochard, Manon and Julien Quatrevaux were all delighted to see him and, to his great pleasure, he learned that the latter two had decided to regularise their liaison by getting married in the spring; so Julien, as Manon's fiancé, now made one of the family party.

They gave him news of the other friends he had made in Rennes, related to him the latest gossip, and brought him up to date on the affairs of the wider world from which, in recent months, he had been almost completely isolated.

The principal topic of interest was still a flood of rumours in connection with the *affaire du Collier*, as the scandal centring round the stolen diamond necklace had come to be called. It appeared that the necklace had been offered to the Queen, but she had publicly refused to buy it; saying that for a million and a half *livres* the King could get him a battleship, and that his need of another ship-of-the-line was greater than her need for more diamonds. But, so rumour ran, she had determined to buy this unique collection of gems privately and, as her agent, had used an ambitious and designing woman called the Countess de Valois de la Motte; then, having entered into the bargain, she had found herself short of funds and resorted to borrowing from the fabulously wealthy Cardinal, who was anxious to gain her favour. There seemed no doubt that the Cardinal had received the necklace from the jewellers and sent it to the Queen, imagining that he was acting on her wishes, by the hand of Madame de la Motte; but the Queen flatly denied having received the necklace and ever having entered into any correspondence with the Cardinal.

Madame de la Motte, an adventurer styling himself Count Cagliostro and a courtesan named Mademoiselle Gay d'Oliva, had been sent to join the Cardinal de Rohan in the Bastille; and he, although as a Prince of the Church not normally subject to the jurisdiction of a secular court, was so determined to prove his innocence that he had agreed to submit to a public trial by the Parliament of Paris. All France was agog for the disclosures which it was expected would be made at the trial, as the honour of not only the Cardinal but also the Queen was now at stake.

One evening towards the end of Roger's stay, Brochard took him down to their old haunt for a chat, and asked him how he spent his evenings at the château.

"Sometimes I work," replied Roger, "but as the Marquis has given me the run of his fine library, I more often make myself comfortable in there with a book."

For a time they talked literature and on Brochard learning that Roger had been entertaining himself with the plays of Corneille, Racine and Molière, the serious-minded Bordelais reprimanded him; saying that if he wished to become a lawyer he should use this opportunity to ground himself in sociology, and read such authors as Montesquieu, Dupont of Nemours, de Quesnay, Rousseau, Voltaire, Mirabeau and Mably.

To become a good lawyer was by no means Roger's final ambition in life, but he said that he would be glad to have a list to take back with him as he had no doubt that many of those authors were on the Marquis's shelves. Brochard then asked him if he still took an interest in international affairs.

"As far as I am able to do so," Roger told him, "but since the departure of the family the news sheets no longer reach us. I heard, though, a few weeks ago, from Monseigneur's bailiff that the Dutch affair had at last been settled."

Brochard nodded. "Yes, by the Treaty of Fontainebleau, signed on November the eighth. By it the Dutch have agreed to demolish their forts on either bank of the Scheldt and open the river to the Austrian traffic. The Emperor, in return, has given up his claim to the sovereignty of Maastricht for a payment of ten million *florins*. The Dutch would go only to five and a half million, so to clinch matters the balance is to be paid out of the French exchequer. 'Tis a great triumph for our Foreign Minister, the Comte de Vergennes, and the peace party."

"I don't quite see why we should have to pay up for the Dutch," said Roger thoughtfully.

"Nor do many other people. There has been a prodigious outcry on that account. Yet had we landed ourselves with a war instead 'twould have cost us a hundred times that sum. 'Twas cheap at the price to my mind. The only trouble is that the Dutch may yet drag us into a conflict if we give full support to their Republican party, who are endeavouring to unseat the Stadtholder, and England comes to his assistance."

"You still feel that another war would spell ruin to France?"

"More so than ever. Since Monsieur de Calonne became Comptroller-General he has launched loan after loan, each offering a higher rate of interest than the last and each less successful than its predecessor. But the country no longer has any faith in the stability of the Government. On the first of this month, as a last desperate measure, he resorted to an attempt to debase our currency. He is offering twenty-five *livres* for every gold *louis* having a face value of twenty-four, which is sent in to the mint; and the gold is to be reminted in new *louis* having a tenth less weight than the old ones. 'Tis the expedient of a bankrupt and it needs but a national calamity of some kind to produce financial chaos."

"Why are the French finances in such a parlous state?" asked Roger. "Cannot the King possibly do something about it?"

Brochard shrugged his broad shoulders. "He could, and has the wish but not the will. He is hopelessly weak and lacks the courage to support those who counsel wise reforms, against the intrigues of the Queen and the nobles."

"Perhaps he fears that if he sponsored measures of too liberal a nature the nobles would rebel against him?"

"They no longer have the power to do so, and the game is in his hands if only he had the strength of mind to play it. When he came to the throne in '74 at the age of twenty, he was full of good intentions. He is of simple tastes and had kept himself unbesmirched by the mire of his grandfather's court. He threw out Louis XV's ministers with the Du Barry and the rest of that licentious rabble. He then had a golden opportunity, but, instead of taking some able economist for his principal minister, he appointed old de Maurepas, a man of over eighty; who had been a minister under Louis XIV, if you please, and had been ousted two generations before by Madame de Pompadour."

Roger nodded as Brochard went on, angrily:

"Then, with the appointment of Turgot as Comptroller-General, he had another chance. Turgot had been Intendant of the Limousin. He was by far the most enlightened of these provincial viceroys, and later was Minister for the Navy. Turgot was, perhaps, the greatest man that France has produced in the present century. He comprehended all the fundamental ills from which the country was suffering and propounded suitable remedies. He was brilliant, broadminded, honest, and the King believed in him; yet he allowed him to be hounded from office. After a period of retrogression, Necker arrived on the scene. He was an incomparably lesser man than Turgot; a slave to his own vanity, and a devotee of compromise who believed in doing things little by little. Yet he was a competent financier and saw the necessity of reform. Again the King had his chance to follow sound advice but, after a few years, he abandoned the Swiss as he had done Turgot. Since then he has allowed himself to be led by a succession of incompetents and, for the past two years, rather than face unpleasant facts he has followed a policy of drift on the advice of Calonne, who is nothing but an unscrupulous speculator."

"What would Turgot have done, had the King maintained him in office?" Roger inquired.

"His policy was no new taxes and no loans. The deficit was to be made good by rigorous economy in the expenditure of the Court and government departments, and the abolition of the hundreds of sinecure offices that carried unjustifiable pensions. He advocated a single tax upon the land and the abolition of all indirect taxation. He wished to remove all restrictions on trade, including corn, and to make all landowners contribute to the public revenue on a scale according to their means."

"That would have meant revoking the privilege by which all persons of noble birth are automatically exempt from taxation."

"Indeed it would. And why not? France now has a population of some twenty-six million. Among them there are a hundred and forty thousand *noblesse* and a hundred and ninety thousand clergy. The first pays no taxes whatever, the second compromises *en bloc* for a purely nominal sum. That thirteen per cent of the population, with the Crown, enjoys two-thirds of the wealth of France; yet it contributes next to nothing. Can you be surprised that the country is on the verge of revolution?"

"You really think so?"

"I do. At my club we professional men now talk of little else. The Court has isolated itself and must reform or perish. The monarchy has become the symbol of oppression, and even the nobles regard the King with contempt. Were he different there might be some hope for the *régime* but his weakness will prove his ruin, and may bring ruin upon all France as well."

Roger was often to remember this conversation, but by the following morning he had dismissed it from his mind and, once more, entered wholeheartedly into the New Year gaieties. He danced a score of minuets, flirted again with several of his past casual inamoratas and enjoyed the hearty laughter at Maître Léger's hospitable table. When he took leave of these good friends he could not know that he would not see them again until their comfortable world was shattered; and that they would then be hunted fugitives, seeking to escape with their lives from the Terror, which was so soon to engulf the *bourgeoisie* as well as the aristocracy.

By the evening of 2nd January, 1786, Roger was back at Bécherel, greatly refreshed by his break and anxious to take up his intriguing work again. A few evenings later, with Brochard's list in hand, he searched the shelves of the Marquis's library and found quite a number of the books that had been recommended to him. Then, while early twilight still forced him to spend most of his leisure hours indoors, he gave himself up to a study of those works which had played such a large part in rendering the *bourgeoisie* discontented, and contributed in no small manner to the Revolution.

Montesquieu's *Persian Letters* he enjoyed; appreciating the spirit of reaction against the vanity and folly of Louis XIV, and his splendid but shallow Court, that animated the book; but he could not get on with the same author's most famous work, *The Spirit of the Laws*. Quesnay, the enlightened physician of Madame de Pompadour, who had been termed by his followers the "Confucius of Europe" appealed to him as a writer of sound commonsense, as did also Quesnay's friend, the Marquis de Mirabeau. Jean Jacques Rousseau he soon discarded, having formed the opinion that the "Sage of Geneva," with his nonsense about everyone returning to nature, was no more than a sloppy sentimentalist. Mably's ideas that all property should be held in common seemed to him those of a dangerous anarchist. But Voltaire proved a mine of unalloyed delight. The great cynic said so clearly and amusingly just what every broadminded and sensible person felt.

As the days lengthened, Roger began to go hawking and coursing with Chenou again, but somehow it seemed that their sport nearly always brought them near the little river on the bank of which he had had his set-to with Athénaïs.

The sight of the stream was enough to recall the memory of her to him with poignant vividness, and whenever he thought of her now it was to excuse her conduct there while condemning his own. He argued that she had behaved only in accordance with her upbringing whereas he should have known better than to take such a mean revenge. The fact that she had refrained from charging him with his crime, and a very heinous crime it was under French law, he put down to her generous and Christian spirit; and that she had returned good for evil by coming to dress his hurts made him see her now as a beautiful martyr turned ministering angel. For her to have done so, he persuaded himself, was a certain sign of her forgiveness and he regretted more than ever that she had left for Paris before he had had a chance to beg her pardon on his knees. With every week that passed his longing to see her again increased, and he felt that he would be prepared to suffer any humiliation if only it would restore him to her good graces. But Paris was a far cry from Bécherel and any hope of his getting there seemed as remote as if he had desired a journey to the moon.

Towards the end of February he had a dream about Georgina. During his first year in France he had often thought of her, sometimes with a keen surge of physical longing engendered by memories of that unforgettable embrace up in the tower, at others with shame at having failed her so lamentably. Then, as time wore on, her image had come to his mind more rarely, but always with tenderness and happy memories of the countless hours of joyous companionship that they had known together as boy and girl. During those early months, when he had thought of her so frequently, he had always put off writing to her in the hope that if he waited a little longer, when he did write, he would have a better report to give of his affairs; but his situation had improved only by such slow degrees, unmarked by any spectacular triumph, that he had never yet reached a point which had seemed to call for a full disclosure to her of his initial folly, later humdrum existence, and still indifferent prospects.

Yet in his dream he saw her with extraordinary vividness. He could see the rich colouring of her ripe, voluptuous beauty and almost feel her warm breath upon his cheek. Her dark eyes were sparkling with excitement as she reached out and, taking his left hand in hers, drew him swiftly along beside her. He had no idea where she was leading him but he saw that in his right hand he held a thick roll of parchment. Then he found himself in a shadowy room standing before the Marquis, and Georgina's voice came clearly from somewhere in his rear.

"Give it to him!" she was saying. "Give it to him, Roger, darling. 'Tis that way your fortune lies."

Then the dream faded and he woke with a start; yet for a minute he had a strong impression that Georgina was still standing there near him in the darkness.

Now fully awake, he could recall every circumstance of the dream, and more, he was suddenly aware that the roll of parchment he had been carrying was the claim to the *Domaine de St. Hilaire*.

The Marquis had said that when the work was finished, but not before, Roger was to report to him wherever he might be. He had meant, Roger felt certain, report in writing; but he had not definitely said so. It now flashed into Roger's mind that he could not be blamed if he chose to interpret the order as one to report in person. That would mean his going to Paris, and in Paris he would see Athénaïs.

He had already translated the greater part of the documents, so the back of the job was broken; but he had yet finally to collate them and make a full, clearly reasoned brief on the whole subject.

From the following morning on he completely abandoned all his other pursuits. Not an hour would he give to hunting, fencing or reading the Encyclopædists; not a moment to day-dreaming about Athénaïs. Shut up in his room at the top of the house he laboured with unflagging energy, hour after hour, day after day, from early in the morning until his eyes were blurred with fatigue at night. He knew that he could not set out for Paris one second before the whole tangled skein had been completely unravelled and its threads laid out in lines plain for anyone to see; and every second spent on the work brought him a second nearer to once again beholding his beloved.

For nearly seven weeks he stuck grimly to his task, grudging even the time he had to give to eating and sleeping, but, at last, it was finished. Every document had been numbered and put back in the big chest. A fat folder contained an index to them and a précis of each; and, with a sense beyond his years, he had composed two briefs instead of one. The first was a twenty-five-thousand word history of the claim, besprinkled with genealogical trees, references and quotations from the original material. It was intended for the lawyers who would handle the case, but, foreseeing that the Marquis would probably have neither the time nor the inclination to wade through this long and complicated argument, Roger had prepared a separate statement for him. It contained a clear, concise summary of all the salient points in less than two thousand words.

On the 16th of April, taking his two briefs and a small valise, Roger set out for Paris. For the first stage, into Rennes, he took one of the Marquis's best horses, but he paused there only to eat a quick meal, then went on by post. Travelling light, as he was, he made good going, and along the main roads he found no difficulty in securing relays. Normally, he would have stopped for a few hours in each of the towns through which he passed to see something of them, but obsessed by the one idea that every mile he covered brought him nearer to Athénaïs he halted only to eat, sleep and change horses. Vitré, Mayenne, Alençon, Chartres and Rambouillet were all passed by him with unseeing eyes, and on the afternoon of the 21st of April he rode into the crowded, smelly streets of Paris.

Aldegonde had told him how to find the Hôtel de Rochambeau, which lay in the *Rue St. Honoré*, hard by the Palace of the Louvre. It was a huge, old-fashioned house with turrets, balconies and upper storeys that overhung a central courtyard.

Handing his horse over to a groom who was lounging there he hurried into the house. He had no thought now for the documents which had cost him such arduous toil, or for the Marquis to whom he was to present them. Yet he dared not ask direct for Athénaïs and had already made up his mind that the quickest way to secure tidings of her was to pay his respects without a moment's delay to Madame Marie-Ange.

Two footmen were standing in the hall and one of them came forward to ask his business.

"Madame Velot," he almost gasped, "I wish to see her—urgently. Please to tell her that Monsieur Breuc is below and craves permission to wait upon her."

The footman bowed: "I regret, Monsieur, but Madame Velot left yesterday with Mademoiselle de Rochambeau to pass the summer at Bécherel."

CHAPTER XVI

THE SECRET CLOSET

I T was a crushing disappointment. With eyes for nothing but the road ahead he must have passed Athénaïs in her coach somewhere between Chartres and Rambouillet the previous afternoon. Evidently her father had altered his plans for her as, after all, she was to spend the summer at Bécherel. If only Roger had known that he might have saved himself the gruelling labour of the past two months. Even had he spread the work over another six months no one could have accused him of idleness, and a whole summer could hardly have passed without his being able to find a means of showing his repentance to the beautiful girl that he loved so desperately. But it was too late to think of that now. His work on the affair of the *Domaine de St. Hilaire* was completed and he must hand it over to the Marquis.

"Is there anyone else that Monsieur would like to see?" inquired the footman.

"Er—yes," Roger murmured, bringing his thoughts back with a jerk. "Kindly take up my name to M. l'Abbé d'Heury."

Five minutes later he was with the stooping, dark-eyed priest, explaining the reason for his arrival in Paris.

D'Heury said that the Marquis had left that morning for Versailles, where he had his own apartments in the palace, but that he transacted most of his business in Paris and did all his entertaining there, so he was certain to return in the course of a few days. Having taken the two reports for submission to the Marquis he then sent for Monsieur Roland, the major-domo of the Paris establishment, and ordered him to provide anything that Roger might require for his comfort during his stay in the capital.

He was given a room at the top of the house that was pleasantly furnished but had an uninspiring outlook, as its casement windows opened on to some leads beyond which a sloping roof cut off any view of the city. Having travelled light from Bécherel he decided to go out at once to buy a few things.

As for many months past he had lived in the depths of the country he found the din and turmoil of the streets a little disconcerting. Paris had seemed huge to him as he had ridden in through its suburbs earlier in the day and on closer inspection it also struck him as having an extraordinarily dense quality. The houses, streets, churches and alleys were packed together as closely as the cells in a honeycomb, and the gabled roofs projected so far over the narrow ways that it was often impossible to glimpse more than a thin strip of sky. The people in the streets had neither the leisurely gait nor the open countenances of the average provincial; with set, intent faces they hurried about their business like a swarm of ants in a nest. Roger lost himself twice in ten minutes, found the façade of the Louvre again and, having completed his purchases, returned to the Hôtel.

That evening he dined with the gaunt Abbé d'Heury and got to know a little about him. It transpired that he was a Molinest, and therefore an enemy of the bigoted, spartan Jansenists who had dominated French religious thought ever since the decline of the power of the Jesuits. He appeared to be an ascetic by nature who had become a broadminded man of the world owing to his occupation, and he displayed a masterful grip of both politics and international relations.

Roger also learned a certain amount about the Marquis. M. de Rochambeau was, it emerged, one of the more serious of the Queen's personal friends and stood high in her favour. Her Majesty frequently consulted him on foreign affairs, which were his principal interest, and nearly always adopted his opinion. Thus, while the Comte de Vergennes was the official Foreign Minister and advised the King, M. de Rochambeau often played a more powerful part in shaping the destinies of France, since the Queen, once having made up her mind about a matter, was infinitely more persistent and determined on its execution than her weak-willed consort.

Towards the end of the meal Roger remarked, with as casual an air as he could manage, how sorry he was not to have had the opportunity of paying his respects to Madame Velot before she left for Bécherel. His fly produced the information he was seeking.

After cutting himself a slice from a pineapple the Abbé replied: "Indeed, yes. You missed the chance of congratulating her on her good fortune. Her post as duenna has been secured to her for another year by Monseigneur's decision that Mademoiselle Athénaïs is still too young to marry."

Striving to keep a tremor from his voice, Roger asked: "Was her marriage under contemplation, then?"

" 'Twas Monseigneur's original intention that she should be married this summer, and on her presentation at Court her beauty raised quite a furore. She will also, of course, bring her husband a very considerable dowry; so a dozen great families put forward candidates for her hand; but she will not be seventeen until June, and, on second thoughts, Monseigneur felt that it would be time enough for him to make a final choice of a husband for her next winter."

In bed that night Roger thought over his situation and was far from happy about it. He had lost his chance of a *rapprochement* with Athénaïs for many months, if not for good; as he had not now the faintest idea where he would be when she returned to Paris next autumn. Somewhat belatedly he realised that by so speedily completing his work on the *Domaine de St. Hilaire* he had cooked his own goose. Now the job was done it seemed most unlikely that the Marquis would have any other similar work for him, so the odds were that he would be paid off. That would put an end to his association with the de Rochambeaue family and he would have to seek fresh employment. By writing to Maître Léger he could, no doubt, get himself taken on as a temporary in Maître Jeurat's office—the point at which he had had the chance of reopening his bid for fortune nine months before—and to become once more a lawyer's clerk seemed doubly hard after the life he had been leading.

During the two days that followed he continued to take his meals with the Abbé and spent the rest of his time exploring the city. He walked all round the vast block of the *Palais du Louvre* and the *Palais des Tuilleries;* went to a Mass in Notre Dame, visited the Churches of St. Roche, St. Sulpice and the Madeleine; and went out to stare at the great pile of the Bastille, with its eight round towers and crenellated battlements that seemed to tower to the skies.

He would have greatly liked to buy himself a new suit, as he had long since grown out of his own clothes and most of the things he was wearing had been bought second-hand from Quatrevaux over a year before, and during the interval he had again grown considerably. However, in view of his once more uncertain future, he thought it better not to risk any major outlay for the moment; but he purchased a pair of smart buckled shoes and had his dark brown hair redressed in the latest style by a barber. On the afternoon of the third day following his arrival the Marquis returned to the capital and, after dinner that night, sent for him.

The Hôtel de Rochambeau in Paris was much older than that in Rennes or the Château de Bécherel, so most of its rooms were neither large nor lofty and Roger was surprised at the spaciousness of the first floor chamber into which he was shown by the servant who had been sent to fetch him. It was low-ceilinged but both long and wide with a row of mullioned windows looking out on to the courtyard. At one end a great map of Europe almost covered the wall; at the other the Marquis was working at a desk inlaid with tortoiseshell. The centre of the room was occupied by a large oval table and on the wall facing the row of windows there were more maps as well as a case filled with sombrely bound reference books; all of which gave the place more the atmosphere of a council chamber than a workroom or library.

On Roger making his bow the Marquis did not invite him to sit down, but the normally haughty expression of his aquiline features relaxed and his voice was affable as he said:

"Monsieur, I have read your abbreviated report and spent half an hour glancing through the big brief that you have compiled. I consider that both are excellent. It will take some months for my lawyers to examine them and pronounce as to if they form a basis for an action which I may hope to win, but you have prepared the ground most admirably. You have also dealt with the matter much more speediy than I had any reason to expect, and I am very pleased with you."

Roger bowed again. "Monseigneur; to some, such work might seem dull, but I have found it of engrossing interest. I am, too, fully convinced that your claim is a sound one, and I wish you all good fortune with it."

"Eh?" The Marquis had opened a drawer in his desk and thrust a hand inside. He was not used to being wished good luck by his employees and looked up with a faint astonishment in his blue eyes.

"Er, thank you,'" he murmured, after a moment; and withdrawing his hand he threw a small, fat leather bag that clinked upon the desk, as he added: "There are a hundred *louis* for you as a reward for your diligence. You will need some new clothes if you are to remain in Paris. Or would you rather return to Brittany and Maître Léger's office?"

As Roger picked up the bag it flashed upon him that the Marquis was offering to retain him there in his employ. The gift and the offer seemed almost too good to be true. Flushing with pleasure, he exclaimed:

"Why, no, Monseigneur! I would much prefer to continue here in your service. And for this generous present I am most grateful."

The Marquis waved his thanks aside. "D'Heury lost his assistant some weeks ago, and I promised I would find him another. Anyone who can write so succinct a report as you have done must be well qualified to fill the post. What salary have you been receiving?"

"Forty *louis* per annum, Monseigneur."

"Tell d'Heury that in future I wish you to receive a hundred and twenty. You will find Paris more expensive in every way than Rennes, and at times you will be required to wait upon me with despatches at Versailles. As one of my secretaries I wish you to make a good appearance. Go now, and place yourself at d'Heury's disposal."

Still overcome by his good luck Roger bowed himself out of the room. D'Heury, who had become quite well disposed towards him in the past few days, received the news with satisfaction and suggested that before settling down to work Roger should take the following day off to equip himself for his new position.

When he awoke next morning Roger thought for a moment that his interview with the Marquis could only have been a dream, but there, under one side of his pillow, was the fat little bag of golden *louis* to confirm the sudden stroke of fortune that had lifted him from the prospect of being an out-of-work lawyer's clerk to a permanent secretaryship with a rich and powerful noble. Recalling his dream in the previous February about Georgina, he felt now that it had clearly been in the nature of a glimpse into the future. It was true that his object in coming to Paris had been to see Athénaïs, and he had failed in that, but in the dream there had been no thought of Athénaïs, only Georgina urging that in completing his work on the *Domaine de St. Hilaire* lay the road to fortune. He felt that now, at last, he could write a full account of himself to her without shame, and determined to spend the next few evenings doing so.

In addition to his hundred *louis* bonus he had over thirty *louis* saved from his time at Bécherel; and now he was to receive a salary of ten *louis* a month—as much as he had been paid a year when he had started with Maître Léger. He had never before possessed so much money and decided that he could well afford to spend lavishly for his own pleasure, as well as to do the Marquis credit. But he also thought that his old things might still come in useful, so, before going out, he wrote to Aldegonde, asking that his sea-chest should be forwarded to Paris.

That day he ordered three new suits with waistcoats of flowered satin, lace jabots and ruffles, silk stockings, a new hat, a pair of evening shoes, ribbons for his hair, a gilt-topped malacca cane, and a quantity of underclothes. With great impatience he waited until all these garments were delivered, then astonished the Abbé one day by appearing like a butterfly that had just emerged out of a chrysalis. From that time on he developed a sudden taste for dandyism and spent a good part of his salary on self-adornment; so that, with his tall, slim figure and dark good looks, he would, had it not been that he wore no sword, have been taken everywhere for a young noble.

Meanwhile, d'Heury was teaching him the minor duties of a private secretary. These proved, at first, a little disappointing, as the Abbé retained all important matters in his own hands, delegating to Roger only such things as purchasing stationery, affixing seals to letters, reporting on appeals for charity and getting out invitations whenever the Marquis entertained; but soon he was entrusted with interviewing casual visitors and occasional missions which took him to other great houses in Paris and out to the Palace at Versailles.

That spring another drought caused a great shortage of meat. Beef had risen from eleven to sixteen *sous* a pound and the butchers in the poorer quarters had been forced to close their shops. There was great grumbling about this and Roger could not wonder when he actually saw something of the unbridled extravagance in which the Court lived.

In order to maintain the standard of splendour first set by Louis XIV hundreds of nobles, thousands of servants, whole regiments of guards and a legion of hangers-on from all classes, fed each day at the King's expense. The dining and mess rooms of the vast palace were never empty, and the food served in each differed only in the degree of culinary art devoted to its preparation; from the highest to the lowest meat, fish, butter, eggs and wine were to be had in unlimited profusion.

As a spectacle the Court never ceased to intrigue him. He had not the *entrée* to the great apartments where the richly-clad host of lords and ladies dined, danced, gambled and flirted each night, but he could watch them arriving and departing at all hours in a never-ending stream of coaches, gaze his fill at them as they made their way up the great marble staircases, and look out upon them from the windows as, more colourful than the flowers, they strolled in little groups about the mile-long formal garden that Le Nôtre had laid out at the back of the palace.

On the 11th of May the King was to inspect the French and Swiss guards, so Roger asked for the day off, and d'Heury gave it to him quite willingly. It was the first time that he had seen Louis XVI and as he had expected, the King did not cut an impressive figure. He was a fat, ungainly man with a large pasty face and, perhaps owing to his bulk, he looked much older than his thirty-two years. The Queen, on the other hand, Roger thought both regal and beautiful. As she drove by in her carriage he was near enough to see that she had blue eyes and an aquiline nose, and he thought that when Athénaïs reached the age of thirty she would be very like her.

Roger was now getting to know most of the Marquis's principal friends by sight, as he shared a workroom with d'Heury which served as an ante-chamber to the Marquis's sanctum, and all visitors had to pass through it.

M. Joseph de Rayneval, the *premier commis* of the Foreign Ministry, was a very frequent caller, and it did not take long for Roger to discover that this high official was working hand-in-glove with the Marquis against the interests of his own master, the Comte de Vergennes. There also came to the house fairly often the Duc de Polignac whose beautiful wife was the avowed favourite of the Queen; the energetic Maréchal de Castries, Minister for the Navy. M. Bérard, head of the French East India Company; the Baron de Breteuil, Minister for Paris; the Duc de Coigny, another close friend of the Queen, and her most trusted adviser, the Comte de Mercy-Argenteau, Austrian Ambassador to France.

There were two others who called with some frequency, to one of whom Roger took an instinctive dislike and to the other an instinctive liking.

The first was the Comte de Caylus. He came of an ancient family and possessed estates both in Brittany and in the French West Indies. His revenues from his slave plantations in Martinique and Saint Domingue were said to be immense, but with them he had also inherited a dash of black blood from a mulatto mother. He was in his late forties; a vigorous and powerfully built man with thick lips, a sallow skin and a flattened nose. He treated his inferior with all the arrogance habitual to the great French nobles and, in addition, had a coarseness of manner quite unusual among them. However, M. de Rochambeau always received him with great cordiality, as they had many interests in common; both came from the same province and both were fervid imperialists, it being de Caylus's most cherished

ambition to bring the whole of the West Indian archipelago under
French domination.

The second was the Abbé de Périgord or, as he was often called,
L'Abbé du Cour. He was of middle height, a little over thirty years
of age and had a curiously attractive face. His eyes were blue-grey,
his nose slightly tip-tilted, his hair fair and his expression piquant.
He never dressed as a churchman but in the height of fashion, and
whenever he moved he leaned gracefully upon a cane, as he was a
permanent cripple, his right leg being shorter than his left.

D'Heury did not care for him, and said that, even in this age,
when it was regarded as normal for a rich prelate to keep a mistress,
de Périgord's life was a flagrant scandal, since he not only lived
openly with the young and beautiful Countess de Flahaut, by whom
he had had a son, but he was one of the most dissolute roués in all
Paris. Moreover, he was an intriguer of the first water who was clever
enough to keep in with the Queen's party on the one hand while being
on the best of terms with the Duc d'Orleans, the most deadly enemy
of the Court, on the other.

Roger, however, took a great liking to the lame Abbé as he thought
him, outwardly at least, all that an aristocrat should be. Not only did
he, with his delicate hands and gentle smile, look the part, but his
manners were a model of easy courtesy and he always had a kind word
for everyone. It was not until some time later that Roger learned that
de Périgord's first names were Charles Maurice de Talleyrand.

Finding Roger willing and intelligent d'Heury began to entrust
him with a certain amount of the Marquis's correspondence. Roger
was given the gist of what was required to be said, wrote the letters
and took them in to M. de Rochambeau for signature. It was this which
led to his being initiated into one of the secrets of the household.

Beyond the ante-room in which the secretaries worked there was
a smaller room which contained a number of presses and had no exit.
Roger had often seen d'Heury disappear into it for ten minutes or
more and had thought that he was busy filing papers there; but, on
Roger's promotion to handling correspondence, the round-shouldered
Abbé revealed to him a short cut to getting the documents signed.
One of the presses had a false back, the wall behind it was very thick
and had been hollowed out to form a small closet; the panel at the
far side of the closet was another secret door, which opened into the
Marquis's sanctum at its far end, just opposite his desk.

As d'Heury explained, this secret entrance enabled the secretary
to communicate with the Marquis, if he wished, about any visitor
who might be in the ante-room without the visitor being aware that
he had done so; and could always be used unless the Marquis had
someone with him. In that case it was M. de Rochambeau's custom
to push over a switch beneath his desk, which had the effect of locking
both the panel in his room and the door of the press, so that no one
could get into the closet and overhear what might be passing between
his visitor and himself.

On the 1st of June the decisions of Parliament regarding the prisoners
on trial for complicity in the affair of the Diamond Necklace were at

last made public. The Cardinal de Rohan, Count Cagliostro and Mademoiselle Gay d'Oliva were declared innocent and set at liberty; but Madame de la Motte was condemned to be whipped, branded upon both shoulders and imprisoned for life.

The populace of Paris received the verdicts with the wildest enthusiasm, and gave the Cardinal as great an ovation on his release from the Bastille as though he were a victorious General returning from the wars. They were inspired to this, not from any especial love for the Cardinal, but because they took the verdict to imply that since he was innocent the Queen must be guilty, and the unfortunate Marie Antoinette had already become the most hated woman in France.

That the Queen was, in fact, blameless there could be little doubt; as the letter purporting to come from her authorising the Cardinal to buy the jewels on her behalf was signed Marie Antoinette de France, and, as even the dull-witted King had pointed out, being by birth an Arch-Duchess of Austria, she always signed herself Marie Antoinette d'Autriche. Nevertheless, the most slanderous rumours were rife, alleging that the Queen had been the Cardinal's mistress, that he had given her the necklace as the price of her virtue and that, when the transaction had come to light, he had nobly allowed himself to be brought to trial and kept his mouth shut in order to save her honour.

The truth, as known to the Queen's intimates, was that she had taken a strong dislike to de Rohan when she was a girl and he the French Ambassador at Vienna. Little thinking that she would later become Queen of France he had made some witty but disparaging remarks about her, and she had sworn never to forgive him. She had, indeed, never done so, but he had tried to buy her favour back by purchasing and sending her the necklace. It had, however, been stolen by his emissary, Madame de la Motte, in transit, and so the Queen had never even known of his intention.

D'Heury, having had the inside story from the Marquis, told it to Roger and they agreed, like everyone else who knew the truth, that the one thing which stood out in the unfortunate affair was the incredible stupidity of the King in ever allowing the matter to form the subject of a public trial, as anyone but a half-wit could have foreseen that, since the Queen could not also be tried and vindicated, it must inevitably lead to her being pilloried.

On the 20th of June, the King set out with his Ministers of War and Marine, the Marshals de Ségur and de Castries, to make a personal inspection of the new harbour-works at Cherbourg, and Roger had good cause to remember the date, as it was on that evening that the most unforeseen events occurred to play havoc with the new routine into which he had now settled.

When the Marquis was in residence and working late it was customary for his two secretaries to take it in turn to go down to supper, so that one or the other should always be available to attend upon him. On this particular evening Roger had already supped and, a little before nine, d'Heury had gone downstairs; but, before handing over, he had neglected to tell his junior that some ten minutes earlier he had shown a visitor in to the Marquis. Having some letters for signature Roger was about to take them in as usual through the secret entrance. It was only when he had stepped into the closet and heard voices on the far side of the panel that he realised that M. de Rochambeau was not alone.

It flashed upon him that he would not have been able to get into the closet had not the Marquis overlooked turning the switch which automatically locked it on both sides, and he knew that he ought to withdraw; but, just as he was about to do so, the visitor who was with the Marquis said:

"I do not agree that the conquest of England is an essential to France achieving undisputed first place in the world's affairs."

The voice came so clearly that Roger recognised it at once as that of the Abbé de Perigord; and the subject of the conversation immediately caused his curiosity to overcome his scruples about eavesdropping, so he remained where he was.

The Marquis replied: "My dear Abbé, whichever way we turn we find the English barring our path. What alternative have we but to build up our strength until in another war we can finally overcome them and make their rich dominions our own. 'Tis that or resigning ourselves to watching France become moribund and bankrupt."

"Nay," said the Abbé, "there are other courses which might yet save us from our present distress. To wage another war with the English would at best be a desperate gamble. Their population is barely the half of ours, yet time and again they have proved terrible antagonists. They have an unreasoning and tenacious courage for which their national bulldog is an admirable symbol. I'd not tempt fate, but seek, as M. de Vergennes is at present doing, a new and better understanding with them."

"But where can that lead us?" the Marquis asked. "Their field of supply is now infinitely more widespread than ours; their industry rests upon a sounder basis; the goods they turn out are of better quality. How can we possibly compete with them? The contemplated treaty for commercial reciprocity which should have been signed over a year ago, would mean virtual free trade between the two nations. For eighteen months I have fought, and succeeded in postponing, this measure, from a most positive conviction that it would prove the final death-blow to French commerce."

"It would not be so," the Abbé remarked quietly, "if it were entered into with a secret understanding that Britain should supply us with all the goods we needed, while leaving us a free hand to market both their wares and ours throughout the rest of Europe."

"You talk in riddles, Abbé," M. de Rochambeau laughed. "'Twould be our salvation, indeed, were we the emporium of Europe; but what possible inducement could we offer Britain to give us a monopoly of her Continental trade?"

"She would have no option if the major portion of the Continent were brought under our control."

"What! Would you have us go to war with half a dozen nations rather than with one?"

219

"Yes; since the one is strong and united, while the others are weak and divided against themselves. Britain is a sea-power, so I would leave her to develop overseas and make her our friend by becoming her biggest customer. France is a land-power, and she should seek new wealth through the expansion of her frontiers."

"Even with England as our ally, 'twould mean a long series of most costly campaigns," demurred the Marquis.

"Not necessarily. Europe is suffering from *fin de siécle* and every country in it now seethes with political unrest, which we could turn to our own ends if we played our cards skilfully. The Catholics of the Austrian Netherlands intensely resent the reforms forced upon them by the Emperor Joseph, and the country is ripe to break away from him. The States-General of Holland is already in open revolt against the Stadtholder and contemplates an attempt to replace his régime with a republic. The King of Prussia is, as we know, on his death-bed. The Great Frederick will wage no more victorious campaigns and there is a strong party that regards his heir-apparent with considerable aversion. The Princelings who rule the German States can always be played off against one another. The Italian States and the two Sicilies are rotten to the core. Hungary is in a state of acute unrest owing to the Emperor's passion for uniformity and his attempt to force German administration and the German language upon it. Russia alone presents no weakness and, like England, should be left to develop outwardly; in her case towards Asia and the dominions of the Grand Turk, whose measure she seems already to have taken."

"And what do you deduce from all this?" the Marquis inquired.

"Why, that France should use the discontented elements in all these countries as her stalking-horse. We should fan the flames of revolt in each until civil war breaks out; then on the pretext that we intend to 'protect' their inhabitants from oppression we should send troops to their assistance. Once in they would not find it easy to turn us out and we could ensure in them the establishment of new governments favourable to our own designs. They would keep their independence, nominally, but, henceforth, they would actually be protectorates, with rulers dependent on the good will of France. By this means, in a dozen years, we could gain control of the greater part of Europe. It would be necessary to support the discontented minorities financially and to supply them in secret with arms; but we should regard each of them as though they were French armies already established in the heart of the countries we mean to dominate. They would, in fact, be the secret columns of France."

There was a moment's silence, then the Marquis said: "What a subtle brain you have, my dear Abbé. You should have been a diplomat instead of a churchman and I wonder that you do not seek office with a view to becoming a minister of the Crown."

The Abbé de Talleyrand-Périgord's voice came again and it was bitter. "I thank you, M. le Marquis, but I have no wish to serve a Court that has already treated me so scurvily."

"To what do you refer?"

"Surely you must have heard of the manner in which I was deprived of my promised Cardinal's Hat. Madame de Brionne obtained the interest of the King of Sweden on my behalf. Gustave III used his influence with the Pope and His Holiness agreed that the vacant Hat should be bestowed upon me. Then the Queen learned of the affair. She instructed the Comte de Mercy to press her brother that he should insist 'twas Austria's turn to receive the dignity; and Pius VI, weakling that he is, gave way to the Emperor. Queens who behave so to their subjects cannot expect their loyal service."

"You must remember," said the Marquis coldly, "that her Majesty is a model wife and mother; and that to maintain a high moral tone at her Court is a thing very near her heart. Your private life, Abbé, is no recommendation to a Cardinal's Hat, and no doubt the Queen quashed it on that account."

"Nay; my life is no worse than that of many another whom family considerations forced into the Church against their will. 'Twas the Queen's vindictiveness, and this accursed affair of the Diamond Necklace. She is not content to have banished de Rohan to an Abbey in Auvergne, although he was declared innocent by his judges; she pursues all who stood by him with her hate. Madame de Brionne is a Rohan by birth, so even I, as her protégé, must suffer for the folly of the King in ever making the matter public. I repeat, I have no further mind to serve a half-witted man and a capricious woman."

When the Marquis next spoke the listening Roger could tell that he was very angry but striving hard to control his temper, as he said:

"A Cardinal's Hat is no small thing to lose, and I sympathise with your disappointment. But, Monsieur l'Abbé, I wish that you would reconsider your decision. We live in most troubled times and 'tis of great importance that, whatever our personal feelings may be about the Sovereigns, we noblemen should give them our fullest support. Otherwise the whole régime may be brought into jeopardy."

"And what if it is?" The Abbé's voice was tinged with a mocking cynicism. "You, Monsieur le Marquis, are now, I fear, too old to adjust yourself to new conditions. But that does not apply to me. Whatever changes may occur I shall find my level at a place for which my abilities fit me; and it may well be that under new masters I shall find the scope to serve France far more effectively."

"So be it then," replied the Marquis in a frigid tone. "Let us revert to the business that brought you here. You persuaded M. de Calonne to send the Comte de Mirabeau to Berlin, on a special mission to report on how long King Frederick can be expected to live, and how Prussian policy may be affected by his death. You arranged that M. de Mirabeau should send you his despatches for transmission to M. de Calonne, and agreed with me that, for a certain price, you would provide me with copies of those despatches before the Minister has sight of them. Are you prepared to carry out our bargain?"

"Yes; since I gave my word upon it and need the money. But 'tis the last thing I'll do which may benefit the Queen."

"Have you the despatches with you?"

"No. They are at my house in Passy. I am come from the Palais

Royale and learnt of their arrival only from a servant who came to find me there upon another matter. But I am told that the packet is a bulky one, so someone may have to give several hours to copying its contents to-night—if the copy is to be of any value—since I must lodge it with M. de Calonne not later than midday to-morrow. I have to return to the Palais to sup with His Royal Highness; and, in any case, I have no mind to copy lengthy documents. My coach is below and I came here to suggest that you should send one of your secretaries back with me to Passy, to do the copying."

"That, I can easily arrange," agreed the Marquis, and he rang a bell on his desk.

Treading gingerly, Roger stepped out of the closet, closed the door of the press and hurried round into the Marquis's room by its main door.

"Where is d'Heury?" the Marquis asked with a frown.

"He is still at supper, Monseigneur," Roger replied. "Shall I fetch him for you!"

"Yes—no! Wait one moment. L'Abbé de Périgord requires some copying to be done at his house in Passy. 'Tis thought it may take several hours and I am anxious to receive the copy as soon as possible. 'Twould halve the time if you and d'Heury both go, and divide the work between you. Tell d'Heury my wishes when you get downstairs."

"Your servant, Monseigneur," Roger laid the letters he was still carrying on the Marquis's desk as the two noblemen took leave of one another; then, adjusting his pace to that of the lame Abbé, he followed him from the room.

Having collected d'Heury they entered the Abbé de Périgord's coach and set out for Passy. It was now about a quarter to ten and, although near the longest day in the year, a bluish dusk obscured the streets except where corner lanterns were already lit. The two Abbés were occupying the rear seat of the coach with Roger seated opposite them, his back to the horses. He knew that they had a drive of between two and three miles before them and while the other two talked in low voices he settled down to think about the long conversation he had just overheard.

It was more than a year since he had sent intelligence of M. de la Pérouse's project of colonising New Zealand to Mr. Gilbert Maxwell, and since doing so he had not encountered anything that he felt might be likely to interest that mysterious gentleman. Then, for an exciting few moments to-night, he had thought that chance was about to reveal to him the inner secrets of France's policy towards Britain. Yet, on consideration, he realised that he had actually learnt nothing. He had already gathered that the Marquis was a rabid imperialist, but he held no official position and represented only the opinion of a small clique of nobles at Court; while the Abbé de Périgord was even further removed from being a Government spokesman, and the full potentialities of his extraordinary scheme for developing "secret columns" devoted to France's interest in other countries had not, as yet, impinged on Roger's mind.

Whatever the Queen's motive for preventing the Abbé from receiving his Cardinal's Hat, Roger could not help feeling that he was no fit candidate for it. Rumour had it that he had recently been caught out using Government funds for improper purposes and that only his great influence with many highly placed ladies had saved him from being consigned to the Bastille. And Roger now knew for certain that he was flagrantly betraying M. de Calonne's confidence by selling copies of secret documents which were intended for the Minister's private eye. Yet, all the same, Roger could not help feeling attracted to the lame Abbé; he was so kind, so gay, so witty, and altogether such a fascinating personality.

At a fast trot the horses drew the well-sprung coach along the north bank of the Seine and right round the great bend of the river to the west of the city, until the streets gave place to tree-lined avenues and big houses set in private gardens. Across the river the lights of the Invalides and the Ecole Militaire could be seen, then, as they came opposite the Isle of Swans, they turned west entering the semi-open country that lay about the little village of Passy.

They were within a few moments of their destination and passing a dark belt of trees when they heard a shout, the horses reared and the coach was brought to a sudden halt.

"*Mort dieu!* We are beset by footpads!" exclaimed de Périgord.

He had scarcely spoken when masked faces appeared at both windows of the coach, the doors were wrenched open and two evil-looking ruffians covered the occupants with their pistols.

CHAPTER XVII

THE ATTACK ON THE COACH

T H E moon had not yet risen and, owing to the overhanging branches of the trees, the afterglow of the summer night did little to lighten the darkness in the lane where the coach had halted. The light was only just sufficient for Roger to make out the faces of the two Abbés opposite him as whitish blurs in the blackness; but he could see a little more of the men who had held them up, as each stood framed in one of the doorways of the coach. Both were masked and each was threatening one of the Abbés with a brace of pistols.

"Out with your purses!" growled the taller of the two, who was standing on d'Heury's side of the vehicle.

D'Heury made a movement to obey; but de Périgord rapped out another oath, and snapped: "Have a care, rogues! I am no rich bourgeois whom you can rob with impunity. Lay a hand on me and I'll have M. de Crosne's police search all Paris for you, and come to see you broken on the wheel for it."

Roger tensed himself. He was unarmed, but if de Périgord meant to put up a fight he was ready to join him in it. He did not think that either of the highwaymen had yet noticed him and kept very still, hoping to be able to take the man nearest him by surprise when the time came to fling himself into the fray.

De Périgord had hardly uttered his threat before the spokesman of the pair took him up.

"So you resist!" he rasped; and, without more ado, pulled the trigger of one of his pistols. A streak of flame issued from its barrel towards d'Heury. By the flash Roger saw the fear in the Abbé's eyes; then heard him cry out. Throwing himself forward he knocked up the other man's pistol, just as he fired, and the bullet thudded harmlessly into the upholstery above de Périgord's head.

With a curse the footpad turned his second pistol on Roger. His companion fired again at d'Heury. Again, by the flash, Roger caught an instant's glimpse of the interior of the coach. D'Heury lay slumped in his corner. De Périgord had pressed a spring in the handle of his cane and was in the act of drawing from it a long, glittering poignard.

As Roger's glance switched, a second before the blackness descended again, he found himself staring down the barrel of the pistol. He jerked himself aside and, at the very second it went off the Abbé's deadly weapon sank into the man's neck. A blinding flash eclipsed Roger's sight, and he felt a blow on the head like a hit from a hammer. It threw him violently backwards, then he seemed to be falling into a pit of blackness.

When he regained partial consciousness he knew that he was lying in a comfortable bed, but he had no idea how he had got there. His head ached intolerably, and someone was adding to its pain by moving it about. From a long way off the voice of the Abbé de Périgord reached him.

"Nay, surgeon," the voice said, "I'll not let you shave off one hair of his head more than is absolutely essential. He is a handsome fellow and those blue eyes of his must play the very devil with the women. But I'd have you know that he saved my life a while back. 'Twould be an ill return on my part to allow his appearance to be spoilt and, maybe, lose him his latest mistress."

Blackness then again engulfed Roger and when next he came to it was morning. On opening his eyes he saw that he was in a pleasant room with a tree outside its low window. Beside his bed sat a rosy-cheeked woman who was busy sewing. When she noticed that he was awake she smoothed out his pillows, gave him a drink of milk and bade him go to sleep again. He obediently shut his eyes and, before he had had time for any but the vaguest thoughts, he dropped off.

When he woke some hours later he felt perfectly well except for a dull pain in his head. He sat up and with a smile at his nurse told her that he felt hungry. She propped his pillows round him, warned him to remain quiet and left him for a while, to return with a light meal of eggs and fruit upon a tray.

After he had eaten he dozed for a little, and when he roused again it was at the rattle of rings as the nurse drew the curtains across the window, so he knew that it was evening. Soon afterwards the Abbé de Périgord came into the room. With a smiling word to the woman he sent her outside; then, leaning gracefully on his cane, he looked down at Roger, and said, slowly:

"*'Ow—do—you do? I 'opes you are better.*"

It was just on three years since Roger had heard a single word of English spoken, but the reflexes in his still woolly brain caused him to reply in that language: "*Thank you; I'm none too bad except that my head still aches.*"

Only after the words were out did he suddenly jerk forward and, staring up at the Abbé, cry in French: "What was that you said?"

The Abbé's delicately modelled mouth twitched with unconcealed humour as he replied in his native tongue: "I only asked you how you were, and I am delighted to see that you are well on the way to recovery."

"But you spoke in English," Roger muttered accusingly.

"What if I did? I do not speak it very well but I know a little of that language. I have English friends. Lord and Lady Grey came to stay with me last year. Also I saw quite a lot of your Prime Minister, Mr. Pitt, when he was over here. He and I had good fun giving one another lessons in our languages. You are an Englishman. I know it, since you raved for a solid hour in that tongue when you were unconscious last night."

"Did I?" faltered Roger lamely, as he strove to grasp the results which this unmasking of his long deception might have upon his fortunes.

"Indeed you did," went on the Abbé, carefully lowering himself ino a chair beside the bed. "But please do not distress yourself on that account. It is clear that for some reason of your own you prefer to pass as a Frenchman, and I would never abuse a confidence obtained in such a manner."

Somewhat reassured, Roger murmured his thanks; then asked the outcome of the affray with the footpads.

"After I had wounded one the other fled," replied the Abbé, "but they were no footpads; they were hired bravos who set upon us in a deliberate attempt to kill me. Of that I now have little doubt. Footpads never use their weapons unless positively forced to it, and those ruffians fired on us before we'd even had a chance to produce our purses. I've a shrewd idea, too, who primed them to it. Unless I'm much mistaken, 'twas the Comte de Caylus."

Roger looked up quickly. "You mean that revolting-looking half-breed who is a close friend of M. de Rochambeau?"

"I do. But let me warn you, my young friend, not to use such expressions in front of anyone who is likely to carry them to M. de Caylus's ears. The fact that his mother was a mulatto does not invalidate his ancient lineage on his father's side, and he is both powerful and vindictive. He is also rich as Crœsus, so 'twas no small triumph on my part to win away from him Mademoiselle Olympe, who is, I think, the loveliest of all our Opera girls."

"You underrate your own good looks, M. le Abbé," Roger laughed. "Between them and M. de Caylus's money how could a woman hesitate, since I can scarce imagine a more horrid fate for any girl than to have to suffer his embraces."

De Périgord bowed. "I thank you for the compliment. He is certainly an oafish fellow and, since my being a churchman prevents his calling me out, he is just the morbid sort of person who might seek redress by attempting to have me murdered. By God's grace those villains cannot have known me by sight, and thinking that every Abbé wears a cassock mistook poor d'Heury for myself; so killed him instead."

"What! Is d'Heury dead!" exclaimed Roger.

"Aye! Shot through the heart. I would be dead, too, had it not been for your prompt action in knocking up the other rogue's pistol. So I owe you a debt that I doubt ever being able to repay. And, believe me, I count my life mighty precious as I get endless amusement from it. I trust that henceforth you will regard me as your friend and allow me to be of service to you whenever occasion offers."

Roger smiled, realising his good fortune in having earned the gratitude of so influential a protector, and said:

"Indeed, M. l'Abbé, I could have done no less; and I count your friendship almost too great an honour, for I am, as you know, but a secretary to M. de Rochambeau."

The Abbé gave him a shrewd look and, being by nature insatiably curious, sought to plumb the mystery of his posing as a Frenchman by replying: "You are at present only a secretary, 'tis true; but that has no bearing on what you may become, particularly in these days; or what you were in the past. It may be that like many others of your countrymen you have been driven abroad by Jacobite sympathies and, having run out of funds, forced to earn your living as best you may."

"I come of a Jacobite family on my mother's side," Roger admitted. "She was a Lady Marie McElfic before her marriage, and my grandfather was the Earl of Kildonan."

"Why; how small the world is!" exclaimed de Périgord, "I know him. But no; it must be your uncle with whom I am acquainted."

Roger nodded. " 'Twould be my uncle Colin. You have the advantage of me there, though, for my mother quarrelled with her family on her marriage and I have never met any of them. He would be about fifty now, and 'tis said that I take after him."

"You do. Now I look at you again I can see the resemblance. Lord Kildonan was in Paris last autumn and again this spring. He broke his journey here for several weeks both going to and coming from Rome, where he spent the winter in attendance on the old gentleman whom you no doubt regard as your lawful Sovereign."

Roger was saved from having to reply to this awkward question by the Abbé standing up, and going smoothly on. "But I am forgetting that you are still an invalid. I must not tire you by gossiping over-much. We'll talk again to-morrow. In the meantime, good night and fair dreams to you, Monsieur le Chevalier de Breuc."

For a moment Roger was nonplussed, but he recovered in time to say good night before his host limped gracefully from the room;

then he gave himself up to thinking over this strange interview. It had not occurred to him before that in France, as the grandson of an Earl, he was fully entitled both to style himself "Chevalier" and place the "de" of the nobility before his name if he wished. He wondered what effect that might have on his affair with Athénaïs. It was the magic pass which would enable him to cross the barrier that lay between them but, even so, it would not raise him to her status. Her father would never allow her to marry a landless Chevalier; moreover, she was still in distant Brittany and he had yet to make his peace with her.

Next day the doctor came to remove his bandages. The bullet had only grazed his scalp and a strip of plaster covering the furrow it had made was now all that was necessary. An inch-wide swathe of his hair had been cut away to cleanse the wound, but the Abbé's barber came in the afternoon to redress his hair in a new fashion which almost concealed the plaster.

In the evening de Périgord paid him another visit and, having thought the matter over during the day, Roger confided to him the major events which had led to his becoming the Marquis de Rochambeau's secretary. He said nothing of Athénaïs and allowed the Abbé to continue in his belief that Jacobite sympathies were one of his principal reasons for coming to France. To this end he laid his quarrel with his father to that account.

It was not that he did not trust the Abbé but he feared that the whole truth might place him in an awkward position. During the past forty years innumerable British subjects of Jacobite sympathies had taken service under the French flag and many of them had held positions of trust in the wars against their own country. So to pose as a Jacobite secured him from any possibility that the Abbé might feel it his duty to inform the Marquis that he had been deceived into employing as his secretary an Englishman who was loyal to King George III. Roger also took the opportunity to say that as long as he had to earn his living as a servant he would greatly prefer that his true lineage should not be made public; and de Périgord readily agreed to the wisdom of this.

When Roger had done the Abbé said thoughtfully: "Would that I had had the courage to do as you did, and break with my family rather than allow them to force me into the Church; but in view of my crippled foot it seemed that no other course was open to me."

"Were you born a cripple?" Roger asked.

"Nay. I came by my lameness through an accident. As a babe I was put out to nurse with poor folk who had not the time to look after me properly, and while still quite young had a fall. The injury was neglected and has cost me dear. As the eldest surviving son of my father, the Count de Talleyrand-Périgord, I was his heir; but when it was found that on account of my lameness I should never be able to bear arms, he secured the King's permission to disinherit me in favour of my younger brother."

"That was hard indeed, and you must have had a most unhappy childhood."

"No worse than falls to the lot of most children of the French

227

nobility. My parents remained almost strangers to me and I never passed a night under their roof; but between the ages of five and eight I spent three wonderful years with my great-grandmother, the Princess de Chalais, at her château near Bordeaux. She and I loved each other fondly, and to live there with her was an education in itself. Her friends were all old people, relics of a past age, but they had known the real glory of the Court of Louis XIV, where integrity and intellect were rated greater virtues than the capacity to tell a dirty story or cheat skilfully at cards. Their manners were impeccable, and they still maintained the old tradition of being a father to their peasants instead of ruining them by a hundred petty taxes to provide for their own extravagance. It almost broke my heart when I was brought back to Paris and put to study in the College d'Harcourt."

"Was it very dreary there?"

"Incredibly so; but the Seminary of Saint Sulpice, where I later spent seven years, was even worse. Before I went there, in an endeavour to reconcile me to entering the Church, my parents sent me to live for a year with my uncle at Hautefontaine, the Court of the Archbishop of Rheims. He was then Coadjutor there and is now Archbishop himself. 'Twas thought that a sight of the pomp, luxury and licence in which these great prelates live would tempt me to follow in their steps with some eagerness, yet even that had no permanent effect on my distaste for the Church as a career. But my latter years at Saint Sulpice were made bearable by a truly charming love affair. When I was seventeen I met a young and lovely actress, named Dorothée Dorinville. She was no common trollop of the stage but loathed its sordidness and was as lonely as myself. She became my mistress, and at our stolen meetings I could forget the endless, nit-picking discourses on theology which for hours each day I was compelled either to listen to or compose. Then at the age of twenty-five I was ordained. At last I had my freedom and not an hour of it have I wasted since. 'Tis a fine life even if we do all live on the edge of a precipice."

Roger smiled at this charming cynic. "I wonder, though," he said after a moment, "that with your high connections you have not yet received greater preferment."

The Abbé took a pinch of snuff, and returned the smile. "Well may you do so, *mon ami*. I wake each morning with amazement on that score myself. So far I have been given but one miserable Abbey, that of Saint Denis in the diocese of Rheims, and been made Vicar-General of the Archbishopric. 'Tis true that I am also *Agent du Chargé* for the Church in the province of Tours, but that brings me little; and I am ever being put to the most shameless shifts to make two ends meet. I should have been given a Bishopric long since, and a rich one at that, but I am past caring overmuch any longer. Great changes are coming to France and in them will lie my real opportunity."

"You think then that the present régime will not last much longer?"

"It cannot, as you would know if you talked with many of my friends; and I do not refer to those who still hide their heads like ostriches in the gaieties of the Court, but men of affairs who are in a position to appreciate the true state and temper of the nation. I am, alas, so poor that I have perforce to eat my dinners at other people's tables, but I give breakfast to a dozen or so of my friends here every morning. At any time you care to take a cup of chocolate with us you will be most welcome. I mean that; and please do not refrain from coming through any fear that you will be cold-shouldered because I may not introduce you by your true rank. The men who meet here are mostly nobles, it is true, but they have the sense to realise that the time is coming when a coat of arms will not be worth a button, and they are interested only in men as men, for what they think and have to say."

"I will certainly avail myself of your kind invitation," Roger replied. "M. le Marquis rarely requires any attendance in the mornings and I can always catch up with my routine work at other hours. But now that I am well enough I feel that I ought to return to the Hôtel de Rochambeau, as with d'Haury's death and my absence there must be a mighty accumulation of matters requiring attention."

"My carriage shall take you back to-morrow morning," said de Périgord. So Roger, having parted from his new friend with many expressions of good will on both sides, returned to his duties on the third day after their unforeseen interruption.

That afternoon he saw his master in an entirely new, and far from pleasant, light. Previously the Marquis had always appeared to him cold, haughty and dispassionate, but just and not unkind. Now, on his arrival from Versailles, he displayed a most evil temper. Its cause was the confusion into which his affairs had been thrown by suddenly being deprived of both his secretaries. He had at once been informed of the reason for this by de Périgord; but, instead of showing the least distress at the unfortunate d'Heury's death and Roger's injury, his mind was entirely taken up with the comparatively slight inconvenience that their absence had caused himself.

For five minutes he ranted at Roger, abusing him for looking no less well than usual, and asserting that clearly he had been fit enough to return to work the day before, instead of idling out at Passy. Then he thrust a great batch of papers at him and snapped:

"Get those into some sort of order and brief me on them by to-morrow morning. With that fool d'Heury getting himself killed I scarce know which way to turn, but you have been here long enough now to take his place temporarily. 'Twas by God's mercy that His Majesty left for Cherbourg on the day you got yourself into trouble, otherwise my affairs would be in a still worse tangle. I had my steward send up two clerks from his department during your absence, but I found them worse than useless, and neither can find me a single paper that I require. Keep them to help you if you wish or send the fools back to Roland. Get out of my sight now and make up for lost time, or 'twill be the worse for you!"

This brief encounter destroyed for Roger all the respect, if not affection, with which he had come to regard the Marquis during the preceding months. He had been granted a glimpse of the man beneath the lace and satin clothing of the aristocrat and for the first time understood his true nature. The Marquis was hard and selfish to the core. All his life he had been in a position to command service but he regarded those who served him merely as convenient machines designed by God to carry out his wishes and, since they could readily be replaced, he did not care one iota if they lived in comfort or died in squalor. It was this revelation which later freed Roger from many serious qualms he would otherwise have felt in his dealings with his master.

Nevertheless, shocked as he was, he was shrewd enough to realise that for the time being his fortune lay in maintaining his place in the de Rochambeau household; so, although by midnight his head was splitting from his recent wound, he worked on until the small hours of the morning, in order to get the Marquis's affairs properly straightened out.

Next day, when he presented the results of his labours, M. de Rochambeau, still in an evil temper, only grunted; but by the end of the week he had resumed his usual haughty placidity and seemed to have forgotten that d'Heury had ever existed.

It was Roger who raised the matter, by saying that he had sent one of the clerks back to the steward but proposed to keep the other, a diligent young man named Paintendre, as he was making himself quite useful.

"Ah yes!" said the Marquis. "That reminds me. I have done nothing about seeking a replacement for d'Heury. But, after all, 'twould be no easy matter to find someone really suitable, and you seem to be managing very well. For a young man your grasp of affairs is quite exceptional. Let us leave matters as they are and if you continue as you are doing I shall have no complaints. What am I paying you?"

"One hundred and twenty *louis* a year, Monseigneur."

"Then take two hundred and forty in future, so that you may properly support your new position."

As Roger thanked him he felt no sense of gratitude. This doubling of his salary was not a generous gesture, as he would earlier have thought it. He knew now that he owed it only to the fact that the Marquis had canons of his own. M. de Rochambeau would have felt himself dishonoured by receiving anything from an inferior for which he had not paid what he considered to be an adequate price, and the maintenance of his own self-esteem demanded that his principal secretary should not live at a lesser standard than those of other nobles of his own status.

All through July Roger had his work cut out to get a full grasp of the confidential affairs into which d'Heury had never initiated him and, when the Marquis's current business did not require his attention, he spent many hours reading through old correspondence so as to fill in the gaps in his knowledge. By the end of August he had mastered all the most important matters and, in the process, had acquired a good general picture of what was going on in most of the principal Courts of Europe, so he was rarely at a loss when M. de Rochambeau asked him about some point that had slipped his own memory.

Horses, carriages and messengers were always at his disposal, so with few expenses other than dressing himself, and ample money with which to indulge his taste, he now became quite a dandy. Once or twice a week he went out to breakfast at the Abbé de Périgord's little house in the Rue de Bellechasse at Passy, and even that exquisite took occasion to compliment him on his choice of waistcoats.

On these visits to Passy he at first kept himself very much in the background, but gradually he was becoming known as one of the circle that gathered there, and he enjoyed the witty conversation of many intellectuals who were, before many years had passed, to exercise great influence on the destinies of France.

Among them were such men as the famous authors, Dupont de Nemours and l'Abbé Delille; the gross and pockmarked but brilliant Comte de Mirabeau; Louis de Narbonne, the elegant and gifted illegitimate son of the King's youngest aunt; August de Choiseul-Gouffier, nephew of Louis XV's Prime Minister; Borthés, Champford, Mathieu de Montmorency, Rulthière and a score of others. They discussed every topic under the sun and nothing was sacred to them. They spared neither women, poets, ministers, playwrights, royalty nor one another. They were mostly under thirty-five, nearly all revolutionaries at heart, and all dissolute of habit. Their conversation sparkled with epigrams and reeked of scandal, yet their thoughts were in the main original and their ideas dynamic.

It was finding that on occasion he could hold his own with the Abbé's brilliant friends that added new impetus to Roger's ambitions. During the past hundred and fifty years by no means all the ministers to the Crown had been nobles; many of the most able had been of humble birth and risen to high office by way of secretaryships and Intendancies. Cardinal Mazarin had been the son of a poor Italian fisherman, yet he had become Prime Minister and a multi-millionaire during the Regency of Anne of Austria, and, so it was said, been secretly married to the Queen. Colbert, Louis XIV's greatest minister, had started life as a clerk, and the Abbé Dubois, from being a poor cleric, had raised himself under the Regency of the Duc d'Orleans to First Minister of the State with a Cardinal's Hat.

Roger was not so conceited as to aspire, as yet, to such high office, but he had acquired sufficient confidence in himself to believe that a wide field of advancement now lay open to him. In the service of the Marquis he was gaining invaluable experience, so he was in no hurry to make a change, but he felt confident that at any time he wished one or other of his new and influential friends would willingly recommend him for some other post which would greatly better his position.

September proved a difficult month for Roger, as the Marquis was much out of humour. The Treaty of Versailles had stipulated that it should be followed by a Commercial Treaty designed to bring Britain and France much closer together, and for the past two years M. de Rochambeau had devoted much of his time to intriguing successfully against all proposals for the development of this trade agreement.

He argued that Britain would gain infinitely more from facilities to export her hardware, cutlery, cottons and woollens to France on

easy terms than France could possibly do from similar facilities to
export her wines and silks to Britain.

In the previous year he had had to combat only a Mr. Craufurd
whom Britain had sent over as a special emissary to negotiate the
Treaty, and Mr. Craufurd had proved both weak and idle. But in May
the British Foreign Secretary, Lord Carmarthen, had recalled Craufurd
and replaced him by the able and active Mr. Eden. In the summer,
therefore, M. de Rochambeau had found himself fighting a losing
battle and this reached its culmination in September.

Owing as much to the apprehensions of the British as the French,
the Treaty in its final form was far from an agreement for "free trade,"
but prohibitions were withdrawn and duties greatly reduced on many
articles; and, as each clause was agreed, the Marquis became more
irritable until, to his extreme chagrin and Roger's secret delight the
Treaty was definitely agreed and signed on the 20th of September.

It was early in October that the Marquis said to him one day:

"M. de Vergenne's wife is seriously ill and the old Count is so
distraught that he has sought leave of absence from the King to remain
at her bedside until she is either dead or better. While he is away no
major decisions on foreign policy will be taken, so I propose to give
myself a holiday and take the waters at Vichy for my health. I have
recently heard from my Paris lawyers that they advise proceeding
with the affair of the *Domaine de St. Hilaire*. As families living in
different provinces are concerned the case will be heard before the
Parliament of Paris. All the original documents that are relevant will
have to be produced in evidence. So, during my absence I wish you
to journey to Bécherel and bring them back with you."

Roger's heart bounded with joy. For some weeks past he had been
very much alive to the fact that Athénaïs would soon be returning to
Paris for the winter season, but that did not open properly until the
Court returned from Fontainebleau in mid-November; and this order
meant that he would see his cherished angel considerably earlier than
would otherwise have been the case.

Within an hour of the Marquis's leaving Paris, Roger was on his
way. Once more he passed through Rambouillet, Chartres, Alençon,
Mayenne, Vitré and Rennes without giving a thought to their historic
interest. The hooves of the many horses he bestrode all rang out the
same magic rhythm: "Ath-én-aïs, Ath-én-aïs, Ath-én-aïs."

When he reached Rennes it was already well on in the afternoon,
but he pushed on and covered the last miles after darkness had fallen.
This time he did not go round to the stable entrance, but rode up to the
front door and hammered upon it with his riding-crop as impatiently as
any young lordling.

From the subdued greeting of the footman who answered it he
sensed that something was wrong. Then he noticed that the man was
wearing a pair of old cloth breeches, that his livery coat was half
unbuttoned, having been pulled on hastily, and that the great hall was
not lit as brightly as was customary when any member of the family
was in residence. Throwing the reins of his horse over an iron hook,

Roger stepped inside. The gloomy shadows seemed to reach out, engulfing him in a cold fear.

"What has been happening here?" he cried to the servant, his voice high with sudden apprehension. "Where is Aldegonde? Why do you stare at me so glumly? Tell me what's wrong; or if you've not the courage, go get him—instantly."

At that moment the fat major-domo came shambling through a door at the back of the hall. He was not in livery but wore an old dressing-gown and heel-less slippers.

"Ah, Monsieur Breuc!" he exclaimed in a doleful voice, as he came forward, "I heard your horse's hooves and wondered who it could be riding up at this late hour. You find us in a poor state to welcome anyone."

Roger slapped his leg impatiently with his riding-crop. "What has befallen you all? Why is the place in semi-darkness? What calamity has plunged you in such gloom?"

"Alas, Monsieur, we have been beset with troubles for a fortnight back. It must be that since Madame Velot slipped upon the stairs and broke her leg."

"Go on, man!" snapped Roger. "One does not douse three-quarters of the lights because a woman breaks her leg. Speak up, or by thunder I'll break my riding-crop across your shoulders!"

Aldegonde had already taken in Roger's new finery, as the dust of the road did not disguise his well-cut, pearl-grey riding suit and doeskin gauntlets. In the past six months he had not only put on an inch in height but grown in mental stature far beyond that proportion. The old major-domo knew the voice of authority when he heard it. Far from showing resentment at this imperious treatment he positively cringed, and wrung his hands together, as he murmured:

" 'Tis no fault of ours, Monsieur; and I mentioned Madame Velot's accident only because 'twas the day she broke her leg that we first heard of the sickness in the village. 'Tis the great pox, no less, and half the staff are now stricken with it."

"Mademoiselle Athénaïs?" croaked Roger.

The major-domo nodded. "She, too, Monsieur, and for the past three days she has been delirious."

CHAPTER XVIII

THE FELL DISEASE

R O G E R had known it. From the very second that the doors of the château had been opened he had felt certain that some terrible calamity had befallen Athénaïs. Up to the last moment he had still hoped against hope that he was wrong and had lacked the courage to pronounce her name. But now he knew the worst, and it was horrible to contemplate.

Owing to the filth in which the peasants lived, crowded together like animals in their miserable dwellings, such sporadic outbreaks were not uncommon. They often halved the younger population of a small community in a month, then died away, leaving the majority of the survivors scarred and disfigured for life. Roger knew that Athénaïs, instead of taking coach to Rennes at the first tidings of the epidemic, must have stayed on to succour her stricken people, as only by actual contact with them could she have caught the disease herself.

"Where is the doctor?" Roger demanded, his voice suddenly quiet again after his outburst.

"We have no doctor living here, Monsieur," replied Aldegonde. "The nearest is Doctor Gonnet of Montfort. 'Twas he who set Madame Velot's leg, and since the sickness came he has ridden over every other day. He will be here again to-morrow."

"Who is looking after Mademoiselle?"

"Mére Sufflot, the midwife from the village. Mademoiselle's maid, Edmée, and several of the younger servants have run away, from fear of catching the sickness."

"Has no attempt been made to get help from Rennes?"

Aldegonde spread out his hands. "I had not thought of that, Monsieur. It seemed to me that Doctor Gonnet was doing all that can be done."

It did not take Roger long to size up the situation. In England, in such a case, the servants would have shown initiative and spirit. They would have taken charge and secured proper medical aid; and no lady's maid worth her salt would have run away. But here in France things were very different. If you had your footman whipped for spilling a cup of chocolate on your gown you could not expect loyal service from him at a time of crisis. Just as the Marquis had been completely unmoved by d'Heury's death, so the servants at Bécherel did not give a straw whether their young mistress lived or died.

"Have my old room prepared," said Roger sharply, "and have all the candles lit. From to-morrow morning the servants are to appear properly dressed in their liveries and go about their usual duties. Since Mademoiselle is still in residence 'tis fitting that the service of the château should be conducted in a normal manner."

For the first time Aldegonde showed resentment at his tone. "Since when," he said sullenly, "has it been Monsieur's place to give orders here?"

"Since the moment I put my foot inside the door," Roger rapped back, assuming an authority to which he had no shadow of right. "I am Monseigneur's emissary. While Mademoiselle remains tied to her bed you'll take your orders from me, or 'twill be the worse for you. Have a bottle of vinegar and some cloves of garlic put in my room, also some cold food and wine. I go now to see Madame Velot."

At this reference to the Marquis the major-domo's attempt to assert himself collapsed like a pricked bubble. He bowed submissively as, without another glance at him, Roger strode with jingling spurs across the great hall.

When he knocked at Madame Marie-Ange's door she called to him to come in and, on entering the room, he saw that she was lying in bed staring at the ceiling. Her surprise at seeing him was only equalled by her pleasure, but he found her in a sad state. In her fall she had fractured her hip as well as her leg. She was still in considerable pain and her injuries having been set in splints it was impossible for her to move the lower part of her body.

On her telling him about her accident he well remembered the treacherous marble stairs that had been the cause of it, as he had narrowly escaped breaking his own nose by slipping on them the preceding autumn.

She was terribly distressed about Athénaïs, but the pain she was in herself appeared to have robbed her of all her powers of concentration. It seemed that she had faith in Dr. Gonnet and could only keep on repeating that with the help of *le bon Dieu* all would be well. Roger learned that it was she who had sent for Mére Sufflot from the village to nurse Athénaïs, as the old woman was the only person in the locality who had any professional experience; and that she was being looked after herself by the head chambermaid.

When Roger announced that he intended to go and see Athénaïs, she made a faint protest, and murmured something about it being most improper for him to enter a young lady's room; but he waved the objection aside and, after having rearranged her pillows for her, marched determinedly off down the corridor.

At his knock, Mére Sufflot opened the door to him. She proved to be a bleary-eyed old crone and stank like a polecat. Looking round he saw that the room was of splendid dimensions. It could have accommodated four full-sized billiard-tables and there would still have been ample space to spare. The heavy-brocaded curtains were drawn and a great wood fire was roaring in the big grate, making the room stiflingly hot. A huge four-poster bed occupied the centre of the wall opposite the windows; but, from where he stood he could not see Athénaïs, as she was hidden from him by a screen.

"How is Mademoiselle?" he asked the old woman, in a low voice.

"The fever has abated, Monsieur," she replied with a cringing leer. "Mademoiselle is out of danger, but I fear that her pretty face will be sadly marked."

"Is she sleeping?"

"No. She has slept most of the day, and 'twas when she woke an hour ago that I knew her to be past the crisis."

"Who relieves you here at night?"

The old woman's bleary eyes showed faint surprise. "Why, no one, Monsieur. I have not left the room for three days. Monsieur Aldegonde sends up trays of food for us which are left outside the door. None of them would come in here while the sickness is still infectious."

"Then go downstairs now and get some fresh air. Be back in an hour."

With an awkward curtsey and a servile grin that showed the gaps between her yellow teeth, Mére Sufflot left him. Then he tiptoed across the soft Aubusson carpet to the foot of the bed.

Athénaïs lay propped up against her pillows. She was awake and fully conscious. Her bright blue eyes seemed larger than ever, but her face smaller, under the great coif of hair that was incongruously piled up on her head. It was only with difficulty that he repressed a start of dismay as he saw the ravages that the disease had made on her lovely features. Great suppurating sores blotched her forehead, cheeks and chin, and she was dabbing at them with a soiled cambric handkerchief.

As she saw him her eyes flickered, then she threw up her hands and pressed them against her face.

"Don't do that!" he said softly. "For goodness sake be careful. It's absolutely imperative that you should not touch those sores."

Slowly she lowered her hands and said in a husky voice: "What brings you here?"

"Monseigneur desired me to bring the papers on which I was working last winter to Paris for him. I arrived but half an hour ago, and words cannot express my distress at the condition in which I find you."

"How come you in my room?" she asked dully.

"I am here to make better arrangements for your attention, Mademoiselle. How long is it since that old woman washed you?"

"She has made no attempt to do so; and I would not let her lay a finger on me if she tried."

"That I can understand; yet you must be washed by someone. I see your sheets need changing too, and the room smells like a charnel house. But I learn that you are past the crisis, so at least we may thank God for that."

"I care not any longer. I have no wish to live now that my looks are ruined."

"Oh, come!" he pleaded with a smile. "Your sores are only just beginning to heal, and if you do not interfere with them they will not mark you. But to start with, you must have clean linen and fresh air, instead of allowing your room to remain a forcing-house for the pestilence." As he spoke, he turned away and walked across the room.

Her husky voice came after him: "What are you about to do?"

"Open two of your windows," he replied.

"Leave well alone," she said sharply. "You are no doctor, and have no right to alter matters here. A draught might kill me."

"Nay. Fresh air never killed anyone," he said over his shoulder. "And I pray you, Mademoiselle, not to make things more difficult for me. My only desire is to serve you and see you well again."

Drawing back the heavy curtains he opened two of the windows and let in the cool night breeze; but he stoked up the fire before returning to her bedside.

As he approached she said, suddenly: "You look different. You have grown; and yes, you are dressed like, like——"

"Like a noble," he supplied the word for her with a smile. "Fine feathers make fine birds, do they not, Mademoiselle? But would you have had me always remain a pettifogging clerk?"

"I am indifferent to what you are or what you may become," she replied coldly.

He bowed slightly. "That, Mademoiselle, is my dire misfortune, but you may depend upon it that I shall never cease to be your most humble and obedient servant."

Turning away from her he quietly left the room, went downstairs, found a footman, and ordered fresh sheets and warm water to be sent up. When they arrived on the landing he carried them into the room and, setting them down, looked through the drawers of a chest until he found a shift of fine linen. Having torn it into strips he picked up the bowl of water and walked over to the bed.

"You are not to touch me," she whispered, her eyes distended with dislike and fear. Then as she saw that he intended to ignore her words she wriggled down in the great bed and drew the sheets up to her chin.

Dipping the linen in the water he began to cleanse the sores upon her face, taking the greatest care not to disturb any of the scabs that were beginning to form round their edges. After a little she eased herself up and let him bathe her neck and hands without further protest. When he had done he found a comb, undid her hair, combed and brushed it and did it up again in two long plaits.

"That is better," he said at last. "And now you must get out of bed for a few minutes while I change the sheets."

"I'll do no such thing," she croaked with a flash of anger. "I'd rather die than let you see me naked."

"Be sensible," he laughed. " 'Tis better that I should do it than that old woman who reeks of brandy and doubtless carries the pox herself. Here's your *robe-de-chambre*. Slip it on, then curl yourself up in the *duvet*. I promise I won't look while you are doing so."

"I won't," she gasped.

He shook his head. " 'Tis that or I'll have you out of that filthy bed as you are. The choice lies with you, Mademoiselle."

"You swear you will not look?"

"I swear it."

He walked away and turned his back. Two minutes later he caught a muffled whisper: "Monsieur Breuc, I am at your disposal."

When he looked he saw that the *duvet* now formed a big ball in the middle of the bed with only one small pink foot showing from it. Slipping his arms under the bundle he lifted it with ease and carrying its precious contents over to the fire deposited it gently in a chair. Then he changed the sheets and pillow-cases, carried the bundle back again and said: "You can get back into bed now. I am going behind the screen."

Having given her a minute or two he emerged to find her sitting up as he had first found her. "Now," he said, "I trust you will at least give me the satisfaction of admitting that you feel more comfortable."

"I do, Monsieur," she replied, a shade more graciously. "And—and, I thank you for it."

He was just about to say something else when the door opened and Mére Sufflot came in.

Momentarily disconcerted he looked at her in silence for a few seconds, then he said: "Please go downstairs again, and ask someone to have hot water placed in my room."

The old woman gave her awkward bob and bustled out again.

Turning back to Athénaïs he once more walked up to the side of her bed and spoke with all the feeling that he could command.

"Mademoiselle. The last thing I wish to do is to tire you with unnecessary talk; but there is something that I must say to you. Something that I have been waiting for nearly a year to say. It concerns the day on which your horse ran away and, through my fault, you were thrown into the river. You were quite right to be angry with me for the liberty I took. I realised that afterwards and I meant to tell you how sorry I was for what I had done; but before I had a chance to do so you had left for Paris. I wish now to offer you my humblest apologies and to assure you that I would never have done such a thing, had I not been near insane from love of you."

Her blotched face remained quite expressionless, as she said slowly: "You did not kiss me because you loved me. 'Twas out of hatred. 'Twas because I had scorned your advances. You wished to humiliate me in return and took a mean revenge."

"Nay, Mademoiselle, I protest," cried Roger. "I have loved you since the very first moment that I set eyes on you. And 'twas love that drove me mad that day."

"Would you then claim that you love me still?" she asked, her eyes over-bright from a return of the fever.

"Indeed, I do!"

"You lie! 'Tis that you have wormed yourself into my father's good graces, and fear that I yet may tell of your assault upon me. You seek my pardon only to protect your place."

"That is not true! I care not a fig if I remain in your father's service, or leave it! Except as it affects my chances of seeing you. 'Tis love alone that made me hasten here at breakneck speed, and 'tis love alone that makes me plead for your forgiveness."

"I'll not believe it!"

"I swear it!"

Her eyes glittered with a feverish light. "Then kiss me again! Now! This very moment; hideous as I am and ridden with disease!"

Without the slightest hesitation he stooped and placed his mouth against her dry and burning lips. He knew full well the danger that he was running but he would have walked through fire to prove his love for her, and he made himself keep his lips pressed against hers for a long moment.

It was the sound of the door opening that made them jerk their heads apart, but Roger had time to step quietly back a pace before Mére Sufflot came round the end of the screen.

Athénaïs's face was now flushed scarlet between the blotches. Her eyes were lowered and she would not raise them as he said:

"There is one more thing, Mademoiselle. An unpleasant one, I fear, but necessary, if we are to save your face from being scarred. Now that your sores are beginning to heal they will itch abominably. Lest the temptation to scratch them prove too much for you we must tie your hands behind your back."

Her mouth went sullen, but she now seemed dazed and did not reply.

Taking a long strip of the linen that he had already prepared for the purpose, he tied one end of it round her left wrist then, having passed the loose end behind her back, he secured it to her right wrist. This single, soft bond still allowed her to raise her hands in front to breast-height and, as it was imperceptible to lie upon, would not, he hoped, seriously interfere with her sleeping.

Fixing Mére Sufflot with a steely glance he said: "You will not untie that bandage even on a direct order from Mademoiselle. On no account are you to let the fire die down, and you are to keep the windows open. Should Mademoiselle grow worse in the night you are to send for me at once. I am the master here now, and these are my orders. If you carry them out fully I will see to it that you are well rewarded, but fail to obey them and I will have you put in the pillory."

Athénaïs's eyes flickered up for an instant and her mouth fell a little open; but she said nothing, and made him only a slight inclination of the head as he bowed formally to her, and wished her good rest, before leaving the room.

Up in his own room he washed his face and hands in vinegar and water and, after gargling with the same simple antiseptic, chewed a clove of garlic to a pulp, then spat out the pieces. He hated the stuff but believed it to be, as in fact is the case, a natural absorbent of poisons, and it was one of the simple hints to the preservation of health that he had picked up from old Aristotle Fénelon.

On getting into bed the familiar room, in which he had slept for so many months, recalled to him his dream about Georgina. He had never received any reply to the long letter he had written to her the previous April, and he wondered if she had, after all this time, become too immersed in her own affairs to bother with him any more, or if it had gone astray. But it was, no doubt, his thinking of her that caused him to dream of her again.

She was standing by his bedside shaking him by the shoulder and saying: "Get up, Roger! Get up, d'you hear! That silly little creature you're so distracted about needs your attention."

He woke with a start, to find himself shouting angrily: "She's not a silly little creature! She's——"

Then he broke off with a laugh. No doubt Georgina would regard Athénaïs as spoilt, stupid, and intolerably conceited, but that did not affect the fact that he loved her; and he had no hesitation in taking the dream as a warning.

On looking at his watch he found it to be one o'clock. Slipping on his bed-robe he went down to the floor below and along to Athénaïs's room. Opening the door he tiptoed inside. On emerging from behind the screen he saw that Athénaïs was asleep, snoring gently through her small, curved nose. But Mére Sufflot was also sleeping soundly; the fire beside which she sat had almost died out, and the chill of the night air coming through the still open windows made him shiver.

Roger could be completely ruthless where the interests near his heart were concerned. Advancing with catlike tread on the old mid-wife, he suddenly thrust out both hands and gripped her firmly round the neck, so that she could not cry out. She woke with a violent start·

Squeezing her neck tighter he gave her a rough shake and, stooping, whispered in her ear:

"Get on your knees and mend that fire piece by piece. If a log falls and wakes Mademoiselle I'll have the hide flayed off you. What is more, if when I come down next she is not still sleeping and you awake I'll strangle you with my own hands."

It was, he knew, the sort of language that a woman of her type, on having failed in her duty, would expect; and the only sort of treatment that would make any impression on her drink-sodden old brain. When her eyes were bulging he released his grip, and with a smothered cough she obediently set to getting the fire back into a blaze.

On returning to his bed he only dozed, and he went down to Athénaïs's room again about four o'clock in the morning. She had turned on her side and was now sleeping quietly. The room was fresh but pleasantly warm and the old harridan, still wide awake, was sitting bolt upright in her chair. As he tiptoed in she gave him a terrified glance but, to her amazement, he patted her gently on the shoulder, and tiptoed out again.

From four to seven he slept soundly, and was roused only by his *petit dejeuner* being brought to him. When he had dressed he sought out Aldegonde and insisted on the major-domo taking him round the servants' quarters. He found that fifteen of the younger members of the staff were down with the sickness, but that several of the older servants, who had already had the disease, were tending them with care. Appropriately enough, he thought cynically, these people are willing to look after one another, but they are quite content to leave their master's daughter in the hands of a besotted old mid-wife.

Relieved of further worry about the sick servants he went up to see Athénaïs. She was awake; but immediately he came in she turned her back to him, so he refrained from speaking to her. To Mére Sufflot he said: "You can doze now if you wish, as I shall be coming in during the morning to keep the fire going." He then went down to the library and waited impatiently for the doctor.

It was half-past eleven before Dr. Gonnet, who had ridden ten miles from Montfort, put in an appearance; and when he did Roger was not impressed by him. He was old, not without shrewd common sense, but a country practitioner who made no secret of the fact that he eked out an existence by attending on the peasantry, and had little leisure to keep abreast with the latest discoveries in medicine. He reported that Athénaïs was progressing favourably, approved Roger's measures for making her more comfortable, but shook his head dubiously over the open windows.

Immediately he had gone Roger went out to the stables in search of Chenou. They greeted one another with their old friendliness and the chief huntsman said feelingly:

"Thank God you are come to us, Monsieur Breuc. We were in a pretty pickle here, and badly needed someone to take charge inside the house. I would have myself but I was loath to trespass on Monsieur Aldegonde's province. If there is any way in which I can help you have but to name it."

"Indeed there is," replied Roger quickly. "I want you to ride into Rennes at once; but before you go give orders for a coach to follow you. When you reach Rennes go to Maître Léger and ask him to recommend the best doctor in the city. Seek out the doctor and offer him any price you like to accompany you back here and remain as resident physician until Mademoiselle Athénaïs is well again. Then go to the Convent of the Sisters of Mercy and see the Superior. Say that you come on behalf of Monseigneur and ask her to furnish you with her two most competent nursing Sisters. Bring the doctor and the nuns back in the coach, and do your damnedest to have them here by nightfall."

"It shall be done, Monsieur; or I will eat my own beard," declared Chenou, and he began to shout for his grooms and stableboys.

During the remainder of the day Roger personally supervised the wants of Athénaïs. She addressed no word to him and he refrained from any approach to her. At ten o'clock that night Chenou returned from his forty-mile trip into Rennes and back, bringing a youngish doctor named Hollier and two Sisters of Mercy. Roger sent Mére Sufflot packing with a *louis* and installed Athénaïs's new attendants. Then he went to bed and slept like a log.

Next day he had all the sick servants moved from their own stuffy quarters to the ballroom of the château, and, having turned it into a hospital ward, placed Dr. Hollier in charge. He then wrote to the Marquis, giving him a full account of the state of affairs at Bécherel, and suggesting that he should remain there until Athénaïs was fully recovered.

The days that followed left him anxious and now a little uncertain of himself. He did not feel justified in any longer going to Athénaïs's room, but waited impatiently each morning for Dr. Hollier's bulletin about her spots. Most days he rode an hour or two with Chenou, and spent the rest of the time with Madame Marie-Angé; reading the novels of Madame de Villedieu to her, these light romances having been her favourites in her youth.

The motherly old soul's leg and hip were gradually mending and, as her pain lessened, she became more alert to what was going on in the household. It was her idea that when Athénaïs was well enough to travel, instead of going to Paris for the winter, she should go to her aunt's château at St. Brieuc, and quietly recuperate there in the good sea air.

Twelve days after his arrival at Bécherel Roger received a reply to his letter to the Marquis. In effect it said little more than: "I approve the measures you have taken regarding my daughter, and you have my full authority to carry out any other measures you may think requisite to her well-being. However, now that she is in good hands there seems no reason why you should linger unduly at Bécherel, so the sooner you return to Paris with the *Domaine de St. Hilaire* documents, the better."

There was no message for Athénaïs, no indication that the stony heart of the Marquis had been touched by his young daughter's affliction;

he still appeared to be entirely wrapped up in his own concerns. In disgust Roger stuffed the missive into his pocket and forgot it.

A week later he received another letter from M. de Rochambeau, this time by personal courier. It said:

> To my great annoyance I have returned to Paris to find you still absent. Why is this? Paintendre is a fool who understands nothing of my affairs. Get to horse at once, and rejoin me here at the earliest possible moment.

Again there was no inquiry as to how Athénaïs was progressing, let alone as to the health of his servants. Yet Roger knew that if he wished to keep his job he must obey the summons without delay. He sat down and wrote a note to Athénaïs, which ran:

> Mademoiselle, I have received your father's command to return immediately to Paris. Having followed the progress of your illness through Dr. Hollier I am greatly rejoiced to know that you are near recovered. I should count it a great favour if you would permit me to take leave of you before my departure.

Five minutes later he received a verbal reply by the footman who had taken up his note. The man bowed to him and said: "Monsieur, Mademoiselle desires you to wait upon her after your evening meal."

The Marquis's courier had not arrived until after mid-day and, for the sake of reaching Paris a few hours earlier, Roger had no intention of forgoing the interview that Athénaïs had granted him. However, he arranged with Chenou to have a coach ready for him at dawn the following morning, and had the great iron chest containing the documents carried down to the front hall in readiness for loading. Early in the evening he dressed himself in his best suit, which he had brought with him, arranged his hair with care and put a beauty patch on his left cheek. When he looked at himself in the mirror he was satisfied that not even the Abbé de Périgord could have surpassed him in his new rôle of a fashionable exquisite.

After he had supped he went upstairs with a beating heart. He felt reasonably confident that Athénaïs would not have consented to see him unless she intended to thank him for the part he had played in bringing order out of chaos at the chateau; but, whether her thanks would be purely formal, or couched in the warmer note of renewed friendship, yet remained to be seen.

One of the Sisters of Mercy admitted him to the room. As he came round the corner of the screen he saw that Athénaïs was sitting up in bed with her hair properly dressed, and that the last traces of her sores had completely disappeared under a dusting of rouge and powder.

For a moment she did not look at him, but addressed the nun: "Sister Angelique, I have business to discuss with my father's secretary. While we are talking you would, no doubt, like to give your mind to your devotions. Pray avail yourself of my oratory."

Without a word the nun obediently crossed the room, and disappeared behind a curtain that concealed an alcove fitted up as a small private chapel. While she knelt there she was still, theoretically, in the room and chaperoning Athénaïs; but, for all practical purposes, Roger was now alone with his divinity.

He thought that she had never looked more beautiful as she turned her big blue eyes on him, and said:

"Monsieur; on learning this afternoon that orders had come for you to return to Paris, I took the opportunity to write to my father. Please convey my missive to him immediately on your arrival."

With a bow Roger took the letter that she held out to him. He had counted more than he knew on being restored to her favour before he left Bécherel; but now it seemed that she had delayed his departure only in order to write this letter, and he was bitterly disappointed.

"It occurred to me," she went on, "that you have long outstayed the purpose of your original mission to Bécherel, and I thought that my father should be informed of the reason for that. Dr. Hollier has told me of all that you have done to restore order and health among the servants here, and we all owe you our gratitude."

He bowed again. "Mademoiselle, I could do no less; and as Monseigneur is angry with me for having delayed so long your letter will prove a boon in modifying his displeasure."

"I trust so." She fiddled with the ribbons of her bed-jacket, and added a little uncertainly: "You wished to say something to me before your departure?"

"Only, Mademoiselle, how happy I am that you are now recovered from your illness and need only rest to restore your full health again."

"Have you no more to say than that?"

"Now that I have seen you, I would add my thanks to God for having preserved your beauty."

Again her words came a little uncertainly: "Under His mercy, Monsieur, I owe that to you. And, since you show no mind to broach a matter that concerns us both, 'tis for me to do so."

His pulses began to race as she lowered her eyes and went on, almost in a whisper. "That night when you arrived here I did a terrible thing; and 'tis generous of you, now that I am well, to spare me your reproaches. By making you kiss me at the height of my fever 'tis a miracle that I did not give you the sickness."

" 'Twas my fault," he said gently, almost overcome by her sudden display of feeling. "I should have waited a more fitting occasion to ask your forgiveness for what had passed before. You were half delirious and knew not what you did. I pray you think no more of it."

"But I must. I knew then that you really loved me, and that I ill deserved it from having been so harsh and wicked towards you."

"Please!" he begged, hardly daring to look at her. But she raised her eyes and her words came more firmly:

"There is only one way in which I can make amends. To wipe away the memory of those other kisses you may, an it please you, kiss me again now."

He was trembling now. Stepping forward he took one of her hands in his and placed his other arm about her shoulders. Stooping above her he took a long breath and, as she raised her face to his, he whispered: "Nay, I'll not do it to pleasure myself alone, but only if you wish it also."

"*Rojé* I do!" she cried suddenly: and flinging her soft arms round his neck she drew his mouth down to hers.

For a space they clung together, then she began to cry softly.

"My loveliness," he murmured, drawing away a little. "Why do'st thou weep?"

"Because—because I am so happy," she sobbed, "yet, at the same time, so sad."

"What troubles thee, my sweet Princess?"

Choking back her tears she smiled fondly up at him. " 'Tis that I would so terribly that I could be thy Princess. Yet, far as thou hast already travelled on the road to fortune, dear miller's youngest son, there can be no hope of that."

"Thou, thou lovest me then?" he breathed.

She nodded. "With all my heart. 'Twas naught but stupid pride that stayed me from confessing it before. For years I have built romance about thee, and thought of thee always as my perfect knight."

Again they kissed, not once but a score of times; and for the next half hour murmured only sweet endearments to one another.

At length Athénaïs placed her hands upon his shoulders and put him gently from her. " 'Tis time for thee to leave me," she said, with a sigh, "or Sister Angelique's curiosity will overcome her piety."

"So soon," he protested. "Nay, she will continue with her devotions for a while yet, and there are still a thousand things that I would say to thee."

"And I to thee. But lest she comes upon us suddenly we must now be circumspect, and thou hadst best sit there in that chair, as though we were in truth discussing business."

As she began to tidy herself and he took the chair, he said: "Tell me, beloved, what are your plans; and when can I hope to see you again?"

" 'Twill be the new year now before I come to Paris," she replied. "In that letter to my father I have asked his consent to travel, when I am well enough, to my aunt's château at St. Brieuc. 'Twas Madame Marie-Angé's idea. She put it in one of the little notes she sends me each day. Though 'tis winter the sea air there will aid my convalescence and 'tis certain my father will agree."

"And when you reach Paris, what then? Think you we will ever find an opportunity to be alone together?"

"Oh, I trust so! Now that I am seventeen my father will, I doubt not, arrange some suitable marriage for me. But 'tis hardly likely that I shall be married before the summer; and in the meantime we shall be living under the same roof."

Roger sighed. "The prospect of your marriage fills me with dismay. Fate has been cruel indeed to separate us by so many barriers."

She shook her head and smiled sweetly. "Think not on that, I beg; for no profit can come to either of us from railing at a decree which was ordained by God. I am overjoyed that you should have won my father's confidence and prospered so; but your lack of lands and quarterings renders any question of marriage between us utterly impossible."

Leaning forward and taking her hand again, Roger said: "Listen, dear love. 'Tis true that I have no lands, and no money other than that which your father gives me; but at least I am of gentle birth and have the right to bear arms. I would have told you of this before but I have had little opportunity and, until this evening, I feared that you might disbelieve me."

While she listened, thrilled with excitement, he then disclosed to her that he was English and how it was that he had come both to leave his own country and, at their first meeting, conceal the truth about himself from her.

"How wondrous strange," she murmured, when he had done. "Just to think 'twas that absurd doll of mine which caused you to conceal your true identity for so long. And 'tis more like a fairy tale than ever that my miller's youngest son should transpire to be a Chevalier."

Although he knew within himself that he was on hopeless ground, the brightness of her eyes encouraged him to say: "Think you that if I disclosed the truth to your father he could be brought to consider me as a suitor to your hand? 'Twould mean our waiting for some years yet, but if he'd agree and give me his countenance I might, by that time, have made enough money to purchase an estate."

"Nay, *Rojé*, nay," she said sadly. "Put such thoughts from your mind, I beg. My father would never consent to have me unmarried for so long. Besides, he will require me to marry into one of the best families in France; so that even if, by some miracle, the King made you a Count to-morrow, he would still not consider you a suitable husband for me. There is, too, another thing. All Englishmen are Protestants, are they not?"

"Not all, but the vast majority; and I am one. I visited Saint Mélaine only to see you; and have gone to other Catholic churches while in France simply so that I should not be thought irreligious."

"Would you be willing to become a Catholic?"

Her question was one that had never even occurred to him and with his upbringing, such a step seemed a terrible one to take. "I— I've never thought about it," he stammered. "But I fear I'd be very loath to change my religion."

"There, you see!" she squeezed his hand. "And, my father apart, I could never bring myself to wed a heretic. 'Twas decreed in heaven that we should never marry, so 'tis best that we should resign ourselves to that."

"Though it breaks my heart, I must confess you right," he murmured sadly. "Yet 'tis more than I can bear, to think of you married to another."

They were silent for a moment then she said softly: " 'Tis time you left me. Kiss me again before you go and think not too gloomily

245

upon the future. Such marriages as mine will be are not of the heart but of convention, and entered into only for the uniting of two great families. What does it matter who I marry so long as you know that my heart is yours and that 'tis you I love.''

CHAPTER XIX

THE BIRTHDAY PARTY

On Roger's arrival in Paris, M. de Rochambeau gave only a moment to Athénaïs's letter. Having read it quickly through he remarked that the delay in Roger's return appeared to have been fully justified, and ordered him to draft a reply to the effect that, under Chenou's escort, Mademoiselle should proceed to her aunt's at St. Briac as soon as she felt well enough to do so. He then plunged into current business.

It was soon clear that the Marquis, having failed in his attempt to block the Anglo-French commercial treaty, had now turned his attention to the United Provinces, and that during the past month, he had informed himself in great detail as to the affairs of that troubled country; so Roger got down to mastering such information on the subject as was at his disposal.

He knew already that it was the French influence with the Republican party that had dragged the Dutch into the war against England in 1780, and that although the war had cost the Dutchmen dear it had done a great deal to strengthen anti-British feeling. French intervention in the dispute over the opening of the Scheldt had saved the Dutch from having to engage in a desperate struggle against Austria, and this had been followed immediately by a Franco-Dutch alliance, which, during the past year, had done much to further strengthen the good will between the two nations to the detriment of Britain.

Meanwhile, with the rise of French influence, the situation of the Stadtholder had become even more precarious. His mother had been an English Princess and his wife, now that Frederick the Great was dead, was the sister of the new King of Prussia, Frederick-William II; but neither power was in a position to sway the councils of his unruly States-General in his favour. Fourteen months before, he had been driven from The Hague and forced to take refuge in Gelderland, the only one of his provinces still loyal to him, and ever since the country had been in a state of increasing unrest.

On going into matters Roger found that a new crisis had occurred just before he had left for Bécherel. The States of Gelderland had advised William V to take military possession of two towns in that province, which, in defiance of his prerogative, had named their own magistrates. His doing so had resulted in the rebellious States of Holland passing a motion suspending him from his office of Captain-General, and he had appealed to his brother-in-law to maintain him in his authority. Instead of sending armed support, the King of Prussia had sent only a special emissary, in the person of Baron Görtz, to argue with the leaders of the Republican party.

These were Mynheers Van Berkel, Gyzlaas and Zeebergen, the Pensionaries of Amsterdam, Dordrecht and Haarlem respectively. With a few others they appeared to be in complete control of the provinces of West Friesland, Holland, Zealand and Utrecht; and were concerned in a plot to deprive the Stadtholder of his office and declare it no longer hereditary in his family.

Any such move, Roger felt, must result in war; since, if England and Prussia were pushed to it they would support the Stadtholder by force of arms; and, for the moment, he could not see what M. de Rochambeau stood to gain by an outbreak of hostilities. France was now nearer to bankruptcy than ever, and could not possibly afford to fight. Civil war in the United Provinces could, therefore, only mean that the Stadtholder, backed by France's enemies, would triumph over the Republicans, and the great influence that France had acquired in the country by peaceable means be lost to her.

That factor was evidently fully appreciated by M. de Vergennes, as it emerged that he was on the point of sending a special mission to the Stadtholders' Court to collaborate with Baron Görtz and the British Minister, Sir James Harris, in an attempt to reconcile William V and his numerous provincial Parliaments. But, as the Marquis was always opposed to M. de Vergennes's pacific policies, Roger felt certain that M. de Rochambeau's sudden preoccupation with Dutch politics was inspired by some deep-laid scheme that boded no good to Britain, and he determined to get to the bottom of it if he possibly could.

His belief was confirmed a few days later when the Marquis, displaying high good humour, informed him that M. de Rayneval had been appointed Ambassador Extraordinary to their High Mightinesses the States-General of the United Provinces; since he already knew that this high official of the French Foreign Ministry was the creature of M. de Rochambeau and his friends, and would follow their secret instructions to the detriment of those given to him by his Minister.

On the 18th of November the Court returned from Fontainebleau to enter on its winter season of endless amusements. The move alone cost a small fortune, as Roger learned in conversation with the secretary of the Duc de Polignac, who, as *Intendant-Général de Postes*, was responsible for arranging such royal journeys. No less than three thousand one hundred and fifty post horses had had to be placed at the Court's disposal for four days or more, to the great detriment of all ordinary travel facilities. Yet this was but a drop in the ocean of money required for the maintenance of the Court.

The Sovereigns seemed to have no idea that money, like grain or any other commodity, was not unlimited, and took time and effort to produce. The establishment of the Queen, exclusive of the salaries of her principal officers of State, had that year amounted to thirty-eight millions of *francs*. The King's expenditure was naturally far greater and, in addition, he was spending huge sums on building additional wings to his palaces at Rambouillet, Compiégne and Fontainebleau, and declared that next year a thorough renovation of the whole of the great palace of Versailles would be absolutely necessary.

Everyone knew that a crash was inevitable, and it was an open secret that M. de Calonne was now at his wits' end to supply the unceasing demands that the King made upon him. For three years he had juggled with the finances of France with all the ability of a super crook, but the day of reckoning was fast approaching. To stave it off he was resorting to the most desperate expedients. The Corporation of Paris decided to spend three millions a year for some time to come on public works, so he forced them to borrow thirty millions at once, left them three and took the other twenty-seven into the Treasury, promising to pay it back as required, as at that junction he could think of no other way of meeting the pensions due to certain courtiers.

The irresponsibility of these favoured few was equalled only by their arrogance, and in December, Roger heard of a particularly flagrant example of it. The Archbishop of Cambrai being out on a shooting party, trespassed on the property of one of his neighbours. Upon the gamekeeper of the adjoining property protesting, the Archbishop did not even deign to reply, but turned his gun on the man and shot him, wounding him grievously.

Yet, even at the height of the Treasury's embarrassments, the King did not cease from ordering new battleships to be built, or M. de Calonne from financing the most wildcat schemes. One, that aroused much public interest, was put forward by a Monsieur Montgolfier who asserted that he had discovered a method of directing the flight of balloons and could run an air-freight service between Paris and Marseilles at a profit.

Roger was reminded by this of M. Joseph Fouché, who had given as his reason for blackmailing old Aristotle Fénelon his need for money to finance balloon experiments; and he wondered what had become of the lanky, corpselike Oratorian teacher. On Roger's remarking one morning to a group of people at the Abbé de Périgord's, on M. de Calonne's folly in adding to his difficulties by backing such harebrained ventures, the Comte de Mirabeau, who was among them, declared with a laugh:

" 'Tis not that he has the faintest hope of profiting by it, but seeks to divert the people's attention from far graver issues. He is endeavouring to buy time by the old expedient of giving the populace 'bread and games.' "

"He would be in no need to provide the latter could he but find the means to purchase the former," smiled de Périgord.

"You have said it, Abbé," agreed the pockmarked Count. " 'Tis certain now that half France will be faced with starvation again this winter; and, whether the King likes it or not, before the year is out he will be forced to call an Assembly of Notables. 'Tis the only resource he has left for pulling the country out of the mess it is in."

"But surely that would be tantamount to a surrender of the Royal prerogative and the granting of a Constitution," Roger objected.

The Count shook his leonine head. "Not necessarily. The nobility, the clergy and the provincial Parliaments would all be represented in an Assembly of Notables, so they would, in the main, express the will of the nation. They would be asked to recommend measures for getting us out of our difficulties; but the monarch would not be bound to accept their advice. Yet it would be a step in the right direction, since once such a body is assembled who knows what powers it might not decide to take into its own hands. Maybe 'twould be the beginning of getting our addle-pated King where we want him."

"Think you the Court is not also aware of that?" said the elegant Louis de Narbonne, with a cynical smile. "And 'tis for that reason the Royal Council will use all their weight to prevent such a project. No Assembly of Notables has been convened since 1626, and after having managed for a hundred and sixty years without consulting the nation 'tis unthinkable that the Court should expose itself to the perils of doing so now."

Nevertheless, de Mirabeau proved the truer prophet, for so desperate were the straits in which M. de Calonne found himself by the end of the year that, on the 30th December, he himself advised the King to convene the Notables.

At this news public excitement reached fever pitch throughout the length and breadth of France, but with Roger it barely registered, as he heard that day that Athénaïs was expected back in Paris early in January.

She arrived on the eighth; Roger's nineteenth birthday. When asked his age he still gave it as two years more than was the fact but in both appearance and manner he now looked all of twenty-one. During his 'teens he had had the good fortune to grow steadily, so that he had developed into a tall, dark young man nearly six feet in height and with shoulders in due proportion.

He was out, on a mission for the Marquis, at the time of Athénaïs's arrival; but, having learned of it on his return, he hung about the upper hall that evening in order to see her on her way to join her father in the drawing-room, before they went in to dinner. As she came down the passage she was giving an arm to Madame Marie-Angé, who, he thought, had aged greatly in the past few months and was walking slowly with the aid of an ebony stick.

They both stopped to greet him with the utmost kindness, and remained talking to him for a few moments. Athénaïs was looking ravishing after her sojourn by the sea, and her eyes sent him the sweetest messages that she could not voice in front of her duenna. He had been puzzling his wits for weeks past as to how he could communicate with her in secret on her return, but he dared not trust any of the servants and had decided that he must wait to see how the land lay when she was actually in residence. To his joy she had evidently been thinking on the same lines and gave him there and then the opportunity that he was seeking.

"Monsieur Breuc," she said sweetly, "you are so knowledgeable about books, and now that I am back in Paris I wish to read all the new ones that have been published during my long absence. I pray you make out a list of the best titles and bring it to me in my boudoir some time to-morrow morning."

"I will do so with pleasure, Mademoiselle," he replied, hiding by a low bow the delight he could not prevent showing in his face.

As they turned away from him the footman-in-waiting threw open the door of the drawing-room, and Roger caught a glimpse of its interior. The Marquis was standing near the fireplace, magnificent as ever in satin and lace, and with him was a younger man, much more plainly dressed.

The visitor was about twenty-five years of age, tall, well-built, and good-looking. Roger could not suppress a twinge of jealousy at the thought that this handsome stranger was about to dine with Athénaïs; and his jealousy was by no means lessened when, on inquiring of Monsieur Roland later that evening, he learned how the young man came to be there.

"He is the son of M. de la Tour d'Auvergne," the major-domo informed him, "and he escorted Mademoiselle from St. Brieuc to Paris. I have it from his valet that he met Mademoiselle at her aunt's and has formed an attachment to her; so decided to accompany her hither."

Somewhat perturbed, Roger made his way to his room. He could not possibly complain of Athénaïs's reception of him, yet it was something of a shock to think that she had actually brought a suitor for her hand to Paris with her. Of the young man he knew nothing, except that his lineage was irreproachable. The family of de la Tour d'Auvergne was as old as that of Hugh Capet who had founded the Royal dynasty of France. There were streets in half the towns of Brittany named after them and Roger recalled having heard it said that, so proud were they of their name that, centuries ago, they had taken for their motto: "I am not Marquis, Duke or Prince; I am de la Tour d'Auvergne," so it seemed unlikely that M. de Rochambeau could have any grounds for refusing to give the young man his daughter.

Roger tried to console himself with the thought that since Athénaïs must marry someone during the coming summer, and it could not be himself, it was fortunate for her that it should be a man of a suitable age and pleasing appearance. He then sat down to write her a long love letter, putting into it all the things he had thought of and would have liked to include in letters to her, had he dared to write to her during the past two months. After which he made out the list of books, and went to bed.

In the morning, as soon as the Marquis had settled himself in his sanctum, he called Roger in and said to him:

"Breuc, we have a visitor staying with us; M. le Vicomte de la Tour d'Auvergne. You will, of course, know the name. His is one of the few great families that have consistently rejected the blandishments of the Court for the past three reigns; preferring to live in the old feudal manner on their estates rather than succumb to the attractions of Versailles. In consequence, M. le Vicomte has never before been in Paris; but he now plans to spend some months here. He will require a lodging, but it should not be too expensive, as his family is only moderately well off. As he does not know the town, I wish you to wait upon him this afternoon and go out with him in search of accommodation suited to his means."

Having assured the Marquis of his diligence in the matter, Roger returned to his work, then at midday went up to Athénaïs's boudoir.

Madame Marie-Angé was there with her and, in front of the duenna. Athénaïs treated him with casual friendliness; but, in the course of ten minutes' conversation on the most successful novels of the day, he managed to pass her his letter and receive one from her.

Immediately he had taken leave of them he rushed up to his room to read it:

Roger, my dear one,

The joy of beholding you again yester 'een was almost unbearable, but I beg you for my sake to use the greatest circumspection. Madame Marie-Angé has I am sure guessed our love but little knows that we have confessed it to one another. She has a great affection for me and a high regard for you. But her sense of duty is stronger than either sentiment and were she to discover that our lips had met she would surely denounce us to my father. For me that would mean confinement within the grey walls of a convent, perhaps for life, and for you such dire punishment as makes me swoon to think upon. Therefore let utmost caution ever be your watchword in all our dealings.

I have give much thought as to how we may at times be together yet keep our secret, and have devised a plan. There is at the top of the house in its east wing an old playroom. 'Tis dusty and neglected and no one ever goes there. I could on occasion, but not too frequently, go up there to seek out some old book or toy without arousing suspicion. Inquire circumspectly as to its situation and seek if there is not a way by which you could reach it, without danger to yourself across the roof. Its window looks out on some leads so can you but reach them unobserved 'twould be easy for me to admit you, and no one could observe me doing so from the street or any other window of the house.

Anxious as I am to hear your dear voice and gaze upon you at my pleasure once again, caution dictates that we should not attempt a meeting until my father next goes without me to spend a night or more at Versailles.

On the first evening of his absence I will await you in the playroom between six of the clock and seven. Come to me if you can, dear Miller's youngest son.

                    Thine in love,

                              Athénaïs Hermonie.

Wild with elation Roger kissed the divine missive a score of times, and could hardly contain his impatience to find out the situation of the playroom which promised him more joys than heaven had to offer. Having thought the matter over during his midday meal he decided that the room probably lay at no great distance from his own, on the far side of the ridge of slates that obstructed the view from his window; since, in the east wing of the house, there seemed no other place where it could be, and he knew that another staircase serving Athénaïs's apartments ran up in that direction.

As soon as he had finished eating he returned to his room, climbed out of his window on to the leads and made his way round the high, sloping roof on their far side. Sure enough, beyond it lay another flat stretch of leads and a dormer window similar to his own. It was very grimy and the inside of its panes were half covered with cobwebs; but on peering through it he could make out an old rocking-horse, and knew that he had found his goal.

In his excitement he had forgotten all about M. de la Tour d'Auvergne, but on going downstairs he found him quietly waiting in the hall. The Vicomte proved to have a good straight nose, prominent chin, clear grey eyes and auburn hair. He was a little under Roger's height and was well but simply dressed.

On Roger introducing himself and apologising for his lateness, the Vicomte said in a pleasant voice: "Please do not distress yourself, Monsieur Breuc. I have oceans of time, whereas you, as M. de Rochambeau's secretary, must be a very busy man. 'Tis I who should apologise for adding myself to your other burdens."

Such words from a noble to a secretary were so unusual that Roger could hardly believe his ears; but his reactions in such circumstances had always been swift, and with a flash of his white teeth he bowed a second time. "Monsieur le Vicomte, your charming consideration makes me doubly eager to be of service to you. I pray you to command me not only this afternoon but at any time during your stay in Paris."

The other laughed. " 'Tis a rash offer, Monsieur; since I hope to be here till summer at the least; and as I like your looks I may take you up on it. But come! I am agog for you to show me this mighty city."

Putting on their top-coats they went out to the waiting coach and drew the warm furs in it about their legs. When the coachman asked for directions the Vicomte declared that there would be ample time for him to find lodgings later and that this afternoon he wished to see something of the capital; so for the next two hours they drove in and out through the narrow streets while Roger pointed out the sights of interest.

On closer acquaintance he fell more than ever under the quiet charm of M. de la Tour d'Auvergne. The Vicomte was so certain of himself that it clearly never even occurred to him to make a parade of his nobility. Whenever the coach stopped and they got out to view a church or monument he asked his questions of vergers, and others to whom they spoke, with simple directness, and never failed to thank them courteously for their trouble. His manner had no resemblance to the exquisite grace which characterised the Abbé de Périgord but was so spontaneous and friendly that Roger was reminded by it of the best type of English gentleman. He was, too, extremely frank about his affairs and, as far as Roger was concerned, somewhat embarrassingly so; since on their way home he took occasion to remark:

"To be honest, I am in no haste to find a lodging; so I trust you will bear with me if I appear difficult upon that score. The fact is that I am most mightily smitten with Mademoiselle de Rochambeau; so the longer I can remain beneath the same roof with her, while not out-staying my welcome, the better I'll be pleased. I scarce dare to hope that, country bumpkin as I am, I'll be fortunate enough to find favour in the eyes of so lovely a lady; but at least while I am in her father's house I'll have some advantage over the more gifted beaux, who are certain to besiege her each time she goes to Versailles."

"I cannot answer for M. de Rochambeau," Roger replied, "but I should imagine that he would be agreeable to your remaining at the hotel as long as you like."

He was about to add: "And it would certainly be sound strategy for you to do so," but refrained, owing to his extraordinarily mixed feelings about his companion. Reason told him that any girl would be lucky to get such a likeable fellow as M. de la Tour d'Auvergne for a husband and that he would be wise to do all he could to aid the match, lest Athénaïs's father chose for her someone much less suitable from the personal point of view. But his whole instinct as a man revolted at the idea of Athénaïs in anyone's arms but his own, and the meaner side of his nature kept whispering that the more attractive the fiancé selected for her the less chance he would have of retaining her affections himself. At present, however, he seemed in no danger of losing them, as her letter to him could not have been more single-hearted, and she had not even made a mention of the Vicomte in it.

Two days later the Marquis went to Versailles and Roger, to his intense relief, learned that Athénaïs was not, on this occasion, to accompany him; as her dressmakers had not yet had time to furnish her with her winter collection, which she was in the process of selecting from the latest fashions.

The winter's night had closed in early and it was snowing with gentle persistence; but Roger scarcely gave a thought to the weather as he climbed out of his window and crossed the roof. He was a good quarter of an hour too early for the rendezvous so he crouched down out of the wind and, warmed by the glow that lay in his heart and brain, let the minutes drift by in glorious anticipation, until, at last, a light appeared behind the cobwebs of the playroom window. Athénaïs opened it and he jumped inside. Next moment, without a word, they were fast in one another's arms.

It seemed that they would never cease from kissing, but, at length, she drew him to an old sofa where they sat down and embraced again. Breathless, unconscious of the cold, they clung together, savouring to the utmost every second of this meeting that both of them had dreamed of for so long. It was many minutes before their words became anything more than hardly distinguishable whispers of love and tenderness; then, when they fell to talking in earnest there seemed so terribly much to say and so desperately little time to say it in.

Each in turn urged the other to be patient and not to jeopardise their happiness by some rash act; then each in turn swore that it would be the death of them if they could not meet soon again. Athénaïs said that she dared not come up to the old playroom with any frequency since Madame Marie-Angé knew that few of the things in it were any concern of hers; the place being really the province of long-dead generations of young de Rochambeaux, who had lived in happier times when it was still fashionable for noble families to bring up their children in their own homes. Yet neither of them could think of any other place where they might meet in safety. Roger suggested that she might have the room cleaned up and say that she had decided to use it as an extra boudoir; but she objected that if she did so Madame Marie-Ange might at any time come up to sit there with her, and so surprise them.

By the burning down of the single candle that Athénaïs had brought with her to light the room, they suddenly realised to their distress that their hour was up, although both of them had been unconscious of the flight of time, and thought it hardly begun. For Athénaïs to linger there longer would make her late for dinner, and so arouse Madame Marie-Ange's curiosity as to what had detained her; and that, in turn, would enhance the risk of arousing suspicion when she said that she was going up to the old playroom again. They could only leave it that each time the Marquis went to Versailles, and did not take her with him, on the first night of his absence they should meet there at six o'clock.

For a further five minutes they clung to one another and kissed with renewed ardour, then Roger stumbled out on to the snowy leads and Athénaïs shut the window of Elysium behind him.

He had to force himself to go downstairs and eat his evening meal with his under-secretary, Paintendre, as though nothing had occurred; but immediately afterwards he excused himself and took refuge in his room. There he could give way to his feelings and think freely of Athénaïs. Trembling with emotion, he passed the rest of the evening, and sat far into the night, reliving in his imagination every moment of that glorious hour with her, again and again.

Two days later he had an unexpected and most unpleasant encounter. He was working at his desk when M. de la Tour d'Auvergne and a young man of about seventeen, wearing the uniform cocked hat, blue cut-away coat and white breeches of a military cadet, entered his office. For a moment Roger did not recognise the youth, then the resemblance to Athénaïs struck him, and he realised that he was once more face to face with Count Lucien.

Having smiled at Roger, M. le Tour d'Auvergne turned to Count Lucien and said: "This is Monsieur Breuc, M. de Rochambeau's secretary, and I doubt not he will advance you the funds of which you stand in need."

"Breuc!" exclaimed the Count. "*Mon dieu!* I thought I knew his face." Then he launched out at Roger: "You miserable upstart! How in the name of perdition did you get here?"

"Monsieur!" said the Vicomte, in a tone of protest.

Roger knew that his whole position—his very life, now that Athénaïs loved him—hung upon his keeping his temper and maintaining an outward air of servility. Bowing before the rising storm he replied in a low voice: "*Monsieur le Comte*, as M. de la Tour d'Auvergne has told you, Monseigneur your father has done me the honour to make me his secretary. Judging by the favour he has shown me he finds my services of some small value. I trust you will allow me the privilege of also serving you."

"Serve me! To hell with you!" cried the young Count. "I'd not have you as a lackey! How dare you show your face again in the house of a de Rochambeau!" And he raised a riding-switch that he was carrying to strike at Roger.

"Monsieur!" repeated the Vicomte sharply, and he seized Count Lucien's wrist. " 'Tis not for me, a guest in your father's house, to question your manners to his servants. But Monsieur Breuc has behaved towards me with every courtesy, and I will not allow you to strike him in my presence unless you can first give some adequate reason for so doing."

"The fellow is a vagabond," blustered Count Lucien. "He dared to raise his eyes to Mademoiselle, my sister, and I had him thrown down the steps of our Hôtel in Rennes for his impudence."

M. le Tour d'Auvergne looked sternly at Roger. "Is this true!"

Roger returned the look squarely. "Monsieur le Vicomte, three years ago, Mademoiselle took pity upon me, and saved me when I was being pursued by a mob for a murder that I had not committed. I naturally conceived a sentiment of deep but most respectful gratitude towards her. Some time later I called at her home and asked to see her, in order that I might express my thanks. Count Lucien met me at the door and, without inquiring the purpose of my visit, took it upon himself to have me thrown out by his servants."

The Vicomte released Count Lucien's wrist, and said: "It seems then that you have but imagined an insult to your sister, Count; and, since it appears that Monsieur Breuc has served your father well, I can scarce think that he would thank you for driving away a useful servant. Be advised by me; forget this baseless prejudice and accept M. Breuc's offer to be of service to you."

The young de Rochambeau shrugged his shoulders. "I have no prejudices where servants are concerned. 'Twas the airs the fellow gave himself when we first met that riled me. And look at him now, dressed up to kill, in clothes far beyond his station."

" 'Twas Monseigneur's own desire that I should do credit to his service," said Roger quietly.

"Then 'tis none of my affair," admitted Count Lucien, grudgingly. "And I'll say no more, provided you keep your place. I am just come from Brienne, where I have completed my three years at the Military Academy, and I have now to spend a year at the finishing school in Paris. My expenses will be much greater here and from time to time I shall require funds. Are you in a position to furnish me with them?"

Roger bowed. "Monseigneur will be returning from Versailles in the course of a day or two. No doubt you will be seeing him and will arrange this matter personally. In the meantime I shall be happy to advance you any sum in reason that you may require."

"A hundred *louis* will do to go on with."

Crossing the room to an iron-bound chest, Roger unlocked it and counted out the money. When he had done M. de la Tour d'Auvergne said to him: "Monsieur Breuc, I should like to discuss further with you the question of my lodgings. If you are at liberty this evening about six o'clock I should be happy if you will take a bottle of wine with me at *La Belle Etoile* hard by here in the *Rue de l'Arbre Sec*."

"Monsieur le Vicomte, I should count it an honour," Roger replied, and his two visitors left him, M. de la Tour d'Auvergne with a smile and Count Lucien with a crestfallen look at the lesson in good manners he had just received from a noble who was not only older but also had more quarterings than himself.

Roger felt that he had been extremely fortunate in that M. de la Tour d'Auvergne had chanced to be present on Count Lucien's arrival in Paris, otherwise an ugly scene might have resulted in his dismissal; but there now seemed little danger of that, and at the *Belle Etoile* that evening he thanked the Vicomte warmly for his intervention.

The Vicomte declared that what Count Lucien needed was for somebody to call him out and teach him manners by a well-directed sword thrust.

"I would that I might be the one to give it him," Roger sighed, "but my position prohibits all thought of such a pleasure."

"Are you a swordsman, then?"

"Several masters have been good enough to say that I am not without skill, and I have fought once, successfully, in earnest."

"Indeed!" The Vicomte raised an eyebrow. " 'Tis unusual to come upon a secretary who can handle a blade."

"I will be honest with you, Monsieur, since I am sure you will not betray my confidence. My story is too long to weary you with in detail, but I am of gentle birth and was brought up to bear arms."

The Vicomte gave him a shrewd look. "Then if you were not brought up to think with the humility of a servant, it may be that there was, after all, something in Count Lucien's allegation, that your sentiments for Mademoiselle Athénaïs were not inspired alone by gratitude."

"Again I will be honest with you," Roger smiled. "I fell in love with Mademoiselle Athénaïs the first moment I set eyes on her. But, of course, I realise that there can be no question of my marrying her, and, since she must marry into a great family I could not wish her better fortune than to find happiness with yourself."

"I thank you, Chevalier, and believe me, loving her as I do, I can well understand your own feelings. You have my deepest sympathy in that your lot denies you the right to become my rival. But, talking of sword-play, I am not without some little skill myself, and, lest when I go to Court I find some quarrel forced upon me, I am anxious to keep my wrist supple. What say you to some practice-bouts?"

"Nothing would please me better; there is a fencing-room behind the stables at the Hôtel."

"We'll meet there then. And now a matter on which I am anxious to consult you. Next week Mademoiselle is to make her appearance at Court, and M. de Rochambeau is to present me to His Majesty. I have a suit or two which will serve for the moment, but I am anxious to possess a better wardrobe. Your taste is admirable, and I would be most grateful for your help in its selection."

"I thank you for the compliment, and 'twould be a pleasure," Roger replied. Then he added thoughtfully. "Since you have done me the honour to consult me, may I say that I think you would be ill-advised to enter into competition with the leading exquisites. You have a personality that few of them possess and would, I believe, make a greater mark if you set a style yourself by keeping to garments with little ornamentation, but of rich material and even, perhaps, of rather sombre colours so that they will stand out in contrast to the sunset hues worn by the majority of the courtiers."

The Vicomte laughed. "How right I was to consult you, *mon chèr* Chevalier. 'Tis a great idea and one that fits well with my modest income, for my purse is by no means as well lined as I would wish."

In the following week Roger had another secret meeting with Athénaïs. The pent-up passion of two months having been partially assuaged at their first meeting, they embraced with no less delight but found a little more time to talk coherently. M. de la Tour d'Auvergne had told her of the help that Roger was giving him in selecting his new clothes and she thanked him for it, saying that she thought it mighty generous in him to behave so to a potential rival.

"My angel," he smiled, caressing her cheek, "If I counted him a rival for your love I think I'd kill him, but for your hand 'tis different. He swears a great devotion to you, I know him to be a true gentleman, and I like him greatly. Tell me, what think you of him yourself?"

"I like him, too," she replied, after a moment. "My love is yours, and no man shall rob you of it. But, since marry I must, I would prefer M. de la Tour d'Auvergne to someone older. The decision lies, though, with my father, and he may not consider that M. le Vicomte is rich enough for me."

"When his father dies he will come into a good estate," hazarded Roger.

She shook her head. "Even then he will have no great fortune. His family have shut themselves away on their lands for so long that they hold no great offices of state, and have none of the fat pensions which fall to those who spend their lives flattering the Sovereigns."

"'Twould be hard on him if he failed in his suit for no other reason than that he is not a millionaire."

"I do not say that my father will reject him; only that his chances would be better had he the income of a man like M. de Caylus."

"That loathsome half-breed!" Roger exclaimed. "Surely your father would never think of giving you to him?"

"Nay, God forbid! I think I'd kill myself rather than be led to the altar by such a man. But be not alarmed. I thought of him only as the richest man of title that I know. There were, though, several good matches proposed for me last winter. The Duc de Vauguyon wants me for his eldest son, and the Comte de Porcin, who is passing rich, would have me replace his Countess who died two years ago. I doubt not, too, that on my return to Versailles overtures from numerous other quarters will be made to my father. Should one be forthcoming where the suitor has lineage equal to M. de la Tour d'Auvergne with greater wealth attached, the poor Vicomte will have to seek a bride else-where."

Roger made a wry grimace. "I am in despair that you should be leaving Paris so soon. What hopes are there of my seeing you at such times as I bring papers out to Versailles for M. le Marquis?"

"None, I fear." Athénaïs sought to soften the blow by speaking very gently. "Madame Marie-Ange will always be with me when I am in our apartments, and when out of them I shall be in the company of other ladies. But take heart, dear love. I shall return to Paris frequently for a night or more, to order new clothes and have them fitted. My father's attendance on the Queen will have no relation to my own and you may be sure that I shall arrange matters so that my visits here will be, as far as possible, during his absence. Each time I come to Paris we will meet in this room at six of the clock and snatch an hour of bliss together."

Greatly consoled, Roger took her in his arms and kissed her fondly. Neither of them had the faintest doubt of the other's eagerness for another meeting at the earliest possible opportunity. She vowed that the balls and parties at Versailles would be a weariness without him, and he that he would be counting the moments until he could breathe the perfume of her hair again. Once more, with a distress that almost amounted to physical pain, they clung to one another for the last few precious seconds, until it became imperative that she should go down to dinner and, half bemused by the heady wine of her caresses, Roger stumbled out of the window.

M. de Rochambeau had, on this occasion, remained longer than usual at Versailles; but when he returned on the 19th of January he was in as good a humour as his cold nature would ever allow him to demonstrate.

By the 11th, M. de Vergennes, worn out with battling against intrigue, and grief for the wife that he had loved so dearly, had become so ill that he could no longer cope with the onerous duties of his post as Foreign Minister. The King, loath to dispense altogether with the services of this wise and upright adviser, had asked him to carry on, but relieved him of the duty of entertaining the Ambassadors to dinner every Tuesday, and delegated this duty to the Baron de Breteuil.

Louis de Breteuil was one of M. de Rochambeau's intimates and, with him, believed that France's best hope of recovery lay in expansion; so his appointment as official host to the *Corps Diplomatique* was a great triumph for French Imperialism.

By the 25th of January, M. de Vergennes's health had become so precarious that the King asked de Breteuil to act for him at the sessions of the Royal Council; and the courtiers, with their noses to every wind that blew, were laying odds that he would be the next Foreign Minister.

Had Roger been of their company he might have made a fine haul by taking such bets, since he knew that de Breteuil did not desire the post, but preferred to continue as Minister for Paris and Keeper of the Seals.

Towards the end of the month there were a number of high-power conferences held in the Marquis's sanctum at the Hôtel de Rochambeau.

De Breteuil, De Castries, De Polignac, De Ségur, and the Marquis d'Adhémar, who was said to be the Duchess de Polignac's lover, and was shortly leaving to take up a new appointment as Ambassador to the Court of St. James, were all present. After much deliberation it was decided, on the Marquis's recommendation, that the Comte de Montmorin should be recommended to the King to succeed M. de Vergennes. M. de Montmorin had served as Ambassador to Spain and later held the office of Royal Governor of Brittany, and it was in the latter capacity that the Marquis had come to know him as an able but pliant man who, lacking powerful family connections, had the wisdom to accept advice from those whose good will could maintain him in office. On the 13th of February, M. de Vergennes, the friend of all peaceful policies, died; on the 14th the King nominated M. de Montmorin to succeed him.

The change meant nothing to the public; from the beginning of the year its whole interest had been centred on the rumour that the King intended to call an Assembly of Notables and hand over to them the direction of the ship of state. After many postponements the vacillating monarch at last brought himself to convene the Assembly on the 22nd of February, but the manner in which he addressed it, when assembled, was a grievous disappointment to the nation. Instead of asking this representative body to consider the desperate state of the country and advise him as to what measures could be taken for its salvation, he simply indicated that his Comptroller-General of Finance had already devised the measures and that their province was to place their weight behind them by an unanimous vote of confidence in the Minister.

M. de Calonne then made a most brilliant hour and a quarter's speech; but, to the amazement of everyone who listened to him, he performed a complete *volte-face* from every principle that he had followed throughout his three years of office. He now proposed, almost in their entirety, the reforms that Turgot had advocated a decade earlier. His revolutionary programme included: The removal of internal customs barriers; the erection of provincial, district and parochial Assemblies; that the hated forced labour of the *corvées* should be commuted for a monetary payment; that a remission of ten millions should be made in the *Gabelle*, and that this loss of income from salt should be recovered by a stamp tax on paper; that all producers of grain should be given a free hand to market it where they would without hindrance; that the nobility and clergy should no longer be exempt from taxation, and that a Land Tax should be instituted to which all property owners, irrespective of class, would be subject.

The next day, the better to deliberate on these matters, the Assembly was divided into seven committees, each of twenty-two members and each having a Prince of the Blood for its chairman. So urgent were the passage of these reforms now considered that all the committees sat every day, except Sundays; but it soon became apparent that opposition to the Royal will was rising in every quarter.

Both the clergy and nobles showed extreme resentment at the

proposal to tax their lands, and the Archbishop of Narbonne led a heated attack upon the measure. The representatives of the ancient provincial Parliaments fiercely opposed the proposals for establishing provincial Assemblies, as they feared that these would usurp their own functions. The trade guilds and entire commercial community of the country raised an outcry about the proposed tax on paper, saying that it would bring ruin to their business. In fact, every class represented in the Assembly had some reason to obstruct the new programme and all united in demanding that a full account should be given of how the national revenues were expended before further taxation was imposed.

M. de Calonne was compelled to admit that the deficit for the current year amounted to one hundred and thirteen millions, but he would give no details. The Princes of the Blood were forced to represent the rebellious attitude of their committees to the King, and one of them, the Prince de Conti, was so impressed by their arguments that he refused to continue his work until forced to do so by a direct order from the Monarch. Another of them, M. de Duc de Orleans, the most bitter enemy of the Court, skilfully slid out of his chairmanship on the plea that he could not be expected to give an impartial judgment on the reduction of the *Gabelle* as it would reduce his income by £30,000 a year. The King's brothers, M. le Comte de Provence and M. le Comte d'Artois, despite their normal preoccupations, the one with learning, and the other with women, worked hard with their committees. Both offered to reduce the cost of their stables by half a million *francs* a year, but this belated gesture was almost overlooked in the general alarm at the appalling state into which the finances had fallen.

In mid-March the Comte de Mirabeau published a broadside openly attacking the administration and, on the 20th a *Lettre de Cachet* was issued for his arrest; but he was warned of it and succeeded in escaping to England. By early April the popular fury against M. de Calonne had risen to such a height that the King could no longer support him and, on the 9th, he was dismissed from office. On the 19th, M. Necker, the ex-Finance Minister, issued a pamphlet, stigmatising M. de Calonne for his three years of mismanagement, and the King ordered the Swiss banker into exile. On the 25th of May the King at last dissolved the Assembly of Notables, which, instead of supporting the Royal Authority, had gone against it on every measure and given vent to the discontent of the whole nation. He was said to have sworn that during his lifetime he would never call another, and he now placed his affairs in the hands of his new Minister, Loménie de Brienne, the Archbishop of Toulouse.

In the meantime, M. de Rochambeau continued to occupy himself with affairs in the United Provinces. The Stadtholder's situation was an extremely difficult one, as the Dutch possessed a very liberal Constitution which rendered him little more than hereditary Chief Magistrate. On the advice of the British Minister, Sir James Harris, he had now formed a bodyguard for his own protection, but he controlled so few troops that it was quite impossible for him to enforce his authority. On the other hand, the States-General were busy secretly recruiting a free-corps throughout the whole country for the maintenance of their independence.

The three Ambassadors, Görtz, Harris and de Rayneval continued their mediation and appeared to be holding the two parties back from an open clash; but all through the spring and early summer the United Provinces remained a powder barrel which, if it went off, was liable to ignite half Europe.

Roger followed every move with the keenest interest but, puzzle his wits as he would, he could still not make out what deep game M. de Rochambeau was playing. It seemed to him beyond belief that the Marquis could be seeking to bring about a war while the finances of France were in such a desperate situation, yet he knew that from the beginning of the year many warlike preparations had been undertaken.

The British Control Commission having evacuated Dunkirk, on the ratification of the Treaty of Versailles, the French had at once begun to refortify the port, and they were now committed to a programme of works there almost as formidable as that for Cherbourg. It had also been decided that a camp of eighty thousand troops should be assembled in the summer for "manœuvres" at Givet, in Flanders. The Navy too, was gradually being got into a state of readiness and the Marshal de Castries had mentioned to the Marquis in Roger's hearing that he had sixty-four ships-of-the-line which could now be made ready for action at short notice.

Having become the repository of such secrets, Roger felt it his duty to pass them on to Mr. Gilbert Maxwell and from early in 1787 a regular correspondence ensued. The information that he sent would actually have been of considerably greater value if he had given with it the attitude and opinions on foreign policy of the many important people with whom he now came in contact; but, not being aware of that, he confined his reports to bare statements of fact which he considered had military significance.

Mr. Maxwell's replies were little more than appreciative acknowledgements, although he occasionally asked in guarded terms if Roger could give him other specific pieces of information. Once he suggested that if Roger could, without endangering his position, get in touch with Mr. Daniel Hailes, the Chargé d'Affaires at the British Embassy in Paris, this might prove useful; and added that Mr. Hailes had been instructed to supply him with funds if he should be in need of them.

Roger still had qualms enough about betraying his employer and, while he was prepared to do so for his country's sake, the idea of selling information for money was highly repulsive to him. So he replied briefly that he was not in need of funds and that he thought it would be most ill-advised for him to have any dealings with the British Embassy.

From Athénaïs's first appearance at Versailles, she became unavoidably involved in the series of endless entertainments that still occupied most of the energies of the feckless Court, but she managed to get back to Paris for a night once every ten days or so. Now and then, to Roger's fury, his work prevented him from taking advantage of her presence to keep their tryst, but the very difficulties that beset their coming together, while still preserving their secret, made them all the more eager for these stolen meetings.

Most of the hours they spent in the old playroom were devoted to kisses, sighs, embraces and mutual vows of devotion, but occasionally they found time to talk for a little of her doings at Versailles. In mid-May she told him that she had now become quite intimate with the Royal circle ás she had recently seen them with less formality.

With the coming of summer the Queen had reopened her Swiss Châlet dairy farm beside the lake near the Petit Trianon. Once or twice a week the Royal family went out there for a picnic meal, with a favoured few of whom Athénaïs was now one. They all wore simple clothes, played at milking the cows, made butter, and cooked their own supper.

Marie-Antoinette loved to throw off the dignity of Queen for a few hours and she was gay and charming with everybody. Athénaïs said that it was a joy to see her acting the farmer's wife and romping with her children, the young Dauphin and the little Princess Royale. Even the heavy-featured, tongue-tied King came out of his shell a little and joined in a game of blind man's buff, when he was not too tired from hunting and fell asleep in his chair.

Athénaïs declared that he was very far from being the fool that many people thought him. He was, she said, a clever geographer, an expert locksmith, and spoke German and English well. It was his misfortune that he would much rather have been a bourgeois family-man than a King, and had it not been for his very simple tastes, gentleness and diffidence, he would have made an excellent Sovereign.

Roger could not question such a first-hand portrait but all the same he accepted it with reservation. He had heard M. de Rochambeau say more than once that the King was so bored by affairs of State that during the meetings of the Royal Council he often drew pictures of locks on his blotting-pad, instead of listening to what his ministers were saying to him; and that on other occasions he returned so exhausted from his favourite pastime of the chase that he slept solidly, snoring his way through discussions of the utmost importance.

Every time Roger saw Athénaïs he asked her if any decision had yet been taken about her marriage, dreading to hear that something definite had been decided which would soon put a period to their meetings; but each time she said that her father seemed in no hurry to dispose of her and, as summer approached, she sought to comfort Roger by saying that, even when her engagement was announced, a further two or three months must elapse while she got her trousseau together, so it was most unlikely that they would have to face separation until the autumn.

M. de la Tour d'Auvergne continued to show the greatest devotion to her, and she freely confessed that, of her suitors whom she had met personally, she favoured him far above the rest; but, as all negotiations for her hand were conducted through her father, there were several that she had not seen and, perhaps, others that she did not even know about.

Roger had helped the Vicomte to find comfortable lodgings in the Rue de Richelieu, soon after Athénaïs had taken up her residence at Versailles, and he had since spent most of his time getting himself invited to every party at which he learned she was to appear; but he often looked in on Roger, or invited him to his apartment for a quiet talk about the object of their mutual devotion, and two or three times a week they fenced together.

It was on the 4th of June that M. de Rochambeau said to Roger: "On the 30th of this month I intend to give a ball. It is Mademoiselle Athénaïs's eighteenth birthday, and on that night I propose to present her to her future husband. Their Majesties have promised to honour me with their presence on this occasion, so I desire that no expense should be spared to give them pleasure. I wish you to go into the matter with my major-domo and make all the necessary arrangements. Everybody of any importance should be invited so I should also like you to get me out a list of guests. I will submit it to the Sovereigns for their approval and when they have made any amendments they may wish, you can employ your assistant on sending out the invitations."

Roger could feel the blood draining from his face, and he prayed that the Marquis would not notice the tremor in his voice as he asked: "Er—is it your desire, Monseigneur, that the name of Mademoiselle's future husband should be given out as yet?"

"No," replied the Marquis, quietly. "The match that I have arranged for Mademoiselle is extremely suitable and she could hardly hope for a better; but 'tis my secret, and I intend to keep it as a pleasant surprise for her on the night of the ball."

At that, Roger had to leave it and, much as he hated the thought of Athénaïs marrying anyone, he could only pray that the pleasant surprise her father planned for her was his consent to the suit of M. de la Tour d'Auvergne.

When he saw her next he found that she was no wiser than himself and, although she knew all about the ball, she had not succeeded in securing even a hint as to whom she was to be affianced. Her own belief was that her father favoured the young Prince de la Roche-Aymon, who was eighteen months her junior, but now that the day of her committal was fast approaching she hoped more than ever that his choice would be her devoted and charming Vicomte.

In the weeks that followed Roger and Monsieur Roland consulted together with great frequency and gave countless orders to ensure the success of the entertainment. The Hôtel was turned upside down and an army of workmen brought in to take down partitions, broaden doorways and erect canopies. The principal *salons* of the mansion were all ear-marked as supper or card rooms; the great courtyard was entirely floored over and tented above, to form a ballroom that would accommodate a thousand dancers. The stables were evacuated, cleaned and converted into a mess for the troops of guards without which the King and his brothers never left their palaces. A hundred new liveries in the de Rochambeau colours were ordered so that every footman might have a brand-new one, and those hired for the evening not appear dissimilar to the permanent staff. Scores of additional candelabra were affixed to light the huge marquee and forty of the best fiddlers in Paris engaged to form the band. The Chef took on fifty additional scullions who worked for days to prepare a superb collation, and the wine butler got up over two thousand bottles of the Marquis's finest wines from the cellars.

The list of proposed guests had been returned from Versailles and the invitations sent out. They included all the Princes of the Blood, except His Royal Highness the Duc d'Orleans, the twenty members of the Royal Council and, excepting the de Rohans, with their kinsmen, the Soubises, Guises and Lorraines, practically every great name that had figured in the history of France for the past three hundred years; Aiguillion, Beaufort, Biron, Bouillon, Bourbon-Condé, Châtillion, Choiseul, Crillon, Epernon, Estrées, Gramont, Guéménée, Lambesq, Longueville, Luynes, Montmorency, Montpensier, Nemours, Nesle, Noailles, Richelieu, Rochefoucault, Soissons, Sully, Trémouille, Villeroy, Vendôme, together with a host of others, and the whole *Corps Diplomatique* as at that date accredited to the Court of Versailles. Monsieur Roland was to be responsible for the service of the guests, and Roger was to be at hand from start to finish, in case during the evening the Marquis wished him to execute any special commission.

On the great night, Athénaïs, her powdered hair ornamented with ostrich feathers and little garlands of fresh flowers, and wearing a dress of cream satin sewn with pearls, took her place beside her father at the top of the grand staircase, to receive her guests. By eight o'clock they were arriving in a constant stream, and soon Cardinals, Duchesses, Ambassadors and Marshals of France were mingling together in a dazzling concourse. At a quarter to nine the Captain of the King's guards arrived to take possession of the house in the name of His Majesty.

At nine o'clock there sounded a loud fanfare of trumpets, announcing the approach of the Sovereigns, and Athénaïs and her father went down to receive them. Bowing or curtseying at every third step, the de Rochambeaus walked backwards before their royal guests right across the parquet floor of the great marquee until they reached the two high thrones, covered in blue velvet spangled with gold *fleur-de-lys*, that had been prepared upon a daïs. When the King and Queen were seated their host and hostess personally offered them refreshments, and they formally broke little cakes on the gold platters and sipped wine from the crystal goblets.

For the entrance of their Majesties the other guests had formed ten deep on each side of the room into a glittering lane, and sunk in a flurry of silks and ribbons, like corn before a gust of wind, in deep obeisance as the Royal couple advanced. Now they formed in a great half-circle, leaving an empty space before the thrones, to the right and left of which the Princes of the Blood and their ladies had seated themselves on brocaded *tabourets*.

The King signed to one of his gentlemen, who handed him a jewelled casket, which he gave to Athénaïs with his good wishes for her birthday. It contained a pair of beautiful emerald drop-shaped ear-rings. One of the Queen's ladies gave her a long, carved ivory box. Beckoning

Athénaïs to her she kissed her lightly on the forehead and laid the box in her arms. On opening it a feather fan was disclosed made with infinite labour from thousands of woodcock points. "Monsieur" the King's eldest brother gave her a pair of diamond buckles; the little son of the Emperor of Cochinchina, then on a mission to the French Court, a beautiful lacquer box; Monsieur Simolin, the Russian Ambassador, a cape of sables; King George's emissary, the Duke of Dorset, a fine pair of Chelsea figures; the Comte de Mercy, a case of Imperial Tokay; and so for an hour it continued, while the splendidly clad denizens of the *ancien régime* paid homage to birth and beauty, laying at her feet enough treasure to keep a thousand poor families from want for a twelvemonth.

When the present-giving was over, at a sign from the King, the band struck up a minuet. Louis of France rose from his throne and led Athénaïs de Rochambeau out on to the floor; Marie Antoinette laid her tapering fingers on the arm of the Marquis, and the two couples took up their positions to open the ball.

For two hours the stately dancing continued; myriads of candles making the jewels of the courtiers scintillate and sparkle as they threaded their way in and out of the complicated evolutions, their silks, satins and velvets blending and merging in a kaleidoscope of riotous colour.

Most of the time Roger stood a little behind the row of *tabourets* to the right of the thrones, glorying in the beauty of his lovely Athénaïs, but always keeping the Marquis in view in case some service was required of him. From time to time various friends came up and chatted to him for a while; M. de la Tour d'Auvergne—as anxious as Roger was to know his fate—Count Louis de Narbonne and the Abbé de Périgord among them.

The lame Abbé, clad in a suit of dove-grey silk, his piquant face alight with animation was, as usual, enjoying himself immensely. The fact that he was lame made other men always get up on his approach and offer him their seats, while he was never expected to extend a similar courtesy to them. In consequence, he gravitated gracefully from one to another of all the loveliest women present, and lingered at their sides whispering amusing immoralities to each of them behind their fans for as long as he listed then, with apparent regret, tore himself away to murmur the latest scandal into the willing ear of another.

Roger proved poor company that night for the people who talked to him. He knew the programme; dancing till midnight, then the announcing of the engagement, then an adjournment for supper, then dancing again until two o'clock, at which hour their Majesties would leave; but the band would play on till four, and by five it was hoped that any lingering drunks would be carried off to their coaches by their servants.

The two hours' dancing before supper seemed an eternity to him and afterwards he only remembered one episode during it. He had moved out a little down one side of the room and was standing behind two men who were some way apart from the crowd.

Suddenly he heard one of them say in English: "I'd give a thousand guineas to know what's inside that damn' fellow's head. If ever there was a mischief-maker, he is one."

The other replied quietly: "Don't worry, Your Grace. We'll know in due course. We have a very reliable agent here. It seems that he is averse to contacting the Embassy, but, no doubt, should any crisis arise he will return home and report to Maxwell personally."

Roger saw that they were both looking intently at the Marquis, and he knew that the first speaker was the British Ambassador, the Duke of Dorset. It flashed into his mind that the other was probably Mr. Daniel Hailes, and that he himself was the "very reliable agent" referred to.

The fact that his King's representatives knew of and counted on him came as a shock, and even more so the intimation that, in the event of a crisis, he was expected to go home and report in person.

At last the band stopped playing, the Sovereigns returned to their thrones and the glittering throng formed again into a great half-circle before them. Under the direction of Monsieur Roland scores of footmen had appeared carrying silver salvers loaded with glasses of champagne. The major-domo himself brought two lovely Venetian goblets on a gold salver to M. de Rochambeau. Going down on one knee the Marquis offered them to their Majesties and each took one.

The King then stood up and addressed the assembled company. "Cousins, my lords and ladies; it is our Royal pleasure this night to er—thank Monsieur de Rochambeau for the very pleasant entertainment he has afforded us. It is also our, er—pleasure to give our Royal consent to a contract of marriage uniting two great and ancient families, both er—distinguished for their services to the Crown. We refer, of course, to the forthcoming nuptials of Mademoiselle de Rochambeau. It will be our Royal pleasure to sign as witness to the marriage contract on a suitable date at—er—our palace of Versailles. In wishing happiness to this couple it gives us special pleasure to know that M. le Marquis has selected for his son-in-law another great landowner in our Province of Brittany."

For Athénaïs's sake Roger's heart leapt for joy. The King's last words could only mean that the Marquis had decided to give her to M. de la Tour d'Auvergne.

After a little pause the King coughed, and went on:

"Mademoiselle de Rochambeau is indeed fortunate, as her husband-to-be is one of the richest men in our realm. But M. le Comte de Caylus is also to be congratulated. . . ."

CHAPTER XX

THE BETROTHAL

A G H A S T, choking with shock and indignation, Roger took in the terrible sentence that had been passed on Athénaïs. As though in a nightmare he heard the heavy-faced, lugubrious King drone on, proposing the health and happiness of M. de Caylus and his future Countess; and saw the burly, sallow-complexioned quadroon step forward from a group of gentlemen on the far side of the thrones.

De Caylus bowed very deeply, first to the Sovereigns, then to Athénaïs. Roger could not see her face but he knew what she must be feeling and he feared that she might faint under the shock. But, with the self-discipline that was one of the virtues of her caste she went through the prescribed formalities without even a tremor. Having sunk almost to the ground in a graceful curtsey she slowly rose to her full height and extended her right hand. The King took it and placed it in M. de Caylus's left. Then raising his goblet the Monarch toasted the affianced pair. A moment later the great marquee was ringing with the cheers of the splendid company.

The King gave his arm to the Queen. With her on his left and M. de Rochambeau one pace behind him to his right they led the way up the grand staircase to supper. Athénaïs and M. de Caylus walked immediately behind them, then came the chastely beautiful Princess de Lamballe, who was in attendance on the Queen, escorted by Comte Lucien de Rochambeau and, after them, the Princes, Ambassadors and nobles followed in strict order of precedence.

It took twenty minutes for the marquee to empty, and for most of that time Roger's brain refused to work. The thought of Athénaïs married to de Caylus made him almost physically sick, yet he knew that the vast majority of those who had witnessed the betrothal took a completely different view of the matter. They would not give a thought to the human, personal side of the affair but regard the alliance as eminently suitable.

Their attitude to such matters was brought home to him afresh by seeing the Abbé de Périgord with the young and lovely Countess de Flahaut, whom everybody openly regarded as his wife in all but name, going upstairs to supper. By right of birth the Abbé should have been the Count de Talleyrand-Périgord but, simply because he had met with an accident when a child, his father had deprived him of his right to inherit both title and estates, and forced him against his will to go into the Church. Yet the Abbé bore no resentment against his father; he recognised that in all things family must come first.

How Roger got through the remaining hours of the ball he never afterwards remembered. At one time he looked everywhere for M. de la Tour d'Auvergne, but could not find him, and so assumed that, overcome with distress, he had gone home. In due course their Majesties, surrounded by their personal attendants, guards and trumpeters, were ushered to the long train of coaches that would bear the Royal party back to the Palais des Tuilleries. Soon afterwards Athénaïs, a fixed, strained smile on her face, which was chalk-white under her rouge, begged to be excused; but the dancing and hollow-sounding laughter seemed to go on interminably. At last the crowd began to thin but, owing to the congestion in the narrow street outside, it could not get away very rapidly. Roger saw that it would be another hour at least before all the guests had gone and, deciding that he could stand it no longer, went up to his room.

When he reached it the summer dawn was already breaking, so he saw at once the small, huddled figure sprawled face downwards on his bed. It took him only a second to guess that when Athénaïs's maids had left her for the night she must have crept up to the play-room and crossed the roof to climb in at his window. Throwing himself on his knees beside the bed, he took her in his arms.

She was so distraught with grief that, for a time, she could only sob her heart out on his chest and murmur:

"Oh, Rojé, Rojé, what am I to do? I cannot bear it. I cannot bear it."

With the comfort of his arms about her, gradually her paroxysms of weeping eased, and she said bitterly: "Why, with half the gentlemen in France to choose from, must my father give me to that loathsome creature. I would have done my best to make de la Tour d'Auvergne happy; I could have borne with de Porcin, or played a mother's part to little de la Roche-Aymon. But the very thought of this beast repels me. Oh, Rojé, what shall I do?"

"Can you not appeal to the Queen," he suggested. "She is said to be kind-hearted, and you say she likes you. Surely she would speak to your father?"

Athénaïs shook her head. "Nay, 'twould be useless, dear love. The Queen is kind, but a martinet where duty is concerned. All the world knows how she must have suffered herself when she first came to Court as a beautiful young bride. The King has never been renowned for his address, and so oafish was he as a young Prince that 'twas seven years before he could bring himself to sleep with her. Everyone knew of her humiliation, yet she bore it with quiet pride, and expects others to face things disagreeable to them in a like manner. She would never interfere in a family matter such as this."

Roger hesitated only a moment, before he said: "Then there is only one thing for it. We must elope together."

She started up and clutched his wrist. "Elope! How can we, Rojé? Where could we go?"

"To England, angel."

"But did you not tell me that your father had forbidden you his house?"

" 'Tis true," he admitted. "But at least I am no servant there. My mother would help us, and in time my father will come round."

"Are you sure of that? I love you, Rojé; oh, I love you dearly; yet I know only too well that I should make but a poor wife for a pauper."

"All will be well. I'm certain of it," he said as firmly as he could manage.

During the past nine months he had thought a hundred times of asking her to run away with him, but he had always put the thought from him because he had so terribly little to offer her. It was for that reason he had hesitated a moment back, before proposing such a desperate expedient. He knew that his mother would help them, as far as she could, but she had not a penny of her own; and, if his father remained adamant, even the best employment he could hope to get would produce an income that, to Athénaïs, would seem little better than penury. Yet, save her he must from de Caylus, and this seemed the only possible way that offered; so he went on with more confidence.

"I've a hundred and fifty *louis* saved, which would keep us in reasonable comfort for a while. Then your jewels, with those you received to-night, must be worth a small fortune. God forbid that I should live on you like some shiftless adventurer; but they would provide a sheet anchor, were there some delay in my obtaining a suitable appointment. That should not be hard, though, after the experience I've had with your father. We would not be rich, but I've confidence in myself now, and once given a decent opening I vow I could earn enough to keep us like gentlefolk. And we'd have each other."

She flung her arms round his neck. "Oh, *Rojé*, dear miller's youngest son; I've not a doubt but that in time you'll make your fortune, and I'd be content to wait for that. I hate the Court, with all its boring ceremonies and stupid etiquette. I'll leave it gladly if you can make enough so that we'll not starve."

"Very well!" he cried, pressing her to him. "Oh, my beloved! I swear you'll not regret it. My father will come round. He could not do otherwise once he sees you. But that apart, we'll make a place for ourselves and have such joy in doing it. With you to work for nothing can stop me."

"I know it," she laughed, turning her tear-stained face up to him. "As for my jewels, they are yours to do as you wish with. At least they would buy and furnish a pleasant little house. Then what you earned could be devoted wholly to food, clothes and servants, and—and children, if they came to us."

"I hope they do. I'd adore to have a daughter just like you."

"Oh, but I must have a son first. A son, *Rojé*, with your blue eyes and those lovely, long dark lashes."

"We'll have both, dear heart; and more if you wish. Would you like lots of children?"

"Yes. And I would keep them with us in our home. I'd not let them be put out to nurse as is the custom here in France."

"I wouldn't let you, anyway," he smiled. "There is little point in having children unless one has the fun of playing with them."

"And telling them stories," she added. "I know so many lovely fairy stories that I shall be able to tell ours."

"Our own story is better than any fairy tale, and you will be able to tell them that, my sweet Princess."

"Dear miller's youngest son! I fear I'll find it very strange in England at first, though. Shall we live in London?"

He nodded. "Yes, since 'tis there that I shall find my best opportunities. And with you for my wife I'll be the proudest man in the whole city.

"Your wife!" she whispered.

Suddenly she gripped his arms with all her strength and her fingers dug into his muscles.

"Your wife!" she breathed again. "But, *Rojé*, I had forgot. I never think of you as one, but—but you are a heretic. I could never marry a heretic."

He too, had temporarily forgotten that last sinister barrier, of man-made bigotry, intolerance and superstition, which, towering high above all others, still separated them.

"You would be an Englishwoman if you married me," he muttered, still dazed from the sudden shock to all the castles in the air they had been building. "And nearly everyone in England is a Protestant."

"Don't ask me to recant!" she cried. "Don't ask me, I beg. I couldn't do it. 'Twould be to imperil my immortal soul."

All Roger's love for her, all the mental pictures of the dream world they had been creating and his acute reluctance to leave her in her present desperate situation, fought within him against the inherited teachings of the Reformation; yet they were not strong enough to prevail entirely.

"I'd give my life for you," he said slowly. "I would lay it down to-morrow; but I hesitate to risk my hopes of salvation."

"Then how can we marry? Oh, *Rojé*, will you not think again, and be received into the Catholic Church?"

"I cannot promise that. I must have time to consider it. But wait! Does not the Pope grant dispensations in special cases? If we could secure one we might yet be married in your Church but each continue in our own religions."

She looked up suddenly, with new hope shining in her eyes. " 'Tis true; and there lies the way out of our difficulty. Such dispensations are costly, I believe; but, if need be, the price of my jewels must go for that. And, for your part, 'twould be necessary only for you to sign a promise that any children of the marriage be brought up in the Roman faith."

"What say you!" he exclaimed. "Commit unborn children to follow a faith of which they have no knowledge! Nay, that I would never do. My soul is my own to jeopardise for love's sake if I wish. Having done so I might still receive God's mercy, but how could I ever hope for that if I signed away the rights of others, who have as yet no minds with which to take decisions of their own."

"But, *Rojé*," she pleaded. " 'Tis natural that children should be brought up to some religion."

"Indeed it is; and as in most cases the parents are of the same faith there arises no question as to what it should be. But where the parents differ 'tis but fair that the children should be left a free choice to decide for themselves, when they are old enough."

Athénaïs sighed. "*Rojé*, dear heart, I am no theologian to argue such questions. I know only the simple facts. The Holy Father will not grant a dispensation for such a marriage as we plan unless you are willing to swear a solemn oath that all children of the marriage should be baptised into the Catholic faith."

He laid his hands on hers and gently drew her arms away from about his neck. "My love," he said softly, "Fate is too strong for us. Even for you I'll buy no dispensation at such a price. Come to England with me if you will and we'll tell everyone that we have been married in France. I pledge you my oath, here and now, never to desert you, and to ever regard you in all things as my wife. But unless you'll marry me by Church of England rites, more I have not the power to offer."

"I cannot," she whispered. " 'Twould make me old before my time to have the ever-present knowledge that I was living in sin; and that my children were bastards, born out of wedlock. No lasting happiness to either of us could ever come of it."

Then with a moan she turned away from him and, burying her face in his pillow, began to sob out her heart.

While he soothed and sought to comfort her he strove to think of some way in which he might yet save her from having to marry de Caylus. It came to him then that there was one possible line of action which he might attempt.

She sat up at last and, still crying quietly, said: "I cannot blame you, *Rojé*. I would feel the same, did you try to bring my babies up as heretics. For a little time we deluded ourselves with a vision of a happiness that we shall never know. Yet I will not submit to marrying de Caylus. There is one escape that even my father cannot deny me. I'd rather put the world and all things in it behind me by casting myself upon the bosom of the Church."

"What! Take the veil?" he exclaimed, aghast.

"Yes. Why not? Had I not known love with you I might have supported that loathsome man's caresses. But now 'tis impossible. If he touched me I would plunge a poignard in his heart; so 'tis better, far, that I should enter a convent."

"You must not do it," he pleaded. "You are so young, so beautiful; 'twould be a sin against nature to let them cut off your golden hair and shut you up for life. Besides, I have thought of a way by which I yet may free you from this hateful marriage. I'll call M. de Caylus out, and kill him."

"Oh, my sweet *Rojé*," she sighed. "The thought is monstrous brave and I know you'd do it, were it possible; but you forget the status you have assumed here in France. M. de Caylus would never accept your challenge. No noble will ever cross swords with one whom he considers to be beneath him."

Carried away by his distress, Roger had forgotten that; yet he knew that she was right, and he could only mutter angrily: "I'd sooner be broken on the wheel than live to think of you in his arms, or suffering a living death in the black robes of a nun."

For a time they fell silent; but full daylight had now come, stressing for both of them the utter exhaustion they felt from the emotions that had torn them during the past night. Athénaïs made Roger swear that he would do nothing rash without first informing her of his intention, and he made her swear that she would likewise take no steps to enter a convent before they had met and talked again.

In the meantime, both knew that her betrothal to M. de Caylus amounted to no more than a formality. He might send her flowers and presents and call upon her, but they would never be left alone together for a moment; so her life would continue just as it had before.

They embraced and kissed sadly once more; then she pulled the

271

thick robe that she was wearing closely round her and Roger, having helped her out of his window, led her across the roof to the old play-room, where they kissed again and parted. When he got back to his room he found that he was dead-beat. Pulling off his clothes he flopped into bed and, laying his head on the pillow, still damp from Athénaïs's tears, he fell unhappily asleep.

Shortly after midday he was roused by a servant coming to tell him that a courier had arrived with urgent dispatches from the United Provinces. On going downstairs he opened them to learn that a match had been struck there well calculated to light the powder-barrel.

Joseph de Rayneval wrote that, since the Stadtholder dared not visit the Hague from fear of an attempt upon his person, his wife, the beautiful and high-spirited Princess of Orange, had resolved to do so, with the intention of putting heart into their supporters there. She had set out a few days previously but, on reaching Schoonhoven, had been stopped by troops belonging to the Province of Holland, treated like a prisoner and, after suffering arrest for a few hours, turned back. For this affront she had demanded that her brother, Frederick-William II of Prussia, should send troops to exact vengeance in her name.

When M. de Rochambeau heard the news he was delighted. He told Roger that he did not think that the King of Prussia would accede to his sister's demand, as his predecessor, Frederick the Great, had already made Prussia's position clear before his death. It was known that when Mr. Pitt had sent Lord Cornwallis to ascertain his intentions during the Dutch crisis of the previous September the old and ailing monarch had declared that an alliance between England and himself to check French ambitions would mean a general war in which England would have to meet the fleets of France, Spain, Holland and perhaps Russia; while he would have on his hands the armies of France, Russia and Austria; and that "although such a contest had been maintained, it was not a game to play often." So the odds were all against the Prussians taking up arms to avenge this insult to the Princess, and their failure to do so would weaken the Stadtholder's position still further.

As soon as Roger was free of the Marquis he hurried round to the lodgings of M. de la Tour d'Auvergne but, to his chagrin, learned that the Vicomte had left that afternoon for Versailles. Why he should have done so Roger could not imagine as, normally, the Vicomte's movements were always governed by those of Athénaïs, and she was still in Paris; but it occurred to him that now she was affianced to M. de Caylus his friend might consider himself in honour bound to cease his attentions to her.

Two days later Athénaïs and her father left again for Versailles. The Hôtel was still in a turmoil with an army of workmen setting it to rights after the ball, so Roger mooned miserably about it tripping over pieces of scaffolding, and unable to settle to anything. Then late that night M. de la Tour d'Auvergne's servant came to ask him to go to his master's lodging.

Roger found the Vicomte pale but calm. He said at once, "I trust that I have not roused you from your bed, but I wished you to know that I fight at dawn."

There was no need to ask who? Roger nodded. "I had the same idea myself, but my position debars me from it."

The Vicomte poured him a glass of wine. "I realise that, and 'twas one of my reasons for not asking you to be one of my seconds. The other was the fact that I do not wish Mademoiselle de Rochambeau's name to be associated with the meeting; and your presence at it might lead to that, owing to your connection with the family. It has taken me three days hanging about Versailles to find a suitable pretext; but this afternoon I learned that M. de Caylus had booked the tennis court. I forestalled him there with M. de Broglie, and refused to give it up. High words followed and to make certain that de Caylus should call me out I taunted him with his black blood. I said: 'de la Tour d'Auvergne does not give way to one who is but three-quarters noble and the other quarter slave'; and those present had to restrain him from having at me there and then."

" 'Twas well done," said Roger. "What think you of your chances?"

" 'Tis hard to say. Physically he is much stronger than myself, and is reputed a most redoubtable antagonist. Yet, as you know, I am well in practice and have the advantage that I have not debauched myself with opera girls these past ten years."

"You will kill him if you can?"

"I must. 'Tis no case for half-measures. Naught but his death can serve to break this monstrous betrothal."

"May God guide your sword. But what of the results? Think you the King will enforce the edicts against duelling in your case?"

The Vicomte smoothed down the lace at his throat. " 'Tis most unlikely that His Majesty will take serious action against a de la Tour d'Auvergne; but he may exile me to my father's estates for a while. For that I care little, providing I can save Mademoiselle Athénaïs from this hideous match. I have a letter here that I wish you to give her in the event of my death; but should I be only wounded, or fortune favour me, I pray you destroy it."

Roger took the letter, and asked after a moment: "How do you intend to spend the hours which yet have to pass before the meeting? If you desire my company I will gladly remain; but if you can sleep it would be the better for your prospects."

"I thank you, *mon ami*," the Vicomte replied, "but I have a quiet conscience, so think that sleep will not de denied me. We meet in the Bois de Vincennes at five o'clock; and M. de Broglie and M. de Melleraie will call for me here at four. Till then I'll doze upon my bed."

"I pray you let your man, Jacques, come to me the moment the duel is over," said Roger, "and if all is well I'll find the means to convey intelligence to Mademoiselle of the great service you will have rendered her. Meanwhile I shall not cease to think of you, and all my prayers will be for your success."

They shook hands firmly, and Roger returned to the Hôtel de Rochambeau in a state of almost unbearable excitement. He knew his friend to be an accomplished swordsman, but also, that this was his first duel, whereas the Comte de Caylus had emerged triumphantly from upwards of a dozen serious engagements. Yet, knowing the Vicomte's feelings as he did, it seemed to Roger that Athénaïs's champion must overcome his opponent through sheer strength of purpose and that, if need be, divine aid would be given to ensure his victory.

The thought that within a few hours Athénaïs might be freed from her horrible commitment filled him with a sense of thanksgiving and elation; but while the issue still remained uncertain he could not escape intermittent waves of apprehension from the knowledge that the Vicomte might be called on to pay a terrible price in his bid to save her, and her position not be bettered after all.

He found sleep quite impossible and by five o'clock was down at the entrance to the courtyard, pacing feverishly to and fro; although he knew that the Vicomte's servant could not bring him tidings of the encounter for another hour, at least.

The meeting was at five but twenty minutes or more would be occupied by the completion of the preliminaries. The seconds would take their time to choose a suitable piece of ground and make certain there were no pitfalls in it; they would discuss such points as to if their principals should fight booted or in stockinged feet, and how they should be placed before engaging so that the light favoured neither party. Then the duel itself might be prolonged by one or other of the protagonists being wounded. The seconds would intervene and a discussion would ensue as to the gravity of the wound and, if it did not appear too serious and the wounded man declared himself still unsatisfied, the combat would be renewed. Then, when a final decision had been reached, it would take a horseman riding fast a good half-hour to cover the distance between the Bois de Vincennes and central Paris. In an agony of mingled hope and fear Roger strove to fight down his impatience.

As the bell of St. Germain l'Auxerrois ceased tolling a quarter after six, he saw M. de la Tour d'Auvergne's servant come cantering down the cobbled street, and ran out to meet him. One look at the man's face was enough and, with a sinking heart, Roger exclaimed:

"Your master! How is he?"

"Bad, Monsieur!" cried Jacques, reining in his horse. "Yet 'tis hoped the wound will not prove fatal. 'Twas over quickly but mighty desperate while it lasted. They fought for but two minutes, then M. de Caylus ran in upon my master and delivered a tricky thrust in the old style, from above. His sword pierced M. le Vicomte under the collar bone and, 'tis thought, passed through the top of his lung. He wished to continue, but his seconds would not permit it. He is being brought back in M. de Broglie's coach, and I go now to warn them at our lodging."

Wheeling his horse about the man cantered off and, sadly downcast, Roger re-entered the Hôtel. His hopes of the past night had proved only wishful thinking and his beloved Athénaïs was still chained by her father's given word to the millionaire quadroon.

That afternoon he went to see the Vicomte and, to his relief, learned that his lung was not affected; but the sword had passed right through the upper part of his body, and the doctors said that it would be two months or so before he would be well enough to get about again.

The story of the duel soon ran round Paris and, in spite of the Vicomte's precautions, Athénaïs's name was freely mentioned as its cause, owing to his having so openly sought her favour. But, as neither of the combatants had been killed, and both were highly placed, the King took no action in the matter.

In the middle of the month Athénaïs returned to Paris, and Roger saw her within a few hours of her arrival. She said that her fiancé now waited on her every morning and that, in Madame Marie-Angé's company, she was compelled to endure his conversation for an hour or more. He was, she admitted, both clever and forceful; but personally, she found him odious and she had come to dread the speculative smile with which he always regarded her.

He had pressed for the marriage contract to be signed in mid-August, but she had protested that she could not possibly have her trousseau ready until well on in September, and her father had compromised by settling the date as Wednesday, the 30th of August.

As there were still seven weeks to go Roger begged her not to take any drastic step as yet, urging that something might occur to prevent the marriage; although M. de la Tour d'Auvergne's attempt to kill de Caylus having failed, neither of them could think of any event likely to do so.

Athénaïs asked him to express to the Vicomte her deep appreciation of the courage and devotion he had shown, and sent him many kind messages; then they embraced and, encouraging one another to hope for a miracle, parted.

Towards the end of July and in early August the Dutch Ambassador Mynheer Van Brantzen and his colleague Mynheer Van Berkenroode, paid a number of visits to the Marquis. They did not represent the Stadtholder, as he was not in the true sense a Monarch, but their High Mightinesses the States-General, and both were strong Republicans. Their visits led to a long correspondence between the Marquis and M. de Ségur, the Minister of War, by which arrangements were made for numerous consignments of French arms to be smuggled over the Dutch frontier. Then, these secret negotiations with the Dutch Emissaries were concluded one night by their arriving accompanied by a strongly armed escort, and removing in two coaches a very considerable sum in gold that the Marquis paid over to them.

It was this which at last gave Roger, as he thought, the clue to M. de Rochambeau's deep-laid scheme. The Marquis had no intention of plunging France into a war which must have proved her final financial ruin. He was, instead, seeking to make French influence paramount in the United Provinces, once and for all, by not only encouraging but actually financing a revolution.

Roger had heard enough of the conversations before the money was handed over to realise that it was to be used to pay the Republican free-corps that had been raised in most of the Dutch cities, since these careful burghers, anxious as they were to abolish their hereditary

Chief Magistrate, would not leave their businesses to take up arms against him unless their expenses were first guaranteed.

That the Marquis and his friends were evidently not, after all, plotting to bring about a general war greatly relieved Roger's anxieties. Civil war was a very different matter and he did not feel that this could bring his country into jeopardy, or seriously weaken her position. British prestige in the United Provinces was already so low that it could hardly be lower. Britain's friend, the weak and inept Stadtholder had for many months past exercised little more than a tenuous authority over a small minority of his cities, so it did not appear that it could materially affect the situation if he were swept away altogether. The thing that did matter and was of vital concern, was that the Dutch ports should not fall into the hands of France, but they certainly could not do so without an outbreak of hostilities between the nations, and of that there now seemed little likelihood.

The King's troubles had by no means been ended by his dissolution of the Assembly of Notables. On the 12th of July certain members of the Parliament of Paris had, for the first time, proposed that, since the Notables had failed, the Estates-General, which had not sat for one hundred and seventy-three years, should be summoned; and declared that they alone had the right to impose fresh taxation. On the 19th the Parliament followed this by flatly refusing to register the Royal edict imposing the new taxes. They were, in fact, little more than a judicial body and had no power to make laws themselves; but they at least possessed a type of negative veto, since no measure ordained by the King actually became law until they had registered it.

The Archbishop of Toulouse, the King's new adviser, proved quite incapable of dealing with the situation and the Monarch, anxious as ever to do the right thing but hesitating between half a dozen different policies, was at length persuaded by his more robust councillors to hold a Bed of Justice. Recourse had not been had to this for many years; it consisted of a formal ceremony at which all the Great Officers of State were present, and, addressing them from the throne, the King spoke his will, such orders as he might give them being considered as imperative.

On the 9th of August the Bed of Justice was held at Versailles, and the King formally ordered the Parliament to register the Edicts. Parliament still refused and demanded the convening of the States-General. Such a situation had never arisen before and on the 16th the King, at his wits' end, exiled the Parliament to Troyes, hoping that this exceptional measure would break down their resistance.

A week in exile having no effect and the exchequer being near empty, on the 23rd the King sent his two brothers to forcibly register the Edicts concerning the Stamp Duty and Land Tax at the *Chambre des Comptes* and the *Cour des Aides* respectively. All through August Paris had been in a ferment, and now rioting broke out in earnest; the guards of the Comte d'Atois were attacked on his reaching the *Cour des Aides*, and many people were injured.

Roger heard from day to day about all these things. Had he given them serious thought he might have realised that so many crises following swiftly on each other, and culminating in mob violence against the retinue of a Royal Prince, could be no less than the first mutterings of the Revolution which had been foreshadowed by so many of his friends. But his whole mind was now given to the thing which engaged his heart—the grim and horrible future which, unless something could be done to avert it, was soon to engulf his beloved Athénaïs.

He dealt automatically with the dispatches which continued to arrive from Holland, but took scant notice of their contents or of any of the conferences that the Marquis frequently held with regard to them. A summer camp for the crack regiments of the French army had been formed, as planned earlier in the year, in Flanders; and the command of this small but efficient force given to the Marquis's brother, M. le Comte de Rochambeau, who was a highly qualified General and had commanded the last French expeditionary force to be sent to America to aid the Colonists against Britain in their war of Independence. M. de Castries, too, had given secret orders for the finest ships of the French fleet to assemble at Brest and to hold themselves in readiness to sail at twelve hours' notice.

Roger had duly sent all such purely military information to Mr. Gilbert Maxwell, but he was a little afraid that it might prove misleading to the British Government, since he was now personally convinced that all these measures were no more than bluff. Standing as he did at M. de Rochambeau's elbow, it seemed perfectly clear to him that the Marquis meant at all costs to avoid war, and the one thing of which he was frightened was that Prussia should intervene in the affairs of the United Provinces by giving military aid to the Stadtholder before the Republicans could pull off their *coup d'etat* and present Europe with a *fait accompli*.

Frederick-Wilhelm II was becoming slightly more bellicose and had moved a certain number of troops down to the Dutch frontier, but the Marquis was convinced that he did not wish to fight, and evidently considered that the best way of preventing him from actually sending troops over the border was for France to show equal readiness and a greater concentration of forces.

Athénaïs was now very frequently in Paris as, to keep up the pretence that she meant to go through with the marriage that had been arranged for her, she had ordered an elaborate trousseau; and this necessitated her dressmakers, furriers, mantle makers and milliners waiting upon her several days a week and occupying hours of her time.

Madame Marie-Angé had long since become accustomed to her charge's strange whim of browsing through the collection of old toys and books in the neglected playroom and, as her hip still pained her when negotiating any flight of stairs, she never came up there. In consequence, from the latter part of July onward, Athénaïs and Roger had met there at least once, and often twice, a week.

Having each sworn to take no rash action without first consulting the other they seemed to have reached a stalemate. At every meeting each snatched at the caresses that the other offered so eagerly and strove to put out of their minds the inexorable approach of the fatal day.

M. de la Tour d'Auvergne's wound had healed well and, by mid-August, he was able to get about again; but he still wore one arm strapped to his side in order to prevent any sudden movement reopening the wound. Roger went often to see him and, again and again, they talked gloomily of Athénaïs's situation. The Vicomte still had no idea that Roger saw her alone in secret, but knew that he was devoted to her and the two of them racked their brains in vain for a way to save her from the nightmare of a marriage with M. de Caylus. The Vicomte said that he would willingly fight again but, having fought him once, the Count was under no compulsion to do so a second time, and, in any case, the wound received in the first combat rendered another out of the question until long after the date fixed for the wedding.

Athénaïs herself brought matters to a head. On the evening of Sunday the 20th of August, after she and Roger had both attended Vespers, they kept a tryst in the playroom. He had hardly taken her in his arms, before she said:

"My dear love, let us make the most of this hour, for 'tis the last we will have together."

Roger began to speak, but she put a soft hand over his mouth, and went on: "There are but ten days left, and I can bear the strain of evading this terrible issue no longer. I have had ample time to search my mind and I cannot face marriage with M. de Caylus. I have now formed a definite resolve to tell my father to-morrow night that it is my intention to seek refuge from the world in a convent."

For a moment Roger did not reply. He had hoped to the last moment that Providence would intervene and provide some way of escape for her; but with only nine clear days left there now seemed little chance of that. He felt as if, somehow, deep down inside himself, he had always known that if she was to be saved it would depend upon himself. He had thought about the awful problem for so long that he knew exactly what he was called on to do. And now, at whatever risk to himself, the time had come when he must do it.

CHAPTER XXI

DOUBLE CRISIS

W H E N Roger did speak, it was firmly. He said: "No. You are not to defy your father yet. I have devised a way in which I can preserve you from M. de Caylus; but it will take a few days to arrange the final details. You must give me till the end of the week. We will meet again on Saturday and if I cannot tell you definitely that there is a fair chance of your not being called on to go through with this hateful marriage you may, that night, declare your intention of retiring to a convent. But you are not to take this most desperate step till then."

His voice held such a ring of authority and confidence that Athénaïs gave in without a murmur; and after an hour of sweet emotion he left her, fully determined on his project.

When the Marquis was in Paris he often worked late at night but he never entered his sanctum before midday, so Roger was under no obligation to be in his office much before that hour. On coming downstairs the morning after he had pledged himself to take desperate measures he ordered his favourite riding-horse to be saddled and, shortly after nine o'clock, took the road to Passy.

M. l'Abbé de Périgord's circle did not gather, to pull the world to pieces over their cups of chocolate at the little house in the Rue de Bellechasse, until eleven o'clock; so Roger planned to get in an hour alone with his friend before any of the others arrived. When he reached the house he was told that M. le Abbé had not yet risen, but Roger had expected that and he sent up a message to the effect that he had come thus early as he particularly desired a private conversation which might occupy some little time.

He was asked to wait in the familiar, sunny morning-room, and a quarter of an hour later the Abbé joined him there. M. de Périgord was still in *déshabille*, wearing a loose gown of shot-blue silk and looking somewhat jaded.

Gracefully smothering a yawn he said: "You're a fine fellow to get me up at this godless hour: I did not get to bed till after seven."

Roger smiled. "You're such a glutton for enjoyment that I thought you never slept, but I suppose you needs must at times."

"Alas, yes! But I spent the night hours with the Du Barry, at her château of Luciennes; and 'twas a riot, but exhausting."

"What, then! Have you now become the lover of Louis XV's old mistress?"

"Nay, I fear I expressed myself badly. 'Tis said that since Lord Seymour left her she has been as faithful as a bourgeois wife to the Duc de Cossé-Brissac. I was but one of the fifteen guests—all of us men, whom they entertained to dinner. And though she must be forty-three or more I vow she did not look a day over thirty. Moreover, although she was bred in the gutter she has ever been a most charming hostess, and she has not lost the art in her retirement. After dinner she gave us a ballet representing the Concourse of the Nations. There were fifteen beauties in it, each of a different nationality, including a Chinese, an Arab, an Indian and a Blackamoor. When the ballet was done they supped with us and we drew lots for their favour. The Spaniard fell to me and she proved no mean performer. But I weary you with all this. Tell me now of this urgent matter which has caused you to rob me of my beauty sleep."

Roger at once plunged into the business he had come upon and, without mentioning any names, gave an account of the situation in which Athénaïs and himself found themselves. He then asked the Abbé what he would advise the hypothetical young man in the case to do.

M. de Périgord's slim hand covered another yawn. "Why, 'tis simple, *mon ami*. If the young man is not a fool he will point out to the young woman that, after three months in a convent she will spend the rest of her life regretting her rash decision, whereas after three

279

months of marriage to her fiancé she will have forgotten how unpleasant he is."

"But those three months!" protested Roger. "Nay! I could never urge the woman I love to surrender herself to such a nightmare."

The Abbé smiled with mild amusement. " 'Twas not for me to dot the "i's" and cross the "t's"; but now that you have let the cat out of the bag, shall we talk of yourself and, quite obviously, Mademoiselle de Rochambeau's betrothal to M. le Comte de Caylus?"

Roger shrugged. "I would have had to name them later, in any case, since I require your help."

"Then, if you have already formed some plan, why ask my advice?"

"Because I thought you might be able to suggest something that I have not yet thought of. I hoped you would see the problem from a different angle."

" 'Tis clear that I do. 'Twould be a crazy act for a lovely creature like Athénaïs de Rochambeau to cut short her life at the age of eighteen."

"I know it. But she herself has selected that course rather than marry de Caylus. And how can one blame her? The very thought of her in the arms of that gross half-breed is a blasphemy."

"Nonsense!" The Abbé rubbed the tip of his retroussé nose angrily. "What matters a man's size to a woman providing he be a good lover; and de Caylus is a healthy enough animal. As for his dash of black blood, 'tis a thing against which you English are prejudiced, I know, but here in France we are more broadminded. If she dislikes his looks tell her to put a pillow over her face and think of the lovely curly-haired children he will give her. Honestly, *mon chér* Chevalier, you are behaving like a child and I needs must speak brutally to bring you to your senses."

Roger had gone slightly pale, and he exclaimed: "He'll give her no children as long as I live!"

De Périgord threw up his hands. "Since, like all advice-seekers, you came here only to have some project you have already formed applauded, let me hear it."

"With God's help I mean to kill him!"

"The devil you do! And how, may I ask?"

"By calling him out, of course; surely you do not consider me capable of stooping to assassination?"

"You appear mad enough at the moment to be capable of anything. But surely you realise that he would never accept a challenge from M. de Rochambeau's secretary?"

"Exactly! And that is where I require your help. I intend to waylay him somewhere, disclose my true status to him, and call on him to fight a duel *à outrance*. My difficulty is that he may not believe me; and you are the only man in France who can convince him that I am of noble blood."

"Why should he believe me, more than another?"

"Because, immediately I told you that Lord Kildonan was my uncle, you exclaimed upon my likeness to him."

De Périgord nodded. "That is true. I would stake all I possess on your being related to the Earl. But do you realise what you are asking of me? You are suggesting that I should act as your second in a duel and, although I may not be a very good one, I am a priest."

"I had not forgotten it; and all I ask is that you should bear witness before M. de Caylus that I have the right to carry arms. I then intend to dispense with all formalities and fight him on the spot."

"*Mort dieu!* But this is utter madness. After encounters in which a death results the edicts against duelling are applied with some severity. So, if you mean to fight to a finish, you would, at the least, expose yourself to a spell in prison. Yet you are not content with that, and propose to place yourself outside all duelling convention by fighting without seconds. Should you kill de Caylus in such circumstances 'twill be counted murder, and the King will make you answer for it with your head."

"I am aware of that; but 'tis a risk that I must take. Were I to indulge in all the usual formalities of a duel, with seconds, doctors, servants and the like, 'twould be bound to leak out; and if it became generally known that I had fought for Athénaïs' twould ruin her prospects of another marriage, so her father would throw her into a convent whether she would or no. I plan to hold up de Caylus in his coach somewhere, at night; and I'll be masked myself, so that his servants will not recognise me. Then, if fortune favours me, 'twill be thought that he was killed defending himself from some highwayman, and no loose tongues will wag a tale that.Mademoiselle de Rochambeau had an affair with her father's secretary."

"The plan is well devised," muttered the Abbé, "but so startling that I have as yet scarce taken it in. Tell me though, if you mean to act the highwayman where is the necessity for me to play a part?"

" 'Twill be for you, Abbé, and you'll do me this great kindness, to speak with him when we halt his coach, while I remain at some little distance. Unless someone whom he knows parleys with him civilly he might think that we are highwaymen in truth, and call on his servants to fire upon us with their blunderbusses. To be filled full of lead would be but a poor ending to such an undertaking. Besides, I am most averse to having him think that he has been set upon by some cut-purse. Though we'll have no seconds I am anxious that all the usual courtesies should be observed, and that we should fight like gentlemen."

De Périgord sighed. "I follow your reasoning, but am most loath to aid you in this desperate business. I know nothing of your ability with the rapier, but I do know that de Caylus is counted one of the finest swordsmen in France. He has fought a score of times, and 'tis scarce two months ago that he made a sorry mess of M. de la Tour d'Auvergne in a matter of minutes."

"I am prepared for the worst," said Roger soberly, "but at least I will stand a better chance than the Vicomte, for I have bested him in many a practice bout."

"But 'tis heads de Caylus wins and tails you lose," protested the Abbé. "All the odds are that you will be killed yourself; but if you are not, and kill him, half the police in France will be after you for murder."

"I know it, I tell you," Roger insisted. "But I see no other chance of preserving Athénaïs from the lust of this abominable quadroon."

"Maybe," the Abbé countered. "But I am by no means convinced as yet that you are justified in throwing away your life on that account. I beg you to consider the facts coolly and to view them in their proper perspective. I cannot believe that Mademoiselle de Rochambeau is either better or worse than most other young women of our aristocracy. They emerge from childhood knowing nothing of men, and so develop romantic ideas about them. Those who are wise do not expect to find romance with their husband, since they know beforehand that he will be some stranger selected for them by their family; but they endeavour to make of him a friend. Once married, society permits them to take as many lovers as they wish, and the husband who seeks to thwart them in that succeeds only in making himself the laughing-stock of his acquaintances.

"Should your beautiful Athénaïs become the Countess de Caylus she will, within a month, have half a hundred attractive men pleading with her to give them a rendezvous; and she would be a freak of nature should she refuse them all. Surely you see that by this marriage taking place you have nothing to lose and everything to gain? In all our lives there come at times unpleasant passages which we are called upon to face. Persuade the girl to put a brave front on her honeymoon. M. de Caylus is far too hardened a roué not to tire of a young and inexperienced bedfellow very quickly. Before October is out she'll be free to console herself with you, and you will have one of the loveliest women in Paris as your mistress. Is that not a better prospect than for her to be immured in a convent, and you to be lying headless in a felon's grave?"

Roger could not know that it was the future Arch-Chancellor of a new French Empire, the bounds of which would spread from the Baltic to the southernmost tip of Italy, and the greatest diplomat of his century, who was exercising all his persuasive arts upon him; but he did know that his friend, the Abbé de Talleyrand-Périgord had given a fair and not overdrawn picture of French society in the age in which they were living. All that the Abbé said was true, plausible and, if his advice was accepted, almost inevitable. Yet Roger could not reconcile himself to it.

"No, Abbé," he said quietly, "I know that you have reason on your side; but there is no evading the fact that neither Athénaïs nor I will accept a continuance of our love upon such terms."

De Périgord regarded him with a smile in which there was no longer any trace of cynicism. "You are mad, of course," he murmured thoughtfully. "All Englishmen are mad, and that, no doubt, accounts for it; but I confess to having a sneaking admiration for your madness. So be it, then. Since you are determined to throw away your life and seek my aid in doing so, I will, however reluctantly, give it you. When and where do you propose to make this suicidal attempt on M. de Caylus?"

"There again, I must crave your help," replied Roger. "I am poorly situated to ascertain his movements, whereas you, owing to your frequent visits to Versailles, should have no great difficulty in finding out when he will next make a journey thence after dark to Paris. But the marriage contract is to be signed in nine days' time, so it is a matter of some urgency."

For a moment the Abbé remained thoughtful, then he said: "De Caylus has a *petit maison* in the Bois de Meudon. 'Tis there that he disports himself with any courtesan to whom he takes a fancy. You may recall my mentioning Olympe, the little Opera girl on whose account he attempted to avenge himself on me last summer. When we had wearied of one another she was tempted back to him by his money, and they still meet with some frequency. Olympe and I have remained good friends and she should be able to tell me when de Caylus will next be passing a night at Meudon."

"I will hold myself in readiness," Roger volunteered, "and be prepared to join you at any time. I only pray that it may be soon."

The Abbé nodded. "I realise the urgency. And while I feel that a meeting on the road 'twixt Versailles and Meudon offers the best prospect of being undisturbed, should that not prove possible I will find out where else de Caylus may be met with on the road at night, before the week is out. Owing to my lameness I must go to the place by coach, but 'tis essential that you should be mounted, and mounted well; since your life will depend on the speed with which you can get away from the vicinity once the affair is over. The best plan, I think, would be for me to send you a simple message giving only the time and place where you are to rendezvous with me. We will then go on in company for the last mile or so, to select a suitable spot at which to hold up de Caylus's coach."

These details having been settled, Roger endeavoured to express his gratitude; but the Abbé waved aside his thanks, yawned once more and said:

"Think nothing of it. 'Tis you who elect to surround your pleasures with so dramatic and dangerous an aura. For myself, I doubt if even a female archangel could woo me into deliberately courting death on her behalf. 'Tis such a marvellous day and hour in which to live. It will not last, alas! Night and darkness are almost upon us. The starving pack is already stirring in its noisome kennels, and within a year or two will, I doubt not, have torn many of us limb from limb. As for those who come after, none will know what the sweetness of life can be who have not lived in Paris before the Revolution."

"*Aprés nous le deluge*, eh?" Roger smiled.

De Périgord stood up and drew his shot-silk gown about him. "It profits one little to swim against the tide, so a wise man swims with it. Now, if you will forgive me, I must make myself presentable to receive those foolish friends of mine, who cannot let well alone; and, instead of rejoicing in all the good things that God has sent them, must ever be striving to bring about some new order of society, which will inevitably put a halter about their own necks."

"He who is forewarned is forearmed," suggested Roger. "I have a feeling that, whatever may befall you, you will find some way to survive it."

Napoleon's future Arch-Chancellor laid a hand upon his shoulder. "May your kind prophecy be true; and, with more immediate cause, I hope the same for you." Upon which, they parted.

That night Roger started putting his affairs in order. He wrote three letters and made a will. The first letter was a very brief one to his father asking forgiveness for the disappointment he had caused him; the second a somewhat longer one to his mother telling her something of his love affair and the circumstances which made it imperative that he should risk his life; the third, a very long one to Georgina, saying that he felt sure that his previous letter to her must have gone astray, and giving a vivid picture, without reservations, of his four years in France. In his will he left his money to his mother, his sword to M. de la Tour d'Auvergne, his books to the Abbé de Périgord, and his clothes to Chenou.

The following evening he went round to see de la Tour d'Auvergne, explained what he planned to do and gave him the four documents, all contained in one large covering envelope, asking that he would deal with them should de Caylus emerge the victor by delivering a mortal thrust.

The Vicomte listened gravely till Roger had finished, then he said: "I honour you greatly for the risk you are about to take. De Caylus is a terrible antagonist and, even if fortune favours you, should you be caught you will certainly be tried for murder."

"I hope to escape that," Roger replied, and went on to explain. "If all goes well only Athénaïs, de Périgord and yourself will ever know who killed the Count. I shall return at once to the Hôtel de Rochambeau and resume my normal activities there next day. There is no reason whatever why anyone should suspect me of the killing. In fact, 'tis of paramount importance that they should not, myself apart, on account of Athénaïs."

"I see your thought," the Vicomte nodded. "If it becomes known that 'twas you who fought on Athénaïs's behalf, 'twill be said that you have been having an affair with her. As an unmarried girl she will be completely ruined and her father is certain to force her to take the veil as the only way of restoring the family honour. But think you de Périgord will be able to induce de Caylus to fight without knowing who it is that sends the challenge?"

"Oh, surely! The Count at least does not lack for courage, and has fought many times. He must by now have superb confidence in his ability to hold his own against any man; so I cannot think for one moment that he would refuse a challenge, once he is assured that it comes from a person whose birth entitles him to send it."

" 'Twill, all the same, be a most unusual meeting; and lest some unforeseen circumstances arise I would fain accompany you to it, to be on hand if needed."

"Nay," protested Roger, "I thank you mightily. But I have no wish to involve you. Besides, you are not yet fully recovered from your wound."

"I am not yet mended to the point of wielding a sword, but I have been riding again recently. You will need someone to hold your horse, and the Abbé being a priest 'tis but right that he should leave the scene as soon as he has assured de Caylus that his challenger is one who has the right to bear arms. Moreover, the Count is much more likely to accept your challenge if he is informed that someone of my status is present to see fair play."

"All that you say is true," Roger admitted, "and I dare take no chances; so I accept your offer gratefully. As soon as I hear from de Périgord about a rendezvous I will let you know it, and when the time comes we will ride thither together."

The following two days, Thursday and Friday, Roger spent both his mornings and evenings at a fencing-school he had occasionally frequented, which lay just off the *Halles*. It was largely a resort of soldiers of fortune, and on each occasion he offered two *louis* to anyone who could best him. Out of ten bouts he lost only three, and two of those were at the end of evening sessions when his wrist was tired, so he felt that he would at least be able to make the redoubtable de Caylus work very hard to obtain a victory.

On the Friday evening he received a brief note from the Abbé, which ran:

"Your man plans to spend Monday night at Meudon with Olympe. His habit on such occasions is to leave Versailles about eight o'clock; but to be on the safe side I will be waiting for you at half-past seven, a half-mile beyond Sevres on the Sevres-Chaville road."

On Saturday morning Roger duly informed de la Tour d'Auvergne of the rendezvous, and got in three more fencing-bouts. Then, at six o'clock, he kept his appointment with Athénaïs.

When he told her his intentions she begged him not to expose himself and said that she would rather take the veil than have him risk his life for her sake. On his proving adamant she declared that she would go straight downstairs and defy her father, and thus render Roger's desperate scheme futile.

"My angel," he said tenderly, "I cannot stop you, but 'twould then be your act which would be futile. Having accepted the help of Monsieurs de Périgord and de la Tour d'Auvergne I cannot now draw back, or they would look upon me as a coward. I beg you not to plead further with me for, whatever you may do, I am now determined to fight de Caylus and kill him if I can."

Plead she did, but without avail; and this, which they knew might be their last meeting, ended by her giving him her kerchief, to wear as her champion, and promising to refrain from burning her boats until Tuesday, the day before the wedding, by which time she would know whether her fiancé or her lover had proved the victor.

It was later that evening that M. de Rochambeau said to Roger: "Although 'tis Sunday to-morrow I intend to hold a conference. M. de Rayneval has returned in secret from the United Provinces and affairs there have now reached a point at which important decisions must be taken without further delay. During the past few months, M. de Montmorin seems to have caught His Majesty's congenital complaint of indecision; but I will have him shilly-shally with us no longer. He is coming here at four o'clock and my friends and I intend to put our views before him in no uncertain manner. We shall be fifteen, all told, so have the conference table prepared and hold yourself in readiness. I wish you to be present in the room to take note of the various viewpoints that may be expressed, and to draft a document which I plan that M. de Rayneval should take back with him."

On numerous previous occasions Roger had attended such conferences for a similar purpose and, apart from the fact that this one was to be somewhat larger than usual, there was no reason to suppose that anything of exceptional interest would transpire at it. Having accepted the Marquis's orders with his habitual quiet deference, he was so wrapped up in his own affairs that he thought no more of it till the following afternoon.

Shortly before four o'clock, M. de Rochambeau's usual collaborators, Messieurs de Breteuil, de Polignac, de Castries and de Ségur arrived with others who were less frequent visitors; the Duc de Normandie, who was governor to the Dauphin, the famous Admiral de Suffren, France's greatest sailor, M. Bérard, the head of the French East India Company, the Duc de Lauzun and the Marquis de Vaudreuil, both close friends of the Queen, the Duc de Châtelet, who had recently been replaced as Ambassador to the Court of St. James's by the Comte d'Adhémar, the Duc de Coigny, the Master of the Royal Horse, and one man that Roger did not know. The party was completed by de Montmorin and de Rayneval.

When they had all seated themselves round the big oval table Roger sat down at a small one near the door, and M. de Rochambeau opened the proceedings.

"Monsieur le Ministre," he said, addressing himself to the Comte de Montmorin, "My friends and I have asked you to meet us here to-day in order that we may put before you the state of affairs in the United Provinces and propose to you certain actions which we recommend in regard to them. M. de Rayneval, very rightly in my view, has taken the exceptional step of returning thence, without being recalled by you, to urge upon us that further procrastination may lose us all that we have been working to achieve for many months past. With him he has brought our distinguished soldier, M. le Comte de Maillebois, whom the Dutch Republican leaders themselves chose to command their free-corps in the event of civil war. It would be best, I think, if these two gentlemen now gave us their first-hand information on the situation that so closely concerns us all."

M. de Rayneval spoke first, and for about twenty minutes gave a dissertation on the attitude of Mynheer Van Berkel, the leader of the Republicans in Amsterdam, and on that of the Pensionaries of the other principal Dutch cities; from which it was clear that the great majority of them were only awaiting a firm promise of French support, in the event of intervention by Prussia, to join in a concerted uprising against the Stadtholder.

Roger listened with only half an ear. His mind was full of lunges, ripostes and foot-movements, and he now knew this old story back-wards. Since France could not possibly afford a war he was convinced that no such promise would be forthcoming; and that while this powerful group of French Imperialists would continue to egg the Dutch Republicans on in secret they would never dare to commit themselves to any step which might lead to a European conflict.

The Comte de Maillebois then took up the tale. He was the one member of the conference whom Roger had not known by sight, and as he began to give facts and figures about the volunteer Republican bands in various cities, Roger listened to him with somewhat more interest. The Count concluded his remarks by expressing the opinion that, while, as a professional soldier, he found the Dutch burghers somewhat poor material, they were sufficiently numerous and keen for him to state with confidence that he could hold the northern frontiers with them against the Prussians until a French army could be marched across the country to his assistance.

The Marquis then called in turn on the Minister of War and the Minister of Marine.

The old Marshal de Ségur said that, as they all knew, the flower of the French regular army was already assembled in Flanders, under the command of that most brilliant soldier, the Marquis's brother, M. le Comte de Rochambeau. The word had only to be given for it to be set in motion and, with the aid of the free-corps controlled by M. de Maillebois, all the strong places of the United Provinces would be in French hands within a fortnight.

The Marshal de Castries added that the Fleet was in a state of instant readiness and, with the aid of the insurgents, could take possession of the Dutch ports within a week.

Roger still saw no cause for alarm, and he wondered vaguely why this group of war-mongers bothered to waste their time discussing what they could do in certain eventualities, when they all knew perfectly well that these vast preparations were no more than a game of bluff, and that in actual fact they dared not move a single man or ship.

The Marquis was now speaking again . . . and so you see, *Monsieur le Ministre*, the stage is set. 'Twas from a man whose politics and private life I deplore, but for whose brain I have a very great respect, that, a little over a year ago, I first had the idea of forming this secret army within the very walls of the cities of a foreign state, and . . . ."

Roger suppressed a start. M. de Rochambeau could only be referring to the Abbé de Périgord, and the conversation between them that he had overheard while standing in the secret closet. For a moment he was so shaken that he did not catch the next few sentences. It was clear now as the sun in a summer sky that the Marquis had adopted the Abbé's subtle scheme and all these months been steadily proceeding with it. Roger recalled the instructions for arms to be smuggled in, the great payment of gold to the Dutch Ambassadors, and a hundred details, all of which had remained unconnected in his mind at the time but now fell into place. He was intensely angry to think that M. de Rochambeau should have fooled him so completely, then followed

287

swift humiliation at the thought that, since the Marquis had concealed nothing from him but the central fact, it was he who had been utterly blind and fooled himself.

" . . . and therefore," the Marquis was going on, "we must not, any longer, regard the Dutch free-corps as groups of political insurgents activated only by a desire to secure certain liberties for themselves. Doubtless they still consider themselves in that light; but, in actual fact, they are now part of the French army; a French Foreign Legion working under French direction who, at our command, will seize the United Provinces and render them, in all but name, a part of France herself."

" 'Twas a stroke of genius," declared de Castries enthusiastically. "The Dutch ports will fall into our hands like ripe plums."

"And the rich trade in the Dutch Indies," added de Coigny.

M. Bérard hit the table. "With France in control of the Dutch settlements at the Cape of Good Hope, I vow we'd drive the British India Company into bankruptcy within three years."

"Come, *Monsieur le Ministre*," urged de Breteuil, "you have but to sign a letter for M. de Rayneval to take back with him, and the thing is as good as done."

M. de Montmorin shook his head. "The King, gentlemen, must first agree to this; and I will confess that I have not yet consulted His Majesty upon it. I dare not give such a pledge to our Dutch friends without his assent, or at least that of the Archbishop of Toulouse."

"The King!" exclaimed de Polignac, with contempt. " 'Twould be fatal to bring him into the business, for he'd not have the resolution to say yea or nay this side of the grave. 'Twas only the other day that *Monsieur*, his brother, said of him, 'When you can keep a number of oiled ivory billiard balls together in your hand, you may then do something with the King.' And 'twas a fair assessment."

"Then the Archbishop must be asked to decide for him," replied de Montmorin firmly. "It will, I fear, come as a shock to you, but as from this evening, His Grace of Toulouse is to formally assume the rôle of Prime Minister. His Majesty informed me personally of this new decision of his at noon to-day."

De Montmorin's announcement caused an extraordinary sensation and was met by a chorus of exclamations.

"Then we're to return to the old days of Prime Ministers, eh?"

"I knew he had gained the King's ear, but hardly suspected this!"

"God save us all if that ambitious prelate is to rule the roost!"

" 'Tis the height of folly to place supreme power in the hands of so vain and fickle a man at such a time as this!"

"I'll not submit to it," declared de Castries angrily. "I have not built up our Navy only to act as the agent of its destruction on the orders of so incompetent a master; I shall resign."

"I, too, shall return my portfolio to His Majesty," de Ségur announced. I am too old now to begin transacting my business with the King through any third party."

"*Monsieurs! Monsieurs!*" The Marquis raised his voice to quell the tumult. "I beg you to take no rash action for the moment. Even in the face of such a sudden and ill-advised decision on the part of the King, I pray that you will place the interests of the country before your own. I ask you for no more than a fortnight. De Rayneval and de Maillebois inform me that, given this letter pledging French support, the Dutch Republicans have already agreed to launch their *coup d'état* against the Stadtholder on the 10th of September. Should you resign before that date our whole plan will be placed in jeopardy. I most earnestly entreat you to retain your Portfolios till then, whatever you may decide to do afterwards."

De Breteuil, De Polignac and De Coigny strongly supported M. de Rochambeau and, after a brief discussion, the other Ministers agreed to do as he asked. De Montmorin then said:

"I regret the concern that my news has caused you, Monsieurs; but I had to make my own position clear. The whole issue must be placed before the Archbishop. If he consents I will do my part as Foreign Minister willingly enough, but not unless."

Roger relaxed again. All was in the melting-pot once more, and, as usual, no definite action would be taken. Besides, he reasoned, even if the Dutch free-corps, having seized power, were fools enough to hand their country over to French domination, that would not stop the Prussians attempting the Stadtholder's restoration; and that meant war, which these sabre-rattlers were not prepared to stomach.

At that very moment M. de Montmorin voiced his thoughts with the words: "Even if M. de Rochambeau's contention is correct and, with the aid of his secret columns, we could seize the country virtually overnight, that is no guarantee that the Prussians and the English will not combine against us in an attempt to restore the Stadtholder; and, if they do, a European conflict is inevitable."

"What if it is?" to Roger's utter amazement, cried the Marquis. "Are you so blind as not to see that violent external action of some kind is now our only hope of saving France from internal collapse and chaos. The country is bankrupt, starving, finished as a great power, and on the verge of revolution. One chance alone remains for us to save the monarchy and save ourselves. The attention of the public must be diverted from the state of affairs at home to great events in which France will triumph outside her frontiers. The possibility of pulling off this coup against the United Provinces is a gift from God in our dire extremity. Should it succeed with little bloodshed, so much the better. Within a few months the vast riches of the Dutch will be diverted to fill our lamentably empty coffers. Should a general conflict ensue we shall enter it with an enormous advantage; since the Dutch ports will already be in our possession and we shall hold them as a pistol pointing at England's breast. Spain, Austria, the Netherlands, Sweden and Russia would all ally themselves with us against Prussia and England; and how could our enemies hope to prevail against such a combination? But 'tis my opinion that they will not dare to fight at all, provided only that we seize the United Provinces before they appreciate what's toward, and so present them with a *fait accompli*."

"I'd not count upon the English standing down," demurred the Duc de Chatelet. "During my time at the Court of St. James's I formed the impression that Mr. Pitt was most anxious to maintain the peace and so put no further drain upon the nation's resources while it is still recovering from the strain of the late wars. Yet he struck me as a young man who will ever stand by his late father's principles and draw the sword, however tattered be the scabbard, should he consider any move in Europe to threaten Britain's security."

"I fear that, too," agreed M. de Montmorin. "And what could be a more flagrant challenge to Britain than this proposed seizure of the Dutch ports?"

" 'Tis a challenge that must be thrown down sooner or later," M. de Rochambeau declared, "and, to my mind, seeing our present overriding need to restore our manufacturers to prosperity, the sooner the better. All of you know how strenuously I fought against the Treaty of Commerce that was signed with Britain a year ago. In that I was bested by M. de Vergennes, and what is the result? To-day twenty-five thousand workmen stand idle in our good city of Rouen alone, owing to the markets having been flooded by cheap Manchester goods."

"Aye, and 'tis the same over half the kingdom," the Duc de Normandie supported him. "Half the factories in Amiens have been forced to close down, and in Nantes scarce a week passes now without half a dozen of our honest merchants going bankrupt as a result of British competition."

Admiral de Suffren leaned forward. "And 'tis on the success of the shipping ventures of the Nantes merchants, and their like, in peace, that we rely for our best reserves to man the fleet in time of war. Let us tackle the English before they can do us further damage. They are not invincible. I have fought them, and I know."

The Admiral's declaration met with almost universal applause and Roger found himself having to entirely readjust his views. It was plain now that these men really wanted war and meant to force the issue to ensure it if they possibly could. M. de Rochambeau's statement had put a completely different complexion on the whole question. Whereas it had previously seemed that France could not fight because she was bankrupt, that now appeared to be the best possible reason for her doing so.

During a further hour every one of them said his piece, and they were unanimous in their opinion that to take advantage of the present situation in the United Provinces, through the secret army that M. de Rochambeau had so skilfully built up there, offered France her only chance of escape from the internal troubles that menaced her.

M. de Montmorin was brought round to agree with them; but he stood firm on his declaration that he could not take the responsibility for committing the country himself, and that the new Prime Minister must be consulted before any written pledge could be transmitted to the Dutch Republicans.

Pressed by the others for an early decision, and now seized with the urgency of the matter himself, he proposed that another meeting should be held the following night at ten o'clock, and promised to bring the Archbishop with him to attend it.

When they had gone Roger was left with his brain in a whirl. During a single conference every theory he had held for the past twelve months on French foreign policy had been smashed to atoms. Nothing was certain yet. Everything still hung on whether the Archbishop would fall a victim to this wave of war fever, on the following night. But if he did it now seemed that war was inevitable; and the French nobles who had gathered there planned a new type of war— a lightning war, unannounced by any ultimatum. Britain and Prussia would be caught off their guard and, before they had time to act, the Dutch ports and strong places would all have been taken by the enemy from within.

Roger knew that the time had now arrived, which had already been envisaged by cleverer people than himself, when no penned account of the situation as he saw it would serve to furnish those who were responsible for his country's safety with a full picture of the enemy's intentions. He must go home and report in person; in order that, in addition to giving his own version of the crisis, he might be questioned and knowledge which he possessed be extracted from him, on points that he might consider of little moment but those who had a broader vision of affairs might consider vital.

On thinking matters over further he realised that if the Archbishop said "No" on the following night there would be no point in hastening to London, since the situation would remain, for the time being at least, unaltered. On the other hand, if he said "Yes" the news must be carried with the utmost speed to Downing Street. Therefore it was imperative that he should be present at the conference that had been arranged to take place an hour or so after the time fixed for his duel.

For a while he even considered if he was not called upon to abandon the duel; but that he could not bring himself to do. He squared his conscience by sitting down and writing a letter to Mr. Gilbert Maxwell in which he divulged the Marquis's whole plot, and added that while no definite decision had been taken as yet, he felt that every possible precautionary measure against the French seizing the United Provinces by surprise should be adopted forthwith.

Another point that exercised him greatly was how, should he emerge successfully from his duel, and the need arose, could he suddenly disappear without leading the de Rochambeau household to suspect that his flight had some connection with the killing of de Caylus.

After deep thought he decided that the best measure would be to give out that he had just heard that his mother was dangerously ill, and that he had decided to leave on the Tuesday morning for Strasbourg. Athénaïs and de Périgord were still the only people who knew that he was an Englishman. and neither of them could possibly connect his departure with the reason that would lay behind it. M. de la Tour d'Auvergne knew only that he was of gentle birth, and again, knew nothing of what had passed at the recent conference. M. de Rochambeau still believed him to be of German extraction but a loyal Frenchman. He could not refuse to let him go to his mother's death-bed and would have no reason to connect his request for immediate leave of absence with de Caylus's death.

If, after all, on the Monday night the Archbishop of Toulouse vetoed M. de Rochambeau's plan, Roger saw that he could always let himself out from having to leave Paris precipitately by saying that he had thought better of it, and had decided to remain until he heard further news of his mother's condition.

On the Monday morning he went to see de la Tour d'Auvergne, and told his story. He also gave him the letter for Mr. Gilbert Maxwell, but in a double envelope concealing its address, and with instructions that the outer one was only to be opened and the inner dispatched in the event of his death.

He hated having to deceive this honest and upright friend, and had already felt many qualms about leaving him to suppose that, as M. de Rochambeau's secretary, he had never ventured to express to Athénaïs the love he felt for her or given him any indication that she returned that love with equal fervour. But, in the latter case, Athénaïs's honour was concerned and, in the former, Roger felt that he was serving the true interests of France as much as of Britain by taking such steps as he could to prevent a war breaking out.

When he got back to the Hôtel he told both Paintendre and Monsieur Roland his story about his mother being seriously ill and, by good luck, he ran into Madame Marie-Angé on the first landing so he told her too, feeling confident that by this channel the story would reach Athénaïs.

That afternoon the Marquis went out, and did not require his services; so he went up to his room and, after a little, slept. At six o'clock, having washed and tidied himself as carefully as though he was going to be presented to the King, he took his sword from its place on the wall. Then, very slowly but resolutely, he walked downstairs; conscious with every step he took that it now lay on the knees of the gods, as to if he would ever walk down a flight of stairs again.

CHAPTER XXII

DESPERATE MEASURES

R o g e r found de la Tour d'Auvergne waiting for him in the Rue de Richelieu. They greeted one another gravely but both endeavoured to act as if their meeting was occasioned only by an arrangement to ride out together to sup with some mutual friend in the suburbs. As they turned their horses into the *Rue des Petits Champs* the Vicomte remarked casually that they were in luck to have such a pleasant evening, and Roger replied that he hoped the dry spell would continue.

They had some eight miles to go, but ample time before them, so they walked their horses a good part of the way, only cantering now and again when they reached the grassy glades of the Bois de Boulogne. Having crossed the river at St. Cloud they turned south towards Sevres and, as they approached the village, Roger took the opportunity to refer again to his fiction about his mother's illness.

"I am still somewhat undecided," he said, "whether to leave Paris to-morrow morning or wait until I receive further news of my mother. On re-reading her letter I think that I at first alarmed myself over-much; yet I would never forgive myself if she died without my having received her blessing."

"In your place I should decide nothing until you have slept upon it," replied the Vicomte. "Your mind will be clearer after to-night's business is settled."

Roger's nerves were very taut, and he repressed an hysterical impulse to laugh at his friend's apt choice of expression. The Vicomte referred, of course, to the duel, but "to-night's business" applied even better to the conference that M. de Rochambeau was to hold at ten o'clock; and whether Roger, if he was still alive, stayed on in Paris or left next day as soon as he had made his excuses to the Marquis, depended on the all-important decision that the Archbishop of Toulouse would be called upon to take that night. However, the Vicomte's advice was on the exact lines that Roger had hoped he would offer, so he accepted it readily.

Half a mile south of Sevres, on the northern outskirts of Bois de Meudon, they came upon the Abbé's coach, drawn up by the side of the road. As they approached it Roger put on his mask, so that the coachman should not afterwards be able to identify him; then, when they were within a hundred yards, they reined in; the Vicomte took Roger's horse, and he went forward on foot to greet de Périgord.

On reaching the coach, Roger saw that the Abbé was not alone; a short, fat man with a thick bandage over his eyes was leaning back beside him. The Abbé put his finger to his lips to enjoin silence, then got out and, taking Roger's arm, limped along with him, back towards the Vicomte.

"I see you have, after all, brought a friend," remarked de Périgord, as soon as they were out of earshot of the coach.

" 'Tis M. de la Tour d'Auvergne," Roger replied. "When I told him what was toward he insisted on accompanying me, to give his assistance should any unforeseen circumstance arise. But I see that you, too, are accompanied."

The Abbé nodded. "My companion is a doctor. His presence will not make it any the less a matter of murder, if you kill de Caylus, but 'twill at least give the meeting more the appearance of an affair of honour, and less that of a ruffianly attack. I have also brought with me two duelling swords from which M. le Comte can choose his length, in the event of his having only a Court sword with him."

"You think of everything," said Roger gratefully; and when the Abbé and the Vicomte had saluted each other, he added: "There is only one thing now which troubles me, and that gravely. 'Tis unavoidable that de Caylus and his servants will recognise you both. Should his death result from the encounter I fear you may be dragged into the matter as accomplice of his unknown killer. I therefore desire that immediately the Count alights you should both leave us, in order that you may not be witnesses to the actual affray."

293

" 'Tis not necessary," declared the Abbé. "I propose that after-wards we should say we accompanied you only for the purpose of enabling you to arrange a meeting with the Count at some other time and place. 'Twas not our fault that you lost your tempers there and then, and once the fight was on there was naught we could do to stop it."

The Vicomte nodded. " 'Tis an admirable explanation to save us from considerable embarrassment."

"Aye, 'tis excellent," Roger agreed. "But there is yet one more fence. An inquiry is certain to be held. Will the Court not press you both to name the masked man for whom you acted? And 'tis as important for Mademoiselle de Rochambeau's sake as for my own that my identity should remain a secret."

"I, too, had thought of that," de Périgord smiled. "If M. de la Tour d'Auvergne is willing I suggest that we should refuse to speak. We are both nobles, so even the King himself cannot give an order for us to be put to the question. But to indicate a reason for our silence we will give the impression that de Caylus's antagonist was a man of such rank that the maintenance of secrecy is imperative to prevent a scandal. We might even infer that it was one of the younger Princes of the Blood, since if the Court thinks that it will at once do its best to hush the matter up."

"You relieve me greatly," said Roger with a sigh. "As for myself, since seeing you last, Abbé, I have received news that my mother is seriously ill, so I may be leaving Paris on that account to-morrow; but I have not made up my mind as yet whether her case is so bad as to warrant my immediate departure. If, having slept upon it, I decide to go, I may have no further opportunity of thanking you for all you have done for me, so I do so now with all my heart."

De Périgord bowed. "I shall regret it if you leave, but I trust that you will write to me in your absence, and soon return to resume a friendship which has given me great pleasure. And now, I think the time has come when we should take up our position on the road that leads to de Caylus's *petite maison.* I will drive on and the two of you can follow my coach at some little distance."

That evening light gave the early autumn tints of the trees a special loveliness as they proceeded at a gentle trot towards the little village of Chaville, but half a mile before reaching it the coach turned off, entering a forest track that led south-eastwards. Three-quarters of a mile along it they came to an open grassy space, in which there was a crossroad. Here the party halted, the coach drawing up where the two roads met while Roger and the Vicomte remained some way away, edging their horses in among the trees so that they should not be seen by anyone approaching. The Abbé got out of his coach and stood by the roadside, as though in some difficulty and waiting to ask assistance of the next passer-by. Under his arm he carried a lengthy package that looked like a roll of silk, and Roger guessed that the two duelling-swords must be concealed within it.

It was very silent in the forest; only the occasional call of a bird, or a scurry in the undergrowth broke the stillness, and the time of waiting seemed interminable. Roger's thoughts were a confused jumble; Athénaïs; the fencing-bouts that he had had in the past few days; his boyhood's home at Lymington; the meeting that M. de Rochambeau was to hold that night; his long-past, drunken, midnight brawl with the Chevalier de Roubec; all drifted and mingled in his agitated mind.

At last there came the drumming of horses' hooves from the track to the west of the clearing. Roger craned forward across his horse's neck, straining with impatience to know if it was actually his enemy's coach approaching, or that of some other wayfarer. Suddenly, between the trees, he glimpsed the vehicle; it was a six-horse coach and the postilion was wearing the Comte de Caylus's green and gold livery.

The Abbé stepped forward into the road and waved his package; the coach rumbled to a halt. What happened next Roger and the Vicomte could not see, as de Périgord was on the far side of the coach and the light was no longer strong enough for them to see through its windows at that distance.

To Roger the next three minutes seemed an eternity. Then the Abbé emerged from behind the coach and came limping quickly towards them. He was only half way across the glade when the coach started into motion. Roger and de la Tour d'Auvergne broke cover and cantered out to meet de Périgord.

"'Tis of no use!" cried the Abbé. "I vowed that you were a person of consequence and would reveal yourself if he would step apart—out of sight of his servants. I told him that M. de la Tour d'Auvergne would see fair play, and that we had a doctor with us; but he was adamant. He says he will not fight, were you the King himself."

De Périgord's coach blocked the way, so de Caylus's coachman had had to urge his horses up on to the grass in order to drive round it, but he was now clear of the other coach and back on the road again beyond it.

Roger cast a reproachful glance at the Abbé. He had banked everything on that subtle tongue of his, which could be either so silver or envenomed at will, taunting de Caylus into accepting the challenge. It now flashed into his mind that de Périgord had, in an endeavour to save him from himself, played a game with him. From the beginning the Abbé had made it so clear that he did not consider it worth risking death to save a girl from being married, just because she did not like her father's choice of husband for her. It must be that, all along, he had intended to deliver the challenge in a manner which would enable it to be refused without loss of face.

Swift as lightning the Abbé saw his thought, and waved it aside. "'Pon my honour I did my best for you. I even flung down the swords at his feet, and they are there still."

De Caylus's coachman had now got his horses into a fast trot, and the coach was just disappearing among the trees that fringed the track leading to the eastwards.

Suddenly de la Tour d'Auvergne urged his horse forward in pursuit, with a cry of: "Quick! Follow me! We'll have him yet!"

"Thanks, Abbé," cried Roger and, turning his mount, he galloped after the Vicomte.

The coach was only a few hundred yards ahead of them but, at the sound of their horses' hooves thundering on the turf, the two footmen riding on the boot turned and saw that they were pursued. There was, too, still sufficient light for them to see that one of their pursuers was masked. Instantly, they began to shout to the coachman and postilion:

"*Allez! Allez!* We are attacked by highwaymen!" And from a canter the six fine horses were lashed into a gallop.

The horsemen had an easy advantage over the heavy, bounding coach and within a couple of minutes were close upon it; but, during them, the two footmen had each pulled a wide-mouthed blunderbuss from under his seat and were endeavouring to take aim with their clumsy weapons.

Roger's heart sank. It seemed near impossible to ride past the coach and bring it to a halt without receiving some of the scattered fusillade of shot that threatened. But, de la Tour d'Auvergne wrenched a pistol from his holster, cocked it, and fired at the man upon the left. The bullet caught him in the shoulder. With a cry, he dropped his blunderbuss.

The other man fired but, at that instant, the coach jolted over a big stone, and the charge of small shot whistled over Roger's head.

Despite the shooting and the shouting, the coachman, now crouching low over his box, flogged his team on. Yet in another minute the two horsemen had drawn level with him, one on each side of the coach.

Pulling his second pistol from its holster the Vicomte thrust it at him and yelled: "Halt, fellow! Halt! Or your life will answer for it!"

The coachman had done his best and, with a shout to the postilion, reined in his horses. Still bumping and bounding the cumbersome vehicle lumbered to a stop.

Roger and de la Tour d'Auvergne rode on some twenty yards and came together again just in front of the steaming leaders.

"Give me your horse!" cried the Vicomte. "I will hold these people in play while you go forward with your intended business. May God guard you and make strong your arm!"

"I thank you!" gasped Roger, throwing over his reins and slipping to the ground. Suddenly he remembered that he was wearing spurs. Stooping he unbuckled them and slipped them into his pocket. By the time he reached the door of the coach the Comte de Caylus had it open and, one heavy hand on its window-sill, was leaning out, a scowl of anger on his dark, ugly features.

While taking off his spurs Roger had got back his breath. Having made a deep, formal bow he said: "Monsieur le Comte. I regret that circumstances prevent me from sending my seconds to you, and offering you the choice of weapons, time and place; but 'tis imperative that we should fight—and now. I pray that you will descend and join me on the grass."

"S'blood! Who are you?" demanded the Count, angrily. "And what is the meaning of this farce?"

"'Tis no farce!" replied Roger coldly. "As you soon will find; I trust to your cost. As to myself, M. l'Abbé de Périgord will have already told you that in crossing your sword with mine you will do it no dishonour. Immediately we are free of prying eyes I will unmask and answer all reasonable questions about myself. Come! The light is failing! Unless you would prefer to fight in semi-darkness, do not delay."

"I'll fight in neither light nor darkness, without a reason," growled de Caylus.

"I'll give you that, once we are apart. And 'tis one that you will answer to readily enough."

"Were I to do so 'twould mean your death, young jackanapes!"

"It suits me that your mind runs in that vein; since, let me warn you, I intend to kill you if I can!"

"You count this affront that I as yet know nothing of as mortal, then?"

"I do. I'll seek no quarter, neither will I give it."

For a moment it looked as if de Caylus was about to spring from the coach; but he kept his temper and evidently thought better of the impulse.

"No!" he exclaimed firmly, "I'll not be dragooned into fighting someone I do not know for something that I may not have done. At any other time I'd skewer you as full of holes as a larded capon, for your impudence; but to-night I have no mind for it." Upon which he suddenly sat back and slammed the door of the coach to in Roger's face.

Seizing the handle of the door Roger wrenched it open and, thrusting his head inside, cried: "Why not to-night as well as any other? You have not the reputation of a coward; since when have you become one?"

De Caylus laughed. "Call me a coward if you will. I care not! I'll not fight to-night, I tell you! In two days' time I am to be wed; and I'll not risk some chance thrust of yours marring my enjoyment of my young wife. After a month with her I'll be your man. If you've a wish to die seek me out again early in October, at any time and place you choose, and I'll cut you to ribbons before I kill you!"

"'Tis your projected marriage that offends me!" cried Roger rashly. "So you'll fight to-night, or I'll slay you where you sit!" And, leaning forward, he seized the Count by his lace jabot, giving a violent tug upon it.

While they had been shouting at one another Roger had been dimly aware that de Caylus was not alone in the coach. Another man occupied the seat opposite him; but Roger's eyes had been riveted on the Count's swarthy face and in the dim light of the interior of the coach the other man's features were obscure.

As Roger's fingers grasped the goffered lace that fell from de Caylus's neckband his vaguely seen companion suddenly thrust out a hand and snatched Roger's mask from his face.

"*Ventre du Pape!*" he shouted to de Caylus, as Roger's features were revealed. "I thought I knew that voice! 'Tis that upstart Breuc; my father's secretary! Your challenger is a fellow that Athénaïs picked up from the gutter!"

Releasing his hold upon the Count, Roger sprang back. But it was too late. The coachman, the postilion and the two footmen must all have heard the shout, so the damage was done, and nothing now could possibly prevent them realising the cause of this deadly quarrel. White with fury and dismay Roger glared into the haughty, handsome face of Count Lucien de Rochambeau.

"You crazy fool!" he burst out. "Since you suspected my identity had you not the sense to realise that its revelation would jeopardise your sister's honour?"

De Caylus was staring at Roger uncomprehendingly. "S'blood! What means all this?" he exclaimed, turning swiftly to Count Lucien. "I've seen this man in your father's office; but why in thunder should you link his name with that of Athénaïs?"

"The dog has been casting sheep's eyes at her since she was fourteen," snapped the young Count. "But he wormed his way into the household and my father remained blind to it. 'Twould now appear that he has the unbelievable impertinence to set himself up as your rival, and would try his hand at killing you to prevent your marriage."

"So that's the way of it," de Caylus growled. "When the Abbé said that de la Tour d'Auvergne was with my unknown challenger methought that having failed to kill me himself he had hired some bravo to attempt it."

"Your thought is worthy of you," cut in Roger. "But neither M. de la Tour d'Auvergne, nor any other true gentleman, would entertain it for a moment."

"And who are you, a dirty, ink-spilling scrivener, to judge what thoughts are becoming to a gentleman?" sneered Count Lucien.

"For that I'll fight you when I've finished with the Count!" flared Roger. " 'Twill be a chastisement long overdue. And I'd have you know that I am of as good a blood as you."

"I'll not believe it! You're naught but an adventurer!"

"Then you give the lie to M. l'Abbé de Périgord as well as to myself. He is acquainted with my uncle, the Earl of Kildonan. My real name is Brook, and my father a Rear-Admiral of the British fleet."

"I care not who you are!" stormed de Caylus. "I'll not now give any man satisfaction till I've possessed Athénaïs. Get hence!"

"And I'll not let you while I live," cried Roger, drawing his sword. "She's for a better man than the debauched grandson of a negro slave!"

De Caylus flushed under his sallow skin. Reaching a hand down to the floor he snatched up one of the swords that de Périgord had thrown in there, and bounded from the coach.

"That's better!" Roger exclaimed, stepping back. "Let's seek an even piece of ground and fight it out."

"I'll not honour you by even the semblance of a proper meeting," bellowed de Caylus, now pale with rage. "I'll kill you where you belong; here in this ditch."

As he spoke he lunged with all his force. Roger leapt sideways— only just in time. He had barely thrown himself on guard when the Count came at him again. To his terror he knew that he had allowed himself to be caught at a terrible disadvantage. A few feet behind him lay a low bank and ditch; if he gave way it was a certainty that he would catch his heel on the bank and go sprawling backwards.

Their blades met, held each other, parted and met again. Up—down. Up—down; at furious speed in clash after clash. De Caylus lunged again. Roger dared not retreat even by a pace. He let his knees go and ducked the thrust. The blade pierced his coat above the shoulder and seared like a hot iron across his skin.

He knew that the Count had drawn first blood, but that the wound was too slight to be of any consequence. For a moment the point of the sword remained caught in the cloth of his coat. Had he been better placed he might have seized the opportunity to stab upward at the Count; but he could not afford to risk it. Instead, before de Caylus had fully recovered, he leapt sideways and pivoted on his left heel. The success of the movement made him gasp with thankfulness. It had brought them round, so that when their swords met again his back was no longer to the ditch; he was facing towards the horses and his adversary towards the back of the coach.

De Caylus was still fighting all out, and Roger knew now what he was up against. The strength exerted against his own blade was so terrific that, every instant, he expected to have it forced down or struck from his hand. He now had enough space between the coach and the ditch to retreat, and he only saved himself from the fierce onslaught by giving back slowly, step by step, as each furious thrust was launched to kill him.

Suddenly he heard de la Tour d'Auvergne's voice, raised in a shout. "Beware! Behind you! *Oh, Mère de Dieu!*"

The Vicomte, still mounted and at the head of the coach-team, was watching the fight with terrible apprehension. From his point of vantage he had suddenly seen something that the two combatants, their eyes fixed upon one another, seeking to divine in them each coming move, had not.

Count Lucien had picked up the other sword from the floor of the coach, slipped out of its far door and come round its back behind Roger.

Aghast with amazement and dread de la Tour d'Auvergne had grasped the fact that the unscrupulous young man, evidently regarding the affray as no ordinary duel but an armed assault, was just about to stab Roger through the back.

The shout put both antagonists off their stroke, and both, involuntarily sprang away from one another to throw a swift glance over their shoulders. De Caylus, seeing nothing, swung back and came charging in again. Roger, finding himself half facing Count Lucien, realised his mortal peril and whipped right round to ward off his new antagonist's first lunge.

He had barely done so when he heard the swift slither of de Caylus's feet behind him. He knew then that he was done. De Caylus alone was a match for any man in France, and the blade, even of a military cadet rising eighteen, added to his was more than any champion could have tackled.

In a wild attempt to save himself Roger abandoned all rules of fence. Pivoting on his right foot he scythed with his sword sideways. Hissing through the air it whipped past Count Lucien's eyes like a lash and, ending in a full half-circle, caused de Caylus to jerk back his head just as he delivered his thrust. Swivelling again, with one swift stroke Roger smashed down Count Lucien's sword, then did a thing he had never dreamed that he would have to do as a result of issuing a challenge. Springing past Count Lucien, he took to his heels and ran.

Instantly, with wild shouts of triumph, the two of them were after, him.

"Let me have him," yelled the young Count. "This scullion should wield a spit and not a sword. I'll teach him to play the highwayman and waylay a coach."

"Leave him to me, boy!" bellowed de Caylus. "He is my affair!"

As Roger fled down the road he was conscious that his face was scarlet. His whole body was aflame with shame, and with it was mingled fear. The back of his scalp prickled. At every step he took he expected to feel a sword pierce his back and sear through his lungs. The thought of the disgrace of being killed in such a way, and, above all, with de la Tour d'Auvergne looking on, was utterly unbearable. Yet he knew that if he faltered for a second, even before he could swing about and throw himself again on guard, he would, within a minute, be choking out his life's blood.

Red-hot tears sprang to his eyes as it flashed into his mind how Count Lucien would gloatingly relate the scene to Athénaïs, and describe to her how they had killed her pasteboard champion like a yellow-livered cur. But, racked as he was with scalding humiliation, he could not bring himself to halt, and offer himself as a sacrifice to honour spitted on the cold steel that was flashing in his rear.

Then it came to him that he was out-distancing his pursuers. Racing on, he forced himself to listen to their steps and attempt to assess how far they had dropped behind him. Another shout from de Caylus, taunting him as a vaunted English aristocrat and calling on him to turn and fight, told him that the Count must be a good twenty paces in his rear.

He risked one swift glance over his shoulder. Count Lucien was running silently and well, no more than six paces from his heels, and had the lead over the heavier de Caylus by some twenty yards.

Suddenly Roger stopped dead and swung about. He did not attempt to throw himself on guard but thrust out his sword and tensed his arm. Count Lucien had just time to make a downward stroke deflecting the point of Roger's blade from his chest to his thigh, then his own impetus carried him right on to it. The steel ripped through the upper part of his leg. With a wild cry, he twisted, dropped his sword and fell.

Roger's blade was caught fast in the muscle, and de Caylus had already covered half the distance between them. Swiftly lifting his left foot, Roger jammed it down hard on Count Lucien's writhing body, gave a sharp tug, and freed his sword. He had one moment's breathing space and he used it to get well clear of the still squirming

Count. Throwing himself on guard in the middle of the road, he panted at de Caylus:

"Now we're man to man again, we'll see if an Englishman's not as good as a French nigger! Kill me if you can!"

Again their blades clashed, clung together, slithered and parted; only to rasp and send the sparks flying again a second later. Up—down. Up—down. Lunge—stamp. Parry—twist. Up—down. Up—down. Feint—stamp—thrust. Clash—clash—clash.

Roger's breath was coming quickly now. In running for his life he had used up his first wind. But de Caylus was no better off, as the pursuit had taken a lot out of his breath too. While giving chase to Roger he had thrown aside the white powdered wig in which he had come from Versailles, and the lingering afterglow of the sunset showed his coarse, crisp black hair, matted in tight curls to his skull. His thick-lipped mouth hung slightly open and two rows of fine white teeth gleamed from it in a ferocious smile. The yellowish whites of his eyes were slightly bloodshot and they glittered like those of a wild boar avid for the kill.

He was still superbly confident and he took risks that Roger would not have dared to take; yet Roger could not get through his guard. Their eyes never left one another's for a second; but both of them knew that de la Tour d'Auvergne had come up with some of de Caylus's people and was ordering them to carry Count Lucien back to the coach.

So far Roger had required every iota of his skill to defend himself from the violence of the Count's attack; but now, de Caylus, realising at last that he was up against an antagonist worthy of him, began to fight more warily, which enabled Roger to attempt some of his favourite thrusts.

Four times they circled round one another, then he delivered a lunge that he had learned from Monsieur St. Paul, the ex-musketeer fencing-master of Rennes. It very nearly did the trick, but de Caylus jerked himself as upright as a matador on tiptoe before a charging bull, and Roger's blade, missing him by a quarter inch, ripped through the satin lapels of his coat.

Again, for a space they circled warily; then again Roger came in, this time with a thrust that had defeated him in one of his practice bouts only a few days before. But the Count must have known it. Quick as lightning he parried, made a swift encircling movement that almost forced Roger's sword from his hand, and stabbed straight at his eyes.

Roger jerked aside his head and the gleaming blade slithered past his ear; but his evasive action had been so violent that it threw him off his balance. For a second he was poised on the ball of one foot, then he tripped and fell.

With a cry of triumph de Caylus was upon him, his sword drawn back to skewer him to the ground. Roger flung himself sideways, rolled over twice and was brought up by the roadside bank edging the ditch. As de Caylus came at him again he squirmed over into the ditch, twisted, and came up with one knee on the bank. Throwing up his sword his luck, and not his judgment, enabled him to parry the thrust.

For a moment they fought with renewed ferocity, the Count

striving with might and main to finish his antagonist while he had him half crouching in the ditch. The very fury of his attack proved his temporary undoing. Instead of confining himself to thrusts he fought wild, using all his giant strength to beat down Roger's guard. Suddenly his sword snapped off short at the hilt.

As de Caylus jumped back it was Roger's turn to give a cry of triumph. Coming to his feet he sprang out of the ditch and rushed upon his adversary. But, before he could get into position to lunge the Count had flung the hilt of his broken sword in his face.

Roger ducked, but just not quickly enough. The sword hilt caught him on the forehead, bounced from it and fell with a clang on to the road. For a moment he was half stunned and stood tottering there. De Caylus meanwhile had leapt back once more and cast a frantic glance round. His eye fell upon Count Lucien's sword, which had been left lying by the roadside some fifteen yards away. Rushing towards it, he snatched it up.

By the time Roger had recovered from his knock on the head sufficiently to advance again, de Caylus was on guard and ready for him. Again the deepening shadows echoed to the clash of swords. Up—down. Up—down. Thrust—stamp—parry. Clash—clash—clash.

But both the combatants were tired now. Neither had had a chance to take off their coats or neckbands, and both were streaming with sweat. Panting, gasping, their clothes disordered, their faces haggard and the perspiration trickling into their eyes, they fought doggedly on. Each thrust they gave grew weaker yet neither could get past the other's guard.

Suddenly de Caylus made a desperate bid to end matters. Charging in on Roger he lifted his sword high and lunged downwards. It was a cunning but unorthodox stroke, since it left its deliverer's breast temporarily exposed; yet it was the one that had defeated de la Tour d'Auvergne two months before.

Having heard the Vicomte describe exactly how it had been administered Roger knew the pass. It was his opportunity. Instead of endeavouring to parry the stroke he delivered a counter thrust himself. Lunging with every ounce of his remaining strength he went almost to his knees as he followed through, his left arm flung straight out behind him. De Caylus's blade passed harmlessly over his shoulder; his own pierced the Count through the heart and came out six inches behind his back.

For a moment de Caylus remained standing there, his eyes goggling. Then the blood gushed from his mouth and, with a horrible choking noise, he crashed to the ground. The falling body wrenched Roger's sword-hilt from his hand; he staggered back, swayed drunkenly, and fell himself.

Almost overcome with exhaustion he lay gasping for breath in the middle of the road; then, dimly, he heard someone shouting at him. De la Tour d'Auvergne had ridden up and, wild with excitement, was congratulating him on his victory. Another voice joined in, and as Roger struggled panting to his knees he saw de Périgord coming at a limping run towards him.

" 'Twas a marvel!" cried the Abbé. "That final thrust of yours was superb! By the most cursed luck I missed the beginning. Before I could get to my coach you had all disappeared, and in following, my fool of a man took the wrong fork of the road a quarter of a mile back. But there is blood on your face. Are you badly hurt?"

"Nay," gasped Roger. "I've naught but a scratch on the shoulder; and a cut on the head—where his sword-hilt struck—when he threw it at me."

The Abbé cast a glance at de Caylus's prostrate body. "He'll throw no more sword-hilts," he said grimly. "I left the doctor in my coach, and the coach just round the bend of the road behind us; since the less he knows the better. Unless you need his ministrations yourself, 'tis pointless to call him."

"I pray you do so, Abbé," cut in the Vicomte. "Count Lucien de Rochambeau is wounded and should have attention."

"What!" exclaimed de Périgord. "Did he then join in the fight?"

Roger nodded. "The young caitiff sought to strike me down from behind. But worse! While I was parleying at the coach door he snatched off my mask and, like an imbecile, cried aloud both my name and his sister's. So all is known. De Caylus's people will be retailing the story to half Paris before another hour is past."

"*Sacré bleu!* Then the question of your returning to your mother is settled for you. You must fly instantly! To horse, man! To horse!"

De la Tour d'Auvergne manœuvred Roger's mount round for him, and cried: "The Abbé is right! Your life will depend on the distance you can put between Paris and yourself before morning."

"One moment!" muttered Roger, and putting his foot on de Caylus's carcase he began to tug upon his sword to get it free.

The Vicomte went on quickly to de Périgord. "I had Count Lucien carried back to their coach. One of the footmen is wounded also. I had to shoot him before we could bring them to a halt. 'Twould be wise to leave your doctor to do what he can for them, and get away from here as quickly as possible yourself. In your place I would go into hiding for a while."

The Abbé considered for a moment, then he said! "Nay, 'tis not necessary. I saw only the end of the fight, not its beginning, and shall maintain that having delivered M. le Chevalier de Brook's message to M. de Caylus I was in no way responsible for what followed. But your case, *mon cher* Vicomte, is very different. Since you pistolled one of the servants, and played a major part in holding up the coach, you have laid yourself open to most serious charges."

"I know it, and intend to seek safety in flight."

Having recovered his sword Roger mounted his horse, and said to the Abbé: "I've no choice now but to bid you farewell; but I thank you mightily for your help in this night's work and pray that no ill will come to you on account of it."

"Fear not for me," de Périgord smiled. "To make my innocence the more plain I intend to drive on to de Caylus's *petite maison* and, with appropriate face, prepare them there to receive his body. Besides, the night is yet young, and the beautiful Olympe should not be deprived of her supper. I'll carry her back to Passy in my coach and do my poor best to console her for the loss of her rich lover."

Roger could not help laughing. "Abbé, you are incorrigible! May your zest for enjoyment never flag; and may we meet again to talk of this night at our ease, over a good bottle."

"We will, *mon ami*. If a warrant is issued to prevent your return I will seek you out when I go to England. In the meantime pray bear my greetings to Lord and Lady Grey, and to Mr. Pitt, should you see him. Take occasion also to wait upon your uncle, and tell my Lord Kildonan to bring me news of you when next he comes to Paris."

De la Tour d'Auvergne had already turned his horse in the direction of Sevres. Roger followed suit, and with shouts of farewell they galloped off into the gathering darkness.

After two miles they eased their pace and walked their horses to give them a breather. It was the Vicomte who broke the silence, by saying a little coldly:

"From de Périgord's parting messages I gather that your mother lives in England, and that you are, in fact, an Englishman?"

"'Tis true," Roger admitted. "My real name is Brook."

"Then may one ask why you have always given yourself out to be a Frenchman from the German provinces?"

"'Twas not through any wish to deceive a good friend such as yourself," Roger assured him quickly. "It came about through my once having narrowly escaped being mobbed by some sailors who had ample cause to hate the English; and, later, to unsay what I had already said to various people seemed to invite too many needless complications. De Périgord discovered the truth only because he heard me babbling while unconscious from a blow on the head, and it then transpired that he is acquainted with my uncle. The story of how I came to France and entered M. de Rochambeau's service is a long one. I have often meant to tell it you, but no suitable occasion ever seemed to occur. I do trust that you are not offended by my having failed to make you this confidence?"

"Nay, not the least, now I understand the reason for your reticence. I was wondering, though, if Athénaïs knows that you are an Englishman and of noble birth."

"Yes, she has done so for a long time past. But why do you ask?"

"Because it seemed to me that if she knew your secret and had long regarded you as her equal, she could not help but love you."

"Monsieur le Vicomte, you pay me a great compliment."

"No more than is your due as a most handsome and gallant gentleman. The romance of your situation, too, could hardly fail to appeal to any maiden, and, since you have told her this long story of yours, I can only assume that at times you must have managed to meet in private. Loving her as you do you would have been scarce human had you not attempted it."

Roger sighed. "Were anyone else to question me on this I'd deny it with my last breath; but, to you, I will avow it. Athénaïs and I have met many times in secret and we love one another very dearly."

"I should have had the wit to guess it," murmured the Vicomte; then, after a moment, he added: "That being so, I find it surprising that you did not attempt to elope together."

"We toyed with the idea," Roger admitted. "But almost from the first both of us knew in our hearts that we could never marry."

"Why so?"

"The sword of religion lies between us. I am a Protestant, and neither of us are prepared to give up our faith for that of the other. We recognised that our love must remain no more than a romantic attachment."

"Yet you knew that she must marry, and marry soon?"

"We accepted that. But both of us pinned our hopes upon her being given a husband who would love her and whom she would grow to love."

" 'Twas a slender hope," remarked the Vicomte cynically, "seeing the manner in which such marriages are arranged."

"Nay, not so slender in her case. Both she and I knew of your devotion to her and discussed it many times. She vowed that she would be mighty pleased to have so true a gentleman as yourself for her husband and would give all her mind to proving a good and loyal wife. 'Twas as savage a blow to us as to you when her father chose M. de Caylus for her."

"Aye, 'twas damnable ill-fortune; and I feel it to be more than ever so in view of what you tell me. Her romantic love for you is a thing apart. If her thoughts were already favourably engaged towards me, I vow I would have won her affections after a few months of marriage, and made her happy. Whereas, instead, her situation has become most desperate."

"I know it," muttered Roger gloomily. "Count Lucien ruined my whole plan. Once 'tis noised abroad that her father's secretary fought on her behalf everyone will put the worst construction on it. Even were it given out that I was a Prince of the Blood, who had been living in the household incognito, it could not save her from the scandal of having had an affair while still an unmarried girl."

The Vicomte nodded. "M. de Rochambeau will force her to take the veil. 'Tis his only possible course, consonant with honour, in such a situation."

"Yes; 'tis a tragedy; and I have but one consolation. She swore to me upon the cross that she would rather enter a convent than wed de Caylus; so my act to-night has burdened her with no worser fate than she would otherwise have decreed for herself."

"Do you really believe that she would have carried out her threat?"

"I am certain of it. 'Twas all I could manage a week back to dissuade her from defying her father; and when I told her I had arranged this meeting she would have burnt her boats to prevent it, had I not vowed that I meant to fight de Caylus whether she did or no."

"Will you attempt to see her before leaving?"

"Nay. We have no rendezvous, and 'twould make her case worse than ever did I force my way in upon her. I had meant to arrange a meeting to-morrow morning but now I dare not stay for that." As he spoke, Roger urged his mount into a canter and added: "Come! Every moment is precious. Now our horses are rested let us push on."

After another long gallop they eased their pace again and the Vicomte said: "*Mon ami*, I cannot keep this up. My old wound is paining me too badly. You must go on alone."

"*Mort dieu!*" exclaimed Roger. "I had forgotten it, and marvel now that you have stayed the pace so far. 'Tis the best of reasons for us remaining together, though; for should it reopen it may cause you to faint."

" 'Twill not reopen, provided I take my time for the rest of the way. But that, you cannot afford to do."

Roger knew it only too well; but, once again, he was not thinking on the same lines as his companion. The Vicomte had in mind the hue and cry that would soon be raised after the slayer of de Caylus, whereas he was concerned with the urgency of his getting back to Paris for the conference at which the Archbishop of Toulouse was to give his fateful decision. The meeting with de Caylus had taken much longer than he had thought would be the case and he still had over half the distance back to the Hôtel de Rochambeau to cover. He would be late anyhow, and if he delayed to keep de la Tour d'Auvergne company he might miss the meeting altogether; yet he felt that he could not leave his friend who was now suffering, as well as in danger on his account; so he said firmly: "I'll not go on and leave you exposed to a greater risk of capture than myself."

"For me, capture would mean, at worst, a reprimand from the King and a spell in the Bastille; whereas for you it would mean death."

"True. Yet seeing the jeopardy in which you have placed yourself for me, I cannot bring myself to leave you."

De la Tour d'Auvergne shook his head impatiently. "I mean to seek sanctuary on my father's estates; as, once there, 'tis most unlikely that anything less than a charge of treason would be pressed against me. But the roads to Brittany and England are divergent, so we would have to part company in another hour or two in any event. I beg, nay, I insist, that you should use the time to the best possible advantage. Otherwise, if you are caught, I'll always believe that but for me you would have got away, and have your death upon my conscience."

"In that case you leave me no option," Roger replied with a feeling of relief that he could not repress. "But I pray you make what haste you can, so as to be well clear of Paris before morning."

" 'Twill be hours yet before warrants can be issued for us."

"I trust so. But since you are in no condition to ride hard 'tis doubly important that you should set out for Brittany with a minimum of delay."

"I shall not ride," the Vicomte announced, "but travel by post-chaise with a team of six; and while my man is making the necessary arrangements I intend to call at the Hôtel de Rochambeau."

"You plan, then, to wait on Athénaïs and tell her what has occurred?" said Roger; and, as de la Tour d'Auvergne nodded, he went on quickly: I'm mighty glad of that. I had been racking my wits without avail, for some means of getting our news to her. I pray you make my adieus and explain the necessity under which I lie to depart without taking leave of her in person."

The Vicomte hesitated. "I intended only to make my own adieus and, whilst doing so, offer formal condolences on her fiancé having been killed in a duel, as though I had but just heard it. Since she knew of your intentions she will realise immediately who killed him."

"Heavens, man! Why stick at that?" Roger expostulated. " 'Tis but half the tale and will not give her warning of the storm which is about to break above her lovely head as a result of her brother's malice and stupidity. 'Twas to prepare her to meet her father's wrath on my account that I was seeking some way to get news to her; and, since you've a mind to say farewell to her before setting out for Brittany, 'tis the perfect opportunity."

"That's sound enough and, could I see her alone, I would willingly both tell her all and give her your messages. But you seem to forget that Madame Marie-Angé is certain to be present at our interview."

"What if she is! She, too, will be in full possession of the truth by to-morrow morning. There is naught to be gained by withholding it from her overnight. I beg you to speak openly before both of them, so that at least Athénaïs may have a little time to take stock of her situation."

"I had not looked at it that way before, but you are right," the Vicomte declared. "Now you must tarry no longer. God speed you, and a safe journey."

"And to you, dear friend!" replied Roger feelingly. "I'll ne'er forget your kindness, and I trust we'll meet again in happier circumstances."

The two young men clasped hands firmly, then Roger pressed his knees into his horse and urged it forward.

It was nearly half-past nine and darkness had fallen. The conference had been called for ten o'clock, and Roger doubted if he could get to it much before half-past. He no longer cared a straw if the Marquis should be angry at his lateness, but he was desperately anxious now lest the meeting should prove a short one and the decision be taken before his arrival. Since he could not have galloped his horse for the best part of nine miles he had so far lost little time unavoidably; but in an endeavour to make up some of the leeway caused by de Caylus's reluctance to fight, he dug his heels into his horse's flanks and forced him to go all out.

In spite of the semi-darkness he made good going all through the outskirts of Paris, and even when he reached the cobbled streets still did not spare his fast-failing mount. A church clock was striking the quarter after ten as he passed the Tuilleries. Five minutes later, he clattered past a long line of waiting coaches outside the Hôtel de Rochambeau, and turned into its courtyard.

Flinging himself off the steaming horse he threw the bridle to a groom, who had come running out of the stable at the sound of the hoof-beats on the *pavé*. Then he ran to the door of the mansion.

As he reached it a sudden thought struck him. It was now too late to go up to his room and tidy himself before the meeting, as he had planned, and, although he could do that downstairs, he could not appear before the Marquis wearing a sword. Swiftly unbuckling his weapon he leant it against the stonework in a dark corner of the porch, where it would be easy for him to reclaim it on his way out.

On his entering the hall the two footmen on duty exclaimed in dismay at the blood on his face, but with a muttered word to them that his injury was nothing to worry about, he dived into the powder-closet. Having washed his face and hands and tidied his hair he called to one of the men to brush the dust off his clothes, then dashed upstairs.

In his office he found his assistant in a state of excited apprehension on his behalf. The Marquis had been furious at Roger's disappearance and had ordered Paintendre to prepare the conference table but refused his offer to take notes.

As the easiest explanation for his lateness, the abrasion on his forehead and the rip in the shoulder of his coat where de Caylus's sword had torn it, Roger said abruptly that he had been set upon by footpads, then asked: "Are they all inside? How long have they been assembled?"

"No more than a quarter of an hour," Paintendre replied. "Most of them were here and arguing well before ten, but the Archbishop of Toulouse was a little late."

That the new Prime Minister had kept the appointment was all Roger wished to know. Taking a piece of paper he hastily scrawled upon it.

Monseigneur,
My service and most humble apologies for such inconvenience as my absence may have caused you. I had the misfortune to be attacked by footpads and was rendered incapable of returning to attend you earlier.

He would not have bothered, but for a sudden fear that unless he offered some explanation the Marquis might, in a fit of cold anger, send him from the room as soon as he appeared. With the paper in his hand he opened the door of the council chamber as noiselessly as he could, slipped quietly inside, and gave a swift look round.

The fifteen nobles who had attended the previous afternoon's gathering were all present and with them, seated on the Marquis's right, was Loménie de Brienne, Archbishop of Toulouse, now Prime Minister of France. The prelate was wearing the violet robes of his ecclesiastical dignity and, with one alabaster hand, was toying with a great diamond and sapphire cross suspended from his neck by a satin ribbon.

As Roger entered de Castries was giving details of the naval preparations at Brest for the seizure of the Dutch ports. The Archbishop was listening to him attentively, but the Marquis was drawing figures on the wad of paper that lay before him and, looking up as the door opened, glowered at Roger. Tiptoeing round the big oval table Roger placed the note he had written by the Marquis's hand, made a low bow, and tiptoed away again towards his own little table beside the door.

On sitting down he was conscious of a sudden wave of relief. It was the last time that he would ever make his "humble service" to this frigid and heartless aristocrat. In another hour or two he would be his own master again, for a time at least; and, within a week, either free for good of this hateful subservience or occupying a condemned cell. Brushing the thought aside he gave all his attention to the meeting.

Within a few minutes he realised that it was, so far, no more than a repetition of that held the previous day. Evidently de Rayneval and the Comte de Maillebois had already made their reports on the situation in the United Provinces, and now the Ministers were outlining the state of immediate readiness of the French armed forces to undertake a lightning stroke.

As the phrases and arguments that he had heard before rolled smoothly from the tongues of de Breteuil, de Polignac and the rest, Roger's mind began to wander. In vivid flashes he saw again the critical phases of the terrible combat in which he had so recently engaged. He recalled de Périgord's cynical smile as he announced his intention of carrying the dead man's mistress off to supper, and the Vicomte's announcement that he meant to wait upon Athénaïs before setting out on his flight to Brittany. He wondered anxiously and sorrowfully what would become of Athénaïs, and if he would ever see her again. To his acute distress he had to admit to himself that it was most improbable, since nothing now could prevent her being immured in a convent, and, if he did succeed in escaping to England, he would never be able to return to France without imperilling his life.

A full hour went by and the Archbishop was asking the opinion of the Foreign Secretary, who had not yet spoken. M. de Montmorin showed none of his hesitation of the previous afternoon but now came out openly on the side of the camarilla that had plotted for war.

As Roger listened with half an ear he realised that the all-important decision would, at last, soon be taken, and that he must pull himself together. For the past half-hour he had been feeling completely exhausted. During his ride back to Paris the excitement of his victory and the urgency of getting to the meeting had prevented him from being fully conscious of his physical state. But, since he had been sitting in the council chamber he had felt with increasing severity the strain he had been through. The duel alone had proved a most gruelling ordeal and in it he had sustained certain injuries, hardly noticed at the time, but now nagging at him. The blood from the cut on his shoulder had dried and his shirt was sticking to it, so that it hurt every time he moved; the place where de Caylus's sword-hilt had struck him on the forehead had swollen into a big lump which throbbed dully.

The Comte de Montmorin had hardly ceased speaking when the Marquis came in to the attack. At first his tone was restrained and as he arrayed his well-reasoned arguments Roger was trying to think what he must do when the meeting ended.

The bulk of the money he had saved while in the service of M. de Rochambeau was in a separate bag, with the Marquis's bullion, in the *coffret-fort* that lay in the office outside, and to it he had the key. As soon as the meeting was over and the Marquis had gone to his own apartments he must collect that, and, he reminded himself with Scottish carefulness, help himself to a further twenty *louis* that were due to him for the month of August that had just expired. Then he would slip downstairs, collect his sword, saddle the best horse in the stable, and so away.

He felt that de la Tour d'Auvergne had been right in his contention that it would be morning before warrants were issued for their arrest, and he wondered if he dared risk attempting to see Athénaïs. The urge to give her what consolation he could, and the longing to hold her in his arms again, were almost overwhelming, but on several counts he decided most reluctantly against it.

In such foreboding circumstances a final meeting, far from consoling Athénaïs, could only harrow her still further; and his own hope of safety lay in reaching one of the Channel ports before his description could be circulated in them, and all captains sailing for England instructed to detain him. To reach Athénaïs at all he would have to wait until the whole household was asleep, then make his way like a burglar to her bedroom. If he was discovered there her father might well kill her, and, even if he got away again undetected, to give several precious hours to such a project would almost certainly result in his own capture and death.

The Marquis's voice had risen and he was now speaking much more rapidly. Roger had never before seen him display such passion and forcefulness. His blue eyes flashing he leaned towards the Archbishop and hammered home his thesis. France was on the verge of irretrievable ruin and open anarchy. Only one thing could save the monarchy, the Church and the nobility. The people's thoughts must be diverted from the hopeless tangle of internal affairs to sudden, unexpected and glorious triumphs beyond the frontiers. The lightning subjugation of the United Provinces would fill France's empty coffers, and give her a breathing space to reorganise. Before the nation had time to consider internal grievances again the Dutch ports could be made the bases of a French Armada and the people worked up to a fever pitch of excitement at the prospect of fresh conquests. By next summer the invasion could be launched and the final blow against England struck. The autumn of 'eighty-eight would see the power of perfidious Albion for ever broken and France rich, prosperous, unchallengeable, the Mistress of the Empire of the World.

The Archbishop's face remained calm and impassive. He continued to toy with his heavy jewelled cross and neither by word nor gesture gave the faintest indication as to if the Marquis's impassioned harangue had made the least impression on him. Yet everyone in the room knew that he was a shallow, vain and intensely ambitious man. M. de Rochambeau was offering him a way of escape from innumerable difficulties with which it was far beyond his very limited capacities to deal. And, far more; for if this audacious and cunningly conceived plan succeeded he would go down to history as greater than Rosney, greater than Mazarin, greater than Colbert, greater even than Richelieu. He would be the most powerful Prime Minister that France had ever known and, if he wished, there would then be few obstacles to his ending his days upon the Papal throne. Could any vain, ambitious prelate possibly resist such a temptation?

As the Marquis ceased speaking there fell a deathly silence in the room. No one moved a muscle and all eyes were riveted with fascinated expectation on the Archbishop's pale face. Slowly he turned to M. de Rochambeau, and said:

"Monsieur le Marquis, you are right. Only a bold course can now save France from hideous disaster. You have won me to your plan and I congratulate you upon it. I give my authority for M. de Montmorin to write a letter in the terms you suggest to the Dutch Republican leaders, pledging them the armed support of France in their rising against the Stadtholder."

Silence fell again for a second. The Marquis was pale as a ghost but his eyes flashed with triumph. Suddenly the others gave vent to their feelings. As the Archbishop stood up to leave the table they broke into a noisy uproar of jubilant congratulation. Fawning upon him and flattering him as the greatest statesman that France had known for a dozen generations they accompanied him downstairs, and for some ten minutes Roger was left alone.

Since he knew that the Marquis and some of the others would return, as soon as they had seen the Archbishop to his coach, he remained where he was, standing by his table, now the prey of almost overwhelming emotions.

The treacherous subjugation of the United Provinces by a *coup d'état* on the 10th of September—the first and all-important step in the plot that must lead to the destruction of Britain—was now inevitable, except for one slender possibility; and he alone, if fortune favoured him, had the power to give his country that chance. He was still convinced that if France was faced with immediate war with England and Prussia she would not dare to implement her promise to the Dutch Republicans. If the British Cabinet had news of what was afoot they still might hesitate to take the plunge and issue an instant ultimatum. If they did hesitate they would be lost. But before they even had a chance to take a decision they must be placed in full possession of the facts, and no one but himself was in a position to carry these facts across the Channel. It was now close on midnight of the 28th-29th August, so there were only twelve clear days before the mine was to be sprung. The Cabinet would need at least six days if effective counter-measures were to be taken to prevent the *coup*. That meant that he had six days in which to get to London—and by morning half the police in France would be hunting him for murder.

He was still immersed in the terrible responsibility that had been thrust upon him when M. de Rochambeau came back into the room, accompanied by Messieurs de Montmorin and de Rayneval.

"Now for the letter!" said the Marquis eagerly. "While we take care of that you, de Rayneval, had best order your baggage to be carried downstairs and get into your travelling things. Not a moment must be lost in transmitting the despatch; and, lest the Archbishop weaken overnight, you must be well on your way to the Hague by morning. Then it will be too late for any last moment shilly-shallying to rob us of our triumph."

"You are right, Marquis!" cried de Rayneval. "I'll make my preparations with all speed and rejoin you here the instant I am done;" and he hurried from the room.

The Marquis glanced at Roger. "You have parchment there? Take down my words in a clear hand. Address the letter to His Excellency, Mynheer van Berkel, Pensionary of Amsterdam; for submission to Their High Mightinesses the States-General of the United Provinces, and all whom it may concern."

Roger tried his quill and wrote the superscription, then he took down the despatch as the Marquis dictated it. The document was short and to the point; a clear and unequivocal promise of armed support by France should this prove necessary for the establishment and maintenance of a new Dutch Republican Government in which for the future all sovereign powers of the United Provinces were to be vested.

When they had done the Comte de Montmorin signed the letter and produced a big seal from a satin-lined box that he had brought with him. Roger fetched wax from his office and the document was duly sealed with the impress of the Foreign Minister to His Most Christian Majesty Louis XVI of France.

It was now close on midnight. M. de Montmorin pleaded fatigue and, having congratulated the Marquis once more, took his departure, leaving M. de Rochambeau and Roger alone together.

For all his iron self-discipline the Marquis could hardly contain his excitement, while he waited for M. de Rayneval to return and collect the letter. Pacing up and down with his hands clasped behind his back he muttered to Roger:

"This is a great night, Breuc, a great night! You have been privileged to witness an historic occasion. For more than twelve months I have laboured tirelessly, and now, on the delivery of this despatch, I shall begin to reap my reward. This time next year you will see the real fruits of my work for France. 'Tis then that we shall witness the downfall of the avaricious, unscrupulous English. 'Tis then that their accursed island will at last be overwhelmed, and the *Fleur-de-Lys* of France fly unchallenged on every sea."

For a moment the veil of the Marquis's aloof passivity was lifted and Roger could see the hatred and ambition seething in his brain. With a flash of intuition he realised that the vain, empty Archbishop must fall like corn before the scythe of the reaper in front of this imperialistic juggernaut. It was not Loménie de Brienne who, if this conspiracy of conquest succeeded, would be the all-powerful Prime Minister of a Europe under the heel of France, or de Breteuil, or de Castries, or de Polignac; it would be the Marechal Duc de Rochambeau.

Suddenly there was a commotion outside in the office. Both Roger and the Marquis turned towards the door. It was flung violently open and Count Lucien staggered in.

312

As his glance fell on Roger he let out a yell of mingled surprise and rage.

"*Mort du diable!* To find you here was beyond my wildest hopes! But for this final audacity you'll pay with your neck!"

Swinging round on his father, he shouted: "Do'st know the snake that thou hast harboured here? He had wounded me and killed de Caylus this very night! Aye, and the cur has brought indelible shame upon our house. He has seduced Athénaïs!"

Roger overturned the small table behind which he stood and jumped for the door. But it was too late. Attracted by Count Lucien's shouts the two footmen had come running upstairs; with them, in the office, were Paintendre and the returning M. de Rayneval. The way was blocked and Roger was unarmed. He knew that he was trapped.

CHAPTER XXIII

THE THREE FUGITIVES

F o r a second all seven men remained absolutely motionless, as though posed in some dramatic *tableaux vivant;* three on the inner side of the open doorway and four on the outer. Suddenly they came to life.

"Seize him!" cried Count Lucien to the footmen. "Seize him, and call the Archers of the Guard!"

The footmen were just behind M. de Rayneval. As they pushed past him to obey, Roger acted. Thrusting Count Lucien aside with one hand he slammed the door to with the other, locked it and pulled the key out. Turning his back to the door, he faced father and son.

The young Count gave a shout: "Break down the door! Break down the door!" And those outside began to hammer upon it.

The Marquis's face was now chalk-white. "It cannot be true," he gasped. " 'Tis like a nightmare! I'll not believe it!"

Roger's shove had sent Count Lucien reeling against a gilded console table fixed to the wall. The blood was seeping through a bandage on his thigh, and with one foot slightly raised he clung to the table for support.

"You'll have ample proof soon enough, Monsieur," he cried. "My own blood is first testimony to what I say, and de Caylus's servants will have carried the story of the fight to a hundred ears by now."

"And whose fault is that?" Roger snapped. "Had you not snatched off my mask and given free rein to your imbecile tongue no one would ever have known who it was that challenged de Caylus to fight, or why."

"Mask! Challenge!" exclaimed the Marquis. "What means all this? For God's sake tell me plainly what has occurred."

"De Caylus and myself were returning from Versailles to his house in the Bois de Meudon," said Count Lucien hurriedly. "Our

313

coach was held up by this churl and some friends of his. They wounded one of the servants then attacked us, forcing us to fight."

"You cowardly assassin! Why not stick to the truth?" Roger cried, trembling with rage. "My friends accompanied me only to see fair play. Since de Caylus refused the civil challenge that I sent I was forced to taunt him to a fight; but when we did fight it was man to man; until you sneaked up on me from the rear and tried to run me through the back. Yet even then I bested both of you single-handed and, having marked you well, slew him in fair fight."

The Marquis stared at him with unbelieving eyes. "You killed de Caylus in single combat? I'll not believe it! He was one of the finest swordsmen in all France."

Roger shrugged. "Disbelieve it then, if you wish. Those who saw it will vouch for what I say."

To make themselves heard they now had to shout, as the people outside had fetched implements and were endeavouring to break down the door; but it was of heavy oak with a good stout lock and at present only quivered at the blows that rained upon it.

"What quarrel had you with de Caylus?" the Marquis asked suddenly, still seeking to grasp the rights of this terrible affair.

Lucien replied for Roger with his accustomed venom. "He killed the Count to prevent his wedding Athénaïs. Did I not tell you, Monsieur, that this viper has become her lover? Had I not unmasked him he would have achieved his end of remaining on here and keeping her for his mistress."

" 'Tis a lie!" roared Roger. "I'll not deny that I love Athénaïs, but I would have been happy to see her wed to any decent man."

The Marquis passed a hand across his eyes. "You!" he stammered. "You, my daughter's lover. *Mort Dieu!* The shame of it will kill me!"

The hammering upon the door forced Roger to raise his voice still higher, as he cried: "I said that I loved her, not that I was her lover; and there is a vast difference in the terms."

"Who would believe you?" sneered the Count. "Not I, for one."

"Thou art right!" moaned the Marquis. "*Marie, Mère de Jesu!* What have I done to deserve this? That my wretch of a daughter should give herself to the embraces of one little better than a serf!"

"Damn you!" snarled Roger, with a sudden flash of vindictiveness. " 'Tis good, for once, to see your arrogance humbled."

Lucien leaned forward. " 'Twas but another lie then, about your being of noble birth?"

The door was creaking now. Someone had found a crowbar and was trying to lever it from its sockets. Roger knew that there was no time to spare for arguments and flung back: "Believe what you like, I care not," and took a step towards the long line of windows.

But the Marquis clutched at this straw which might salve his injured pride. Side-stepping to bar Roger's path, he cried: "What is this story? Since you killed de Caylus you must be a remarkably fine swordsman. Have you the right to bear arms?"

Roger ignored the question and shouted: "Stand from my path, or 'twill be the worse for you."

Count Lucien's voice came, now from his rear. "He says he's the nephew of an Earl, and that his father is an Admiral of the English Fleet. The Abbé de Périgord swore to that on his behalf."

Suddenly the Marquis's whole attitude changed. From a distraught and humiliated parent he became again the imperialist statesman. His whole body tensed from the swift realisation that his precious plans were now in vital peril. His mighty scheme might yet be undone if, in ignorance, he had taken an enemy into his employ. Drawing himself up, he cried above the din: "I demand the truth! Have you deceived me as to your origin?"

"Yes," Roger shouted back. "I am an Englishman, and proud of it. Now get from my path, or I'll no longer let the fact that you are Athénaïs's father weigh with me."

De Rochambeau's reply was a sharp command: "Lucien! Have at at him! He must not leave the room alive!"

The door creaked and groaned; one hinge had given way and the corner above it gaped open. Rhythmic thuds upon the panels told that those who were trying to break it down were now using a heavy piece of furniture as a battering-ram.

At the Marquis's order the Count drew the frail Court sword that he had been wearing ever since leaving Versailles. As Roger heard it slither from its scabbard he swung round. Only two paces separated them. Before Lucien could poise himself for a lunge Roger clenched his fists and went sailing in. The slender sword hovered, still pointing towards the ceiling, as he struck out with his right. The blow took the young man fair and square beneath the chin.

His head shot backwards, his feet slid from under him; and, as he fell, the edge of the console table struck him sharply behind the ear. His body hit the highly-polished floor with a thud, then slithered along it. His sword flew from his hand and clattered away across the parquet. He rolled over once, groaned, and lay still.

As Roger's eye followed Lucien's fall, it suddenly lit upon the letter for the Dutch Republican leaders. It had been lying on his own small table, but had been wafted from it to the floor, when he knocked the table over on Count Lucien's sudden appearance. Previously it had not even occurred to him that he might get away with the vital document. Now, it flashed upon him that, if he could, it would provide incontestable proof of all he meant to say if he ever succeeded in reaching England.

Stooping, he snatched it up, and thrust it into his pocket. Then he turned again, and ran towards the windows.

But in the half-minute occupied by Roger's encounter with Lucien the Marquis had not been inactive. The second he had ordered his wounded son to the attack he had swung about and raced for the far end of the room. The dress sword that he had been wearing before the meeting lay there on a chair. Seizing the shagreen scabbard with one hand and its diamond-studded hilt with the other, he wrenched it out.

Roger had reached the long line of low windows and flung one of them open, but a glance over his shoulder told him that he dared not attempt to wriggle through it. Before he could possibly do so the Marquis would be upon him from the rear.

For the second time that night the horrible thought of a glittering steel blade searing through his back seized him. Turning again he left the window in a bound and sped across the room towards Lucien's limp body.

As he ran his eyes were on the door. The din of blows upon it now half deafened him. Stout as it was, he could see from its swaying that it could not hold much longer. And once the mob of servants broke into the room all chance of escaping by the window would be gone. They would pull him down as surely as a pack of deer hounds founder an exhausted stag at bay.

The impetus of his dash across the room caused him to come up with a crash against the console table. He grabbed at it, missed its edge, and fell. As he rolled over he saw the Marquis coming at him sword in hand. De Rochambeau's blue eyes were as hard and cold as the steel he held. There was not a trace of mercy in them, and he lunged downwards with all his force, intent to kill.

Roger jerked himself violently aside. The point of the sword stabbed through his coat within an inch of his ribs and buried itself quivering in the floor.

For a moment it was stalemate. Roger was pinned down by his clothes, but the Marquis could not free his blade from the wood that gripped its point; the one strove to wrench himself away, the other tugged with all his strength upon his sword. Simultaneously, Roger's coat ripped and the wood yielded up the steel.

The weapon came free with such suddenness that its release nearly sent the Marquis over backwards. As he staggered, and strove to regain his balance for a second thrust, Roger had time to roll over again. His hand shot out and clutched the hilt of Count Lucien's sword. Squirming under the big oval table, he came up on his knees, bumped his head violently, fell forward, recovered, and stumbled to his feet on its far side.

Silent, grim, merciless, the Marquis came round its edge at him. Roger stepped back a pace and threw himself on guard. The swords of both combatants were light, but none the less deadly. They met with a "ting," bent, slithered and circled, catching the rays from the steadily-burning candles.

Now that Roger was armed his hopes of getting away had risen. His victory over de Caylus had given him immense confidence in his sword-play. He did not believe that a man of fifty, who rarely took any exercise, could stand up to him for more than half-a-dozen passes; but he soon found that he had been counting his chickens before they were hatched.

De Rochambeau was no mean swordsman, and he fought with cool, calculated cunning. He made no attempt to disable his antagonist but simply sought to keep him in play while warily defending himself. After he had parried three rapid thrusts Roger divined his intent. He was taking no chances but playing for time, till the door should collapse and the shouting mob outside come streaming in to his assistance.

Roger knew then that he must finish matters or be captured. Suddenly closing in he ran his blade along that of the Marquis until the two swords were hilt to hilt, then he gave a violent twist of his wrist. The stroke was an extremely risky one, as, to make it, he had had to throw himself off balance, but he was gambling on the Marquis's wrist proving weaker than his own. For a second the decision lay in the lap of the gods, then de Rochambeau's wrist gave way. His hand doubled back and his weapon sailed across the room to strike with a clang against his ornate desk.

For an instant only, the Marquis's eyes showed indecision, then, risking a thrust, he stretched out clawing hands and rushed right in on Roger. Short of killing him there was only one thing to do. Throwing up his sword so that it slanted back across his shoulder, Roger drove the butt of its hilt into his aggressor's face. The gilded ball of the pommel struck the Marquis above the left eye.

With a loud cry, the first sound he had uttered since he had snatched up his sword, he sagged at the knees, and fell sprawling at Roger's feet.

Turning about Roger threw a swift look at the door. The lock and one hinge still held but both the upper panels had been stove in, and one of the footmen was striving to wriggle through one of the jagged holes. Full of apprehension now as to what reception he might meet with in the courtyard, Roger ran back to the window.

Normally at this hour the stable hands would have been asleep, but it was not much over a quarter of an hour since the nobles attending the conference had departed, so in the past few minutes someone might easily have mustered them.

Throwing a section of the window open, he peered out. With infinite relief he saw that it was not occupied, as he had feared it would be, by another group of M. de Rochambeau's people waiting to set upon him. Evidently it had not occurred to any of those upstairs that he might risk the drop into the courtyard.

It was dark down there and the place was full of shadows but there was no sign of life except near the gate, where a coach was standing. It sped through his mind that it must be the one which was to carry M. de Rayneval to The Hague.

Taking his sword between his teeth he threw one leg over the low sill. As he did so a figure moved out of the patch of shadow at the back of the coach, and called something up to him; but he did not catch the words as, at that moment, the door gave with a crash behind him.

Drawing his other leg over the sill he squirmed round and, gripping the woodwork with his hands, lowered himself, letting his feet dangle.

He was now looking into the room. The door had given way with the wretched footman still halfway through the smashed panel. His head and shoulders were buried beneath it while his legs kicked grotesquely in the air. But none of the others were attempting to help him. With M. de Rayneval at their head eight or ten members of the household were scrambling over the wrecked door and coming straight at Roger.

He sent up a fleeting prayer that the man by the coach would not be upon him before he could recover from his fall, took the sword from his mouth with his right hand, hung for a second suspended by his left, then let go of the sill.

With a frightful jolt he landed on his feet. He let his knees go slack in an effort to take up the shock, but overbalanced and fell backwards. For a moment the wind was knocked out of him and he lay there gasping. But the sound of running feet upon the cobbles made him force himself to turn over and struggle to his knees.

De Rayneval and the rest had reached the windows above him. They were now shouting to attract the attention of the stable hands, and anyone else who might yet prevent Roger's escape. As he heard their cries he knew that if he did not get away in the next few moments he would certainly be overwhelmed. His one hope now lay in overcoming the man who was running at him, then making a dash for the street.

Count Lucien's unexpected arrival had deprived him of the chance of collecting his savings, and now this outcry rendered it impossible for him to saddle a horse. Instead of riding away on a fast mount with a full purse and several hours' start of his pursuers, he must now take to his heels and seek to avoid an immediate hue and cry as best he could. And he was not yet even clear of the courtyard. Unless he could deal speedily with the man who was now almost on him, the driver of the coach would close the gates, and he would be trapped there.

These frantic thoughts all jostled through his brain as, still shaken by his fall, he came to his feet, and turned to face the figure that was running at him out of the darkness. Staggering back against the wall he threw himself on guard to gain a moment's breathing-space.

Suddenly, as his sight adjusted itself to the darkness, he saw that the man had a sword at his side but had not drawn it. Next second a familiar voice cried: "To the coach, man! To the coach! Don't linger there or they'll have you yet!"

Only then, with a gasp of mingled amazement and thankfulness, did Roger recognise his friend de la Tour d'Auvergne.

Giving a cry of relief he started forward. But before he had covered three paces he suddenly remembered his own sword, which he had left in a corner of the porch, close by. The fine old Toledo blade had been his companion through good fortune and ill from the very first day that he had landed in France, over four years before; and that night it had served him supremely well. For the sake of another few moments he could not bring himself to abandon it.

318

The light of torches now came from the stable end of the courtyard. Above him shouts and cries still rent the stillness of the night. Answering shouts came from the grooms and ostlers only a hundred paces away, as they streamed out into the yard. But Roger ignored both them and de la Tour d'Auvergne's frantic appeals to hurry. Swerving as he ran he dashed towards the porch, flung down Count Lucien's gilded rapier and snatched up his own plain but deadly blade.

As he leapt down the steps the crowd of stablemen were only fifty paces from him; but de la Tour d'Auvergne had now drawn his sword, and stood ready to come to his assistance. A moment later the two friends were running side by side for the coach.

"Bless you!" panted Roger, as they ran. " 'Twas a marvellous thought of yours to bring a coach, and stand by here lest I found myself in some extremity."

The Vicomte laughed. "I can take no credit for that, *mon ami*. I had thought you on your way to England. 'Twas but five minutes back that I heard your voice and that of M. de Rochambeau, raised in altercation, above there—and delayed my departure to learn the outcome."

As they reached the coach Roger saw that it was only a one-horse hired hackney; but they were still forty paces ahead of the yelling mob of stable hands, and the coachman was on the alert, ready to drive off the instant they were inside it.

Separating for a moment as they reached the back of the coach they sped along its sides. Each seized a door, wrenched it open and, simultaneously, flung themselves into its dark interior. The coachman's whip cracked, the horse jerked on the traces and the vehicle jolted forward.

Roger stumbled and fell to his knees. As his head went forward it hit a yielding but solid substance. Thrusting out a hand to steady himself it fell upon folds of rich heavy silk. There came a quick excited cry but, even before he heard it, Roger had recognised the fragrant scent that partially overcame the musty odour of the old hackney. There, in the pitch darkness, sat Athénaïs.

The Vicomte, knowing of her presence, had thrown himself into the place beside her. Levering himself up as the coach turned into the street, Roger dropped on to the seat opposite them. The lamp on the gate lit their faces for a moment and they were both smiling at him.

"What—what means this?" he exclaimed, almost overcome with excitement.

De la Tour d'Auvergne's rich voice came out of the darkness: "We are eloping. 'Twas a decision taken on the spur of the moment, but I vow we'll not regret it."

Athénaïs's clear treble followed close upon his words. "Nay, may I die if I do! To your inspiration, Monsieur, and your trust in me I'll owe my escape from the veil." She leaned forward and placed a hand on Roger's knee. "And to you, dear miller's youngest son, for the slaying of the dragon this night we both owe a debt that we shall ne'er be able to repay."

As the coach careered swiftly down the street, leaving M. de Rochambeau's people behind, Roger strove to readjust his thoughts. He did not doubt that Athénaïs still loved him, yet he knew that she had been right beyond all question to accept the Vicomte's proposal that they should elope.

" 'Twas a marvellous impulse," he said quickly. "Since for both of you it means all that offered a few months back, before any of us gave a thought to de Caylus. But what led you to conceive it?"

"We are your debtors there again," replied the Vicomte. " 'Twas born of the converse I had with you when we were returning from the fight. You told me that Athénaïs would be happy to have me as a husband, while concealing nothing of your own relations with her. After you had left me I realised for the first time how she felt and how I stood. 'Twas but a jump then to the thought of snatching her from her father's vengeance."

"You owe me nothing," Roger demurred. "The swift and audacious decision was entirely yours. It needed courage, too, seeing that you can have had no time to make any preparations and M. de Rochambeau may yet pursue you."

"Nay, I doubt that," Athénaïs chimed in. " 'Tis no small part of the genius of M. le Vicomte's stroke that it will muddy the waters of the affair. By carrying me off he protects me from the scandal to which I would otherwise have been subject on your account. Since he accompanied you to the encounter before eloping with me, 'twill now be said that you plotted the whole business together. People will believe that 'twas out of friendship for him that you killed de Caylus, and not from love of me. And my father is no fool. He'll not let his anger against me deprive him of this chance to save the family honour."

Roger felt that her reasoning was sound. For her father to catch her if he could, and drag her back to throw her into a convent, would be as good as an admission that any rumours de Caylus's servants might spread about the cause of the duel were true; whereas a runaway match with a noble of de la Tour d'Auvergne's quality would give the whole matter an acceptably romantic twist, and save her reputation.

"I think you're right," he said, after a moment, "but none the less, if M. le Vicomte is to be saddled with such full complicity in the slaying of de Caylus, 'tis more than ever important that you should use the utmost speed in reaching Brittany. Our good hackney coachman has served us well in carrying us clear of the Rue St. Honoré without trouble, but you must secure some far swifter vehicle with a minimum of delay."

" 'Tis all arranged," the Vicomte announced. "As soon as I reached my lodging I gave instructions to Jacques about our journey. We are now on our way to a rendezvous with him at the Red Mill, up on Montmartre. While I took this hackney to the Hôtel de Rochambeau he was to pack for me, then engage a post-chaise with a team of six and be waiting for us there."

"Why at Montmartre?" asked Roger. " 'Tis to the north of Paris and the road to Brittany lies to the west."

De la Tour d'Auvergne smiled in the darkness. "I promised our coachman a good reward to do as he was ordered without argument; but that will not stop his tongue wagging should he later be questioned by the police. If he thinks that we took the Amiens road it may fox them somewhat, for a few hours at least; and the detour to bring us round on to our true course is not considerable."

" 'Twas well planned," Roger agreed. "But tell me now, how you succeeded in carrying Athénaïs off with so little fuss? I'd have thought that Madame Marie-Angé would have brought the whole Hôtel about your ears."

Athénais laughed. "Poor Marie-Angé! We left her locked up in a toilette."

" 'Twas amazingly simple," the Vicomte added. "By the time I reached the Hôtel 'twas near half-past eleven; but I sent up a message that I had urgent news for Athénaïs and by good fortune she had not yet retired. She received me with Madame Velot and, just as you had urged me to, I related all that had passed without reserve."

" 'Tis cruel of me to laugh," Athénaïs took up the tale, "but 'twas vastly diverting, now that one can look back upon it. No sooner did Marie-Angé learn that for near a year past you and I had been carrying on a clandestine affair beneath her nose than she fainted dead away. Whether from shock to her sensibilities or from fear of what my father would say to her, I know not; but it gave M. le Vicomte the chance he was seeking to beg me to save myself and make him happy."

"And on Mademoiselle consenting to entrust herself to me, I carried her duenna to the closet and locked her in," de la Tour d'Auvergne went on. " 'Twas an anxious ten minutes while my newly-betrothed collected her jewels and a night-bag, but all went well. I feared, too, that on seeing her about to leave the house alone with me at night the servants would run to acquaint M. le Marquis with so unusual an occurrence, and that he would order them to detain us before we could reach the coach. But not a soul did we see; the hall was empty and we made our exit without anyone being aware of it."

" 'Twas my unconscious good fortune to have cleared the way for you," Roger smiled. "The servants had all congregated in my office, and were striving to break down the door between it and M. le Marquis's sanctum."

"But what in the world possessed you to return to the Hôtel. I thought you well upon the road to Le Havre or Calais."

Roger felt a horrid qualm about deceiving his friends; but they knew nothing of the intricacies of international affairs and he doubted if he could persuade them that his betrayal of M. de Rochambeau was justified by the chance it offered of preventing war. So he said a little hurriedly:

"I returned to collect my money and some other things. But, alas! I accomplished neither. Though, fortunately, I took the precaution of putting ten *louis* in my pocket against an emergency before I left for the Bois de Meudon. On my return I became involved in a conference that M. le Marquis was holding, and 'twould have provoked the most awkward questions had I attempted to leave before 'twas over. The affair was not concluded till midnight; then, just as I was hoping to get away, Count Lucien came on the scene. He told his father everything and 'twas that which precipitated the riot that you heard."

The coach had now dropped into a walking pace and, as it mounted the steep hill toward Montmartre, Roger related the outcome of Count Lucien's denunciation. He had hardly done when it breasted the rise and turned towards Clichy. A quarter of a mile further on it pulled up in an open space beneath the shadow of the big red windmill that dominated the height. A figure appeared at the window and threw the coach door open. It was Jacques, who announced that he had the post-chaise there in readiness.

They got out and while Roger escorted Athénaïs over to the chaise the Vicomte paid off the hackney coachman liberally. The two friends then moved aside out of earshot of the servants.

"How do you now intend to proceed?" asked de la Tour d'Auvergne.

"I shall make for Dieppe, since 'tis the nearest port to Paris," replied Roger.

" 'Tis a hundred miles and you will have to ride all night, unless you are to be passed by the couriers that will be despatched to close the ports against you. Count Lucien's wound not having proved serious enough to keep him at Meudon has deprived us of the long start we thought was ours. By now he and his father may be at the Ministry of Police, and if M. de Crosne proves readily available warrants will be issued for our arrest within an hour or so."

"I know it," Roger agreed glumly. "And I have yet to find a horse to carry me the first stage of my journey."

"Jacques has brought my two mounts as well as his own. The best of the pair I used to take me to Meudon and back so he is not fit for much else to-night, but you are welcome to the other."

"A thousand thanks. I'll not refuse your offer."

"Allowing for only brief halts to change horses on the road, 'tis a twelve-hour ride. Do you think that after what you have already been through to-night you can keep the saddle for so long?"

" 'Tis that which gives me most concern," Roger agreed. "Could I but rest for a few hours before making a start I'd do it easily enough; but that is impossible."

De la Tour d'Auvergne considered for a moment, then he said: "Why not come with us to Brittany? Once there you could hide for a while. My people would never betray you, and within a week or so I would find a trustworthy Captain to take you across to England."

Roger was tempted to accept, but the imperative necessity of reaching London by the 3rd, or at latest, the 4th of September, and the additional danger that he would bring upon his friends by remaining with them, made him feel that he ought to gamble everything on attempting to get through on his own, and at once.

" 'Tis mighty generous of you," he said. "But for all our sakes 'tis best that we should separate. The main hue and cry will be after me. If M. de Crosne's people pick up traces of me in my dash into Normandy 'tis unlikely that they will bother themselves so much about you. But if they learn that I am with you in the chaise they'll concentrate on that. Then, if they catch us, Athénaïs, as well as we two, would be hauled back to Paris."

"There's sense in that," the Vicomte nodded. "Yet I fear you may fall off your horse from fatigue on the last stage to Dieppe. Wait, though! I have it! I'll order the chaise to take us to Mantes. 'Tis midway between your route and ours. Thus we shall leave no tidings of our passing to our pursuers on either of the roads they would expect us to take. On reaching there we will separate; but 'tis a good thirty miles and while we cover them you can rest yourself in the chaise. 'Twould give you a far better chance of reaching Dieppe without collapsing."

Roger barely hesitated. If he did collapse and was forced to halt on the road it was certain that M. de Crosne's couriers would pass him while he slept. His chances of getting safely across the Channel would then be enormously reduced as, by the time he reached the port, every Captain would have been warned to be on the look-out for him.

"Yes," he said, " 'twould not only give me a few hours free from exertion, but also reduce the distance I have to ride to seventy-five miles. I will gladly come with you as far as Mantes."

As they turned towards the post-chaise Roger took a last look at Paris. Despite the lateness of the hour lights were still shining from many dormer windows and there was no sense of repose about that city of violent contrasts. Underneath the myriad roofs down there in the valley many hundreds of nobles and several thousand wealthy *bourgeois* would-be-nobles, clad in their rich silks and satins, with powdered hair, patches and quizzing-glasses, were gambling at innumerable tables or supping off the fat of the land with their latest mistresses; while five times their number of servants aped their ways yet hated and envied them; and fifty times their number of fellow human beings, overworked, underpaid, half-starved, were taking such rest as they could get in conditions of the utmost misery and squalor.

The moon emerging from behind a bank of scudding cloud silvered the uneven, close-packed ranks of gables and threw the open spaces up as blanks of deep shadow. Following the bend of the river Roger picked out the Ile de la Cité, the vast quadrangle made by the Palace and, beyond it, the empty blackness of the Tuileries' gardens. It was there, before the trees shed their leaves many times again, that *Madame la Guillotine* would be set up to do her deadly work, striking down the innocent as well as the guilty with blind impartiality.

Had Georgina been present her strange gift might have enabled her to see its sinister shadow; but Roger was simply wondering whether he would ever see Paris again as a free man, or be brought back there within the next few days, as a manacled prisoner, to meet an infamous death upon the scaffold.

323

"Come! 'Tis no time to dally," called de la Tour d'Auvergne; and, running over to the post-chaise, Roger scrambled in. Jacques was already mounted, and holding the bridles of the two led horses. As Roger slammed the door of the carriage the postilion cracked his whip and they were off.

For a little while, as they drove between the scattered farms and windmills on the heights of Clichy, they talked; but by the time they reached the village of Asnières they had fallen silent. All three of them were now feeling the reaction from the hours of strain and excitement through which they had passed, the post-road was broad and even, and the chaise a well-sprung one; its rhythmic rocking had a soporific effect on their over-wrought minds, and before they passed south of the bend in the Seine to the east of St. Germain they were asleep.

Two hours later they shook themselves awake and descended in the yard of the *Auberge du Grand Cerf* at Mantes. Such post-houses were well used to travellers with urgent business arriving at all hours, and the night ostlers had already run out to change the horses. The door of the inn was unbolted after a few moments by a sleepy serving man who had just pulled on his jacket. Lantern in hand, he invited them to enter and take a cup of wine while the chaise was being furnished with its relay.

De la Tour d'Auvergne pulled out his watch, glanced at it, and said: " 'Tis barely half-past three, so we have made good time, and I confess to being plaguey hungry. We can well afford twenty minutes for a scratch meal before we take the road again. What say you to it?"

Athénaïs smiled as she took the arm he offered. " 'Tis said that a wife's first duty is to see her husband lacks not for his creature comforts, so I pray you, Monsieur, order what you will and I'll encourage you by partaking of a few tid-bits."

"Whatever they can give us will be welcome," Roger supported her. "For I, too, am now remembering the fact that to-night I missed my supper."

The serving man led them into the inn parlour; then produced part of a cold ham, bread, butter, cheese and two bottles of Corton. Although the night was not cold they ate and drank standing round the smouldering ashes of the fire, conscious that they dared not linger, yet finding little to say to one another now that the time for Roger to leave the others had so nearly come.

After the Vicomte had swallowed a few mouthfuls of the food and a single glass of wine he said to Athénaïs: "I have some further arrangements to make for our journey, Mademoiselle, so I pray you excuse me. I shall be away for some ten minutes."

Roger realised then that the Vicomte had only pleaded hunger as an excuse to bring them into the inn, and that he had done so with the most generous intention of giving his companions an opportunity to say their farewells in private.

As the door closed behind de la Tour d'Auvergne the two lovers made an instinctive movement towards each other, but both checked it almost instantly, and Roger shook his head.

324

Athénaïs smiled sadly, having the same thought. " 'Tis true. My lips are no longer mine to give you; yet you will ever hold a great part of my heart."

"And you of mine, my most beautiful Princess," He replied. "I would, though, that I had the courage to beg you to forget me; for your betrothed surely deserves that you should make him happy."

"And I will make him so, never fear. Having gone contrary to the fashion by taking a lover before my marriage, 'tis my intent to continue in my eccentric course, and be faithful to my husband afterwards."

" 'Tis a wise decision," Roger agreed gravely. "If he were not so fine a man I would be sick with envy; but honesty compels me to admit that he is more worthy of you than myself."

"Say not so, dear miller's youngest son. No gentleman of France or England could have shown greater devotion to his lady, or more gallantry on her behalf, than you have done."

He smiled. "That is as it should be in an old romance; but when it comes to marriage more sterling qualities are of greater worth. He, too, fought on your behalf. I was more fortunate, that is all. He loves you as devotedly as I have ever done, and in addition has qualities that I lack. I often lie to gain my ends and that is a thing he would never do. I am an adventurer by instinct and, though I was sorely tempted in your case, I doubt if I shall ever marry; whereas he is the very pattern of upright manhood best suited to be the father of a woman's children and give her a constant love."

It had cost Roger a lot to say that, but he wanted to leave an impression with her that she had not, after all, lost so much by losing him; and thus cause her heart to incline the more speedily towards her husband.

He was all the more disconcerted when she suddenly cried in a tone of reproach: "Oh, *Rojé, Rojé!* You have no need to praise his qualities and decry your own. Have I not told you that I will be a good wife to him; and this marriage gives both him and me a better prospect of contentment than any our parents would have made for us. But 'tis not for their worthiness that women love men. If aught could make me love him 'tis his generosity in having left us here expressly that you might take me in your arms again. Yet you waste these precious minutes in talking like a fool!"

Her eyes were swimming with tears as she swayed towards him and, all his better resolutions gone, he caught her to his breast. For a few moments they clung together, then she took from her middle finger a great sapphire ring and put it on the little finger of his left hand.

"Take this," she said, smiling wanly. "You'll not need it to remember me by, but it may serve you in some emergency. 'Twas the ring de Caylus gave me on my betrothal to him, so in any case I would wear it no longer. And 'twould pleasure me to think that his gift had saved you in a time of trouble."

As he thanked her she went to the table and poured two glasses of wine. Giving him one she lifted the other, and said: "Should we meet again 'twill be only as friends, so I give a toast. To our memories and our future friendship."

"To our memories and our future friendship," he repeated, and they both drank down the wine.

Their empty glasses were still in their hands when de la Tour d'Auvergne re-entered the room.

She turned away to hide her tear-dimmed eyes, but he did not even glance at her, and said to Roger with a smile: "I have chosen and vetted the best fresh mount in the stables, and 'tis outside ready saddled for you. What we owe to one another no words can express so let us not attempt it. Instead we'll wish each other God-speed and a renewal of our friendship. May it not be too long before we meet again. Let's drink a glass of wine to that."

"You put my own thoughts better than I could have put them myself," Roger smiled back; and filling the glasses he drank again with de la Tour d'Auvergne. Then all three of them went out into the night.

As they reached the yard the Vicomte murmured: "Your best road is to Gisors, and thence to Gournay."

"And yours?" asked Roger. "I would like to know as I shall be thinking of you."

"We shall make for Evreux and should reach the town by six o'clock. 'Tis there I hope to find a priest to marry us."

"My prayers for your happiness go with you."

"And mine with you for your good fortune."

Athénaïs was already seated in the chaise. As the Vicomte settled himself beside her she extended a slender hand to Roger. Bowing over it he kissed her fingertips. Then he took one last look at the beautiful face that four years before, when still that of a child, had thrown an instant enchantment over him. He had seen it proud, angry, sullen, disfigured, and finally, as the adoring face of a most lovely woman. The magnificent blue eyes were still dim with tears but they smiled bravely, and serenely now, upon him. He released her hand and closed the door.

Before the chaise was out of the yard he had mounted the horse that the ostler was holding for him. A moment later his love and his friend were being whirled along the road to the north-west as fast as six fresh horses could carry them; while he had turned his mount on to the road to the north-east and was settling down to ride for his life—and to reach England with the letter that might prevent a war.

CHAPTER XXIV

ONE THOUSAND *LOUIS* REWARD

I T was just on four in the morning when Roger galloped out of the courtyard of the *Grand Cerf* at Mantes; at a quarter to six he drew rein in that of the *De Blanmont* at Gisors. In the stable he changed his horse for a chestnut gelding and, within five minutes, was on his way again.

Now that the morning light had come the peasants were wending their way out into the fields, but he took no notice of them or of the countryside through which he passed. His every thought was concentrated on choosing the best ground for his mount, and seeing that each time he adjusted its pace it should not jolt and tire him needlessly.

By seven o'clock he reached Gournay, changed his chestnut for a bay mare at the *Auberge du Nord*, and took the road to Neufchatel. This stage was longer than the last and the vigour of the good wine he had drunk in Mantes had now passed out of him. Moreover, shortly after eight o'clock it began to rain, which soon made the going heavier; so he did not reach Neufchatel until a quarter past nine.

He had now covered over fifty miles and still had twenty-five to go; the fourth and last stage of his journey being considerably the longest; so, on dismounting in the yard of the *Lion d'Or*, he decided to give himself a rest before undertaking it.

Going into the inn he ordered coffee, laced it well with cognac and, lying back in an elbow chair with his long legs stretched out before him, drank it slowly. At a quarter to ten he went out into the rain, mounted a mettlesome strawberry roan that had been saddled for him and took the road to Dieppe.

A wind had now got up and was blowing the rain against his face in gusty squalls. Before he covered half the distance he was feeling both tired and dejected. His knees and thigh muscles were aching acutely from their hours of constant pressure on his mounts, in two places he was saddle-sore and the slippery reins were hurting where he gripped them with the gloved fingers of his left hand. Despite these physical afflictions he had no doubts about his ability to reach Dieppe, but he was now extremely perturbed by the state of the weather. The fine spell had clearly broken and with every mile he covered towards the sea conditions worsened, so he was desperately afraid that all sailings might be cancelled on that account.

At a quarter past twelve he urged the flagging, foam-flecked roan past the turnpike at the entrance to Dieppe and asked the way down to the harbour. He was aching in every limb and soaked to the skin, but he had done the journey from Paris well under twelve hours and he felt confident that no ordinary courier would do it under eighteen; so, with the hour or two's start he must have had over any agent that M. de Crosne might have despatched to Dieppe, he felt that he still had a clear field for the best part of eight hours, and would get clean away if only a boat were leaving before nightfall.

But on reaching the pier from which the packets left for Newhaven, his worst fears were realised. He was told that the boat that would normally have left at six that evening would not be sailing, owing to the storm in the Channel.

He knew that the first inquiries for him would be made at the official posting-house; so instead of going there he went to a small inn on the *Quai Henri IV*, called *Le Bon Matelot* and stabled his horse. Then, tired, wet and sore as he was, he went out and spent two hours dragging himself round the harbour district from one drinking-booth to another, frantically endeavouring to find a Captain who would put out for England in the storm.

Normally, the money he had on him would have been ample to induce some poor fisherman to undertake the trip, but none of them would do so in such weather. It occurred to him then that this was just the sort of emergency that Athénaïs had had in mind when she had given him de Caylus's ring; so he showed it to several of the fishing-masters and offered it in exchange for an immediate passage to England.

It was a beautiful sapphire, surrounded with small diamonds and he thought that it must be worth at least a hundred *louis;* but all of them shook their heads. One after another they pointed out that neither gold nor jewels were of use to any man if he was lying rotting at the bottom of the sea, and that as the waves were riding too high for the packet it would be suicide to attempt the crossing in one of their much smaller craft.

A little before three, Roger realised that further efforts were useless. Neither prayers nor bribes would induce any master to leave Dieppe harbour that night. In the dram-shops that he had visited he had had several cognacs to whip up his failing energies but now he felt utterly done, and knew that when he did sleep it would be for many hours.

By morning it was as good as certain that the authorities would be hunting him. De Crosne's agent would have picked up the fact overnight that the fugitive had left the *Lion d'Or* at Neufchatel on a roan horse, and the steed not having been handed in at the Dieppe posting-stage would be searched for throughout the public stables of the town. It would be found at *Le Bon Matelot*, so for him to spend the night there obviously involved a considerable risk. In consequence, he went to another small inn, near the *Eglise St. Jacques*, called the *Chapon Fin*, and took a room there.

Going straight upstairs he emptied his pockets, pulled off his soaking clothes, and gave them to the chambermaid to be dried at the kitchen fire, then flopped naked into bed. He was utterly exhausted and, despite his anxieties, was overcome almost instantly by a deep and dreamless sleep.

He slept for sixteen hours, waking a little before eight the following morning. He was terribly stiff, but his head was clear and he felt ravenously hungry. Giving scarcely a thought to any of these things, he jumped out of bed and ran to the window. In a second he saw that the rain was sheeting down and being driven in violent gusts against the panes. With a curse, he turned away; but, none the less, seeing that the maid had brought back his dried clothes while he slept he began to hurry into them.

On getting downstairs he at once questioned the landlord about the prospects of the packet sailing that day, but the man said that the weather had worsened during the night and it was certain that no ships would be leaving port while the gale continued. Roger could only attempt to console himself by ordering two boiled eggs and a fillet steak to be served in the coffee-room with his *petit déjeuner*.

The astounded landlord gave him a nasty jar by declaring that he "must be an Englishman in disguise." For a second he thought that he had aroused the man's suspicions in connection with a description of himself which might have been circulated to innkeepers during the night; then he remembered that he was, after a lapse of years, once more on a coast where the habits of the English were well known, and realised that the man was only joking.

Yet, all the same, while Roger was eating his eggs and steak he knew he must face the fact that M. de Crosne's courier would have reached Dieppe the preceding night, and the odds were that the police would be combing the town for him that morning. As he had arrived at the *Chapon Fin* hatless, coatless and without baggage of any kind, it seemed certain that suspicion would swiftly fall on him in the event of any inquiry being made there. So after breakfast he paid his bill and left the inn.

In spite of the rain and the blustering wind he went along to the harbour to make quite certain that no ships were leaving. He found it practically deserted and an old salt who was splicing a rope under a lean-to told him that, even if the wind dropped, which he thought unlikely, the seas would be running too high for any vessel to venture out into them for another twenty-four hours at least.

Cursing the weather that, by its foulness, was placing his life in jeopardy, Roger set about endeavouring to alter his appearance. After buying a large canvas grip he visited a secondhand clothes' shop, where he bought a tattered cloak and a seaman's stocking-cap. Putting these on outside, to conceal the clothes in which he had left Paris and hide his hair, he visited another secondhand shop in a better part of the town and bought there a more expensive outfit. It included sea-boots, blue trousers and reefer coat, a topcoat with a triple collar and a low, square-crowned bowler hat with a shiny leather band, of a type often worn by the officers of merchant ships.

Having crammed his purchases into the bag he carried it to the far side of the channel leading from the harbour to the sea, where he had noticed that morning a number of sheds and half-built boats on stocks. No one was working there in the teeming rain so he entered one of the wooden sheds and, without fear of interruption, changed into his new clothes. Next, he plaited his back hair and, doubling the thin end under, tied it with a piece of ribbon in a nautical queue. Then he made a bundle of his Paris clothes, weighted it with stones and, carrying it to the water's edge, threw it in.

It was only with the greatest reluctance that he parted with his elegant, soft-leather riding-boots and the expensive lace at his wrists and throat, but he knew that it would have been madness to keep them, as they were just the sort of things that would have given him away.

329

Returning to the town side of the harbour it struck him that, since he must remain in Dieppe for at least one more night, he would be seen by fewer people if he took lodgings rather than a room at another inn; so he set about hunting for something suitable. Happening to notice a street sign reading *"Rue d'Ecosse"* he thought that a good omen and turned along it. Sure enough a hundred yards from its entrance he came upon a neat little house with a card bearing the carefully-drawn words *Apartement à Louer* in its ground-floor window.

The door was opened to him by an immensely fat woman who, puffing and wheezing, took him upstairs to a sparsely furnished but clean-looking bedroom and sitting-room. For appearance sake he haggled a little over the price and made her include his *petit déjeuner* in it; then he took the rooms, paid her a deposit and went out again, to get himself a midday meal.

After eating reasonably well in an unpretentious restaurant he bought a bottle of wine and some cold food for his supper, and a few toilet articles; then he returned to the house in the *Rue d'Ecosse* and, since he had nothing else to do and would at least not be seen there, went to bed.

For the first time since leaving the *Rue St. Honoré* to fight his duel with de Caylus he had leisure to think over the tornado of events in which he had been caught up. The duel seemed to him to have taken place at least a week ago, yet, curiously enough, he was under a vague impression that it was only that morning that Athénaïs, if all had gone well, had married de la Tour d'Auvergne in Evreux. But after a minute's thought he realised that while the duel had taken place less than forty-four hours ago, Athénaïs had most probably been Madame la Vicomtesse for thirty hours or more. It was actually Wednesday the 30th of August, the day that she was to have married de Caylus, and while the long hours of Monday night had been crammed with happenings that stood out in Roger's mind Tuesday had passed him by almost unnoticed, owing to his exhausted state in the morning and his having slept through the whole of the latter part of the day.

As he thought again of the fateful conference, he got out the letter signed by the Comte de Montmorin and re-read it. When he had done so it struck him more forcibly than ever how extraordinarily fortunate he was to have secured such a document. Despite his periodical communications to the mysterious Mr. Gilbert Maxwell, the British Government might well hesitate to accept his bare word as conclusive evidence on a matter of such extreme significance. In view of the Commercial Treaty with France and their greatly improved relations with that country, it seemed certain that his revelations would come as an appalling shock to them; and doubt that he could possibly be right would almost certainly prevent them from taking any positive action until his statements could be verified. Yet in some immediate *démarche*, such as an ultimatum, lay their only hope of preventing the French from seizing the Dutch ports.

He realised now that, had he arrived in London as he had originally planned, he would have had little hope of saving the situation; whereas if he could do so with the letter, so damning were its contents and the signature of the Foreign Minister whoever saw it could not possibly require any further evidence of France's intentions, and there would be a real hope of averting war.

Rolling the precious parchment up into a thick tubular spill he tied a piece of string round it and then made a loop of the string to go round his neck, so that it should hang there like a locket and there would be no risk of it being lost by being inadvertently jerked out of one of his pockets. Then he took off the sapphire ring as being too valuable a gem for an ordinary ship's officer to wear, and tied that also to the string about his neck.

About seven o'clock he had his cold meal and drank the bottle of rich white Château Coutet, from the estate of the Marquis de Lur Saluces, that he had bought to wash it down. Then at half-past eight he blew out his candle and soon fell asleep.

He woke as the first pale streaks of dawn filtered through the flimsy curtains and, scrambling out of bed, went to the window. It was still raining, but gently, and the wind had dropped. His impulse was to dress at once but, knowing that no boats would put out until the sea had gone down, he restrained his impulse and went back to bed.

At seven o'clock a slatternly maid brought his *petit déjeuner*. After eating it he got up, dressed, and went down to the port. There was still little activity there and the packet-boat, lying alongside her jetty, showed no signs of preparing to put to sea. Near the landward end of the jetty there was a large notice-board and, thinking that a notice might have been put up there giving some information about sailings, he walked over to it.

A thick-set, middle-aged man with heavy eyebrows, was already standing in front of the board, reading a large placard occupying nearly half its area, which, from its cleanness, could only recently have been pasted up. As Roger came up beside the man and his eyes fastened on the notice, his stomach seemed to turn over. It read:

ONE THOUSAND LOUIS REWARD

Attention! A felon of exceptional ferocity and baseness is urgently sought by the Government. Five hundred Louis d'Or will be paid by M. le Comte de Crosne, His Majesty's Lieutenant of Police, or by any accredited agents of the Crown, for information leading to the securing of the person, dead or alive, of one

ROGER BROOK

The above is an Englishman, giving himself out to be the son of a British Admiral, and a nephew of the Earl of Kildonan. Yet he speaks French with the fluency of one born in this country and has passed for several years

as a native of the province of Alsace, under the name of
BREUC.

The man wanted is tall and slim. He is about twenty-
one years of age, having a fine figure, pleasant, expressive
countenance and good complexion. His hair, worn long,
is dark brown, his eyes a striking deep blue with dark
lashes. His nose is straight, his chin firm and he has good
teeth.

He dresses with elegance and has the manners of a
person of quality. When last seen he was wearing a plum-
coloured satin coat, flowered waistcoat, red twill riding
breeches, brown Hessian boots, and lace ruffles and jabot.

A further reward of five hundred Louis d'Or will be
paid to anyone returning a stolen document that the
above-described felon is believed to be carrying on his
person. The said document is a letter signed by M. le
Comte de Montmorin, His Majesty's Foreign Minister.

The aforesaid ROGER BROOK alias BREUC, is
required to answer to charges of murder, theft and treason.
Attention!

ONE THOUSAND LOUIS REWARD

The reward offered was an extraordinarily high one, showing how
concerned Roger's enemies were to effect his capture, and he had
to admit that the de Rochambeaux had been generous enough in their
description of him; but for all that the portrait was damnably accurate
and he was conscious of a rising wave of fright at the thought that
everyone he met could hardly fail to recognise him from it.

On remembering that he had at least had the sense to change his
clothes he gave vent to a sigh of relief; but, next second, he was seized
with consternation. The thick-set man beside him had turned and was
staring at his face.

Suddenly the man spoke: "You fit that description strangely well,
Monsieur. I've rarely seen such deep blue eyes as yours."

With an effort Roger forced a smile. "Nay. I'm an honest seafarer,
and my purse has never run to satin coats or lace folderols."

"You might have shed those overnight," said the man, meditatively.
"You're the right height, too, and have just shown me two sets of
good even teeth."

Roger could not divine if the fellow really suspected him or regarded
his likeness to the description as pure coincidence; until, with a sudden
narrowing of his close-set eyes, the man went on:

"What would you be doing down here at the jetty in this weather,
eh? *Sang de Dieu!* I believe you're this English murderer, trying to
get away to your own damned island!"

332

With his heart in his boots Roger gave a swift glance round. They were hidden from the greater part of the quay by the wooden offices of the Packet Boat Company. At the moment there was no one in sight, but the man looked tough and brawny. He might put up an ugly fight and raise the alarm before he could be knocked out; and Roger knew how swiftly a mob could suddenly congregate at the least excitement in an apparently empty street. He decided that he must keep his head and try to bluff it out.

"Listen to me, *mon ami*," he said, with sudden sternness. "You have this matter wrong. If you wish I will accompany you to the office of police and prove to them before you that I am one Julien Quatrevaux of Rennes, a Breton by birth and second officer of the India trader, *Tobago Queen*, now lying in Le Havre. But to do so it will be necessary to send for papers to my lodgings, which are at the far end of the town, and my whole morning will be lost. I have a seat booked in the diligence to carry me back to Le Havre. If I miss it I'll not be there by nightfall and my ship may sail without me. That would put me to considerable loss as well as great inconvenience. Should I be so subjected on account of your wild fancies I will not only sue you for detaining me without warrant and for the loss I shall sustain, but seek you out later with a seaman's cudgel and beat you to within an inch of your life. Now! Do you wish to gamble your absurd imaginings against these penalties, or not?"

The man hesitated. One thousand *louis* was an enormous reward; to a poor man it was a fortune. But the account given by his *vis-à-vis* of himself seemed solidly circumstantial and, if true, threatened to land him in endless trouble. After a moment he shrugged, and said:

"Monsieur, I meant no offence. But you must admit that you are like enough to the description of this felon to raise anyone's suspicions."

"That may be!" replied Roger tersely, "but I am not he. Good day to you," and, turning on his heel he walked firmly, but unhurriedly, away.

His bluff had worked; nevertheless the encounter had shaken him badly. It was all he could do to control his pace and prevent himself looking back to see if the man had run off in search of an *agent de ville*. Turning into the first side street he came to, the instant he was out of sight round the corner, he took to his heels.

When he eased his pace half a mile farther on, and dropped into a walk, he was white and breathless. He knew now that whether the packet sailed or not from Dieppe that evening it would be fatal for him even to go near her jetty again; as the man might be lying in wait for him there with a police agent. Moreover, although the storm had passed, he dared not seek out the fishing-masters and ask one of them to take him across. Too many of them had seen him on the Tuesday in the clothes in which he had come from Paris and, on seeing him again, would undoubtedly connect him with the description of the wanted felon, which must now be the talk of the harbourside. By now, too, the roan horse must have been found, proving that he had chosen Dieppe for his attempt to reach England; so every moment he remained there he would be in imminent peril of recognition and capture. Clearly he must get away from the town at the earliest possible moment.

During his flight he had lost himself, but glimpsing the sea through a narrow alley he turned along it and, having reached the esplanade, soon found his way back to his lodgings. On his way there he made up his mind to move along the coast, in the hope of finding a vessel in a smaller harbour, where there were no trails of his presence to make the place so piping hot for him. Having collected his bag he settled with the fat landlady and, leaving the town by its south-western exit, took the road to Fécamp.

As soon as he was out of sight from the last houses of Dieppe he climbed over some sand dunes until he found a convenient hollow and set about redisguising himself as well as he could. His alarming experience with the thick-set man had convinced him that he still looked too like a gentleman and that he would do better to give himself a more villainous appearance. Taking off his topcoat and the square-crowned bowler he buried them in the sand, and put on again the old cloak and the stocking-cap; but, before adjusting the latter he tied a folded silk handkerchief round his forehead and pulled it down over one of his tell-tale blue eyes as though it was a bandage.

Proceeding on his way again he endeavoured to think up further measures by which he might trick M. de Crosne's bloodhounds. The fact that he had been advertised as an Englishman speaking French like a native, suddenly struck him. Clearly they would be inquiring for a man who appeared to be a Frenchman, and certainly not one who admitted to being English. Therefore, he might fox them by a double bluff if he gave out that he was English and spoke only a little very bad French.

After another mile or so he had supplemented this idea by deciding to infer that he was an English smuggler who had got left behind on a recent trip. The fact that he had decided against parting with his sword, and the bandage that he now wore over one eye, already lent him the air of a seafaring desperado. The smugglers brought good money to the coastal villages and so were regarded as friends by the fisher-folk; and, wanting to get home, would provide him with an excellent reason for seeking a passage across the Channel.

Having spent so many hours in bed during the past two days and nights he was fully recovered from the fatigue of his long ride and, the sun having come out, he tramped along in better spirits than he had been for some time. Soon after midday he stopped for a meal at a wayside inn and, having rested for an hour, pushed on. By five o'clock in the afternoon he had walked eighteen miles and entered the little port of St. Valéry-en-Caux.

To his intense annoyance he saw that the harbour was almost empty and standing out to sea a cluster of about fifteen vessels. It could only be the fishing-fleet, and must have sailed about an hour before.

As he approached the quay he saw that a couple of longshoremen were in the process of loading fresh vegetables on to a two-masted barque. To reach it he had to pass the customs office and, on the notice board outside it, he caught sight of another of those damnable placards offering one thousand *louis* for his capture, dead or alive.

The sight of it almost unnerved him and caused him to turn tail; but he realised that by this time there would be one of them posted up on every quayside from Dunkirk to Brest and that if he was to get away at all he must, sooner or later, chance recognition in endeavouring to secure a passage. He knew that by far his safest course would have been to go into hiding for a few weeks; but that was impossible, unless he were prepared to give up his attempt to prevent the seizure of the Dutch ports, and that, nothing would have induced him to do.

Bracing himself for the encounter he slouched up to the bigger of the two longshoremen, and asked in mangled French and English when the barque was bound.

"She'll sail on the night tide, round four of the morning," the man replied. "That is, if the weather holds; but it's none too promising and the fishing-fleet has put out for a few hours only because it's been weather-bound these past two days. The barque is carrying a mixed cargo to Falmouth."

Roger pretended not to fully understand and while the man repeated the information for him more slowly he was thinking; 'Falmouth is a devilish long way from London and I have already been three days on my journey. The crossing will take the best part of two days, and from Cornwall to London thirty hours at least. Allowing for unforeseen delays 'tis unlikely that I'll get to Whitehall before the morning of the 5th of September. That will leave the Cabinet a margin of only four clear days in which to act. Still, better that than no chance at all, and I suppose I'll be lucky if I can induce the Captain to take me.'

Having thanked the man he inquired the Captain's name and, on being told that it was Rapenot, he walked with a rolling gait up the gang-plank.

Captain Rapenot was in his cabin. He proved to be a tall, grizzled fellow with gold rings in his ears and a hook in place of a left arm. He looked up from his bills of lading and greeted Roger with a none-too-friendly stare.

To maintain his rôle of seaman, Roger opened the conversation by asking if he could do with an extra hand.

The captain shook his grizzled head. "No. I've a full crew for this trip; and you're an Englishman, aren't you?"

On Roger admitting it, he went on gruffly: "I've no love for the English. 'Twas a round shot from an English frigate that took off my left arm, so I never take on an English hand unless I'm forced to. Get you gone!"

Seeing his chance slipping Roger broke into a swift, garbled version of his story. Then he urged that the war had been over for nearly five years and that malice for ills inflicted in it should not be allowed to rankle for so long; and finally, producing his purse, offered to pay for his passage.

"How much have you there?" asked Captain Rapenot, in a slightly mollified tone.

"Seven *louis* and a few odd *francs*," replied Roger in the atrocious French that he was using. "I can ill afford to part with my savings, but I'll give you five *louis*."

"Nay; but I'll take you for the seven."

"Then I'd land near penniless," Roger protested. "Make it six?"

"Seven, and not a *sou* less," insisted the Captain.

"If I agree will you give me a cabin to myself, and treat me as a passenger?"

"Yes. I'll do that. I'm not shipping a third mate, so you can have his cabin, and feed at my table. You must pay me the money now, though. I'll not risk your skipping ship when we reach port."

So the harsh bargain was struck. With great reluctance Roger counted out the coins on the table, knowing that if anything prevented the barque from sailing it was highly unlikely that he would be able to induce the avaricious Captain to give them back; and that he would then find himself in the most desperate straits that any man can be— a fugitive without resources.

Having swept up the money and thrust it into his pocket Rapenot took him along a narrow passage under the low poop, kicked open a door exposing a cubby hole three-quarters of which was occupied by a bunk, and left him.

Roger's relief at having secured a passage was only equalled by his anxiety to see the barque leave port. Each hour up to nightfall seemed as long as a day, and those that followed scarcely less so. He had nothing with which to occupy himself and while, on the one hand, he feared to show his face to more people than was positively necessary, on the other he felt that as long as daylight lasted to shut himself up in his miserable little cabin might arouse suspicion.

From hanging about the extremities of the ship in a seemingly endless ordeal of waiting he had only one respite. At six o'clock he was summoned aft to sup with the Captain and the two mates. The first officer was a taciturn Norman and the second a short, black-bearded Marseillaise. Both of them obviously went in dread of the hook-armed Rapenot, so the meal was not a convivial one.

At midnight Roger thought of turning in; but he knew that he would not be able to sleep until the ship was well on her way, so he remained up and spent the remaining hours pacing the deck. As he did so he was in constant anxiety about the weather, knowing that if it showed signs of deteriorating Rapenot would not sail. It seemed to him that the wind was freshening a little but, to his overwhelming relief, shortly before four o'clock the bosun piped all hands to their stations.

St. Valery was only a little harbour, so ships of even the barque's moderate size were infrequent visitors to it, and it took nearly an hour of careful manœuvring before she was clear of the bar; but by five o'clock her sails were set and she was feeling the swell of the sea. At last Roger was able to go to his narrow cabin and, worn out with anxiety, flung himself down fully dressed on the bunk to sleep.

He slept till nearly midday and, when he woke, his first conscious thought was that they were in for a bad crossing. The ship was rolling with a nasty twist and rain was spattering on the porthole. Getting up he lurched along to the filthy wash-place, freshened himself up as well as he could, then made his way to the main cabin, which also served as the officers' dining-room.

The Captain and the second mate were just sitting down to their midday meal, and both appeared to be in an evil temper. It transpired that the barque would not have sailed the previous night had she not already been overdue at Falmouth, and now Rapenot was regretting his decision. Roger remained silent and pretended not to understand most of what was said. He was thanking all his gods that some perishable cargo had forced Rapenot to sail against his better judgment and felt that he, personally, would not mind if the ship made the voyage on her beam ends, provided only that she landed him in England. But he was destined to feel very differently about it before many hours were gone.

During the early part of the afternoon he could think of little else than the miracle of his preservation through the past few days, and his ruminations on his escape from death at the hands of de Caylus, being seized by the de Rochambeaux, or captured by M. de Crosne's agents, did much to stifle his awareness of the increased heaving of the deck. But as the day wore on sail after sail was lowered, until with bare masts and the wind howling through the naked rigging the barque was driving before the storm.

As the wave-crests grew higher the horizon became ever more limited, so that by dusk the ship seemed to be the centre of a tiny world apart and utterly isolated in a cauldron of foaming, boiling waters.

Roger had imagined himself to be a good sailor, but now he knew that he was not. As he clung to a stanchion for support he was desperately sick. Miserable, and furious at his lack of control over himself, he crawled to his cabin; but worse was to follow for, although he had unloaded his midday meal, he found that he continued to strain and vomit in bouts of soul-shattering nausea.

The next twenty-four hours proved a worse nightmare than anything he could conceivably have conjured up in his wildest imagination, and he was not even left alone in his agony. At some time in the early hours of the following morning Captain Rapenot kicked open the door of his cabin and called on him to lend a hand manning the pumps as the forward hatch cover had been torn off by the gale and every wave that now hit the ship was slopping over into the hold.

It was not from any lack of willingness to help, but from exhaustion, that Roger remained deaf to the Captain's shouts and continued to lay inert. But his condition did not save him. Asking him what kind of a sailor he pretended to be, Rapenot came at him with a curse and, lifting a length of rope with a spliced Turk's-head at the end of it, he struck him half a dozen savage blows about the legs and body.

With a moan, Roger struggled to his feet and strove to ward off further punishment; but in his present state he was no match for the brutal Captain, who, still beating him about the back and shoulders, drove him forward along the slanting deck.

While he laboured with his last strength at the pumps the water swirled terrifyingly round his knees, and his anguish was such that he genuinely wished that the ship would founder, so that he might escape his torment in death. How long he stuck it he never knew, but he must have collapsed and been carried back to his cabin for, when he was next conscious of his surroundings, he found himself sprawled on his bunk again.

All day the storm continued and twice, during it, Rapenot mercilessly drove him out to do further spells at the pumps. But before he started on his third spell one of the crew gave him a mug of black coffee laced with brandy, which he managed to keep down, and after that he felt better.

The storm had eased and as he churned the iron handles of the creaking pump with three stalwart *matelots* his sense of humour came back to him. It crossed his mind how incongruous it was that the elegant M. le Chevalier de Breuc, whose name must by now be the talk of Versailles as the conqueror in single combat of the redoubtable Comte de Caylus, should find himself being kicked around like a galley-slave. He also had another thought. It was, how incredibly right he had been in refusing to go to sea; since, if it could be like this at the beginning of September, it must hold the torments of the seventh hell for those who had to face it during the icy months of winter.

That night he was called on no further and slept right through till eleven o'clock next morning. When he awoke, to his surprise, he felt none too bad and soon discovered that he was hungry. On going out on deck he saw that the sea had gone down and that the barque was now riding on an oily swell under half sail. One glance across the slippery green waters showed him, too, that they were in sight of land. His heart leapt with the knowledge that it must be England.

Eight bells sounded soon afterwards, so he went in to the main cabin. The black-bearded Marseillais was there, and while they waited for Rapenot to appear, so that the service of the meal could begin, he gave Roger the situation. The sou'-wester had driven them many miles off their course and they were now beating west along the coast of Sussex.

Roger had again temporarily lost count of time but a swift check up told him that to-day was Sunday the 3rd. To his consternation he realised that it would be six full days that night since he had left Paris, yet, owing to the storm he was no nearer to reaching London than he had been when at St. Valery, and it would now be the seventh before he could get his precious paper to Whitehall. Even if the Cabinet acted instantly it seemed highly improbable that they would be able to get instructions to the British Minister at The Hague in time for him to make a bid to stop the revolt planned for the tenth.

Rapenot came in and, while they were eating, made some sarcastic references to Roger's poor showing as a seaman, but he took refuge in his avowed scant knowledge of French and pretended not to understand. And he was much too perturbed about the delay, which now threatened to wreck the object of his journey, to care.

When he went out on deck again all sail was set and, owing to the configuration of the coast, the barque was now considerably nearer to it than she had been in the morning. By two o'clock she was off the eastern end of the Isle of Wight and Roger was picking out familiar beauty spots with a futile longing for wings with which to reach them. Yet it was not until they were passing St. Catherine's Point, at the southern extremity of the island, that he was suddenly seized with a brilliant idea. Why should he not get Captain Rapenot to turn into the bay to the west of the island, lower a boat, and put him ashore.

The instant the idea came to him he realised that the advantages it offered were immense. From Lymington he could, at a push, ride to London overnight, and give the Cabinet a clear six days in which to make their intentions known with regard to the United Provinces. More, if he landed at Falmouth, it would be with only a few *francs* in his pocket. He knew no one there and might suffer the most infuriating delays and difficulties in raising the money or credit necessary before he could even set out for London. Whereas Lymington was his home. His mother was certain to have a few guineas in the house that she could lend him. He could borrow a horse from the stables and be off within the hour. To land there would make all the difference between success and failure.

Then his mind flashed to Rapenot. The grizzled, hook-armed Captain was a surly devil and about as disobliging as any man could be. There seemed only one way to get round him, which was to buy his complaisance, and Roger's pockets were near empty. Suddenly he thought again of de Caylus's ring. That ought to do the trick.

Undoing his coat he pulled out the end of the string that hung round his neck, undid it, took off the ring and slipped it into his pocket; then he retied the string and thrust back the precious document that was still attached to it. Walking over to the deck-house, in which the Captain was talking to his Marseillais second mate, he thrust in his head and said: "Captain, a word with you, if you please."

Rapenot got up from the wooden bench on which he was sitting and came to the door. "Well?" he said, "what would you?"

Roger politely touched his stocking-cap, then jerked a thumb over his shoulder. "My home is no great distance from here, not far from Southampton, and 'twould be a great boon if you could put me ashore somewhere in the neighbourhood of the Needles."

The Captain's lip curled. "Why should I go out of my way for such as you? This unseasonable weather has already lost me five days on my trip to Falmouth, and a part of my cargo is rotting in the hold. I've not time to give to landing passengers."

"Oh, come!" expostulated Roger, pointing to a small, broad-beamed yacht that was lapping briskly through the water off their starboard beam. "You have but to slacken sail a little and hail yonder yacht. Those in it will come alongside and take me off without a doubt."

"I'll slacken sail for no one," declared Rapenot gruffly, "I bargained to take you to Falmouth and I'll take you there; but I'll be damned if I'll lose a breath of this wind to pleasure anyone."

Roger produced the sapphire ring. "'Tis worth a lot to me to reach my home speedily. I'm mighty loath to part with this, but I'll give it you if you'll do as I wish."

Rapenot's eyes narrowed at the sight of the valuable jewel. "If that is a genuine stone 'tis worth the profits on a dozen voyages," he said slowly.

"'Tis genuine!" declared Roger. "I'll take my oath on that."

The Marseillais had come up behind his Captain. With a suspicious glance at Roger, he remarked: "The Englishman must have some desperately urgent business ashore to offer such a gem."

"The Englishman!" exclaimed Rapenot, a sudden light dawning in his eyes. "*Mort de ma vie!* He is the felon mentioned in the proclamation that we read!"

"*Ventre du diable!* You are right!" cried the Marseillais. "I recognise him from the description now."

"Seize him," Rapenot bellowed, starting forward. "If we throw him in the hold and take him back to France we'll reap the thousand *louis* reward!"

For a second Roger was dumbfounded by this unexpected and horrifying outcome of his plan. During all the agonising discomforts of the past two days he had thought himself safe at least from meeting his end on a French scaffold. Yet now he was menaced once again by the ignominious doom of a felon. If they got him they would bind and gag him and he might lie for days in Falmouth harbour, a prisoner in some stinking hole, without a hope of escape. The thought of being taken when so near his goal and actually within sight of England was unendurable. As they came at him he thrust the ring into his pocket, leapt back, and drew his sword.

Both the Frenchmen had drawn their knives. Rapenot threw a glance over his shoulder and called to the helmsman. "Antoine! Leave the wheel! Summon the bos'n! Tell him to get the muskets!"

Roger knew then that he had not a moment to lose. Without waiting to be attacked he sailed in with a lightning lunge at Rapenot.

To his joy the blade pierced the Captain through the shoulder, causing him to drop his knife with a screech of pain.

But the wily Marseillais, crouching low, ran in under Roger's sword and thrust upwards with his knife.

Only the roll of the ship saved Roger from taking the stab in the stomach. The dip of the swell caused him to take a pace backward as he wrenched free his sword. Then, with a swift recovery, he turned to face his second antagonist.

Shouts and calls now came from the body of the vessel. Few of the crew who had been standing there knew what the fracas was about, but, on seeing their officers attacked, they came swarming towards the ladders that led up to the poop.

His eyes gleaming Roger lunged again. The point of his sword caught the Marseillais beneath the chin, and, with a howl, the man staggered back, clasping at his bleeding neck.

Having temporarily freed himself from his two attackers Roger turned and jumped for the ship's side. The nearest member of the crew had only just tumbled on to the break of the poop, but Rapenot had picked up his knife and was coming at him again.

Throwing one leg over the low bulwark Roger suddenly swung round, leaned inboard and delivered another thrust. Rapenot threw up his hook, but too late; the flashing blade, forced upwards by his own gesture of defence, ripped his face from the chin to the corner of his eye.

Roger jerked back his sword, seized its sheath with his left hand, fumbled for a moment, then rammed it home. As he did so the foremost sailor came at him brandishing a heavy belaying-pin, but·when he lashed out it whistled through empty air. Ducking the blow Roger heaved himself over the side and fell with a splash into the water.

He went down, down, down; steadied, came up and, as his head emerged, gave a gasp. He knew that he was far from being out of danger. As he had swung himself overboard several of the crew, led by the bos'n, had been running across the deck with muskets and pistols in their hands; and he was over a mile from the shore.

His only hope lay in the little yacht that had been bobbing along a quarter of a mile off their beam. He had glimpsed it just before he hit the water. Their attention caught by the shouts and fighting on the poop of the barque the yacht's crew had put her over on a leeward tack, in order to get closer and see what was happening.

Striking out towards her Roger raised himself in the water and gave a shout: *"A moi! A moi!"*

Then he suddenly remembered that he was swimming in his own home waters, and yelled: "Help! Help! I am an Englishman! Help! Rescue!"

A musket banged in his rear, then another. One of the balls sent up a spurt of water within a foot of his head; but the people in the yacht had heard him, and were now urging him on with cries of encouragement.

A wave slapped into his face and momentarily blinded him. For no accountable reason a mental picture of Georgina passed before his physically sightless eyes. He saw her as he had seen her over four years before, on that unforgettable afternoon, telling his fortune by gazing into a glass of water. She was saying: "You are in great danger. You are swimming with a valuable document held between your teeth."

Instantly he recalled the vital letter. If it got soaked through the ink would run and it might become illegible. Turning on his back he fumbled with the buttons at his neck, undid them and pulled out the little roll of parchment. As two more of the men in the barque fired at him he gripped it with his teeth, rolled over, and struck out for the yacht again.

341

She was almost on him now and he recognised the man who was standing at the tiller in her stern. It was old General Cleveland of Vickers Hill. The veteran had gone purple in the face with rage. He was shaking his fist at the sailors in the barque and roaring at them.

"Damn you for a lot of besotted Frogs! How dare you take up arms in British waters! I'm a Magistrate! I'll have the law on you! I'll have the Navy out, and have you flogged, keel-hauled and shot for this. So help me God, you bloody pirates, I'll teach you to fire on an Englishman!"

The old man's bellowing came as the most divine music to Roger's ears. A moment later a young man whom he did not know, hauled him in over the yacht's bow. Flopping on to the bottom boards he lay there panting.

The General, still quivering with indignation, continued to roar curses and threats at the men in the barque. He appeared entirely oblivious of the fact that he was unarmed and a fine target for their bullets, or that it was improbable that they understood one word of what he was yelling at them. His attitude was enough. As the barque sailed on and the yacht dropped astern they leaned over the side, their weapons in their hands, gazing stupidly at him; but they did not fire again.

Still gasping, Roger got to his feet and scrambled aft. With a wide grin he panted: "You were just in time, Sir; and I'm mightily grateful to you. The rough side of the tongue of a British General was the very thing those rogues needed."

The General stared at him in surprise. "So you know me, eh? Who the hell are you?" Then the light of recognition dawned in his eyes. "Why! God bless my soul if it's not Christopher Brook's boy! Well, I'll be damned!"

The crew of the yacht proved to be the General's two nephews and, as the old man turned his craft back towards the Solent, Roger gave them the most abbreviated version of his story that he could think of; which was little more than that he had been chased out of France on account of a duel that he had fought and that the Captain of the barque had attempted to prevent his landing at Lymington.

At a quarter to six he was thanking his rescuers once more, and a moment later, he stepped ashore on to British soil, glowing with the knowledge that he had now pulled off his great coup, and could reach London in ample time for the Cabinet to take action.

Half walking, half running, he hurried up the short hill and along the avenue of limes towards his home. The postern gate in the high west wall was ajar. As he slipped inside he saw his mother only thirty feet away cutting dahlias in her flower border. Slamming the door too behind him he ran forward shouting: "Mother! Mother, darling!"

Lady Marie turned, gave one look at the tall, wet, bedraggled, looking stranger, dropped her basket, and cried: "My bairn! My bairn!"

Next moment she was weeping for joy in her big son's arms.

Five minutes later Roger was stripping off his sopping outer garments in the kitchen of the house, while the cook, Polly, and another maid, whom he did not know, all fussed round preparing a hot posset, that his mother insisted he must drink at once to ward off a chill.

When he asked if she had any of his old things still that he could slip on, she laughed up at him: "My darling, thou hast forgotten the passing of the years. So fine a man could ne'er get into the things of the dear, headstrong boy I lost so long ago. Go to thy father's room, rub thyself down well and borrow one of his dressing-gowns; then join me in my drawing-room, for I can scarce bear to wait to hear thy news."

Having done as she bid him, the moment he entered the drawing-room, he said: "I see my father's things about upstairs, so take it he is in residence. How are his feelings now towards me?"

Her smile gave place to an anxious look. "I fear, m'dear, that they remain unchanged. After you left us he forbade me ever to mention your name to him again. He is over at Pylewell now, dining with Mr. Robbins, and will not be back till half-past eight or nine. Yet now that you are returned I beg that you will face him, Roger, and strive to heal the breach. It breaks my heart that my two dear ones should remain divided by this old quarrel."

"I will," he promised. "But not to-night; for I must be on my way to London within the hour."

"So soon!" she cried.

He nodded. "Yes, dearest. I'll need to borrow a suit of my father's clothes and a horse from the stables, also such money as you can lend me; for my need is desperately urgent. But I promise you I will come back as soon as my business is completed and do my best to make my peace, for your sake even more than for my own."

"This business, Roger," she hazarded. "Can you tell me of it? Up to last month your letters have kept me informed of your doings. But 'tis mighty surprising that you should return like this, in a poor seaman's clothes and involved in some desperate matter."

He told her then about his duel and that just before he had been compelled to fly from Paris he had secured certain information which he believed would prove of great value to the Government.

She smiled when he had done. " 'Twas just like my brave lad to save that poor maid from so loathsome a marriage. And I cannot think that your returning penniless will adversely affect the prospects of your healing the breach with your father. In fact, it may soften him more than if you had come back to us a rich man, bringing us splendid presents."

"Apart from the immediate future I'll have no need to beg of him or you," Roger assured her. "My four years in France have at least taught me how to support myself. And from the experience I've gained, I doubt not that I'll soon secure a good position with some man of affairs. But, much as I would love to, I must not linger now. While I go up and dress I pray you, dearest, have prepared for me some sort of meal."

Half an hour later, booted and spurred for the road, he was tucking into good honest English fare while his mother fussed about him.

When he had done she gave him fifteen guineas and said: "I've not been able to have a mount saddled for you, as Jim Button is attending his cousin's wedding over at Beaulieu. But there is the brown mare you used to ride in the stable, and a fine chestnut that your father bought recently. Best take the mare, though, for I think the chestnut needs shoeing."

Having thanked her he kissed her fondly and hurried from the house. It was getting on for eight o'clock, and dark now; but he knew from of old where the stable lantern hung, and that on the shelf below it he would find flint and tinder.

Inside the stable it was pitch-black, but his fumbling fingers soon found what they sought and, striking a light, he lit the lantern.

As he took it from its hook he heard a sudden movement in his rear. Swinging half round he glimpsed a tall figure coming at him. For a second the flickering candle in the lantern threw up a monstrous shadow on the wall and ceiling. Its upper part outlined cloaked shoulders, a hard, conical, flat-crowned hat, and a hand holding a bludgeon.

The blow caught Roger on the side of the head. He reeled, dropped the lantern and fell. As the light went out the figure hurled itself on top of him. Hands grabbed his throat and, lifting his head bashed the back of it again and again against the stones. With each crack his efforts to defend himself grew weaker. His consciousness slipped from him and his body went limp.

When he came to, a few minutes later, his hands and feet were tied with stout cord and a handkerchief, its ends tied behind his head, gagged his widely stretched mouth. His attacker was kneeling above him softly cursing in French as he thrust his hands into one after the other of his victim's pockets.

Finding nothing he undid the top of Roger's waistcoat and, with a cry of triumph, pulled out the little roll of parchment. As he severed the string he muttered to himself: "Praises be that my instinct was right. By to-morrow morning I'll have earned me more than two year's income from this."

Roger was still only half conscious and incapable of movement. As the man left him he strove to collect his wits, but only one coherent thought flickered in his bemused mind. In some utterly inexplicable manner he had been beaten at the post, and that with the loss of the document his best hopes of saving his country had been shattered.

CHAPTER XXV

THE MYSTERIOUS FRENCHMAN

R o g e r ' s head felt as though it was splitting. Both its back, and the side on which he had received the first blow, hurt intolerably. He heard the clopping of a horse's hoofs as his attacker led one of the animals out of the stable and a faint light filtered in through the doorway. Then the door was closed, the darkness became pitch again; there came the faint clink of the horse's shoes on the cobbles of the yard and, after a moment, silence.

Making an effort he jerked at his bonds; but each time he did so a spasm of pain shot through his head; so that he was forced to give up and lie quite still for a while, until the throbbing of his temples gradually eased. At length the stabs became less insistent and gave way to a dull ache.

Wriggling up into a sitting position he tried again to free first his hands, then his feet; but both seemed to have been tied by an expert. The thin, tough cord bit into his wrists and ankles and all his efforts failed to loosen its painful grip.

Forced to give up he relaxed and fell to wondering who it could conceivably have been that had attacked him. The expert knotting of the cords that bound him made him suspect one of the sailors from the barque. He could not imagine how any of them had managed to get ashore and trace him to his home, yet that seemed the only possible explanation.

One thing was plain; for the best part of two hours that evening, since his landing at Lymington, he had held a trump card for preventing disaster to his country firmly in his hand. He could have taken it straight to the Mayor, or one of the local justices, for safe keeping and had a sworn copy made; and now he had lost it. Yet he could not feel himself to blame, since, having once stepped ashore, he had had not the remotest reason to suppose there was any risk of having the document taken from him.

Its loss was all the more infuriating in that he had, after all, made good time in reaching England. The journey from Paris had taken him just under six days. It was still only the 3rd of September, and the Dutch Republicans were not due to rise until the 10th, so had he been able to get the letter to Whitehall by the following morning the Government would have had ample time to act. Whereas now, without the letter to verify his statement, it was a hundred to one that they would lose their opportunity while seeking confirmation from other sources of his seemingly incredible story.

He wondered how long he had been lying there, and thought that it must be at least an hour, although it seemed much longer. Then he heard the ring of iron horseshoes on the cobbles again. The stable door was pushed open, the starlight filtered in, and he saw two shadowy forms come through the opening.

At first they did not see him and, since he was tightly gagged, he could not cry out. One of them groped for the lantern and swore at not finding it in its accustomed place. After a moment the flint was struck and a dim glow from the tinder revealed the lantern lying smashed upon the floor.

The figure swore again, picked it up and lit the candle. As he did so the light flickered on Roger's bound feet.

"Hell's bells!" exclaimed his father's voice. "Jim! There's a man here and he's trussed like a fowl. What in thunder's been going on here in our absence! 'Tis as well we met at the gate. Hitch the horses' bridles to the door latch, and take this lantern while I cut the fellow free."

As the Admiral got out his pocket knife Jim Button raised the lantern so that it shone on Roger's face.

"Swelp me, Bob!" he cried suddenly. "I believe he be Master Roger!"

"Shiver my timbers!" bellowed the Admiral, "so it is!"

With swift, sure strokes he severed the cords that bound Roger, then undid the knot of the handkerchief that gagged him. Roger lurched to his feet but his mouth was so sore that he could not speak for a moment. His father caught his arm and said:

"Steady, boy! Take it easy! Yours is the strangest home-coming that ever was. But, by God, your dear mother will be mightily pleased to see you. Let's to the house."

It was true enough that, however either of them might have envisaged a reunion, neither had ever dreamed that it would occur in such extraordinary circumstances, and one which made it so natural that the Admiral should accept his errant son's return without loss of dignity.

Roger ran his tongue round his sore mouth and muttered: "I've already seen her, Sir. I was about to saddle a horse and set out for London when I was attacked, an hour or so ago."

"What!" boomed the Admiral. "Dost mean to say that having returned after all these years you meant to shear off again without seeing me?"

"I'd intended to return as soon as possible," said Roger warmly, giving his father's arm a quick squeeze. "But I landed from France only at six o'clock, and must get with all speed to London on Mr. Gilbert Maxwell's business."

His father gave him a sharp glance. "Ah! That's different; and 'tis good to hear that you put nothing before your duty, lad. But come to the house and tell me how it is I came to find you in such dire straits."

Jim Button suddenly broke in. "The last time I seed 'e, Master Roger, was the day the Admiral come home from the wars. 'Tis good to see 'e ag'in, an' here's hopin' 'e'll be with us for as long a spell as he."

"Thanks, Jim," Roger took the groom's hand and shook it. "I'll be back by mid-week, I trust; and we'll have some great rides together. When you've watered the horses and rugged them up, would you saddle my mare and bring her round to the front, so that I can get off without delay?"

"That I will, Master Roger," came the cheerful response, and, with linked arms, father and son left the stable yard.

Lady Marie's distress at Roger's unexpected return in such a battered state was almost instantly overcome by her joy at seeing her two loved ones arm-in-arm like two long-lost brothers. Having quickly examined Roger's head, she pronounced his injuries only superficial, but hurried off to fetch warm water, lint and bandages.

The Admiral was in a high good humour. He had dined well at Pylewell and his face was ruddy with port and good cheer. As the door closed behind his wife, he said, jokingly, to Roger: "Well, boy; hast fortune favoured thee on thy travels? Are thy pockets bursting with good golden *louis?*"

Roger laughed. " 'Twould ill become me to complain against the dame; since for a year past I've enjoyed an income of two hundred and forty *louis* with all found, horses to ride and servants to wait on me, in the house of a powerful noble. But, through a twist of the wheel, I had to leave all that behind me and I return to you like the proverbial bad penny, a veritable pauper. So I'll be dependent on your generosity for a month or two, till I can secure new employment."

"Think not a thing of that," smiled the Admiral, with a wave of his hand. "You did monstrous well to achieve such a position unaided. But you have no call to seek another. I'm a rich man now, my lad, and can well afford to support an only son. I can give you an income of three hundred and not miss the money."

"Have you come into a fortune, then?" exclaimed Roger in amazement.

"Nay," the Admiral grinned. " 'Tis prize money, accruing from the sale of all the ships that I captured during the long years of war. Their Lordships were plaguey slow in paying it out; but what with Frenchmen, Spaniards, Dutchmen, and the rest, I've netted thousands; as have most other British Captains. You'll not have noticed in the dark, maybe, but I'm building two more rooms on to the house; a fine, lofty dining-room, and an equally spacious bedroom above it for yourself."

"For me!" Roger gasped. "That will be the meaning of the scaffolding I saw, then, as I entered the house with my mother. But how could you know that I'd return, Sir?"

"I knew you'd come back sooner or later," averred the Admiral. "I'll not deny that your refusing to enter the Navy was a bitter blow to me. But since you had the spirit to go your own way, 'twas as good as certain that you'd not haul down your flag, and one day come sailing into port like a good mariner. I'd not encourage your mother to hope on that, but I've been waiting to splice the mainbrace with you this many a long day."

Like King Charles II before him Roger could only marvel that he had been fool enough to remain away from home so long.

"But tell me," went on his father. "What led to your abandoning your good position in such haste, and this dastardly attack upon you to-night?"

Roger had only just started to recount his Odyssey when his mother returned with the dressings. Having bathed the wounds she made a poultice of Grains of Paradise and bound it round his head. While she was doing so he continued with his story and brought it up to date.

When he had done, the Admiral frowned, and said: "But who can this villain be, that attacked you? How could any of your enemies have known that they would find you here, and so lie in wait for you in the stable?"

" 'Tis a problem that utterly defeats me," Roger declared. "At first, from the efficacy of the knots that tied me, I inclined to think it one of the seamen from the barque. Yet I cannot now see how it could be. 'Twas certainly not Captain Rapenot, for he had a hook to his left arm and the man who pounced on me grasped my throat with two hands. Besides, I wounded both Rapenot and his second mate too seriously for either of them to venture such an undertaking."

"They might have sent the first mate or a member of their crew ashore," hazarded the Admiral.

Roger shook his head. "I don't believe it possible, Sir. The barque sailed straight on to the west. While General Cleveland was bringing me ashore I watched her for more than an hour, and she neither lowered a boat nor showed any signs of dropping anchor."

"She might have put into Christchurch."

"Nay. If she had, there'd not have been time enough for one of them to get back here by half-past seven. Moreover, although they guessed who I was, I had told them only that my home lay near Southampton. How could a foreign seaman have found out so swiftly where I lived. 'Twas not one of the men from the barque, I'm now convinced of that."

"Think you it might have been a vagrant, or perhaps an Egyptian from the forest come in to rob our hen-roost and, seeing you, thought he might snatch a purse as well?"

" 'Twas no vagrant, Sir. This fellow knew what he was after. I can hear his cry of triumph now as he came upon the letter, and he muttered to himself in French about collecting the reward."

"Then it must have been someone from France who caught the packet on Thursday afternoon, and sailed some twelve hours ahead of you."

"You're right, Sir," Roger agreed. " 'Tis the only explanation. Yet I am still foxed completely, for how could anyone in France have thought it probable that I might make for Lymington?"

"The de Rochambeaux might have done so, and told M. de Crosne's people."

"Athénaïs alone knew the situation of my home, and she would never have betrayed me. Her father and brother did not even know that I was an Englishman until a few hours before I left Paris."

"You told them your name, though; and that you were my son."

"True; and, knowing that, an agent, having got to London, might have obtained your address through the Admiralty. But that is no explanation in this case. In view of the storm no boat leaving a French port on Thursday afternoon could have entered a British harbour until the weather eased this morning. She would have been bashed to pieces on the piers in the attempt. My attacker cannot possibly have stepped ashore in England earlier than an hour after dawn to-day, and 'tis humanly impossible for him to have reached London, found out where we lived and got here by seven o'clock this evening."

The Admiral nodded. "Well reasoned, lad! Wherever he landed such a proceeding could not mean less than a hundred and fifty mile ride. Dick Turpin himself could not have done it in the time."

" 'Tis an impenetrable mystery," Roger sighed, "and I fear we'll never learn the solution to it; though I'd give de Caylus's sapphire to know the fellow's identity, and for a chance to get even with him."

Suddenly the Admiral slapped his thigh. "Damme! What in thunder are we thinking of, to be swopping theories like a couple of schoolmarms, when we should be about hunting the villain down."

"That will be no easy task, seeing how poor is the description I can give of him."

" 'Twill be no easy task for him to get back to France, either; once I am gone into action. We know he's a Frenchie, and tall, you say? What else can you recall about him?"

"He had the thin hands of a well-bred man, though they were muscular. I think that he was clean-shaven; but of that I cannot be certain, since I glimpsed his face only as a pale blur. From his shadow I should say that he was wearing a coat or cloak with a heavy cape-collar, and his hat was in the modern style, a hard felt, flat-topped and conical-sided."

While Roger was giving his description his father had snatched up a piece of paper and was swiftly making notes. When he had done, he said: " 'Tis well! I'll go up to the Mayor and have his constables circulate this description locally. The King of France is not the only man whose purse is long enough to offer five hundred guineas' reward for a capture, and by morning all South Hampshire will be hunting for this dog. Meanwhile, 'tis no time to stand on ceremony. C.-in-C., Portsmouth, will bear me no grudge if I poach his territory in a case like this, and my signature as Rear-Admiral, Channel Squadron, will be honoured from Dover to Land's End. 'Tis my intention to close the ports."

"Well done, Sir!" Roger exclaimed, his despair giving place to hope. He had never before seen his big, rubicund father at work in a crisis, and realised now how well fitted he was to hold a high command.

"Give me now the words you heard him mutter," the Admiral went on. "Maybe we'll get something from them."

Roger endeavoured to recall the expressions used, but he could not, and replied: "He said something to this effect: Thank God my instinct proved right. By to-morrow morning this will have earned me as much as I make in two years."

"To-morrow!" his father repeated. "Surely you could not have heard aright? He could not reach a port and make the crossing in the time. Perhaps, though, he had a boat awaiting him in some smuggler's cove along the coast. If so, we're sunk."

"That may be it, Sir; but, even if he had, he'd not be able to reach France before to-morrow night, and I'll take my oath that he said to-morrow morning."

"The fellow is a positive will-o'-the-wisp!" cried the Admiral in exasperation. "One thing is clear; he knew this to be your home and came here on a sudden inspiration; thinking that if you landed anywhere between Poole and Southampton you would come here first before proceeding to London, and hoping for a chance to waylay you. The odds are that he is one of M. de Crosne's agents. But as for his returning to France to reap the reward by to-morrow morning, no man born of woman could do it."

Lady Marie had been sitting listening to her men. For the first time since she had finished bandaging Roger's head, she spoke. "Think you there is anywhere in this country where he could collect the money?"

Roger jumped to his feet. "Mother, I believe you have it! The notice said that M. de Crosne *or any accredited agent of the French Crown* would pay out the reward. The French Ambassador is such a one. Could it possibly be that our man is on his way to London?"

"Nonsense!" laughed his father. " 'Tis too far-fetched. Having done his business, a French police-agent's first thought would be to get back to France."

"Not necessarily! If he is a cunning one, as this fellow seems to be. He would know that you, as a British Admiral, would have special facilities for swiftly closing the ports against him. 'Twould be a clever move to ride unmolested through the night to London while we remained here organising parties to scour the coast. In any event, 'tis time now that I was off. I'd meant to take the journey easily, but I shall ride hard now, since there is just a chance that I may pick up his trail and overhaul him."

"Oh, Roger!" exclaimed Lady Marie, "Are you recovered enough to face such an ordeal. 'Tis over ninety miles."

He smiled at her. "I pray you be not concerned on that score. Your Grains of Paradise have already done wonders for my head; and now that I am once again on our own good soil I'd ride to Scotland, had I a mind to it."

"So be it then," the Admiral agreed. "But 'tis my belief that you misunderstood what the fellow said, and will be on a wild goose chase. For my part I shall cast a wider net by taking the measures I have outlined. But I wish you fortune, and if you catch your man the five hundred guineas I intend to offer shall be yours."

"Thanks, Sir!" cried Roger. "If my instinct proves as good as my enemy's I'll hope to claim it. Though, even if I'm right, I'll have but an outside chance of catching him. He has well over two hours' start, and the only way I can hope to make that up is with your assistance."

"How so?"

"In aiding me to obtain all possible facilities on my journey. I pray you write me a note giving me priority at all posting-houses for remounts and the like; and add a line enabling me to call for assistance in attempting his capture."

The Admiral moved quickly over to Lady Marie's secretaire, took quill and paper, and wrote:

To all whom it may concern.

The bearer of this is Mr. Roger Brook, and he rides upon His Majesty's business. Every possible aid that he may require is to be rendered to him. In the event of his calling for assistance to secure the person of a French agent for detention and examination such assistance is to be afforded him without question.

Christopher Brook,
Rear-Admiral, Channel Squadron.

Roger thrust the paper into his pocket, kissed his mother fondly and, followed by his father, hurried from the room.

Outside the front door Jim Button was walking the mare up and down. As they came out, he cried:

"The chestnut be gone from the stable, Sir. That varmint must have took 'e."

"God rot his guts!" bellowed the Admiral; and Roger remembered then that, as he struggled back to consciousness, he had heard his attacker lead a horse out into the yard.

"He be no good picker," Jim went on. "The chestnut be overdue for shoeing. He'll not get five miles afore a shoe comes loose; or my name's not Jim Button."

"A thousand thanks for such good tidings, Jim," cried Roger, as he mounted. Then, with a shout of good-bye to his father, he turned the mare and cantered through the already open gates on his way to London.

Trotting up the lane he turned left at the church and out of the town towards Boldre. The hamlet was only two miles away and he reached it in under ten minutes. Pulling up outside the smithy, without dismounting, he hammered with his crop upon the door. It was now close on ten o'clock and the smith was in bed asleep. Roused by Roger's shouts he opened an upper window and thrust out a head crowned by a white, tasselled nightcap. But Roger's swift inquiry drew a blank; no traveller had halted there to have a chestnut shod within the past two hours.

Ten minutes later he galloped into Brockenhurst and knocked up the smithy there; but with the same result.

Between Brockenhurst and Lyndhurst he made splendid going through the lovely stretch of forest, but he was now wondering if his father had not been right, and that he had set out on a wild goose chase. If Jim was correct about the chestnut the horse should have cast a shoe before this. Roger had to confess to himself that his guess had been a long shot. In the cold light of reason it was much more probable that his unknown enemy would endeavour to slip back to France. In that case there was still a chance that the Admiral's net might close upon him at one of the ports. On the other hand, so astute a rogue might well have prepared his retreat beforehand, and already be well out to sea in some smuggler's lugger that had been waiting to carry him home. Again, having secured the letter, there was no urgent reason why he should hurry back. He might consider discretion the better part of valour, and decide to go into hiding for a time, then make the crossing when the hue and cry had died down. It would be easy for a Frenchman to lie low for weeks in the foreign quarter of a great seaport like Southampton without the least risk of discovery.

Yet Roger was absolutely positive that he had heard aright, and that, somehow, his attacker planned to collect the reward next morning. If that were so there was only one place that he could do it, and that was at the French Embassy in London.

At twenty minutes to eleven Roger cantered into Lyndhurst. With a catch of the breath he saw that there was still a light behind the curtains of the blacksmith's upstairs window. It might have been any belated traveller who had kept him up, but the augury seemed good, and so it proved.

Roger had no sooner attracted the smith's attention and put his question, than the man replied:

"Yes, Master. I re-shod the off-fore of a chestnut and looked to his other shoes for a foreign gentleman not an hour back."

"Can you describe him?" cried Roger.

"He were a tall chap, wearing a long riding-coat and a flat-crowned steeple hat."

"But his face?"

"Ah, I'd not swear to that. He kept hisself well in the shadow. But he were clean shaven, and somewhat pasty looking. Seeing he were a furriner it crossed me mind that he'd maybe landed only a few hours back, and bin down with the sea-sickness in yesterday's storm."

"His age?"

"On the youngish side. Maybe thirty, but not more."

"Did he say where he was going?"

"Nay. His English were poor. He spoke little and not a word of that."

"How long since he left here?"

"Three-quarters of an hour."

"Thanks," shouted Roger, and wheeling his mare, he sped out of the town along the road to Totton.

It was his man without a doubt. Moreover, his prospects of overtaking him were far better than he had ever dared to hope. It could not have taken over two hours for his enemy to reach Lyndhurst and have his horse reshod; he must have halted on the way, either at Lymington or Brockenhurst, to take a meal at one of the inns before setting out for London. That argued his complete confidence that he would elude any hue and cry that might be raised after him by making for the capital instead of one of the ports. He could not have known, either, that Roger's father would return so soon and release him, and probably thought that his victim would remain trussed in the stable until someone found him in the morning. All the odds were now that, without the least suspicion that he was being pursued, the Frenchman was riding on at quite a moderate pace. And he was only three quarters of an hour ahead. His heart high with elation, Roger spurred on his mare, and rode all out along the springy turf that bordered the road across the more open part of the forest, east of Lyndhurst.

He reached Totton a quarter of an hour before midnight and flung himself off his steaming mount in the yard of the posting-house. The night ostler told him that the traveller for whom he inquired had changed horses there half an hour earlier. His description of the Frenchman was as vague as that of the smith. He could only remember that he had been tall and sickly looking. But Roger felt it pointless to waste time in pressing for details. He had enough to go on and felt certain now that his enemy was one of M. de Crosne's agents, and that he would not know him even if he saw him. How de Crosne, or his man, had known that the home of the Englishman they were pursuing was at Lymington remained a mystery over which Roger continued to puzzle his wits in vain; and, had he needed any added incentive to overtake his enemy the prospect of solving the problem would have provided it. But he needed none. Having had his saddle transferred to a mettlesome grey from the posting-stables, he left the address to which his own mare was to be returned, and pushed on.

In his first stage he had covered fourteen miles; his next, to Win-chester, was fifteen. At first the road ran up and down a series of switchback hills then through flattish farm country. The weather had cleared and the September moon had risen above the trees. The grey proved a good steed and Roger was in no mood to spare him. He was fond of horses but fonder of his country and he was now determined to catch his man, even if he had to kill several of his mounts under him. Just before one in the morning he rode over the chalk hills into Winchester.

At the Black Swan he inquired again. His man had changed horses there and trotted out of the yard only ten minutes before his arrival. While his saddle was being changed from the exhausted grey to a bay mare he took stock of the situation. He had little doubt now that he could catch his unsuspecting enemy on the next lap; but it was as good as certain that the Frenchman would be armed. Jim had put a pair of pistols into Roger's holsters as a normal precaution against his encountering a highwayman; and he was not afraid to face any man in a fight. But in this case if he came off worst it was not only himself, but his country, that would be the loser. He positively dared not risk being left wounded in a ditch while his enemy got clean away with the letter. In consequence, he decided that the time had now come when he must make use of his father's warrant. Winchester was a garrison town so he felt that there would be no difficulty in securing military aid there.

Mounting the bay he rode at a quick trot to the barracks of the Hampshire Regiment. The sentry at its gate called the Sergeant of the guard. The Sergeant said that he thought some of the officers were still up, and, having handed his mount over to an orderly, Roger hurried with him to the mess.

After an infuriating wait of five minutes in the hall a heavily-moustached Captain, who was half-seas-over, came out to see him. Roger did not mince matters. Politely but swiftly he stated his business, produced his warrant, and requested that a mounted escort should be furnished for him with the minimum possible delay.

The Captain sobered up at once, and said: "This is an infantry barracks, so normally I'd only be able to help you by asking some of the officers to turn out with their grooms. But 'tis your good fortune that we've been on manœuvres recently, and a squadron of Dragoons are quartered here as our guests. Have the goodness to wait here a few moments and I'll fetch one of their officers. He is having the devil's own luck at the cards to-night, so you'll be doing us a favour, Sir, if you'll relieve us of him and prevent his further inroads on our pockets"

Again Roger had to submit to seeing a few more precious moments slip away. Then one of the big double doors of the ante-room opened again and the Captain returned, accompanied by a thick-set, red-faced young man with a crop of ginger curls. To Roger's amazement he found himself face to face with his old enemy of Sherborne days, George Gunston.

Recognition was mutual for, at that second, Gunston cried: "Why, damn my soul! If it isn't Bookworm Brook!"

Roger flushed slightly and replied: "I have no time for exchanging compliments, but if you have a mind to it I will find plenty later on at any time and place you may suggest."

"I see that you are already acquainted," murmured the Captain, a trifle uneasily.

"By God! The fellow's challenging me!" exploded Gunston, going redder in the face than ever.

"Not at the moment," said Roger sharply. "The Captain, here, will have told you what's afoot. I am on the King's service and require a troop of horse to accompany me instantly. I pray you, Mr. Gunston, let our personal prejudices lie dormant for this night, at least; and give me your aid without demur."

"On the King's service," muttered Gunston, bringing his heels together with a click and bowing. "So be it, Mr. Brook. Be pleased to come with me."

Much as Roger disliked Gunston he had to admit that he was a good officer. Within twelve minutes he had his troop of Dragoons roused from their sleep, out of their barrack room and mounted. He gave a sharp word of command and, with Roger beside him, wheeled his horse. With the clatter of hooves and the jingling of sabres behind them, they trotted out of the barrack gates and took the London road.

Roger reckoned that his enforced delay to secure an escort had cost him a little over twenty minutes, so his enemy now had half an hour's lead over him again; but he thought that with luck they might catch up with him before he reached Alton.

The road ahead lay through water meadows, and on their right meandered the river Itchin, in which Roger's father had occasionally taken him, while still a boy, to fish for the wily brown trout.

For the first mile or so they held their pace while Roger satisfied Gunston's curiosity as briefly as he decently could. Then, when he had described the foreigner that he was endeavouring to catch, Gunston shouted an order and the whole troop settled down to get the best out of their chargers.

For ten miles they rode hard, without exchanging a word, and, going at a steady canter, mounted the long slope that lies some way to the south of Alton. As they breasted its crest a mile of open country lay before them. Simultaneously Roger and George caught sight of a solitary horseman walking his horse half a mile ahead. The bright moonlight showed quite plainly that he was the man they were after. Even at that distance they could make out the lankiness of his figure, the heavy collared riding-coat and his truncated, steeple-crowned hat.

Having visualised just such a situation, Roger had intended that the troop should reduce its pace to a trot, ride up alongside the unsuspecting Frenchman as though about to pass him, halt, wheel and surround him; thus taking him prisoner before he even had a chance to attempt to escape.

But Lieutenant George Gunston had very different ideas. With the instinct of a born fox-hunting squire he instantly rowelled his horse and gave vent to a loud: "Tally ho! Tally ho! Tally ho!"

Taken completely by surprise Roger could only choke back his fury. His mount automatically leapt forward beside its companion, while the whole troop of Dragoons followed their excited officer with wild shouts of enthusiasm and glee.

The man ahead turned to throw one glance over his shoulder, then set spurs to his horse. The hunt was up, and there was nothing that Roger could do about it now but to crouch low over his mare's neck and attempt, with the rest, to ride down his quarry.

As he had foreseen the attempt was a failure. The Frenchman had too good a lead, and the road now sloped down towards some beech-woods. Urging his steed on to the grass at the side of the road he veered off to the right at a gallop and, a few minutes later, was lost to sight in the deep shadow of the woods.

After their ten miles at a pressing pace, and final mile-long burst of speed, the horses were now badly winded; and, as they reached the valley bottom where the thick beechwoods came right up to both sides of the road, Gunston threw up his hand to halt his men. Then, as the sweating horses stumbled to a standstill, he called in an aggrieved tone to Roger: "Damme! The Frog has cheated us of our sport. He's gone to earth!"

"And whose fault is that?" snarled Roger, white with rage. "You besotted oaf! What the hell did you expect, having given him ten minutes' warning?"

"Hey!" Gunston bellowed back. "King's business or no, I'll not have anyone hold such language to me. I take you up in earnest now on your invitation to meet you at another time and place."

Roger's lip curled. "That suits me well. I've a long score to settle with you that I've not forgot. And God help you if you cannot use a sword or pistol better than you do your head."

"We'll see about that," Gunston snapped. "Send me your seconds when your business in town is done; and I'll show you that I can use either as well as I do my fists. But since you are in command here at the moment, what are your wishes now that we have lost our man?"

"Please to remain here with your men, and have them scour the woods till dawn," Roger replied coldly. "I fear the odds are now very great against your making a find, but should you catch him take instant action to secure the document that he carries before he can destroy it; then bring him on to London. As I act under Naval orders 'twould be best if you deliver him and the paper to the Admiralty. I shall ride on alone, and if I have no luck, I will call there later in the day to learn if there is news of you."

Swivelling his mare, Roger flogged the poor brute into a trot and rode on into Alton. Already, while galloping at a breakneck speed after the vanishing Frenchman, he had decided that if, through Gunston's folly, he lost his quarry, the best course would be for him to ride on as fast as possible. It was certain that his man would lie up in the woods for a bit before venturing back on to the road, so by passing him while he hid and getting to the capital first there was still a chance that he might be headed off before he could reach the French Embassy.

At Alton Roger changed his exhausted mare for another bay and continued on, now through flattish country, towards Farnham. The middle of the stage was about half-way between Lymington and London and he was already feeling the strain. Yet he dared not let up for a moment. He had never been to London and had no connections there upon whom he could call at a moment's notice. If his last card was to be of any value careful arrangements would have to be made for the playing of it and, as he would have to appeal for help to strangers, that would take time. He did not even know where the French Embassy was situated; and his man, now thoroughly alarmed, would probably approach it by a circuitous route, so he reckoned that if an effective ambush was to be organised he must reach the capital at least an hour ahead of his quarry.

He got to Farnham at three-thirty, changed his horse again and cantered up the slope on to the Hog's Back. The road now ran along the crest of a high ridge and the sinking moon lit a weird and splendid panorama of pine forests stretching away into the distance. But he

356

had no eyes for it and swaying automatically with his mount pressed on to Guildford.

As his horse walked him up the steep high street of the old city he decided that, having covered two-thirds of his journey, he must rest for a while, at least. While his saddle was being changed to a piebald in the yard of the White Hart, he went inside and asked the serving man to bring him some coffee laced with rum. It seemed days ago since he had woken on the barque that morning, but he was thankful now that he had slept on till eleven o'clock. He was not feeling the least tired mentally, but his back and thighs were protesting strongly at the strain his sixty-mile ride had put upon them.

It was a quarter to five by the time he had drunk his coffee and two minutes later he was on his way to Cobham. To his intense annoyance the piebald proved an awkward brute, being one of those mounts that always seem reluctant to break cleanly from a trot to a canter and vice versa. The jolting he received during the ten-mile stretch took it out of him more than his hard ride with Gunston over a longer distance had done; and he was much relieved when he was able to change it at Cobham for the fourth bay that he had ridden that night.

The Ladies' Mile on to Esher offered him a good clear gallop, but by the time he reached Kingston he felt terribly done. There, he changed horses for the last time and set out on the final eleven-mile stage. His mount was a good one but he was no longer capable of getting the best out of it. Yet he continued to do his damnedest.

He knew that his enemy had ridden at leisure for the first half of the journey and so must be in much better shape than himself. The odds were that within half an hour of taking to the woods the Frenchman would have regained the road and was now riding all out behind him. He had thought of endeavouring to prevent him being furnished with relays, but to do so would have meant stopping at each posting-house while somebody in authority was found to whom he could show his father's warrant, and he had decided that he dared not risk such a series of delays.

As dawn broke he was riding at a slow trot over Putney Heath, then he walked his horse down the slope towards the bridge, crossed the Thames, and began to trot again through the village of Fulham. Nerving himself to a last effort he cantered up the slope beyond Knightsbridge and pulled up at the tollgate on Hyde Park Corner, at eight o'clock.

Having inquired his way to Queen Anne's Gate, he trotted the last half-mile past Buckingham House and through St. James's Park, to rein in and almost fall from his saddle in front of Mr. Gilbert Maxwell's house.

His ring at the door was answered by a smooth-faced servant in plain livery, to whom he said that he must see Mr. Maxwell immediately, on a most urgent matter.

"I am sorry, Sir," the man answered, "but Mr. Maxwell has already gone out."

This was the one thing that Roger had not foreseen, and it came as a desperate blow.

"Where can I find him" he gasped. "I come on the King's business, and 'twill not wait."

The servant shook his head regretfully. "Mr. Maxwell never leaves word where he is to be found when he walks abroad."

"How soon will he be back?"

"That is more than I can say, Sir. But if you care to leave your name, or write to him——"

"I tell you my business is of most desperate urgency," Roger cried, "and the day would be gone before a letter could be delivered."

"Oh, no, Sir," the man replied blandly. "If you care to enter and write your letter here, I can promise you that it will reach him with very little delay."

Roger was in no state to ponder this paradox and assess its meaning. Instead he stood leaning against the iron railing for a moment, frantically searching his mind for some other source where he might secure the urgent help he needed. Suddenly he had an inspiration, and asked: "Where is Amesbury House?"

"In Arlington Street, Sir. Just off Piccadilly. You have but to ride north across the Park and you will come to it."

"I pray you help me to my horse."

The man obliged and Roger trotted across Birdcage Walk towards St. James's Palace. As he did so it crossed his mind that perhaps, after all, Mr. Gilbert Maxwell was at home but, owing to the highly secret nature of his work, made it a rule never to reveal himself to anyone If so, a note left for him might have produced the required action in time to be effective; but that was only speculation, and Roger's need was too urgent for him to consider turning back now that he had thought of another possibility.

Outside the Palace he inquired again, of a man in a cocked hat, for the exact situation of Amesbury House, and, on learning it, pushed on up St. James's Street. Having turned left near its top end another moment brought him into the courtyard of the great mansion he was seeking.

Flinging himself off his horse he stumbled up the steps and shouted to the liveried footman on the door: "Lord Edward Fitz-Deverel! Is he at home?"

"Why, yes, Sir," replied the astonished servant. "But His Lordship is not yet risen."

"No matter! Take me to him!" panted Roger.

His dishevelled state and bandaged head now proved a talisman. The footman was sensible enough to see that this was no time to stand on ceremony. Acting with an initiative that no French servant would have dared to show, he grabbed Roger by the arm and hurried him up the broad marble staircase, then along a corridor to a heavily-carved door. Banging on it with his fists, he cried: "My Lord! There's a gentleman here who has travelled in great haste to see you."

"Let him come in then," called a voice; and, throwing open the door, Roger staggered forward towards Droopy Ned.

Droopy did not seem to have grown any older. He still had the curiously ageless look of a young man old before his time. He was dressed in a magnificent flowing robe of Indian silk and wore a turban round his head. With his feet stretched out before him, he reclined at ease on a gilded chaise-longue while toying with a breakfast tray set on a low table at his side.

As his pale blue eyes fell on Roger, he said languidly: "Egad, Sir! You seem in a plaguey hurry. Who are you? I seem to know your face."

Collapsing in a chair, Roger grinned at him. "We last met on leaving Sherborne. You told me then to call upon you if ever I needed assistance and, by God, if ever any man needed it, I need it now."

"Why! Strap me, if it's not young Roger Brook!" Droopy grinned back. "And I'll honour the pledge willingly. If you need a poor sword or a fat purse, either are at your service."

In five minutes Roger had given the salient points in the affair that concerned him so desperately. Droopy's quick brain seemed to leap ahead of the tale at almost every stage; and, well before it was done, the languid fop had given place to the man of action. Throwing off his robe and turban he began to pull on his outdoor clothes; then he took two long strides to the door and hollaed for his servants.

One he sent to order his coach, another to collect four footmen armed with pistols to accompany him, and a third to request his father to ask an audience of Mr. Pitt for him at noon.

As they ran off to execute his orders he hastily completed his dressing, then fetched a decanter of some foreign cordial from a bureau and made Roger swallow a couple of glasses of it. The liquor revived him wonderfully and when, a few minutes later, they ran downstairs he felt that, if put to it, he could yet have ridden another stage. Within a quarter of an hour of his having reached Amesbury House, they were in the coach and off, with two armed footmen on the box and another two inside the vehicle with them.

"Whither are we going?" Roger asked, as the coach trundled across Piccadilly.

"To Portland Place," replied Droopy. " 'Tis in that fine new thoroughfare that the French Embassy is situated."

Ten minutes later they were driving up the beautiful broad street, with open country at the far end of it.

"How do you plan to take him? inquired Roger, thrusting his head out of the window. But this time he had no need to be apprehensive.

"We'll lie in wait for him in front of the house next to the Embassy," Droopy said, pulling him back by the skirt of his coat. "I'll send two of my men round to the back entrance lest, perchance, he elects to attempt getting in that way. Should he do so one of them can hold him covered with a pistol while t'other comes round to fetch us. From your description of his figure and dress 'tis impossible that they should fail to recognise him. Henry and Thomas, here, shall take the back of the house while James and John remain on the boot to render us assistance should we need it. I will give all of them their instructions; since you must not show yourself, lest he recognise you, even from a distance, and gallop off once more."

" 'Tis well planned," Roger agreed. "But he'll not recognise me, for I've never been face to face with the fellow, except in the dark."

"Of that, you cannot be certain," Droopy remarked shrewdly. "In any event, 'tis wisest that you should remain in a corner of the coach and not emerge until I give the word."

The dispositions were soon made, and they settled down to wait. Excited and overwrought as he was, Roger soon found his head nodding and, after sitting still for ten minutes, he was sound asleep.

Over an hour and a half elapsed, and when one of the footmen rapped sharply on the roof of the coach Roger did not hear him. Droopy peered out of the window and watched a thin, lanky figure come riding up the street. He waited patiently until the man had dismounted and stood in the road some ten paces away. Then he shook Roger awake, thrust a pistol into his hand and, levelling his own, sprang out of the coach.

At the sound the horseman turned, started, and made a move as though to dash for the doorway of the Embassy; but he knew that it was too far off for him to reach it. He had seen instantly that he was covered by the two footmen on the boot of the coach as well as by Droopy, and he heard the latter shout in French:

"Stand! In the King's name! One move and I shoot to kill!"

Shaking the sleep from his eyes, Roger sprang into the road beside Droopy, and found himself staring into the pale, corpse-like face of Joseph Fouché.

CHAPTER XXVI

WARRANT FOR EXTRADITION

" ' H o w positively extraordinary that I should have clean forgot all about that man," said Roger, some quarter of an hour later, as the coach rumbled south towards Downing Street. "That strange, colourless personality of his had left no impression on my mind; yet when I was searching my memory last night I should have recalled him, seeing that he is the only man in all France to whom I gave not only my father's name and my own but also the place where lay my home. 'Tis amazing, too, that he should have carried them in his memory for close on four years."

"Nay, 'tis not so amazing in view of what he said," Droopy Ned replied in his careless drawl. "It seems he prides himself on his astuteness as an amateur in detection, and a fine memory is an essential requisite for that. The name, too, of a foreign Admiral would be apt to stick in any man's mind more readily than that of one of his own countrymen. 'Tis little wonder that on seeing the notice about you on the docks at St. Malo he recalled you, and decided to gamble the price of a return fare on the packet to Southampton against the earning of so handsome a reward."

Roger nodded. "Yes, the five hundred *louis* offered for the letter would mean a lot to a poor school teacher, and as his pupils have not yet assembled for the autumn session, he no doubt felt that even if the venture failed 'twould prove a pleasant diversion before returning to his dreary work. I wonder though that a man so fond of intrigue does not take up something else."

"He will. Believe me, Roger, that pale, sickly-looking fellow has prodigious strength of character concealed beneath his corpse-like countenance. I'll swear to that, or I'm no judge of men. 'Tis the very colourlessness of his personality that will make him both powerful and dangerous. Did'st nòtice that he would not look us in the eye. That was not shame, nor fright, nor modesty. 'Twas because he was determined to hide from us the ambition that consumes him inwardly and his fury at our having thwarted him."

"Yet he spoke me fair enough. An apology was the last thing I expected; but he vowed that he'd meant me no harm personally and was tempted to the venture only on account of the reward."

"And, like a softy, you repaid him royally for it," laughed Droopy. "Instead of clapping him in jug for the assault upon you, and for stealing your father's horse, you let him go. Yet should you ever meet Monsieur Joseph Fouché again I vow your generosity will avail you nothing. That man would strangle his own mother, and crave her pardon while accomplishing the act from a fixed conviction that a soft answer ever turneth away wrath."

"Ah, well!" Roger shrugged. "We have the document intact. 'Tis that alone that matters."

Yet he had made a terrible enemy, and in later years was often to recall Droopy's shrewd judgment; since Joseph Fouché, his pale hands dripping with the blood he had shed during the Terror, was to emerge from it as the dreaded Chief of the Secret Police under the Consulate; and, having served and betrayed many masters, was to become in due course millionaire, Minister and Duke of Otranto, the most unscrupulous, hated and feared of all Napoleon's servants.

*   *   *   *   *

On their arriving at No. 10, Downing Street, a secretary confirmed that Mr. Pitt had agreed to the Marquess of Amesbury's request that he would receive Lord Edward at noon; but they were a little early for the appointment, and were taken through to wait in the back portion of the long, narrow hall. Then, presently, the secretary led them up to the front room on the first floor, which Mr. Pitt used as his office.

Droopy introduced Roger, who pleaded his overnight journey as excuse for appearing in such a dirty and dishevelled condition and, while doing so, took swift stock of the remarkable man to whom at the age of twenty-four King George III had entrusted the destinies of Britain.

He was taller than Roger had expected, and dressed in a high-collared coat the top button only of which was fastened, so that the filmy lace of his shirt showed above and below it. His fair hair was brushed back from his high forehead, his mouth was sensitive and his almond-shaped eyes were grave; his long oval face already showed the cares of office and his manner seemed a little awkward. On the table in front of him stood a decanter of port and some glasses, from one of which he was already drinking. With shy abruptness he invited them to join him, and, when they had poured two glasses, asked their business.

Without a word Roger produced the letter and laid it before him.

Having read it the Prime Minister said: "I like the directness of your methods, Mr. Brook. How did you come by this, and what do you know concerning its contents? Tell me everything you can. In a matter of such gravity my time is yours."

Roger then told his tale and, afterwards, spent a further half-hour answering a series of shrewd questions fired at him by Mr. Pitt, who was now pacing restlessly about the room holding his glass in one hand and swinging the decanter in the other.

At length he returned to his chair and said with a smile: "How old are you, Mr. Brook?"

"I shall be twenty in January, Sir."

Mr. Pitt nodded. "That is but a little more than a year younger than I was when I first created some stir in Parliament. I mention this so you may know that I am not one who considers that good counsel can come only from old age, and that I shall give a certain weight to your opinion. What would you do were you in my place?"

Roger did not hesitate, but accepted the honour done him as he was meant to do. He said firmly: "I see only one thing for it, Sir. If you wish to avert a war that may well prove disastrous to Britain later, you must risk one now. 'Tis my conviction that if challenged at the present juncture the French will not dare to fight; but, if they are once allowed to gain control of the Dutch ports and the wealth of the United Provinces, 'twill be a very different matter."

"You opinion marches with my own, Mr. Brook," the Prime Minister declared. "I am not altogether uninformed regarding the state of affairs in the United Provinces, and they have given me considerable concern for some time. Of this devilish French plot, of which you have brought us such timely warning, I confess I was in complete ignorance. Yet I now see many pointers to it, of which I have hitherto failed to recognise the significance. Sir James Harris, our Minister at The Hague, has twice returned to London for special consultations with the Cabinet, and he has repeatedly urged upon me the necessity for an alliance with Prussia to check the ambitious designs of the French in the Dutch Netherlands. Unfortunately, the old King of Prussia, who died last year, rejected my overtures to that end; but the new King, his nephew, seems more amenable."

Mr. Pitt paused to swallow another swig of port, then went on: "King Frederick-William II is brother to the Stadtholder's wife, and he most strongly resents the insolence of these Dutch Republicans to his sister and her husband. He has even mobilised an army of thirty thousand men under the Duke of Brunswick on the Dutch border in an attempt to overawe them without bloodshed; yet further he does not seem prepared to go. If, by sending him information of this French conspiracy, we could induce him to march in, half our battle would be already won. And 'tis that which I intend to do. I shall despatch a courier by fast ship to-night with letters to both Sir James and the Duke. The one, I know, will do his utmost to check the French designs; with regard to the other, we can only hope that he will realise the necessity for prompt action."

To Roger's surprise, and somewhat to his consternation, Droopy Ned suddenly said: "Permit me to propose, Sir, that Mr. Brook should be your messenger. He knows the ins and outs of this affair better than any other man, and might well turn the balance in our favour with His Grace of Brunswick."

"I thank you, Lord Edward, 'tis an admirable thought," replied the Prime Minister; then he swung round on Roger: "May I count upon you for this mission, Mr. Brook?"

Roger had passed through a week of trial that would have lasted most men a lifetime, but he did not hesitate in his reply: "I am His Majesty's loyal servant, Sir; and yours."

Mr. Pitt smiled. " 'Twas well said, seeing the ordeals you have survived so recently, and you merit all your country's gratitude."

He helped himself to another glass of port, stood up and went on slowly: "Our course is set then. 'Tis monstrous hard that after having used my utmost ingenuity for near four years to preserve the peace of Europe, and in the meantime once again built up Britain's prosperity, that I should now be called on to invite a war. Yet there is clearly no alternative. I will have despatches ready for you by eight o'clock this evening and make all arrangements for your journey. I pray to God that He may aid you to persuade the Prussians to act in this emergency; but, meanwhile, we will take our measures here. If Prussia acts not with us, England will act alone. I intend this day to give orders for the mobilisation of the British Fleet."

*　　　*　　　*　　　*　　　*

Late that evening Roger went aboard a frigate that was lying off Gravesend, and sailed in her on the night-tide. He found himself in the extraordinary position of not only carrying Mr. Pitt's despatches but with letters of marque recommending him as a person whose opinion should be asked and given due weight. A little over twenty-four hours later he was in The Hague, and having the British Minister roused from his bed.

363

When Sir James Harris had read the despatches addressed to him he exclaimed: "Thank God that Mr. Pitt has at last decided to support the Stadtholder by force of arms. 'Tis the policy that I have been urging on him through our Foreign Secretary, my Lord Carmarthen, for these past two years."

Roger found Sir James extremely well informed, immensely competent and, to him personally, kindness itself. They immediately took a great liking to one another and, within two hours of his arrival, the Minister asked him to accompany him to an early morning conference with Baron Göetz, with whose collaboration he had been striving to stave off the French domination of the United Provinces.

That same morning Roger left with Baron Göetz in his travelling coach for Munster, the headquarters of the Duke of Brunswick's army. There followed forty-eight hours of almost uninterrupted conferences at which the Duke consulted with his senior commanders and numerous German Princes who were on his staff. Roger played little part in these deliberations, but he found his German good enough to understand the gist of what was going on and, at times, was able to corroborate a point through an interpreter.

On the 9th of September the Duke acted and launched his army into the rebellious provinces. The free companies came out, but France did not honour her promise to support them and withdrew the Comte de Maillebois, who was replaced by the Rhinegrave von Salms. He and his Dutch volunteers proved no match for the well-disciplined Prussian army trained by Frederick the Great, and the Dutch nobility declared for the Stadtholder.

On the 16th the French Government issued a declaration that it would not suffer the Constitution of the United Provinces to be violated, and for a few days it looked as if France was going to fight. But Roger had learned that at the beginning of the month both de Castries and de Ségur, refusing to serve under the Archbishop, had resigned; so he knew that M. de Rochambeau and the war party no longer had the direction of affairs, and his contention that the French were bluffing proved correct.

On the 20th, after an absence of two years, the Stadtholder entered The Hague with his friends in triumph and to the plaudits of the great mass of the common people. Roger participated in the rejoicings as Sir James's guest. On the 28th he returned to London, his mission accomplished.

* * * * *

After having signed the book at No. 10, he spent two hectic nights with Droopy Ned, then went down to Lymington. His parents could not make enough of him and his father insisted that he must accept the five hundred guineas reward for his capture of Joseph Fouché, so he was well in funds. The Admiral also was most averse to his seeking any fresh employment for at least a year.

On his first morning at home he rode over to seek news of Georgina but there he met with a disappointment. Both Colonel Thursby and his lovely daughter proved to be abroad, and the butler told Roger that Georgina was now Lady Etheredge, having married Sir Humphrey Etheredge some three years before.

While in London Roger had asked Droopy Ned and another gentleman to act for him in the matter of George Gunston, and on the 10th of October he learned that a meeting had been arranged for the 17th.

The duel took place in a secluded part of St. John's Wood, and Gunston had chosen pistols. Both principals refused all offers of mediation on the ground, but agreed that on neither side was the offence mortal. Roger put his bullet into George's shoulder, and George neatly nicked Roger's arm; but neither wound was at all serious.

Both agreed that honour had been satisfied and, like good Englishmen, promised in front of their seconds to bear no malice after the affair. Three nights later they dined together but the evening was a complete frost. Neither of them had a single idea in common and they parted disliking one another every bit as cordially as they had before their duel.

*   *   *   *   *

After fulfilling his dinner engagement with George, Roger returned home. Four days later he was just about to go out shooting, with his father, when the Chief Constable of the district was announced, and old Ben said that it was Roger the gentleman had come to see.

The thought that leapt to Roger's mind was that it must be in connection with the duel. He knew that the edicts against duelling were being enforced with considerable rigour, but his ex-adversary had assured him when they had dined together that since both their wounds were slight no action would be taken. However, as Gunston might lose his commission in the event of an official inquiry, Roger was much more concerned for him than for himself, as he went into the library to interview his visitor.

For a few moments they exchanged courteous platitudes, then the Chief Constable came to the point and said: "The present is one of the most disagreeable tasks I have ever been called on to perform, Mr. Brook. 'Tis for that reason I decided to wait upon you myself. It would appear that you are but recently returned from France and fell into some trouble while in that country?"

"Yes," Roger agreed quietly. In the back of his mind he had always feared that something of this kind might arise, but did not feel that any good purpose could be served by denying it.

The Chief Constable hesitated awkwardly. "The fact is, Mr. Brook, although it distresses me mightily, I have here a warrant for your extradition to face a charge of murder."

Roger smiled a little nervously. " 'Tis true that I killed a man, but 'twas the outcome of a duel. I pray you give me a moment to consult my father on what course I should pursue in this."

365

"With pleasure, Mr. Brook. In fact"—the Chief Constable winked a knowing brown eye—"if 'twould be of any service to you I'll willingly forget the matter for twenty-four hours and return to learn, er—your decision then."

" 'Tis monstrous kind of you," Roger smiled as he left the room, "but I would like to speak with my father first."

When Admiral Brook heard what was afoot he nearly exploded. But he agreed with Roger's own view, that the music should be faced and an appeal made to Mr. Pitt for his intervention.

In consequence, Roger surrendered himself there and then; but on his appearing before the local justices they immediately accepted bail for him, on his father's surety, at the nominal sum of one hundred guineas.

At home once more he immediately wrote a full account of his meeting with de Caylus and sent it to the Prime Minister. But the days that followed were very anxious ones. He knew better than most people the relations which now existed in such matters between England and France. Ever since the signing of the Commercial Treaty in the summer of '86 such warrants for extradition had been promptly honoured in both countries. Contrary to immemorial custom, even debtors who had fled abroad were now being returned in considerable numbers to answer to their creditors; and in a case where murder was the charge only the most exceptional circumstances were likely to hold up the execution of the warrant.

On the 30th he received a reply from the Prime Minister's secretary. It simply said that Mr. Pitt would be pleased if Mr. Brook would wait upon him at No. 10 at 4 o'clock in the afternoon of the 4th of November.

The letter could hardly have been more non-committal and, still feeling a considerable degree of anxiety, Roger proceeded to London on the 2nd.

*　　*　　*　　*　　*

The 3rd of November proved to be a sunny autumn day and that afternoon Roger decided to go for a walk in Hyde Park. As he was strolling beside the drive that led towards Kensington Palace his eye roved over the handsome equipages in which numerous belles of the town were taking an airing.

Suddenly he caught sight of Georgina, being bowled along behind two high-stepping greys. At the same moment she saw him and called to her coachman to bring her barouche to a halt beside the railings. Leaning out from it, she exclaimed:

"Why! Roger Brook! Odds life! Can it in truth be you; or is it a ghost I see?"

"Nay, 'tis indeed myself!" Roger cried. "And prodigious glad I am at this chance meeting. Egad! You look more ravishing than ever."

Her billowing skirt of striped taffeta showing beneath a rich fur cloak, and her lovely face aglow from the fresh air, under a great picture hat decked with ostrich feathers, she was indeed a ravishing sight. At his words she dropped her black eyes in mock coyness and said: "I vow you flatter me, Sir. Yet I had cause to think you had quite forgotten me."

" 'Tis not so!" he protested quickly. "I swear to that. I inquired for you the first day I was home, and learned that you were then abroad. But did you never receive my letter?"

"Nay!" she cried, with sudden vehemence; her whole manner changing as she looked him squarely in the face. "Roger, thou art a very swine! Not one single line in four whole years have I had from thee!"

"Georgina," he smiled, "You have not changed one iota, and the violent variation of your moods is as bewitching as ever. But I had reason for my non-communicativeness, since in the first years I had little to tell you that was to my credit. When can we meet so that I may crave pardon for my shortcomings? for I would go on bended knee to retrieve my place in your good graces."

Her eyelashes fluttered and she pretended to become coy again. "I am a wife, Sir; and owe a duty to my husband."

Roger knew quite well that she was only acting, and he found her mummery enchanting. Playing up to it, he said: "Then needs must I seek your window, and bring a scaling ladder to it on the next dark night."

Suddenly she sat back and roared with laughter. Then, her dark eyes mocking, she replied: "I think you are improved and show a readier wit than when last we met; and 'twould intrigue me to learn what life has made of you. For old time's sake I will cancel all my engagements this night and give you supper."

"You will!" he cried eagerly. "Where shall I wait upon you, and at what hour?"

Putting a finger to her red lips she leaned right out of the barouche, and whispered: "Be on the corner of Charles Street and St. James's Square at nine o'clock. I'll see to it that there is a plain carriage waiting there, and 'twill bring you to me."

Before he could reply she had pulled the string attached to her coachman's little finger. Then she waved her muff to Roger and gave him a glowing smile. The coachman cracked his whip and, as Roger made a gallant leg, the spanking pair of greys bore Georgina swiftly away.

For the next few hours Roger's thoughts were so full of the mysterious assignation he had been given by his first flame that it took them completely off his anxieties as to what Mr. Pitt might have to say to him the following afternoon.

Returning to Amesbury House, where he was staying with Droopy, he donned the best suit in his new wardrobe, had Droopy's barber do his hair, and availed himself of some of Droopy's most expensive scent. At a quarter to nine, malacca cane in hand and looking as fine a figure as the most exquisite French Marquis who ever graced the galleries of Versailles, he took up his position on the corner of St.

James's Square. A few minutes later a closed carriage without arms on its door panels drove up, and he got into it.

At a smart trot the vehicle carried him along to Hyde Park Corner, down the vale into Knightsbridge and out to Kensington village. There, it turned right and mounted a steep hill, then it entered the private grounds of a small villa and drew up before the porch.

The moment he had stepped out of the carriage and closed its door it turned on the gravel sweep and drove away. As he approached the porch the door opened to disclose a trim female figure. Recognising the girl as Georgina's personal maid at Highcliffe, Roger cried:

"Why, Jenny! 'Tis good to see you again. How fares it with you?"

She bobbed him a curtsey. "The better for seeing you, Mr. Brook, and well, considering the hours we keep. Milady awaits you, Sir, if you'll be pleased to follow me."

The girl crossed the hall and ushered him into a room the size of which surprised him, seeing the smallness of the house. It was very lofty; the far end of it was shut off completely by heavy red curtains falling from the ceiling to the floor. Opposite them a cheerful wood fire roared in a wide grate. Before it was set a table for two, laid with crystal, silver and white napery. On one side of the fireplace there was a big generously-cushioned sofa and on it, dressed in a low-cut crimson gown that made a perfect foil to her dark beauty, sat Georgina.

As Roger entered she regally extended her hand, on which there flashed a huge solitaire diamond, and, bowing low, he kissed it.

"Come sit by me, and tell me all about yourself," she smiled up at him.

"Nay," he declared as he sank on to the sofa cushions, " 'Tis the privilege of the fair sex to have their innings first; and if I am to conceal nothing from you 'twill take all of two hours to relate my story. So let us save it till after we have supped. But be pleased to tell me of this strange little house. 'Tis a most agreeable spot, but quite a way from the city. Do you live here?"

"Lud, no!" she ejaculated, "I've a mansion in St. James's Square. This is but a *pièd-a-terre*. There is a lovely view, though, from Campden Hill, here, and 'tis no great distance from the Metropolis. I come here when I am wearied of the madding crowd, and wish to be alone."

"Only then?" Roger cocked a wicked eyebrow.

"For shame, Sir! If you let your glances imply such things I shall turn you out. 'Twas built by an artist as his studio, and now 'tis mine. I paint here when the spirit moves me."

"That sounds good cover for other amusements," he smiled, undeterred.

"Indeed, 'tis true. Both Mr. Gainsborough and Sir Joshua Reynolds come here to give me lessons, and the rivalry between the two old gentlemen is vastly amusing. But, strap me! I do believe, Sir, from the impudent look upon your face, that you still question my veracity."

He made her a mocking little bow. "Madame, 'twould never enter my mind to doubt a thing you say. 'Twas only—well, the seclusion of the spot, and the mysterious manner in which I was conveyed hither.

368

You must forgive me, if in my poor debased mind I found some resemblance to those charming *petit maisons* outside Paris, in which the French nobles entertain the ladies of the Opera."

"Damn you, Roger!" she laughed. " 'Tis true enough, and from you I have no desire to conceal it. The paintings are there behind the curtain; but the place has other uses. As you well know, I have never been a subscriber to the view that the male of the species should alone be privileged to indulge in such diversions."

"And your husband?" Roger grinned. "Is he then complaisant, or is he liable to interfere with my digestion, by leaping in through the window with a drawn sword, after supper?"

"Oh, Humphrey!" She shrugged. "His pack of hounds mean more to him than his wife. He has a box in Leicestershire, and is there now. If he has had a good day's cubbing, he will be dead drunk ere this."

"Was it a love match when it started, that has gone cold upon you since?" asked Roger. "Or was it the other thing?"

"The other thing; although we liked one another well enough, and are still good friends."

"I thought, though, that you'd vowed you'd take nothing less than an Earl," Roger twitted her; "and he's a mere baronet."

Her eyes became serious. "Fret not over that, my friend. I am but twenty-one and have ample time ahead of me. If Humphrey does not break his neck over the sticks, the poor fellow will burst himself like a rotten barrel, ere long. I'll still be a Duchess before I die. I swear it."

"What induced you to marry Sir Humphrey, then?"

At Roger's question her face changed to a glowing enthusiasm. " 'Twas Stillwaters, his place in Surrey. The first moment I set eyes on it, I knew I had to have it. 'Twas designed by William Kent. It has a terrace a quarter-mile long and a great Palladian portico with forty-foot pillars. The house overlooks lawns that slope down to a fine lake, and the whole is surrounded by birchwoods. You must come down to stay, Roger, and you will fall in love with it just as I did. 'Tis near Ripley, and not far from London. Just the right distance for week-end parties; and it gives me the perfect setting in which to entertain the great world that I have always hankered after."

He smiled. "I think I understand; and I see that you have been true to your original design. Do you get all the pleasure you anticipated from playing the great hostess?"

"Indeed I do! To stick a mental pin into one statesman's bottom, and let another kiss me behind a screen, gives me the greatest satisfaction when the planned intentions behind such acts become apparent."

They were silent for a moment, then he said: "Since your husband is so wrapped up with country pursuits, how did you manage to drag him abroad; or did you go alone?"

"Lud, no!" she exclaimed with a laugh. " 'Twas to Italy I went, and had I been unescorted I verily believe those passionate Italians would have raped me in the street. As it was I had to have a footman sleeping outside my door each night. But Humphrey would have made a poor companion for such a journey. I travelled with my father, and I'd sooner see the sights with him than I would with most men."

"You're monstrous fortunate," Roger told her. "Or perhaps I should say, clever. Since it seems to me you both have your cake and eat it."

" 'Tis the art of life to know what one wants and have at it," she smiled. "And if I am any judge, dear Roger, I think from the fine figure you now cut, that you have become not altogether inept at that."

"If so, I owe more than I can ever repay to you," he said seriously. "You not only made me a man, but by your gift of yourself to me showed me what was worth having and what to cast aside. Had things been otherwise my first experiences might well have been so sordid as to alter my whole outlook."

She leaned over and kissed him lightly on the cheek. " 'Tis good to hear that you are fastidious in your loves, and not become a rake. I hate a man who turns up the skirts of every wench he meets in a dark passage."

For a further ten minutes they talked of old times. Then Jenny came in with a tray of hot dishes that she put upon a heater, on a side table, and left them to help themselves.

While Roger opened the champagne, Georgina served the food, then they sat down to supper.

They ate well but with long pauses between each dish for talking over their wine. Halfway through the meal Georgina urged him to keep her in suspense no longer about his doings, so he began with their parting four years before and his meeting with Dan, the smuggler. He told her how he had narrowly escaped both becoming a prisoner in the French galleys, and drowning; of his meeting with De Roubec and how the Chevalier had swindled him out of her jewels; of old Doctor Aristotle Fenélon and their disastrous meeting with Joseph Fouché; of how Athénaïs had rescued him and he had then become the whipping boy of a lawyer's apprentices; of the Légers' kindness to him and his hopeless longing for Athénaïs; of his employment by the Marquis de Rochambeau to go into the matter of the *Domaine de St. Hilaire;* of his becoming the Marquis's junior secretary and his friendship with the Abbé de Périgord; of his promotion on the Abbé d'Heury's death and of Athénaïs's illness; of her love for him and the international intrigues of her father; of the appearance of de la Tour d'Auvergne upon the scene and of Athénaïs's engagement; of his duel with de Caylus and his flight with the eloping couple; of his escape from France and the assault that Fouché had made upon him; of his dash to London and recovery of the letter; of his interview with Mr. Pitt and his mission to the United Provinces; of his duel with George Gunston and of his present danger of being extradited to France on a warrant for murder.

When he had done it was nearly midnight, although Georgina had hardly spoken a word, except from time to time to encourage him to go on. So fascinated was she by his story that they had not even moved, and were still sitting over the table. At length, when the tale was told, she said:

"Thou hast fulfilled all thy promise, Roger. 'Twas a hard, uphill road that thou wast forced to tread, but having breasted the hill I foresee a great future for thee."

He made a grimace. "I pray you may be right; but unless Mr. Pitt is prepared to divert the normal course of justice on my behalf I may yet find myself handed over to the tender mercies of the French; and if that occurs M. de Rochambeau will make it his business to see that I die upon a scaffold."

"Have no fear," she smiled. "In view of your services, Billy Pitt could never look in his own mirror again did he refuse to intervene. But he is a good and loyal friend, so I have no doubt at all that he will do so without pressing. Even if he did not you have no cause to worry. It so chances that the Count d'Adhémar, who is the French Ambassador here, is one of my beaux. I vow that at my request he will get the charge against you withdrawn from the French Courts."

Roger looked up quickly. "Could you really do that? Mr. Pitt will protect me, I am convinced, by staying the execution of the warrant here. But if you could get the charge withdrawn in France that would be a boon indeed. 'Twould mean that I could return there as a free man, if I wished."

"And 'tis your wish to return to France, Roger?" she asked.

"Why, yes; I'd like to, sometime."

"Not now, at once, to rejoin Athénaïs?"

He shook his head. "Nay, she is married, and to my friend. That is over and done with."

"Do you miss her very much?"

"Yes, damnably."

"You loved her very deeply, then?"

"I did indeed. She was wondrous beautiful."

"Was she more beautiful than I am, Roger?"

He smiled. "I would be a most ungracious guest were I to tell you so. But I will tell you something else. You have some quality that she lacked. Maybe 'tis your vitality, your good-fellowship, your warmth, your forthright mind, or maybe, 'tis nought but your infectious laughter. I do not know. Yet there it is. You have some gift, some power, some touch, that will attract men to you long after your beauty fades, and Athénaïs has become the pleasant but quite uninteresting mother of a grown-up family."

"I thank thee, Roger," she smiled back. "It seems then that thou wert in love with her beauty rather than herself; yet that makes no difference to the longing one can feel in such a case. Many a poor girl, knowing nothing of your mind, is yet destined to suffer the most desperate cravings for kind looks from those damnably attractive blue eyes of thine. Dost know that thou hast grown monstrous handsome, Roger?"

"I have no cause to quarrel with my looks," he said slowly; "so we must make a pretty pair. For if I'll not say that thou art the loveliest creature in the world, I'll say that thou hast no rival in the length and breadth of Britain."

371

Georgina stood up. Although the room was still pleasantly warm she threw another log on the fire. Then she came round behind him and, laying a hand on his shoulder, checked his movement to rise from the table.

For a moment she remained there in silence. Then she began to stroke his cheek softly with the tips of her fingers, as she whispered: "Yes, thou hast grown monstrous handsome, Roger darling; and 'tis pleasant to think that thou doest not find me ill to look upon. Dost know that we two are marooned here for the night? That is, unless thou hast the wish to undertake a plaguey long walk back to London. Thinkest thou that it lies within my power to console thee a little for the loss of Athénaïs?"

*   *   *   *   *

At four o'clock on the following afternoon Roger was shown into Mr. Pitt's office. The Prime Minister greeted him kindly, offered him a glass of port and, when he was seated, said at once:

"Mr. Brook, I pray you concern yourself no further about this warrant for your extradition. I have had it quashed; and would have written to tell you so, had I not wished to express my thanks to you in person for all that you have done; and let you have, in confidence, the final outcome of the affair in which you were so deeply involved."

"I am most grateful to you, Sir," Roger murmured, but the Prime Minister waved his thanks aside.

"Sir James Harris wrote Lord Carmarthen of the assistance you gave us on your trip abroad, so I know you to be informed of events in the United Provinces up to the end of last month. Since then, Amsterdam, the last stronghold of the rebels, surrendered on the 10th of October, and the French have entirely come to heel. Unable to face a war they have suffered the humiliation of being compelled to entirely reverse their policy. Last week the Court of Versailles exchanged declarations with us, agreeing for the future to sustain the Stadtholder in the full rights of his office."

Roger nodded. "Then there is no longer any fear of a European conflagration?"

"None, I am happy to say; and that is very largely due to Sir James Harris and yourself. You will, I know, be pleased to hear that His Majesty is rewarding Sir James for his long and arduous toil on the nation's behalf, by elevating him to the peerage under the title of Baron Malmesbury. As to yourself, your case presents certain difficulties, since it is contrary to all practice to confer a public award for work of a secret nature. But if I can be of service to you in any way you have but to name it."

Mr. Pitt paused for a moment, then added: "I have no desire to pry into your private affairs, but if a gift of money would be of any assistance to you——?"

"I thank you, Sir." Roger smiled. "But my father has recently made me an allowance of three hundred a year, and that is ample for my needs."

The Prime Minister took a swig of port, and said: "None the less, I shall feel aggrieved unless I can do something for you. Surely, now that you are returned to England, you intend to take up some career. With gifts such as yours you should go far."

"Ah, there's the rub, Sir," Roger replied. "My father set his heart upon my entering the Navy, but four years ago I ran away to France rather than be sent to sea. I've no wish to remain idle, yet those four years are now entirely lost to me. I am not trained to anything except secretarial work and I've no desire to do that all my life. Yet no other opening seems to offer."

Mr. Pitt stood up, and began to walk about the room, as he asked: "What type of work would really hold your interest, and what qualifications have you?"

"I am said to have a flair for languages, Sir. I now speak French as well as most Frenchmen and know a little German. I have proved to myself that I do not lack for courage or resource and would meet any man with either sword or pistol, were I called upon to do so. As to the type of work I would prefer, 'tis hard to put a name to it, but I would like to retain my independence of action as far as possible, and I've a strong desire to travel again. But I fear I shall find it monstrous hard to launch myself in any manner that will fulfil those wishes."

"I think not," said young Mr. Pitt, laying a kindly hand on Roger's shoulder. "Consider yourself launched, Mr. Brook. England and I have a hundred uses for a man like you."